READER'S DIGEST
SELECT EDITIONS

The condensations in this volume
are published with the consent of the authors
and the publishers © 2008 Reader's Digest.

www.readersdigest.co.uk

The Reader's Digest Association Limited
11 Westferry Circus Canary Wharf London E14 4HE

For information as to ownership of
copyright in the material of this book,
and acknowledgments, see last page.

Printed in Germany
ISBN 978 0 276 44287 2

SELECTED AND CONDENSED
BY READER'S DIGEST

THE READER'S DIGEST ASSOCIATION LIMITED, LONDON

CONTENTS

If you were one of the millions of people who enjoyed *Kane & Abel*, you probably won't want to wait before getting stuck into the pages of this new Jeffrey Archer novel. Very much in the vintage mould of that earlier book, *A Prisoner of Birth*

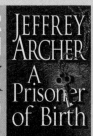

revolves around two individuals from different ends of the social scale. Their fortunes connect in London, with surprising consequences, and before long they face each other in a courtroom, in a trial that will have lifelong repercussions for them both.

Rarely does a book come along that is exceptional in terms of story, character *and* emotional power, but *Child 44* hits the spot. Leo Demidov, an officer in Stalin's State Security force, refuses to denounce his wife as a traitor and is banished from Moscow to Siberia to work in the local militia. There, Leo is drawn into the investigation of a suspicious death. He suspects it's the work of a serial killer, but in a regime that won't admit to the existence of such evil, he has no choice but to pursue the truth alone—and on the run.

ON THE EDGE
RICHARD HAMMOND

315

On September 20, 2006, much loved *Top Gear* presenter Richard Hammond suffered serious brain injury and coma following a high-speed crash, and the nation held its breath. This is the compelling account, in 'the Hamster's' own words and those of his wife Mindy, of his hospitalisation and drama-filled journey to recovery. The couple's courage and unwavering devotion in the face of overwhelming odds are an inspiration to anyone, *Top Gear* fan or otherwise.

A Mayan legend has it that thirteen crystal skulls are hidden across the globe; if they can be reunited, they will stave off the destruction of mankind. This belief, and the existence of one of the skulls in the British Museum, were enough to spark novelist Manda Scott's imagination and she's used them to write a beguiling adventure with a romantic twist. The tale moves between Cambridge and a cave beneath the Yorkshire Moors, taking us back in time to the fifteenth century and deep into the heart of South America.

THE CRYSTAL SKULL
MANDA SCOTT

435

JEFFREY ARCHER

A PRISONER OF BIRTH

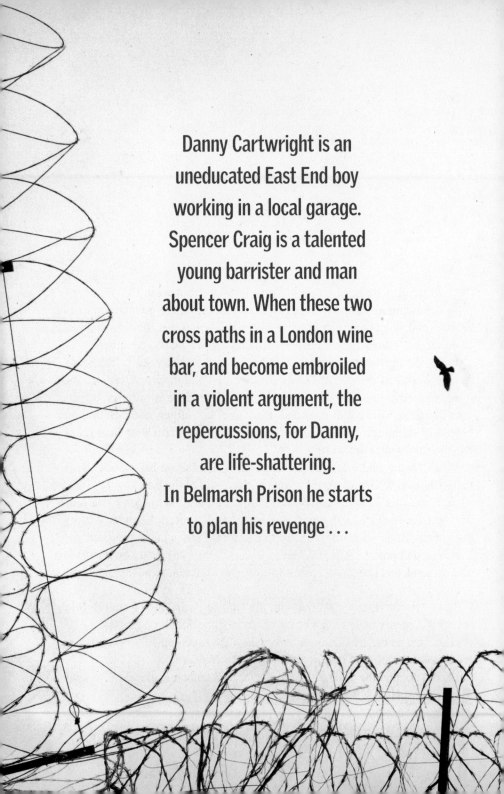

Danny Cartwright is an uneducated East End boy working in a local garage. Spencer Craig is a talented young barrister and man about town. When these two cross paths in a London wine bar, and become embroiled in a violent argument, the repercussions, for Danny, are life-shattering. In Belmarsh Prison he starts to plan his revenge . . .

PROLOGUE
September 18, 1999

'Yes,' said Beth. She tried to look surprised, but wasn't all that convincing as she had already decided that they were going to be married when they were at secondary school. However, she was amazed when Danny fell onto one knee in the middle of the crowded restaurant.

'Yes,' she repeated, hoping he'd stand up before everyone in the room turned to stare at them. But Danny remained on one knee and, like a conjuror, he produced a tiny box from nowhere. He opened it to reveal a gold band boasting a single diamond that was far larger than Beth had expected—although her brother had already told her that Danny had spent two months' wages on the ring.

When Danny finally got up, he tapped in a number on his mobile. Beth knew only too well who would be on the other end of the line.

'She said yes!' Danny announced into the phone. 'Why don't you join us?' he added before Beth could stop him. 'Let's meet at that wine bar off the Fulham Road—the one we went to after the Chelsea game last year.'

Beth didn't protest. After all, Bernie was not only her brother but Danny's oldest friend, and Danny had probably already asked him to be his best man.

WHEN BETH AND DANNY strolled into the Dunlop Arms, they found Bernie seated at a corner table with a bottle of champagne and three glasses.

'Fantastic news,' he said even before they had sat down.

'Thanks, mate,' said Danny, shaking him by the hand.

Bernie popped the cork and filled the three champagne glasses. 'To long life and West Ham winning the cup.'

'Well, at least one of those is possible,' said Danny.

'I think you'd marry West Ham if you could,' said Beth with a smile.

Danny laughed. 'I'll be married to you and my team for the rest of my life.'

'Except on Saturday afternoons,' Bernie reminded him.

'And you might even have to sacrifice a few of those once you take over from Dad,' added Beth.

Danny frowned. He had been to see Beth's father during his lunch break and had asked him for permission to marry his daughter—some traditions die hard in the East End. Mr Wilson couldn't have been more enthusiastic about Danny becoming his son-in-law, but went on to tell him that he had changed his mind about something they'd agreed on.

'And if you think I'm gonna call you Guv when you take over from my old man,' said Bernie, breaking into Danny's thoughts, 'you can forget it.'

'Is that who I think it is?' said Beth, looking across the room.

Danny took a closer look at a man standing in a group of four at the bar. 'It certainly looks like 'im.'

'Looks like who?' asked Bernie.

'That actor what plays Dr Beresford in *The Prescription.*'

'Lawrence Davenport,' whispered Beth.

'I think you fancy him,' said Bernie, as he topped up their glasses.

'No, I don't,' said Beth a little too loudly, causing one of the men at the bar to turn round. 'And in any case,' she added, smiling at her fiancé, 'Danny's far better-looking than Lawrence Davenport.'

Bernie roared with laughter. 'Just because Danny's shaved and washed his hair for a change, don't think it's gonna become a habit, sis. Try to remember that your future husband works in the East End, not the City.'

'Danny could be anything he wanted to be,' said Beth, taking his hand. 'He's got plans for the garage that will make you—'

'He'd better have, 'cos gettin' spliced don't come cheap,' said Bernie. 'To start with, you're gonna have to find somewhere to live.'

'There's a basement flat round the corner that's for sale,' said Danny.

'We've saved enough between us to put down a deposit,' said Beth, 'and when Danny takes over from Dad—'

'Let's drink to that,' said Bernie, only to find that the bottle was empty. 'I'd better order another.'

'No,' said Beth firmly. 'I've got to be on time for work tomorrow.'

'To hell with that,' said Bernie. 'It's not every day that my little sister gets engaged to my best mate. Another bottle!' he shouted. The barman smiled as he removed a second bottle of champagne from the fridge.

One of the men standing at the bar checked the label. 'Pol Roger,' he said, before adding in a voice that carried, 'Wasted on them.'

Bernie jumped up from his seat, but Danny pulled him back down.

'Ignore them,' he said, 'they're not worth the space.'

The barman walked smartly across. 'Don't let's be havin' any trouble, lads,' he said, as he removed the cork. 'One of them's celebratin' his birthday, and they've had a bit too much to drink.'

Beth took a closer look at the four men while the barman filled their glasses. One of them was staring at her. He winked, opened his mouth and ran his tongue around his lips. Beth quickly turned back, relieved to find that Danny and her brother were chatting.

'So where you goin' on honeymoon?'

'St Tropez,' said Danny.

'And you're not coming along this time,' said Beth.

'The slut's quite presentable until she opens her mouth,' said a voice from the bar.

Bernie leapt to his feet again. Two of the men stared defiantly at him.

'They're drunk,' said Beth. 'Just ignore them.'

'Oh, I don't know,' said one of the other men. 'There are times when I quite like a slut's mouth to be open.'

Bernie grabbed the empty bottle and it took all of Danny's strength to pull him back down.

'I want to leave now,' said Beth firmly. 'I don't want a bunch of public school snobs ruining my engagement party.'

'Come on, Bernie, let's get out of here,' Danny said, getting up. Bernie stood up and reluctantly followed his friend. Beth was pleased to see that the four men at the bar had turned away from them, but as Danny opened the back door one of them swung round and said, 'Leaving, are we?' He then took out his wallet and said loudly, 'When you've finished with her, my friends and I have just enough left over for a gangbang.'

'You're full of shit,' said Bernie.

'Then why don't I join you and we can sort it out?'

'Be my guest, Dickhead,' said Bernie, but Danny shoved him through the door and out into the alley. Beth followed and slammed the door quickly behind them and began walking down the alley. Danny gripped Bernie by the elbow, but they had only gone a couple of yards before his mate shook him off, saying, 'Let's go back inside and sort them.'

'Not tonight,' said Danny, leading his friend on down the alley.

Beth had reached the main road when she saw the man Bernie had called

Dickhead standing there, one hand behind his back. He leered at her and began licking his lips again, just as one of his friends came round the corner.

'Let's go back inside,' she shouted at Danny, only to see that Lawrence Davenport and the fourth member of the group were now standing by the back door of the wine bar, blocking the path.

'No, no,' she pleaded, as Dickhead came charging up the alley.

'You take him,' said Bernie, 'and I'll deal with the other three.'

Beth looked on in horror as Dickhead threw a punch that caught Danny on the side of the chin and sent him reeling back. He recovered in time to block the next punch, feint, and then land one that took Dickhead by surprise.

As the two men standing by the back door didn't seem willing to join in, Beth hoped the fight would be over fairly quickly. She could only watch as her brother landed an uppercut to the other man, the force of the blow almost knocking him out. As Bernie waited for him to get back on his feet, he shouted to Beth, 'Do us a favour, sis, get a cab. This ain't gonna last much longer and then we need to be out of here.'

Beth didn't move until she was certain Danny was getting the better of Dickhead, who was lying spreadeagled on the ground. Then she ran down to the main road and began searching for a taxi. After a couple of minutes she spotted a familiar yellow FOR HIRE sign and flagged down the cab.

'Where to, luv?' asked the cabbie.

'Bacon Road, Bow,' said Beth as she opened the back door, 'and there'll be two friends joining me in a moment.'

The cabbie glanced over her shoulder and down the alley. 'I don't think it's a taxi you'll be needing, luv,' he said. 'If they were my friends, I'd be phoning for an ambulance.'

BOOK ONE: The Trial
Chapter 1

'Not guilty.'

As he spoke, Danny Cartwright could feel his legs trembling as they sometimes did before the first round of a boxing match he knew he was going to lose. The clerk of the court recorded the plea and said, 'You can sit down.'

Danny collapsed onto the little chair in the dock. He looked up at the judge, who was seated on the far side of the courtroom in a high-backed green leather chair behind a long bench littered with case papers. Mr Justice Sackville removed a pair of half-moon spectacles from the end of his nose and said in an authoritative voice, 'Bring in the jury.'

Danny took in the unfamiliar sights and sounds of Court Number Four at the Old Bailey. He looked at the two men who were seated at either end of what he'd been told was counsel's bench. His young advocate, Alex Redmayne, gave him a friendly smile, but the prosecution counsel, an older man, short and rotund, never glanced in his direction.

Suddenly, a door in a far corner of the courtroom opened and the usher appeared, followed by the seven men and five women of the jury.

Once they had settled, the clerk of the court rose. 'Members of the jury,' he began. 'The defendant, Daniel Arthur Cartwright, stands before you charged on one count of murder. He has pleaded not guilty. Your charge is to listen to the evidence and decide whether he be guilty or no.'

Mr Justice Sackville glanced down at the bench below him. 'Mr Pearson, you may open the case for the Crown.'

Mr Arnold Pearson, QC, rose slowly from the counsel's bench and opened the thick file that rested on a lectern in front of him. He touched his well-worn wig, then tugged on the lapels of his gown. 'If it please Your Lordship,' he began, 'I appear for the Crown in this case, while my learned friend, Mr Alex Redmayne, appears for the defence. The case before Your Lordship is one of murder. The cold-blooded, calculated murder of Mr Bernard Henry Wilson. During the course of this trial, you will learn how the defendant lured Mr Wilson to a public house in Chelsea, London, on the night of Saturday, September the 18th, 1999, where he carried out this brutal and premeditated murder. He had earlier taken Mr Wilson's sister, Elizabeth, to Lucio's Restaurant in Fulham Road. The court will learn that Cartwright made a proposal of marriage to Miss Wilson after she had revealed that she was pregnant. He then called her brother Mr Bernard Wilson on his mobile phone and invited him to join them at the Dunlop Arms so that they could celebrate.

'The Crown will suggest that Cartwright knew the layout of the wine bar well and had selected it for one purpose and one purpose only: its back door opens onto a quiet alleyway, an ideal location for someone with murderous intent. Cartwright would later blame the murder on a complete stranger who just happened to be a customer at the pub that night.

'But unfortunately for Cartwright,' continued Pearson, 'the other four customers who were in the Dunlop Arms that night tell a different story, a story that has been corroborated by the barman. The Crown will present all five as witnesses and they will tell you that they overheard a dispute between the two men. All five saw Daniel Cartwright leave by the back door, followed by Bernard Wilson and his sister Elizabeth. Moments later, a scream was heard. Mr Spencer Craig, one of the customers, left his companions and ran out into the alley, where he found Cartwright repeatedly thrusting a knife into Mr Wilson's chest. Mr Craig immediately dialled 999 on his mobile phone. A few minutes later, two police officers arrived on the scene and found Cartwright kneeling over Mr Wilson's body with the knife in his hand.

'Members of the jury,' continued Pearson, again tugging at his lapels, 'every murderer has to have a motive and in this case envy, greed and ambition were the sordid ingredients that provoked Cartwright to remove the one rival who stood in his path.

'Members of the jury, both Mr Cartwright and Mr Wilson worked at Wilson's Garage in Mile End Road. The garage is owned and managed by Mr George Wilson, the deceased's father, who had planned to retire at the end of the year, handing over the business to his only son, Bernard.

'Members of the jury, you will discover that these two young men had a long history of rivalry and antagonism that stretched back to their schooldays. With Bernard Wilson out of the way, Cartwright planned to marry the boss's daughter and take over the business himself. However, everything did not go as planned, and so he tried to place the blame on an innocent bystander.' Pearson smiled. 'Once you have heard the evidence you will be left in no doubt that Daniel Cartwright is guilty of murder.' He turned to the judge. 'That concludes the prosecution opening for the Crown, M'lord. With your permission I shall call my first witness.'

Mr Justice Sackville nodded, and Pearson said, 'I call Mr Spencer Craig.'

Danny Cartwright watched as a tall man, not much older than Danny, and dressed in a blue pinstriped suit, entered the courtroom.

Craig stepped into the witness box, picked up the Bible and delivered the oath without looking at the card the usher held in front of him.

Pearson smiled at his principal witness. 'Is your name Spencer Craig?'

'Yes, sir,' he replied.

'And do you reside at forty-three Hambledon Terrace, London SW3?'

'I do, sir.'

'And what is your profession?' asked Mr Pearson, as if he didn't know.

'I am a barrister-at-law.'

'I should like to take you back to the evening of September the 18th, last year. Perhaps you could take us through what happened that night.'

'My friends and I were celebrating Gerald's thirtieth birthday—'

'Gerald?' interrupted Pearson.

'Gerald Payne,' said Craig. 'An old friend from my days at Cambridge. We were enjoying a glass of wine in celebration of Gerald's birthday, when I became aware of raised voices. I turned and saw a man seated at a table in the far corner of the room beside a young lady.'

'Do you see that man in the courtroom now?' asked Pearson.

'Yes,' replied Craig, pointing at Danny.

'What happened next?'

'He jumped up,' continued Craig, 'and began shouting and jabbing his finger at another man seated at the table. I heard one of them say to the other, "If you think I'm gonna call you Guv when you take over from my old man, you can forget it." The young lady was trying to calm him down. The defendant shouted, "Then why don't I join you and we can sort it out?" After that he grabbed a knife from the bar—'

'You saw the defendant pick up a knife from the bar?' asked Pearson.

'Yes, I did.'

'And then what happened?'

'He marched off in the direction of the back door, which surprised me.'

'Why did it surprise you?'

'Because the Dunlop Arms is my local, and I'd never seen the man before.'

'I'm not sure I'm following you, Mr Craig,' said Pearson.

'The rear exit is out of sight if you're sitting in that corner of the room, but he seemed to know exactly where he was going.'

'Ah, I understand,' said Pearson. 'Please continue.'

'The other man got up and chased after the defendant, with the young lady following close behind. Moments later we all heard a woman scream.'

'And what did you do?'

'I left my friends and ran into the alley in case the woman was in danger.'

'And was she?'

'No, sir. She was screaming at the defendant, begging him to stop attacking the other man.'

'They were fighting?'

'Yes, sir. The chap I'd earlier seen shouting now had the other man pinned against the wall and was thrusting the knife into his chest.'

'What did you do next?' asked Pearson quietly.

'I phoned the emergency services. They assured me that they would inform the police and send an ambulance immediately. They told me not to approach the man with the knife, but to return to the bar and wait until the police arrived.'

'How did your friends react when you went back into the bar and told them what you had seen?' asked Pearson, looking down at his notes.

'They wanted to go outside to help, but I told them what the police had advised and that I also thought it might be wise for them to go home. I was the only one to witness the whole incident and I didn't want them to be in any danger should the man with the knife return to the bar.'

'And how long did you have to wait before the police arrived?'

'It was only a matter of moments before I heard a siren, and a few minutes later a detective entered the bar through the back door. He introduced himself as Detective Sergeant Fuller, and informed me that the victim was on his way to the nearest hospital.'

'What happened next?'

'I made a full statement, and then DS Fuller told me I could go home.'

'And did you?'

'Yes, I returned to my house, which is only about a hundred yards from the Dunlop Arms, and went to bed, but I couldn't sleep. So I got up and wrote down everything that had taken place earlier that evening as I knew I would be called as a witness in any forthcoming trial.'

'Thank you, Mr Craig.'

The two men smiled at each other before Pearson said, 'No more questions, M'lord.'

Mr Justice Sackville turned his attention to the defence counsel. He was well acquainted with Alex Redmayne's distinguished father, Sir Matthew Redmayne, but the young man had never appeared before him. 'Mr Redmayne, do you wish to cross-examine this witness?'

'I most certainly do,' replied Redmayne, as he gathered up his notes.

After he'd been arrested, Danny had been advised by an officer to find himself a lawyer. He quickly discovered that lawyers, like garage mechanics, charge by the hour and you only get what you can afford. He could afford £5,000 pounds, the sum he had saved as the deposit on a flat for when he and Beth were married. Every penny of it had been swallowed up in fees he had paid up-front to his solicitor and the young barrister who was to represent him in court.

But Danny had liked Alex Redmayne from the day he met him. He had a posh accent and had been to Oxford University, but he never spoke down to his client. He asked Danny to go over what had taken place that night again and again, as he searched for inconsistencies in the story. He found none, and when the money ran out he still agreed to conduct Danny's defence.

'Mr Craig,' began Alex Redmayne, 'what time did you and your friends arrive at the Dunlop Arms that evening?'

'I don't recall the exact time,' Craig replied.

'Let me try to jog your memory. Was it seven? Seven thirty? Eight?'

'Nearer eight, I suspect.'

'So you had already been drinking for some three hours by the time my client, his fiancée and his closest friend walked into the bar. And how much drink had you consumed by, let's say, eleven o'clock?'

'I've no idea. It was Gerald's thirtieth birthday so no one was counting.'

'Well, as you had been drinking for over three hours, shall we settle on half a dozen bottles of wine? Or perhaps it was seven, even eight?'

'Five at most,' retorted Craig. 'That's hardly excessive for four people.'

'I would normally agree with you, Mr Craig, had not one of your companions said in his written statement that he drank only Diet Coke, while another claimed to have had only one or two glasses of wine because he was driving.'

'But I didn't have to drive,' said Craig. 'The Dunlop Arms is my local and I live only a hundred yards away.'

'Isn't it the truth, Mr Craig, that it was you who started this quarrel when you delivered an unforgettable remark to my client as he was leaving.' He glanced down at his notes. '"When you've finished with her, my friends and I have just enough left over for a gangbang"?' Redmayne waited for Craig to reply, but he remained silent.

'I also suggest that when Mr Wilson told you that you were "full of shit", it was *you* who said, "Then why don't I join you and we can sort it out?"'

'I think that sounds more like the kind of language one would expect from your client,' responded Craig.

'Or from a man who had had a little too much to drink and was showing off to his friends? I suggest, Mr Craig,' Redmayne continued, 'that you left by the front door and ran round to the back because you wanted a fight.'

'I only went into the alley after I'd heard the scream.'

'Did any of your friends follow you into the alley?' Redmayne enquired.

'No, they did not.'

'So they didn't witness the fight you had with Mr Cartwright?'

'How could they, when I did not have a fight with Mr Cartwright?'

'Did you get a boxing Blue when you were at Cambridge, Mr Craig?' Craig hesitated. 'Yes, I did.'

'And while at Cambridge,' Redmayne continued, 'were you rusticated after being involved in a drunken brawl with some locals whom you later described to the magistrates as a "bunch of yobs"?'

'That was years ago, when I was still an undergraduate.'

'I'm curious to discover why, Mr Craig, after you returned to the bar, you advised your friends to go home.'

'They had not witnessed your client stabbing Mr Wilson, and so weren't involved,' said Craig. 'And I thought they might be in danger if they stayed.'

'But if anyone was in danger, it would have been you, the only witness to the murder of Mr Wilson, so why didn't you leave with your friends?'

Craig remained silent.

'Perhaps the real reason you told them to leave,' said Redmayne, 'was because you needed them out of the way so that you could run home and change out of your blood-covered clothes before the police turned up?'

'You seem to have forgotten, Mr Redmayne, that Detective Sergeant Fuller arrived only a few minutes after the crime had been committed,' responded Craig scornfully.

'It was seven minutes after you phoned the emergency services that the detective sergeant arrived on the scene. However, he then spent some considerable time questioning my client before he entered the bar.' Turning to the judge, Redmayne said, 'No more questions, M'lord.'

'Mr Pearson,' said the judge, 'do you wish to re-examine this witness?'

'Yes, M'lord,' said the counsel for the prosecution. 'Mr Craig, when Scotland Yard's forensic experts examined the murder weapon, was it your fingerprints they identified on the knife handle, or those of the defendant?'

'They weren't mine,' said Craig, 'otherwise I would be in the dock.'

'No more questions, M'lord,' said Pearson.

THE COURT ROSE for lunch, then at two o'clock the proceedings began again. Gerald Payne was the next witness to be called.

Danny didn't immediately recognise the man who entered the courtroom. He was around five foot nine inches tall, prematurely bald, and his well-cut beige suit failed to disguise the fact that he'd lost a stone since Danny had last seen him. The usher handed Payne a copy of the New

Testament and held up the oath. Although Payne read from the card, he displayed the same self-confidence that Spencer Craig had shown earlier.

'Gerald David Payne, what is your profession?' asked Pearson.

'I am a land management consultant.'

Redmayne wrote down the words *estate agent* next to Payne's name.

'And which firm do you work for?' enquired Pearson.

'I am a partner with Baker, Tremlett and Smythe.'

'You are very young to be a partner in such a distinguished firm.'

'I am the youngest partner in the firm's history,' replied Payne.

Pearson patiently took Payne through the events of the night in question. Yes, he had been at the Dunlop Arms. No, the witness confirmed, he had not ventured out into the alley when he heard the scream. Yes, he had gone home when advised to do so by Spencer Craig.

'Thank you, Mr Payne,' concluded Pearson. 'Please remain on the stand.'

Redmayne rose slowly from his place. 'Mr Payne,' he said, looking up at the witness, 'when you were an undergraduate at Cambridge, were you a member of a society known as the Musketeers?'

'Yes,' replied Payne, looking puzzled.

'And was that society's motto: "All for one and one for all"?'

'Yes, it was,' replied Payne, with a slight edge to his voice.

'What else did the members of that society have in common?'

'An appreciation of Dumas, justice and a bottle of fine wine.'

'Or perhaps several bottles of fine wine?' suggested Redmayne as he extracted a small, blue booklet from the pile of papers in front of him and began to turn its pages. 'Was it not one of the society's rules that if any member found himself in danger, it was the duty of all other members to come to his assistance?'

'Yes,' replied Payne. 'I consider loyalty to be the benchmark by which you can judge any man.'

'Do you indeed?' said Redmayne. 'Was Mr Spencer Craig also a member of the Musketeers?'

'He was,' replied Payne. 'In fact, he's a past chairman.'

'No more questions, M'lord,' said Redmayne.

THE FOLLOWING MORNING, Lawrence Davenport entered the court stage right, and followed the usher to the witness box. He was about six foot tall, but so slim he appeared taller. He wore a tailored navy-blue suit and a cream shirt that looked as if it had been unwrapped that morning. But it was not his garments that caused women to turn their heads: it was the piercing blue eyes and thick, wavy, fair hair.

Davenport had built his reputation playing a heart surgeon in *The Prescription*. For an hour every Saturday evening, he seduced an audience of over nine million. His fans didn't seem to care that he spent more time flirting with the nurses than performing coronary artery bypasses.

The usher handed him a Bible and held up a cue card so that he could deliver his opening lines. As he recited the oath, Alex Redmayne couldn't help noticing that all five women on the jury were smiling at the witness.

Mr Pearson rose. 'Lawrence Andrew Davenport, can you confirm that you were at the Dunlop Arms on the evening of September the 18th, 1999.'

'Yes,' said Davenport. 'I joined a few friends to celebrate Gerald Payne's thirtieth birthday. We were all up at Cambridge together,' he added.

Pearson intended to keep Davenport in the witness box for as long as he could, for his answers were word-perfect and exactly mirrored Spencer Craig's version of events. When Pearson came to the end of his questions he said, 'Please remain in the witness box, Mr Davenport, as I'm sure my learned friend will wish to cross-examine you.'

'Do you wish to cross-examine this witness, Mr Redmayne?' the judge asked, sounding as if he were looking forward to the encounter.

'No, thank you, M'lord,' replied Redmayne, barely shifting in his place.

Few of those present in the court were able to hide their disappointment.

Alex remained unmoved, recalling his father's advice never to cross-examine a witness the jury like, for they will want to believe anything the person has to say. Get them out of the witness box as quickly as possible, in the hope that by the time the jury comes to consider the verdict, the memory of their performance might have faded.

TOBY MORTIMER, SEATED in the corridor outside, had been dreading his spell in the witness box for weeks, despite Spencer's reassurance that even if Redmayne found out about his drug problem, he would never refer to it.

Mortimer was sweating. His craving had got stronger after what happened that night. How long before the shakes would begin? As long as he was called next, a surge of adrenaline should get him through.

The courtroom door opened and the usher reappeared. 'Reginald Taylor!' he bellowed, then led the manager of the Dunlop Arms into the courtroom.

Mortimer gripped the edge of the bench as he felt the shakes coming on.

He wasn't sure how much longer he could last before he fed his addiction. And in his head he could hear Spencer Craig saying, 'Pull yourself together,' even though he was now a mile away, sitting in his chambers, probably chatting to Lawrence about how well it had gone so far. They would be waiting for him to join them: the last piece in the jigsaw.

By the time Reginald Taylor re-emerged from the courtroom, Mortimer's shirt, pants and socks were soaked in sweat. He began pacing up and down the corridor and smiled hopefully at the usher when the man reappeared to summon the next witness, but it was not his turn.

'Detective Sergeant Fuller!' the usher bellowed.

Mortimer, now shaking uncontrollably, headed unsteadily to the washroom and locked himself inside a cubicle. He took a small pouch from his jacket pocket, unfolded it and laid it out on the lavatory seat, then picked up a phial of liquid, plunged a hypodermic needle into it and drew back the plunger. As he inserted the needle into his leg he breathed a deep sigh of relief as he drifted into another world—a world not inhabited by Spencer Craig.

'I AM NOT WILLING to discuss the subject any longer,' said Beth's father as he took his seat at the table and Mrs Wilson put a plate of eggs and bacon in front of him.

'But, Dad, you can't seriously believe that Danny would kill Bernie. They were best friends since their first day at Clem Attlee.'

'I've seen Danny lose his temper. Besides, do you expect me to believe a complete stranger stabbed your brother to death?'

'Have you forgotten,' said Beth, 'that Danny was the man you were so keen for me to marry, and who you asked to take over the garage when you retired? So what's suddenly stopped you believing in that man?'

'There's something I haven't told you,' said Beth's father. 'When Danny came to see me that morning, to tell me he was going to ask you to marry him, I thought it was only fair to let him know that I'd changed my mind about who would be taking over the garage when I retired.'

'I CALL MR TOBY MORTIMER,' Mr Pearson said reluctantly.

The usher stepped into the corridor and roared, 'Toby Mortimer!' He checked up and down the benches, but there was no sign of the man.

A pregnant young woman looked up, and the usher's eyes settled on her. 'Have you seen Mr Mortimer, madam?' he asked.

'Yes,' she replied, 'he went off to the toilets, but he hasn't returned.'

'Thank you, madam.' The usher disappeared for a few moments, then came back into the courtroom. He hurried over to the associate, who listened before briefing the judge.

'Mr Pearson,' Mr Justice Sackville said. 'It appears your final witness has been taken ill, and is now on his way to hospital. I therefore intend to close proceedings for the day.'

ALEX REDMAYNE HAD HOPED that Mortimer would be the one Crown witness who might buckle under pressure—the chink in the armour of the four Musketeers—but now he knew his trump card had been removed from the pack. As he closed his file, he accepted that the fate of Danny Cartwright now rested in the hands of his fiancée, Beth Wilson. And he still couldn't be sure if she was telling the truth.

Chapter 2

They didn't grant Danny bail, and so he had spent the past six months locked up in Belmarsh high-security prison in southeast London, languishing for twenty-two hours a day in a cell eight foot by six, the only furnishings a single bed, a Formica table, a plastic chair, a small steel washbasin and a steel lavatory. A tiny, barred window high above his head provided his only view of the outside world. Every afternoon they allowed him out of the cell for forty-five minutes, when he would jog around a yard surrounded by a sixteen-foot wall.

When Beth entered the courtroom on the first morning of the second week of the trial, it was the first time Danny had seen her for two weeks. She gave him a warm smile before taking the oath.

'Is your name Elizabeth Wilson?' enquired Alex Redmayne.

'Yes,' she replied, 'but I'm known as Beth.'

'And you live at twenty-seven Bacon Road in Bow, east London.'

'Yes, I do.'

'And Bernie Wilson, the deceased, was your brother?'

'Yes, he was,' said Beth.

'Miss Wilson,' continued Redmayne, 'would you tell the court what your relationship is to the accused.'

'Danny and I are going to be married next week,' she replied.

'Next week?' repeated Redmayne, trying to sound surprised.

'Yes, the final banns were read yesterday by our parish priest.'

'But if your fiancé were to be convicted—'

'You can't be convicted for a crime you didn't commit,' responded Beth.

Alex Redmayne smiled. 'How long have you known the defendant?'

'As long as I can remember,' replied Beth. 'We went to the same school, Clement Attlee Comprehensive.'

'When is the baby due?' asked Redmayne.

'In six weeks,' Beth said, bowing her head.

'Did your brother get on well with Danny?'

'Danny was his best friend,' said Beth. 'They played together in all the school teams—football, cricket, even boxing.'

'Did they regularly quarrel, as my learned friend has suggested?'

'Only about West Ham, or Bernie's latest girlfriend.'

Alex noticed one or two of the jury members were smiling.

'So there was no bad feeling between them, as has been suggested by my learned friend, Mr Pearson.'

'How could *he* know?' asked Beth. 'He never met either of them.'

'I'm now going to take you back to September the 18th last year,' said Redmayne. 'I want you to tell the jury in your own words exactly what took place that night.'

Beth nodded. 'It was Danny's idea'—she was smiling at the defendant now—'that we should go for dinner in the West End as it was a special occasion . . .'

Alex Redmayne took her through the events of that evening, how they'd met Bernie at the Dunlop Arms in Chelsea after their meal, and how Spencer Craig had provoked her brother into a fight in the alley, during which her brother had told her to go and get a taxi as he was confident it would all be over quickly.

'How long did it take you to find a taxi?'

'Only a few minutes,' said Beth, 'but when the cabbie drew up, to my surprise he said, "I don't think it's a taxi you'll be needing, luv. If they were my friends, I'd be phoning for an ambulance." And without another word he shot off.'

'Has any attempt been made to locate the taxi driver concerned?' asked the judge.

'Yes, M'lord,' replied Redmayne, 'but so far no one has come forward.'

'So how did you react when you heard the taxi driver's words?'

'I swung round to see my brother Bernie lying on the ground. He appeared to be hurt, and Danny was holding his head in his arms. I ran back down the alley towards them.'

'And did Danny give an explanation as to what had happened?'

'Yes. He said that they had been taken by surprise when Spencer Craig produced the knife. Danny had tried to wrestle it from him when he started stabbing Bernie.'

'And did Bernie confirm this?'

'Yes, he did.'

'So what did you do next?'

'I phoned the emergency services.'

'Who turned up first? The police or an ambulance?'

'Two paramedics,' said Beth without hesitation.

'And how long was it before they arrived?'

'Seven, perhaps eight minutes.'

'How can you be so sure?'

'I never stopped looking at my watch.'

'And how many more minutes passed before the police arrived?'

'I can't be certain,' said Beth, 'but it must have been at least another five.'

'And how long did Detective Sergeant Fuller remain with you in the alley before he went into the bar to interview Mr Craig?'

'At least ten minutes,' said Beth. 'But it might have been longer.'

'Miss Wilson,' continued Redmayne, 'while you were waiting for the police, did the paramedics take your brother to the nearest hospital?'

'Yes, they did everything they could,' said Beth, 'but I knew it was too late. He'd already lost so much blood.'

'Did you and Danny accompany your brother to the hospital?'

'No, I went on my own because Detective Sergeant Fuller wanted to ask Danny some more questions.'

'Did that worry you?' Redmayne enquired.

'Yes, because Danny had also been wounded. He'd been—'

'That's not what I meant,' said Redmayne. 'Were you anxious that the police might consider Danny to be a suspect?'

'No, it never crossed my mind,' Beth said. 'I had already told the police what happened. He always had me to back up his story.'

'Thank you, Miss Wilson. No more questions, M'lord.'

The judge turned to Beth and said, 'Would you remain in the witness box? I have a feeling Mr Pearson may have one or two questions for you.'

Mr Pearson rose slowly from his seat. 'Miss Wilson, what did you have for breakfast this morning?'

'I had a cup of tea and a boiled egg.'

'Nothing else, Miss Wilson?'

'Oh, yes, some toast.'

'How many slices of toast?'

She hesitated. 'I can't remember.'

'You can't remember what you had for breakfast *this morning*, and yet you can recall in great detail every sentence you heard six months ago.' Beth bowed her head. 'Not only can you recall every word Mr Spencer Craig uttered that night, but you can even remember such details as him leering at you and rolling his tongue round his lips.'

'Yes, I can,' insisted Beth. 'Because he did.'

'Then let's go back and test your memory even further, Miss Wilson. 'Who was it who said'—Pearson leaned forward to check his notes—'"There are times when I like a slut's mouth to be open"?'

'I'm not sure if that was Mr Craig or one of the other men.'

'You're "not sure"? "One of the other men"? The defendant, perhaps?'

'No, one of the men at the bar.'

'You told my learned friend earlier that you didn't react because you'd heard worse in the East End,' Pearson reminded Beth.

'Yes, I have.'

'In fact, that's where you heard the phrase in the first place, isn't it, Miss Wilson?' said Pearson, tugging the lapels of his black gown.

'What are you getting at?'

'Simply that you never heard Mr Craig deliver those words in a bar in Chelsea, Miss Wilson, but you have heard your fiancé, Danny Cartwright, say them in the East End many times, because that's the sort of language he would use.'

'No, it was Mr Craig who said that.'

'You also told the court that you left the Dunlop Arms by the back door. Why didn't you leave by the front door, Miss Wilson?'

'I wanted to slip out quietly and not cause any more trouble.'

'So you had already caused *some* trouble?'

'No, *we* hadn't caused any trouble.'

'Then why didn't you leave by the front door, Miss Wilson? If you had, you would have found yourself on a crowded street and could have "slipped away", to use your words, "without causing any more trouble".'

Beth remained silent.

'Then you say Cartwright pushed Mr Wilson towards the back door. Was that when Mr Craig heard your brother say, "Then why don't I join you and we can sort it"?'

'It was Mr Craig who said: "Then why don't I join you and we can sort it *out*," because that's the kind of language they use in the West End.'

Bright woman, thought Alex, delighted that she'd picked up his point and rammed it home.

'And when you were outside,' said Pearson quickly, 'you found Mr Craig waiting for you at the other end of the alley?'

'Yes, I did.'

'How long was it before you saw him standing there? Less than a minute?'

'I don't remember,' replied Beth. 'But it wasn't that long.'

'"It wasn't that long,"' repeated Pearson. 'Miss Wilson, if you were to leave the Dunlop Arms by the front door, make your way through a crowded street, then down a long lane, before finally reaching the end of the alley, you'd find it's a distance of two hundred yards. Are you suggesting that Mr Craig covered that distance in a minute?'

'It could have been more than a minute.'

'But you were keen to get away,' Pearson reminded her. 'So if it had been more than a minute you would have had time to reach the main road and disappear long before they could have got there.'

'Now I remember,' said Beth. 'Danny was trying to calm Bernie down, but my brother wanted to go back into the bar and sort Craig out, so it must have been more than a minute.'

'Or was it Mr Cartwright he wanted to sort out?' asked Pearson. 'Leaving him in no doubt who was going to be the boss once his father retired?'

'If Bernie had wanted to do that,' said Beth, 'he could have flattened him with one punch. He'd always been the better boxer.'

'Not if Mr Cartwright had a knife,' responded Pearson.

'It was Craig who had the knife, and it was Craig who stabbed Bernie.'

'How can you be so sure, when you didn't witness the stabbing?'

'Because Bernie told me that's what happened.'

'Are you sure it was Bernie who told you, and not Danny?'

'Yes, I am.'

'Perhaps you can remember who had the knife in his hand when you ran back to join your brother?'

'It was Danny. He explained that he had to wrestle it away from Craig when he was stabbing my brother.'

'But you didn't witness that either?' Pearson asked.

'No, I didn't.'

'And your fiancé was covered in blood?'

'Of course he was,' said Beth.

'So if it was Mr Craig who stabbed your brother, he must also have been covered in blood.'

'How could I know? He'd disappeared by then.'

'Into thin air?' said Pearson. 'So how do you explain that, when the police arrived a few minutes later, Mr Craig was sitting at the bar, waiting for the detective, and there was not a sign of blood anywhere?' This time Beth didn't have a reply. 'And may I remind you,' continued Pearson, 'who it was that called for the police in the first place? Not you, Miss Wilson, but Mr Craig. A strange thing to do moments after you've stabbed someone, when your clothes are covered in blood.'

He paused to allow the image to settle in the jury's minds.

'Let us move on. Is it true that Mr Cartwright was hoping to become the manager of Wilson's Garage when your father retired?' said Pearson.

'Yes, my dad had already told Danny he was being lined up for the job.'

'But didn't you later discover your father had changed his mind and told Cartwright he intended to put your brother in charge at the garage?'

'Yes, I did,' said Beth, 'but Bernie never wanted the job in the first place. He always accepted that Danny was the natural leader.'

'Possibly, but as it was the family business, wouldn't it have been understandable for your brother to feel resentful at being passed over?'

'No, Bernie never wanted to be in charge of anything.'

'Then why did your brother say that night, "And if you think I'm going to call you Guv if you take over from my old man, you can forget it"?'

'He didn't say "if", Mr Pearson, he said "when".'

'Sadly, we only have your word for that, Miss Wilson, while there are three other witnesses who tell a completely different story.'

'They're all lying,' said Beth, her voice rising.

'And you're the only one who's telling the truth although you didn't actually witness what took place,' responded Pearson. 'No more questions, M'lord.'

'ARE YOU GOING to put Cartwright in the witness box?' Alex's father asked, when Alex went to see his parents in Bath at the weekend. He'd started quizzing him about the trial even before he'd shut the front door. Not out of character for the old man. After all, that was what he did during the week. On Monday they would both be at the Old Bailey, just serving in different courts.

'Of course,' said Alex. 'Why wouldn't I?'

'Because it's the one element of surprise you have left,' the old judge said, putting down his whisky. 'Pearson will be expecting Cartwright to be in the witness box for the rest of the week, but if you were to close your case tomorrow morning without any warning, he'd be on the back foot. He's assuming that he'll be cross-examining Cartwright towards the end of the week, not that he'll be asked to sum up for the prosecution first thing tomorrow.'

'But if Cartwright doesn't give evidence, the jury will assume the worst. You've warned me about that so many times in the past.'

'Perhaps, but one or two of the jury will assume you've advised him not to face Pearson, especially after the grilling the man gave his fiancée.'

'Cartwright is every bit as bright as Pearson,' said Alex.

'But you mentioned that he has a short fuse.'

'Only when someone attacks Beth.'

His father nodded. 'Then you can be sure that once Cartwright's in the witness box, Pearson will keep on attacking Beth until he lights that fuse.'

'But Cartwright doesn't have a criminal record, he's been in work since the day he left school, and he was about to get married to his long-term girl-friend who just happens to be pregnant.'

'So we know four subjects Pearson won't mention in cross-examination. But you can be sure he has surprises in store for Danny Cartwright.'

'True, but perhaps I've also got one or two surprises for him to worry about,' said Alex.

'Such as?'

'Craig stabbed Danny in the leg, and he's got the scar to prove it.'

'Pearson will blame it on Bernie Wilson.'

'So you are advising me *not* to put Cartwright in the box?'

'Not an easy question to answer, my boy,' his father replied. 'I wasn't in court, so I don't know how the jury responded to Beth Wilson's testimony. Sleep on it and don't decide anything until the morning.'

ALEX ARRIVED at the Old Bailey moments after the night porter had unlocked the front door. Following a consultation with Danny in the cells below, he went to the robing room and changed into his legal garb, then made his way to Court Number Four. Alex entered the empty courtroom, took his seat at the end of the bench and placed three files marked *Cartwright* on the table in front of him. It was 9.35 a.m.

At ten minutes to the hour, Arnold Pearson and his junior strolled in and took their places at the other end of the bench.

Danny Cartwright was next to appear, accompanied by two policemen. He sat on a wooden chair in the centre of the dock.

On the stroke of ten, Mr Justice Sackville entered and called for the jury to be brought in.

Once the jury members were settled, the judge turned to defence counsel. 'Are you ready to call your next witness, Mr Redmayne?'

Alex rose, smiled up at the judge and said, 'My Lord, that concludes the case for the defence.'

Mr Justice Sackville looked across at Pearson, who now resembled a startled rabbit caught in the headlights of an advancing lorry. 'You may begin your closing speech for the Crown,' he told the barrister.

'I wonder, M'lord,' he spluttered, as he stood to address the judge, 'if Your Lordship would allow me a little more time to prepare my closing remarks. May I suggest that we adjourn in order that—'

'No, Mr Pearson,' interrupted the judge, 'I will not adjourn proceedings. It is a defendant's right to choose not to give evidence. The jury and the court officials are all in place, and I need not remind you how crowded the court calendar is. Please proceed with your closing remarks.'

Pearson's junior passed a file across to his leader. The barrister opened it, aware that he had barely glanced at its contents during the past few days. 'Members of the jury . . .' he began. He stumbled from paragraph to paragraph as he read from his script, until even his junior looked exasperated. It was evident that thinking on his feet was not one of Pearsons's strengths. By the time he came to the last page, two hours later, even Alex was dozing off.

When Pearson finally slumped back down, Mr Justice Sackville suggested that this might be a convenient time to take a lunch break.

An hour and a half later, Alex presented his carefully crafted closing argument. He had no way of knowing how his most important points were playing with the jury, but at least he felt he could reply 'yes' should his father ask if he had served his client to the best of his ability.

MR JUSTICE SACKVILLE'S SUMMARY was masterful. He suggested the jury should take seriously the testimony of three witnesses who had stated unequivocally that only Mr Craig had left the bar to go out into the alley, and only after he'd heard a woman scream. Craig had stated on oath that he had seen the defendant stab Wilson several times and that he had then immediately returned to the bar and called the police.

Miss Wilson, on the other hand, claimed that it was Mr Craig who had drawn her companions into a fight, and it was he who must have stabbed Wilson. However, she did not witness the murder, but did say it was her brother who told her what had happened before he died. If they accepted *this* version of events, the judge said, they might ask themselves why Mr Craig contacted the police and, perhaps more importantly, why there was no sign of blood on any of his clothes when DS Fuller interviewed him some twenty minutes later.

'Members of the jury,' Mr Justice Sackville continued, 'there is nothing in Miss Wilson's past to suggest that she is other than an honest and decent citizen. However, you may feel that her evidence is somewhat coloured by her devotion to Cartwright, whom she intends to marry. You must put aside any natural sympathy you might feel because Miss Wilson is pregnant. Your responsibility is to weigh up the evidence and ignore any irrelevant side issues.'

The judge went on to emphasise that Cartwright had no previous criminal record, and that for the past eleven years he had been employed by the same company. He warned the jury not to read too much into the fact that Cartwright had not given evidence. That was the defendant's prerogative, he explained, although, if he had nothing to hide, the jury might find it a puzzling decision.

The judge ended by advising the jury to take their time. After all, a man's future was in the balance. However, they should not forget that another man had lost his life, and if Danny Cartwright had not killed Bernie Wilson, who else could possibly have committed the crime?

At twelve minutes past two, the jury filed out to begin their deliberations.

TWO DAYS LATER, at twelve minutes past three, an announcement came over the tannoy. 'All those involved in the Cartwright case, please make their way back into Court Number Four, as the jury is returning.'

Once the jury was seated, the judge leaned forward and asked the foreman, 'Have you been able to reach a unanimous verdict?'

'No, M'lord,' came back the immediate reply.

'Would it help if I were to consider a majority verdict, and by that I mean one where at least ten of you are in agreement?'

'That might solve the problem, M'lord,' the foreman replied.

'Then I'll ask you to reconvene and see if you can come to a verdict.' The judge nodded to the usher, who led the jury back out of court.

The men and women were back in their places a few minutes later.

'Have you reached a verdict?' the judge asked the foreman.

'We have, M'lord,' he replied.

'And is it a majority of you?'

'Yes, M'lord, a majority of ten to two.'

The judge nodded in the direction of the usher, who bowed. 'Members of the jury,' he said, 'do you find the prisoner at the bar, Daniel Arthur Cartwright, guilty or not guilty of murder?'

'Guilty,' the foreman pronounced.

A gasp went up around the court. In the public gallery there were cries of 'No!' and the sound of sobbing.

Once the courtroom had come to order, the judge delivered a long preamble before passing sentence. The only words that would remain indelibly fixed in Alex's mind were *twenty-two years*.

His father had told him never to allow a verdict to affect him. After all, only one defendant in a hundred was wrongly convicted.

Alex was in no doubt that Danny Cartwright was the one in a hundred.

BOOK TWO: Prison
Chapter 3

'Welcome back, Cartwright.' The officer seated behind the desk in Reception looked down at the charge sheet. 'Twenty-two years,' he said with a sigh. 'I'm sorry, lad.' It was not a sentiment he often expressed.

'Thanks, Mr Jenkins,' Danny said quietly.

'Now you're no longer on remand,' said Jenkins, 'you're not entitled to a single cell any more.' He opened a file, which he studied. 'I'm going to put you in block three, cell number one-two-nine. They should make interesting company,' he added, nodding to an officer standing behind him.

'Follow me, Cartwright,' said the officer.

Danny followed him down a long brick corridor. They came to a halt at a double gate. The officer selected a large key from the chain that hung round his waist, unlocked the first gate and ushered Danny through. He joined him before locking them both in, then unlocked the second gate. This process was repeated four more times before Danny arrived at Block 3. It wasn't hard to see why no one had ever escaped from Belmarsh. Danny's keeper handed him over to the unit officer.

'Right, Cartwright,' said his new minder, 'this is going to be your home for at least the next eight years, so you'd better settle down and get used to it. If you don't give us any trouble, we won't give you any. Understood?'

'Understood, Guv,' repeated Danny, using the title every con gives a screw whose name he doesn't know.

As Danny climbed the iron staircase to the first floor, he didn't come across any other inmates. They were all locked up—as they nearly always were, sometimes for twenty-two hours a day. Outside cell number 129, the unit officer selected another key from yet another ring, this time one heavy enough to open the lock of a two-inch-thick iron door.

Danny stepped inside and the heavy door slammed shut behind him. He looked suspiciously at the two cons who already occupied the cell. A large, overweight man was lying half asleep on a single bed, facing the wall. He didn't even glance up at the new arrival. The other man was seated at a small table, writing. He put down his pen, rose from his place and thrust out a hand, which took Danny by surprise.

'Nick Moncrieff,' he said, sounding more like an officer than an inmate. 'Welcome to your new abode,' he added with a smile.

'Danny Cartwright,' Danny replied, shaking his hand. He looked across at the unoccupied bunk.

'As you're last in, you get the top bunk,' said Moncrieff. 'You'll get the bottom one in two years' time. By the way,' he said pointing to the giant who lay on the other bed, 'that's Big Al.' Danny's other cellmate grunted, but didn't bother to turn round to find out who'd joined them. 'Big Al doesn't say a lot, but once you get to know him, he's just fine.'

Danny heard the key turning in the lock once again, and the heavy door was pulled open.

'Follow me, Cartwright,' said a voice. Danny stepped back out of the cell and followed another officer he'd never seen before. The screw led him back down the iron staircase, along another corridor, and through a further set of double gates before coming to a halt outside a set of doors marked STORES. The officer gave a firm rap on them, and a moment later they were pulled open from the inside.

'CK4802 Cartwright,' said the officer, checking his charge sheet.

'Strip off,' said the stores manager. 'You won't be wearing any of those clothes again'—he looked down at the charge sheet—'until 2022.'

Once Danny had stripped, he was handed two pairs of boxer shorts (red and white stripes), two shirts (blue and white stripes), one pair of jeans (blue), two T-shirts (white), one pullover (grey), one donkey jacket (black), two pairs of socks (grey), one pair of shorts (blue gym), two singlets (white gym), two sheets (nylon, green), one blanket (grey), one pillow case (green) and one pillow (circular, solid). The only items he was allowed to keep were his trainers.

The stores manager gathered up all of Danny's clothes and dropped them into a large plastic bag, which he sealed, filling in the name *Cartwright CK4802* on a little tag. He then handed Danny a smaller plastic bag, which contained a bar of soap, a toothbrush, a plastic disposable razor, one flannel (green), one hand towel (green), one plastic plate (grey), one plastic knife, one plastic fork and one plastic spoon. He ticked several boxes on a green form before swivelling it round for Danny to sign.

'You report back to the stores every Thursday afternoon between three and five,' said the stores manager, 'when you'll be given a change of clothes.' He slammed the doors closed.

Danny picked up the two plastic bags and followed the officer back down the corridor to his cell, where he was locked up moments later. Big Al didn't seem to have stirred in his absence and Nick was still seated at the table, writing.

Danny decided to make his bed. He took his time, as he was beginning to discover just how many hours there are in each day, how many minutes in each hour, and how many seconds in each minute when you're locked up in a cell twelve foot by eight, with two strangers to share your space.

Once he'd made the bed, Danny climbed back onto it and stared up at the white ceiling. One of the few advantages of being on the top bunk was that his head was opposite the tiny barred window. As Danny looked through the iron bars to the exercise yard below, his thoughts turned to Beth. He hadn't even been allowed to say goodbye to her.

Next week, and for the next thousand weeks, he'd be locked up in this hellhole. His only chance of escape was an appeal. Mr Redmayne had warned him that that might not be heard for at least a year. Surely a year would be more than enough time for the lawyer to gather the evidence he needed to prove that Danny was innocent?

A KLAXON PROCLAIMED that the forty-five minutes set aside for 'Association'—a stroll round the perimeter yard, a game of dominoes, or just slumping in front of the television on the ground floor—was over. The prisoners were herded back into their cells, block by block.

Big Al was already slumbering on his bunk by the time Danny walked back into the cell. Nick followed a moment later, the door slamming behind him. It wouldn't be opened again until tea—another four hours.

Nick returned to the plastic chair behind the Formica table. He was just about to start writing again, when Danny asked, 'What are you scribblin'?'

'I keep a diary,' replied Nick, 'of everything that goes on in this place.'

'Why would you want to be reminded of this dump?'

'It whiles away the time. And as I want to be a teacher when I'm released, it's important to keep my mind alert.'

'Will they let you teach after you've done a stretch in this place?'

'You must have read about the teacher shortage?' said Nick.

'I don't read a lot,' admitted Danny.

'Perhaps this is a good chance to start,' said Nick, putting his pen down.

'Can't see the point,' said Danny, 'if I'm banged up in 'ere.'

'But you'd be able to read your solicitor's letters, which would give you a better chance of preparing your defence when the appeal comes up.'

'Are you two ever goin' to stop talkin'?' asked Big Al in a Glaswegian accent.

'Not much else to do,' replied Nick with a laugh.

Big Al sat up and removed a pouch of tobacco from a pocket in his jeans. 'So wha' you in for, Cartwright?' he asked.

'Murder,' said Danny. He paused. 'But I was stitched up.'

'That's wha' they all say.' Big Al took out a packet of cigarette papers from his other pocket, extracted one and laid tobacco on top of it.

'Maybe,' said Danny, 'but I still didn't do it. What about you?'

'Me, I'm a bank robber,' said Big Al, licking the edge of the paper.

'So how long have you been banged up in Belmarsh?'

'Two years. They transferred me to an open prison for a while, but I tried to abscond. So they won't be takin' tha' risk again. Got a light?'

'I don't smoke,' said Danny.

'No' you as well. Whit a pair of muppets. Now I won't be able to have a smoke till after tea.'

'So you'll never be moved out of Belmarsh?' asked Danny in disbelief.

'No' until my release date,' said Big Al. 'Once you've absconded from a cat D, they send you back to a high-security nick.' He placed the cigarette in his mouth. 'Still, I've only go' another three years to go,' he said as he lay back down and turned to face the wall.

'What about you?' Danny asked Nick. 'How much longer have you got?'

'Two years, four months and eleven days. And you?'

'Twenty-two years,' said Danny. 'Unless I win my appeal.'

'Nobody wins their appeal,' said Big Al. 'So you'd better get used to it.'

'TEA!' HOLLERED A VOICE as the door was unlocked for the second time that day. Danny picked up his plate and mug and followed a stream of prisoners as they made their way downstairs to join the queue for the hot plate.

Standing behind the counter were five prisoners dressed in white overalls and white hats. 'What is it tonight?' asked Nick, handing over his plate.

'You can 'ave sausages with beans, beef with beans or spam fritters with beans, squire,' said one of the inmates serving behind the counter.

'I'll have spam fritters without beans, thank you,' said Nick.

'I'll 'ave the same, but with beans,' said Danny.

'And who are you?' asked the server. 'His bleedin' brother?'

Danny and Nick both laughed. Although they were the same height, around the same age and didn't look unalike in prison uniform, neither of them had noticed the similarity. After all, Nick was always clean-shaven with every hair neatly in place, while Danny only shaved once a week and his hair, in Big Al's words, 'looked like a bog brush'.

'How do you get a job workin' in the kitchen?' asked Danny as they made their way slowly back up the spiral staircase to the first floor.

'You have to be enhanced.'

'And how do you get *enhanced*?'

'Just make sure you're never put on report,' said Nick. 'In about a year's time you'll be enhanced, but you still won't get a job in the kitchen.'

'Why not?'

'Because there are a thousand other cons in this prison,' said Big Al, 'and nine hundred of 'em want to work in the kitchen—logic, right? You're out of your cell for most of the day, and you get the best choice of grub. So you can forget it, Danny Boy.'

'What other jobs are goin'?' asked Danny.

'You could get a job in the stores,' said Nick, 'or become a cleaner or a gardener but most likely you'll end up on the chain gang.'

'The chain gang?' Danny said. 'What's that?'

'You'll find out soon enough,' replied Nick.

'So what job 'ave you got?' asked Danny.

'You ask too many questions,' replied Big Al.

'Big Al is the hospital orderly,' said Nick.

'That sounds like a cushy number,' said Danny.

'I have to polish the floors, empty the bins, and make tea for every screw tha' visits matron. I never stop movin',' said Big Al.

'Very responsible job that,' said Nick. 'You have to have an unblemished record when it comes to drugs, and Big Al doesn't approve of junkies.'

'Is there any other job worth considerin'?' asked Danny desperately.

'Education,' said Nick. 'If you decided to join me, you could improve your reading and writing. And you'd get paid for it.'

'True, but only eight quid a week,' chipped in Big Al. 'You get twelve for every other job. No' many of us can turn our noses up at an extra four quid a week baccy money like the Squire here.'

A KEY TURNED in the lock and the heavy iron door was pulled open.

'Cartwright, you're on the chain gang. Report to the duty officer.'

'But—' began Danny.

'Stick with me,' said Nick, as the officer left. 'I'll show you the drill.'

Nick and Danny joined a stream of silent prisoners. When they reached the end of the corridor, Nick said, 'This is where we part company. I'm off to Education. The chain gang is in the opposite direction.'

Danny nodded and followed a group of prisoners to the end of a corridor, where an officer carrying a clipboard ushered all of them into a large, rectangular room. Inside were six Formica tables, with about twenty plastic chairs lined up on each side. Danny found a vacant seat.

'Liam,' announced the man seated on his left.

'Danny.'

Brown plastic buckets were placed in front of each seated prisoner by inmates with yellow armbands. Danny's bucket was full of tea bags. Liam's contained sachets of butter. There was a stack of plastic bags at one end of each table and they were passed along from prisoner to prisoner so that a packet of Rice Crispies, a sachet of butter, a tea bag, and tiny containers of salt, pepper and jam were dropped into each one. At the end of the table, another prisoner stacked them.

'They'll be sent off to another prison,' Liam explained, 'and end up as some con's breakfast about this time next week.'

Danny was bored within a few minutes, and would have been suicidal by the end of the morning, if Liam hadn't provided an endless commentary on everything from how to get yourself enhanced to how to end up in solitary.

'Don't look up,' whispered Liam as a fresh bucket of tea bags was placed in front of Danny. Liam waited until the prisoner wearing a yellow armband had removed their empty buckets before he added, 'If you ever come across that bastard, make yourself scarce.'

'Why?' asked Danny, glancing across to see a thin-faced man with a shaven head and tattooed arms leave the room carrying the stack of buckets.

'His name's Kevin Leach,' said Liam. 'He's trouble—big trouble.'

'What kind of trouble?' asked Danny.

'He caught his wife in bed with his best mate. After he'd knocked them both out, he tied 'em to the bedposts. When they came round, he stabbed 'em with a kitchen knife—once every ten minutes, starting at their ankles, and ending up at the heart. He's a nutter. He won't see the outside of this place until they carry him out feet first.' Liam paused. 'So be careful. They can't add another day to his sentence and he doesn't care who he cuts up.'

'YOU NEED A HERRCUT,' said Big Al. 'Book yourself in with Louis.'

'And who's Louis?' asked Danny.

'Prison barber,' said Big Al. 'He gets through about five cons in forty minutes durin' Association, but he's so popular you might have to wait for a month before he can do you. As you're no' going anywhere soon, tha' shouldn't be a problem. But if you want to jump the queue, he charges three fags for a bullet head, five for a short back and sides. And the Squire,' he said, pointing to Nick, 'has to hand over ten fags on account of him still wishin' to look like an officer and a gentleman.'

'A short back and sides will suit me just fine,' said Danny. 'But what does he use? I don't fancy having my hair cut with a plastic knife and fork.'

Nick put down his book. 'Louis has all the usual equipment—scissors, clippers, even a razor.'

'How does he get away with that?' asked Danny.

'He doesn't,' said Big Al. 'A screw hands over the stuff at the beginning of Association then collects it before we go back to our cells.'

'Is this Louis any good?' asked Danny.

'Before he ended up in here,' said Big Al, 'he used to work in Mayfair, chargin' the likes of the Squire fifty quid a head. That was before he was caught with his trousers down on Hampstead Heath.'

'TWO LETTERS FOR YOU, Cartwright,' the unit officer said as he passed a couple of envelopes across to Danny.

The smaller of the two envelopes was handwritten, so Danny assumed it was from Beth. The second letter was typed. He lay silently on his bunk considering the problem for some time before he finally gave in.

'Nick, can you read my letters to me?' he asked quietly.

'I can and I will,' replied Nick.

Danny passed across the two letters. Nick unfolded the handwritten letter first, and checked the signature. 'This one's from Beth,' he said.

'Dear Danny,

It's only been a week, but I already miss you so much. How could the jury have made such a terrible mistake? Why didn't they believe me, when I was there and saw everything? I will come and visit you next Sunday afternoon. Your mum and dad are both well and send their love, and so does my mother. I'm sure Dad will come round given time, especially after you win the appeal. I miss you so much. I love you, I love you, I love you.

See you on Sunday, Beth.'

Nick unfolded the second letter. 'It's from an Alex Redmayne,' he said.

'Dear Danny,

Just a line to bring you up to date on your appeal. I have completed all the necessary applications and today received a letter from the Lord Chancellor's Office confirming that your name has been entered on the list. However, I must warn you that the process could take anything up to two years. I am still following up all leads in the hope that they might produce some fresh evidence, and will write again when I have something more tangible to report.

Yours sincerely, Alex Redmayne.'

Nick put the letters back in their envelopes and returned them to Danny. He picked up his pen and said, 'Would you like me to reply to them?'

'No,' said Danny firmly. 'I'd like you to teach me to read and write.'

SPENCER CRAIG WAS beginning to think it had been unwise to choose the Dunlop Arms for the Musketeers' monthly get-together. He had persuaded his fellow members that it would show that they had nothing to hide, but was already regretting his decision.

He wasn't surprised that Toby Mortimer hadn't shown up—he was probably lying in a gutter somewhere with a needle sticking out of his arm—and Lawrence Davenport had made some lame excuse for not attending, claiming he had to be at an awards ceremony. At least Gerald Payne had made an appearance. Craig emptied the remainder of the Chablis into Payne's glass. 'Another bottle, barman,' he said.

'The '95, Mr Craig?'

'Of course. Nothing but the best for my friend.'

'No need to waste your money on me, old fellow,' said Payne.

Craig didn't tell him that it hardly mattered what was in the bottle, because the barman had already decided exactly how much he was going to charge Craig for 'keeping shtum', as he put it.

BIG AL'S SNORING sounded like a cross between an elephant drinking and a foghorn. Nick managed to sleep through rap music emanating from nearby cells, but he still hadn't come to terms with Big Al's snoring.

He lay awake and thought about Danny's decision to give up the chain gang and join him at Education. While Danny may not have had much of a formal education, he was brighter than anyone Nick had taught in the past two years. He was always asking questions, rarely satisfied with the answers. And although he may not have been literate, he was clearly numerate, and had a grasp of figures that Nick knew he would never equal.

'Are you awake?' asked Danny, breaking into Nick's thoughts.

'Big Al's probably preventing anyone in the next three cells from sleeping,' Nick replied.

'I was just thinking that since I signed up for Education, I've told you a lot about me, but I still know almost nothin' about you.'

'I've told you a lot about *myself*, while I know almost *nothing* about you,' Nick corrected. 'What do you want to know?'

'For a start, how did someone like you end up in prison?'

'I was court-martialled while my regiment was serving with the NATO forces in Kosovo. My platoon was ordered to protect a group of Serbs who had been charged with ethnic cleansing. A band of Albanian guerrillas drove past the compound firing their Kalashnikovs into the air, to celebrate the Serbs' capture. When a car full of them came dangerously close to the compound, I warned their leader to stop firing. He ignored me, so my staff sergeant fired a few warning shots, which resulted in two of them ending up with gunshot wounds. Later, one of them died in hospital.'

'And you got eight years for that?'

'I was the officer in charge.'

'How come you don't get any letters?'

'I've made no attempt to stay in contact with my family since the court-martial, and they've made no effort to get in touch with me.'

'Even your mum and dad?' said Danny.

'My mother died giving birth to me.'

'I'm sorry. Is your father still alive?'

'As far as I know, yes, but he was colonel of the same regiment I served in. He hasn't spoken to me since the court-martial.'

'That's a bit rough.'

'Not really. The regiment is his whole life. I was meant to follow in his footsteps and end up as commanding officer, not be court-martialled.'

'Any brothers or sisters?'

'No.'

'Aunts and uncles?'

'One uncle who lives in Scotland, and an aunt in Canada.'

'No other relations?'

'*Relatives.* Relations has a double meaning. No. The only person I've ever really cared for was my grandfather, but he died while I was in Kosovo.'

'And was your grandfather an officer too?'

'No,' said Nick laughing. 'He was a pirate. He sold armaments to the Americans during the Second World War, made a fortune—enough to retire on, buy a large estate in Scotland and set himself up as a laird.'

'A laird?'

'Clan leader, master of all he surveys.'

'Does that mean you're rich?'

'Unfortunately not. My father managed to squander his inheritance while he was colonel of the regiment—"keeping up appearances".'

'What's hanging from the chain round your neck?' asked Danny.

At that moment Big Al woke with a start, grunted, climbed out of bed and plonked himself on the lavatory. Once he'd pulled the flush, Danny and Nick tried to get to sleep before he started snoring again.

DR BERESFORD KILLED IN CAR ACCIDENT read the headline on the front page of the *Mail on Sunday*. The article went on to tell its readers that Lawrence Davenport's star was on the wane, and the producers of *The Prescription* had decided to write him out of the script . . . The phone rang in Spencer

Craig's study. He wasn't surprised to find it was Gerald Payne on the line.

'Have you seen the papers?' Payne asked.

'Yes,' said Craig. 'The show's ratings have been going south for the past year, so they're looking for some gimmick to give them a boost.'

'But if they ditch Larry,' said Payne, 'he's not going to find it that easy to get another part. We certainly don't want him going back on the bottle.'

'I don't think we should be discussing this over the phone, Gerald. Let's meet up soon.' Craig opened his diary, in which several days were blank. He didn't seem to be getting quite as many briefs as he had in the past.

SEVEN LINES OF TABLES were set out in rows, marked A to G. The prisoners had to sit on one side on red chairs that were bolted to the floor. Their visitors sat on the other side on green chairs, also bolted to the floor, making it easier for the staff to carry out surveillance. Danny walked down the rows until he came to row E. At last he saw her, sitting on a green chair. Despite having Beth's photo up on his wall, he had forgotten quite how beautiful she was. She was carrying a parcel.

Danny quickened his pace. He threw his arms round her and the parcel let out a cry. Danny stepped back to see Christy for the first time.

'She's beautiful,' he said taking his daughter in his arms. He looked at Beth. 'I'm going to get out of here before she ever finds out her father was in jail.'

He sat down on the red chair and began to tell Beth about his cellmates as he tucked into the two Mars bars and two cans of Diet Coke that Beth had purchased for him from the canteen, aware that he wouldn't be allowed to take them back to his cell once the visit was over.

'Nick is teachin' me to read and write,' he told her. 'And Big Al is showin' me how to survive in prison. What's happenin' back in Bacon Road?'

'Some of the locals are collecting signatures for a petition to have you released, and *DANNY CARTWRIGHT IS INNOCENT* has been sprayed on the wall outside Bow Road tube station.'

Danny listened to Beth's news until a voice announced over the tannoy, 'All visitors must now leave.'

Danny wondered where the shortest hour in his life had gone, as he rose slowly from his seat and took Beth in his arms, kissing her gently.

'Goodbye, my darling,' she said when he eventually released her.

'Goodbye,' said Danny, who watched as Beth walked away, carrying his daughter. His eyes never left them until they had disappeared out of sight.

'SHORT BACK AND SIDES?' asked Louis as the next customer took his place in the barber's chair.

'No,' whispered Danny. 'I want you to make my hair look more like your last customer's.'

'It'll cost you,' said Louis.

'How much?'

'Same as Nick, ten a month.'

Danny removed an unopened packet of Marlboros from his jeans.

'First thing you'll have to do is let your hair grow,' Louis said. 'And cut your sideboards a lot higher, because Nick's don't fall much below the top of his ears. And his hair's a shade lighter than yours, but nothing a little lemon juice won't take care of.'

'OK. Book me in for the first Monday of every month,' said Danny. 'My appeal comes up in July and my lawyer seems to think that it matters how you look when you're in the dock.'

Chapter 4

Minutes turned into hours, hours became days, days ended up being weeks in the longest year of Danny's life. Though, as Beth regularly reminded him, it hadn't been entirely wasted. In a couple of months' time Danny would take six GCSEs, and his mentor seemed confident that he would pass them all with flying colours.

Beth and Christy visited Danny on the first Sunday of every month, and lately she could talk of little other than his upcoming appeal. Mr Redmayne was still searching for fresh evidence, because without it, he admitted, they didn't stand much chance.

Danny tried to concentrate on the essay he was writing on *The Count of Monte Cristo*—his GCSE set text. Perhaps, like Edmond Dantès, he would escape. But you can't build a tunnel when your cell is on the first floor, and he couldn't throw himself into the sea because Belmarsh wasn't on an island. So, unlike Dantès, unless he won his appeal he had little hope of gaining revenge on his four enemies. After Nick had read his last essay, he had given Danny a mark of 73 per cent, with the comment: *Unlike Edmond Dantès, you won't need to escape, because they'll have to release you.*

How well the two of them had come to know each other during the past year. In truth they had spent more hours together than he and Bernie had ever done. Some of the new prisoners even assumed they were brothers—until Danny opened his mouth. That was going to take a little longer.

Danny looked up from his essay when he heard the key turning in the lock. Mr Pascoe pulled the door open to allow Big Al to stroll in.

'Got some news for you, Danny Boy,' said Big Al, once the door had been slammed shut. 'Ever come across a bastard called Mortimer?'

Danny's heart began to race. 'Yes,' he eventually managed. 'He was in the bar the night Bernie was murdered, but he never showed up in court.'

'Well, he's showed up here, hasn't he?' said Big Al. 'He reported to the hospital this afternoon. Needed some medication, if you know whit I mean. Checked his file. Possession of a class-A drug. Two years. I've got a feelin' he's gonnae be a regular visitor to the hospital, and it's just possible he might be able to supply tha' new evidence your lawyer has been lookin' for.'

'SO, WHAT CAN I DO for you, Mr Craig?'

'I believe you'll find it's what I can do for you.'

'I don't think so, Mr Craig. I've been banged up in this shit-hole for eight years and during that time I haven't heard a dickybird out of you. You know I couldn't afford even an hour of your time, so why don't you just come to the point and tell me what you're doin' here?'

Spencer Craig had carefully checked the interview room for any bugs before Kevin Leach, the shaven-headed prisoner Liam had warned Danny about, joined him for a 'legal visit'. He knew he was taking a risk—but the prospect of a long spell in prison was an even less attractive proposition.

'Got everything you need, have you?' asked Craig.

'I get by,' said Leach. 'Don't need a lot.'

'But no one is sending you in any little extras,' said Craig. 'And you haven't had a visit for over four years. In fact you haven't even made a phone call during the past two years—not since your Aunt Maisie died.'

'Well-informed as ever. Where's all this leading, Mr Craig?'

'Aunt Maisie might have left you something in her will.'

'Now why would she bother to do that?'

'Because she's got a friend whom you're in a position to help. Her friend has a problem—a craving, not to put too fine a point on it.'

'Let me guess. Heroin, crack or cocaine?'

'Right first time,' said Craig. 'And he's in need of a regular supply.'

'And how much has Aunt Maisie left me to cover this considerable outlay, not to mention the risk of being caught?'

'She hoped that fifty pounds a week would be enough to make sure her friend wouldn't need to look elsewhere.'

'Tell her if she makes it a hundred, I might just think about it.'

'I think I can say on her behalf that she accepts your terms.'

'So what's the name of Aunt Maisie's friend?'

'Toby Mortimer.'

'ALWAYS FROM THE OUTSIDE IN,' said Nick. 'It's a simple rule to follow.'

Danny picked up the plastic spoon and began to scoop up the water that Nick had poured into his breakfast bowl.

'No,' said Nick. 'You always tilt a soup bowl away from you, and push the spoon in the same direction.' He demonstrated, then removed the bowl and replaced it with a plastic plate on which he had put a thick slice of bread and a helping of baked beans. 'Now, I want you to think of the bread as a lamb chop, and the baked beans as peas.' He picked up the knife and fork on his side of the table and demonstrated how Danny should hold them. 'And I want you to eat the piece of bread as if it were a lamb chop.'

'How would you like it, sir?' grunted Big Al. 'Medium or rare?'

'You will only be asked that if you order a steak,' said Nick.

Danny dug into his slice of bread. 'No,' said Nick. 'Cut your meat, don't tear it apart, and only a small piece at a time.' Danny carried out his instructions, but once he had swallowed the piece of bread, he scooped up some beans on the end of his fork. 'No, no, no,' said Nick. 'A fork isn't a shovel. Just pierce a few peas at a time.'

'But it'll take for ever if I carry on this way,' said Danny.

'And don't speak with your mouth full,' replied Nick.

It was some time before Danny was able to finish his meagre meal.

'Place your knife and fork together, so your waiter knows you've finished.'

'I don't eat in restaurants that often,' admitted Danny.

'Then I shall have to be the first person to invite you and Beth out for a meal as soon as you've been released. Now, tomorrow I'll show you how to taste wine after the waiter has poured a small amount into your glass . . .'

'And the day after tha',' said Big Al, his word accompanied by a long fart, 'I shall allow you to sip a sample of my piss, a rare vintage which will remind you tha' you're in prison and no' in the bloody Ritz.'

'IT'S NOT WHA' I'D CALL a coincidence,' said Big Al, one morning a few days later. He was glad to have a private word with Nick while their cell-mate was taking a shower. 'Leach ends up in Segregation and the next morning Mortimer's back, desperate to see the doctor.'

Nick stopped writing. '*Not* a coincidence? You think Leach was his supplier?'

'Mortimer's got the shakes. Tha' always happens when you start a detox programme. Anyway, we'll soon find out if Leach is involved.'

'How?' asked Nick.

'He gets out of solitary in a couple of weeks. Got banged up there for supplyin' when they realised he didnae have an Aunt Maisie providing his monthly income. If Mortimer stops turnin' up for treatment the moment Leach gets out, we'll know for sure.'

'So we've only got another fortnight to gather the evidence we need from Mortimer,' said Nick. 'You have to borrow Danny's tape recorder and set up an interview as soon as possible.'

'Yes, sir,' said Big Al, standing to attention by the side of his bed. 'Do I tell Danny about this, or keep my mouth shut?'

'You tell him everything, so he can pass on the information to his barrister. In any case, three brains are better than two.'

'Just how bright is he?' asked Big Al as he sat back down on his bunk.

'Far brighter than me,' admitted Nick. 'But don't tell him I said so, because with a bit of luck I'll be out of this place before he works it out for himself.'

'LETTERS,' SAID THE OFFICER. 'Two for Cartwright, one for Moncrieff.' He passed the single letter to Danny, who checked the name on the envelope.

'No, I'm Cartwright,' said Danny. 'He's Moncrieff.'

The officer frowned at his mistake, and handed the single letter to Nick and the other two to Danny.

'And I'm Big Al,' said Big Al.

'Fuck off,' said the officer, slamming the door behind him.

Danny began to laugh, but then looked at Nick and saw that he had turned ashen grey. He couldn't remember when Nick had last received a letter. 'Do you want me to read it first?' he asked.

Nick shook his head, and continued reading. As he read, his eyes began to water. He passed the letter to Danny, who saw that it was from a solicitor.

Dear Sir Nicholas,

I am sorry to have to inform you that your father has passed away. He died from a heart attack yesterday morning, but the doctor assures me that he suffered little or no pain. I will make an application for compassionate leave in order that you may attend the funeral.

Yours sincerely,

Fraser Munro

'CAN YOU TAKE CARE of this while I'm away?' asked Nick, unfastening the silver chain from around his neck and handing it to Danny.

'Sure,' said Danny, as he studied what looked like a key attached to the chain. 'But why not take it with you?'

'Let's just say I trust you more than most of the people I'm going to meet up with later today,' said Nick, without further explanation.

'I'm flattered,' said Danny, putting the chain round his neck.

They heard a key turning in the lock. It was the first time they had ever seen Mr Pascoe and Mr Jenkins dressed in civilian clothes.

'Follow me, Moncrieff,' said Mr Pascoe. 'The governor wants a word with you before we set off for Edinburgh.'

'Do give him my best wishes,' said Danny, 'and ask him if he'd like to pop in for afternoon tea some time.'

Nick laughed at Danny's imitation of his accent. 'If you think you can pass yourself off as me, why don't you try taking my class this morning? After all, we've got to put all those GCSEs you passed with flying colours to some use.'

LAWRENCE DAVENPORT'S PHONE was ringing, but it was some time before he emerged from under the sheets to get it. 'Who the hell is this?' he mumbled.

'Gibson,' announced the familiar voice of his agent.

Davenport was suddenly awake. Gibson Graham only rang when it meant work. Davenport prayed it would be a film or another television role.

'I've had an availability enquiry,' said Gibson. 'It's a revival of *The Importance of Being Earnest*, and they want you to play Jack. Four weeks on the road before it opens in the West End. The pay's not great, but it will remind all those producers out there that you're still alive.'

Davenport didn't warm to the idea. He remembered only too well what it was like to spend weeks on the road followed by night after night in the West End. But it was his first serious offer for nearly four months.

'I'll think about it,' he said, and put the phone down. He checked his bedside clock. It was ten past ten. He groaned and slid back under the sheets.

DURING THE MORNING BREAK, Danny took over Nick's duties as the prison librarian. After completing his tasks, he picked up a copy of *The Times* from the newspaper shelf and sat down to read the obituary of Sir Angus Moncrieff Bt, MC, OBE. He read the details of Sir Angus's life from his schooldays at Loretto School through Sandhurst, to his commission with the Cameron Highlanders. After winning the MC in Korea, Sir Angus had gone on to become Colonel of the Regiment in 1994. The final paragraph reported that the title now passed to his only son, Nicholas Alexander Moncrieff.

'See you later, Nick,' said a voice, but the prisoner had already left the library before Danny could correct his mistake.

As Danny played with the key on the end of the silver chain, wishing, like Malvolio in *Twelfth Night*, that he could be someone else, he thought about the mistake his fellow prisoner had made, and wondered if he could get away with it when he came face to face with Nick's class.

Nick's group were already seated at their desks waiting for him when Danny entered the Education Department. Clearly they had not been told that their usual teacher was attending his father's funeral. Danny marched boldly into the room and smiled at the dozen expectant faces.

'Open your books at page nine,' he said, hoping he sounded like Nick.

'I can't find page nine,' said one of the prisoners, as an officer strolled into the room. A puzzled expression appeared on his face.

'Moncrieff?'

Danny looked up.

'I thought you were on compassionate leave?' he said checking his clip-board.

'You're quite right, Mr Roberts,' said Danny. 'Nick's at his father's funeral in Scotland, and he asked me to take over his class this morning.'

'Are you taking the piss, Cartwright?'

'No, Mr Roberts.'

'Then get yourself back to the library before I put you on report.'

NICK'S TRAIN PULLED in to Waverley Station in Edinburgh a few minutes after twelve. A police car was waiting to drive him, Pascoe and Jenkins from Edinburgh to Dunbroath.

The car drew up outside the church fifteen minutes before the service was due to begin. An elderly gentleman, who Nick remembered from his youth, stepped forward as the policeman opened the back door. He wore a black tailcoat, wing collar and a black silk tie and he looked more like an undertaker than a solicitor. He raised his hat and gave a slight bow. Nick shook hands with him and smiled. 'Good afternoon, Mr Munro,' he said.

'Good afternoon, Sir Nicholas,' he replied. 'Welcome home.'

DANNY WANTED TO TELL Nick the good news, but he knew that he wouldn't be back from Scotland until after midnight.

Alex Redmayne had written to confirm that the date of his appeal had been set for May 31st, only two weeks away. Danny would have liked Beth to be the first to learn that Mortimer had made a full confession and that Big Al had recorded every word of it on Danny's tape recorder, but he couldn't risk putting anything in writing. The tape was secreted in his mattress and he would hand it over to Mr Redmayne during his next Legal Visit.

THE CHURCH WARDEN accompanied the new head of the family down the aisle to the front pew on the right-hand side. Mr Pascoe and Mr Jenkins took their places in the row behind. Nick turned to his left, where the rest of the family were seated in the first three rows on the other side of the aisle. During the service not one of them even glanced in his direction; they were all clearly under his uncle Hugo's orders to ignore him.

Once the priest had administered the final blessing, the congregation gathered in the churchyard to witness the burial. Nick noticed a man who must have weighed more than twenty-five stone, and who didn't look at home in Scotland. Nick returned his smile and tried to recall when they had last met. Then he remembered: Washington DC; the opening of an exhibition at the Smithsonian to celebrate his grandfather's eightieth birthday, when his fabled stamp collection had been put on public display. But Nick still couldn't recall the man's name.

After the coffin had been lowered into the grave and the final rites administered, the Moncrieff clan departed, without a single member offering their condolences to the deceased's son and heir. One or two of the locals, whose livelihoods did not depend on his uncle Hugo, walked across and shook hands with Nick, while the senior officer representing the Regiment stood to attention and saluted. Nick raised his hat in acknowledgment.

As he turned to leave the graveside, Nick saw Fraser Munro talking to Mr Jenkins and Mr Pascoe. Mr Munro came over to him. 'They've agreed that you can spend an hour with me to discuss family matters, but they'll not allow you to accompany me back to the office in my car.'

'I understand.' Nick thanked the chaplain then climbed into the back of the police car. Pascoe and Jenkins took their places on either side of him.

As the car moved off, Nick looked out of the window and saw the large man lighting a cigar. 'Hunsacker,' he said to himself. 'Gene Hunsacker.'

'WHY DID YOU WANT to see me?' demanded Craig.

'A little bird tells me that Aunt Maisie's friend has started singing like a canary,' said Leach.

'Then shut him up,' spat out Craig.

'It may be too late for that. I'm told there's a tape.'

Craig stared across the table. 'And what's on this tape?' he asked quietly.

'A full confession . . . with names, dates and places.' Leach paused. 'It was when I was told the names that I felt I ought to consult my lawyer.'

Craig didn't speak for some time. 'Do you think you can get your hands on it?' he asked eventually.

'At a cost.'

'How much?'

'Ten grand.'

'That's a bit steep.'

'Bent screws don't come cheap,' said Leach. 'In any case, I bet Aunt Maisie doesn't have a plan B, so she hasn't got much choice.'

Craig nodded. 'All right. But if it's not in my possession before May the 31st, you won't get paid.'

'YOUR FATHER MADE a will, which this firm executed,' said Mr Munro. 'It was witnessed by a Justice of the Peace, and I have to advise you that, however you feel about its contents, you would be unwise to dispute it.'

'It would not cross my mind to oppose my father's wishes,' said Nick.

'The bulk of your father's estate has been left to his brother, Mr Hugo Moncrieff. He has left nothing to you except the title, which of course was not his to dispose of.'

'Be assured, Mr Munro, this does not come as a surprise.'

'I'm relieved to hear that, Sir Nicholas. However, your grandfather, a shrewd and practical man, made certain provisions in *his* will, of which you are now the sole beneficiary. Your father made an application to have that will rescinded, but the courts rejected his claim.' Munro rummaged around the papers on his desk until he found a yellow parchment. 'Here's what I'm looking for. Your grandfather's will.' He placed a pair of half-moon spectacles on the end of his nose and searched for the relevant clause. '*I leave my estate in Scotland, known as Dunbroathy Hall, as well as my London residence in The Boltons, to my grandson Nicholas Alexander Moncrieff,'* he read. *'My son Angus will be allowed full and free use of both of these properties until his demise, when they will come into the possession of the aforementioned grandson.'* Mr Munro placed the will back on his desk. 'I have to inform you that your father took advantage of the words "full and free use", and borrowed heavily against both properties. In the case of the Dunbroathy estate, he secured a sum of one million pounds, and for The Boltons, a little over a million. In accordance with your father's will, once probate has been agreed, that money will pass to your uncle Hugo.'

'So despite my grandfather's best intentions I end up with nothing.'

'Not necessarily. I believe you have a legitimate case against your uncle to retain the money he procured by this little subterfuge.'

'You may well be right, Mr Munro, but I will not call my father's judgment into question.'

'So be it. I also have to report,' Mr Munro continued, 'that your uncle, Hugo Moncrieff, has offered to take both properties off your hands, and with them the responsibility for both mortgages.'

'Do you represent my uncle Hugo?' Nick asked.

'No, I do not,' said Mr Munro firmly.

'In that case, may I enquire if you would be willing to represent me?'

'I would be proud to continue my association with the Moncrieff family.'

'How would you advise me to proceed?'

Mr Munro gave a slight bow. 'Anticipating that you might seek my counsel, I have on your behalf set in motion a train of enquiries. I am advised that the price of a house in The Boltons is currently around three million pounds. With regard to the Dunbroathy estate, my brother, who is a local councillor, tells me that Hugo Moncrieff recently made enquiries at the town hall as to whether planning permission might be granted for a hotel development on the estate, despite the fact that your grandfather hoped it would be handed over to the National Trust for Scotland.'

'Was your brother able to put a value on the estate?' asked Nick.

'Not officially, but he said that similar properties are currently trading at around three and a half million pounds. However, you must not forget that both properties are encumbered with mortgages that have to be serviced. I am assured, though, that if you were willing to lodge a second charge on both properties you would have no problem in meeting the payments.'

'You have been most solicitous on my behalf,' said Nick. 'Thank you.'

Munro placed several documents on the table. 'I will have to ask you to sign these agreements even though you will not have time to consider them in detail. However, if I am to proceed while you complete . . .' he coughed.

'My sentence,' said Nick.

'Quite so, Sir Nicholas,' said the solicitor, passing him a fountain pen.

'I also have a document of my own that I wish you to witness,' said Nick. He took out several pieces of lined prison paper from an inside pocket and gave them to his solicitor.

NICK WAS SURPRISED to find Danny still awake when the cell door was opened by Mr Pascoe just after midnight. Although he was exhausted, he was pleased to have someone to share his news with, and Danny listened attentively.

'You would have been so much better at handling Munro than I was,' said Nick. 'To begin with, I doubt if you would have allowed my uncle to get away with stealing all that money.' He was about to go into more detail about the meeting with his solicitor when he suddenly stopped and asked, 'What are you looking so pleased about?'

Danny climbed off the bunk, slipped a hand under his pillow and extracted a small cassette tape. He put it in the cassette player Beth had sent in on his birthday, and pressed PLAY.

The tape ran through the events surrounding the murder, then Mortimer's voice added, 'That was a year and a half ago, and not a day goes by when I don't think about that lad. I've warned Spencer that as soon as I'm fit enough to give evidence . . .' The tape stopped.

'Well done!' exclaimed Nick, but Big Al only grunted. He had stuck to the script Danny had written for him, which covered all the points Mr Redmayne needed for the appeal.

'I still have to get the tape to Mr Redmayne somehow,' said Danny as he removed it from the cassette player and tucked it under his pillow.

'That shouldn't prove too difficult,' said Nick. 'Send it in a sealed envelope marked LEGAL. No officer would dare to open it unless he was convinced the lawyer was dealing in money or drugs directly with an inmate, and no barrister would be stupid enough to take that sort of risk.'

'Unless tha' inmate had a screw working on the inside,' said Big Al, 'who just happened to find out about the tape.'

'But that's not possible,' said Danny, 'not while we're the only three who know about it.'

'Don't forget Mortimer,' said Big Al, finally deciding it was time to sit up. 'And he's no' capable of keeping his mouth shut, especially when he needs a fix.'

'So, what should I do with the tape?' said Danny. 'Because I have no chance of winning my appeal without it.'

'Don't send it by post,' said Big Al. 'Make an appointment to see Redmayne, then hand it over to him in person. 'Cause who d'you think just happened to have a meeting with *his* lawyer yesterday?'

Nick and Danny didn't speak as they waited for Big Al to answer his own question. 'Tha' bastard Leach,' he said.

'That could just be a coincidence,' said Nick.

'No' when tha' lawyer is Spencer Craig.'

NEXT DAY, they all heard the key turning in the lock, which took them by surprise, as there was still another hour before Association.

When the cell door was pulled open, Mr Hagen was standing in the doorway. 'Cell search,' he said. 'You three, in the corridor.'

Nick, Danny and Big Al made their way onto the landing and were even more surprised when Hagen marched into their cell and pulled the door closed behind him. The surprise was not that a screw was carrying out a pad search. They were common enough—officers were always on the lookout for drugs, drink, knives and even guns—but usually there were three officers present, so that prisoners couldn't claim something had been planted.

A few moments later the door swung open and Hagen reappeared, unable to hide the grin on his face. 'OK, lads,' he said, 'you're clean.'

'BANG UP! Everyone back in your cells immediately!' bellowed a voice. Whistles were blowing, klaxons were blaring and officers appeared from every corridor and herded any stray prisoners back into their cells.

'But I have to report to Education,' protested Danny as the cell door was slammed in his face.

'Not today, Danny Boy,' came the answer.

It was twenty-seven hours before he, Nick and Al heard a key turning in the lock.

'What was that about?' Nick asked the officer who opened their cell door.

'No idea,' came back the regulation response.

'Some poor bastard's topped himself,' said a voice from the next cell.

'Anyone we know?' asked another.

'A druggie,' said a third voice, 'only been with us for a few weeks.'

GERALD PAYNE ASKED the man at the porter's lodge in the Inner Temple to direct him to Mr Spencer Craig's chambers. He had left his office in Mayfair as soon as Craig had phoned saying, 'If you come to my chambers around four, you won't be suffering any more sleepless nights.'

'Mr Payne?' asked a young woman, who introduced herself as Craig's secretary. 'He's just phoned to say that he's left the Old Bailey and should be with you in a few minutes. Perhaps you'd care to wait in his office?'

'Thank you,' said Payne as she ushered him into a large room.

She closed the door behind her, and Payne sat down facing Craig's desk; it was almost bare, just a large blotting pad, a tape recorder and a bulky, unopened envelope addressed to Mr S. Craig and marked *Private*.

A few minutes later, Craig came bursting into the room.

'Is that what I think it is?' asked Payne, pointing to the envelope.

'We're about to find out,' said Craig. 'It arrived in the morning post while I was in court.' He ripped open the envelope from Belmarsh and tipped its contents—a small cassette tape—onto the blotting pad.

'How did you get hold of it?' asked Payne.

'Better not to ask,' said Craig. 'Let's just say I've got friends in low places.' He smiled, picked up the tape and slotted it in the cassette player. 'We are about to find out what Toby Mortimer was so keen to share with the rest of the world,' he said as he pressed the PLAY button.

'I can't be sure which one of you will be listening to this tape,' said a voice Craig didn't recognise. 'It could be Lawrence Davenport—but that seems unlikely. Gerald Payne is a possibility. But I suspect it's most likely to be Spencer Craig. Whichever of you it is, I want to leave you in no doubt that if it takes me the rest of my life, I'm going to make sure that all three of you end up in jail for the murder of Bernie Wilson. And let me assure you that you'll never find the tape you were hoping for. It is somewhere you'll never find it, until you're locked up in here.'

IT WAS MAY 31. Danny took his place in the dock and waited for the three judges to appear. He had been driven out of Belmarsh at 7 a.m. in a prison van. On arrival at the Royal Courts he'd been locked in a cell and told to wait. It gave him time to think. Not that he would be allowed to say anything in court. Alex Redmayne had explained to him that an appeal was very different from a trial.

Danny looked up to where Beth and her mother were seated in the front row of a gallery that was packed with the good citizens of Bow, all of whom were in no doubt that he would be released later that day.

At ten o'clock, the three judges considering the appeal trooped into the courtroom. The court officials rose, bowed to Their Lordships and then waited for them to take their places on the bench.

Once the court had settled, the senior judge, Lord Justice Browne, invited Alex to begin his summation.

Alex steadied himself. 'My Lords, I am in possession of a tape recording that I should like you to consider. It is a conversation with Toby Mortimer, who was unable to give evidence at the original trial as he was indisposed.' Alex picked up the tape and placed it in a cassette player on the table in front of him. He was about to press the PLAY button, when Lord Justice Browne leaned forward and said, 'One moment please, Mr Redmayne.'

The three judges whispered among themselves, then Lord Justice Browne asked, 'Will Mr Mortimer be appearing as a witness?'

'No, M'lord, but the tape will show—'

'Why will he not be appearing before us, Mr Redmayne?'

'Unfortunately, M'lord, he died quite recently.'

'May I enquire what was the cause of death?'

'He committed suicide, M'lord, after taking an overdose of heroin.'

'Was he a registered heroin addict?' continued Lord Justice Browne.

'Yes M'lord, but this recording was made during a period of remission.'

'No doubt a doctor will appear before us to confirm this?'

'Unfortunately not, M'lord.'

'Am I to understand that a doctor was not present when the tape recording was made?'

'Yes, M'lord.'

'I see. And were you present at the time?'

'No, M'lord.'

'Then I am curious to know, Mr Redmayne, exactly who was present.'

'A Mr Albert Crann, more familiarly known as "Big Al".'

'What was his position at the time?'

'He is a prisoner of Belmarsh Prison.'

'Is he indeed? I am bound to ask, Mr Redmayne, if you have any proof that this recording was made without Mr Mortimer being coerced or threatened.'

'No, M'lord. But I'm confident you will be able to make a judgment concerning Mr Mortimer's state of mind once you have listened to the tape.'

'Allow me a moment to consult with my brethren, Mr Redmayne.'

Once again the three judges whispered among themselves.

Lord Justice Browne turned back to defence counsel. 'Mr Redmayne, we are of the opinion that we cannot allow you to play the tape, as it is clearly inadmissible. Let me warn you, if the contents of this tape were ever to become public, I would be obliged to refer the matter to the CPS.'

Alex cursed himself under his breath. He should have released the tape to the press the day before the appeal was due to be heard, and then the judge would have had no choice but to consider the conversation to be admissible as fresh evidence.

The three judges retired and it was only a short time before they returned with a unanimous verdict. Alex lowered his head when Lord Justice Browne uttered the words, 'Appeal dismissed.'

Danny had just been condemned to spend the next twenty years of his life in jail for a crime Alex was certain he had not committed.

Chapter 5

By the time they reached his cell, the damage had been done. The table had been smashed to pieces, the sheets ripped to shreds and the little steel mirror wrenched from the wall. As Mr Hagen heaved open the door, he found Danny trying to pull the washbasin from its stand. Three officers came charging towards him and he took a swing at Hagen, who ducked the punch just in time. The second officer grabbed Danny's arm, while the third kicked him sharply in the back of the knee. Hagen cuffed his arms and legs while his colleagues held him down.

They dragged him out of his cell and down the iron staircase, keeping him on the move until they reached the corridor that led to the segregation unit. They came to a numberless cell. Hagen opened the door and the other two threw him in.

Danny lay still on the cold, stone floor for some considerable time. Had there been a mirror in the cell, he would have been able to admire his black eye and the patchwork of bruises across his body. He didn't care; you don't when you've lost hope and have another twenty years to think about it.

'WE DIDN'T HAVE any choice, sir,' said Pascoe.

'I'm sure that's right, Ray,' said the governor, 'but we all know how lifers can react if their appeal is turned down: they either become loners, or tear the place apart.'

'A few days in the slammer will bring him to his senses,' said Pascoe.

'Let's hope so,' said the governor, 'because Cartwright's a bright lad. I'd hoped he'd be Moncrieff's natural successor.'

'Two or three days in Segregation will sort him out,' said Pascoe.

'I hope so, Ray. And have a word with Moncrieff. He's Cartwright's closest friend. See if he can knock some sense into him. Who's next?'

'Leach, sir. One of my informers tells me he overheard Leach saying he was going to get even with Cartwright, if it was the last thing he did. Something to do with a tape, but I can't get to the bottom of it.'

'That's all I need,' said the governor. 'You'd better keep a twenty-four-hour watch on both of them. I don't want a repeat of what happened to the poor bastard at Garside—and all he did was give Leach a V-sign.'

DANNY SAT at the small Formica table and stared down at a blank sheet of paper. He was alone in the cell as Nick was taking a shower and Big Al was over at the hospital. It was some time before he wrote the first sentence.

Dear Beth,

This will be the last time I write to you. I have given a great deal of thought to this letter and have come to the conclusion that I cannot condemn you to the same life sentence that has been imposed on me. As you know, I am not due to be released until I'm almost fifty and with that in mind, I want you to start a new life without me. If you write to me again, I will not open your letters; if you try to visit, I will remain in my cell. On this nothing will change my mind.

Do not imagine even for a moment that I don't love you and Christy, because I do, and I will for the rest of my life. But I am in no doubt that this course of action will be best in the long run.

Goodbye, my love, Danny

He glanced at the photograph of Beth on the wall in front of him, then folded the letter and placed it in an envelope.

The cell door swung open.

'Letters,' said an officer standing in the doorway. 'One for Moncrieff, and one for . . .' he spotted the silver chain around Danny's neck and hesitated.

'Nick's taking a shower,' Danny explained.

'Right,' said the officer. 'There's one for you and one for Moncrieff.'

Danny recognised Beth's neat handwriting immediately. He didn't open the envelope, just tore it up and flushed the pieces down the lavatory.

When Nick came back from the shower room, Danny handed him back the things he'd been keeping safe for his friend: his watch, ring and silver chain.

'Thanks,' said Nick. He then spotted the brown envelope on his pillow. He grabbed it, opened it up and read the contents.

Dear Mr Moncrieff,

I am directed by the Parole Board to inform you that your request for early release has been granted. Your sentence will therefore be terminated on July 17, 2002. Full details will be sent later.

Yours sincerely,

T. L. Williams

THE GOVERNOR had decided the prisoners would be allowed out of their cells to watch the World Cup match between England and Argentina. At five minutes to twelve, the doors were unlocked and the men flooded out of their cells, all heading in one direction.

Danny was among those seated at the front, waiting for the game to start. The prisoners were clapping and shouting, with one exception, who was standing silently at the back. He wasn't looking at the TV, but at an open cell door on the first floor. The man he was looking for must still be in his cell. He didn't move. Officers don't notice prisoners who don't move. He was beginning to wonder if the man had broken his usual routine because of the match. But he wasn't watching the match. His mate was sitting on a bench at the front, so he must still be in his cell.

After thirty minutes, with the score nil–nil, there was still no sign of him.

Then, just before half-time, an English player was brought down in the Argentine penalty area. The crowd surrounding the TV seemed to make as much noise as the 35,000 spectators in the stadium. Background noise was all part of the plan. His eyes were still fixed on the open cell door when, without warning, the rabbit came out of his hutch. He was wearing boxer shorts and flip-flops with a towel over his shoulder. He didn't look down; he clearly had no interest in football.

The man detached himself from the group and walked slowly to the far end of the block, before climbing stealthily up the spiral staircase to the first floor. No one looked round.

He came to a halt outside the shower room. It was steamed up. Relieved to find that only one person was taking a shower, he padded silently over to the wooden bench on the far side of the room, where a towel lay neatly folded in the corner. He picked it up and twisted it into a noose. The prisoner in the shower rubbed some shampoo into his hair.

Everyone on the ground floor had gone silent. There was not a murmur as David Beckham placed the ball on the penalty spot.

The man in the shower room took a few paces forward as Beckham's right foot connected with the ball. The roar that followed sounded like a prison riot, with all the officers joining in.

The prisoner, who had just finished rinsing his hair under the shower, was about to step out when a knee landed in his groin, followed by a clenched fist into his spine, which propelled him against the tiled wall. Another hand grabbed his hair and jerked his head back. Though no one heard the bone snap, when he was released his body sank to the ground like a puppet whose strings had been cut.

His attacker bent down and placed the noose round his neck, then lifted the dead man up and held him against the wall while he tied the other end of the towel to the shower rail. He lowered the body into place, then returned to the entrance of the shower room. On the floor below the celebrations were almost out of control.

He was back in his cell in less than a minute. Laid out on his bed were a towel, a clean T-shirt and a pair of jeans, a fresh pair of socks and his trainers. He stripped off his wet gear, dried himself and put on the clean clothes. He then slipped back outside and rejoined his fellow inmates unnoticed.

When the final whistle eventually blew, there was another eruption of noise. Officers shouted, 'Back to your cells!' but the response was slow.

He turned and walked purposefully towards one particular officer, knocking against his elbow as he passed by.

'Look where you're going, Leach,' said Mr Pascoe.

'Sorry, guv,' said Leach, and continued on his way.

DANNY MADE his way back upstairs. He knew that Big Al had reported to surgery because as a Scotsman he had no interest in the game and had volunteered for the shift. But he was surprised that Nick wasn't in the cell.

Suddenly the shriek of a klaxon echoed round the block, accompanied by the sound of officers screaming, 'Back to your cells!' Moments later the cell door was pulled open and an officer stuck his head in. 'Moncrieff, where's Big Al?'

Danny didn't bother to correct him—after all, he was still wearing Nick's watch, ring and silver chain again while Nick was taking a shower—and simply said, 'He'll be at work in the hospital.'

When the door slammed shut, Danny wondered why he hadn't asked where *he* was. A few minutes later the door was pulled opened again by the same officer, and Big Al ambled in.

'Hi, Nick,' he said in a loud voice before the door was slammed shut. Then he placed a finger on his lips, walked across to the lavatory and sat down on it. 'Look as if you're workin' and don't open your mouth, just listen.' Danny picked up his pen and pretended to be concentrating on his essay. 'Nick's topped himself.'

Danny thought he was going to be sick. 'But why—'

'I said don't speak. They found him hangin' in the showers.'

Danny began to pound the table with his fist. 'It can't be true.'

'Shut up and listen. I was in the surgery when two screws rushed in—one of them said, "Sister, come quickly, Cartwright's topped himself." I knew that was balls, 'cause I'd just seen you at the football. It had to be Nick.'

'But why—'

'Don't worry about why, Danny Boy,' Big Al said firmly. 'The screws and the sister ran off, so I was left on my own for a few minutes. Then another screw turns up and marches me back here.'

'But they'll find out it wasn't me as soon as—'

'No, they won't,' said Big Al, 'because I had enough time to switch the names on your two files, didn't I.'

'You did *what*?' said Danny in disbelief. 'I thought the files are always locked up.'

'They are, but not during surgery, in case the sister needs to check on someone's medication. And she left in a hurry, didn't she?'

'But why did you do that?' Danny asked.

'Once they check his fingerprints an' his blood group, they're goin' to go on thinkin' it's you who topped himself because you couldnae face another twenty years in this shit-hole. And as long as they think tha', there's no' going to be an inquiry.'

'But that doesn't explain *why* you switched . . .' Danny went silent for some time before saying, 'So I can walk out of here in six weeks' time?'

'You catch on fast, Danny Boy. There are only about half a dozen people in this place who can tell you apart, and once they've checked the files, even they're going to be programmed to thinkin' you're dead.'

Danny was silent again. He'd have to spend the rest of his life pretending to be Nick Moncrieff. 'I'll have to think about it. I'm not sure that I can pull it off.'

'You've probably got twenty-four hours—until that door opens again. And let's face it, you'll have a better chance of clearin' your name—not to mention gettin' those bastards who murdered your mate—on the outside.'

'I'VE BEEN BLIND for the past two years, when all the time it was staring me in the face.' Danny looked up from Nick's diary. 'I've just reached the point where I turn up in this cell and you two have to decide what story you're going to tell me.' Big Al frowned. 'You were the staff sergeant under Nick's command who shot those two Albanians in Kosovo when Nick's platoon was ordered to guard some Serbian prisoners.'

'Worse,' said Big Al. 'It was after Captain Moncrieff had given a clear order *not* to fire until he'd first issued a warnin' in Serbo-Croat.'

'But you chose to ignore that order, and Nick ended up carryin' the can.'

'Yes,' said Big Al. 'Despite the fact that I told the court-martial exactly whit happened, they chose to take Nick's word rather than mine.'

'Which resulted in you being charged with manslaughter.'

'And being sentenced to ten years rather than twenty-two for murder.'

'Nick writes a lot about your courage, and how you saved half the platoon, including himself, while you were serving in Afghanistan.'

'He exaggerated.'

'Not his style,' said Danny, 'although it does explain why he was willing to shoulder the blame, even though you had disobeyed an order.'

'I told the court-martial the truth,' repeated big Al, 'but they still stripped Nick of his commission and sentenced him to eight years for bein' negligent in the course of duty. Do you imagine a day goes by when I don't think about the sacrifice he made for me? But I'm certain of one thing—he would've wanted you to take his place.'

'How can you be so sure?'

'Read on, Danny Boy, read on.'

'SOMETHING DOESN'T RING TRUE about this whole episode,' said Pascoe.

'What are you getting at?' asked the governor. 'You know as well as I do that it's not uncommon for a lifer to commit suicide within days of his appeal being turned down.'

'But not Cartwright. He had too much to live for.'

'We can't even begin to know what was going on in his mind,' said the governor. 'Don't forget that he broke up his cell and ended up in Segregation. He also refused to see his fiancée or his child.'

'True. But is it just a coincidence that this happens within days of Leach threatening to get him?'

'You wrote in your report that there's been no contact between them.'

Pascoe shook his head. He admitted, 'It's still just a gut feeling . . .'

'You'd better have a little more to go on than a gut feeling, Ray, if you expect me to open a full inquiry. And the first question we'd be asked is why, if we knew about Leach's threats to Cartwright, didn't we recommend that he was transferred to another prison the same day.'

PAYNE WAS SHOWING a client round a penthouse apartment in Mayfair when his mobile phone began to ring. When the name 'Spencer' appeared on the screen he excused himself and went into the next room to take the call.

'Good news,' said Craig. 'Cartwright's dead. It's on page seventeen of the *Evening Standard*. He committed suicide. He was found hanging in the showers. So that's the end of our problems.'

'Not while that tape still exists,' Payne reminded him.

'There'll be no interest in a tape of one dead man talking about another.'

THE CELL DOOR swung open and Mr Pascoe walked in. He stared at Danny for some time, but didn't speak. Danny looked up from Nick's diary.

'OK, lads, grab a meal and then get back to work. And Moncrieff,' said Pascoe, 'I'm sorry about your friend Cartwright. I for one never thought he was guilty.' Danny tried to think of a suitable reply, but Pascoe was already unlocking the next cell.

'He knows,' said Big Al quietly.

'Then we're done for,' said Danny.

'I don't think so,' said Big Al. 'For some reason he's goin' along with the suicide. By the way, what made you decide to go along with my idea?'

Danny picked up the diary, flicked back a few pages and read out the words: '*If I could change places with Danny, I would. He has far more right to his freedom than I do.*'

DANNY STOOD as inconspicuously as possible at the back of the churchyard as Father O'Connor raised his right hand and made the sign of the cross.

The governor had granted Nick's request to attend Danny Cartwright's funeral at St Mary-le-Bow. He had reminded Moncrieff that though he had only five weeks left to serve, he would be accompanied by two officers who would never leave his side. And if he were to disobey any of the strictures placed upon him, the governor would not hesitate to recommend to the Parole Board that they rescind their decision to allow early release. This, of course, rather suited Danny, as he was not permitted to speak to anyone other than the accompanying officers until he was back inside the prison.

Danny was relieved to find that Nick's clothes were almost tailor-made for him, and although he had never worn a hat before, it had the advantage of shielding his face from any curious onlookers.

He watched a gathering that was larger than he had anticipated. His mother looked pale and drawn, and Beth was very thin. Only his daughter, Christy, was oblivious to the occasion as she played quietly by her mother's side.

Danny was touched to see Beth's father standing by her side, head bowed, and, just behind the family, the tall, elegant figure of Alex Redmayne in a black suit, his lips pursed, a look of smouldering anger on his face. Danny suddenly felt guilty that he hadn't replied to any of Redmayne's letters since the appeal.

Father O'Connor delivered his eulogy, sprinkling holy water around the grave and, as the coffin was lowered into the ground, intoned, 'May eternal rest be granted unto Danny, O Lord.'

Danny wasn't allowed to move until the last mourners had departed. When Mr Pascoe finally turned to tell him that they should leave, he found him in tears.

DANNY SPENT EVERY spare moment reading and re-reading Nick's diaries, until he felt there was nothing left to know about the man.

Big Al, who had served with Nick for five years, was able to fill in several gaps, including how Danny should react if he ever bumped into an officer of the Cameron Highlanders, and he also taught him how to spot the regimental tie at thirty paces. They discussed endlessly the first thing Nick would have done the moment he was released.

'He'd have gone straight up to Scotland,' said Big Al.

'But all I'll have is forty-five pounds and a rail voucher.'

'Mr Munro, Nick's family lawyer, will be able to sort all that out for you. Just be sure that when he sees you for the first time—'

'The second time.'

'—but he only saw Nick for an hour after Nick's father's funeral, and he'll be expectin' to see Sir Nicholas Moncrieff, not someone he's never met before. The bigger problem will be what to do after that.'

'I'll come straight back to London,' said Danny.

'So what will you do once you're back in London?'

'One thing's for sure, I will not be satisfied until I've had revenge on the men whose lies have ruined my life.'

'Bit like that Frenchman you told me about, what's his name . . .?'

'Edmond Dantès,' said Danny.

'You're going to kill them all?'

'No, they must suffer, to quote Dumas, "a fate worse than death".'

'Perhaps you should add Leach to tha' list,' said Big Al.

'Leach? Why should I bother with him?'

'Because I think it was Leach who killed Nick. I keep askin' myself, Why would Nick have topped himself six weeks before bein' released?'

'But why would Leach kill Nick?'

'I don't think it was Nick he was after. Don't forget you were wearing Nick's silver chain, watch and ring while he was taking a shower.'

'But that means—'

'Leach killed the wrong man. You can be sure that Craig wouldnae have paid up for the wrong tape.'

Danny tried not to think about the fact that he might have been unknowingly responsible for Nick's death.

'But don't worry yourself, Nick. Once you're out of here, a fate worse than death isn' what I have planned for Leach.'

MR PASCOE MARCHED him into the governor's office.

'Why did you want to see me, Moncrieff?' asked the governor.

'It's a delicate matter,' Danny replied. 'It concerns Big Al.'

'Who, if I remember correctly, was a staff sergeant in your platoon?'

'Yes, sir. That's why I feel somewhat responsible for him. I overheard a heated row between Big Al and Leach. Of course, it's possible that I'm over-reacting, and I'm confident I can keep the lid on it while I'm still around, but if anything were to happen to Big Al after I left, I would feel responsible.'

'Thank you for the warning,' said the governor.

'HOW MUCH LONGER has Moncrieff got to serve?' asked the governor after Danny had closed the door behind him.

'Ten more days, sir,' said Pascoe.

'Then we'll have to move quickly if we're going to ship Leach out.'

'There is an alternative, sir,' said Pascoe.

HUGO MONCRIEFF TAPPED his boiled egg with a spoon while he considered the problem. Then he sifted through the morning post until he came across the letter he was looking for. It was from his lawyer, Desmond Galbraith.

Galbraith was able to confirm that, following Angus Moncrieff's funeral, Hugo's nephew, Sir Nicholas, had attended a meeting with his solicitor, Fraser Munro. Munro had called Galbraith the next day and had not raised the subject of the two mortgages. This led Galbraith to believe that Sir Nicholas would not be disputing Hugo's right to the £2 million that had been raised using his grandfather's two homes as security.

Hugo smiled. Since his brother Angus had left the regiment, single malt had become his constant companion, and towards the end of his life, Angus was willing to sign almost any document placed in front of him: first a mortgage on the London property he rarely visited, followed by another on the estate, which Hugo convinced him was in need of urgent repair. Finally, Hugo persuaded him to end his professional association with Fraser Munro, who in Hugo's opinion had far too much sway over his brother, and appoint Desmond Galbraith to take over the family's affairs.

Hugo's final triumph had been Angus's Last Will and Testament, signed only a few nights before his brother passed away and, thankfully, just months before Nick was due to be released. However, Galbraith had failed to prise out of Mr Munro the original copy of Sir Alexander's earlier will, as the old solicitor had pointed out that he now represented the main beneficiary, Sir Nicholas Moncrieff.

Hugo reread the last paragraph of Galbraith's letter and cursed. His wife Margaret, who was sitting at the other end of the table reading the *Scotsman*, looked up from her paper.

'Nick is claiming he knows nothing about the key his grandfather left him,' Hugo muttered. 'Yet we've seen him wearing the thing round his neck.'

'He didn't wear it at the funeral,' said Margaret. 'I looked carefully.'

'Do you think he knows what that key unlocks?' said Hugo.

'He may do, but that doesn't mean he knows where to look for it.'

'Father should have told us where he had hidden the collection.'

'You and your father were hardly on speaking terms towards the end,' Margaret reminded him. 'And he considered Angus to be weak and too fond of the bottle. The time has come for us to resort to more direct tactics.'

'What do you have in mind, old gal?'

'Once Nick is released, we can have him followed. If he does know where the collection is, he'll lead us straight to it.'

IT WAS DANNY'S LAST night at Belmarsh and he lay awake on the lower bunk. Big Al had been shipped out of the prison the previous day and transferred to Wayland Prison in Norfolk. By the time Danny had returned to his cell from the library in the afternoon, there was no sign of him.

By now Big Al would have worked out that Danny had been to see the governor, and he'd be fuming. But Danny knew that he'd calm down once he settled into the Category-C prison, with a television in every cell. His thoughts moved on to the plan that had begun to form in his mind over the last six weeks, then he drifted into sleep.

Next morning, Danny shaved and put on his prison clothes for the last time. When eventually the door opened, Mr Pascoe had a broad grin on his face. 'It's time for you to pick up your personal belongings, Moncrieff.'

They walked down the corridor to the storeroom.

'Morning, Moncrieff,' said Webster, the stores manager, placing two plastic bags on the counter. He disappeared into the back, returning with a large leather suitcase covered in dust and bearing the initials N.A.M.

Eventually Pascoe and a heavily laden Danny arrived back at the cell. 'I'll be back in about an hour to fetch you,' Pascoe said.

Danny emptied the contents of the bags onto the bed: two suits, three shirts, two ties and two pairs of shoes. Danny selected the suit he'd worn at his own funeral, a cream shirt, a striped tie and a pair of smart black shoes.

He stood in front of the mirror and stared at Sir Nicholas Moncrieff, officer and gentleman. He felt like a fraud.

He packed the rest of the clothes in the suitcase before retrieving Nick's diary from under the bed, along with a file of correspondence marked *Fraser Munro*. All that remained were a few of Nick's personal belongings, which Danny had put on the table, and the photo of Beth, which he took off the wall and put into a side pocket of the suitcase.

Danny looked at his friend's personal belongings. He strapped on Nick's slim Longines watch with 11.7.91 stamped on the back—a gift from his grandfather on his twenty-first birthday—then slipped on a gold ring which bore the Moncrieff family crest. He stared at a black leather wallet containing seventy pounds in cash and a Coutts's chequebook, and finally put them in an inside pocket. He reached inside his shirt and touched the small key that was hanging from the chain round his neck. After searching the diaries for the slightest clue, he was no nearer to discovering what it unlocked.

Now a very different key was turning in the lock of his cell door, which opened to reveal Mr Pascoe.

Danny picked up Nick's suitcase, walked out onto the landing and followed Mr Pascoe down the spiral staircase. He'd forgotten how many double-barred gates there were between B-Block and Reception, where Mr Jenkins was seated behind his desk waiting for him.

'Good morning, Moncrieff,' he announced cheerfully. He checked the ledger in front of him. 'I see that over the past four years you have saved two hundred and eleven pounds and, as you are also entitled to forty-five pounds discharge allowance, that makes in all two hundred and fifty-six pounds.' He counted out the money before passing it over to Danny. 'Sign here.'

Danny wrote Nick's signature and put the money in his wallet.

Mr Jenkins handed him a rail warrant to Dunbroath in Scotland, then Danny picked up the suitcase and followed Mr Pascoe out of Reception, down the steps and into the yard. Together they walked to the gatehouse.

'Name and number?' demanded the gate officer.

'Moncrieff,' Danny replied. 'CK1079.'

'Ah, yes,' said the officer, checking his clipboard. 'Sign here.'

Danny scribbled Nick's signature in a little rectangular box, then the officer checked the name against the prison number and the photograph, before looking up at Danny and pressing a red button under his desk. The first of the massive electric gates slowly began to open.

Once the first gate had slipped into its housing in the wall, Pascoe finally offered, 'Good luck, lad; you'll need it.'

Danny shook him by the hand. 'Thank you, Mr Pascoe' he said. 'For everything.' Danny picked up Nick's suitcase and stepped into the void between two different worlds. The first gate slid back into place behind him, and the second one began to open. Danny Cartwright walked out of prison a free man. The first inmate ever to escape from Belmarsh.

BOOK THREE: Freedom
Chapter 6

At King's Cross, Nick faced his first test. He spotted a row of phone booths, took out his wallet—Nick's wallet—extracted a card and dialled the number in the bottom right-hand corner.

'Munro, Munro and Carmichael,' announced a voice.

'Mr Fraser Munro, please,' said Nick.

'Who shall I say is calling?'

'Nicholas Moncrieff.'

'Good morning, Sir Nicholas,' said the next lilting voice Danny heard.

'Good morning, Mr Munro. I'm travelling up to Scotland later today and I wondered if you might be free to see me some time tomorrow?'

'Of course, Sir Nicholas. Would ten o'clock suit you?'

'Admirably,' said Danny, recalling one of Nick's favourite words.

'Then I'll look forward to seeing you here in my office.'

'Goodbye, Mr Munro.' Danny put the phone down. He was covered in sweat. But Big Al had been right. Munro was expecting Nick.

THE TRAIN ARRIVED at Waverley Station at three thirty. Half an hour later Danny climbed on board the train to Dunbroath, trundling into the little station at four thirty. He was relieved to see a taxi waiting on the stand outside.

'Where to?' asked the driver.

'Perhaps you can recommend a hotel?'

'There is only one.'

Three pounds fifty later, plus a tip, Danny was dropped outside the Moncrieff Arms.

'I need a room for the night,' he told the receptionist.

'Would you sign the booking form, sir?' Danny could now sign Nick's name almost without thinking. 'And may I take your credit card details?'

'But I don't . . .' began Danny. 'I'll be paying cash,' said Nick.

'Of course, sir.' She swivelled the form round and checked the name. 'I'll have a porter take your case up, Sir Nicholas.'

DANNY WOKE to a cacophony of bird tunes. He climbed out of bed and walked across the soft carpet to the bathroom and stepped into the shower. He washed himself in the steady stream of hot water and dried himself with a large fluffy towel. He felt clean for the first time in years.

After a breakfast of kippers, he paid his hotel bill and walked to the newsagent's next door.

'Am I far from Argyll Street?' he asked the girl behind the counter.

'A couple of hundred yards. Turn left out of the shop, go past the Moncrieff Arms . . .'

Danny walked quickly back past the hotel until he finally saw the name Argyll Street carved on a stone slab above him. He checked his watch: 9.54.

He had a few minutes to spare, but he couldn't afford to be late. Nick was always on time.

His pace slowed as he approached number twelve. A brass plate on the wall displayed the faded imprint of Munro, Munro and Carmichael. Danny took a deep breath, opened the door and marched in. The girl in Reception said, 'Good morning, Sir Nicholas. Mr Munro is expecting you.'

'FOLLOWING THE DEATH of your partner,' said a woman officer standing behind the counter, 'I'm authorised to pass Mr Cartwright's personal belongings to you. If you'd be kind enough to sign here, Miss Wilson.'

Beth signed her name and glanced inside the box. On top were Danny's light blue jeans and when she noticed the tear where the knife had entered Danny's leg she almost burst into tears.

'Thank you,' she said softly. As she turned to leave she came face to face with another prison officer.

'Good afternoon, Miss Wilson,' he said. 'My name is Ray Pascoe.'

Beth smiled. 'Danny liked you,' she said.

'And I admired him,' said Pascoe. 'Allow me to carry that for you.' He took the box from her as they walked down the corridor. 'I wanted to find out if you still intend to try to have the appeal verdict overturned.'

'What's the point,' said Beth, 'now that Danny's dead?'

'Would that be your attitude if he were still alive?' asked Pascoe.

'No, of course it wouldn't,' said Beth sharply. 'I'd go on fighting to prove his innocence for the rest of my life.'

When they reached the front gates Mr Pascoe handed the box back to her and said, 'I have a feeling Danny would like to see his name cleared.'

'GOOD MORNING, MR MUNRO,' said Danny, thrusting out his hand.

'I trust you had a pleasant journey, Sir Nicholas,' Munro replied.

Nick had described Mr Munro so well that Danny almost felt he knew him. 'Yes, thank you. The train journey allowed me to go over our correspondence once again, and to reconsider your recommendations,' said Danny as Munro ushered him into a chair by the side of his desk.

'My latest letter may not have reached you in time,' said Munro. 'I fear it's not good news. A writ has been issued against you by your uncle Hugo. It claims that your father left the estate in Scotland and the house in London to Hugo and that you have no legal claim over them.'

'But that's nonsense,' said Danny.

'I agree with you and, with your permission, I will reply that we intend to defend the action vigorously. To add insult to injury,' Munro continued, 'your uncle's lawyers have come up with what they describe as a compromise. If you were to accept your uncle's original offer, namely that he retains possession of both properties along with responsibility for the mortgage payments, he will withdraw the writ.'

'He's bluffing,' said Danny. 'If I recall correctly, Mr Munro, your original advice was to take my uncle to court and make a claim for the money my father borrowed against both houses, a matter of two million pounds.'

'That was indeed my advice,' continued Mr Munro. 'But if I recall your response at the time, Sir Nicholas'—he opened a file—'your exact words were, "If those were my father's wishes, I will not go against them."'

'That was how I felt at the time, Mr Munro,' said Danny, 'but circumstances have changed since then. I do not believe my father would have approved of Uncle Hugo issuing a writ against his nephew.'

'I agree,' said Munro, unable to hide his surprise at his client's change of heart. 'So, can I suggest that we issue a counterwrit asking the court to make a judgment on whether your father had the right to borrow money against the properties without consulting you? However, I must warn you that the matter may not be resolved quickly. It could be a year, perhaps even more, before the case comes to court.'

'That might be a problem,' said Danny. 'I'm not sure there's enough money in my account at Coutts' Bank to cover . . .'

'No doubt you will brief me after speaking to your bankers.'

'Certainly,' said Danny.

'There are one or two other matters I feel we ought to discuss, Sir Nicholas.' Munro extracted a document from the bottom of a pile of papers. 'You recently executed a new will.'

'Remind me of the details,' said Danny, recognising Nick's familiar handwriting on lined prison paper.

'You have left the bulk of your estate to one Daniel Cartwright.'

'Oh my God!' said Danny.

'Am I to assume that you wish to reconsider your position, Sir Nicholas?'

'No,' said Danny, recovering quickly. 'It's just that Danny died recently.'

'Then you will need to make a new will at some time in the future. But frankly, there are far more pressing matters for us to consider.'

'Like what?' asked Danny.

'There is a key that your uncle seems most anxious to get his hands on. It seems that he is willing to offer you one thousand pounds for a silver chain and key that he believes are in your possession. He realises that they have little intrinsic value, but he would like them to remain in the family.'

'And so they will,' responded Danny. 'I wonder if I might ask you in confidence, Mr Munro, if you have any idea what the key opens?'

'No, I do not,' admitted Munro. 'On that particular subject your grandfather did not confide in me. Though I would suggest that if your uncle is so keen to lay his hands on it, I think we can assume that the contents of whatever the key opens will be worth far more than a thousand pounds.'

'Quite so,' said Danny. 'Tell him that you are not aware of the existence of such a key.'

'As you wish. May I enquire if it is your intention to settle in Scotland?'

'No, Mr Munro. I shall be returning to London shortly.'

'Then you will require the keys to your London residence,' said the solicitor, handing over a bulky envelope.

'Thank you,' said Danny.

'There is one further matter I should bring to your attention, Sir Nicholas.' He turned to a safe, and extracted a small envelope. 'Your grandfather asked me to hand this to you in person, but not until after your father had died. I should have carried out his wishes at our previous meeting, but with all the, er, constraints you were under at that time, it quite slipped my mind.'

He passed the envelope to Danny who looked inside, but found nothing. 'Does this mean anything to you?' Danny asked.

'No, it doesn't,' confessed Mr Munro. 'Perhaps the name and address might be of some significance.'

Danny studied the envelope. It was addressed to *Baron de Coubertin, 25 rue de la Croix Rouge, Genève, La Suisse*. He placed the envelope in an inside pocket without further comment.

Mr Munro rose from his chair, accompanied Sir Nicholas to the door, shook him warmly by the hand and bade him farewell. As he watched his client stride back in the direction of the hotel, he couldn't help thinking how like his grandfather Sir Nicholas had turned out to be.

ON THE TRAIN to London, Danny looked at the envelope that Nick's grandfather must have wanted him to have without his father knowing. But why?

The stamp on it was French, value five francs, and showed the five circles of the Olympic emblem. The envelope was postmarked Paris, 1896. Danny knew from Nick's diaries that his grandfather had been a keen collector, so the stamp might possibly be rare and valuable, but he had no idea who to turn to for advice.

From King's Cross, Danny took the tube to South Kensington. With the aid of an *A to Z* bought from a station kiosk, he walked down Old Brompton Road in the direction of The Boltons.

Once there, Danny came to a halt outside number twelve, pushed open a squeaky iron gate and walked up a weed-covered path to the front door.

He made several attempts at turning the key in the lock before the door opened reluctantly. He switched on the hall light. Inside, the house was exactly as Nick had described it in his diary: a thick green carpet, faded; red patterned wallpaper, faded; no pictures on the walls; and long, dusty antique lace curtains that hung from ceiling to floor. Uncle Hugo must have removed anything of value while Nick was away in prison.

Once he'd explored the ground floor, Danny climbed the stairs. Having checked all seven bedrooms he selected one of the smaller ones in which to spend his first night. He concluded that it must have been Nick's old room, because in the wardrobe there was a rack of suits and a row of shoes that fitted him perfectly. He looked out of the window onto a large garden. Even in the fading light of dusk he could see that the lawn was overgrown from years of neglect.

NEXT MORNING, Danny leapt out of bed to dress. He chose the least conservative garments he could find, but still felt he ended up looking like a Guards captain on furlough.

As eight o'clock struck on the church clock in the square, Danny picked up the wallet from the bedside table, put it in his jacket pocket, and left the house. He walked in the direction of South Kensington tube station, only stopping to drop into a newsagent's and pick up a copy of *The Times*. As he was leaving the shop, he spotted a notice board offering various services. 'Cleaner, five pounds an hour, references supplied. Call Mrs Murphy on . . .' Danny made a note of the number.

He got off the tube at Charing Cross and walked along the Strand looking for Coutts' Bank. He had not gone far before he spotted a large glass-fronted bronze building, discreetly displaying three crowns above the name Coutts. He was about to find out the extent of his wealth.

He entered through the revolving doors and took an escalator up to the banking hall. Several tellers, dressed in black frock coats, were serving customers at a counter that ran the length of the room. Danny walked up to a window and said, 'I would like to make a withdrawal.'

'How much do you require, sir?' the young teller asked.

'Five hundred pounds,' said Danny, handing over a cheque he had written out earlier that morning.

The teller checked the name and number on his computer. 'Would you be kind enough to wait for one moment, Sir Nicholas?' he asked. A few moments later an older man appeared and gave him a warm smile.

'Sir Nicholas?' he ventured. 'My name is Mr Watson. I'm the manager.' He offered his hand, which Danny shook warmly. 'It's a pleasure to meet you. Perhaps we could have a word in my office?'

'Certainly, Mr Watson,' said Danny. He followed him through a door that led into a small wood-panelled office.

'I see that you haven't made a withdrawal for the past four years, Sir Nicholas,' Mr Watson said looking at his computer screen.

'That's correct,' said Danny. 'But in future I will be a more regular customer. Would you mind telling me how much is in my current account?'

The manager glanced at the screen again. 'Seven thousand, two hundred and twelve pounds. Is there anything else I can do for you, Sir Nicholas?'

'Yes, I'll need a credit card.'

'Of course,' said Watson. 'If you fill in this form,' he added, pushing a questionnaire across the table, 'we'll send one to your home address.'

'There's one other thing,' said Danny once he'd completed the form. 'Would you have any idea where I can get this valued?' He took out the little envelope from an inside pocket and slid it across the desk.

'Stanley Gibbons,' the manager replied without hesitation. 'They are leaders in the field, and have a branch just up the road. I would recommend that you have a word with Mr Prendergast.'

'I'm lucky that you're so well informed.'

'Well, they have banked with us for almost a hundred and fifty years.'

DANNY WALKED OUT of the bank with an extra five hundred pounds in his wallet, and continued down the road until he saw the Stanley Gibbons sign over a door. A tall, thin man stood behind the counter turning the pages of a catalogue.

'Mr Prendergast?' asked Danny.

'Yes,' he said. 'How may I help you?'

Danny took out the envelope and put it on the counter. 'Mr Watson at

Coutts suggested that you might be able to value this for me.'

Mr Prendergast picked up a magnifying glass and studied the stamp and postmark. 'It's a first-edition five-franc imperial, issued to mark the founding of the modern Olympic Games—of little value, perhaps a few hundred pounds. But there are two factors that could add to its importance.'

'And what are they?' asked Danny.

'The postmark date is April the 6th, 1896, which was the date of the opening ceremony of the first modern Olympic Games.'

'And the second factor?'

'The person the envelope is addressed to, Baron de Coubertin. It was the baron who founded the modern Olympics, and that is what makes your envelope a collector's item.'

'Are you able to place a value on it?' asked Danny.

'That would be rather difficult, sir, as the item is unique. But I would be willing to offer you two thousand pounds for it.'

'Thank you, but I'd like a little time to think,' replied Danny.

MOLLY MURPHY, CLEANER for hire, hailed from County Cork. She must have been about a foot shorter than Danny, and was so thin that he wondered if she had the strength to manage more than a couple of hours' work a day. Her first words to him were, 'I charge five pounds an hour, cash. And if you don't think I'm up to it, I'll leave at the end of the week.'

Danny kept an eye on Molly for the first couple of days, but it soon became clear that she had been forged in the same furnace as his mother. By the end of the week he was able to sit down anywhere in the house without a cloud of dust rising, climb into a bath that didn't have a watermark, and open the fridge to grab something without fearing he'd be poisoned. By the end of the second week, Molly had started making his supper as well as washing and ironing his clothes. By the end of the third week he wondered how he had ever survived without her.

During the third week Danny had bought a laptop and a printer, reams of paper, several files and pens and pencils. He had already begun to research the lives of the three surviving men who had been responsible for Bernie's murder.

Fraser Munro had submitted a bill for £4,000 for work done since the funeral, and that had arrived the same day as the new credit card, as well as his bank statement. Four thousand pounds would make a very large dent on the bottom line, and Danny wondered how long he could survive.

THE IMPORTANCE OF BEING EARNEST was showing at the Garrick Theatre and the previous day, Danny had telephoned to book a seat for a matinée performance. He had never been to a West End theatre before.

In the interval, Danny followed the crowd into one of the bars and became distracted by a high-pitched conversation between two girls.

'What did you think of Larry Davenport?' asked the first.

'He's wonderful,' came back the reply. 'Pity he's gay.'

'But are you enjoying the play?'

'Oh, yes. I'm coming again on closing night.'

'How did you manage to get tickets?'

'One of the stagehands lives in our street.'

'Does that mean you'll be going to the party afterwards?'

'Only if I agree to be his date for the night.'

After the final curtain call, Danny made his way back to the box office. The box-office manager smiled. 'Enjoy the show?'

'Yes, thank you. Do you have a ticket for the closing night?'

'I have a single seat in row W.'

'I'll take it,' said Danny, passing over his credit card. 'Does that allow me to attend the party afterwards?'

'No, 'fraid not,' said the manager. 'That's invitation only.' He swiped the card. 'Sir Nicholas Moncrieff,' he said, looking at him more closely.

'Yes, that's right,' said Danny.

The manager printed out a single ticket, took an envelope from below the counter and slipped the ticket inside.

On the tube journey back to South Kensington, Danny opened the envelope to check his ticket: C9. He looked inside the envelope and pulled out a card, which read:

THE GARRICK THEATRE
invites you to the closing-night party of
The Importance of Being Earnest
at the Dorchester
Saturday, September 14, 2002

Danny suddenly realised the importance of being Sir Nicholas.

'HOW VERY INTERESTING,' said Mr Blundell of Sotheby's. 'In thirty years in the business I've never come across anything quite like this.' He picked up his magnifying glass again and studied the envelope more closely.

'Could you give me a rough estimate of its value?' asked Danny.

'If the envelope were purchased by a dealer, two thousand two hundred to two thousand five hundred would be my guess. But at auction, should two collectors want it badly enough, who can say?'

'And when will your next stamp sale be?' asked Danny.

'September the 16th,' replied Mr Blundell. 'Six weeks' time.'

Danny picked up the envelope, handed it to Mr Blundell and said, 'Then I'll leave you to find the two people who want my envelope.'

'I'll do my best,' said Mr Blundell. 'And may I add how much I always enjoyed assisting your grandfather in the building of his great collection.'

'His great collection?' repeated Danny.

'Should you wish to add to that collection, or indeed to sell any part of it, I would be only too happy to offer my services.'

'Thank you,' said Danny. He left Sotheby's without another word—he couldn't risk asking questions to which he would be expected to know the answers. But as he strolled along Bond Street he thought about the significance of Blundell's reference to his grandfather's 'great collection'.

He didn't notice that someone was following him.

HUGO MONCRIEFF picked up the phone.

'He went to a meeting with his probation officer first thing this morning, then he went to Sotheby's. He left there twenty minutes ago and now he's standing at a bus-stop in Piccadilly,' said the voice on the line.

'So?' said Hugo. 'Why did he go to Sotheby's?'

'He left an envelope with the head of the Philatelic Department. It will come up for auction in six weeks' time. On September the 16th.'

'I'll have to be there. What was on the envelope?'

'A stamp issued to mark the first modern Olympics, which Blundell estimated to be worth between two and two and a half thousand.'

'Thank you,' said Hugo, and put down the phone.

'How unlike your father to allow one of his stamps to be put up for sale. Unless . . .' said Margaret as she folded her napkin.

'I'm not following you old gal. Unless what?'

'Your father devotes his life to putting together one of the world's finest stamp collections, which disappears on the day he dies and isn't even mentioned in his will. What *are* mentioned are a key and an envelope, which he leaves to Nick. I may be wrong, but I suspect that the key and the envelope are connected in some way.'

'But we still don't have the key,' said Hugo.

'The key will be of little importance, I suppose, if you can prove that you are the sole heir to the Moncrieff fortune.'

Chapter 7

D anny rose and joined the standing ovation, so engrossed in the play that he almost forgot his real purpose for being there.

After Lawrence Davenport had taken countless curtain calls, the audience slowly made their way out of the theatre. As it was a clear night, Danny decided he would walk to the Dorchester. He couldn't afford a cab.

He had begun to stroll towards Piccadilly Circus, when a voice behind him said, 'Sir Nicholas?' He looked round to see the box-office manager hailing him with one hand, while holding a taxi door open with the other. 'If you're going to the party, why don't you join us?'

'Thank you,' said Danny, and climbed in to find two young women sitting on the back seat.

'This is Sir Nicholas Moncrieff,' said the box office manager as he unfolded one of the seats and sat down to face the women.

'Nick,' preferred Danny, as he sat on the other folding seat.

'Nick, this is my girlfriend Charlotte. She works in props. And this is Katie, who's an understudy. I'm Paul.'

'Which part do you understudy?' Nick asked Katie.

'I stand in for Eve Best who's playing Gwendolen. I've only done one performance during the entire run. Still, it beats being out of work. What about you, Nick, what do you do?'

'I used to be a soldier,' Danny said.

Katie smiled at Danny as the cab drew up outside the Dorchester. He remembered so well the last young woman who had looked at him that way.

Danny was the last to climb out of the taxi. He heard himself saying, 'Let me get this one.'

'Thanks, Nick,' said Paul, as he and Charlotte strolled into the hotel. Danny took out his wallet and parted with ten pounds he could ill afford.

Katie hung back and waited for Nick. 'Paul tells me this is the second time you've seen the show,' she said, as they made their way into the hotel.

'I came on the off-chance you'd be playing Gwendolen,' said Danny.

She smiled and kissed his cheek. Something else Danny hadn't experienced for a long time. 'You're sweet, Nick,' she said, as she took his hand and led him into the ballroom.

'So what are you hoping to do next?' asked Danny, almost having to shout above the noise of the crowd.

'Three months of rep with the English Touring Company. This is going to be my chance to be on stage, and your chance to come and see me. Take your choice—Newcastle, Birmingham, Cambridge or Bromley.'

'I think it will have to be Bromley,' said Danny. He looked round the room in search of Davenport. His eyes rested on another man he should have realised might be there that evening. He was chatting to a couple of girls who were hanging on his every word.

Danny took a pace towards him, then another, until he was just a few feet away. Spencer Craig looked straight at him and Danny froze. Then he realised Craig was looking over his shoulder, probably at another girl.

Danny stared at the man who had killed his best friend and probably thought he'd got away with it. *Not while I'm still alive,* said Danny to himself. He took another pace forward, emboldened by Craig's lack of interest, and a man in Craig's group, who had his back to Danny, instinctively turned round to see who was invading his territory.

Danny came face to face with Gerald Payne. He'd put on so much weight since the trial that it was a few seconds before Danny recognised him. Payne turned back, uninterested. Even in the witness box, he hadn't given Danny a second glance.

Danny helped himself to a smoked-salmon blini while listening to Craig's conversation with the two girls. He was delivering an obviously well-rehearsed line about the courtroom being rather like the theatre.

'Very true,' said Danny in a loud voice. Craig and Payne both looked at him, but without a flicker of recognition. In any case, why should they give Danny Cartwright a thought? After all, he was dead and buried.

'How are you getting on, Nick?' Danny turned to find Paul, the box-office manager, by his side.

'Very well, thank you,' said Danny. 'Better than I expected,' he added.

A burst of applause erupted around the room, and all heads turned to see Lawrence Davenport as he made his entrance, with a beautiful girl at his side. He smiled and waved as if he were visiting royalty.

'Would you like to meet him?' asked Paul.

'Yes, I would,' said Danny.

'Then follow me.' They made slow progress across the crowded ball-room towards Davenport.

'Larry, I want you to meet a friend of mine, Nick Moncrieff.'

Davenport didn't bother to shake hands with Danny—he was just another face in the crowd. Danny smiled at Davenport's girlfriend.

'Hello,' she said. 'I'm Sarah.'

'Nick. Nick Moncrieff,' he replied. 'You must be an actress.'

'No, far less glamorous. I'm a solicitor.'

'Hi, Sarah,' said another young man. 'You are without question the most gorgeous woman in the room,' he said before kissing her on both cheeks.

Sarah laughed. 'I'd be flattered, Charlie, if I didn't know that it's my brother you really fancy, not me.'

'Are you Lawrence Davenport's sister?' said Danny in disbelief.

'Someone has to be,' said Sarah. 'But I've learned to live with it.'

'What about your friend?' said Charlie, smiling at Danny.

'I don't think so,' said Sarah. 'Nick, this is Charlie Duncan, the play's producer.'

'Pity,' said Charlie, shaking Danny's hand then turning his attention to the young men who were surrounding Davenport.

'I think he fancies you,' said Sarah.

'But I'm not . . .'

'I'd just about worked that out,' said Sarah with a grin.

Danny continued to flirt with Sarah, aware that this woman could undoubtedly tell him everything he needed to know about her brother.

'Perhaps we might—' began Danny, when another voice said, 'Hi, Sarah, I was wondering if . . .'

'Hello, Spencer,' she said coldly. 'Do you know Nick Moncrieff?'

'No,' he replied, and after a cursory handshake, continued his conversation with Sarah. 'I was hoping to have a word with you.'

'I was just about to leave,' said Sarah, checking her watch.

'But the party's only just begun, can't you hang around a little longer?'

'I'm afraid not, I have to be in court at ten o'clock sharp, and I need to go over some papers before briefing counsel.'

'It's just that I was hoping—'

'Just as you were on the last occasion we met,' she said, turning her back on Spencer Craig.

'Sorry about that, Nick,' said Sarah. 'Some men don't know when to take no for an answer, while others . . .' She smiled. 'I hope we'll meet again.'

'How do I . . .' began Danny, but Sarah was already halfway across the ball-room, the kind of woman who assumes that if you want to find her, you will.

'HI, STRANGER. Where did you disappear to?'

'Ran into an old enemy,' said Danny. 'And you?'

'The usual bunch. So boring,' said Katie. 'I've had enough of this party. How about you?'

'I was just leaving.'

'Good idea,' said Katie. 'Why don't we jump ship together?'

They walked across the ballroom and headed towards the swing doors. Once Katie had stepped out onto the pavement, she hailed a taxi.

'Where to, miss?' asked the driver.

'Where are we going?' Katie asked Nick.

'Number twelve The Boltons.'

'Right you are, Guv,' said the cabbie.

Danny hadn't even sat down before he felt a hand on his thigh. Katie's other arm draped around his neck, and she leaned across and kissed him.

By the time the taxi drew up outside Nick's home, there were very few buttons left to undo. It took Danny some time to get the key in the lock, but once inside the front door, Katie pulled off his jacket. They left a trail of clothes all the way from the front door to the bedroom.

AT SOTHEBY'S some weeks later, Danny decided to sit at the far end of the back row so that he could keep his eye on those who were bidding, as well as on the auctioneer. As he leafed through the catalogue, he noticed a man who must have weighed over twenty-five stone waddling into the room, carrying a large unlit cigar in his right hand. The man made his way slowly down the aisle before taking a seat, on the end of the fifth row, which appeared to have been reserved for him.

When Mr Blundell spotted the individual he walked across to greet him. To Danny's surprise they both turned and looked in his direction. Mr Blundell raised his catalogue in acknowledgment and Danny nodded. The man with the cigar smiled as if he recognised Danny, who hoped it meant his interest was in the de Coubertin envelope.

By the time the auctioneer announced lot number 37, Danny was nervous.

'This is a unique envelope showing an 1896 first edition of a stamp issued by the French government to celebrate the opening ceremony of the modern Olympic Games,' Blundell began. 'The envelope is addressed to the founder of the games, Baron Pierre de Coubertin. Do I have an opening bid of a thousand pounds?' Several paddles were raised.

'Fifteen hundred?' Almost as many.

'Two thousand?' Not quite as many.

'Two thousand five hundred?'

'Three thousand?'

When the bidding reached £6,000, the big man removed his cigar.

'Sold, to the gentleman in the front row, for six thousand pounds,' said the auctioneer as he brought the hammer down.

Danny tried to see who was seated in the front row, but he couldn't work out which one of them had bought his envelope. He felt a tap on his shoulder, and looked round to see the man with the cigar towering over him.

'My name is Gene Hunsacker and I'm from Texas,' he said in a loud voice. 'If you'd care to join me for a coffee, Sir Nicholas, it's possible that we may have something of mutual interest to discuss.' He shook Danny by the hand. 'I had the honour of knowing your grand-daddy,' he added as they walked downstairs to the restaurant, where Hunsacker headed for a seat that appeared to be his by right.

'Two black coffees,' he said to a passing waiter, without giving Danny any choice. 'Now, Sir Nicholas. I'm puzzled.'

'Puzzled?' said Danny, speaking for the first time.

'I can't work out why you let the de Coubertin come up for auction, and then allowed your uncle to outbid me for it. Unless you and he were working together and hoped you could force me to go even higher.'

'My uncle and I are not on speaking terms,' said Danny, choosing his words carefully. 'Were you a friend of my grandfather's?'

'Friend would be presumptuous,' said the Texan. 'Pupil and follower would be nearer the mark. He once outfoxed me for a rare Two Penny Blue, back in 1977 when I was still a rookie collector, but I learned quickly from him and he was a generous teacher. I keep reading in the press that I have the finest stamp collection on earth, but it ain't true. That honour goes to your late grand-daddy. Years ago he tipped me off that he'd be leaving the collection to his grandson, and not to either of his sons. When I saw the de Coubertin for sale I realised he had kept his word and left it all to you.'

'I don't even know where the collection is,' admitted Danny.

'Maybe that explains why Hugo was willing to pay so much for your envelope,' said the Texan, 'because he has absolutely no interest in stamps.

There he is now.' Hunsacker pointed his cigar at a man standing at the reception desk.

So that was Uncle Hugo, thought Danny. He could only wonder why Hugo wanted the envelope so badly that he'd been willing to pay three times its estimated value. Danny watched as Hugo passed a cheque to Mr Blundell, who in return handed over the envelope.

'You're an idiot,' muttered Danny, rising from his seat.

'What did you say?' asked Hunsacker, the cigar falling out of his mouth.

'Me, not you,' said Danny quickly. 'It's the address he's after, not the envelope, because that's where Sir Alexander's collection has to be. I have to go Mr Hunsacker, I apologise. I should never have sold the envelope.'

'I wish I knew what in hell's name you were going on about,' said Hunsacker taking a wallet from a pocket. He passed a card across to Danny. 'If you ever decide to sell the collection, at least give me first option.'

Danny tucked Hunsacker's card into Nick's wallet. His eyes never left Hugo Moncrieff, who put the envelope into his briefcase, walked across the lobby and joined a woman who linked her arm in his. The couple left the building quickly and Danny followed them to their Mayfair hotel. Thirty minutes later, they emerged and got into a taxi, so Danny jumped into the next cab that came along and followed them to Heathrow.

HUGO PRESSED the green button on his mobile just as the tannoy announced, 'Final call for all passengers travelling to Geneva on Flight BA0732.'

'He followed you from Sotheby's to the hotel and then to Heathrow,' reported the tail that Hugo had put on Danny earlier.

'Is he on the same flight as us?' asked Hugo.

'No, he didn't have his passport with him so they wouldn't sell him a ticket.'

'Typical Nick. Where is he now?'

'On his way back to London, so you should have a twenty-four-hour start on him.'

'Let's hope that's enough. Don't let him out of your sight for a moment.'

'HAVE YOU COME across another heirloom, Sir Nicholas?' asked Mr Blundell hopefully.

'No, but I do need to know if you have a photo of the envelope from this morning's sale,' said Danny.

'Yes, of course,' replied Mr Blundell. 'Is there a problem?'

'No,' Danny replied. 'I just need to check the address on the envelope.'

'Of course,' repeated Mr Blundell. He tapped some keys on his computer, and a moment later an image of the letter appeared on the screen. He swivelled the screen round so that Danny could see it.

Danny copied down the name and address. 'Do you by any chance know if Baron de Coubertin was a serious stamp collector?' asked Danny.

'Not to my knowledge,' said Mr Blundell. 'But of course his son was the founder of one of the most successful banks in Europe.'

THE FIRST THING Danny did when he arrived back at The Boltons was to search for Nick's passport. Molly knew exactly where it was. 'And by the way,' she added, 'a Mr Munro called and asked you to phone him back.'

Danny retreated to the study, called Munro and told him everything that had happened that morning.

'I'm glad you phoned back,' the old solicitor eventually said, 'because I have some news for you, although it might be unwise to discuss it over the phone. I was wondering when you next expected to be in Scotland.'

'I could catch the first train tomorrow morning,' said Danny.

'Good. It might be wise for you to bring your passport with you.'

'For Scotland?' said Danny, puzzled.

'No, Sir Nicholas. For Geneva.'

MR AND MRS MONCRIEFF were ushered into the board room.

'The chairman will be with you in a moment,' the secretary said. 'Would you care for coffee or tea while you're waiting?'

'No, thank you,' said Margaret, as her husband began pacing around the room. The secretary left and closed the door behind her.

'Calm down, Hugo. The last thing we need is for the chairman to think we're unsure about your claim. Now, come and sit down.'

A door at the far end of the room opened and an elderly gentleman entered. Although he stooped and carried a silver cane, such was his air of authority that no one would have doubted he was the bank's chairman.

'Good morning, Mr and Mrs Moncrieff,' he said in perfect English and shook hands with them. 'My name is Pierre de Coubertin.' He took a seat at the head of the table. 'How may I assist you?'

'Rather simple, really,' responded Hugo. 'I have come to claim the inheritance left to me by my father, Sir Alexander Moncrieff.'

'And what makes you think he conducted any business with this bank?'

'It was no secret within the family,' said Hugo. 'He told both my brother

Angus and myself about his long-standing relationship with this bank, which, among other things, was the guardian of his stamp collection.'

'Do you have any evidence to support such a claim?'

'No, I do not,' said Hugo. 'My father considered it unwise to commit such matters to paper, given our country's tax laws, but he assured me that you were well aware of the situation.'

'I see. Perhaps he furnished you with an account number?'

'No. But I have been briefed on my legal position by the family's solicitor, and he assures me that as I am my father's sole heir following my brother's death, you have no choice but to release what is rightfully mine.'

'That may well be the case,' confirmed de Coubertin, 'but I must enquire if you possess any documents that would substantiate your claim.'

'Yes,' said Hugo, placing his briefcase on the table. He flicked it open and produced the envelope he had bought from Sotheby's the previous day. 'This was left to me by my father.'

De Coubertin studied the envelope addressed to Hugo's grandfather. 'Fascinating,' he said, 'but it does not prove that your father held an account with this bank. Please excuse me for a moment while I ascertain if that was indeed the case.' The old man rose and left the room.

'GOOD MORNING, Sir Nicholas,' said Fraser Munro as he rose from behind his desk. 'I trust you had a comfortable journey?'

'It might have been more comfortable if I hadn't been aware that my uncle is at this moment in Geneva, trying to relieve me of my inheritance.'

'Rest assured,' responded Munro, 'that in my experience, Swiss bankers do not make hasty decisions. Now, we will come to Geneva in good time. For the moment, we must deal with more pressing matters that have arisen on our own doorstep.'

'Is this the problem you felt unable to discuss over the phone?'

'Precisely,' said Munro. 'Your uncle is now claiming that your grandfather made a second will, only weeks before his death, in which he disinherited you and left his entire estate to your father.'

'Do you have a copy of this will?' asked Danny.

'I do,' replied Munro, 'but I was not satisfied with a facsimile so I travelled to Edinburgh to attend Mr Desmond Galbraith in his chambers in order that I could inspect the original. Naturally, the first thing I did was to compare your grandfather's signature with the one on the original will. I was not convinced, but if it is a fake, it's a damned good one. Also, I could find no fault with the paper or the typewriter ribbon, which appeared to be of the same vintage as those of the original will.'

'Can it get any worse?'

'I'm afraid so. Mr Galbraith also mentioned a letter purportedly sent to your father by your grandfather a short time before he died.'

'Did he allow you to see it?'

'Yes. It was typewritten, which surprised me, because your grandfather always wrote his letters by hand. In it he wrote that he had decided to disinherit you, and that he had accordingly written a new will, leaving everything to your father. Clever. If the estate had been divided between both of his sons, it would have looked suspicious. Too many people knew that he and your uncle hadn't been on speaking terms for years.'

'But this way,' said Danny, 'Uncle Hugo still ends up with everything, because my father left his entire estate to him. But you used the word "clever". Does that mean that you have your doubts about whether my grandfather actually wrote the letter?'

'I most certainly do,' said Munro, 'and not only because it was typed. It was on two sheets of your grandfather's personal stationery, which I recognised immediately, but for some inexplicable reason the first page was typed, while the second was handwritten and bore only the words: *These are my personal wishes and I rely on you both to see they are carried out to the letter, Your loving father, Alexander Moncrieff.* The first page, the typewritten one, detailed those personal wishes, while the second was not only handwritten, but was identical in every word to the one that was attached to the original will. Quite a coincidence.'

'But surely that alone must be enough proof . . .?'

'I fear not. Although we may have reason to believe the letter is a fake, the fact is the writing on the second page is unquestionably in your grandfather's hand. I doubt there's a court in the land that would uphold our claim. And if that weren't enough,' continued Munro, 'your uncle served a trespass order on us yesterday. Not satisfied with being the rightful heir to both the estate in Scotland and the house in The Boltons, he is also demanding that you vacate the latter within thirty days, or he will serve you with a court order demanding rent, backdated to the day you took occupation.'

'So I've lost everything,' said Danny.

'Not quite,' said Munro. 'You still have the key, and I suspect that the bank will be loath to hand over the stamp collection to anyone who is unable to produce that.'

THE CHAIRMAN RETURNED after a few minutes, and resumed his place opposite his would-be customers. 'Mr Moncrieff,' he began. 'I have been able to confirm that Sir Alexander did indeed conduct business with this bank. We must now attempt to establish your claim to be the sole heir to his estate. First, I must ask you if you are in possession of a passport?'

'Yes, I am,' replied Hugo, who opened his briefcase, extracted his passport and handed it across the table.

De Coubertin studied the photograph before returning the passport to Hugo. 'Do you have your father's death certificate?' he asked.

'Yes,' replied Hugo, taking a second document from his briefcase.

The chairman studied the document. 'And do you also have your brother's death certificate?' he asked. Hugo passed over a third document. Once again de Coubertin took his time before handing it back. 'I will also need to see your brother's will, to confirm that he left the bulk of the estate to you.' Hugo handed over the will.

De Coubertin studied Angus Moncrieff's will. 'And are you in possession of your father's will?' he said eventually.

'Not only am I able to supply you with his Last Will and Testament,' said Hugo, 'signed and dated six weeks before his death, but I am also in possession of a letter he wrote to my brother Angus and myself that was attached to that will.' Hugo slid both documents across the table, but de Coubertin made no attempt to study either of them.

'And finally, Mr Moncrieff, was there a key among the bequests?'

'There most certainly was,' said Margaret, 'but unfortunately it has been mislaid, although I have seen it many times over the years. It's quite small, silver, and if I remember correctly, it has a number stamped on it.'

'And do you recall that number, Mrs Moncrieff?' asked the chairman.

'Unfortunately, I do not,' Margaret admitted.

'I will ask one of our experts to study the will,' said de Coubertin. 'Should they consider it to be authentic, we will hand over any possessions we are holding in Sir Alexander's name.'

'But how long will that take?' asked Hugo.

'A day, a day and a half at the most,' said the chairman. 'Would you like to return at three p.m. tomorrow?'

DANNY AND MR MUNRO touched down at Geneva Airport later that evening. The short journey into the city ended when the taxi driver pulled up outside the Hôtel Les Armeurs, situated in the old town, near the cathedral.

Munro had called de Coubertin before leaving his office. The chairman of the bank had agreed to see them at ten o'clock the following morning.

Danny rose early, showered and dressed, and over breakfast Munro went over questions he thought de Coubertin might ask. Danny stopped listening to his lawyer when a fellow guest entered the room and went straight to a window table—another seat that he clearly assumed would be kept for him.

'I think the world's leading stamp collector has decided to join us for breakfast,' whispered Danny.

'From that I assume your friend Mr Gene Hunsacker is among us?'

'No less. I can't believe it's a coincidence that he's in Geneva.'

'Certainly not,' said Munro. 'Hunsacker will circle like a vulture until he discovers which of you has been anointed as the legitimate heir to the collection, and only then will he swoop.'

DANNY AND MUNRO ARRIVED at the bank a few minutes early. The chairman's secretary was waiting to accompany them to the board room.

Danny was admiring a portrait of the founder of the modern Olympic Games, when the door opened and the present holder of the title entered.

'Good morning, Sir Nicholas,' he said, walking up to Danny. 'Like me, you are the grandson of a great man.' He invited Sir Nicholas and Mr Munro to join him at the board-room table. 'What can I do for you gentlemen?'

'I had the great honour of representing the late Sir Alexander Moncrieff,' Munro began, 'and I now have the privilege of advising Sir Nicholas. We have come to claim my client's rightful inheritance,' he continued, opening his briefcase and placing on the table one passport, one death certificate and Sir Alexander's will.

'Thank you,' said de Coubertin. 'Sir Nicholas, may I ask if you are in possession of the key that your grandfather left you?'

'Yes, I am.' Danny undid the chain that hung round his neck and handed the key to de Coubertin, who studied it carefully before returning it. The old man stood up and said, 'Please follow me, gentlemen.'

They walked down a long corridor until they came to a small lift. When the doors slid open, de Coubertin stood to one side to allow his guests to step in, then joined them and pressed a button marked −2. The lift came to a stop two floors down and when the doors opened, they stepped out into a brick-walled corridor. At the end of the corridor was a steel barred gate. A guard unlocked the gate the moment he spotted the chairman, then accompanied the three of them until they came to a massive steel door with two locks. De Coubertin took a key from his pocket, placed it in the top lock and turned it slowly. He nodded to Danny, who put his key in the lock below and also turned it. The guard pulled open the heavy steel door.

Danny stepped into a small square room whose walls were covered from floor to ceiling with shelves that were crammed with leather-bound books.

'Perhaps you would be kind enough to inform the guard when you wish to leave,' de Coubertin said, 'and then join me back in the board room.'

DANNY SPENT the next half-hour turning the pages of album after album, and began to understand why Gene Hunsacker had flown all the way from Texas to London, and then on to Geneva.

'I'm none the wiser,' said Munro, looking at forty-eight Penny Blacks.

'You will be after you've had a look at this one,' said Danny, passing him the only leather-bound book in the entire collection that was not dated.

Munro turned the pages: column after column listing when, where and from whom Sir Alexander had acquired each new item and the price he'd paid.

MR AND MRS MONCRIEFF WERE shown into the board room at 3 p.m. Baron de Coubertin was seated at the far end of the table, with three colleagues on either side of him. All seven men rose as the Moncrieffs entered the room, and didn't resume their places until Mrs Moncrieff had sat down.

'Thank you for allowing us to inspect your late father's will,' said de Coubertin, 'as well as the attached letter.' Hugo smiled. 'However, I must inform you that in the opinion of our experts, the will is invalid.'

'Are you suggesting that it's a fake?' said Hugo, rising angrily.

'We are not suggesting, Mr Moncrieff, that you were aware of this. However, we have decided that these documents do not stand up to the scrutiny required by this bank.' He passed the papers across the table.

'Are you able to tell us what in particular prompted you to reject my husband's claim?' asked Margaret quietly.

'No, madam, we are not.'

'Then you can expect to hear from our lawyers later today,' said Margaret as she gathered up the documents and rose to leave.

'MR GALBRAITH, PLEASE. This is Hugo Moncrieff.'

'How did you get on in Geneva?' were Galbraith's first words.

'De Coubertin said the will was a fake.'

'But I don't understand,' said Galbraith, sounding genuinely surprised. 'I had it examined by a leading authority, and it passed every known test.'

'Well, de Coubertin clearly doesn't agree with your leading authority.'

'I'll call de Coubertin and advise him to expect service of a writ. That will make him think twice about doing business with anyone else until the authenticity of the will has been resolved in the courts.'

'Perhaps the time has come for us to set in motion the other matter we discussed before I flew to Geneva.'

'All I'll need, if I'm to do that, is your nephew's flight number.'

WHEN MUNRO JOINED DANNY in his hotel room the next morning, the lawyer found his client surrounded by sheets of paper, a laptop and a calculator.

'I think you should hear about Mr Hunsacker's movements,' he said.

'How did you find out?' asked Danny.

'The room-service waiter was happy to give me a great deal of information about the gentleman in return for ten Swiss francs. It appears that Mr Hunsacker booked into the hotel two days ago. The management sent a limousine to the airport to pick him up from his private jet. The young man was also able to tell me that Mr Hunsacker's hotel booking is open-ended.'

'A sound investment,' said Danny.

'Even more interesting is the fact that the same limousine drove him to the Banque de Coubertin yesterday morning.'

There was a knock on the door.

'Sooner than I thought,' said Danny. 'I'll need a moment to clear up these papers. Can't have Hunsacker thinking I don't know what the collection is worth.' Danny knelt down on the floor and Munro joined him as they began gathering up reams of scattered papers.

There was another knock on the door, a little louder. Danny disappeared into the bathroom with the papers, while Munro went to open the door.

'Good morning, Mr Hunsacker, how nice to see you again. We met at Sir Alexander's eightieth—' He was offering his hand, but the Texan barged past him, clearly looking for Danny.

The bathroom door opened a moment later, and Danny reappeared, wearing a hotel dressing gown. He yawned and stretched. 'What a pleasant surprise, Mr Hunsacker. To what do we owe this unexpected pleasure?'

'Surprise be damned,' said Hunsacker. 'You know very well why I'm in Geneva. How much do you want?'

'I confess I was discussing that very subject with my legal advisor only moments before you knocked on the door, and he wisely recommended that I should wait a little longer before I commit myself.'

'Why wait? You don't have any interest in stamps.'

'True,' said Danny, 'but perhaps there are others who do. Mr Watanabe for example,' suggested Danny, remembering an article he'd found among his grandfather's papers that suggested Hunsacker had a rival in his claim to possess the finest collection in the world.

'Name your price,' said Hunsacker.

'Sixty-five million dollars,' said Danny.

'You're crazy. I'd be willing to pay fifty million,' said Hunsacker.

Danny didn't blink. 'I'd be willing to drop to sixty.'

'You'd be willing to drop to fifty-five,' said Hunsacker.

'Let's settle on fifty-seven and a half,' said Danny.

'It's a deal,' said Hunsacker. 'Now, give me the key, Nick, so I can inspect the goods.'

'I will allow you to have my grandfather's ledger,' said Danny. 'As for the key,' he added with a smile, 'Mr Munro will deliver it to you the moment the money is lodged in my account.'

DANNY AND MUNRO were among the first to disembark from flight BA737 after it landed at Heathrow. As they walked down the steps they were surprised to see three policemen standing on the tarmac. When Danny's foot touched the bottom step, two of the policemen grabbed him, while the third pinned his arms behind his back and handcuffed him. 'You're under arrest, Moncrieff,' he said as they marched him off.

Danny had spent most days since his release wondering when they'd catch up with him. The only surprise was that they'd called him Moncrieff.

'WHEN I TOLD you that I hoped we'd meet again,' said Sarah Davenport, 'an interview room at Paddington Green Police Station wasn't exactly what I had in mind.'

Danny smiled ruefully as he looked across the small wooden table at his new solicitor.

Mr Munro had blamed himself for not remembering that Sir Nicholas was not allowed to leave the country as he was still on probation. The lawyer had gone on to explain that he could not represent his client in an English court of law. However, he could recommend . . . 'No,' Danny had responded, 'I know exactly who I want to represent me.'

'I'm flattered,' Sarah continued, 'that when you found yourself in need of legal advice I was your first choice.'

'You were my only choice,' admitted Danny. 'I don't know any other solicitors.' He regretted his words the moment he'd said them.

'And to think I've been up half the night—'

'I'm sorry. That's not what I meant. It's just that Mr Munro told me—'

'I know what Mr Munro told you,' said Sarah with a smile. 'Now we don't have any time to waste. I have a number of questions to ask before you appear before the judge at ten o'clock.'

'GOOD MORNING, Mr Galbraith,' said Munro. 'I apologise for not returning your call earlier, but I have a feeling that you are well aware of what caused me to be detained,' he said sourly.

'Indeed I am,' responded Galbraith, 'which is precisely the reason I needed to speak to you so urgently. You will have been informed that my client has withdrawn all pending actions against Sir Nicholas regarding the two properties, so I'd assumed that your client will wish to respond in the same magnanimous manner, and withdraw his writ disputing the validity of his grandfather's most recent will.'

'You can assume nothing of the sort,' retorted Munro sharply.

'May I suggest, then, that as there is now only one dispute outstanding between the two parties, namely whether Sir Alexander's most recent will is valid, it might be in the interest of both parties to expedite matters by making sure this action comes before the court at the first opportunity?'

'May I respectfully remind you, Mr Galbraith, that it has not been this firm that has been responsible for holding up proceedings. Nevertheless, I welcome your change of heart, even at this late juncture.'

'I am delighted that that is your attitude, Mr Munro, and I'm sure you will be pleased to learn that Mr Justice Sanderson's clerk rang this morning to say that His Lordship has a clear day in his diary on the last Thursday of the month, and would be happy to sit in judgment on this case.'

'But that gives me less than ten days to prepare my case,' said Munro.

'Frankly, Mr Munro, you either have proof that the will is invalid, or you do not,' said Galbraith.

'MY LORD,' began Sarah as she rose to face Mr Justice Callaghan. 'My client does not deny his breach of licence, but he did so only in order to establish his rights in a major financial case, which he anticipates will shortly be coming before the High Court in Scotland. I should also point out, My Lord, that my client was accompanied at all times by his solicitor Mr Fraser Munro, who is representing him in that case. You may also consider it to be relevant, My Lord, that my client was out of the country for less than forty-eight hours, and returned to London of his own volition. The charge that he failed to inform his probation officer is not entirely accurate, because he rang Ms Bennett at her office, and when he received no reply, left a message on her answering machine. That message was recorded and can be supplied to the court if Your Lordship pleases.

'My Lord, this uncharacteristic lapse has been the only occasion on which my client has failed to abide by his licence conditions, and he has never missed a meeting with his probation officer. I would add that since being released from prison, my client's behaviour, with the exception of this one blemish, has been exemplary. Not only has he abided by his licence, but he has continued his efforts to further his education. He has recently been granted a place at London University, which he hopes will lead to an honours degree in business studies. My client unreservedly apologises for this lapse, and he has assured me that it will never happen again.

'In conclusion, My Lord, I would hope that after you have taken all these matters into consideration you will agree that no purpose will be served by sending this man back to prison.' Sarah bowed and resumed her place.

'Thank you, Miss Davenport,' the judge said. 'I would like a little time to consider your submission before I pass judgment. Perhaps we could convene again at noon.'

'COULD I SPEAK to the chairman, please? My name is Fraser Munro.'

'Mr Munro,' said de Coubertin. 'How can I assist you on this occasion?'

'I thought I would let you know that the matter which concerns us both will be resolved on Thursday of next week.'

'Yes, I am fully aware of the latest developments,' replied de Coubertin.

Munro coughed. 'Might I have a word with you off the record?'

'Not an expression we Swiss have come to terms with.'

'Then perhaps in my capacity as a trustee of the late Sir Alexander Moncrieff's estate, I could seek your guidance.'

'I will do my best,' replied de Coubertin.

'I understand,' said Munro. 'I have reason to believe that Mr Hugo Moncrieff has shown you the documents that constitute the evidence in this case.' De Coubertin did not respond. 'As you were willing to see Sir

Nicholas after your meeting with Mr Moncrieff, I can only assume that the reason you rejected his uncle's claim was because the bank, like myself, is not convinced that the second will is valid. In the name of justice, what was it that convinced you that the second will was invalid, but that I have failed to identify?'

'I'm afraid I am unable to assist you, Mr Munro, as it would break client confidentiality.'

'Is there anyone else that I can turn to for advice?' pressed Munro.

There was a long silence before de Coubertin eventually said, 'We sought a second opinion from an outside source, and much as I might like to divulge the name of that source, that would also be contrary to the bank's policy. However, the gentleman who advised us and who is unquestionably the leading authority in his field, hasn't yet left Geneva.'

'ALL RISE,' said the usher as twelve o'clock struck and Mr Justice Callaghan walked back into the courtroom. Sarah turned to smile encouragingly at Nick, who was standing in the dock with a look of resignation on his face.

Once the judge had settled in his chair, he peered down at defence counsel. 'Miss Davenport, I have taken into consideration your client's record since his release. This is commendable, but does not alter the fact that he abused his position of trust.' Danny bowed his head. 'Moncrieff,' said the judge, 'I intend to sign an order today which will ensure that you will be returned to prison for a further four years should you break any of your licence conditions in the future. For the period of your licence you may not under any circumstances travel abroad. You are free to leave the court.'

As the judge rose, bowed and shuffled out of the courtroom, the usher opened the gate to allow Danny to step out of the dock.

He walked over to Sarah, smiling. 'Can you join me for lunch?' he asked.

'No,' said Sarah, switching off her mobile phone. 'Mr Munro has just spoken to me. He wants you to take the next flight to Edinburgh.'

THE CASE of Moncrieff v. Moncrieff was to be tried before a high court judge in Chambers, as both sides agreed it would not be wise to air any family disagreements in public.

'Gentlemen,' Mr Justice Sanderson began. 'In my opinion the only question to be settled in this dispute is the validity of the second will, which Mr Galbraith claims, on behalf of his client, was Sir Alexander Moncrieff's Last Will and Testament. Mr Munro believes, without putting too fine a point on it, that the document is a fake. I hope that both sides consider this to be a fair assessment of the present position. If so, I will ask Mr Galbraith to present his case on behalf of Mr Hugo Moncrieff.'

Desmond Galbraith rose from his place. 'My Lord, my client and I would like to present a witness who will put this matter to rest once and for all.'

'By all means,' said Mr Justice Sanderson. 'Please call your witness.'

'I call Professor Nigel Fleming,' said Galbraith.

A tall, elegant, grey-haired man walked into the room and took the oath. He was Professor Fleming, an expert in inorganic chemistry from Edinburgh University and he testified that the same paper and ink had been used to produce both wills.

'Thank you, Professor,' said the judge when Fleming's cross-examination was finished. 'If you would be kind enough to wait there, I have a feeling that Mr Munro will have some questions for you.'

Munro rose slowly. 'I have no questions for this witness, My Lord.'

'Will you be presenting any other witnesses, Mr Galbraith?' asked the judge.

'No, My Lord. I can only assume that my learned friend's refusal to cross-examine Professor Fleming means that he accepts his findings.'

Munro didn't rise, in any sense of the word.

'Mr Munro,' said the judge, 'will you be calling any witnesses?'

'Yes, My Lord. Like my esteemed colleague, I will be calling only one witness.' Munro paused for a moment. 'I call Mr Gene Hunsacker.'

The door opened and the vast Texan ambled slowly in.

Hunsacker took the oath, his voice booming around the small room.

'Have a seat, Mr Hunsacker,' said the judge. 'Proceed, Mr Munro.'

Munro rose and smiled at Hunsacker. 'For the record, would you be kind enough to state your name and occupation?'

'My name is Gene Hunsacker the third, and I'm retired.'

'And what did you do before you retired?' asked the judge.

'Not a lot, sir. My pa was a cattle rancher, but I myself never took to it. When oil was discovered on my land I sold up and since then I've spent my time pursuing my hobby.'

'Mr Hunsacker,' said Munro, 'would I be right in suggesting that you are considered the world's leading authority on postage stamps?'

'It's either me or Tomoji Watanabe,' Hunsacker replied.

The judge said, 'Can you explain what you mean by that Mr Hunsacker?'

'Both of us have been collectors for over forty years, Your Honour. I have the larger collection, but to be fair to Tomoji, that's possibly because I'm a darn sight richer than he is, and I keep outbidding the poor bastard. I sit on the board of Sotheby's, and Tomoji advises Phillips Auctioneers. I can't tell you who's the world's leading authority, but whichever one of us is number one, the other guy is certainly number two.'

'Thank you, Mr Hunsacker,' said the judge.

'Mr Hunsacker, have you studied the will involved in this case?' said Munro.

'I have, sir.'

'And what is your professional opinion of the will?'

'It's a fake.'

Desmond Galbraith was immediately on his feet.

'Yes, yes, Mr Galbraith,' said the judge, waving him back in his place. 'I do hope, Mr Hunsacker, that you can support that assertion.'

'I shall prove, Your Honour, that Sir Alexander's second will is a fake. In order to do so, I require you to be in possession of the original document.'

Mr Justice Sanderson turned to Galbraith, who shrugged, rose from his place and handed the second will across to him.

'Now, sir,' said Hunsacker, 'if you would be kind enough to turn to the second page of the document, you will see Sir Alexander's signature written across a stamp.'

'What exactly are you suggesting Mr Hunsacker?'

'Her Majesty the Queen was crowned at Westminster Abbey on June 2nd, 1953,' said Hunsacker. 'The Royal Mint produced a stamp to mark that occasion. That stamp shows the Queen as a young woman, but because of the remarkable length of Her Majesty's reign, the Royal Mint has had to issue a new edition every so often, to reflect the fact that the monarch has grown a little older. The edition that is affixed to this will was issued in March 1999.' Hunsacker swung round in his chair to look at Hugo Moncrieff, wondering if the significance of his words had sunk in.

'Your Honour,' he concluded, 'Sir Alexander Moncrieff died on December 17, 1998—three months *before* the stamp was issued. So one thing is for certain: that sure can't be his signature scrawled across Her Majesty.'

MR JUSTICE SANDERSON wasn't given the opportunity to pass judgment in the case of Moncrieff v Moncrieff as one of the parties had withdrawn its claim soon after Mr Gene Hunsacker had left the judge's chambers.

Over dinner in Edinburgh, Munro advised his client not to press charges, even though Danny had no doubt who was responsible for the policemen waiting for him at Heathrow. 'However,' Munro added, in one of those rare moments when his guard came down, 'if your uncle Hugo causes any trouble in the future, then all bets are off.'

Danny had asked Mr Munro to become a trustee of the family estate and had made it clear that he wanted Dunbroathy Hall and the surrounding land to be handed over to the National Trust for Scotland, just as Nick's grandfather had wanted.

BOOK FOUR: Revenge
Chapter 8

The next morning, when the taxi drew up outside his house in The Boltons, Danny opened the gate to find a tramp lounging on his doorstep.

'This is going to be your lucky day,' Danny said as he took out his wallet. The dozing figure stirred and raised his head.

'Hi, Nick.'

Danny threw his arms round him, just as Molly opened the door. 'He said he was a friend of yours,' she said, 'but I still told him to wait outside.'

'He is my friend,' said Danny. 'Molly, meet Big Al.'

He led the Glaswegian into the kitchen. 'So tell me everything,' he said once they were seated at the table.

'No' a lot to tell, Nick,' said Big Al between mouthfuls of Molly's Irish stew. 'Thank God they shipped me out of Belmarsh, otherwise I might have been there for the rest of my life.' He added with a smile, 'An' we know who was responsible for tha'.'

'So what have you got planned?' asked Danny.

'Nothin' at the moment, but you did say to come and see you once I got out. I hoped you'd let me stay for a night.'

'Stay as long as you like,' said Danny. 'Molly will prepare the guest room.'

'Thanks,' said Big Al. 'But I'll be out of here as soon as I find a job.'

'You were a driver in the army, weren't you?' said Danny.

'I was *your* driver for five years,' whispered Big Al, nodding his head in the direction of Molly.

'Then you've got your old job back,' said Danny.

'But you haven't got a car,' Molly reminded him.

'Then I shall have to get one,' said Danny. 'And who better to advise me?' he added, winking at Big Al.

DANNY WAS READING Milton Friedman's *Why Governments Always Raise Taxes*, when the phone rang. He picked it up and heard a woman's voice.

'Hi, Nick. It's a voice from your past.'

'Hi, voice,' said Danny, desperately trying to put a name to it.

'You said you were going to come and see me while I was on tour.'

'So where are you performing at the moment?' asked Danny, still racking his brains for a name.

'Cambridge, the Arts Theatre. In *A Woman of No Importance*.'

'Oscar Wilde again,' said Danny, aware that he didn't have much longer.

'Nick, you don't even remember my name, do you?'

'Don't be silly, Katie,' he said, just in time. 'How could I ever forget my favourite understudy?'

'Well, I've got the lead now, and I was hoping you'd come and see me.'

'Sounds good,' said Danny flicking through the pages of his diary, although he knew that almost every evening was free. 'How about Friday?'

'Couldn't be better. We can spend the weekend together.'

'I have to be back in London for a meeting on Saturday morning,' said Danny, looking at a blank page in his diary.

'So it will have to be another one-night stand,' said Katie. 'I can live with that. Curtain's up at seven thirty. I'll leave a ticket for you at the box office.'

Danny put the phone down and stared at the photograph of Beth that was in a silver frame on the corner of his desk.

THE THREE MEN who arrived on Danny's doorstep the next day looked identical in every way except for their age. They wore well-tailored dark blue suits, white shirts and anonymous ties, and each carried a black leather briefcase.

'How nice to see you again, Baron,' said Danny. 'Do come in.'

De Coubertin bowed low. 'May I introduce Monsieur Bresson, the bank's chief executive, and Monsieur Segat, who handles our major accounts.' Danny shook hands with all three and led them into the living room. Molly appeared soon after, carrying a tray laden with tea and biscuits.

'Perhaps I could begin by asking you to bring me up-to-date on the current state of my account?' Danny said, as they all sat down.

'Certainly,' said Monsieur Bresson, opening an unmarked brown file.

'Your account is showing a balance of just over fifty-eight million dollars, which is currently accumulating interest at the rate of 2.75 per cent per annum.'

'I have to say, Monsieur Bresson, that I find a return of 2.75 per cent unacceptable. In future I shall put my money to better use.'

'Can you tell us what you have in mind?' asked Segat.

'Yes,' said Danny. 'I shall be investing in three areas—property, stocks and shares, and possibly bonds. I will also set aside a small amount, never more than ten per cent of my total worth, for speculative ventures.'

Segat nodded. 'May I ask whether you will wish to make use of the bank's expertise in managing your investments? I mention this because our property department, for example, employs over forty specialists in the field—seven of them in London alone.'

'I shall take advantage of everything you have to offer,' said Danny. 'However, I do intend to act aggressively. And I will expect you to move quickly if immediate payment will secure a better price.'

Bresson handed over a card. It had no name on it, just a phone number embossed in black. 'That is my private line. We can wire any amount of money you require to any country at the touch of a button. And when you call, you need never give your name, as the line is voice activated.'

'Thank you,' said Danny. 'I also require your advice on my day-to-day living expenses. I have no desire for the tax man to be prying into my affairs, and as I live in this house and employ a housekeeper and driver, while apparently subsisting on nothing more than a student grant, it may be that I will pop up on the Inland Revenue's radar.'

'If I might make a suggestion?' said de Coubertin. 'We used to send one hundred thousand pounds a month to an account in London for your grand-father. It came from a trust we set up on his behalf. He paid tax on this income in full, and carried out some of his smaller transactions through a company registered in London.'

'I should like you to continue that arrangement,' said Danny.

De Coubertin extracted a file from his briefcase, removed a sheet of paper and said, pointing to a dotted line. 'Then if you would sign here, Sir Nicholas.'

THE FRIDAY EVENING traffic was heavy and Big Al drove up to the Arts Theatre in Cambridge only ten minutes before the curtain was due to rise. Danny picked up his ticket from the box office, and followed a group of fellow latecomers into the stalls.

When the curtain rose, Danny became lost in another world, and resolved that in future he would go to the theatre on a regular basis. How he wished that Beth was sitting next to him and sharing in his enjoyment. Katie was on stage, giving a polished performance, but all he could think about was Beth.

When the curtain came down, Danny made his way to the stage door and asked if he could see Miss Benson.

'What's your name?' the doorman demanded, checking his clipboard.

'Nicholas Moncrieff.'

'Ah, yes. She's expecting you. Dressing room seven, first floor.'

Danny walked slowly upstairs and knocked on the door marked '7'.

'Come in,' said a voice.

He opened the door to find Katie sitting in front of a mirror wearing only a black bra and pants. She was removing her stage make-up.

'Shall I wait outside?' he asked.

'Don't be silly, darling; I've nothing new to show you, and in any case, I was hoping to arouse a few memories,' she added turning to face him.

She stood up and stepped into a black dress, which, strangely, made her look even more desirable. 'You were wonderful,' he said lamely. 'I really enjoyed the play.'

'Are you sure, darling?' she asked looking at him more closely. 'You don't sound altogether convinced. Is something wrong?'

'I have to get back to London. I have some urgent business.'

'It's another woman, isn't it?'

'Yes,' admitted Danny.

'Then why did you bother to come in the first place?' she said angrily.

'I'm sorry. I'm very sorry.'

'Don't bother to call again, Nick. You couldn't have made it more obvious that I'm a woman of no importance.'

'SORRY, BOSS, but I thought you said no' before midnight,' said Big Al, quickly finishing his hamburger.

'I changed my mind,' said Danny, who was soon fast asleep in the passenger seat of his new BMW. He didn't wake until the car came to a halt at a traffic light on Mile End Road.

Then he leaned back and closed his eyes again, though he knew that there were some familiar landmarks he wouldn't be able to pass without at least a sideways glance: Clement Attlee Comprehensive, St Mary-le-Bow Church and, of course, Wilson's Garage.

He opened his eyes, then wished he'd kept them closed. 'It can't be possible,' he said. 'Pull over, Al.'

Big Al brought the car to a halt.

'Wait here,' said Danny, opening the door.

He walked across the road, then stood on the pavement and stared up at a sign that was attached to the wall. He took a pen and a piece of paper out of an inside pocket and wrote down the number below the words FOR SALE. When he saw some locals spilling out of a nearby pub, he ran quickly back across the road and joined Big Al in the front of the car.

'Let's get out of here,' he said without explanation.

A PLAN BEGAN to form in Danny's mind and by Sunday evening it was nearly in place. Every detail would have to be followed to the letter; one mistake and all three of them would work out what he was up to. But the bit-part players, the understudies, had to be in position long before the three lead actors could be allowed to walk on stage.

When Danny woke in the house in The Boltons on Monday morning he retreated to his study, picked up the phone and dialled the number on the card. 'I will need to move a small amount of money some time today, and very quickly,' he said.

'Understood.'

'I will also need advice on a property transaction.'

'Someone will be in touch with you later today.'

Danny replaced the phone and took the piece of paper out of his pocket and dialled the number.

'Roger Parker,' said a voice.

'You have a property for sale on Mile End Road,' said Danny. 'Wilson's Garage.'

'Oh, yes, first-class property, freehold.'

'How long has it been on the market?'

'Not long, and we've already had a lot of interest.'

'How long?'

'Five, perhaps six months,' admitted Parker.

Danny cursed to himself as he thought about the anxiety Beth's family must have been going through, and he'd done nothing to help them. 'What's the asking price?'

'Two hundred thousand,' said Parker, 'or nearest offer, which of course includes the fixtures and fittings. Can I take your name, sir?'

Danny quickly replaced the receiver. He stood up and walked across to a shelf that had three files on it marked respectively *Craig*, *Davenport* and *Payne*. He took down Gerald Payne's file and checked the phone number of Baker, Tremlett and Smythe, where the Musketeer was the firm's youngest-ever partner. But Danny had no plans to speak to Payne today. Payne had to come to him, desperate to make the deal. Today was saved for the messenger. He dialled the number.

'Baker, Tremlett and Smythe.'

'I'm thinking of buying a property on Mile End Road.'

'I'll put you through to the department that handles East London.'

There was a click on the line. 'Gary Hall. How can I help you?'

'Mr Hall, my name is Sir Nicholas Moncrieff and I wonder'—slowly, very slowly—'if I've got the right man.'

'Tell me what it is you need, sir, and I'll see if I can help.'

'There's a property for sale in Mile End Road that I'd like to buy, but I don't want to deal directly with the vendor's estate agent.'

'You can be assured of my discretion, sir.'

I hope not, thought Danny. You are my messenger.

'What number in Mile End Road is it?'

'One-three-seven,' Danny replied. 'It's a garage—Wilson's Garage.'

'Who are the vendor's agents?'

'Douglas, Allen, Spiro.'

'I'll have a word with my opposite number there and find out all the details,' said Hall, 'then give you a bell back.'

'I'll be in your area later today. Perhaps you could join me for a coffee?'

'Of course, Sir Nicholas. Where would you like to meet?'

Danny could think of only one place he'd ever been to that was anywhere near Baker, Tremlett and Smythe's offices. 'The Dorchester,' he said. 'Shall we say twelve o'clock?'

Danny remained at his desk. He still needed some other players to be in place before midday if he was going to be ready for Gary Hall. But before he could use the phone again, it began to ring. Danny picked it up.

'Good morning, Sir Nicholas,' said a voice. 'I manage the bank's property desk in London.'

BIG AL DREW UP outside the terrace entrance of the Dorchester just after 11.30. A doorman opened the back door of the car and Danny stepped out.

'My name is Sir Nicholas Moncrieff,' he said as he walked up the steps.

'I'm expecting a guest to join me around twelve—a Mr Hall. Could you tell him I'll be in the lounge?' He handed the doorman a ten-pound note.

'I certainly will, sir,' said the doorman, raising his top hat.

'And your name is?' asked Danny.

'George.'

'Thank you, George,' said Danny, and walked into the hotel.

He paused in the lobby and introduced himself to the head concierge, whose name was Walter. After a conversation with Walter, he parted with another ten-pound note.

On Walter's advice, Danny made his way to the lounge and waited for the maître d' to return to his post. This time Danny took a ten-pound note out of his wallet before he'd made his request.

'Why don't I put you in one of our more private alcoves, Sir Nicholas? I'll see that Mr Hall is brought across to you the moment he arrives. Would you care for anything while you're waiting?'

'A copy of *The Times* and a hot chocolate,' said Danny.

'Of course, Sir Nicholas.'

'And your name is?'

'Mario, sir.'

At two minutes to twelve, Mario was standing by his side. 'Sir Nicholas, your guest has arrived.'

'Thank you, Mario,' Danny said, as if he were a regular customer.

'It's a pleasure to meet you, Sir Nicholas,' said Hall, taking the seat opposite Danny. He opened his briefcase and took out a file. 'I think I have all the information you require,' he said, opening the cover. 'One-three-seven Mile End Road—it used to be a garage, owned by a Mr Albert Wilson who died recently.' The blood drained from Danny's face.

'Are you feeling all right, Sir Nicholas?' asked Hall.

'Yes, yes, I'm fine,' said Danny, quickly recovering. 'You were saying?'

'The business continued trading for a couple of years but in that time it ran up large debts, so the owner decided to cut her losses and sell up.'

'*Her* losses?'

'Yes, the site is now owned . . .'—he once again checked his file—'by a Miss Elizabeth Wilson, the daughter of the previous owner. The site is approximately five thousand square feet, but if you are considering making an offer, I could do a survey. There's a pawnshop on one side, and a Turkish carpet warehouse on the other.'

'What's the asking price?'

'Two hundred thousand, including fixtures and fittings, but I'm fairly confident you could pick it up for a hundred and fifty. There hasn't been much interest shown, and there's a far more successful garage trading on the other side of the road.'

'I can't afford to waste any time haggling,' said Danny, 'so listen carefully. I'm prepared to pay the asking price, and I also want you to make an offer for the pawnshop and the carpet warehouse.'

'Yes, of course, Sir Nicholas,' said Hall writing furiously. He hesitated. 'I'll need a deposit of twenty thousand pounds before we can proceed.'

'By the time you get back to your office, Mr Hall, two hundred thousand pounds will have been deposited in your client account. As soon as you know about the other two properties, call me. And I must make one thing clear: the owner must never find out who she is dealing with.'

'I understand,' said Hall. 'How do I get in touch with you?'

Danny took out his wallet and handed him a freshly minted card.

Hall rose from his chair. 'I'll get straight back to the office and talk to the vendor's agents.'

Danny watched Hall as he scuttled away, then he opened his mobile phone and dialled Coutts's number. 'I want two hundred thousand pounds to be transferred to the client account of Baker, Tremlett and Smythe in London,' he instructed.

'Understood.'

Danny closed the phone and wondered how quickly Gary Hall would discover that Mr Isaac Cohen had wanted to sell the pawnshop for years, and that the owners of the carpet warehouse wanted to retire to Ankara so that they could spend more time with their grandchildren.

Mario placed the bill discreetly on the table by his side. Danny left a large tip. He needed to be remembered. As he passed through Reception he paused to thank Walter, the head concierge. Then he pushed his way through the swing doors and walked out onto the terrace. George rushed across to the waiting car and opened the back door.

Danny extracted another ten-pound note. 'Thank you, George.'

George, Walter and Mario were now all paid-up members of his cast, although the curtain had only just fallen on the first act.

BACK AT THE BOLTONS, Danny took the file marked *Davenport* off the shelf. Another bit-part player was about to become involved in Lawrence Davenport's next production. Danny dialled his number.

'Charles Duncan Productions.'

'Mr Duncan, please.'

'Who shall I say is calling?'

'Nick Moncrieff.'

'I'm trying to remember where we met,' said the next voice on the line.

'The Dorchester. *The Importance of Being Earnest* closing-night party.'

'Oh, yes, now I remember. So what can I do for you?'

'I'm thinking of investing in your next production,' said Danny. 'A friend of mine put a few thousand in *Earnest* and he tells me he made a handsome profit, so I thought this might be the right time for me to—'

'You couldn't have called at a better time,' said Duncan. 'I've got the very thing for you, old boy. Why don't you join me at the Ivy for a spot of lunch tomorrow, if you happen to be free, and we can discuss it?'

'No, you must let me take you, old boy,' said Danny. 'Why don't you join me at the Dorchester. Shall we say one o'clock in the Palm Court Room?'

'Yes, of course. One o'clock,' said Duncan. 'It's *Sir* Nicholas, isn't it?'

'Nick's just fine,' said Danny, making an entry in his diary.

Chapter 9

'Good morning, George,' said Danny as the doorman opened the back door of the car for him.

'Good morning, Sir Nicholas.'

Danny strolled into the hotel, waving at Walter as he passed through reception. Mario's face lit up the moment he spotted his favourite customer.

'A hot chocolate and *The Times*, Sir Nicholas?' he asked, once Danny had settled into his alcove seat.

'Thank you, Mario. I'd also like a table for lunch at one o'clock tomorrow, somewhere I can't be overheard.'

'That won't be a problem, Sir Nicholas.'

Danny leaned back and thought about the meeting that was about to take place. His advisors from de Coubertin's property department had called. They had come up with a realistic price for the pawnshop and the carpet warehouse, but they had also drawn his attention to a barren plot of land that ran behind the three properties and which was owned by the local council. Apparently, the planning committee had for years wanted to build 'affordable housing' on that land, where Danny remembered playing football with Bernie when they were kids, but with a garage so close to the site, the Health and Safety Committee had vetoed the idea.

Danny had plans to solve their problem.

'GOOD MORNING, Sir Nicholas.'

Danny looked up from his newspaper. 'Good morning, Mr Hall,' he said, as the young man took the seat opposite him. Hall opened his briefcase, took out a document and handed it to Danny.

'These are the deeds for Wilson's Garage,' he explained. 'Contracts were exchanged when I met up with Miss Wilson this morning.'

Danny thought his heart would stop beating at the mention of Beth's name. 'And the buildings on either side?' he asked.

'Mr Cohen says he'd let the pawnshop go for two hundred and fifty thousand, while Mr Kamal is asking three hundred and twenty thousand for the carpet warehouse.'

'Offer Mr Cohen two hundred and twenty thousand for the pawnshop and settle for two hundred and forty. Pay Mr Kamal his asking price. I want you to close both deals on the same day. Once you've closed the deals, let me know so I can open negotiations with the council. Meanwhile, I'll deposit five hundred and forty thousand pounds in your client account today. Neither side must know about the other sale.'

'I won't let you down,' said Hall.

'I hope not,' said Danny. 'Because if you succeed in this little enterprise, I've been working on something far more interesting. But as there is an element of risk involved, it will need the backing of one of your partners, preferably someone young, who's got balls and imagination.'

'I know exactly the right man,' said Hall.

DANNY WAS SEATED at a quiet corner table fifteen minutes before Charlie Duncan was due to appear.

At two minutes to one, Duncan entered the Palm Court Restaurant wearing an open-necked shirt. The head waiter had a discreet word with him before offering him a striped tie that clashed with his salmon-pink shirt.

Danny suppressed a smile as Mario accompanied Duncan across the room to his table. He rose to shake hands with the theatrical producer, whose cheeks were now the same colour as his shirt. 'You're obviously a regular here,' said Duncan, taking his seat. 'Everyone seems to know you.'

'My father and grandfather always used to stay here whenever they came down from Scotland,' said Danny. 'It's a bit of a family tradition.'

'So you've never invested in the theatre before?' asked Duncan as the wine waiter showed Danny a bottle of wine. He studied the label and nodded.

'The answer to your question is no,' Danny said as the wine was poured. 'So I'd be fascinated to learn how your world operates.'

'The first thing a producer has to do is identify a play,' said Duncan. 'Your next problem is to find a star.'

'Like Lawrence Davenport?' said Danny.

'No, that was a one-off. Davenport's not a stage actor. He can just about get away with light comedy as long as he's backed up by a strong cast.'

'But he can still fill a theatre?'

'We were running a little thin towards the end of the run,' admitted Duncan, 'once his Dr Beresford fans had dried up. Frankly, if he doesn't get back on television fairly soon, he won't be able to fill a phone box.'

'And how much are the stars paid?' asked Danny.

'Sometimes as little as two or three thousand a week. We only paid Larry Davenport three thousand.'

'Three thousand a week? I'm amazed he got out of bed for that.'

'So were we,' admitted Duncan. 'Soap stars get used to earning thousands of pounds a week, not to mention the lifestyle that goes with it. But once that tap is turned off, they can quickly run out of cash, even if they've accumulated some assets.'

'So what are you planning to do next?' asked Danny.

'I'm putting on a piece by a new playwright called Anton Kaszubowski. He won several awards at the Edinburgh Festival last year. It's called *Bling Bling*,' he said. 'What sort of figure would you be thinking of investing?'

'I'd begin with something small,' said Danny, 'say ten thousand. If that works out, I could well become a regular.'

'I'll be in touch when I've signed up a lead actor. By the way, I always throw a drinks party for the investors when I launch a new show. You'll be able to see Larry again. Or his sister, depending on your preference.'

'JAPANESE KNOTWEED?'

'Yes, we believe that Japanese Knotweed is the answer,' said Bresson. 'Although I'm bound to say that Monsieur Segat and myself were both puzzled by the question.'

Danny made no attempt to enlighten them, as he was just beginning to learn how to play the Swiss at their own game. 'And why is it the answer?'

'If Japanese Knotweed is discovered on a building site, it can hold up planning permission for at least a year. Experts have to be brought in to destroy the weed, and building cannot commence until the local health-and-safety committee deem the site to have passed all the necessary tests.'

'So how do you get rid of Japanese Knotweed?' asked Danny.

'A specialist company moves in and sets fire to the whole site. Then you have to wait another three months to make sure that every last rhizome has been removed before you can re-apply for planning permission.'

'That wouldn't come cheap?'

'No. We came across an example in Liverpool,' added Segat. 'The council discovered Japanese Knotweed on a thirty-acre site with planning permission for a hundred houses. It took more than a year to remove it, at a cost of three hundred thousand pounds.'

'Why is it so dangerous?' asked Danny.

'If you don't destroy it,' said Bresson, 'it will eat its way into the foundations of any building and, ten years later, without warning, the whole edifice comes crumbling down. In Osaka, in Japan, it destroyed an entire apartment block, which is how it acquired its name.'

'So how do I get hold of some?' asked Danny.

'I have no idea, but I suspect that any company that specialises in destroying it could point you in the right direction. It would of course be illegal to plant it on someone else's land,' Bresson added.

'But not on your own land,' Danny replied, silencing both bankers. 'Have you come up with a solution for the other half of my problem?'

Segat answered. 'My team has identified a piece of land in East London that fulfils your criteria. London, as you will be aware, is bidding to host the 2012 Olympics, with most events planned to take place at Stratford in East London. This has already created a speculative market for sites in the area. My contacts inform me that six potential sites for the velodrome have been identified, of which two will be short-listed by the Olympic Committee. You are in the happy position of being able to purchase both of them.'

'We have valued the two sites,' continued Bresson, 'at around a million pounds each, but the current owners are asking for a million and a half. If they were to make the short list, they could end up being worth as much as six million. You've got a month to make up your mind because that's when the short list will be announced.'

'Thank you,' said Danny. 'I'll let you know. Now, I'd like an update on your negotiations with the council over the Wilson's Garage site.'

'Our lawyer had a meeting with the chief planning officer last week,' said Segat, 'to discover what his committee would regard as acceptable were you to apply for outline planning permission. The council has proposed that if seventy flats were to be built on the site, one third of them would have to be classified as affordable dwellings. If we were to agree that in principle, they would sell us the plot for four hundred thousand pounds, and grant outline planning permission at the same time. On that basis, we would recommend that you accept their offer, but try to get the council to allow you to build ninety flats. The chief planning officer felt that this would cause heated debate in the council chamber. However, if we were to raise our offer to, say, five hundred thousand, he could see his way to recommending our proposal, thereby allowing you to obtain the whole site for just over a million pounds.'

'You've done well,' said Danny. 'Once we've agreed terms and provisional planning permission has been granted, just sell the site on to the highest bidder.'

WHEN DANNY PUSHED THROUGH the swing doors of Baker, Tremlett and Smythe, he found Gary Hall waiting in the foyer.

'He's an exceptional man,' Hall enthused as they walked to the lifts. 'The youngest partner in the history of the company,' he added, as he pressed a button that would whisk them to the top floor. 'And he's landed a safe parliamentary seat, so I don't suppose he'll be with us much longer.'

Danny smiled. His plan only involved Gerald Payne being sacked. His having to resign a parliamentary seat as well would be a bonus.

When they stepped out of the lift, Hall led his most important client along the partners' corridor until they reached a door with the name GERALD PAYNE printed in gold. Hall knocked softly, opened it and stood aside to allow Danny to enter.

Payne leapt up from behind his desk, thrust out his hand and gave Danny an exaggerated smile. 'Have we met before?' he asked, looking at Danny closely.

'Yes,' said Danny. 'At Lawrence Davenport's closing-night party.'

'Oh, yes, of course,' said Payne, and invited Danny to take a seat.

'Let me begin, Sir Nicholas—'

'Nick,' said Danny.

'Gerald,' said Payne. 'Let me begin by expressing my admiration for your little coup with Tower Hamlets council over the site in Bow.'

'Mr Hall did most of the spadework,' said Danny. 'I'm afraid I've been distracted by something far more demanding.'

'Will you be involving our firm in your latest venture?' Payne enquired.

'I need someone to represent me when it comes to putting in an offer.'

Payne smiled. 'Are you able to take us into your confidence at this stage?'

Danny returned the smile. 'Everyone knows that if London is awarded the 2012 Olympics, there will be a lot of money to be made. I've identified an opportunity that hasn't attracted press attention. The Olympic Committee has been considering six sites for the building of a velodrome, and in a fortnight's time we'll learn which two sites are short-listed. My bet is that even after the announcement is made, it won't get more than the odd paragraph in the local paper. But I have some inside information which I acquired at a cost of four pounds ninety-nine.'

'Four ninety-nine?' repeated Payne, looking mystified.

'The price of *Cycling Monthly*,' said Danny, removing a copy from his briefcase. 'In this month's issue, the editor leaves no doubt as to which two sites the Olympic Committee will be short-listing, and he clearly has the ear of the minister. The next edition won't be on the stands for another ten days, but for a sum that was admittedly a little more than four pounds ninety-nine, I managed to get my hands on this early proof. There's an article on page seventeen by the President of the British Cycling Federation, in which he says that the minister has assured him that only two sites are being taken seriously. The minister will be making an announcement to that effect in the House of Commons the day before the magazine goes on sale. He goes on to say which of the two sites his committee will be backing.'

'Brilliant,' said Payne. 'But surely the owners of that site must be aware that they may be sitting on a fortune?'

'Only if they can get their hands on next month's *Cycling Monthly*, because at the moment they still think they're on a short list of six.'

'So what are you planning to do?' asked Payne.

'The site favoured by the Cycling Federation as the most likely to be selected changed hands recently for three million pounds, although I haven't been able to identify the buyer. However, once the minister has made her announcement, it could be worth fifteen million. While there are still six sites on the short list, if someone were to offer the present owner four or five million, they might be tempted to take a quick return rather than risk ending up with nothing.'

'If there are only two sites in contention,' said Payne, 'why not purchase both of them? It would be impossible for you to lose.'

'Good idea,' said Danny, 'but there's not much point in doing that until we've found out if the site we're really interested in can be purchased. That's where you come in.'

'I'll be back in touch with you as soon as I've tracked down the owner.'

As Danny turned to leave, he spotted an invitation on the mantelpiece. 'Will you be at Charlie Duncan's drinks party this evening?' he asked.

'Yes, I will. I occasionally invest in his shows.'

'Then I may see you there,' said Danny. 'You can update me then.'

'Will do,' said Payne.

BIG AL DROPPED his boss at Charlie Duncan's offices a few minutes after eight. The room was so crowded, the guests could hardly move. Someone touched Danny's arm and he turned to find Gerald Payne by his side.

'Nick,' he said. 'Good news. I've tracked down the bank representing the owner of one of the sites tipped for the velodrome. The banker, a Monsieur Segat, is calling in the morning to let me know if his client is willing to sell.'

'Gerald.' Davenport suddenly appeared and leaned over to kiss Payne on both cheeks.

Danny was surprised to see that Davenport was unshaven, and wearing a shirt that had clearly already been worn more than once that week.

'Do you know Nick Moncrieff?' asked Payne.

'We met at your closing-night party,' said Danny.

'Oh, right,' said Davenport, showing a little interest.

'Will you be starring in Charlie's next production?' asked Danny.

'No,' replied Davenport. 'Much as I adored being in *Earnest*, I can't afford to devote my talents to the stage alone.'

'That's a pity,' said Danny. 'I would have invested considerably more if you'd been a member of the cast.'

'How nice of you to say so,' said Davenport. 'Perhaps you'll have another opportunity at some time in the future.'

'I do hope so.'

'Well, if you really did want to make a shrewd investment, I have—'

'Larry!' said a voice. Davenport turned away and kissed another, far younger man.

The moment had gone, but Davenport had left Danny's path to success wide open.

'Hi, Nick,' said Charlie Duncan.

'Hi, Charlie,' replied Danny.

'Are you still thinking of investing in *Bling Bling*, old boy?'

'Oh, yes,' said Danny. 'You can put me down for ten thousand. Is Lawrence Davenport doing a film at the moment?'

'What makes you ask that?'

'The unshaven look and the shabby clothes. I thought they might be involved in some part he's playing.'

'No, no,' said Duncan laughing. 'He's only just got out of bed.' He lowered his voice. 'I'd steer clear of him, if I were you. He's on the scrounge. But don't lend him any money, because you'll never get it back.'

MOLLY HAD already served Monsieur Segat with a cup of tea by the time Danny arrived back at The Boltons after his regular meeting with his probation officer, Ms Bennett. The banker rose from his seat as Danny entered the room and apologised for being late.

Segat gave a slight nod before sitting back down. 'In accordance with your instructions, you are now the owner of both sites that are in serious contention for the Olympic velodrome.'

'Has Payne called back?' was all Danny wanted to know.

'Yes. He phoned again this morning and put in a bid of four million pounds for the site most likely to be selected. I presume you want me to turn down his offer?'

'Yes. But tell him that you would accept six million, on the understanding that the contract is signed before the minister announces her decision.'

'But the site will be worth at least twelve million if everything goes to plan.'

'Be assured, everything is going to plan,' said Danny. 'Has Payne shown any interest in the other site I've bought?'

'No. Why should he,' said Segat, 'when everyone is in agreement as to which site will be selected?'

Having gained the information he needed, Danny switched subject. 'Who put in the highest offer for the Wilson's Garage site on Mile End Road?'

'It was Fairfax Homes. I've studied their proposal,' said Segat, handing Danny a glossy brochure, 'and have no doubt that, subject to a few modifications, the scheme should get the green light within the next few weeks.'

'How much?' asked Danny, trying not to sound impatient.

'Ah, yes,' said Segat. 'Fairfax came in at one point eight million pounds, giving you a profit of half a million pounds.'

Danny studied Fairfax's plans for a block of luxury flats on the site where he had once worked as a garage mechanic.

'Shall I call Mr Fairfax and let him know his was the winning bid?'

'Yes, do,' said Danny. 'And once you've spoken to him, I'd like a word.'

While Segat made the call, Danny continued to study Fairfax Homes' impressive plans for the new apartment block. He only had one query.

'I'll just pass you over to Sir Nicholas, Mr Fairfax,' said Segat. 'He would like to have a word with you.'

Danny took the phone. 'I've just been studying your plans, Mr Fairfax,' said Danny, 'and I see you have a penthouse on the top floor.'

'That's right,' said Fairfax. 'Just over three thousand square feet.'

'And you're putting it on the market at six hundred and fifty thousand?'

'Yes, that will be the asking price,' Fairfax confirmed.

'I'll close the deal at a million three if you throw in the penthouse.'

'A million two and you've got yourself a deal,' said Fairfax.

'On one condition.'

'And what's that?'

Danny told Fairfax the change he wanted, and the developer agreed.

DANNY HAD CHOSEN the hour carefully: 11 a.m. Big Al drove round Redcliffe Square twice before stopping outside number 25.

Danny walked up the path and rang the bell. There was no reply. He banged the brass knocker twice, but still no one answered the door. He decided to try again in the afternoon, and had almost reached the gate when the door swung open and a voice demanded, 'Who the hell are you?'

'Nick Moncrieff,' said Danny, walking back up the path. 'You asked me to give you a call, but you're ex-directory. As I was passing . . .'

Lawrence Davenport was wearing a silk dressing gown. He clearly hadn't shaved for several days and was blinking in the morning sunlight like an animal coming out of hibernation on the first day of spring.

'You hinted you had an investment I might be interested in,' said Danny.

'Oh, yes, I remember now,' said Davenport. 'Yes, come in and have a seat in the drawing room while I change. I'll only be a moment.'

Danny didn't sit. He walked round the room admiring the paintings and fine furniture, even if they were covered in a layer of dust. He peered through the back window to see a large but unkempt garden, and remembered the anonymous voice on the line from Geneva that morning. Houses in the square were currently changing hands at around £3 million, and Mr

Davenport had purchased number twenty-five in 1996, when eight million viewers were tuning in to *The Prescription* every Saturday. 'He has a mortgage of one million pounds with Norwich Union,' the voice had concluded, 'and for the last three months he's fallen behind with his payments.'

Davenport walked back into the room. He was wearing an open-necked shirt, jeans and trainers. Danny had seen better-dressed men in prison.

'Can I fix you a drink?'

'It's a little early for me,' said Danny.

'It's never too early,' said Davenport as he poured himself a large whisky. He took a gulp and smiled. 'I'll get straight to the point. I'm a little strapped for cash at the moment, just until someone signs me up for another series. In fact my agent phoned this morning with one or two ideas.'

'You need a loan?' said Danny.

'Yes, that's the long and the short of it.'

'And what can you put up as collateral?'

'Well, my paintings for a start. I paid over a million for them.'

'I'll give you three hundred thousand,' said Danny. 'Assuming you can provide evidence that you did pay over a million.'

Davenport took another gulp of whisky. 'I'll think about it.'

'You do that,' said Danny. 'And if you repay the full amount within twelve months, I'll return the paintings at no extra charge.'

'So what's the catch?' asked Davenport.

'No catch, but if you fail to pay the money back within twelve months, the paintings will be mine.'

'I can't lose,' said Davenport, a broad grin on his face.

'Let's hope not,' said Danny. 'I'll instruct my lawyers to draw up a contract.'

Chapter 10

Danny read *The Times* as Molly poured him a black coffee. An exchange had reportedly taken place on the floor of the House between the Minister for Sport and the Member for Stratford South.

Cormack (Lab, Stratford South): 'Is the minister aware that the president of the British Cycling Federation has written to me pointing out that his

committee voted unanimously in favour of the site in my constituency?'
Minister: 'Yes, I am, partly because my honourable friend kindly sent me a
copy of that letter (laughter). Let me assure him that I shall take the views
of the federation very seriously before I make my final decision.'

Molly put two boiled eggs in front of Danny just as his mobile phone rang
and Payne's name flashed onto the screen. 'Good morning,' said Danny.

''Morning, Nick. I wanted you to know that I've had a call from the
Swiss this morning and they've turned down your offer of four million. But
they made it clear that they would accept six mill, as long as the full amount
is paid before the minister announces her final decision.'

'That's still a good deal,' said Danny. 'But I've got news too, and I'm
afraid it's not so good. My bank's not willing to advance me the full amount
just now.'

'But surely they can see what an opportunity this is?' said Payne.

'Yes, they can, but they still consider it's a risk. Perhaps I should have
warned you that I'm a little overstretched at the moment. I can put up a million,' said Danny. 'Which means we'll still be five million short.'

A long silence followed, then Payne said, 'Nick, I don't suppose you'd
allow me to offer this deal to some of my other clients?'

'Why not,' said Danny, 'considering all the work you've put in. I'm just
livid that I have to miss out on the best deal I've come across for years.'

'That's very magnanimous of you,' said Payne. 'I owe you one.'

'You sure do,' said Danny, as he snapped his mobile closed.

He was about to attack his egg when the phone rang again. He checked
the screen. The word *voice* flashed up. He opened the phone and listened.

'We've had several calls with offers for your site this morning, including
one of eight million. What do you want me to do about Mr Payne?'

'You'll be getting a call from him, in which he'll make an offer of six
million. You will accept his offer,' Danny said before the voice could comment, 'on two conditions. He must deposit six hundred thousand with the
bank before close of business today and he must pay the full amount before
the minister makes her announcement in ten days' time.'

SPENCER CRAIG LEFT chambers at five o'clock, as it was his turn to host the
quarterly Musketeers' dinner. They still got together four times a year,
despite the fact that Toby Mortimer was no longer with them.

Gerald Payne had rung him earlier in the day to say that he had some
exciting news to share that could change all their lives. Payne had gone

from strength to strength in his firm, and now that he had been selected for a safe Conservative seat in Sussex, he looked certain to be an MP after the next election. Larry Davenport appeared more relaxed recently, and had even paid back the £10,000 Craig had lent him a couple of years ago; perhaps Larry also had something to tell the team. Craig had his own piece of news to share with the Musketeers this evening, and although it was no more than he had expected, now that the Danny Cartwright trial was just a hazy memory in his colleagues' minds, it was nevertheless gratifying.

He had put some champagne in the fridge and had just started uncorking a bottle of wine in the dining room, when the doorbell rang.

He couldn't remember when he'd last seen Gerald so buoyant, and assumed it must be because of the news he'd called about that afternoon.

'How are you enjoying the constituency work?' Craig asked as he hung up Payne's coat and led him through to the drawing room.

'Great fun, but I can't wait for the general election so I can take my place in the Commons.' Craig poured him a glass of champagne and asked if he'd heard from Larry lately. 'I popped round to see him one evening last week, but he wouldn't let me inside the house, which I thought was strange.'

'The last time I visited him, the place was in a dreadful state,' said Craig.

'He must be working though,' said Payne. 'He sent me a cheque last week for a loan I'd given up on long ago.'

'You too?' said Craig, as the doorbell rang a second time.

When Davenport strolled in to join them, all the self-confidence and swagger seemed to have returned. Craig offered him a glass of champagne and couldn't help thinking that Larry looked ten years younger.

'Let's begin the evening with a toast,' said Craig. 'To absent friends.'

The three men raised their glasses and cried, 'Toby Mortimer!'

'So, who shall we drink to next?' asked Davenport.

'Sir Nicholas Moncrieff,' said Payne, without hesitation.

'Who the hell is he?' asked Craig.

'The man who's about to change all our fortunes.'

'How?' asked Davenport, unwilling to reveal the fact that Moncrieff was the reason he'd been able to pay off all his debts.

'I'll tell you the details over dinner,' said Payne. 'And tonight I insist on going last, because this time I'm confident you won't be able to trump me.'

'I wouldn't be so sure of that, Gerald,' said Davenport.

A young woman appeared in the doorway. 'We're ready when you are, Mr Craig.' Spencer always employed caterers.

The three men strolled through to the dining room and Craig took his place at the head of the table. Portions of smoked salmon were placed in front of his guests. Once he had tasted the wine and nodded his approval, the young woman filled their glasses. Craig turned to Davenport and said, 'I can't wait any longer, Larry. Let's hear your news first. You've clearly had a change of fortune.'

Davenport leaned back in his chair. 'A couple of days ago I had a call from the BBC. It was the senior producer of *Holby City*, who told me that they were going to write a new character into the series and I was their first choice. They've asked me to do a screen test next week.'

'Bravo,' said Craig, raising a glass.

'Not bad, I must admit,' said Payne, 'but I'm still confident I can beat you.'

Craig drank some wine, then set his glass down on the table again. 'The Lord Chancellor has asked to see me next week.'

'Is he going to offer you his job?' asked Davenport.

'All in good time,' said Craig. 'But the only reason he asks to see someone of my humble status is when he's going to invite them to take silk and become a QC.'

'And well deserved,' said Davenport, as he and Payne rose from their places to salute their host.

'It hasn't been announced yet,' said Craig, waving them back down, 'so whatever you do, don't breathe a word.'

Craig and Davenport turned to Payne. 'Your turn, old chum,' said Craig. 'So what is it that's going to change all our lives?'

BIG AL STOOD in the doorway, clutching a large parcel. 'It's just been delivered, Boss. Where shall I put it?'

'Just leave it on the table,' said Danny, continuing to read his book on the theory of free-market economics. But as soon as he heard the door close, he put down the book and walked across to the table. He looked at the package marked *Hazardous, Handle with Care* for some time before removing the wrapping to reveal a cardboard box. He had to peel off several layers of tape before he was finally able to lift the lid.

He took out a pair of black rubber boots, a black nylon jumpsuit and a mask and tried them on—a perfect fit. The only thing Danny left in the box was a plastic container covered in bubble wrap and marked *Hazardous*. He didn't unwrap it because he knew what was inside. Like any good farmer planting his seeds, he would have to choose the day, even the hour, carefully for his 'night ops' at the site in Stratford. He'd already worked out that he should be able to cover the three acres in just over three hours of painstaking, backbreaking work.

'AND HOW MUCH will *you* be contributing to this enterprise?' asked Craig.

'About a million of my own money,' said Payne, 'of which I've already transferred six hundred thousand in order to secure the contract.'

'Won't that stretch you?' asked Craig.

'To breaking point,' Payne admitted, 'but I'm unlikely to come across an opportunity like this again in my lifetime.'

'Let me try to understand what you're proposing,' said Davenport. 'Whatever sum we put up, you'll guarantee to double it in a month?'

'You can never guarantee anything, but in simple terms this is a two-horse race, and ours is the favourite. I have the opportunity to pick up a piece of land for six million, which will be worth fifteen to twenty million once the minister announces which site she's selected for the velodrome.'

'That's assuming she chooses your site,' said Craig.

'I've shown you the Hansard entry reporting her exchange with MPs.'

'OK, I'm willing to risk two hundred thousand,' said Craig.

'If Gerald's willing to risk a million, so am I,' said Davenport. 'I'm fairly confident I can raise that amount on my house.'

'How are you going to raise the rest of the money?' Craig asked Payne.

'My chairman is stumping up half a million and I've approached a few chums for whom I've made money over the years.'

MOLLY APPEARED in the doorway of Danny's study. She was shaking and unable to speak.

'What's the matter, Molly?' asked Danny, jumping up. 'Are you OK?'

'It's him,' she whispered. 'That actor. That Dr Beresford. You know, Lawrence Davenport.'

'Is it, indeed?' said Danny, laughing. 'Show him into the drawing room.'

He picked up the Davenport file and brought himself quickly up to date, then went downstairs to join his uninvited guest.

Davenport leapt up as Danny entered the room. As they greeted one another, Danny was momentarily taken aback by the actor's smart, clean-shaven appearance.

'Sorry to barge in on you like this,' the actor said. 'I wouldn't have done if it wasn't a bit of an emergency.'

'Please don't worry,' said Danny, sitting down in the chair opposite. 'Do sit down. How can I help?'

'I want to invest a rather large sum of money in a business venture. Only temporary, you understand. Not only will I repay you within a few weeks at the outside, but,' he said, looking up at the McTaggart above the fireplace, 'I'll also be able to reclaim my paintings at the same time.'

Danny was suddenly aware that the room was full of Davenport's pictures. 'Rest assured, they will be returned the moment the loan is repaid.'

'That could turn out to be sooner than I had anticipated,' said Davenport. 'Especially if you were able to help me out with this little enterprise.'

'What sort of sum did you have in mind?' asked Danny.

'A million,' said Davenport tentatively. 'The problem is that I've only got a week to come up with the money.'

'And what would your collateral be this time?' asked Danny.

'My house in Redcliffe Square.'

'And you say that you will pay the full sum back within a month, using your home as collateral?'

'Within a month, it's guaranteed—a racing certainty.'

'And if you fail to pay back the million in that time?'

'The house is yours.'

'We have a deal,' said Danny. 'I'll get onto my lawyers straight away.'

'NICK, HOW LOVELY to see you,' said Sarah as she took her seat in the theatre. She leaned across and whispered, 'Now, tell me you've been a good boy.'

'Depends what you mean by good,' said Danny as he sat next to her.

'You haven't missed a meeting with your favourite lady?'

Danny thought about Beth, even though he knew Sarah was referring to Ms Bennett, his probation officer. 'Not one,' he said.

'And you haven't even thought about going abroad?'

'Not unless you count travelling up to Scotland to visit Mr Munro.'

'Good. So what else have you been up to that's safe to tell your other solicitor?'

'Not a lot,' said Danny. 'How's Lawrence?'

'Never better. He's doing a screen test for *Holby City* next Thursday.'

A familiar voice said, 'Hello, Sarah,' and Charlie Duncan bent and kissed her cheek. He turned to Danny. 'Good to see you, Nick. Enjoy the show.'

The lights went down and the curtain rose. Danny had read the script of *Bling Bling*, but hadn't been able to follow it, so he was curious to see how the show in which he had invested £10,000 would work on stage. By the interval, he was stifling a yawn.

'What do you think?' he asked Sarah, wondering if he had missed something.

Sarah put a finger to her lips and pointed to the critic in front of them, who was writing furiously. 'Let's go and have a drink,' she whispered.

Danny followed her into the stalls bar. As they entered the crowded room, he spotted Gerald Payne standing by a table, pouring a glass of champagne for Spencer Craig. He wondered if Craig had yet been tempted to invest in his Olympic site.

'Hey, Sarah, Nick! We're over here!' shouted Payne, waving furiously at them. 'Come and have a glass of bubbly.'

Danny walked reluctantly across to join them. 'You remember Nick Moncrieff,' said Payne, turning to Craig.

'Of course,' said Craig. 'The man who's about to make us all a fortune.'

'Let's hope so,' said Danny—his question answered.

'We'll need all the help we can get after tonight's performance,' said Payne, with a grimace.

'Oh, it could have been worse,' said Sarah.

'It's shit,' said Craig. 'So that's one of my investments down the drain.'

'You didn't put too much into it, I hope?' said Danny.

'Nothing compared to what I've invested in your little enterprise,' said Craig, who couldn't take his eyes off Sarah.

Payne whispered to Danny, 'I transferred the full amount this morning. We'll be exchanging contracts some time in the next few days.'

'I'm delighted to hear it.'

'By the way,' added Payne, 'I've managed to get a couple of tickets for Parliamentary Questions next Thursday. So if you'd like to join me for the minister's statement, you'd be most welcome.'

'That's kind of you, Gerald, but wouldn't you rather take Lawrence or Craig?' He still couldn't bring himself to call him Spencer.

'Larry's got a screen test that afternoon, and Spencer has an appointment with the Lord Chancellor at the other end of the building. We all know what that's about,' he said, winking.

'Do we?' asked Danny.

'Oh, yes. Spencer's about to be made a QC,' Payne whispered.

'Congratulations,' said Danny, turning to his adversary.

'It's not official yet,' said Craig.

'But it will be next Thursday,' said Payne. 'So, Nick, why don't you meet me outside the St Stephen's entrance of the House at twelve thirty and we can listen to the minister's statement before going off to celebrate.'

WHEN THE CURTAIN FELL, Danny turned to Sarah. 'If you're going to the opening-night party, why don't I give you a lift?'

'I'm not going,' said Sarah, linking her arm in his. 'How do you feel about taking a lonely girl out to dinner?'

Danny recalled the last time he'd taken up such an offer, and how that evening had ended. He didn't want to have to explain to another girl, and particularly not this one. 'I'm sorry,' he said, 'but . . .'

'You're married?' asked Sarah.

'I only wish,' said Danny.

'I only wish I'd met you before she did,' said Sarah, unlinking her arm.

'That wouldn't have been possible,' said Danny, without explanation.

'Bring her along next time,' said Sarah. 'I'd like to meet her. Good night, Nick.' She kissed him on the cheek and drifted off to join her brother.

ALEX REDMAYNE WAS LOOKING across the Thames at the London Eye when she arrived. He rose from the bench to greet her.

'Have you ever been on the Eye?' he asked as she sat down beside him.

'Yes, once,' said Beth. 'You used to be able to see our garage from the top.'

'It won't be long before you'll be able to see Wilson House,' said Alex.

'Yes. It was kind of the developer to name the building after my dad. He'd have enjoyed that.'

'I have to be back in court by two o'clock,' said Alex. 'But I needed to see you urgently, as I have some news. I had a letter this morning from the Lord Chancellor's office, and he's agreed to re-open the case.' Beth threw her arms round him. 'But only if we can supply some fresh evidence.'

'How can we possibly do that?' asked Beth.

'I've been thinking. Do you remember that Danny and Big Al shared a cell with a man called Nick Moncrieff?'

'Of course,' said Beth. 'He taught Danny to read and write.'

'Well, some weeks before Moncrieff was released, he wrote to me offering to help in any way he could, as he was convinced Danny was innocent.'

'But how could he help after all this time?'

'Danny once told me that Moncrieff kept a diary while he was in prison, and there may be something in it that we could use to help clear Danny's name. Courts take such diaries very seriously, because they're contemporaneous evidence.'

'Then all you have to do is get in touch with Moncrieff,' said Beth, unable to hide her excitement.

'It's not that simple,' said Alex. 'He might not welcome a letter from a lawyer he's never met, asking him to become involved in another court case.'

'Danny said you could always rely on Nick, come hell or high water.'

'Then I'll write to him today,' said Alex.

DANNY MET GERALD PAYNE outside the St Stephen's entrance of the Palace of Westminster. It was his first visit to the House of Commons.

'I have two tickets for the public gallery,' Payne announced in a loud voice to the officer stationed at the entrance.

Once they had passed under the metal detector, Payne guided Danny down a marble corridor to the Central Lobby. He showed his tickets to a policeman on the desk, who directed them to the Strangers' Gallery.

When the Speaker rose at 12.30 and bellowed, 'Statement by the Minister for Sport,' Payne leaned forward to get a better view. The minister rose from the front bench and placed a red file on the dispatch box.

'Mr Speaker, I will make a statement concerning the site of a prospective Olympic velodrome. Members will recall that I informed the House earlier this month that I had short-listed two locations but would not make my final decision until I had received surveyors' reports on both sites.' Danny glanced round at Payne; a bead of sweat had appeared on his forehead. 'Those reports were handed in to my office yesterday.

'Having read the reports, all the parties concerned agreed that only one site could possibly be considered.' A flicker of a smile appeared on Payne's lips. 'However, the surveyor's report revealed that it is infested with a plant known as Japanese Knotweed, which, once it takes hold, renders the land unsuitable for any building project. I am therefore left with no choice but to select the excellent, alternative site for this project.' Payne's skin turned chalk white when he heard the word 'alternative'. The minister resumed her place and waited for questions.

Danny looked at Payne, whose head was resting in his hands.

An usher came running down the steps. 'Is your friend feeling all right?' he asked, looking concerned.

'I'm afraid not,' said Danny, looking unconcerned. 'Can we get him to a lavatory? I have a feeling he's going to be sick.'

Danny took Payne by the arm and helped him to his feet, and the usher guided them both up the steps and out of the gallery.

As Payne bowed his head and clung to the edge of the basin in the wash-room, Danny loosened the estate agent's tie and helped him off with his jacket. He removed Payne's mobile from a pocket of his jacket and scrolled through the address book until he reached the name 'Lawrence'. As Payne fell onto his knees, sobbing, Danny checked his watch. Good. Davenport would be preparing for his screen test. He began to tap out a text message: *minister didn't select our site. Sorry. Thought you'd want to know.* He smiled and touched the SEND button, before returning to the list of contacts. He scrolled down again, stopping at the name 'Spencer'. . .

SPENCER CRAIG LOOKED at himself in the full-length mirror. He had pur-chased a new shirt and silk tie especially for the occasion. He'd also booked a car to pick him up from chambers at 11.30 a.m. He couldn't risk being late for the Lord Chancellor.

'First he'll offer you a glass of dry sherry,' a senior colleague had told him. 'Then he'll chat for a few minutes about the dire state of English cricket, and then suddenly he'll tell you in the strictest confidence that he will be making a recommendation to Her Majesty that your name should be included in the next list of barristers to take silk.'

The car stopped outside the entrance to the House of Lords, where an officer checked his name on a clipboard and waved them through. The driver came to a halt outside the Lord Chancellor's office, where Craig was escorted up a red-carpeted staircase to a heavy oak door.

The escort tapped on the door and a voice said, 'Come in.'

Craig could feel the sweat on the palms of his hands as he walked into the magnificent oak-panelled room that overlooked the River Thames.

'Have a seat, Mr Craig,' said the Lord Chancellor, now opening a red folder on the centre of his desk. There was no suggestion of a glass of dry sherry. 'I thought, given the circumstances, Mr Craig, I should have a word in private rather than you becoming aware of the details in the press.'

No mention of the state of English cricket either.

'We have received an application,' the Lord Chancellor continued, 'for a Royal Pardon in the case of Daniel Arthur Cartwright. Three Law Lords have advised me that having reviewed the evidence, it is their recommenda-tion that I should advise Her Majesty to allow a full judicial review of the case. As you were a prosecution witness in the original trial, I felt I should warn you that Their Lordships are minded to call you to appear before them in order to question you concerning your evidence at the original hearing.'

Before he could continue, Craig jumped in. 'But I thought that before Their Lordships would even consider overturning an appeal, it was necessary for new evidence to be presented for their consideration?'

'New evidence has been forthcoming. There is a claim from Cartwright's former cellmate.' He peered at the folder. 'A Mr Albert Crann, who states that he was present when Mr Toby Mortimer asserted that he had witnessed the murder of Mr Bernard Wilson.'

'But this is nothing more than hearsay, coming from the lips of a convicted criminal. It wouldn't stand up in any court in the land.'

'I would have to agree with that judgment, had not a fresh piece of evidence been presented, a diary kept by another cellmate who recorded everything that he witnessed in prison, including conversations in which he took part.'

'So the sole source of these accusations is a diary that a convicted criminal wrote while he was in prison?'

'No one is accusing you of anything, Mr Craig,' said the Lord Chancellor, 'and you will, of course, be given every opportunity to present your side of the case.'

'Who is this criminal with the diary?' demanded Craig.

The Lord Chancellor looked up and said, 'Sir Nicholas Moncrieff.'

Chapter 11

Danny sat in his usual alcove seat inside the Dorchester reading *The Times*. An out-of-breath Gary Hall appeared by his side.

'Sorry to be late,' he gasped, 'but the senior partner called me in just as I was about to leave. Quite a bit of flak flying around following the minister's statement. Everyone is blaming everyone else.' He took a seat.

'Well, at least no one appears to be blaming you, Gary,' said Danny.

'Oh, no one thinks I was even involved,' said Hall. 'Which is why I've been promoted.'

'Promoted?' said Danny. 'Congratulations.'

'Thank you, but it wouldn't have happened if Gerald Payne hadn't been sacked. He was summoned to the senior partner's office first thing this morning and told to clear his desk and be off the premises within an hour.'

'Didn't they realise we took the idea to Payne in the first place?'

'No, once it turned out you couldn't raise the full amount, it suddenly became Payne's idea. In fact you're regarded as someone who's lost his investment and may have a claim against the company.'

Danny managed to stifle a smile. 'I have another job for you,' he said. 'I need you to dispose of a property in Redcliffe Square—'

'Hi, Nick,' said a voice.

A tall, heavily built man whom Danny had never seen before was towering over him. He was wearing a kilt and had a shock of brown wavy hair.

'Hello,' said Danny, standing up and shaking the stranger's hand warmly, pretending to know him. 'Can I introduce you to a business associate of mine, Gary Hall?'

The man bent down and shook hands with Hall, saying in a strong Scottish accent, 'Pleased to meet you, Gary, I'm Sandy, Sandy Dawson.'

'Sandy and I go back a long way,' said Danny, hoping to find out how long.

'Sure do,' said Dawson. 'But I haven't seen Nick since we left school.'

'We were at Loretto together,' Danny said, smiling at Hall. 'So what have you been up to, Sandy?' he asked, desperately searching for another clue.

'Still in the meat business,' said Dawson. 'What about you, Nick?'

'I've been taking it pretty easy since . . .' said Danny, attempting to discover if Dawson knew that Nick had been to prison.

'Yes, of course,' said Sandy. 'Terrible business, most unfair. I'm delighted to see you've come through the whole experience unscathed. Anyway, sorry to interrupt you but I couldn't just walk by without saying hello.'

'Quite right,' said Danny. 'It was good to see you after all this time.'

'You too,' said Dawson, as he turned to leave.

Danny sat back down, and began to take some papers from his briefcase, Dawson turned back. 'Oh . . . did you know that Squiffy Humphries died?'

'No, I'm sorry to hear that,' said Danny.

'Had a heart attack on the golf course while playing a round with the headmaster. The fifteen has never been the same since Squiffy retired.'

'Yes, poor old Squiffy. Great coach.'

'The whole of Musselburgh turned out for his funeral.'

'No more than he deserved,' said Danny. Dawson nodded and walked away.

Danny passed over the deeds of Lawrence Davenport's house in Redcliffe Square to Gary Hall.

Hall studied the document for some time before he asked, 'What sort of price are you expecting the property to fetch?'

'Around three million,' said Danny. 'There's a mortgage of just over a million, and I've put up another million, so anything above two point two, two point three should show me a profit.'

'The first thing I'll have to do is arrange for a survey.'

'Pity Payne didn't carry out a survey on the Stratford site.'

'He claims he did,' said Hall. 'My bet is the surveyor had never heard of Japanese Knotweed. To be fair, neither had anyone else in the office.' He turned the last page of the deeds. 'I say, is that who I think it is?'

'Yes, Lawrence Davenport, the actor,' said Danny.

CRAIG HAD SENT OUT for four pizzas and there would be no waitresses to serve wine for this particular gathering of the Musketeers.

Since leaving the Lord Chancellor's office, he had spent every spare moment trying to find out everything he could about Sir Nicholas Moncrieff. He had soon discovered that Moncrieff had been released from prison a couple of weeks after Cartwright's death. But what Craig couldn't work out was why anyone would be willing to devote his entire existence, as Moncrieff had done, to tracking down and then attempting to destroy three men he had never met. Unless . . .

It was when he placed the photographs of Moncrieff and Cartwright next to each other that Craig's suspicions were seriously aroused.

There was a knock on the front door. Craig went to open it, to be greeted by the forlorn figure of Gerald Payne, clutching a bottle of cheap wine.

Craig led him into the drawing room. 'So where have you been hiding?'

'I'm staying in Sussex with my mother until this all blows over. I'm telling everybody I resigned from Baker, Tremlett and Smythe to devote more time to my constituency work.'

'I have no doubt you'll survive,' said Craig. 'Frankly, I'm far more worried about Larry. He not only failed to land the part in *Holby City*, but he's telling everyone that you texted him about the minister's statement just as he was about to take the screen test.'

'But that's just not true,' said Payne. 'I was in such a state of shock I didn't get in touch with anyone, not even you.'

'Someone did,' said Craig. 'And I now realise if it wasn't you who sent us both a text, it had to be someone who knew about Larry's screen test.'

'The person who had access to my phone at that time.'

'The ubiquitous Sir Nicholas Moncrieff.'

'The bastard! I'll kill him!' said Payne.

'That must be Larry,' said Craig as the doorbell rang.

Payne couldn't believe the change in Larry when he went to let him in. He was wearing a pair of faded jeans and a crumpled shirt, and clearly hadn't shaved since he'd heard about the announcement. He slumped down in the nearest chair. 'Why, why, why?' were his opening words.

'No need to panic,' said Craig. 'I think I've come up with a way of finishing off Moncrieff once and for all. And there's a possibility that we can all get our money back, too.'

'But what I still don't understand,' said Payne, 'is why he put us through all this. It can't just be because he shared a cell with Cartwright.'

'I agree, there has to be more to it than that,' said Davenport.

'There is,' said Craig. 'And if it's what I think it is, Moncrieff won't be bothering us for much longer. Ever heard of oldschoolchums.com?'

'Yes, but who have you been trying to get in touch with?' asked Payne.

'Anyone who knew Moncrieff when he was at school or in the army.'

'Did anybody contact you?' asked Davenport, as the doorbell rang again.

'Seven people, but only one had all the necessary qualifications,' said Craig, as he left to answer the door. When he reappeared moments later, he was accompanied by a tall, heavily built man.

'Gentlemen, allow me to introduce Sandy Dawson,' said Craig. 'Sandy was in the same house at Loretto College as Nicholas Moncrieff.'

Dawson shook hands with Payne and Davenport.

'When Sandy got in touch,' interrupted Craig, 'thinking I was Moncrieff, I told him my reservations about the man claiming to be his old school friend, and he agreed to put him to the test. Gerald told me that Moncrieff had an appointment with one of his colleagues, Gary Hall, at the Dorchester, so Sandy turned up there.'

'When I first spotted him I felt certain it was Nick,' said Dawson. 'But when I walked over to have a word with him, he didn't show the slightest sign of recognition, and it's not as if I'm that easy to forget.'

'That's one of the reasons I selected you,' said Craig. 'But it still doesn't constitute proof, not after fifteen years or more.'

'Which is why I decided to test him,' explained Dawson. 'I told him that Squiffy Humphries had died, and the man said "Great coach". That was his mistake. Squiffy Humphries was our house matron. There was no way he could have forgotten her. I don't know who the man at the Dorchester was, but I can tell you one thing for certain, he wasn't Nicholas Moncrieff.'

'Then who the hell is he?' asked Payne.

'I know exactly,' said Craig. 'And what's more, I will be able to prove it.'

BETH EMERGED from Knightsbridge tube station. The pavements were busy with window shoppers and locals walking off Sunday lunch.

Alex Redmayne could not have been more supportive over the past weeks, and when she had left him less than an hour ago, she had felt confident. But now, as she walked to The Boltons, that confidence began to fade.

Nick Moncrieff was a decent man who had become a loyal friend of Danny's when they were in prison together, so she couldn't understand why he wouldn't even consider an off-the-record meeting with Alex Redmayne to discuss giving evidence before the tribunal, particularly as his diaries had been delivered to Alex's chambers the day after Alex wrote to him. It must have something to do with Moncrieff wanting to avoid any confrontation with the police until he had completed his probation order. But Alex wasn't willing to give up easily. He had convinced Beth that if she could get Moncrieff to give evidence before the Law Lords, it might be the deciding factor in having Danny's name cleared.

DANNY WAS READING through his essay on J. K. Galbraith's theories on a low-tax economy when the doorbell rang. He walked along the corridor and pulled open the door.

'My name is Beth Wilson. I apologise for disturbing your Sunday . . .'

Danny stood there, speechless, staring at the woman he loved.

Beth turned white. 'It can't be,' she said.

'It is, my darling,' Danny replied as he took her in his arms.

Gerald Payne, sitting in a car opposite, continued taking photographs.

'MR HUGO MONCRIEFF?'

'Who is this?'

'My name is Spencer Craig. I'm a barrister, and I have a proposition.'

'And what might that be, Mr Craig?'

'If I were able to restore your fortune, what would that be worth?'

'Name your price.'

'Twenty-five per cent.'

'That sounds a bit steep.'

'To give you back your estate in Scotland, kick out the occupant of your house in The Boltons, restore the full amount paid for your grandfather's stamp collection and reclaim your bank accounts in Geneva and London? No, I don't think that's particularly steep, Mr Moncrieff. In fact it's quite reasonable when the alternative is a hundred per cent of nothing.'

'But how could this be possible?'

'Once you've signed a contract, Mr Moncrieff, your father's fortune will be restored to you.'

'And there will be no fees or hidden charges?' asked Hugo suspiciously.

'No fees or hidden charges,' promised Craig. 'In fact, I'll throw in a little bonus, which I suspect will even please Mrs Moncrieff.'

'And what's that?'

'Sign my contract, and by this time next week she'll be Lady Moncrieff.'

'DID YOU GET A PHOTO of his leg?' asked Craig.

'Not yet,' replied Payne.

'That's your priority now. Let me know the moment you do.'

'Hold on,' said Payne. 'He's coming out of the house with the woman who went inside with him yesterday.'

'Describe her.'

'Late twenties, five foot eight, slim, brown hair. They're getting into the back of Moncrieff's car.'

'Stay with them,' said Craig, 'and keep me briefed on where they go.' He put the phone down, turned on his computer and pulled up a photo of Beth Wilson, which confirmed that she fitted the description.

Once Payne had got the photograph of Cartwright's left leg, Craig would make an appointment to see Detective Sergeant Fuller. He would then let the policeman take the credit for capturing an escaped murderer.

DANNY WONDERED how much time he had left before Craig found out his true identity, if he hadn't done so already. Only a couple more days, that was all Danny needed, and then the whole world would know the truth.

He put on his running kit. He had decided to go on an extended run as he needed to think about his meeting with Alex Redmayne the following morning.

As he ran past Cheyne Walk, he avoided looking up at Sarah's apartment, where he knew her brother, Lawrence Davenport, was now living. If he had done so, he might have spotted another man, who he would have recognised, standing by an open window taking a photograph of him.

Danny continued towards Parliament Square, and, when he passed the St Stephen's entrance to the House of Commons, he thought about Payne and wondered where he was, little realising he was standing on the opposite side of the road focusing his camera, trying to look like a tourist taking a picture of Big Ben.

'DID YOU GET a half-decent photograph?' asked Craig.

'Enough to fill a gallery,' replied Payne.

'Well done. Bring them over to my place now.'

Craig put the phone down, poured himself a drink and thought about what he was going to say to the man he'd been looking forward to calling all week.

'Could I speak to Detective Sergeant Fuller?' he said when the phone was answered.

'*Inspector* Fuller,' said a voice. 'Who shall I say is calling?'

'Spencer Craig. I'm a barrister.'

'I'll put you through, sir.'

'Mr Craig, it's been a long time since I've heard from you. I'm unlikely to forget the last occasion you called.'

'Nor me,' said Craig, 'and that's the reason I'm phoning this time, *Inspector.* Many congratulations, but I have a piece of information that might make your promotion to chief inspector even quicker.'

'You have my full attention,' said Fuller.

'But I have to make it clear, Inspector, that you didn't get the information from me. And I'd rather not talk about it over the phone.'

'Of course. So where and when would you like to meet?'

'The Sherlock Holmes, twelve fifteen tomorrow?'

'How appropriate,' said Fuller. 'I'll see you there, Mr Craig.'

Craig was about to make another call when the doorbell rang. He opened the door to find Payne standing under the porch, grinning. Payne walked straight past him without uttering a word, marched into the kitchen and spread six photographs out on the table.

Craig looked down at the images and understood immediately why Payne was so smug. Just above the knee on Danny's left leg was a scar from a wound that Craig remembered inflicting.

'ARE YOU AWAKE?'

'Yes,' said Beth.

'Are you still hoping I'll change my mind?'

'Yes, but I know it's pointless to try to persuade you, Danny. You've always been as stubborn as a mule. I only hope you realise that if it turns out to be the wrong decision, this could be our last night together.'

'But if I'm right,' said Danny, 'we'll have ten thousand nights like this.'

'But we could have a lifetime of nights like this without you having to take such a risk.'

'You have no idea what it's like to be continually looking over your shoulder, waiting for someone to say, "The game's up, Danny Boy, you're going back to jail for the rest of your life." When I saw you standing in the doorway, I realised that I no longer wanted to be Sir Nicholas Moncrieff. I'm Danny Cartwright, and I'm in love with Beth Wilson of Bacon Road. Besides, if three Law Lords believe my case is strong enough to consider a Royal Pardon, perhaps they'll feel that I have an even stronger case if I'm willing to give up so much to prove my innocence.'

'I know you're right, Danny, but the last few days have been the happiest of my life.'

'Mine too, Beth, but they'll be happier still when I'm a totally free man. I've had my last meeting with my probation officer. That was the first step. And I have enough faith in human nature to believe that Alex Redmayne, Fraser Munro and even Sarah Davenport will not rest until they see justice done.'

As Danny leaned across and kissed her gently on the lips, a noise like a clap of thunder reverberated from the floor below.

'What the hell was that?' Danny switched on the bedside light and heard the sound of footsteps pounding up the stairs. He swung his legs out of bed as three police officers dressed in flak jackets and carrying batons burst into the bedroom, three more following close behind. The first three grabbed Danny and threw him to the floor. Two of them pressed his face into the carpet while the third held his arms behind his back and snapped a pair of handcuffs on him. Out of the corner of his eye, he could see a policewoman pinning Beth against the wall, while another handcuffed her.

When Inspector Fuller walked in they yanked Danny to his feet.

'Caution them,' Fuller said as he sat on the bed and lit a cigarette.

Once the ritual had been completed, Danny and Beth were dragged downstairs and out through the front door where three police cars, lights flashing, back doors open, awaited them.

Danny, just a towel covering him, was thrown into the back of the middle car, to be sandwiched between two officers. He could see Big Al suffering the same treatment in the car in front.

'YOU HAVEN'T ARRIVED a moment too soon,' said Alex's mother.

'That bad?' said Alex, strolling into the drawing room.

'Worse,' replied his mother. 'When will the Home Office realise that when judges retire, the only people they have left to judge are their innocent wives?'

Alex smiled. 'Did His Lordship tell you that I sent him the details of a case I'm currently working on, and that I could do with his advice?'

'If he turns you down, Alex, I won't feed him again.'

'Then I must be in with a chance,' said Alex, as his father strolled in.

'A chance of what?' the old man asked.

'A chance of some help on a case that—'

'The Cartwright case?' said his father. 'I've just finished reading the transcripts. As far as I can make out, there aren't many more laws left for the lad to break; murder, escaping from prison, theft, cashing cheques on bank accounts that didn't belong to him, selling a stamp collection he didn't own, travelling abroad on someone else's passport, and even claiming a baronetcy that should rightfully have been inherited by someone else. You can't blame the police for throwing the book at him.'

'Does that mean you're not willing to help me?' asked Alex.

'I didn't say that,' said Justice Redmayne, turning round to face his son. 'On the contrary. I'm at your service, because I'm absolutely certain of one thing: Danny Cartwright is innocent.'

BOOK FIVE: Redemption
Chapter 12

Danny Cartwright sat on the wooden chair in the dock and waited for the trial to begin. He looked down into the well of the court to see his two counsel deep in conversation as they waited for the judge to appear.

Danny had spent an hour with Alex Redmayne and his junior in an interview room below the court earlier that morning. They had done their best to reassure him, but he knew all too well that, although he was innocent of murdering Bernie, he had no defence to the charges of fraud, theft, deception and escaping from prison. A combined tariff of eight to ten years seemed to be the general consensus, from the barrack-room lawyers of

Belmarsh to the eminent silks plying their trade at the Old Bailey. And the sentence would be added to Danny's original tariff, which would mean that he would be eligible for his old-age pension before he could hope to see the light of day again.

The press benches to Danny's left were packed with reporters waiting to add to the thousands of column inches they had written over the past six months. The story of Danny Cartwright, the only man ever to escape from Britain's top high-security prison, fascinated the public, and the first day of the trial was taking on the status of an opening night in the West End, with queues having begun to form outside the Old Bailey at four that morning.

Alex Redmayne and his junior, The Rt Hon Sir Matthew Redmayne, KCMG, QC, had refused to charge a penny for their services, although Sir Matthew had warned Danny that if they were able to convince the jury that the profits he'd accrued during the past two years belonged to him and not to Hugo Moncrieff, he would be presenting a hefty bill plus expenses.

Beth had been released on bail the morning after she had been arrested, as Alex had been able to convince the court that, although Beth was technically guilty of aiding and abetting, she had been aware that Danny was still alive for only four days, and she and her fiancé had already made an appointment to see Alex in his chambers on the morning she had been arrested. The judge gave Beth a six months' suspended sentence.

The judge did not taken quite as lenient a view when it came to the role Big Al had played in the conspiracy. Alex had pointed out that his client, Albert Crann, had made no financial gain from the Moncrieff fortune, other than to receive a salary as Danny's driver while being allowed to sleep in a small room on the top floor of his house in The Boltons. But Mr Arnold Pearson, QC, representing the Crown, had then produced a bombshell.

'Can Mr Crann explain how the sum of ten thousand pounds was deposited in his private account only days after he'd been discharged from prison?'

Big Al had no explanation, and even if he had, he wasn't about to tell Pearson where the money had come from. The judge sent Big Al back to Belmarsh to serve another five years—the rest of his original sentence. Danny made sure he became enhanced, and that he behaved impeccably during his period of incarceration. Glowing reports from Senior Officer Ray Pascoe, confirmed by the governor, meant that Big Al would be released on a tag in less than a year.

Beth had had one good piece of news to tell Danny on one of her Sunday afternoon visits to Belmarsh while he was awaiting trial. 'I'm pregnant.'

'Let's hope it will be a brother for Christy,' Danny had said as he took her in his arms. 'If it is, we can call him Bernie.'

'No, we're going to call him . . .' The klaxon had signalled the end of visits and drowned out her words.

MR JUSTICE HACKETT had called both counsels to his chambers before proceedings began, to warn them to steer clear of any reference to the original murder trial, the verdict of which had been reached by a jury and later upheld by three judges at the Court of Appeal. He went on to stress that should either party attempt to place on record the contents of a particular tape as evidence, or mention the names of Spencer Craig, QC, Gerald Payne, MP, or the well-known actor Lawrence Davenport, they could expect to face his wrath. Now he peered around the courtroom, much as an opening batsman does when checking to see where the fielders have been placed.

He turned his attention to the opening bowler for the home team, Arnold Pearson, QC. 'Mr Pearson, are you ready to make your opening?'

'I am, M'lord,' replied Pearson, rising slowly from his place. 'Members of the jury, the defendant is charged with five counts. The first is that he escaped from Belmarsh Prison while in custody for a previous offence.

'The second count is that the defendant did steal, from Sir Hugo Moncrieff, an estate in Scotland, comprising a fourteen-bedroom mansion and twelve thousand acres of arable land.

'The third count is that he occupied a house, namely number twelve The Boltons, London SW10, which was not lawfully his.

'The fourth count relates to the theft of a unique stamp collection and the sale of that collection for the sum of over fifty-five million pounds.

'And the fifth count is that the defendant cashed cheques on a bank account at Coutts in the Strand, London, and transferred money from a private bank in Switzerland, neither of which actions he was entitled to do, and that he profited by so doing.

'The Crown will show that all these counts are linked, and were committed by the defendant, Daniel Cartwright, who falsely passed himself off as Sir Nicholas Moncrieff. In order to prove this, members of the jury, I will first have to take you back to Belmarsh Prison to show how the defendant was able to place himself in a position to commit these audacious crimes. To do that, it may be necessary for me to mention in passing the original offence of which Cartwright was convicted.'

'You will do no such thing,' interjected Mr Justice Hackett. 'The original crime committed by the defendant has no bearing on the offences that are being tried in this court. You may not refer to that earlier case unless you can show a direct and relevant connection between it and this case.'

Sir Matthew frowned. Alex would have to develop an ingenious argument if he didn't want to arouse the wrath of Mr Justice Hackett.

'I will tread more carefully in future,' Pearson said, as he turned to the next page of his file and continued his lengthy opening speech.

'. . . So NOW THAT as a result of his audacious and premeditated deception, Cartwright is a multimillionaire, you may well ask yourselves what he could possibly do next. I will tell you,' said Pearson. 'He bought himself a top-of-the-range BMW, employed a chauffeur and a housekeeper, settled down in The Boltons and carried on the myth that he was Sir Nicholas Moncrieff. And, members of the jury, he would still be living that myth today if it were not for the professionalism of Chief Inspector Fuller, the man who arrested Cartwright for his original offence in 1999, and who now single-handedly tracked him down, arrested him and finally brought him to justice. That, members of the jury, is the case for the prosecution.'

'Not bad,' admitted Alex to his father, as Pearson resumed his seat.

'I agree, though Arnold did make one mistake he may live to regret.'

'And what was that?' asked Alex.

Sir Matthew passed his son the piece of paper on which he had written the words *single-handedly*.

'THERE'S ONLY ONE THING you have to get this witness to admit,' said Sir Matthew. 'But at the same time, we don't need the judge or Arnold Pearson to realise what you're up to.'

'No pressure,' said Alex with a grin, as Mr Justice Hackett re-entered the courtroom after the lunch break.

The judge bowed low before resuming his place in the high-backed, red leather chair. He nodded in the direction of Mr Pearson who rose from his place and said, 'I call Chief Inspector Fuller.'

Chief Inspector Fuller took the oath without even glancing at the card.

'Detective Chief Inspector Fuller,' said Pearson, 'can I place on the record that you were the arresting officer when Daniel Cartwright committed his previous offence for which he received a prison sentence?'

'That is correct, sir.'

'How did you learn that Cartwright might have escaped from Belmarsh

Prison and was passing himself off as Sir Nicholas Moncrieff?'

'On October the 23rd last year I received a telephone call from a reliable source who told me that he needed to see me on an urgent matter.'

'Did he go into any detail at that time?'

'No, sir. He's not the sort of gentleman who would commit himself over the telephone.'

Sir Matthew wrote down the word 'gentleman', not a word a policeman would normally use when referring to a snitch. His second catch in the slips. He wasn't expecting many of those while his old adversary Arnold Pearson was on his feet bowling the Chief Inspector gentle off-breaks.

'So a meeting was arranged?' said Pearson.

'Yes, we agreed to meet the following day.'

'And when you met the next day, he informed you that he had some information concerning Daniel Cartwright?'

'Yes. Which came as a bit of a surprise,' said Fuller, 'because I was under the misapprehension that Cartwright had hanged himself.'

'So what did you do next?'

'I placed a twenty-four-hour surveillance team on number twelve The Boltons, and quickly discovered that the resident who was claiming to be Sir Nicholas Moncrieff did bear a striking resemblance to Cartwright.'

'But surely that would not have been enough cause for you to arrest him?'

'No,' replied Fuller. 'I needed more tangible proof than that.'

'And what form did this tangible proof take?'

'On the third day of surveillance, the suspect received a visit from a Miss Elizabeth Wilson, and she stayed the night.'

'Miss Elizabeth Wilson?'

'Yes. She is the mother of Cartwright's daughter and she visited him on a regular basis while he was in prison, which made me confident that the information I had been given was accurate.'

'And that was when you decided to arrest him?'

'Yes.'

'Thank you, Chief Inspector. I have no more questions at present.'

'Thank you, Mr Pearson,' said the judge. 'Do you wish to cross-examine this witness, Mr Redmayne?'

'I certainly do, M'lord,' said Alex, rising. 'Chief Inspector, you told the court it was a member of the public who volunteered the information that made it possible for you to arrest Daniel Cartwright.'

'Yes, that is correct,' said Fuller, gripping the rail of the witness box.

'So it wasn't, as my learned friend suggested, a "single-handed" piece of police ingenuity?'

'No. But as I'm sure you appreciate, Mr Redmayne, the police rely on a network of informers.'

'So this "gentleman", as you described your informant, called you and you arranged to meet him. Where did that meeting take place, Chief Inspector?'

Fuller turned to the judge. 'I would prefer, M'lord, not to identify the location.'

'Understandably,' said Mr Justice Hackett. 'Move on, Mr Redmayne.'

'So there would be no point in my asking you, Chief Inspector, to name your paid informant?'

'He wasn't paid,' said Fuller, regretting the words immediately.

'Well, at least we know that he was an unpaid, professional gentleman.'

'Well done,' whispered Alex's father. 'Go for the jugular, Alex.'

'Chief Inspector, you told the court that it was after you had seen Miss Wilson enter the house that you became convinced that it was Daniel Cartwright and not Sir Nicholas Moncrieff who was living there.'

'Yes, that's correct,' said Fuller.

'But once you had taken my client into custody, didn't you have a moment's anxiety about whether you might have arrested the wrong man?'

'No, Mr Redmayne, not after I'd seen the scar on his . . .'

'Not after you'd seen the scar on his—'

'—checked his DNA on the police computer,' said the Chief Inspector.

'Sit down,' whispered Alex's father. 'You've got everything you need, and Hackett won't have worked out the significance of the scar.'

'Thank you, Chief Inspector. No more questions, M'lord.'

'Do you wish to re-examine, Mr Pearson?' asked Mr Justice Hackett.

'No, thank you, M'lord,' said Pearson, trying to work out the significance of Fuller's evidence.

'Thank you, Chief Inspector,' said the judge. 'You may leave the box.'

Alex leaned over to his father as Fuller left the court and whispered, 'But I didn't get him to admit that the "professional gentleman" was Craig.'

'He was never going to name his contact, but you still managed to trap him twice,' said Sir Matthew. 'And don't forget, there's another witness who must also know who reported Danny to the police, and he's not going to feel at home in a courtroom, so you should be able to corner him before Hackett works out your real purpose.'

MR JUSTICE HACKETT said in a loud voice, 'Are you ready to call your next witness, Mr Pearson?'

Pearson rose from his place. 'Yes, M'lord. I call Sir Hugo Moncrieff.'

The usher guided Sir Hugo into the box and handed him a Bible. Once he'd taken the oath, Pearson gave him a smile and said, 'Sir Hugo, when did you last see your nephew, Nicholas Moncrieff?'

'On the day we both attended his father's funeral.'

'And did you have an opportunity to speak to him on that sad occasion?'

'Unhappily not,' said Hugo. 'He was accompanied by two prison officers who said that we were not to have any contact with him.'

'What sort of relationship did you have with your nephew?'

'Cordial. We all loved Nick. He was a fine lad.'

'So there was no ill feeling when you and your brother learned that he had inherited the bulk of the estate from your father?'

'Certainly not,' said Hugo. 'Nick would automatically inherit the title on his father's death, and along with it the family estate.'

'So it must have come as a terrible shock to discover that he had hanged himself in prison and that an impostor had taken his place.'

Hugo lowered his head for a moment, then said, 'It was a massive blow for my wife Margaret and myself, but thanks to the rallying round of friends and family, we are slowly trying to come to terms with it.'

'Word perfect,' whispered Sir Matthew.

'Can you confirm, Sir Hugo, that the Garter King of Arms has established your right to the family title?' asked Mr Pearson.

'Yes, I can. The letters patent were sent to me some weeks ago.'

'Can you also confirm that the estate in Scotland, along with the house in London and the bank accounts in London and Switzerland are once again in the custody of the family?'

'I'm afraid not.' Sir Hugo turned to the judge. 'It's the policy of both the banks concerned not to acknowledge ownership while a court case is still in progress, M'lord. The legal transfer cannot take place until this case is concluded.'

'Fear not,' said the judge, giving him a warm smile. 'Your long ordeal is coming to an end.'

Sir Matthew was on his feet instantly. 'I apologise for interrupting Your Lordship, but does your response to this witness imply that you have already come to a decision in this case?' he asked with a warm smile.

The judge looked flustered. 'No, of course not, Sir Matthew,' he replied.

'I was merely stating that whatever the outcome of this trial, Sir Hugo's long wait is finally coming to an end.'

'I am obliged, My Lord. It is a relief to discover that you have not made up your mind before the defence has been given a chance to present its case.'

'No more questions, My Lord,' Pearson said, before resuming his place.

'Mr Redmayne,' said the judge, 'is it your intention to cross-examine this witness?'

'Yes, M'lord. Sir Hugo,' Alex began, 'you told the court that your relationship with your nephew, Nicholas Moncrieff, was a close one—"cordial" was the word I think you used to describe it—and that you would have spoken to him at his father's funeral had the prison officers not prevented it.'

'Yes, that is correct,' said Hugo.

'When was it that you first discovered that your nephew was in fact dead, and was not living, as you had believed, at his home in The Boltons?'

'A few days before Cartwright was arrested,' said Hugo.

'In that case, I am bound to ask, Sir Hugo, how many times during that eighteen-month period did you and your nephew, who you were so close to, meet up or speak on the phone?'

'But that's the point: it wasn't Nick,' said Hugo.

'No, it wasn't,' agreed Alex. 'But you have just told the court that you didn't become aware of that fact for eighteen months.'

'Well, we both lead busy lives,' Hugo said, trying to think on his feet. 'He was living in London and I spend most of my time in Scotland.'

'I understand that they now have telephones in Scotland,' said Alex. A ripple of laughter went round the court.

'What are you implying?' asked Hugo.

'I'm not implying anything,' replied Alex. 'But can you deny that when you both attended a stamp auction at Sotheby's in London in September 2002 and then spent the next few days in Geneva at the same hotel as the man you believed to be your nephew, you made no attempt to speak to him?'

'He could have spoken to me,' said Hugo, his voice rising.

'Perhaps my client didn't want to speak to you, as he knew only too well what sort of relationship you had with him. Perhaps he knew that you had not written or spoken to him once during the past ten years. Perhaps he knew that your own father had cut you out of his will?'

'I see that you are determined to take the word of a criminal before that of a member of the family.'

'No, Sir Hugo. I learned all of this *from* a member of the family.'

'Who?' demanded Hugo defiantly.

'Your nephew, Sir Nicholas Moncrieff,' replied Alex.

'But you didn't even know him.'

'No, I didn't,' admitted Alex. 'But while he was in prison, where you never once in four years visited or wrote to him, he kept a daily diary.'

Pearson leapt up. 'M'lord, I must protest. These diaries to which my learned friend refers were only placed in the jury bundle a week ago, and although my junior has struggled manfully to go through them line by line, they consist of over a thousand pages.'

'My Lord,' said Alex, '*my* junior has read every word of those diaries, and for the convenience of the court he has highlighted any passages we might later wish to bring to the attention of the jury.'

'They may be admissible,' said Mr Justice Hackett, 'but I do not consider them to be relevant. It is not Sir Hugo who is on trial, nor his relationship with his nephew, so I suggest you move on, Mr Redmayne.'

Sir Matthew tugged his son's gown.

'May I have a word with my junior?' Alex asked the judge.

'If you must,' replied Mr Justice Hackett, still smarting from his last encounter with Sir Matthew. 'But make it quick.'

Alex sat down. 'You've made your point, my boy,' whispered Sir Matthew, 'and in any case, the most significant line in the diaries ought to be saved for the next witness. Added to that, old man Hackett is wondering if he's gone too far and given us enough ammunition to apply for a retrial. As this will be his last appearance in the High Court before he retires, he won't want to be remembered for a retrial. So, when you resume, say that you accept His Lordship's judgment, but you hope that your learned friend will find time to consider the few entries that your junior has marked for his convenience.'

Alex rose from his place and said, 'I accept Your Lordship's judgment without question, but as I may need to refer to certain passages in the diary at a later date, I can only hope that my learned friend will find enough time to read the few lines that have been marked up for his consideration.' Sir Matthew smiled. The judge frowned and Sir Hugo looked mystified.

Alex turned his attention back to the witness. 'Sir Hugo, can I confirm that it was your father's wish, as clearly stated in his will, that the estate in Dunbroath should be handed over to the National Trust for Scotland, with a sufficient sum of money to be put aside for its upkeep?'

'That was my understanding,' admitted Hugo.

'Then can you also confirm that Daniel Cartwright abided by those wishes, and that the estate is now in the hands of the National Trust?'

'Yes, I am able to confirm that,' replied Hugo, somewhat reluctantly.

'Have you recently found time to visit number twelve The Boltons and see what condition the property is in?'

'Yes. I couldn't see a great difference from how it was before.'

'Sir Hugo, would you like me to call Mr Cartwright's housekeeper in order that she can tell the court in graphic detail what state she found the house in when she was first employed?'

'It may well have been somewhat neglected, but as I have already made clear, I spend most of my time in Scotland and rarely visit London.'

'That being the case, Sir Hugo, let us move on to your nephew's account at Coutts Bank in the Strand. Are you able to tell the court how much money was in that account at the time of his tragic death?'

'How could I possibly know that?' Hugo replied sharply.

'Then allow me to enlighten you, Sir Hugo,' said Alex, extracting a bank statement from a folder. 'Just over seven thousand pounds.'

'But surely what matters is how much there is in that bank account at the present time?' retorted Sir Hugo triumphantly.

'I couldn't agree with you more,' said Alex, taking out a second bank statement. 'At close of business yesterday, the account stood at a little over forty-two thousand pounds. Next, we should consider the stamp collection that your father, Sir Alexander, left to his grandson, Nicholas.'

'Cartwright sold it behind my back. I would never have agreed to part with something that the family has always regarded as an heirloom.'

'I wonder if you would like a little time to reconsider that statement,' said Alex. 'I am in possession of a legal document drawn up by your solicitor, Mr Desmond Galbraith, agreeing to sell your father's stamp collection for fifty million dollars to a Mr Gene Hunsacker of Austin, Texas.'

'Even if that were true,' said Hugo, 'I never saw a penny of it, because it was Cartwright who ended up selling the collection to Hunsacker.'

'He did indeed,' said Alex, 'for a sum of fifty-seven and a half million dollars—seven and a half million more than you managed to negotiate.'

'Where is all this leading, Mr Redmayne?' asked the judge. 'However well your client has husbanded the Moncrieff legacy, it was still he who stole everything in the first place. Are you trying to suggest that it was always his intention to return the estate to its rightful owners?'

'No, My Lord. However, I am attempting to demonstrate that perhaps Danny Cartwright is not quite the evil villain that the prosecution would have us believe. Indeed, thanks to Cartwright's stewardship, Sir Hugo will be far better off than he could otherwise have expected to be.'

Sir Matthew offered up a silent prayer.

'That's not true!' said Sir Hugo. 'I'll be worse off.'

Sir Matthew sat bolt upright and whispered, 'There is a God in heaven after all. Well done, my boy.'

'I am now completely at a loss,' said Mr Justice Hackett. 'If there is over seven and a half million dollars more in the bank account than you had anticipated, Sir Hugo, how can you possibly be worse off?'

'Because I recently signed a legal contract with a third party who was unwilling to reveal the details of what had happened to my nephew unless I agreed to part with twenty-five per cent of my inheritance.'

The judge called loudly for order, and Alex didn't ask his next question until silence had been restored.

'When did you sign this agreement, Sir Hugo?'

Hugo removed a diary from a pocket, and flicked over the pages. 'October the 22nd last year,' he said.

Alex checked his notes. 'The day before a professional gentleman contacted Chief Inspector Fuller to arrange a meeting at an unknown location.'

'I have no idea what you're talking about,' said Hugo.

'Of course you had no way of knowing what was going on behind your back. But I am bound to ask, Sir Hugo, what this gentleman offered in exchange for your signature once you had signed the contract.'

'He told me that my nephew had been dead for over a year and that his place had been usurped by that man sitting in the dock.'

'And what was your reaction to this incredible piece of news?'

'I didn't believe it,' said Hugo, 'but then he showed me several photographs of Cartwright and Nick, and I had to admit they did look alike.'

'I find it hard to believe, Sir Hugo, that that was enough proof for a shrewd man to part with twenty-five per cent of his family fortune.'

'No, it wasn't enough. He also supplied me with several other photographs to back up his claim.'

'Several other photographs?' prompted Alex, hopefully.

'Yes. One of them was of the defendant's left leg, showing a scar above his knee that proved he was Cartwright and not my nephew.'

'Stay calm,' whispered Sir Matthew, 'stay calm.'

'Perhaps the time has come, Sir Hugo, for you to name this professional gentleman who demanded twenty-five per cent of what was rightfully yours in exchange for that information?'

'I can't do that,' said Hugo.

'Why not?' demanded the judge.

'Because one of the clauses in the agreement,' said Hugo, mopping his brow, 'was that under no circumstances would I reveal his name.'

Mr Justice Hackett placed his pen down on the desk. 'Now, listen to me, Sir Hugo. If you don't want a contempt of court order brought against you, and a night in a cell to help jog your memory, I suggest that you answer Mr Redmayne's question and tell the court the name of this professional gentleman who demanded twenty-five per cent of your estate before he was willing to expose the defendant as a fraud. Do I make myself clear?'

Hugo began to shake. He peered up into the gallery, to see Margaret nodding. He turned back to the judge and said, 'Mr Spencer Craig, QC.'

'That's what they call a double whammy,' whispered Sir Matthew. 'Now our esteemed judge has no choice but to allow you to subpoena Spencer Craig, unless of course he wants a retrial.'

Chapter 13

The judge addressed the jury. 'Good morning, members of the jury. Yesterday you heard Mr Pearson complete the case for the prosecution, and now the defence will put its side of the argument to you. After a consultation with both sides, I shall be inviting you to dismiss the charge that the defendant attempted to steal the Moncrieff estate in Scotland. Sir Hugo confirmed that this was not the case, and that in accordance with his father's wishes, the estate has been taken over by the National Trust for Scotland. However, the defendant still faces four other serious charges.'

He smiled benignly at the jury before turning his attention to Alex. 'Mr Redmayne, please call your first witness,' he said.

'Thank you, M'lord,' said Alex, rising. 'I call Mr Fraser Munro.'

THE FIRST THING Munro did when he entered the courtroom was to smile at Danny in the dock. He was dressed in a black tailcoat and pinstripe trousers, a white shirt with a wing collar and a black silk tie. He gave the judge a slight bow before delivering the oath.

'Would you please state your occupation for the record,' said Alex.

'I am a solicitor of the High Court of Scotland.'

'Can I confirm that you are a past president of the Scottish Law Society?'

'I am, sir.' That was something Danny didn't know.

'Would you please explain to the court, Mr Munro, what your relationship is to the accused?'

'Certainly, Mr Redmayne. I had the privilege, as my father did before me, of representing Sir Alexander Moncrieff, the first holder of the baronetcy.'

'Did you also represent Sir Nicholas Moncrieff?'

'I did, sir.'

'Did you have any reason to believe that the person who visited you after he had been released from Belmarsh was not Sir Nicholas Moncrieff?'

'No, sir. I had only seen him for one hour during the past twelve years, and the man who walked into my office not only looked like Sir Nicholas, but was wearing the same clothes as he had on the previous occasion we'd met. He was in possession of the correspondence that had taken place between us, and was wearing a silver chain and key that his grandfather had shown me years before.'

'Looking back with the benefit of hindsight, did you ever suspect that the man you believed to be Sir Nicholas Moncrieff was in fact an impostor?'

'No. In all matters he conducted himself with courtesy and charm.'

'Can I confirm, Mr Munro, that since Danny Cartwright's arrest, the responsibility for the Moncrieff estate has returned to your stewardship?'

'That is correct. However, I must confess that I have not conducted the day-to-day business with the flair that Danny Cartwright displayed.'

'Would it be right to say that the estate is in a stronger financial position now than it has been for some years?'

'Without question.'

'I do hope,' interrupted the judge, 'that you are not suggesting, Mr Munro, that that diminishes the severity of these charges?'

'No, My Lord, I am not,' said Munro. 'But I have discovered with advancing years that few things are entirely black or white. I can best sum it up, My Lord, by saying that it was an honour to have served Sir Nicholas Moncrieff and it has been a privilege to work with Mr Cartwright. They are both oaks, even if they were planted in different forests. But then, M'lord, we all suffer in our different ways from being prisoners of birth.'

'The jury cannot have failed to notice, Mr Munro,' continued Alex, 'that you retain the greatest respect and admiration for Mr Cartwright. But with that in mind, they may find it hard to understand how the same man became involved in such a nefarious deception.'

'I have considered that question endlessly for the past six months, Mr Redmayne, and have come to the conclusion that his sole purpose must have been to fight a far bigger injustice that had—'

'Mr Munro,' interrupted the judge sternly, 'as you well know, this is neither the time nor the place to express your personal opinions.'

'I am grateful for your guidance,' said Munro, 'but I took an oath to tell the whole truth, and I presume you would not wish me to do otherwise?'

'No, I would not, sir,' snapped the judge, 'but I repeat, this is not the appropriate place to express such views. Please move on, Mr Redmayne.'

'I have no more questions for this witness, My Lord,' said Alex.

'Mr Pearson,' said the judge, 'is it your intention to cross-examine this witness?'

Pearson rose. 'Yes, My Lord. Mr Munro, when your client was arrested, did you not feel that you had been negligent in the pursuance of your duty? This man had stolen the family silver, to quote a fellow Scot, and you had done nothing to prevent it.'

'No, sir, he had not stolen the family silver. The only thing Danny Cartwright had stolen, Mr Pearson, was the family name.'

'You can no doubt explain to the court,' said the judge, 'the moral dilemma I am facing under your hypothesis.'

'Your Lordship need not trouble himself with any moral dilemma,' said Munro, 'because I was interested only in the legal niceties of the case.'

'The legal niceties?' said Mr Justice Hackett, treading carefully.

'Yes, M'lord. Mr Danny Cartwright was the sole heir to the Moncrieff fortune, so I was unable to work out what law, if any, he was breaking.'

'Can you explain to the court, Mr Munro,' asked Pearson, 'just what you mean by that?' The judge leaned back, happy to allow Pearson to be the one who sank deeper into the Munro mire.

'It's simple really, Mr Pearson. The late Sir Nicholas Moncrieff made a will in which he left everything to Daniel Arthur Cartwright of Bacon Road, London E3, with the sole exception of an annuity of ten thousand pounds which he bequeathed to a Mr Albert Crann.'

Pearson collapsed onto the bench, forgetting to say, 'No more questions.'

An outbreak of whispers filled the court as Munro stepped out of the box, walked across to the dock and shook hands with the defendant.

'My Lord, might I address you on a point of law?' enquired Alex.

'Of course, Mr Redmayne, but first I will have to release the jury. Members of the jury, as you have just heard, defence counsel has asked to discuss a point of law with me. It may not have any bearing on the case, but should it do so, I will fully brief you on your return.'

When the court had been cleared the judge said, 'How can I assist you, Mr Redmayne?'

'My Lord, following the evidence given by the estimable Mr Munro, the defence would suggest that there is no case to answer on counts three, four and five, namely the occupation of the house in The Boltons, benefiting from the sale of the stamp collection, and the issuing of cheques on the Coutts bank account. We would ask that all these counts be dismissed, as it is self-evidently quite difficult to steal that which already belongs to you.'

'You make a fair point, Mr Redmayne. What is your view, Mr Pearson?'

'The Crown has no objection,' said Pearson.

'I will so inform the jury when they return. However, I'm sure you don't need reminding, Mr Redmayne, that the most serious offence, that of escaping from prison while in custody, remains on the indictment.'

'I am aware of that, M'lord,' said Alex. 'There is a related matter.'

'Yes, Mr Redmayne?' said the judge, putting down his pen.

'My Lord, following Sir Hugo Moncrieff's evidence, we have subpoenaed Mr Spencer Craig, QC to appear before you as a witness. He has asked for Your Lordship's indulgence as he is currently leading in a case taking place in another part of this building, and will not be free to appear before Your Lordship until tomorrow morning.'

'When the jury returns, after I have directed them on these two matters, I shall release them for the rest of the day.'

'As you wish, My Lord,' said Alex, 'but before you do so, may I alert you to a slight change in tomorrow's proceedings? My Lord, you will be aware that it is a tradition of the English bar to allow one's junior to examine one of the witnesses in a case, in order that they may gain from the experience and indeed be given the chance to advance their career.'

'I think I can see where this is leading, Mr Redmayne.'

'Then with your permission, M'lord, my junior, Sir Matthew Redmayne, will lead for the defence when we examine the next witness, Mr Craig.'

COURT NUMBER FOUR was already packed by the time Danny took his place in the dock. The press benches were filled with crime correspondents who, during the past week, had written hundreds of column inches on the case, and had warned their editors to expect a lead story for tomorrow's first editions. They couldn't wait for 'the encounter between the greatest advocate since F. E. Smith and the most brilliant young QC of his generation' (*The Times*), or 'the Mongoose versus the Snake' (the *Sun*).

Danny looked up at the public gallery and smiled at Beth, sitting with her mother. Sarah Davenport, who had been in attendance most days, was seated at the end of the front row, her head bowed. At five minutes to ten, a policeman opened the courtroom door and a hush fell over the assembled gathering as Alex Redmayne and his junior made their way to counsel's bench.

The noise of chatter ceased again when Mr Justice Hackett took his seat at the centre of the stage.

'Good morning,' he said, once the jury had settled. 'Members of the jury, the first witness today will be Mr Spencer Craig, QC. You will recall his name being raised during the cross-examination of Sir Hugo Moncrieff. Mr Craig does not appear as a witness for either the prosecution or the defence, but has been subpoenaed to attend this court, meaning that he does not do so willingly. Your only duty is to decide if the evidence Mr Craig presents has any bearing on the case being tried in this court, namely, did the defendant unlawfully escape from custody? On that count, and that count alone, you will be asked to deliver your verdict.'

Mr Justice Hackett beamed down at the jury before turning his attention to junior counsel. 'Sir Matthew,' he said, 'are you ready to call the witness?'

Matthew Redmayne rose. 'I am indeed, My Lord,' he responded. 'I call Mr Spencer Craig.' His words sounded like a death knell.

A policeman stepped into the corridor and bellowed, 'Mr Spencer Craig!'

A moment later, Spencer Craig, dressed in his legal garb, strode into the courtroom as if it was just another day in the life of a busy advocate. He stepped into the witness box, delivered the oath in a confident manner, and turned to face Sir Matthew.

'Mr Craig,' Sir Matthew began. 'When did you first discover that Sir Nicholas Moncrieff was in fact Mr Daniel Cartwright?'

'A friend of mine who had been at school with Sir Nicholas bumped into him at the Dorchester Hotel. He soon realised the man was an impostor.'

'And why should this friend decide to inform *you*, in particular, of this remarkable discovery?'

'He didn't; it simply arose in conversation over dinner one night.'

'Then what was it that caused you to take a gigantic leap in the dark and come to the conclusion that the man posing as Sir Nicholas Moncrieff was in fact Daniel Cartwright?'

'I didn't for some time,' said Craig, 'not until I was introduced to the supposed Sir Nicholas at the theatre one evening and was shocked by the similarity in looks, if not in manner, between him and Cartwright.'

'Was that the moment when you decided to contact Chief Inspector Fuller and alert him to your misgivings?'

'No. I felt that would have been irresponsible, so I first made contact with a member of the Moncrieff family.'

'Which member of the family did you contact?' asked Sir Matthew.

'Mr Hugo Moncrieff, Sir Nicholas's uncle, who informed me his nephew had not been in touch with him since the day he'd been released from prison some eighteen months before, which added to my suspicions.'

'Was that when you reported those suspicions to Chief Inspector Fuller?'

'No, I still felt I needed more concrete evidence.'

'But the chief inspector could have relieved you of that burden, Mr Craig. I am at a loss to understand why you chose to remain involved?'

'I felt it was my responsibility to make sure I wasn't wasting police time.'

'How very community-spirited of you. But I'm bound to ask who it was that alerted you to the possible advantages of being able to prove that the man posing as Sir Nicholas Moncrieff was in fact an impostor?'

'The advantages? I'm not sure I follow you,' said Craig.

'Then allow me to assist you,' said Sir Matthew. He put out his right hand and Alex handed him a single sheet of paper. Sir Matthew ran his eye slowly down the page. 'Would I be right in suggesting, Mr Craig, that if you were able to prove that it was Nicholas Moncrieff and not Danny Cartwright who committed suicide while in Belmarsh Prison, Mr Hugo Moncrieff would not only inherit the family title, but a vast fortune?'

'I was not aware of that at the time,' said Craig, not flinching.

'So you were acting with entirely altruistic motives?'

'Yes, I was, as well as the desire to see a dangerous criminal locked up.'

'Allow me to ask you when your acute sense of public duty was overcome by the possibility of making several million pounds?'

'When Sir Hugo invited me to act on his behalf in a private capacity.'

'And do you consider it ethical for a QC to charge twenty-five per cent of a man's inheritance in exchange for a piece of secondhand information?'

'It is now quite common, Sir Matthew, for barristers to be paid on results,' said Craig calmly. 'But perhaps I should point out that I did not charge a fee or any expenses, and that had my suspicions been proved wrong I would have wasted a considerable amount of my time and money.'

'Then you will be delighted to learn, Mr Craig, that the altruistic side of your nature has won the day. As you will be aware, the court has recently been informed by Mr Fraser Munro, the late Sir Nicholas Moncrieff's solicitor, that his client bequeathed his entire estate to his close friend Mr Danny Cartwright. So you have, as you feared might be the case, wasted a considerable amount of your time and money. But despite my client's good fortune, let me assure you, Mr Craig, that I shall not be charging *him* twenty-five per cent of his inheritance for my services.

'Which brings me neatly to your meeting with Chief Inspector Fuller. The chief inspector informed the court that he would require a little more proof than photographs revealing a close similarity between the two men before he could consider making an arrest. In an answer to one of my leader's questions, he confirmed that you supplied him with that proof.'

Sir Matthew knew that he was taking a risk. Had Craig responded by saying that he had no idea what he was talking about, and that he had simply passed on his suspicions to the chief inspector, Sir Matthew had no follow-up question. But Craig did not respond immediately, which gave Sir Matthew the confidence to take an even bigger risk. He turned to Alex and said, 'Let me have those photographs of Cartwright running along the Embankment, the ones that show the scar.'

Alex handed his father two large photographs.

After a long pause, Craig said, 'I may have told the chief inspector that if the man living in The Boltons had a scar on his left thigh, just above the knee, that would prove that he was in fact Danny Cartwright.'

Alex's face revealed nothing, although he could hear his heart beating.

'And did you then hand over some photographs to the chief inspector to prove your point?'

'I may have done,' admitted Craig.

'Perhaps if you were to see copies of the photograph they might refresh your memory?' suggested Sir Matthew. The biggest risk of all.

'That won't be necessary,' said Craig.

'I would like to see the photographs,' said the judge, 'and I suspect the jury would as well, Sir Matthew.'

'Certainly, M'lord,' said Sir Matthew. Alex handed a pile of photographs to the usher, who gave two to the judge before distributing the remainder to the jury, to Pearson and finally to the witness.

Craig stared at the photos in disbelief. They were not the ones Gerald Payne had taken during Cartwright's evening run. If he had not admitted to knowing about the scar, the defence would have crumbled and the jury would have been none the wiser. Sir Matthew had landed a blow, but he, Spencer Craig, would not fall for a sucker punch a second time.

'My Lord,' said Sir Matthew, 'you will see the scar that the witness referred to is on Mr Cartwright's left thigh, just above the knee. Chief Inspector Fuller stated that this was the evidence on which he relied before taking the decision to arrest my client.' Sir Matthew paused before he asked a question he was confident Craig could not have anticipated.

'When did you first phone Chief Inspector Fuller?'

'I'm not sure I understand,' Craig replied eventually.

'Mr Craig, you phoned Chief Inspector Fuller on October the 23rd last year, the day before you met him at an undisclosed location to hand over the photographs showing Danny Cartwright's scar. But when was the first occasion you came into contact with him?'

'He was the policeman who came to the Dunlop Arms when I called 999 after I had witnessed Danny Cartwright stabbing his friend to death.'

'His friend,' said Sir Matthew quickly, getting it on the record. 'On the first occasion you met Chief Inspector Fuller, following the death of Bernard Wilson, you made a statement. In fact, Mr Craig, you ended up making three statements: the first, thirty-seven minutes after the stabbing had taken place; the second, which you wrote later that night because you couldn't sleep; and a third, seven months later, when you appeared in the witness box at Danny Cartwright's trial. I am in possession of all three of those statements, and I must admit, Mr Craig, that they are admirably consistent. However, what I am puzzled by is the scar on Danny Cartwright's left leg because you said in your first statement'— Alex handed his father a single sheet of paper, from which he read—'"I saw Cartwright pick up the knife from the bar and follow the woman and the other man out into the alley. A few moments later I heard a scream. I ran out into the alley and saw Cartwright stabbing Wilson in the chest. I then returned to the bar and *immediately* phoned the police."' Sir Matthew looked up. 'Do you wish to make any amendments to that statement?'

'No,' said Craig firmly, 'that is exactly what happened.'

'Then I am bound to ask, Mr Craig, exactly what you meant by the word *immediately*, because according to your evidence, you phoned the police seventeen minutes after Danny Cartwright's fiancée, Beth Wilson, had called for an ambulance. One wonders what you might have been up to during—'

'Sir Matthew,' interrupted the judge. 'Are you able to show that this line of questioning is relevant, remembering that the only offence left on the charge sheet concerns your client escaping from custody?'

'No, I am not, M'lord. However, I do wish to pursue a line of questioning that is relevant to this case, namely the scar on the defendant's left leg.' He made eye contact with Craig. 'Can I confirm, Mr Craig, that you did not witness Danny Cartwright being stabbed in the leg?'

It was some time before Craig eventually said, 'No, I did not.'

'So, Mr Craig, allow me to put forward three scenarios for your consideration. You can then tell the jury which of them you consider to be the most likely. The first scenario: Danny Cartwright grabs the knife from the bar, follows his fiancée into the alley, stabs himself in the leg, pulls out the knife, and then stabs his best friend to death.'

Laughter broke out in the court. Craig waited for it to die down before he responded. 'That's a farcical suggestion, Sir Matthew, and you know it.'

'I'm glad we have something on which we can agree, Mr Craig. Let me move on to my second scenario: it is in fact Bernie Wilson who grabs the knife from the bar; he and Cartwright go out into the alley, he stabs Cartwright in the leg, pulls out the knife and then stabs himself to death.'

This time even the jury joined in the laughter.

'That's even more farcical,' said Craig. 'I'm not quite sure what you imagine this charade is proving.'

'This charade is proving,' said Sir Matthew, 'that the man who stabbed Danny Cartwright in the leg was the same man who stabbed Bernie Wilson in the chest, because only one knife was involved—the one picked up from the bar. So I agree with you, Mr Craig, my first two scenarios are farcical, but before I put the third to you, allow me to ask you one final question. If you did not witness Cartwright being stabbed in the leg, how could you possibly have known about the scar?'

Everyone's gaze was transferred to Craig, who no longer looked calm.

'I must have read about it in the transcript of the trial.'

'One of the problems that an old warhorse like myself faces once he's pensioned off,' said Sir Matthew, 'is that he has nothing to do with his spare time. So for the past six months, my bedside reading has been this transcript.' He held up a five-inch thick document. 'Let me assure you, Mr

Craig, there is no mention from the first page to the last of a wound to Danny Cartwright's left leg.' Sir Matthew turned to face the jury and added, 'Which, I confess, is my fault. You see, in the original trial, my son was defending only his second case as leader and came to me for advice. I suggested he shouldn't put Danny Cartwright in the witness box, when in fact the scar on his leg might well have proved his innocence.'

Sir Matthew turned back to the witness and said, 'And so I come to my final scenario, Mr Craig. It was *you* who picked up the knife from the bar before running out into the alley. It was *you* who thrust the knife into Danny Cartwright's leg. And it was *you* who stabbed Bernie Wilson in the chest and left him to die in the arms of his friend.'

Uproar broke out in the courtroom and the judge had to wait until the usher had called for silence before saying, 'I feel I should give Mr Craig the opportunity to answer Sir Matthew's accusations at this point.'

'I will be only too happy to do so, M'lord,' said Craig evenly, 'but first I should like to suggest to Sir Matthew a fourth scenario.'

'I can't wait,' said Sir Matthew, leaning back.

'Given your client's background, isn't it possible that the wound to his leg was inflicted at some time before the night in question?'

'But that still doesn't explain how you could possibly have known about the scar in the first place.'

'I don't have to explain,' said Craig defiantly, 'because a jury has already decided that your client didn't have a leg to stand on.'

'I wouldn't be so sure about that,' said Sir Matthew, turning to his son, who handed him a cardboard box. Sir Matthew removed a pair of jeans from the box and held them up. 'These are the jeans that the prison service returned to Miss Elizabeth Wilson when it was thought that Danny Cartwright had hanged himself. Jeans that he was wearing the night he was taken into custody. I am sure that the jury will be interested to see that there is a bloodstained tear in the left lower thigh region, which matches . . .'

The outburst that followed drowned out the rest of Sir Matthew's words. Everyone turned to look at Craig, wanting to find out his answer, but he wasn't given the chance to reply, as Pearson finally rose to his feet.

'M'lord, I must remind Sir Matthew that it is not Mr Craig who is on trial,' Pearson declared, 'and that this piece of evidence'—he pointed at the jeans—'has no relevance when it comes to deciding if Cartwright did or did not escape from custody.'

Mr Justice Hackett was no longer able to hide his anger. Once silence had returned to his court, he said, 'I couldn't agree with you more, Mr Pearson, that a bloodstained tear in the defendant's jeans is not relevant to this case.' He looked down at the witness with disdain. 'However, I have been left with no choice but to abandon this trial and send the transcripts of this and the earlier case to the DPP for his consideration, because I am of the opinion that a miscarriage of justice may have taken place in the case of the Crown versus Daniel Arthur Cartwright.'

This time the judge made no attempt to quell the uproar that followed as journalists bolted for the door.

Alex turned to congratulate his father, who looked at his son and remarked, 'It's far from over yet, my boy.'

EPILOGUE: Final Judgment

Once Father O'Connor had blessed the bride and groom, Mr and Mrs Cartwright joined the rest of the congregation of St Mary-le-Bow as they gathered around the grave of Danny Cartwright. It was the bride's wish that a service be held in memory of the man whose death had made it possible for Danny to prove his innocence.

Apart from Danny, only two people present had known Nicholas Moncrieff. One of them stood upright on the far side of the grave, dressed in a black tailcoat, wing collar and black silk tie. Fraser Munro had travelled down from Dunbroath to honour the last in the line of Moncrieffs that he would serve. Danny had tried to thank him for his wisdom and strength at all times, but all Mr Munro had said was, 'I wish I'd had the privilege of serving you both, but that was not to be. By the way,' added Munro sheepishly, 'I must admit to having hit one of your adversaries below the belt while you were safely locked up in Belmarsh.'

'So what have you been up to in my absence?' said Danny, trying to keep a straight face.

'I sent all the papers concerning the validity of Sir Alexander's second will to the Procurator Fiscal's office, alerting them to the fact that I felt an offence may have been committed. As nothing happened for several months, I assumed that Galbraith had managed to have the whole escapade swept under the carpet. That was until I read this morning's *Scotsman* on the plane down to London.' He opened his briefcase, took out a newspaper and passed it across to Danny.

Danny stared at the front-page headline. *Sir Hugo Moncrieff Arrested for Forgery and Attempted Fraud.* When Danny finished reading the article, he smiled and said to Mr Munro, 'Well, you did warn him that if he caused me any further trouble "all bets were off".'

'Did I really utter those words?' said Munro in disgust.

BIG AL HAD BEEN granted compassionate leave to attend the funeral of his friend and he stood to attention between prison officers Ray Pascoe and Alan Jenkins. Danny smiled when their eyes met, but Big Al quickly bowed his head. He didn't want these strangers to see him weeping.

Danny turned his attention to Alex Redmayne, who hadn't been able to hide his delight when Beth had invited him to be godfather to their new son.

Danny gripped his wife's hand, and couldn't resist looking across the road, where a new sign had recently been put in place: CARTWRIGHT'S GARAGE, UNDER NEW MANAGEMENT. Tomorrow they would fly to Rome for a much-delayed honeymoon, during which they would try to forget that when they returned they would have to face the ordeal of another long trial, relating to the murder of Bernie, another much-loved person who was buried in St Mary-le-Bow's churchyard. Their ten-week-old son chose that moment to express his feelings by starting to cry, and not in memory of Sir Nicholas Moncrieff, but just because he felt that the service had gone on for too long.

'Shh. It won't be much longer before we can all go home,' his mother promised soothingly, as she took Nick in her arms.

'BRING UP THE PRISONERS.'

Court Number Four at the Old Bailey was packed long before ten o'clock in the forenoon, but then, it was not every day that a Queen's Counsel, a Member of Parliament and a popular actor were arraigned on charges of murder, affray and conspiracy to pervert the course of justice.

All three defendants were being represented by the most eminent legal minds their solicitors could instruct, and the talk in the corridors of the Old Bailey was that as long as they all stuck to their original story, it was doubtful if any twelve jurors would be able to reach a unanimous verdict. The chatter subsided when Spencer Craig, Gerald Payne and Lawrence Davenport took their places in the dock.

Craig was dressed in his court apparel, making it appear as if he had entered through the wrong door, and that it should have been he who was seated on counsel's bench waiting to deliver the opening speech.

Payne was wearing a dark blue suit, striped silk tie and a cream shirt, as befitted a Member of Parliament representing a rural seat.

Davenport wore faded jeans, an open-necked shirt and a blazer. He was unshaven and looked as if he hadn't slept for several days. While Payne and Craig chatted, Davenport glanced up towards the public gallery. Once he had checked to see she was in her place, he stared blankly in front of him.

Mr Justice Armitage took his seat on the bench and instructed the court usher to bring in the jury. As the twelve men and women took their places, Craig studied them, aware that they would decide his fate. He'd already briefed Larry to make eye contact with the women jurors, as they needed only three who couldn't bear the thought of Lawrence Davenport being sent to jail to ensure that they would all be set free. But Craig was annoyed to see that the actor was staring fixedly in front of him.

'Will the defendants please rise.' All three of them stood up.

The clerk of the court read out the charges. 'Spencer Malcolm Craig, you are charged that on the night of September the 18th, 1999 you did murder one Bernard Henry Wilson. How do you plead, guilty or not guilty?'

'Not guilty,' said Craig defiantly.

'Gerald David Payne, you are charged that on the night of September the 18th, 1999 you were involved in an affray that ended in the death of Bernard Henry Wilson. How do you plead, guilty or not guilty?'

'Not guilty,' said Payne firmly.

'Lawrence Andrew Davenport, you are charged that on the night of September the 18th, 1999 you were a witness to the murder of Bernard Henry Wilson, and that you later gave false evidence in court. How do you plead, guilty or not guilty?'

Lawrence Davenport raised his head and looked up into the public gallery, where his sister was seated at the end of the front row.

Sarah gave her brother a reassuring smile.

Davenport lowered his head, and for a moment seemed to hesitate before saying in a whisper that was barely audible, 'Guilty.'

JEFFREY ARCHER

Homes: London and Cambridge
Favourite author: Charles Dickens
Blog: www.jeffreyarchers.blogspot.com

It has often been said that Jeffrey Archer's own story would make an international best seller. He was born in London, brought up in Somerset, the son of a printer, and educated at Wellington School and Brasenose College, Oxford, where he gained an athletics blue, was President of the University Athletics Club, and went on to run the 100 yards in 9.6 seconds for Great Britain in 1966.

After leaving Oxford he was elected to the Greater London Council, and three years later, at the age of twenty-nine, he became MP for Louth. After five years in the House of Commons and with a promising political career ahead of him, he invested heavily in a Canadian company called Aquablast, on the advice of the Bank of Boston. The company went into liquidation and three directors were later sent to jail for fraud. Left with debts of £427,727, and on the brink of bankruptcy, Jeffrey Archer resigned from the Commons.

Aged thirty-four, and determined to repay his creditors in full, he sat down to write his first novel *Not a Penny More, Not a Penny Less*. Written at the home of his former Oxford principal, it was taken up by the literary agent, Debbie Owen, and sold to seventeen countries within a year. It was also made into a successful serial for BBC Radio 4, and was later televised in 1990 by the BBC. *Shall We Tell the President?*, his second novel, was published in 1977, and from that point on Archer produced almost a book a year for the next twenty years. In literary terms, he has gone from strength to strength and is now published in sixty-three countries and more than thirty-two languages, with international sales totalling over 125 million copies.

After resigning from the House of Commons, his political career continued, and from September 1985 to November 1986 he was Deputy Chairman of the Conservative Party. Alongside his writing, he was active in many fields, co-ordinating the Campaign for Kurdish Relief, and raising money for charity—more than £10 million in the last ten years—as an amateur auctioneer. For his achievements he was made a Life Peer in the Queen's Birthday Honours List of 1992.

Having run a successful campaign for Mayor of London for two-and-a-half years, from 1997, in 1999 Jeffrey Archer was selected, by an overwhelming majority, as the official Conservative Party Candidate for London's Mayor. In November that same year, he withdrew his candidacy, having been charged with perjury and conspiracy to pervert the course of justice. He was sentenced to four years imprisonment and was released in July 2003, having served two years. Three published volumes of his *Prison Diary* recount that time of his life. Volume I, *Hell*, is a searing account of his first three weeks in the high security prison, HMP Belmarsh; Volume II, *Purgatory*, is set in HMP Wayland, a C category prison; and the third and final volume, *Heaven*, is about his final transfer to an open prison.

Jeffrey Archer completed the Flora London Marathon on April 18, 2004, in five hours twenty-six minutes, raising money for the Make-A-Wish Foundation UK, the British Heart Foundation, the Fund for Addenbrooke's and the Facial Surgery Research Foundation. He recalls being overtaken by a camel, a phone box and a girl walking, and says he has no plans to repeat the experience, but nevertheless likes to stay fit. He still trains six days a week with the help of an Australian coach, and he won't let travel interfere. On a recent trip to Australia to publicise his previous book, *False Impression*, he even had his programme sent ahead so that he could continue his workouts without missing a beat.

Seemingly indefatigable in every area of his life, he describes his writing regime as follows: 'I am very disciplined and usually go abroad to try and eliminate any distractions. I work in two-hour blocks—and I have a huge hourglass, which was a present from Mary, on my desk to ensure that I work for the full 120 minutes of each session. I write from six to eight a.m., breaking for two hours for breakfast and to read the morning newspapers, or catch up on the cricket scores; then, from ten a.m. until twelve p.m., when I break to go to the gym or for a long walk before a light lunch. Back to work at two until four p.m., after which I might relax by watching an episode of my favourte TV show, *The West Wing*, and then my final session is from six till eight p.m. I find that my morning sessions are usually the most productive.'

And at the outset, does he always know how his books will end? 'I usually know the first four or five chapters in detail, and the next ten in outline, which will take me to the middle of the book. Then it's time to pray. As I write, I'm wondering what will happen on the next page. My theory is: if I wonder what will happen on the next page, there's a good chance you will as well . . . '

Jeffrey has been married for forty years to Dr Mary Archer, who is chairman of Cambridge University Hospitals NHS Foundation Trust (incorporating Addenbrooke's and the Rosie Hospitals in Cambridge). They have two sons, William and James.

Taken from: www.jeffreyarcher.co.uk

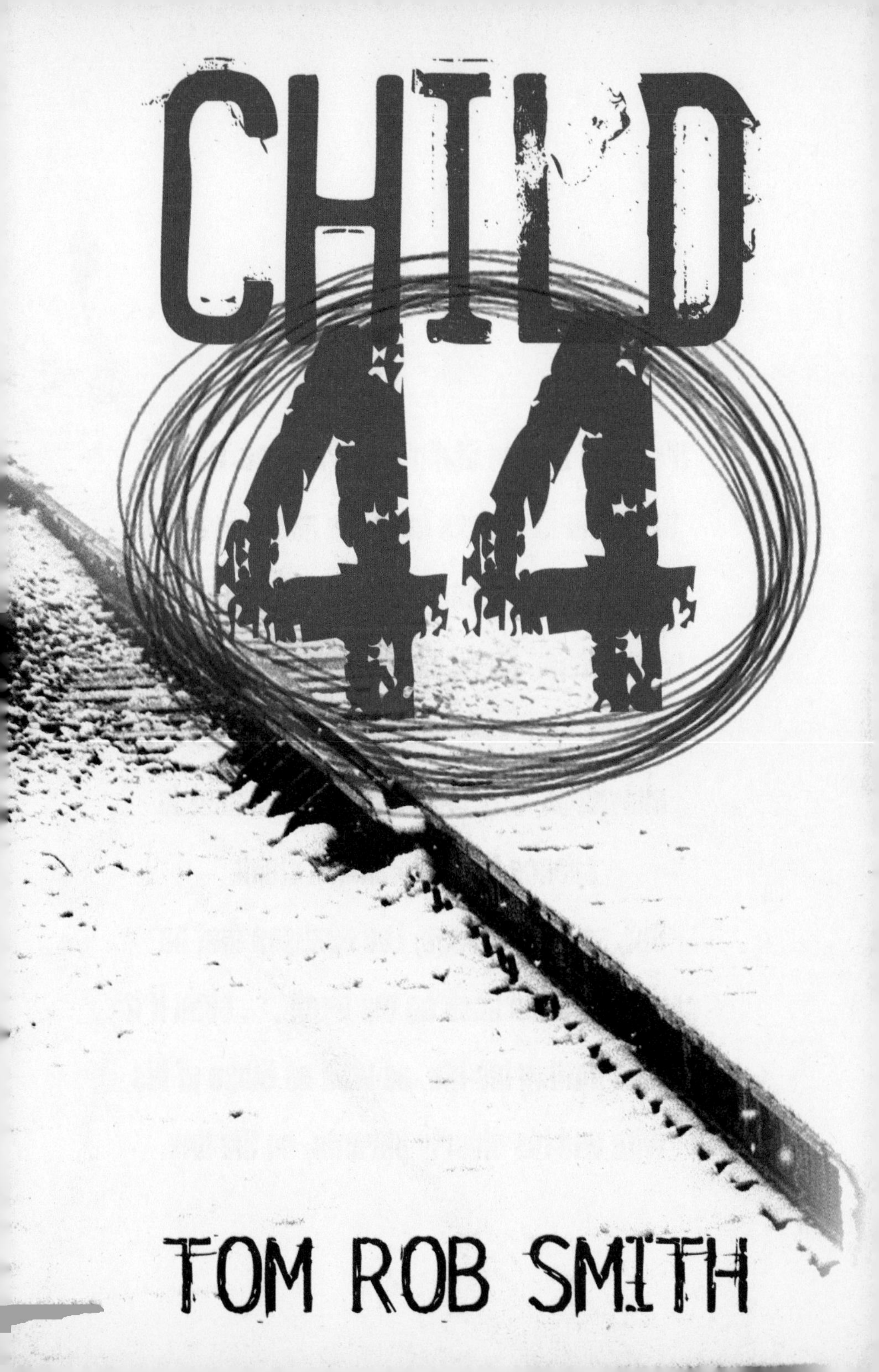
CHILD 44
TOM ROB SMITH

It's 1953 and, in Stalin's 'crime-free' Russia, the security forces have the nation in their grip: the State commands and controls what people think. So when the Andreevs suspect that their four-year-old son, Arkady, has been murdered, Officer Leo Demidov is sent to silence their outlandish claim.

But, as time passes, Leo realises that he cannot turn his back on the truth . . . even if it means putting his life, as well as those of his wife and his elderly parents, on the line.

The village of Chervoy, Ukraine, Soviet Union, January 1933

Since Maria had decided to die, her cat would have to fend for itself. She'd already cared for it far beyond the point where keeping a pet made any sense. Rats and mice had long since been trapped and eaten by the villagers. Domestic animals had disappeared shortly after that. All except for one, this cat, which she'd kept hidden. Why hadn't she killed it? She needed something to live for; something to protect and love—something to survive for. She'd made a promise to continue feeding it up until the day she could no longer feed herself. That day was today. She'd already cut her leather boots into thin strips, boiled them with nettles and beetroot seeds. She'd already dug for earthworms, sucked on bark. This morning in a feverish delirium she'd gnawed the leg of her kitchen stool, chewed and chewed until there were splinters jutting out of her gums. Upon seeing her the cat had run away, hiding under the bed, refusing to show itself even as she'd knelt down, calling its name, trying to coax it out. That had been the moment Maria decided to die, with nothing to eat and nothing to love.

Maria waited until nightfall before opening her front door. She reckoned that under the cover of darkness her cat stood a better chance of reaching the woods unseen. If anyone caught sight of it they'd hunt it. Even this close to her own death, the thought of her cat being killed upset her. She comforted herself with the knowledge that surprise was on its side. In a community where grown men chewed clods of earth in the hope of finding ants or insect eggs, where children picked through horse shit in the hope of finding undigested husks of grain and women fought over the ownership of bones, Maria was sure no one believed that a cat could still be alive.

PAVEL COULDN'T BELIEVE his eyes. It was awkward, thin, with green eyes and black speckled fur. It was unmistakably a cat. He'd been collecting firewood when he saw the animal dart from Maria Antonovna's house, cross the snow-covered road and head towards the woods. Holding his breath, he glanced around. There was no one else about, no lights at the windows. It was as though his village had been snuffed out by the heavy snowfall. Much of the snow lay undisturbed, there were hardly any footprints and not a single path had been dug. Days were as quiet as the nights. No one got up to work. None of his friends played, staying in their houses where they lay with their families huddled in beds. Most had given up scavenging for food. In these circumstances, the appearance of a cat was nothing short of miraculous.

Pavel closed his eyes and tried to remember the last time he'd eaten meat. When he opened his eyes he was salivating. Excited, he dropped his pile of sticks and ran home. He had to tell his mother, Oksana, the news.

OKSANA SAT WRAPPED in a blanket, staring at the floor, conserving energy as she devised ways of keeping her family alive. She was one of the few who'd not given up. She would never give up. Not as long as she had her sons. But determination wasn't enough. She had to be careful. A misjudged endeavour could mean exhaustion, and exhaustion invariably meant death. Some months ago, Nikolai Ivanovich, a neighbour, had embarked on a desperate raid on a State granary. He had not returned. The next morning Nikolai's wife and Oksana found his body by the roadside. He was lying on his back—his belly pregnant with the uncooked grain he'd swallowed in his dying moments.

Her recollections were interrupted by the sound of someone running. No one ran unless there was important news. She stood up, fearful.

Pavel burst into the room. 'Mother, I saw a cat.'

She gripped her son's hands, hoping he wasn't imagining things; hunger could play tricks. But his face showed no sign of delirium; his eyes were sharp, his expression serious. He was only ten years old and already a man. Circumstances demanded that he forgo his childhood. His father was almost certainly dead. He'd set off for the city of Kiev in the hope of bringing back food and had never returned. Now Oksana depended upon her son as much as he depended upon her. Pavel had sworn that he'd keep his family alive.

Oksana touched her son's cheek. 'Can you catch it?'

He smiled, proud. 'If I had a bone.'

The pond was frozen. Oksana rooted through the snow to find a rock. She punctured a small hole in the ice. Bracing herself for the freezing water, she reached in, moving quickly. Her hand touched the bottom and clutched nothing but silt. Where was it? Panicking, she leaned down, submerging her arm, searching. Her fingers brushed glass. Relieved, she grasped the bottle and pulled it out. Her skin had turned blue, but she'd found what she was looking for—a bottle sealed with tar. Inside was a collection of small bones.

She found Pavel had stoked the fire. She warmed the seal over the flames, tar dripping onto the embers in sticky globs. While they waited, Pavel rubbed her arm, restoring the circulation. With the tar melted, she tipped the bottle upside-down. Several bones snagged on the rim. She pulled them free, offering them to her son. Pavel studied them, scratching the surface, smelling each one. Having made his selection he was ready to leave.

She stopped him. 'Take your brother.'

Pavel thought this a mistake. His younger brother was clumsy and slow. And anyway the cat belonged to him. He'd seen it, he'd catch it.

His mother pressed a second bone into his hand. 'Take Andrei.'

ANDREI WAS NEARLY eight years old and he loved his older brother very much. Rarely going outside, he spent most of his time in the back room, where the three of them slept, playing with a pack of cards. The cards had been made by his father from squares of paper pasted together, before he'd set off for Kiev. Andrei was still waiting for him to come home. No one had told Andrei to expect anything different. Whenever he missed his father, which was often, he'd deal the cards out on the floor, sorting them by suits and numbers. Of course, Andrei preferred playing with his brother but Pavel had little time for games. He was always busy helping their mother.

Pavel entered the room. Andrei smiled, hoping he was ready to play a hand, but his brother crouched down and swept the cards together.

'Put these away. We're going out. Where are your *laptys*?'

Andrei crawled under the bed, retrieving two strips cut from a tractor tyre and a pile of rags, which, when bound together with string, served as boots. Pavel helped tie them, explaining that tonight they had a chance of eating meat as long as Andrei did exactly as he was told.

'Who's bringing us meat?'

'We're going to catch it ourselves.'

Andrei knew his brother was a skilful hunter. He'd trapped more rats than any other boy in the village. This was the first time Andrei had been invited to accompany him on such an important mission.

Outside in the snow, Andrei paid special care not to fall over. He often stumbled and tripped, for the world appeared blurred to him. The only things he could see clearly were objects he held very close to his face. If someone was able to make out a person in the distance, he put it down to intelligence or experience or some attribute he'd yet to acquire. Tonight he wouldn't fall over and make a fool of himself. He'd make his brother proud.

By the edge of the woods, Pavel bent to examine the cat's tracks.

Andrei crouched down, watching. 'Is this where the cat walked?'

Pavel nodded. 'The tracks are faint, which means the cat isn't heavy, so there'll be less food for us. But if it's hungry it's more likely to go for the bait.'

Andrei tried to absorb this information, but his mind drifted. 'Brother, if you were a playing card, what card would you be?'

Pavel sighed. 'If I answer, do you promise not to talk any more?'

'I promise. I'll be quiet.'

'I'd be a knave, a knight, the one with a sword. Now, not a word.'

Andrei nodded. Pavel stood up. They entered the woods.

They walked for a long time—it felt like hours to Andrei. His brother seemed to have little difficulty following tracks in the moonlight. They went deep into the woods, further than Andrei had ever gone before. He often had to run to keep pace. His legs ached, his stomach ached. He was cold and hungry. The string binding the rags to the tyre strips had come loose and snow was edging under the soles of his feet. He didn't dare ask his brother to stop and retie them. To take his mind off the discomfort he snapped a twig from a sapling and chewed the bark, grinding it into a coarse paste. His brother had told him that bark paste sated feelings of hunger.

Suddenly Pavel gestured for him to remain still. He must have seen the cat. Andrei stopped. Pavel crouched down. Andrei copied him, peering into the forest, trying to bring the trees into focus.

Pavel drew his knife, cutting his finger and daubing blood on the chicken bone their mother had given him. He did the same with Andrei's bait, a broken rat skull. Without saying a word the brothers parted, heading in opposite directions. Pavel had already given Andrei detailed instructions. Once they were some distance apart, they placed the bones in the snow.

As instructed, Andrei took the length of string from his pocket. Pavel had tied the end into a noose. All Andrei had to do was position it around the rat's skull. He did this, then stepped back as far as the string would allow, getting down onto his stomach. He lay in wait. But he could barely see his bait. It was a blur. Suddenly afraid, he hoped the cat would go towards his brother. Pavel would catch it and they could go home and eat.

But now he could see something: a black shape moving towards him. The cat had chosen him. Of course, if he caught it then Pavel would play cards with him and never get cross again. His mood changed to anticipation. Yes, he'd be the one to catch this cat. His brother warned against pulling the snare too early. So Andrei decided to wait, just to be sure. He could almost bring the black fur and four legs into focus. He'd wait a little longer . . .

He heard his brother hiss. 'Now!'

Andrei panicked. He'd heard that tone many times before. It meant he'd done something wrong. He squinted hard and saw that the cat was standing in the middle of his snare. He pulled the string. But too late, the cat had leapt away. Overcome with anger, he was ready to chase the cat and catch it and smash its skull. But he saw that his brother remained flat on the ground. And Andrei, who'd learned always to follow his brother's lead, did the same. The blurred black outline was now moving towards his brother's trap.

Suddenly Andrei saw the black shape spring forward. A moment later, Pavel leapt up, yanking the string round the cat's paw. Screeching filled the forest as the creature thrashed in the snow. Pavel was afraid the knot would break. Andrei heard his brother cry out, his voice frantic: 'Kill it! Kill it!'

Now he was being given instructions. He jumped up, ran forward and threw himself on top of the cat's writhing body. He could feel the animal wriggling beneath his stomach. Keeping himself flat on the cat, Andrei looked behind him, his eyes pleading with Pavel to take charge.

'It's still alive!' he shouted.

Pavel ran to him and dropped to his knees. Andrei remained motionless, feeling his brother reach under his body. Pavel jerked his hands out; he must have been bitten. Then he clambered to the other side and slid his hands under again, this time arriving at the tail. Andrei felt his brother's fingers creeping up the cat's back, nearing its head, closer and closer. Crazed with fear, the cat began biting at anything—his jacket, the snow.

Imitating his brother, Andrei cried out, 'Kill it! Kill it!'

Pavel snapped the animal's neck. Neither of them did anything for a moment, just lying still, breathing deeply. Finally Pavel stood up. Andrei remained in the snow, not daring to move.

'You can stand up now.'

He could stand up now. He could stand side by side with his brother. He could stand proud. Andrei hadn't disappointed. He reached up, took his brother's hand and got to his feet. Pavel couldn't have caught the cat without him. Andrei laughed, clapping his hands and dancing on the spot. He felt as happy as he'd ever felt in his entire life. His brother hugged him.

Now they had to transport their prize back to the village unseen.

Pavel picked the cat out of the snow. 'I'm going to carry it hidden under a pile of sticks,' he said, 'so it will look like we've been collecting firewood. But if we'd really been collecting firewood, you'd be carrying sticks too.'

Andrei was impressed by his brother's logic—he'd never have thought of that. He set about gathering wood. Finding loose sticks in the snow was difficult, and he was forced to rake through with his bare hands. After each sweep he rubbed his fingers together, blowing on them. His nose had begun to run, snot collecting on his top lip. He didn't mind, though, not after their success. He began to hum a song his father used to sing.

EXPERIENCING THE SAME shortage of sticks, Pavel had moved away from his brother. Some distance away he saw a fallen tree. He hurried towards it, and placed the cat in the snow so he was free to snap off all the dead wood. There was plenty here and he glanced around, looking for Andrei. He was about to call out when there was a noise. He turned sharply. The woods were dense, dark. He shut his eyes, concentrating on that sound: the *crunch*, *crunch*, *crunch* of snow. It was getting faster, louder. Adrenaline shot through his body. He opened his eyes. A man was running straight towards him, holding a thick branch. He'd heard them kill the cat and now he was going to steal their prize. Pavel began kicking snow over the cat, trying to conceal it.

'We're collecting . . .'

Pavel's voice trailed off as the man burst through the trees, raising the branch. Only now, seeing this man's gaunt face and wild eyes, did Pavel realise that he didn't want the cat. He wanted him.

Pavel's mouth fell open at more or less the same time as the branch arched down, the end slamming against the crown of his head.

ANDREI STOPPED HUMMING. He hadn't found that many sticks and he didn't want to be told off, not after he'd done so well. He stood up, squinting into the forest. 'Pavel?'

There was no reply. Andrei walked in the direction he'd last seen his brother but he could see nothing. He called again, louder. Why wasn't his brother answering? Something was wrong. Andrei wiped his nose on his sleeve and wondered if this was a test. What would his brother do in this situation? He'd follow the tracks in the snow. Andrei dropped his sticks and searched the ground on his hands and knees. He found his own footprints and traced them back to the point where he'd left his brother. Proud of himself, he switched to his brother's footsteps. If he stood up he couldn't see the prints, so he crouched, his nose only an arm's length from the snow, and carried on.

He arrived at a fallen tree, sticks scattered all around, footsteps everywhere—some deep and large. The snow was red. Andrei took a handful, crushing it between his fingers, squeezing it and watching it turn to blood.

'Pavel!'

He didn't stop shouting until his throat hurt and his voice disappeared. Whimpering, he just wanted his brother back. But it was no good. His brother had left him. And he was alone.

OKSANA HAD HIDDEN a small bag of powdered cornstalks, pigweed and crushed potato peelings behind the bricks of her oven. During inspections she always kept a small fire burning. Collectors sent to check that she wasn't hoarding grain never looked beyond the flames.

Tonight the family would have a feast. She melted clumps of snow, bringing it to the boil and thickening it with the powdered cornstalks. Of course she was getting ahead of herself. Pavel hadn't succeeded yet. But she felt sure he would. If God had given her hardship he'd also given her a son to help. All the same, if he didn't catch the cat she wouldn't become angry. Anger was a waste of energy. Even as she tried to brace herself for disappointment, she felt giddy at the prospect of a meat and potato borscht.

Andrei stood in the doorway, his face cut, snow on his jacket, snot and blood running from his nose. His *laptys* had completely come apart.

Oksana ran over. 'Where's your brother?'

'He left me.' Andrei started to cry. He didn't know where his brother was. He didn't understand what had happened. He couldn't explain.

Oksana brushed Andrei aside and hurried out of the house, looking to the woods. There was no sign of Pavel. Maybe he'd fallen and injured himself. She ran back inside, only to see Andrei standing by the borscht with a spoon in his mouth, soup dribbling from his lip. Overcome with anger—at her dead husband, her missing son—she ran forward, knocking Andrei to the ground.

'You useless, clumsy, stupid boy. Where is my son? What happened?'

He couldn't talk; he just kept crying, and so she hit him, pounding her hands on his tiny chest. Only when the borscht was in danger of boiling over did she stop. She stood up, moving the soup off the fire.

Andrei whimpered on the floor. Oksana looked down at him, her anger melting away. He was so small. He loved his older brother so much. She bent down, picked him up and sat him on a chair. She wrapped her blanket round him and poured him a bowl of borscht. She offered him the spoon. He stopped crying and began to eat. When he'd finished she filled the bowl again. She told him to eat slowly. He ignored her, finishing a second bowl. Very quietly she asked what had happened and listened as he explained the blood in the snow, the dropped sticks and the heavy footprints.

She closed her eyes. 'Your brother is dead. He's been taken for food. Do you understand? Just as you hunted that cat, someone was hunting you.'

Andrei remained silent. He didn't understand. Oksana stood up and left the house. She fell on her knees in the snow, and stared up at the full moon. 'Please, God, give me back my son.'

Only God could bring him home now. It wasn't so much to ask. All she wanted was her son, her reason to live.

Some of the neighbours appeared at their doors. They stared at Oksana. They listened to her cries. But there was nothing unusual about this kind of grief and people did not watch for long.

TWENTY YEARS LATER

Moscow, February 14, 1953

Leo stared up at Apartment Block 18—a low-rise, squat slab of grey concrete. It was late afternoon, already dark. An entire working day had been lost to a task that was as unpleasant as it was unimportant. According to the militia incident report, a boy aged four had been found dead on the railway lines. The boy had been playing on the tracks, and was caught by a passenger train; his body was cut up by the wheels. The driver of the 21.00 to Khabarovsk had communicated at his first stop that he'd caught a glimpse of someone or something on the tracks shortly after leaving Yaroslavskiy Vokzal station. Whether that train had actually hit the boy wasn't yet established. But there was no need to press the issue; it was a tragic accident with no question of blame. The matter should have already been closed.

Ordinarily, Leo Stepanovich Demidov—an up-and-coming member of the MGB, the State Security force—would not have become involved in this kind of incident. The loss of a son was heartbreaking for the family, but not a State Security concern. However, this particular situation had grown unexpectedly complicated. The parents were unable to accept that their son,

Arkady, had been responsible for his own death. They'd been telling people that he'd been murdered. By whom, for what reason, they had no idea. But they had an emotive power on their side, and it was possible that they were convincing other gullible people: neighbours, friends and strangers.

To aggravate the situation further, the boy's father, Fyodor Andreev, was himself a low-ranking member of the MGB and, as it happened, one of Leo's subordinates. He was bringing the MGB into disrepute by using his authority to give credibility to this assertion. Had the circumstances not been mitigating, Leo's task here might well have been this man's arrest. The whole thing was a mess. And Leo had been forced to leave a sensitive, genuine assignment in order to straighten the matter out.

He was not looking forward to the confrontation with Fyodor, so Leo took his time walking up the stairs, contemplating how he had ended up here. He'd never intended to join the State Security Department; the career had grown out of his military service. During the Great Patriotic War he'd been selected from the Central Institute of Physical Culture, where he'd been a student, to join a special-forces battalion. Handpicked for athleticism and physical prowess, the new recruits were taken to a camp at Mytishchi, just north of Moscow, where they were trained in close combat, low-altitude parachuting and the use of explosives. The battalion came under the direct authority of the NKVD—as the secret police was known before State Security became the MGB—rather than the military, and its missions reflected this. Sent behind enemy lines, destroying infrastructure, collecting information, carrying out assassinations—they were clandestine raiders.

Leo had flourished. As a result he'd been awarded the Order of Suvorov 2nd Class. His levelheadedness, military success and above all absolute belief in his country had resulted in him becoming a poster boy—quite literally—for the Soviet liberation of German-occupied territory. He and a gaggle of soldiers from a patchwork of divisions were photographed surrounding the burning wreck of a German panzer, guns in the air, victory on their faces; in the background, smoke rose from smouldering villages. Leo, with his good looks, was ushered to the front of the photograph. One week later the photograph had made the front page of *Pravda* and Leo, symbol of victory, was being congratulated by strangers, troops, civilians.

After the war, Leo had moved into the NKVD itself. His only ambition was to serve his country, a country that had defeated Fascism, a country that provided free education and healthcare, that trumpeted the rights of workers around the world. Although his employment in the State Security force was frequently unpleasant, he understood the necessity of guarding their revolution from enemies both foreign and domestic, from those who sought to undermine it and those determined to see it fail. To this end Leo would lay down his life. To this end he'd lay down the lives of others.

None of this heroism or military training had any relevance today. This was a colleague, a friend, a grief-stricken father. But Leo needed to tread carefully. He couldn't allow himself to be swayed by the same feelings that were blinding Fyodor. This hysteria was putting a good family in danger. Left unchecked, the groundless chatter about murder could grow like a weed, spreading through the community, making people question one of the fundamental pillars of their new society: *There is no crime.*

Few believed this absolutely. There were blemishes: this was a society in transition, not perfect yet. It was every citizen's duty to study the works of Lenin, and Leo knew that crime would wither away as poverty disappeared. They hadn't reached that plateau yet. Things were stolen, drunken disputes became violent; there were the *urki*—the criminal gangs. But people had to believe they were moving towards a better state of existence. To call this murder was to take a giant step backwards. The Party's enemies were not only saboteurs, spies and wreckers of industry but also doubters of the Party line, doubters of the society that awaited them. By that rule, Fyodor, Leo's friend and colleague, had indeed become an enemy.

Leo's mission was to guide the family back from the brink. They were upset, that was all. They weren't thinking straight. He wasn't here to threaten them, at least not immediately; he was here to help them, to restore faith.

He knocked, and Fyodor opened the door.

Leo bowed his head. 'I'm very sorry for your loss.'

Fyodor stepped back, allowing Leo into the room.

Every seat was taken. There were elderly people, children—obviously the entire family had gathered. It was easy to imagine how they'd encouraged each other to think that some mysterious force was to blame for the little boy's death. Maybe that made their loss easier to bear.

Leo turned to Fyodor. 'It might be easier to talk if it was just us two.'

'Please, this is my family; they want to hear what you have to say.'

Leo glanced around—twenty or so sets of eyes were fixed on him. They already knew what he was going to say and they did not like him for it. They were angry that their boy had died, and Leo would simply have to accept that he was the focal point for their anger.

'I can think of nothing worse than the loss of a child,' he began. 'I remember congratulating you when you and your wife celebrated the birth of your son. And it is with terrible sadness that I find myself consoling you.'

A little stiff perhaps but Leo meant it sincerely. It was met with silence.

'I've never experienced such a loss,' he continued. 'I don't know how it would make me react. Perhaps I'd feel the need to blame someone. But, with a clear head, I can assure you that the cause of Arkady's death is not in dispute. I have brought with me the report, which I can leave with you. I've been sent also to answer any questions you might have.'

'Arkady was murdered. We want your help in investigating. We would like the MGB to place pressure on the procurator to open a criminal case.'

It was the worst possible beginning to their discussion. The father was calling for the impossible.

Leo nodded, trying to maintain an air of reconciliation. 'Arkady was caught by a passing train. His death was an accident, a terrible accident.'

'Then why was he naked? Why was his mouth stuffed with dirt?'

The boy was naked? That was the first Leo had heard of it. He opened the report. *The boy was found clothed.* Now that he read the line again it struck him as odd. But there it was. He continued to scan the document: *Having been dragged along the ground his mouth contained dirt.* He closed the report. The room was waiting.

'Your boy was found clothed. Yes, there was dirt in his mouth. But his body was dragged by the train; some dirt in his mouth is to be expected.'

An elderly woman stood up. Although stooped by age, her eyes were sharp. 'That is not what we were told. The man who found the body—Taras Kuprin—told us Arkady was not wearing a single item of clothing. A collision with a train doesn't undress a boy.'

'Kuprin's statement is in this report,' Leo said. 'He claims the body was found on the tracks, fully clothed. He's quite clear about that.'

'Why did he tell us differently?'

'Maybe he was confused. I don't know. But I have this man's signature on his statement. I can read you the entire report aloud if you like.'

The elderly woman spoke again. 'That report is a lie.'

Everyone tensed. Leo remained silent, struggling to stay calm.

Fyodor stepped forward. 'Leo, new evidence has come to light today. A woman who lives in an apartment looking out over the tracks saw Arkady with a man. We know no more than that. This woman is not a friend of ours. We've never met her. She heard about my son's death. And if what we've been told is true, she can describe this man. We're waiting for her now.'

'She's coming here? I'd be interested to hear what she has to say.'

Leo was offered a chair. He waved it away. He'd stand.

Everyone was waiting for the knock on the door. Leo regretted not taking that chair. Almost an hour passed, in silence, before a faint knock was heard. Fyodor opened the door, introduced himself and showed the woman in. She was in her thirties, with a kind face and large, nervous eyes.

'These are my friends and family,' said Fyodor. 'No need to be alarmed.'

But she wasn't listening. She was staring at Leo.

'My name is Leo Stepanovich. I'm an MGB officer. What is your name?'

Leo took out his pad, finding a fresh page. The woman didn't reply. He glanced up. Leo was about to repeat the question when she finally spoke.

'Galina Shaporina.' Her voice was a whisper.

'And what did you see?'

'I saw . . .' She looked about the room, then back at Leo.

'You saw a man?' Fyodor prompted, tension evident in his voice.

'Yes, a man.'

Fyodor sighed with relief.

'A man,' she continued, 'a worker perhaps, on the railway—I saw him through my window. It was very dark.'

Leo tapped his pad with his pencil. 'You saw him with a young boy?'

'No, there was no boy.'

Fyodor's mouth dropped. 'But we were told you saw a man holding my little boy's hand.'

'No, no, no—there was no boy. He was holding a bag, I think—a bag full of tools. He was working on the tracks, perhaps. I didn't see very much, a glimpse, that's all. I'm very sorry your son died.'

Leo shut his pad. 'Thank you.'

The woman looked about the room, at all the eyes on her. She turned to Leo. 'Will there be any further questions?'

'No. You can go.'

As Galina hurried to the door, the elderly woman called out, 'You lose your nerve so easily?'

Fyodor approached the elderly woman. 'Please, sit down.'

She nodded, neither disgusted nor approving. 'Arkady was your son.'

'Yes.'

Leo couldn't see Fyodor's eyes. He wondered what silent communication was passing between these two people. Whatever it was, she took her seat. Galina had slipped away. Leo hoped that they'd reached a turning point.

Fyodor returned to Leo's side. 'Forgive my mother, she's very upset.'

'This is why I'm here. So we can talk this through within the confines of this room. But once I leave this room, the conversation cannot continue. If anyone asks you about your son you cannot say he was murdered. Not because I order you to but because it is not true.'

'We understand.'

'Fyodor, I want you to take tomorrow off. This has been authorised. If there's anything more I can do for you . . .'

'Thank you.' Fyodor shook Leo's hand. 'We're all very upset. Forgive us any outbursts.'

'They'll pass unrecorded. But as I said, this ends here.'

Fyodor's face stiffened. He nodded. As though the words were bitter he forced them out: 'My son's death was a terrible accident.'

Leo walked down the stairs, breathing deeply. He was glad the matter had been resolved. Fyodor was a good man. Once he came to terms with his son's death, the truth would be easier to accept.

The village of Kimov, 160 km north of Moscow

Anatoly Brodsky hadn't slept for three days. He was so tired that even the most basic tasks required concentration. The barn door in front of him was locked. He knew he'd have to force it open, but he simply didn't have the energy. Snow had begun to fall. He looked up at the night sky; his mind drifted, and when he eventually remembered where he was, snow was settling on his face. He realised that if he didn't get inside he was going to die. Concentrating, he kicked the door. Timbers splintered. Encouraged, he summoned the last sparks of energy and kicked again. The wood cracked, the door swung back. He stood at the entrance, adjusting to the gloom. On one side of the barn there were two cows; on the other side there were tools, straw. He spread some coarse sacks on the frozen ground and lay down.

FROM HIS BEDROOM window, Mikhail Zinoviev could see that the barn door was open. It was swaying back and forth in the wind, and snow was swirling into his barn. He turned round. His wife was in bed, asleep. Quietly, he put on his coat and his felt boots and went outside.

The wind had picked up, whipping snow into Mikhail's face. He raised his hand to his eyes. As he approached the barn, he could see through his fingers that the door had been kicked open. Peering inside, he saw the outline of a man lying on the ground. Without any clear sense of what he was doing, he entered, grabbed a pitchfork, stepped up to the sleeping figure.

The man opened his eyes and looked up at Mikhail. The prongs of the pitchfork quivered above his stomach. Neither of them moved.

They remained like this, frozen mid-frame, until a feeling of shame overcame Mikhail. He dropped the pitchfork and sank to his knees.

'Please forgive me.'

ANATOLY SAT UP. The adrenaline had jolted him awake but his body ached. How long had he been asleep? Not long, not long enough.

'I understand,' he said hoarsely, his throat dry. 'I shouldn't have come here. I shouldn't have asked for your help. You have your family to think of. I've put you in danger. It is I who should be asking for your forgiveness.'

Mikhail shook his head. 'I was afraid. I panicked. Forgive me.'

'There's nothing to forgive. I might have done the same.' Anatoly glanced out at the snow. He couldn't leave now. He wouldn't survive. 'Listen: I want you to forget that I ever came here. Forget that I ever asked for your help. Remember us as we were. Remember us as the best of friends. By first light I'll be gone. I promise.'

Mikhail's head dropped; he wept.

When Anatoly arrived unannounced that evening, Mikhail had seemed understandably surprised. All the same, Anatoly had been welcomed warmly, offered food, drink, a bed. Only when his hosts heard that he was making his way north to the Finnish border did they understand the reason for the sudden arrival. He was wanted by the State Security Police, the MGB. As that fact became clear, the welcome evaporated. The punishment for aiding and abetting a fugitive was execution. He knew this, but had hoped his friend would accept the risk. True, it was an enormous amount to ask, but Anatoly had once saved Mikhail's life, and though he'd never considered it a debt, that was only because he'd never thought he'd need to call it in.

During their discussion it had become apparent that Mikhail wasn't prepared to take that risk. His wife had glared at Anatoly with unmasked venom, frequently interrupting their conversation to ask to speak with her husband in private. Circumstances demanded prudence and caution in everyday life. And there was no denying he'd brought danger to his friend's family, a family he loved. Lowering his expectations sharply, Anatoly had told Mikhail that he wanted nothing more than a night's sleep in their barn. He'd be gone by tomorrow morning. It'd been his idea to smash the lock to the barn. In the unlikely event that he was caught, the family could claim there'd been an intruder. He'd believed that these precautions had reassured his hosts. But clearly Mikhail had thought that killing Anatoly and reporting him as an intruder was the only way to guarantee the safety of his family.

Unable to watch his friend cry, Anatoly leaned close. 'There's nothing to feel guilty about. We're all just trying to survive.'

Mikhail looked up, wiping his tears away. Realising that this would be the last time they would ever see each other, the two friends hugged.

'You're a better man than me,' Mikhail said, pulling back.

He left the barn, wedging the door shut behind him. Anatoly heard the fading crunch of snow as Mikhail trudged back to the house.

Moscow

The table had been smashed, the bed turned upside-down, the mattress shredded and floorboards ripped up, yet the search of Anatoly Brodsky's apartment had yielded no clue so far as to his whereabouts. Leo crouched down to examine the fireplace. Stacks of papers had been burned. Using the muzzle of his gun he raked the remains, hoping to find some fragment untouched by fire. Everything was black ash. The traitor had escaped.

Leo was to blame. He'd given this man the benefit of the doubt; he'd presumed he was innocent. He'd disregarded a fundamental principle of their work: the presumption of guilt. *Better to let ten innocent men suffer than one spy escape.* His first serious misjudgment since joining State Security. Few officers got an opportunity to make a second mistake.

He hadn't thought much of the case: Brodsky was educated, with some competence in the English language, and dealt with foreigners on a regular basis. This was grounds for vigilance, but the man was a respected vet in a city with few trained vets. Foreign diplomats had to take their cats and dogs to someone. Furthermore, this was a man who'd served in the Red Army as a field doctor. His background was impeccable. According to his military records, despite not being technically qualified as a doctor he'd worked in several field hospitals and subsequently received two commendations.

Major Kuzmin, Leo's mentor, had reminded him that those who appear the most trustworthy deserve the most suspicion. The duty of an investigator was to scratch away at innocence until guilt was uncovered. If no guilt was uncovered, they hadn't scratched deep enough. In the case of Brodsky, the question was whether this suspect had become a vet so that foreign diplomats could meet him openly. Why did he establish his practice within walking distance of the American Embassy? Why—shortly after he opened this practice—did several employees of that embassy obtain pets? Finally, why did the pets of foreign diplomats seem to require more frequent attention than pets belonging to a typical citizen?

Having considered the case, Leo decided not to arrest the suspect outright but to have him followed, reasoning that if this citizen was working as a spy it was an opportunity to discover who he was working with. Though he never said as much, he was uncomfortable about making an arrest without more evidence. That was a qualm he'd lived with throughout his professional life. He'd arrested many citizens knowing only that someone mistrusted them; evidence would be acquired during interrogation. But Leo was no longer a lackey, and he'd decided to make use of his authority and do things a little differently. He wanted proof, something more than conjecture. In short, he wanted to feel OK about arresting Anatoly Brodsky.

As part of the surveillance operation, Leo had taken the day shift, following the suspect from eight in the morning till eight in the evening. For three days he'd observed nothing out of the ordinary. The suspect worked, ate lunch out and went home. He seemed a good citizen. When, this morning, Leo had been ordered to fix the Fyodor Andreev situation immediately, he didn't protest that he had more important things to do. Yet while he was meeting relatives, stamping out rumours, this suspect was making his escape. The idiot delegated to maintain watch had thought nothing of the fact that there hadn't been a single customer at the veterinary practice all day. It wasn't until dusk that the agent had become suspicious and entered, intending to pose as a customer. He'd found the premises empty. A back window had been prised open. The suspect could have escaped at any time.

Brodsky is gone. When Leo had heard those words he'd felt sick. He'd called an emergency meeting with Major Kuzmin. Leo now had the proof of guilt he'd been looking for, but he no longer had the suspect. His mentor instructed him to catch this traitor at all costs. Leo was not to sleep, eat, rest, do anything until that man was in their custody.

He stared out of the window at the snow that had begun to fall over the city. What had gone wrong? The suspect must have sighted the agents tailing him and planned his escape, burning documents relating to his espionage or his destination. Leo had to find some fragment of his escape plan.

The neighbours were a retired couple in their seventies, their married son, his wife and their two children. All six were sitting in the kitchen of their two-room apartment. A junior officer stood behind them for the purpose of intimidation. Leo could see their fear as he walked up to the table.

'Anatoly Brodsky is a traitor,' he said. 'If you help him in any way, even by saying nothing, you will be treated as an accomplice. The pressure is on you to prove your loyalty to the State.'

The elderly man, the grandfather, was quick to offer information. Copying Leo's choice of words, he claimed the traitor had gone to work that morning a little earlier, carrying the same case as usual, wearing the same coat and hat. He also offered suggestions as to where this traitor could be, all of which Leo sensed were nothing more than desperate guesswork. The grandfather concluded by saying how much everyone in their family disliked and mistrusted Brodsky as a neighbour, and how the only person who liked him was Zina Morosovna, who lived downstairs.

Zina Morosovna, a woman in her fifties, was trembling like a child, and failing to hide it by smoking. Leo found her standing beside a reproduction of a famous Stalin portrait—smooth skin, wise eyes—hung prominently over her fireplace. Perhaps she thought it might protect her.

Leo didn't bother to introduce himself, cutting straight to the chase. 'Why is it you're such good friends with Anatoly Brodsky when everyone else in this building disliked and mistrusted him?'

Zina was caught off guard. 'Anatoly was a good man.'

'Brodsky is a spy. Yet you call him good? Treachery is a virtue?'

Realising her mistake, Zina began to qualify her comment. 'All I meant was that he was very considerate with the noise. He was polite.'

Leo took out a pad and wrote down her ill-chosen words in large letters: *HE WAS A GOOD MAN.* He wrote clearly so that she could see exactly what he was writing: those words were more than enough to convict her as a collaborator. At her age she had little chance of surviving the Gulags.

Zina retreated to the corner of the room. 'I don't know where Anatoly has gone but I do know that he has no family. His wife was killed in the war. His son died of tuberculosis. He rarely had any visitors. As far as I could tell, he had few friends . . .' She paused, clearly caught up in her own recollections.

Leo wasn't impressed. 'I want to know where he is,' he prompted. 'I don't care about his wife or son.'

She appeared to come to a decision. 'Anatoly kept himself to himself. However, he did receive and send letters. Occasionally he left them with me to post. The only regular correspondence was addressed to someone in the village of Kimov. It's somewhere north of here, I think. He mentioned that he had a friend there. I don't remember the name of the friend. That's the truth. That's all I know.'

Her voice was choked with guilt. While no outward display of emotion could ever be taken at face value, Leo's instincts told him that she was betraying a confidence. He ripped out the incriminating page from his notebook and handed it to her. She accepted the sheet as payment for a betrayal. He saw contempt in her eyes. He didn't let it bother him.

The name of a rural village to the north of Moscow was a tenuous lead. It was much more likely that Brodsky was being sheltered by the people he was working for. The idea of a foreign-funded traitor falling back on a personal connection ran contrary to the notion that he was a professional spy. And yet Leo felt sure this was a lead he should pursue. It was the only clue he had. Equivocation had already cost him.

He hurried to the truck parked outside and began rereading the case file. He was interrupted by the return of his second-in-command, Vasili Ilyich Nikitin. Aged thirty-five, five years older than Leo, Vasili had once been one of the MGB's most promising officers. In his early days as an investigator he had signalled his dedication to the MGB by denouncing his only brother for making anti-Stalinist remarks. Apparently the brother had made a joke at Stalin's expense. He'd been drunk at the time, celebrating his birthday. The brother had been given a twenty-year labour sentence. But three years later he had escaped, killing several guards in the process. He was never caught, and if Vasili hadn't strenuously helped in the search his career might not have survived. Still, the embarrassment of the incident hung round his neck. Leo knew that his deputy, with no more brothers to denounce, was on the lookout for some other way of getting back in favour.

Vasili had just finished his search of the veterinary practice. He handed Leo a crumpled letter that, he explained, he'd found caught behind the traitor's writing desk. All other correspondence had been burned, yet in his hurry the suspect had missed this one. Leo read it. The letter was from a friend telling Anatoly he was welcome to stay with him at any time. The address was partially smudged but the name of the city was clear: Kiev.

Leo handed the letter back to his deputy. 'This was written by Brodsky. He wanted us to find it. He's not heading to Kiev.'

The letter had been hastily written. The handwriting was inconsistent, poorly disguised. The content seemed intended solely to convey that the writer was a friend to whom Brodsky could turn in an hour of need. The address was deliberately smudged to prevent a quick identification of the genuine occupant. The location of the letter—behind the desk—seemed staged.

Leo returned his attention to the file. According to the records, Brodsky was friends with a man called Mikhail Sviatoslavich Zinoviev, who had been discharged from the Red Army suffering chronic frostbite. Several of his toes had been amputated; Brodsky had performed the operation. Leo's finger ran along the document, searching for a current address.

Kimov.

Leo turned to his men, catching Vasili's sour expression.

'We're leaving.'

THE ROADS OUT OF MOSCOW were covered with icy mulch, and despite the truck's tyres being fitted with snow chains their speed rarely rose above twenty-five kilometres per hour. Snow gusted around them; the windscreen wipers struggled to keep even the smallest patch of window clear. With visibility less than ten metres the truck pushed forward. It was nothing less than desperation on Leo's part to attempt a journey in these conditions.

Leo was seated beside Vasili and their driver. The steel cabin was heated only by the residual warmth from the rattling engine. But at least the cabin offered some protection from the weather. In the back his nine heavily armed agents travelled in no such luxury. The ZiS-151 trucks had tarpaulin roofs that cold air and even snow whipped through. Since temperatures could fall to minus thirty, all rear compartments of the ZiS-151s were fitted with wood-burning stoves, but they warmed only those within touching distance. Leo had sat there many times himself: every ten minutes the two nearest the stove reluctantly moved away from the heat, relegated to the coldest position at the ends of the benches while the rest of the team shuffled up.

For the first time in his career, Leo could sense dissent among his team. The reason wasn't the discomfort. His men were used to tough conditions. No, there was something else. Tonight he felt hostility, resistance. Aside from Vasili he wasn't used to it. He pushed the thoughts aside. Right now his popularity was the least of his concerns.

If the suspect was in Kimov, Leo thought it likely that he'd be on the move at first light. Leo was taking a chance betting that they'd get to the village in time. Brodsky's escape had embarrassed Leo and he was determined to make amends, determined to be the one to make the arrest. But if Brodsky wasn't in Kimov, Vasili would be the first in line with a testimonial detailing how his superior officer disregarded the promising Kiev lead. Sensing his weakness, others in the directorate would come forward to denounce him as a poor leader while Vasili positioned himself as Leo's logical successor. For both men, much depended upon the location of this traitor.

Leo glanced across at his deputy, a man both handsome and repulsive in equal measure—as if his good looks were plastered over a rotten centre. There were just the tiniest fractures in his attractive façade, visible at the corners of his mouth: a slight sneer that hinted at dark thoughts. Perhaps sensing that he was the subject of attention, Vasili turned and smiled a thin, ambiguous smile. Something pleased him.

Suspicious, Leo checked the map. With a population of less than a thousand, Kimov was a speck of dust on the Soviet canvas. He'd warned the driver not to expect any road signs. Yet Leo began to suspect that they'd missed their turning. They were still travelling north when they should be travelling west. The driver had overshot the mark.

'Turn round!' he ordered.

Neither the driver nor Vasili seemed surprised by the request.

'But we didn't see the exit,' the driver mumbled.

'We've missed it. Stop the truck.'

Pumping the brake in short bursts to avoid sliding on the ice, the driver slowed to a stop. Leo jumped out and in blizzard conditions began to direct the truck through an awkward U-turn. The driver exhibited an improbable level of incompetence. Vasili had organised the truck, the driver. Leo wondered how many other members of his team had invested more in his failure than his success. Feeling isolated, he sent the driver to sit in the back and took the wheel himself. He'd get them there. He could trust no one.

By the time they were on the correct road, the storm had passed. A weak winter sun was rising. They were passing through the rural heartlands—fields, forests. Turning into a gentle valley, Leo saw the village: a cluster of wooden farmhouses with square bases and high triangular roofs, a vista unchanged for a hundred years. This was old Russia: communities built round bucket wells and ancient myths, where the health of cattle was decided by the grace of the *Dvorovoi*, the yard spirit, where parents told their children that if they misbehaved spirits would steal them and turn them into bark. Their country's ideological revolution had done little to dislodge this primitive folklore.

Exhausted, Leo stopped the truck at the first farmhouse. From his jacket pocket he took out a glass vial of white crystals—pure methamphetamine. He'd been introduced to it while fighting on the Eastern Front. Now it was prescribed to Leo by the MGB doctors, and he used it whenever he couldn't afford to rest. Its usefulness couldn't be underestimated. But its price was a crash about twenty-four hours later: complete exhaustion that could be offset only by taking more. Side effects were manifesting themselves. He'd lost weight; his powers of recall had faded, and he had to write notes to himself. It was impossible to judge whether he'd become more paranoid as a result of the drugs, since paranoia was an essential asset, a virtue to be cultivated. If it had been amplified by the methamphetamines, that was all to the good.

He tapped a small amount onto his palm, then washed it down with the contents of a hip flask. The vodka stung his throat, failing to hide the acrid chemical taste, which made him want to gag. He waited for the sensation to pass, surveying his surroundings. Fresh snow covered everything. Leo was pleased. Outside Kimov itself there were few places to hide. A person would be visible for kilometres, their tracks through the snow easy to follow.

He had no idea which of these farms belonged to Mikhail Zinoviev. Since a military truck parked in the road took away any element of surprise, Leo jumped out, drew his gun and moved towards the nearest house.

Before he'd even knocked on the door, an elderly woman appeared. She was wearing a blue dress and an embroidered shawl round her head.

'I'm looking for Mikhail Sviatoslavich Zinoviev. Where is he?'

She clearly didn't care for Leo, or his gun or his uniform. She cocked her head to one side and made no response. It was the second time in two days that an elderly woman had squared up to Leo, held him in open contempt.

The stalemate was broken when the woman's son hurried out of the house. 'Excuse her,' he said. 'She's old. What can I do for you?'

'Mikhail Sviatoslavich. Where is he? Which is his farm?'

With what seemed like great relief, the son pointed out his friend's farm.

Leo returned to the truck. He split the assembled men into three groups. Two of them would advance on the house from different sides, one each from the front and back, while the third team would surround the barn. Each man was armed with a 9mm Stechkin APS automatic pistol. In addition, one man in each group carried an AK-47.

'We take the traitor alive,' Leo told each team. 'We need his confession. If you're in any doubt, any doubt at all, you don't fire.'

He repeated this command with particular emphasis to the group headed by Vasili. Killing Anatoly Brodsky would be a punishable offence. Their own safety was secondary to the life of the suspect. In response, Vasili took command of his group's AK-47.

Attempting to limit Vasili's potential to sabotage this operation, Leo gave them the least important area to secure. 'Your group will search the barn.'

They moved off. Halfway towards the house, the groups broke off in different directions. Thirty paces from the door, Leo paused, allowing the other two groups to get in position. Vasili's team encircled the barn while the third group arrived at the back of the house. There was no sign of life outside. A whisper of smoke rose from the chimney. Ragged cloth hung in front of the small windows. Except for the click of AK-47 safety catches there was silence. Suddenly a little girl stepped out from a small rectangular building, the pit toilet—set back from the main house. The three officers nearest Leo swung round, training their guns on her. The girl froze, terrified.

Leo raised his hands. 'Don't shoot!'

No one moved. Then the girl broke into a run, sprinting towards the house as fast as she could, screaming for her mother.

Leo felt the first amphetamine kick—his fatigue evaporated. He leapt forward; his men followed, moving in on the house. The little girl threw open the front door, scampered inside. Leo was seconds behind, raising his gun and barging through to a small, warm kitchen. Two young girls, aged maybe ten and four, were standing by a fire. Their mother was shielding them with one hand on each of their chests. A man in his forties entered from the back room.

Leo turned to him. 'Mikhail Sviatoslavich?'

'Yes?'

'My name is Leo Stepanovich Demidov, officer of the MGB. Your friend Anatoly Brodsky is wanted for questioning. Tell me where he is.'

'Anatoly? Anatoly lives in Moscow. I haven't seen him for years.'

'Don't lie. If you tell me where he is, I will forget that he ever came here. You and your family will be safe.'

Mikhail's wife glanced at her husband; she was tempted by the offer. Leo felt an overwhelming sense of relief. He'd been right. The traitor was here. Without waiting for an answer, Leo gestured for his men to search the house.

VASILI ENTERED THE BARN, gun raised, finger against the trigger. He stepped towards the pile of straw, which was high enough to conceal a man. He fired several short bursts. Wisps of straw flew up. The cows behind him snorted, shuffled away, kicking the ground. But no blood seeped out. There was no one here; they were wasting their time. He went outside and lit a cigarette.

Alerted by the sound of gunfire, Leo ran out of the house.

Vasili called to him, 'There's no one here.'

Leo hurried towards the barn, his jaw clamped tight.

Annoyed at being ignored, Vasili tossed the cigarette into snow. 'Unless he can disguise himself as a cow, he's not in there. Maybe you should shoot them just in case.'

Vasili glanced around for laughter and the men obliged. He wasn't deluded; he recognised that none of them thought he was funny. Their laughter was an indication that the balance of power had begun to shift. Their allegiance to Leo was weakening. Maybe it was the exhausting journey. Maybe it had been Leo's decision to let Brodsky remain free when he should have been arrested. But Vasili wondered if it had something to do with Fyodor and the death of his boy. Leo had been sent to clear that matter up. Many of the men here were Fyodor's friends. If there was resentment, it could be manipulated.

LEO BENT DOWN, examining the tracks in the snow. Fresh boot prints led out from the barn, heading for the fields. He stood up and entered the barn.

'I've searched there already!' Vasili called out after him.

Ignoring him, Leo touched the smashed lock on the door. He saw the grain sacks spread on the ground and returned outside.

'I want three men to follow me, the fastest three. Vasili, you'll remain here. Continue searching the house.'

He took off his heavy winter jacket and gave it to his deputy. Unimpeded, able to run, he began following the tracks towards the fields. The three agents didn't remove their coats, but followed sluggishly.

Leo was already several hundred metres ahead, and picking up speed. The amphetamines focused him; nothing else existed except the tracks in the snow. Though he guessed the suspect had at least an hour's head start, that didn't concern him. The man had no idea he was being followed.

Up ahead was the crest of a gentle hill and Leo hoped that from there he'd be able to see the suspect. Reaching the top he paused, surveying the landscape. There were snow-covered fields in every direction. Some distance ahead was the edge of a dense forest but before that, a kilometre away, downhill, a man was shuffling through the snow. This was no farmer or labourer. It was the traitor. Leo was sure of it. He was making his way towards the forest. If he reached the trees he'd be able to hide. Leo checked over his shoulder—his three agents were lagging. They couldn't be counted on. He'd have to catch the traitor himself.

AS THOUGH SOME sixth sense had alerted him, Anatoly stopped walking and turned round. There, running down the small hill towards him, was a man. There could be no doubt that this was an officer of the State. Anatoly had been certain that all evidence connecting him to this remote village had been destroyed. He stood for a moment, mesmerised by the sight of his pursuer.

He'd been found. He felt his stomach heave, his face flush red, and then he spun round and began running towards the woods. His first few steps were clumsy and panicked. Realising that his coat was a hindrance, he pulled it off, dropping it on the ground, running for his life.

Anatoly no longer made the mistake of glancing behind him. He was concentrating on the woods ahead. They offered a chance to hide. And if it came to a fight he'd have a better chance in there, where there were branches and stones, than unarmed and out in the open.

LEO INCREASED HIS SPEED, sprinting as though on a running track. Some part of his mind remembered that the terrain was treacherous and running at this speed precarious. But the amphetamines made him believe anything was possible—he could leap this distance between them.

Suddenly Leo lost his footing, and tumbled face down into a snowdrift. Dazed, he rolled onto his back, wondering if he was hurt. He felt no pain. He got up, brushing the snow from his face and hands. He looked for Brodsky, expecting to see him disappearing into the forest. But to his surprise, the suspect was standing still. Confused, Leo hurried forward. Barely a hundred metres now separated them. Leo drew his gun, slowing to a walk. His heart was pounding, two thumps for each footstep. His fingers trembled; sweat seeped down his back. There were scarcely fifty paces between them. Brodsky turned round. He wasn't armed. It was as though he'd inexplicably given up. Leo continued, closer and closer. Finally he could see what had stopped Brodsky. There was a river some twenty metres wide between him and the woods. It hadn't been visible from the hill, hidden under a blanket of snow that had settled across the frozen surface.

Leo called out, 'It's over!'

Brodsky turned back to the river and stepped out onto the ice, his feet sliding across the surface. The ice sheet creaked under his weight, but he didn't slow down. Black, crooked lines formed on the surface, fanning out from underneath his feet. Icy water seeped up through them.

Leo reached the edge of the riverbank, holstered his gun, stretched out his hand. 'The ice won't hold. You won't reach the woods.'

Brodsky stopped and turned. 'I'm not trying to reach the woods.'

He raised his right leg, and with a sudden movement brought his boot crashing down. Water rushed up, the ice broke apart and he fell through.

The traitor wasn't going to surface, Leo decided. No doubt he was swimming away from the air hole in an attempt to kill himself and protect his accomplices. Hurrying down the riverbank, he estimated where under the ice Brodsky might be. Leo unfastened his heavy leather belt and gun, dropped them on the ground and stepped out onto the frozen river. Almost immediately the ice began to strain. He kept moving, trying to keep his footsteps light, but the ice was splintering under his weight. Reaching the middle of the river, he crouched, frantically brushing away the snow. But the suspect was nowhere to be seen. Leo moved further downstream but fracture lines were surrounding him from all sides. Water began to swell, the cracks came together. He filled his lungs, bracing himself as he heard a snap.

The ice collapsed.

Although he didn't feel the full extent of the cold, doped up as he was, he knew he had to move fast. There were shafts of light where the ice had broken, but beyond that the water was dark, shielded from the sun by a canopy of snow. He swam downstream, blindly groping right and left, his body screaming for air. Realising he wouldn't get a second chance, realising that returning empty-handed might mean death, he took another stroke downstream. His hand brushed something: cloth, a trouser leg. It was Brodsky. Leo swam underneath him, gripped him round the neck. The pain inside Leo's chest was sharp. He had to get back to the surface. With one arm round the motionless suspect's neck, he tried punching the ice above him, but his blows glanced off the smooth hard surface.

Leo focused on the shafts of sunlight upstream. He kicked hard, propelling them both towards the light. Leo took another kick—felt sunlight across his face—pushed upwards. The two men broke the water's surface.

Leo gasped and gasped again. But Brodsky wasn't breathing. Leo pulled himself up onto the bank, dragging his prisoner with him. Their skin was pale blue. Leo couldn't stop shaking. In contrast, the suspect remained perfectly still. Leo opened the man's mouth, tipping the water out, blowing air into his lungs. He pushed down on his chest, blew more air into his lungs.

'Come on!'

Brodsky spluttered back into consciousness, doubling over and vomiting up the icy water that filled his stomach. Leo didn't have time to feel relief. They had minutes before they'd die from hypothermia. He stood up.

He could see his three officers in the near distance, running fast. The men had evidently spotted Leo disappearing into the river.

Leo dropped down to the prisoner's side. Brodsky's eyes were closing—he was drifting back into unconsciousness. Leo hit him across the face. The suspect opened his eyes but almost immediately began to close them again.

Leo hit him again and again and again. They were running out of time.

He stood up, calling to his men. 'Hurry!'

His energy was sapping as finally the cold caught up with him and his chemical invincibility began to melt away. An extraordinary fatigue was repossessing his body. His officers arrived.

'Take off your jackets,' he ordered. 'Get a fire started.'

All three took their jackets off, wrapping one round Leo and the other two round Brodsky. They needed wood. There was a picket fence some distance away and two of the agents ran towards it while the third agent began ripping the sleeve of his coarse cotton shirt into strips. Leo remained focused on his prisoner, hitting him to keep him awake.

The two officers returned with planks. They cleared an area of ground, kicking aside the snow and laying the timbers across the frozen soil. They placed the strips of cotton on the planks, then balanced thin wooden shards around them. One of the officers took out his lighter, tipping the fluid over the cotton. The flint sparked, the cotton caught light. The wood smouldered. But it was damp and refused to catch. Leo ripped the lining from the inside of the jacket, adding this to the fire. If it went out they'd both die.

Between them they only had one lighter remaining. The officer carefully tipped the last of the lighter fuel over the struggling fire. The flames grew, aided by a crumpled cigarette carton. All the officers were on their knees, stoking the fire. The timbers began to burn.

Brodsky opened his eyes, staring in confusion at the flames in front of him. Leo's gaze returned to the fire's centre. Steam rose from his clothes. Two of the officers carried on collecting firewood. The third stood guard.

'Are you well enough to walk?' Leo asked his prisoner.

'I used to go fishing with my son. At night we'd build fires like this and sit round them. He didn't much like to fish but I think he enjoyed the fires. Had he not died he would have been roughly the same age as you are now.'

Leo said nothing.

'If it's all right with you,' Brodsky added, 'I'd like to stay a little longer.'

Leo added some more wood to the fire. They could wait a little longer.

ON THE WALK BACK, none of the men spoke. The distance Leo had covered in thirty minutes took them almost two hours to retrace. Each footstep seemed heavier and heavier as the methamphetamines disappeared from his system. Only the fact of his success sustained him now. He'd stood on the brink of failure and stepped back from it.

As they neared the farmhouse, the prisoner turned to Leo. 'When I arrived last night the family wanted nothing to do with me,' he said urgently. 'They threatened to call the authorities. That's why I was forced to break into their barn. They thought I'd gone. The family has done nothing wrong.'

Leo tried to imagine what had really happened last night. The traitor had sought his friend's help but that help had not been forthcoming. It was certainly not the escape plan of a competent spy.

'I have no interest in your friends,' he said.

They reached the farm. Lined up on their knees outside the barn were Mikhail Zinoviev, his wife and their two young daughters. Their hands were tied behind their backs; they were shivering. Mikhail's face was battered: blood dripped from his smashed nose; his jaw was broken. The officers were in a loose, uncertain ring around them. Vasili stood behind the family. Leo was about to speak when Vasili lined up his gun and fired a shot into the back of Zinoviev's head. The man's body fell forward into the snow.

Only Brodsky reacted, making a noise, an inhuman noise—no words but grief and anger mixed together. Vasili took a step to the side and positioned his gun behind the wife's head.

Leo raised his hand. 'Lower your gun! That's an order.'

'These people are traitors. We need to make an example.'

Vasili pulled the trigger, a second shot rang out and the woman's body slumped into the snow beside her husband's. Brodsky tried to break free but the two officers escorting him kicked him to his knees. Vasili took another side step, positioning the gun behind the head of the elder daughter.

Leo drew his gun, pointing it at his deputy. 'Lower your gun.'

Outrage and adrenaline swept through him. He took aim. If he fired now the girl would survive. Both girls would survive—no one would be murdered.

The word had sprung into his head: *murdered*.

Vasili was no fool. He lowered his gun. 'The girls have learned a valuable lesson. Maybe they'll grow up to be better citizens than their parents.'

Leo moved towards his deputy, passing the two corpses, leaving a boot print in the bloody snow. In a swift arc he swung his gun, cracking the edge against the side of Vasili's head. Vasili fell back. There was a trickle of blood where the skin had broken. But before he could straighten up he felt the barrel of Leo's gun against his temple. Everyone watched.

Very slowly, Vasili tilted his head and looked up, his jaw quivering. He was afraid of death, this man to whom the death of others was so casual. Leo's finger touched the trigger. But he couldn't do it. Not in cold blood.

Let the State punish him. Trust in the State. He holstered his gun.

'You'll remain here and wait for the militia. You'll explain what has happened and assist them. You can make your own way back to Moscow.'

Leo helped the two girls to their feet and walked them to the house.

Three agents were needed to carry Anatoly Brodsky to the truck. His body was slack as though life had been sucked out of it. He was muttering incomprehensibly, insane with grief.

Inside the house, the two girls said nothing, seemingly unable to comprehend that the bodies outside were their parents. Leo asked if they had any other family. Neither girl said a word. He told the elder girl to pack—they were coming to Moscow. Neither of them moved.

He went to the bedroom and began to pack for them, looking for their things, their clothes. His hands began to shake. He stopped, sat on the bed and looked down at his boot. He clumped his heels together and stared at the thin, compact ridges of blood-soaked snow that fell to the floor.

Moscow, February 16

Though it had been his place of work for the past five years, Leo had never felt comfortable in the Lubyanka, the headquarters of the MGB. There was something about the building itself that made people uneasy, as if fear had been factored into the design, although Leo knew that it had been nothing more than an insurance office before the Revolution. Still, its façade created the impression of watchfulness: rows of windows crammed together, rising to a clock at the top that stared out over the city like a single beady eye.

Leo handed over his identity card: a card that meant he could not only enter the building but also leave. The cardless men and women led through these doors were often never seen again. The system might carry them into the Gulags or to a building just behind this one, on Varsonofyevsky Lane, another State Security compound fitted with sloping floors, log-panelled walls to absorb bullets and hoses to wash away the blood. Leo didn't know the precise execution capacity but it was up to several hundred a day.

Entering the main corridor, Leo wondered how it would feel to be led down to the basements with no leave to appeal and no one to call for help. The judicial system could be bypassed entirely. Leo had heard of prisoners lying abandoned for weeks and doctors who served no other purpose than the study of pain. He'd taught himself to accept that these things existed for a reason, a greater good. They existed to terrify. Terror protected the Revolution. Without it, Lenin would have fallen; Stalin would have fallen.

The Lubyanka held a special place in the people's psyche, representing the place where those guilty of anti-Soviet agitation, counterrevolutionary activity and espionage were processed. No one could be sure they weren't guilty of such crimes since no one, including Leo, could be sure exactly what they were. In the 140 articles of the criminal code, Leo had to guide him just one article, defining the political prisoner as a person engaged in activity intended to *overthrow, subvert, or weaken the Soviet Power*. Not even those who worked within the Lubyanka's walls could be certain that the system they sustained would not one day swallow them too.

Although Leo was still wearing his leather gloves and long woollen overcoat, he was shivering. Dizzy spells came over him, lasting for several seconds. He hadn't eaten in two days, yet the thought of food made him sick. Even so, he stubbornly refused to consider the possibility that he was ill; he was a little tired, perhaps, but he just needed to sleep. He couldn't take a day off today, not when there was the matter of Anatoly Brodsky's interrogation.

Interrogations were technically not part of his duties. The MGB had specialists who did nothing but interview suspects, moving from cell to cell, extracting confessions. They were motivated, like most employees, by simple things such as the prospect of a performance-related bonus, awarded if the suspect signed promptly and unconditionally, without amendments. Interrogators formed something of a clique, working as a team. Many of their more extreme operations were confined to the basement, where they could control environmental elements such as heat and light. In contrast, Leo's role as investigator meant he spent most of his time upstairs or outside. The basement was a world he preferred to keep under his feet.

After a short wait, Leo was called in. Unsteady, he entered Major Kuzmin's office. The walls were decorated with framed propaganda posters and black and white photographs, including one taken at the Leader's seventieth birthday in which Stalin was shaking Kuzmin's hand.

Kuzmin stood by the window overlooking Lubyanka Square. He was wearing a uniform one size too small for his squat frame. His glasses were thick and often slid down his nose. In short, he was a ridiculous-looking man, and not even the supreme power of life and death had bestowed upon him any gravitas. It was rumoured that in his day he'd been something of an expert in interrogations. Looking at him now, it was hard to believe.

Leo sat down. Kuzmin remained standing by the window. He'd become adept at appearing to gaze out at the view while actually watching people in the reflection. The usefulness of this trick was reduced by the fact that almost everyone, including Leo, was aware they were being watched.

'Congratulations, Leo,' Kuzmin began. 'I knew you'd get him. The experience was a valuable lesson for you.'

Leo nodded.

'Are you ill?'

Leo paused. Evidently he looked worse than he imagined. 'It's nothing. A cold, perhaps, but it will pass.'

'My guess is that you think I was wrong to take you off the Brodsky case to make you deal with Fyodor Andreev.'

'No, Major. I should have arrested Brodsky immediately. It was my fault.'

'That's evasive of you. My point is simply this: Fyodor's family wasn't a trivial issue. One of your men had become twisted by grief and unwittingly made himself and his family enemies of the State. While I'm pleased you caught Brodsky, I considered your work with Fyodor the more important.'

'I understand.'

'Then we come to the matter of Vasili Nikitin.'

Leo had known that his actions would be reported. Vasili wouldn't hesitate to try to use them against him.

'You pointed a gun at him?' Kuzmin went on. 'And then you hit him? He says you were out of control. He says you were taking narcotics. They made you irrational. He's pushing for your suspension. He's upset, you understand.'

Leo understood perfectly; the executions were not the issue here.

'I was ranking officer and I gave an order. Vasili disobeyed. How can any of us maintain command if orders are ignored? Perhaps it's my military background. In military operations, disobedience is punishable by death.'

Kuzmin nodded. Leo had chosen his defence wisely—the principles of military decorum. 'You're right, of course. Vasili is hotheaded. He disobeyed an order. This is true. But he was enraged by the family's collaboration. I'm not condoning what he did, you understand. We have a system in place for such violations. They should have been brought here. As for the drugs—'

'Prescribed by the doctors here. I hadn't slept in twenty-four hours.'

'They don't concern me in the least. I told you to do whatever it takes. But I wish to give you a word of warning. Hitting a fellow officer gets you noticed. People will quickly forget that your reasons were sound. You took justice into your own hands. That is not acceptable.'

'I apologise.'

Kuzmin moved away from the window, and put a hand on Leo's shoulder. 'Consider the matter closed. I have a different challenge for you: Brodsky's interrogation. I want you to handle it personally. You may call on whoever you like to assist you—a specialist interrogator—but I want you to be present when he cracks. It's important that you see this man for who he really is.'

It was an unusual request. Kuzmin noted Leo's surprise.

'Do you have any objection?'

'None.' Leo stood up. 'I'll begin immediately.'

'One last thing: I want you and Vasili to work together on this.'

THERE WERE THREE types of cell. There were the holding cells: square rooms, a floor covered with straw, with enough space for three men to lie side by side. There were always five men in any one cell, packed so tightly that one man couldn't scratch himself without the others also moving. Since there was no latrine, space also had to be made for the bucket. Once it was brimming, prisoners were made to carry it to the nearest drain and told that if they spilled even the smallest drop they would be shot. Barbarity, certainly, but barbarity for a reason, barbarity for the greater good.

The Greater Good. It was necessary to repeat it, to carve it onto every thought, so that it ran like ticker tape across the bottom of your mind.

After the holding cells, there were punishment cells. Some were ankle deep in freezing water, the walls covered in mould and slime. After a five-day stretch the body never recovered. There were narrow closets, like coffins, where bedbugs had been left to multiply and in which a prisoner would remain, naked, feasted upon, until ready to sign a confession. There were rooms with hooks, chains, electric wires, punishments of all kinds. But these horrors seemed small beside the magnitude of the greater good. The survival of their political system, the promise of a golden age of plenty where poverty would be a memory, justified anything.

Finally, there were the interrogation cells. Leo had arrived at one such cell. He knocked. The plate-steel door was unlocked by a boy barely seventeen years old. The cell was small and rectangular, with stark concrete walls and a stark concrete floor, but brightly lit. Five powerful bulbs hung from the ceiling. Against the back wall, incongruous in the bleak setting, was a sofa. Anatoly Brodsky was sitting on it, his wrists and ankles tied with rope.

'He keeps shutting his eyes, keeps trying to sleep. But I keep hitting him,' the young officer proudly explained. 'He hasn't had a moment's rest, I promise you. That sofa's the best part. It's comfortable, really soft. All he wants to do is sit back and doze off. But I won't let him.'

Leo nodded and could see the young officer was a little disappointed not to receive more gushing praise of his dedication. The officer took up position in the corner of the room, armed with his black wooden baton.

Brodsky was sitting on the edge of the sofa, hunched forward, his eyes half closed. Leo sat beside him. Vasili would be here any minute and Leo hoped that the prisoner could be persuaded to cooperate before he arrived.

Brodsky looked up, his eyes widening a fraction. It took him a moment to recognise Leo. 'Mikhail's daughters?' he slurred. 'Where are they?'

'They've been placed in an orphanage. They're safe.'

'Have you ever been to an orphanage? They'd have had a better chance of surviving if you'd left them on their own.'

'The State is looking after them now.'

To Leo's surprise, the prisoner reached up and, with his wrists still bound, felt Leo's brow. The junior officer sprang forward. Leo waved him away.

'You have a fever,' Brodsky said. 'You should be at home. You men have a home? Where you sleep and eat and do all the things normal men do?'

Leo wondered at this man. He was brave and rude, and Leo couldn't help but like him. He pulled back, wiping his clammy forehead with his sleeve.

'You can save yourself unnecessary suffering by talking to me. There's not a person we've questioned who didn't wish they'd admitted everything straight away. What will you gain by silence?'

'I will gain nothing.'

'Then will you tell me the truth?'

'Yes.'

'Who are you working for?'

'Anna Vladislovovna. Her cat is going blind. Dora Andreyeva. Her dog refuses to eat. Arkadi Maslow. His dog has broken its front leg.'

'If you're innocent, why did you run?'

'I ran because you were following me, no other reason. Once you're followed you're always arrested. Once you're arrested you're always guilty.'

'Which officials from the American Embassy are you working with?'

A flash of understanding crossed Brodsky's face and he sighed deeply. 'I have no doubt that I'll eventually say whatever it is you want me to say but right now I will say this: I—Anatoly Tarasovich Brodsky—am a vet. Soon your records will say that I was a spy. You will have my confession and you will force me to give you names. But whatever I eventually tell you will be a lie because I am a vet.'

Leo grew impatient. 'Are you aware of what will happen to you if you don't talk to me?'

'Even children are aware of what goes on in here. But I will not make this easy for you. If you want me to say I'm a spy, you will have to torture me.'

'I'd hoped this could be avoided. All I need is a list of names.'

'There's nothing more stubborn than a fact. That is why you hate them so much. I am a vet. My innocence offends you because you wish me to be guilty. You wish me to be guilty because you've arrested me.'

There was a knock on the door. Vasili had arrived.

Leo stood up. 'You should have taken my offer,' he muttered.

'Perhaps one day you'll understand why I could not.'

Vasili entered. He was wearing a sterilised dressing at the point where he'd been hit, which Leo suspected was intended only to trigger conversation and enable him to describe the incident to as many people as possible. Vasili was accompanied by a balding middle-aged man dressed in a crumpled brown suit. Seeing Leo and Anatoly together, Vasili seemed concerned.

'Has he confessed?' he asked.

'No.'

Evidently relieved, Vasili signalled for the junior officer to get the prisoner to his feet. The middle-aged man in the brown suit stepped forward, smiling, offering Leo his hand.

'Dr Roman Hvostov. I'm a psychiatrist.'

'Leo Demidov.'

'Pleased to meet you.'

They shook hands. Hvostov led them to his surgery, unlocking the door.

The surgery was small and clean. There was a red leather chair bolted to the white-tiled floor. On the walls were glass cabinets filled with labelled bottles and jars. Hanging beneath the cabinets was an array of steel surgical instruments. Brodsky didn't struggle as he was strapped to the chair. His wrists, ankles and neck were fastened with black leather straps. Leo tied his feet while Vasili tied his arms. Hvostov scrubbed his hands at the sink.

'For a time I worked in a Gulag hospital,' he said. 'It was full of people pretending to be mentally ill. They would do anything to get out of work. They would run around like animals, screaming obscenities, tearing their clothes off, anything to convince me they were deranged. My job was to identify who was lying and who was genuine. There were numerous academic tests but prisoners quickly caught on and shared information and soon everyone knew how to cheat the system. In the end there was only one way of getting to the truth.'

Hvostov filled a syringe with thick yellow oil, then placed it on a steel tray and carefully cut away part of the prisoner's shirt, tying a rubber tourniquet round the top of his arm in order to expose a wide blue vein.

'I'm about to inject camphor oil into your bloodstream,' he told the prisoner. 'It will induce a seizure. While you are in this seizure you will be unable to lie. In fact you will not have the ability to do very much at all. If you are able to speak, you will only be able to speak the truth.'

'Then go ahead. Inject your oil. Hear what I have to say.'

Hvostov placed a rubber gag in the prisoner's mouth. 'This is to stop him biting off his tongue during the most intense part of the seizure,' he explained to Leo. 'Once he has calmed down, we can remove it.'

The doctor inspected the syringe—there was a yellow dewdrop of oil at the needle's tip. Satisfied, he sank the needle into Brodsky's vein.

'We need to do this slowly. Too quick and he'll suffer an embolism.'

He pushed down on the plunger and the treacle-thick yellow oil began to move from the syringe into the prisoner's arm.

Suddenly all intelligence left Anatoly Brodsky's eyes; they rolled back in his head and his body shook. Only a fraction of the oil had been injected.

'And now we inject a little more.'

Another five millilitres was injected and bubbles appeared at the corners of Brodsky's mouth, small white bubbles.

'And now we inject the rest.'

Hvostov injected the remaining oil, then pulled the needle out and pressed a cotton pad against the entry point on the arm. He stepped back.

'And now we wait.'

Brodsky was less like a human and more like a machine gone wrong, an engine pushed past its limits. His body was pulling against the restraints in a way that suggested that there was some external force acting upon him.

Hvostov glanced at his watch. 'Wait a little longer.'

Streams of foam dribbled down from either side of the prisoner's mouth, running underneath his chin. The vibrations were slowing down.

'OK. Ask your questions. See what he says.'

Vasili stepped forward and untied the rubber gag. Brodsky vomited foam and saliva onto his lap. Vasili turned round with an incredulous look.

'What the fuck is he going to tell us like this?'

'Try.'

'Who are you working with?'

In response, the man's head slumped against the restraint. He gurgled. Blood ran out of his nose.

Hvostov used a tissue to wipe away the blood. 'Try again.'

'Who are you working with?'

Brodsky's head rolled to the side, like a puppet. His mouth opened and shut, but there was no sound.

Vasili shook his head, turning to Leo. 'This is stupid. You try.'

Leo stepped forward. 'Who are you working with?'

A noise came from Brodsky's mouth, like a baby's spluttering.

Hvostov peered into Brodsky's eyes. 'Try again. Ask simple questions to start off with. Trust me. He's coming out of it.'

Leo stepped closer. 'What is your name?'

His lips moved. 'Anatoly.'

'Who are you working with?'

He was no longer shaking. His eyes rolled forward. And then he spoke, faint, hurried—as a man might speak in his sleep. 'Anna Vladislovovna. Dora Andreyeva. Arkadi Maslow.'

Vasili reached for his notepad, scribbling down the names. 'Recognise any of those names?' he asked.

Yes, Leo recognised those names. A seed of doubt, sitting dormant and undigested in the pit of Leo's stomach, cracked open.

Anatoly Tarasovich Brodsky was a vet.

Anatoly Tarasovich Brodsky was nothing more than a vet.

February 17

Dr Zarubin put on his mink-fur-lined hat, picked up his leather bag and nudged his way off the crowded tramcar. On the opposite side of the road, stretching hundreds of metres above him, was a set of four U-shaped apartment blocks. Somewhere in one of these buildings was apartment 124—the home of MGB officer Leo Stepanovich Demidov.

The doctor had been briefed by Major Kuzmin on the details of Leo's sudden departure. He'd left at the beginning of a crucial interrogation, claiming to feel feverish and unable to continue his duties. The major was concerned by the timing of the departure. Was Leo really sick? Or was there another reason for his absence? Why had he given assurances that he was well enough to work only to change his mind after being set the task of interrogating the suspect? The doctor had been dispatched to investigate.

Zarubin supposed that Leo's poor health was due to his prolonged exposure to icy water, exacerbated by his use of narcotics. If this was the case, the doctor was to facilitate his recovery. If he was feigning sickness, then

Zarubin was to dope him with a powerful sedative, which he would administer by pretending it was a medicine or tonic. Leo would be bedridden for twenty-four hours, giving the major time to decide how best to proceed.

Apartment number 124 was located in the third block on the fourteenth floor. The elevator rattled its way up to the top, and Zarubin needed both hands to pull the stiff grate sideways. The wind over the exposed concrete walkway brought tears to his eyes.

The door of apartment 124 was opened by a young woman. The doctor had read Leo's file and knew that he was married to a woman called Raisa Gavrilovna Demidova: twenty-seven years old, a schoolteacher. The file hadn't mentioned that she was beautiful. She was, notably so, and it should have been in the file. These things mattered. He hadn't prepared himself for it. She'd made every effort to play down her beauty. Her hair and her clothes were styled in the most common of fashions. Evidently she did not seek the attention of men, a fact that made her all the more attractive to the doctor.

He smiled at her, showing a set of stained teeth, yellow from years of heavy smoking. 'I'm Dr Zarubin. I've been sent to look in on Leo.'

Raisa smiled in response. She'd clearly been expecting the MGB to send someone. 'I'm Raisa, Leo's wife. You have identification?'

The doctor took off his hat, found his card and presented it.

There were candles burning in the apartment. Raisa explained that there was only intermittent power at the moment—there was a recurrent problem with the electricity on all floors above the tenth.

'He'll survive,' joked Zarubin. 'If he's kept warm. He's not a flower.'

She asked if the doctor wanted a hot drink, since it was cold outside. He accepted her offer, touching the back of her hand as she took his coat.

In the kitchen, the doctor watched as she prepared tea.

'I hope the water is still hot,' she said, her voice soft and calm.

She brewed loose leaves in a small pot. As she poured the liquid into a tall glass, Zarubin's eyes drifted down her body, roaming over the outline of her breasts, her waist. Her clothes were dowdy—a grey cotton skirt, thick stockings, a knitted cardigan over a white shirt. He wondered why Leo hadn't used his position to dress her in foreign tailored luxuries.

'Tell me about your husband,' he said.

'He has a fever. He claims to feel cold when he's hot. He refuses to eat.'

'If he has a fever, it's best that he doesn't eat for the time being. However, his lack of appetite might also be due to his use of amphetamines. Do you know anything about this?'

'If it's to do with his work, I know nothing.'

'Have you noticed any changes in him?'

'He skips meals. And after working long stretches he tends to become a little absent-minded.' She handed the doctor his glass. 'Would you like sugar?'

'Jam would be nice.'

As she reached for the top shelf, the back of her shirt lifted up, revealing a patch of pale, perfect skin. Zarubin felt his mouth go dry. She took down a jar of dark purple jam, unscrewed the lid and offered him a spoon. He scooped out a clump of jam, placed it on his tongue and sipped the hot tea, feeling the jam dissolve. With a deliberate intensity he stared into her eyes.

She blushed. 'Perhaps you'd like to get on with the examination?'

He didn't move. 'I'd like to drink my tea first. There's no rush.'

She seemed flustered. He enjoyed making her wait.

The windowless bedroom was hot, the air stale. Zarubin sat down on the bed, beside Leo. He took his temperature. It was high but not dangerously so. He listened to Leo's chest. There were no indications that this was anything more than a cold. Raisa stood beside him, watching. He took a bottle from his bag and measured out a spoonful of thick green liquid.

'Please lift his head.'

She helped Leo into a sitting position. Zarubin tipped the liquid down his throat. Once he'd swallowed, she lowered Leo's head onto the pillow.

'What was that for?' she asked.

'It's a tonic—to help him sleep.'

'He needs no help with that.'

The doctor didn't reply. He couldn't be bothered to think up a lie. The drug was in fact a combination of a barbiturate, a hallucinogenic and, to disguise the taste, sugar syrup. Its purpose was to incapacitate the body and mind.

An idea had taken hold of Zarubin. If he reported that Leo wasn't sick, he would almost certainly be arrested and would probably be imprisoned. His beautiful wife would end up alone and vulnerable, in need of an ally. Zarubin felt sure he could offer her an acceptable, comfortable alternative as a mistress. He was convinced that Raisa's survival instinct was highly tuned. Yet there might be a less complicated way of getting what he wanted.

He stood up. 'Can we speak in private?'

In the kitchen, Raisa crossed her arms. There was a furrow in her brow— a tiny crinkle in her otherwise perfect pale skin. 'Will my husband be OK?'

'He's suffering from a fever. And I would be prepared to say that.'

'You'd be prepared to say what?'

'I'd be prepared to say that he was genuinely sick.'

'He *is* genuinely sick. You just said so yourself.'

'Do you understand why I'm here? I've been sent to discover if your husband is genuinely ill or if he's merely trying to avoid work.'

'But it's obvious that he's sick. Doctor or not, anyone could see that.'

'Yes, but I'm the one who decides. And I'd be prepared to say that he was suffering from a fever, on the record, if you were prepared to sleep with me.'

Remarkably she didn't even blink. No visible reaction. 'And if I said no?'

'I'd say that your husband was a liar. I'd say that he was desperate to avoid work. I'd recommend that he be investigated.'

Taking her silence as acceptance of his offer, Zarubin stepped towards her and pressed his hand against her leg. 'Don't worry. Your husband is fast asleep. He won't disturb us.' His hand moved under her skirt. 'You might even enjoy it. Many other women have.'

He leaned towards her, his lips parting, as though she were an apple he was about to bite into. He pulled her closer, his grip tightening.

Suddenly he let go, raising both his hands in the air. Raisa had a knife against his throat.

'If you're unsure of my husband's condition, please inform Major Kuzmin to send another doctor. A second opinion would be welcome.'

The two of them sidestepped round each other, the knife against his neck, until Zarubin backed out of the kitchen. Raisa remained at the entrance, holding the knife at waist height. The doctor put on his coat, picked up his leather bag and opened the door, squinting as he stepped out into the bright winter sunlight. Raisa snatched his hat from the peg and tossed it at his feet. When he bent down to pick it up, she slammed the front door shut.

AS SHE LISTENED to him walk away, Raisa saw that her hands were shaking. Perhaps she'd given him some reason for thinking she'd sleep with him. She ran the events through her mind: opening the door, smiling at his ridiculous joke, making tea. Zarubin was deluded. There was nothing she could have done about that. But maybe she could have flirted with his proposition, pretended that she was tempted. She rubbed her brow. She'd handled that badly. They were in danger.

She entered the bedroom and sat down beside Leo. His lips were moving. She leaned closer, trying to make sense of his words. They were barely audible fragments. He was delirious. He gripped her hand. His skin was clammy. She pulled her hand free and blew the candle out.

LEO WAS STANDING in a drab government office. Raisa was beside him, wearing a pale red dress; the dress she'd borrowed from a friend on the day of their wedding. In her hair she wore a single white flower, picked from the park. He was wearing an ill-fitting grey suit, borrowed from a colleague. At the table in front of them, a balding man was hunched over paperwork. Raisa presented their documentation and they waited. There were no vows, no ceremony or flowers, no guests. No fuss; it was bourgeois to make a fuss. The balding civil servant entered their details into a ledger. Paperwork completed, he handed them a marriage certificate. They were man and wife.

Back at his parents' old apartment, there were friends, neighbours, all keen to celebrate their wedding. Elderly men sang unfamiliar songs. Yet something was wrong with this memory. There were faces that were cold and hard. Fyodor's family was here. Leo was still dancing but the wedding had become a funeral. Everyone was staring at him. There was a tap at the window. He turned to see the outline of a man, pressed up against the glass. It was Mikhail Sviatoslavich Zinoviev, a bullet through his head. Leo turned back. The room was now empty except for two young girls—Zinoviev's daughters, dressed in filthy rags. Their stomachs were swollen, their skin blistered. Lice crawled in their matted black hair. Leo closed his eyes.

Shivering, freezing cold, he opened his eyes. He was underwater. The ice was above him and the current was pulling him down. An intense pain burned in his lungs. Unable to hold his breath, he opened his mouth.

LEO GASPED, opening his eyes. Raisa was seated beside him, trying to calm him. He looked around, confused, his mind still half in the dream world. But this was real: he was back in his apartment, back in the present.

Relieved, he took hold of Raisa's hand. 'Remember the first time we saw each other?' he whispered. 'You thought I was rude, staring at you. I got off at the wrong metro stop just to ask your name. And I wouldn't leave until you did. So you told me your name was Lena. For a week all I could talk about was this beautiful woman called Lena. When I finally saw you again and convinced you to walk with me, I called you Lena the entire time. At the end of the walk I was ready to kiss you and you were only ready to tell me your real name. The next day I told everyone how wonderful this woman Raisa was and they laughed at me, saying last week it was Lena, this week it's Raisa and next week it'll be someone else. But it was always you.'

Raisa wondered where this sudden sentimentality had come from. She made him lie back and before long he was asleep again. It had been almost twelve hours since Dr Zarubin had left. A slighted, vain old man was a dangerous enemy. To take her mind off her anxieties she made chicken broth. It bubbled on a slow heat, ready for Leo when he was able to eat again. She stirred the soup, then filled a bowl for herself. There was a knock on the door. It was late. She wasn't expecting visitors. She picked up the knife, placing it behind her back before moving closer to the door.

'Who is it?'

'It's Major Kuzmin.'

Her hands shaking, she opened the door. Kuzmin was standing outside with two tough-looking soldiers.

'Dr Zarubin has spoken to me,' he announced.

Raisa blurted out, 'Please, take a look at Leo for yourself—'

Kuzmin seemed surprised. 'No, that isn't necessary. I trust the doctor on medical matters.'

Zarubin had told the truth. She bit her lip, trying not to let her relief show.

'I've spoken to your school,' the major continued. 'I've explained that you'll be taking leave in order to help Leo recover. We need him fit. He's one of our finest officers.'

'He's lucky to have such concerned colleagues.'

Kuzmin waved this comment aside. He gestured at the officer standing beside him. He stepped forward, offering her a large paper bag.

'This is a gift from Dr Zarubin. So there's no need to thank me.'

Raisa tucked the knife down the back of her skirt, then reached forward, accepting the bag. 'Will you come in?'

'Thank you, but it's late and I'm tired.' Kuzmin bade Raisa good night.

She shut the door and walked to the kitchen, putting the bag on the table. It was filled with oranges and lemons, a luxury in a city of food shortages. They were Zarubin's way of saying that she should feel indebted to him for reporting that Leo was genuinely sick. Had another whim taken him, he might have had them both arrested. She emptied the bag into the bin, then stared at the bright colours before picking out every piece of fruit.

February 19

For three days, Leo hadn't left his apartment. He'd stayed in bed, sipping hot lemon and sugar water, eating borscht and playing cards with his wife. For the most part he'd slept, and after that first day he'd suffered no more nightmares. But in their place he'd felt a dull melancholy. He'd expected the feeling to fade, convinced that it was a side effect of the methamphetamine slump. The feeling had got worse. He'd taken his supply of the drug and tipped it down the sink. No more narcotic-fuelled arrests. Was it the drugs? Or was it the arrests? As he'd grown stronger he found it easier to rationalise the events of the past few days. Brodsky had been a mistake, an innocent man caught up and crushed in the cogs of a vital and important but not infallible State machine. A single man didn't dent the meaningfulness of their operations. The principles of their work remained sound. The protection of a nation was bigger than one person. It was essential that Leo keep matters in proportion. The only way to carry on was to keep things in proportion.

The reasoning was sound, and now, as Leo approached the doors to the Lubyanka after three days away, he realised that he believed none of it.

Leo was shown into Kuzmin's office. The major was seated. He indicated that Leo should take the chair opposite.

'You're feeling better?'

'Yes, thank you. My wife told me that you visited.'

'We were concerned about you. It's the first time you've been ill.'

'I apologise.'

'It wasn't your fault. You were brave, swimming in that river. And we're glad you saved him. In your absence, Brodsky confessed. It took two days, two camphor shock treatments. But in the end he broke. He gave us the name of seven Anglo-American sympathisers. He was executed last night.'

Leo concentrated on keeping his expression still.

Kuzmin handed Leo a thin black file. 'Inside you have the full transcript of his confession.'

Leo opened the file. His eyes caught the first line: *I—Anatoly Tarasovich Brodsky—am a spy.* Leo flicked through the typed pages: opening with an apology, expressing regret before describing the nature of his crime. He'd seen this template a thousand times. They varied only in the details.

Kuzmin handed him a sealed envelope. 'He named seven collaborators working with foreign governments. I've given six of the names to other agents. The seventh is yours to investigate. As you're one of my best officers, I've given you the hardest. Inside that envelope is all the information we currently hold on the individual, which, as you will see, is not very much. Your orders are to collect further information and, if this person is a traitor, to arrest them and bring them here.'

Leo ripped open the envelope, pulling out several large black-and-white surveillance photographs, taken from across a street.

They were photographs of Leo's wife.

RAISA WAS RELIEVED to be nearing the end of the day. She'd spent the past eight hours teaching exactly the same lesson to all her year groups. Normally she taught political studies, but this morning she'd received instructions from the Ministry of Education ordering her to spend the day discussing with each class how much Stalin loved his country's children. As part of that love, Stalin wanted all children to be reminded of certain basic precautions. They were not to cross roads without looking twice, they were to be careful when travelling on the metro and they were not to play on the railway tracks. Over the past year there had been several tragic accidents on the railways. The safety of the State's children was paramount. They were the future.

As a rule, Raisa's classes were tiring. Every pronouncement she made regarding Generalissimo Stalin or the state of the Soviet Union was expected to be met with applause. Students were competitive, none wanting to seem less dedicated than his or her neighbour. Every five minutes the class would come to a halt as the children rose to their feet, stamping on the floor or banging their desks with their fists. Initially she'd suspected that they enjoyed this raucous behaviour, but she'd come to realise this was not the case. They were afraid. Consequently, discipline was never a problem. She rarely needed to raise her voice. From the age of six, the children understood that to disrespect authority was to take your life into your own hands. Youth provided no protection. The age at which a child could be shot for their crimes, or their father's crimes, was twelve.

Among her colleagues at Secondary School 7, Raisa counted only one friend—Ivan Kuzmitch Zhukov, a language and literature teacher of about forty. One day he'd casually lamented the size of the school library—a cupboardlike room in the basement stocked with pamphlets, back issues of *Pravda*, approved texts and not a single foreign author. Hearing him, Raisa had whispered that he should be more careful. That whisper had been the beginning of an unlikely friendship that, from her point of view, might have been strategically unwise. Ivan was in many people's eyes already a marked man. Other teachers were convinced that he hoarded forbidden texts under his floorboards or, far worse, he was writing a book of his own and smuggling the subversive pages out to the West. It was true that he'd loaned her an illegal translation of *For Whom the Bell Tolls*, which she'd never dared take back to her apartment. Raisa could afford the association only because her own loyalty had never been closely scrutinised. She was, after all, the wife of a State Security officer. Logically, Ivan should have kept his distance. No doubt he had deduced that if Raisa had wanted to denounce him she would have done so already, considering how many imprudent things she'd heard him say. He was married, with three children. All the same, she suspected he was in love with her. It was not something she dwelt on and she hoped for both their sakes that it was not something he dwelt on either.

OUTSIDE THE MAIN ENTRANCE to the school, across the road, in the foyer of a low-rise apartment block, stood Leo. He was wearing civilian clothing he'd borrowed from work. In the Lubyanka there were cupboards full of coats, jackets, shirts and trousers kept for this purpose. In an ankle-length grey woollen coat and a thick fur hat pulled down over his forehead, Leo was convinced his wife wouldn't recognise him if she glanced in his direction.

This wasn't the first time his wife had been followed. Leo had arranged surveillance three years ago. They'd been married less than a year. She'd become increasingly distant. They were working long hours, glimpsing each other briefly in the morning and evening. He couldn't understand why she'd changed. Whenever he broached the subject she'd claimed she felt unwell, yet she refused to see a doctor. The only explanation he could come up with was that she was in love with another man.

Leo had dispatched a newly recruited, promising young agent to follow his wife for a week, justifying this course of action because it was motivated by love. If his colleagues had found out, they might have interpreted this matter differently. If Leo couldn't trust his wife sexually how could they trust her politically? But Raisa hadn't been having an affair and no one ever found out about the surveillance. Relieved, he had accepted that he simply needed to be patient and help her with whatever difficulty she was going through. Over the months, their relationship had gradually improved. Leo had transferred the young agent to Leningrad on a promotion.

This mission, however, was entirely different. It was a matter of national security. At stake was not their marriage but their lives. There was no doubt in Leo's mind that Raisa's name had been inserted into Anatoly Brodsky's confession by Vasili. Leo blamed himself. Taking time off work had given Vasili an opportunity, which he'd exploited ruthlessly. Leo couldn't claim the confession was a lie—it was an official document. All he could do was register his profound disbelief, suggesting to Kuzmin that Brodsky was trying to incriminate Raisa as an act of revenge. He'd accepted the case on the basis that he was simply trying to clear his wife's name.

Across the road, children poured out of the school, breaking off in all directions. Leo knew that Raisa wasn't timetabled for any extracurricular activities—she'd be leaving soon. There she was, standing at the entrance with a male colleague. He had a trim grey beard, round glasses. Leo noted that he was not an unattractive man. He looked educated, cultivated, refined. This must be Ivan; Raisa had mentioned him.

Leo willed them to separate at the gates, but instead they set off together, side by side. He waited, allowing them to get ahead. They were familiar with each other; Raisa laughed at a joke and Ivan seemed pleased. Did Leo make her laugh? Not really, not often. He didn't object to being laughed at when he was foolish or clumsy, but no, he didn't tell jokes. Raisa did. She was playful, verbally, intellectually. Leo had never been in any doubt that she was smarter than him. But he'd never been jealous—until now.

Glad to be on the move, Leo trailed his wife at a distance of about fifty metres. In the weak orange glow of the streetlights it wasn't difficult—there were hardly any other people on the street. That changed when they turned onto Avtozavodskaya, the main road. Queues of people were lined up outside grocery stores, clogging the pavements. Finding it hard to keep track of his wife, Leo quickened his pace. Then Raisa and Ivan turned into Avtozavodskaya metro station, disappearing from view.

Leo hurried forward, then descended the stone steps to the lower hall. It was rush hour, and thousands of people hustled in line at the ticket barriers. Going against the flow, Leo backtracked up the steps and surveyed the crowd. Raisa and Ivan had passed through the barrier and were waiting for a place on the escalator. Leo rejoined the throng, edging forward.

He passed through the ticket barrier, then took the first available position on the escalator. Raisa was maybe fifteen steps below him. In order to talk to Ivan, who was standing on the step behind and above her, she'd turned round. Leo was in her line of view. He pulled back behind the man in front of him and waited until he was almost at the lower level before looking again. The passageway divided into two tunnels, for trains travelling north and south, each filled with passengers. Leo couldn't see his wife anywhere.

If Raisa was en route home she'd be heading north on the Zamoskvoret-skaya line to Teatral'naya, where she'd change to the Arbatsko–Pokrovskaya line and travel eastwards. Leo moved down the platform, studying the faces. Raisa wasn't here. Could she have taken a train in the other direction? Suddenly a man moved and Leo caught a glimpse of Ivan. Raisa was by his side. He was almost certainly in her peripheral vision; if she hadn't seen him it was only because she wasn't expecting to see him. With nowhere to hide, he continued down the platform, then came to a stop by the edge. Slowly he turned his head. Raisa was talking to Ivan. She hadn't seen him. A gust of warm air blew down the crowded platform. The train was approaching.

As everyone turned to watch, Leo caught sight of a man looking away from the oncoming train, directly at him. It was the briefest of glances, eye contact for a fraction of a second. Leo had never seen this man before. Yet he knew immediately that he was a fellow State Security operative.

The crowd surged forward towards the train doors. The agent was gone, out of sight. The doors opened. Leo hadn't moved; he was still staring at the point where he'd seen those cool, professional eyes. Why did they need a second agent following his wife? They didn't trust him, of course. But he hadn't expected them to take such measures. Brushed aside by disembarking passengers, he recovered and boarded the train, one carriage down from Raisa. He pushed his way towards the door to the adjoining carriage. Through the window he could see Raisa's hand, holding the side bar.

The second agent boarded the same carriage as Leo, taking up position several metres away. He was well trained, calm. This agent wasn't following Raisa. He was following Leo.

He should have guessed that this operation wouldn't have been left entirely in his hands. His superiors had an obligation to make sure he did his job properly. They might even suspect he was working with Raisa if she was a spy. Anything he reported back would be crosschecked with the other agent. For this reason it was essential for Raisa to go straight home; if she went anywhere else, she'd be putting herself at risk. Her only chance of escape was by doing nothing, meeting nobody. She could work, shop and sleep. Any other activities were liable to be misconstrued.

If Raisa was going home she'd remain on this train for the next three stops, then change at Teatral'naya. Leo saw that the agent had slipped into a vacant seat. He was casually staring out of the window, no doubt watching Leo out of the corner of his eye.

The train pulled into the second station—Novokuznetskaya. The doors opened. Leo watched Ivan disembark. Please stay on the train, he thought.

Raisa got off. She wasn't going home. To follow her would expose her to the scrutiny of the agent. Not to follow her would put his life in jeopardy. Leo turned his head. The agent hadn't moved. From that position he couldn't have seen Raisa get off the train. He was taking his cue from Leo. The doors were about to shut. Leo stayed where he was.

Leo glanced through the connecting window, as though he was still checking on Raisa. His plan depended on the agent believing that she was on the train. Leo hadn't counted on the crowds. Raisa and Ivan were still on the platform, moving towards the exit with excruciating slowness. Since the agent was staring out of the window, he'd see them as soon as the train moved.

The locomotive began to roll forward. Raisa was standing in plain view. Leo felt the blood rush from his stomach. He slowly turned his head. A sturdy middle-aged man and his sturdy middle-aged wife were standing in the aisle, blocking any view the agent might have of the platform. The train rattled into the tunnel. Barely able to conceal his relief, Leo resumed his pantomime of staring into the adjoining carriage.

At Teatral'naya station, Leo waited for as long as possible before getting off the train. Glancing back, he saw that the agent had also disembarked.

The passage funnelled out into a thoroughfare with access to the different lines. Leo turned right, to eastbound trains on the Arbatsko–Pokrovskaya line, the route home. If he could get far enough ahead, he might be able to board the next train before the agent caught up.

There were crowds of people in front of him in the tunnel. Suddenly he heard the sound of an approaching train. He reached into his jacket pocket, taking out his State Security identity card and tapping it on the shoulder of the man in front of him. As though scalded, the man stepped aside, the crowd parted. He was able to hurry forward. The train was there, its doors open. He boarded, then turned to see how close his tail was.

The people who'd moved out of the way had closed ranks. The agent was stuck behind them, pushing people out of the way. He was catching up. Why weren't the doors closing? The agent was now at the platform, only metres away. The doors began to close. His hand darted out, grabbing the side of the door. But the mechanism wouldn't be pulled back and the man had no choice but to let go. Leo watched out of the corner of his eye as the agent was left behind. In the darkness of the tunnel, he took off his sweat-sodden hat.

THE ELEVATOR came to a stop on the fifth floor, the doors opened and Leo stepped out into the narrow corridor. The hallway smelt of cooking. It was seven in the evening, the time at which many families ate *uzhin*, the last meal of the day. As he walked towards his parents' apartment he felt tired. He'd spent several hours crisscrossing the city. After losing the agent he'd returned home, turned on the lights and drawn the curtains—a necessary precaution even though they were on the fourteenth floor. Then he'd changed his clothes and left again, taking a deliberately circuitous route to the metro and travelling back into the city, to ask his parents' advice.

That was something he hadn't done in a long time. The balance of their relationship had shifted—he now helped his parents far more than they helped him. Leo liked it that way. He enjoyed being able to secure them easier jobs. With just a polite enquiry his father had become a foreman at the munitions factory, taken off the assembly line, while his mother, who spent her days stitching parachutes, had been given a similar rise in status. He'd improved their access to food—they no longer had to queue for several hours for basics such as bread and buckwheat; instead they were given access to the *spetztorgi*, the special shops not intended for the general public, selling exotic delights such as fresh fish, saffron and real dark chocolate.

The apartment he'd managed to have allocated to them was in a low-rise block in a pleasant residential area. It boasted a private washroom and its own small balcony. They shared it with no one—extraordinary in this city. Their old apartment had been shared with his father's uncle and his family. There had been two bedrooms, one for each family. The apartment had no inside toilet or bathroom, and the outdoor facilities were without hot water. After fifty years of hardship his parents finally enjoyed a privileged life, a fact they keenly appreciated. And it all hung by the thread of Leo's career.

Leo knocked on the door. When his mother, Anna, opened the door she seemed surprised. She stepped forward excitedly, hugging her son.

'Why didn't you tell us you were coming? We heard you were ill. We came over to see you but you were sleeping like a child.'

'Raisa told me you came round. Thank you for the fruit.'

'We didn't bring any fruit. At least I don't think we did. I'm getting old. Maybe we did!'

Having heard the conversation, his father, Stepan, appeared from the kitchen. They'd both gained a little weight recently. They looked well.

Stepan embraced his son. 'Are you better?'

'Yes, much. How's your back?'

'It hasn't hurt for a while now. One of the benefits of an administrative job. All I do is oversee other people's hard work.'

In the kitchen a head of cabbage was bubbling in a copper pot of water. His parents were in the middle of preparing *golubsty* and Leo told them to carry on, they could talk in the kitchen. He stood back and watched as his father mixed together mince (fresh meat, not dried, possible only because of Leo's job), fresh grated carrots (again, possible only because of him) and cooked rice. His mother set about peeling the leaves from the cooked cabbage head. His parents knew something was wrong and waited for Leo to begin.

'Have any of your acquaintances been arrested?' he asked at last.

Stepan and Anna glanced at each other. Anna shrugged.

'Everyone knows someone who's been arrested. But we don't question it. I say to myself: you officers are the ones with the evidence. I know only what I see of people and it is very easy to appear to be nice and normal and loyal. It is your job to see past that. You know what's best for this country.'

Leo nodded. 'This country has many enemies. We must protect it. Unfortunately even from ourselves.'

He paused. He hadn't come here to repeat State rhetoric. His parents stopped working, turning to face their son.

'My superior officers believe Raisa's a traitor. They believe she's a spy working for a foreign agency. I've been ordered to investigate.'

'Is she a traitor?' Stepan asked.

'Father, she's a schoolteacher. She works. She comes home. She works. She comes home.'

'Then tell them that. Why do they even think such a thing?'

'There's the confession of an executed spy. He claimed he'd worked with her. But that confession is a lie. In reality the spy was just a vet. We made a mistake in arresting him. I believe his confession to be the fabrication of another officer trying to implicate me. I know my wife is innocent.'

Stepan wiped his hands on Anna's apron. 'Tell them the truth. Expose this officer. You are in a position of authority.'

'This confession has been accepted as the truth. If I defend Raisa I'm contesting the validity of a State document. If they admit one is flawed they admit all of them are. They cannot go back. The repercussions would be enormous.'

'Can you not say that this spy—this vet—was mistaken?'

'I intend to. But if they don't believe me, they'll arrest me as well as her. And there's a strong chance they'll arrest both of you. Part of the judicial code targets any family members of a convicted criminal.'

'And if you denounce her?'

'We'll survive. She won't.'

The water was still bubbling on the stove. At last Stepan spoke.

'You're here because you're unsure what to do, because you're a good man and you want us to tell you to do the right thing. Which would be to tell them that Raisa is innocent. And to brave the consequences.'

'Yes.'

Stepan nodded, looking at Anna. After a moment he said, 'But I can't give you that advice. How can I? I want my wife to live. I want my son to live.

And I want to live. I'd do whatever it takes to ensure that. It's one life for three. I'm sorry. But we're old, Leo. We wouldn't survive the Gulags. We'd be separated. We'd die alone. And what purpose would our deaths serve? Would your wife be saved? If that were the case I'd gladly give up my life for the two of you. But that isn't the case. All that would happen is that we'd die—all four of us—but you'd die knowing that you'd done the right thing.'

Leo looked at his mother. Her face was pale but she was quite calm.

'When do you have to decide?' she asked.

'I have two days to gather evidence. Then I must report back.'

His parents continued with the preparation of dinner, wrapping mince in the cabbage leaves, laying them side by side in a baking tray.

'You'll eat with us?' Stepan asked when the tray was full.

Following his mother into the living room, Leo saw that there were already three place settings. 'You're expecting a guest?'

'We're expecting Raisa. When you knocked on the door we thought you were her.' Anna laid a fourth plate on the table. 'She comes almost every week. She didn't want you to know how lonely she finds it, eating with only the radio for company. We've become very fond of her.'

It was true that Leo was never home at seven. A culture of long working days had been fostered by Stalin, who slept for no more than four hours a night. Leo had heard that no one left the Politburo until the lights of Stalin's study were turned off, normally some time past midnight. Though this didn't apply to the Lubyanka, few officers worked less than ten-hour days.

There was a knock. Stepan opened the door, allowing Raisa into the hallway. She was as surprised as his parents to see Leo.

'He was working nearby,' Stepan explained. 'For once we can eat together as a family.'

While the *golubsty* finished baking in the oven, they had *zakuski*, plates of pickles, mushroom salad and, for each of them, a thin slice of veal tongue served with horseradish. It was a generous spread. Leo couldn't help calculating the cost of each dish. Whose death had paid for that slice of tongue?

Feeling sick, he remarked, 'I can see why you come here every week.'

Raisa smiled. 'Yes. They spoil me. I tell them *kasha* would be fine but—'

'It's an excuse to spoil ourselves,' Stepan interjected.

'You come here straight after work?' Leo asked, trying to sound casual.

'That's right,' Raisa replied.

That was a lie. She'd gone somewhere with Ivan first. But before Leo could consider it further, Raisa corrected herself.

'That's not true. Normally I come here straight after work. But tonight I had an appointment, which is why I'm a little late.'

'An appointment?'

'With the doctor.' Raisa began to smile. 'I'd meant to tell you when we were on our own, but since it has come up . . .'

'Tell me what?'

Anna stood up. 'Would you like us to leave?'

Leo gestured for her to be seated. 'Please. We're family. No secrets.'

Raisa nodded. 'I'm pregnant.'

February 20

Leo couldn't sleep. He lay awake, listening to the slow breathing of his wife, her back pressed against his side not out of any deliberate expression of intimacy but through chance movements. Finally he got out of bed and stood by the living-room window, which had a view of the apartment block opposite. A wall of windows with only three lights on, three out of a thousand or so, and he wondered what was keeping the occupants from sleeping. It was four in the morning, arresting hour—the best time to seize a person, to grab them from sleep. They were vulnerable, disorientated. Unguarded comments made as officers swarmed into their homes were often used against suspects in their interrogations. It was not easy to be prudent when your wife was being dragged across the floor by her hair. How many times had Leo smashed a door open with the sole of his boot? How many people had he pulled from their beds? How many apartments had he torn apart? He couldn't remember. But he had always been confident that it wouldn't happen to him.

His wife was pregnant. Did that change anything? It might change the attitude of his superiors to Raisa. They'd never liked her. In these times it was expected, demanded, that couples have children. After the millions who'd died fighting, children were a social obligation. Why had Raisa not become pregnant? The question had dogged their marriage. The pressure had been cranked up recently: questions asked with greater frequency. Perhaps he could mention that she was pregnant? He dismissed the idea. A traitor was a traitor; there were no exonerating circumstances.

Leo showered. The water was cold. He made a breakfast of oatmeal. He had no desire to eat, and watched it harden in the bowl. Raisa entered the kitchen, sat down. He got up. Neither of them spoke as he waited for the oatmeal to warm up. He put a bowl before her. She said nothing. He made a glass of weak tea, placed it on the table alongside the jar of jam.

'I'll try to be home a little earlier,' he said.

'You don't have to change your routine for me.'

'I'll try anyway.'

Leo shut the front door. He made his way to the elevator. Once it had arrived he pressed the button for the top floor. On the thirtieth floor, the top floor, he stepped out and walked down the passage to the service door at the end marked NO ENTRY. The lock had been smashed a long time ago. It led to a flight of stairs that in turn led to the roof. He'd been here before, when they'd first moved in. Facing west you could see the city. Facing east you could see the edge of the countryside, where Moscow gave way to snow-covered fields. Four years ago, admiring this view, he'd thought himself one of the luckiest men alive. He had a powerful job, a beautiful wife. His faith in the State had been unquestioning. Did he miss that feeling? Yes, he did.

He took the elevator down to the fourteenth floor, returning to his apartment. Raisa had gone to work. He took off his jacket and boots, warmed his hands, ready to begin his search.

Leo had overseen the searches of many apartments. They were treated competitively by those who worked in the MGB. Officers demonstrated extraordinary thoroughness to prove their dedication. Works of art were cut from the frames, books ripped apart, entire walls knocked down. Leo proposed to treat the search of his home no differently. He ripped off the bed linen, turned the mattress upside-down and felt every square inch. Paper documents could be stitched into a mattress. Finding nothing, he moved to the shelves. He checked every book to see if anything had been placed inside. He opened the drawers and looked down at Raisa's neatly folded clothes. He picked up each garment, feeling and shaking it before dropping it on the floor. He ran his fingers along the walls to see if there was the outline of a safe. He took down the framed newspaper clipping, the photo of himself beside the panzer, and took the frame apart. The slip of newspaper floated to the floor. He put the clipping and the frame back together, then turned the bed on its side. He got a screwdriver from the kitchen and took up every floorboard. Underneath there was nothing but dust and pipes.

He went into the kitchen, washed the dirt off his hands. There was a knock on the front door. He rinsed his hands. There was a second knock. Water dripping from his arms, he moved into the hallway. 'Who is it?' he called.

'It's Vasili.'

Leo closed his eyes, feeling his heart rate quicken, trying to control the surge of anger. Vasili knocked again. Leo stepped forward, opened the door.

Vasili was accompanied by two men. The first was a pale young officer Leo didn't recognise. The second officer was Fyodor Andreev.

'We're here to help. Major Kuzmin sent us.'

'Thank you, but I have the investigation under control.'

'I'm sure you do. We're here to assist.'

'Thank you, but that's not necessary.'

'Come on, Leo. We've travelled a long way. And it's cold out here.'

Leo stepped aside, letting them in. None of the three men took off their boots, which were encrusted with ice; chunks dropped from their soles, melting into the carpet. Leo shut the door, aware that Vasili was here to bait him. He offered his guests tea, or vodka if they preferred.

Vasili dismissed Leo's offer with a shake of his head and glanced into the bedroom. 'What have you found?' Without waiting for a reply, he entered the room, staring at the upturned mattress. 'You've not even cut it open.' He leaned down, drawing his knife, ready to slice open the mattress.

Leo caught hold of his hand. 'There's a way to feel for items stitched into the material. You don't have to cut it.'

'So you're going to put the place back together again?'

'That's right.'

'You still think your wife is innocent?'

'I've found nothing to suggest otherwise.'

'May I give you some advice? Find another wife. Maybe you'd be better off with one who wasn't so beautiful.' Vasili reached into his pocket, pulling out a set of photographs of Raisa outside the school with Ivan, the literature teacher. 'She's fucking him, Leo. She's a traitor to you and the State.'

'These were taken at the school. They're both teachers. It proves nothing.'

'Do you know his name?'

'Ivan, I think. I've never met him.'

'We've had an eye on him for some time.'

Seeing the heap of clothes on the floor, Vasili bent down and picked up a pair of Raisa's panties. He rubbed them between his fingers, placing them under his nose and never taking his eyes off Leo. Instead of feeling anger at this provocation, Leo contemplated his deputy in a way he'd never bothered to before. Who exactly was this man who hated him so much? Was he motivated by professional jealousy or by raw ambition? Watching him now, Leo realised there was something personal about this hatred.

'May I take a look around the rest of your apartment?' Vasili asked.

Fearing a trap of some kind, Leo replied, 'I'll come with you.'

'No, I'd prefer to do it by myself.'

Leo nodded. Vasili moved off.

Hardly able to breathe, his throat constricted with anger, Leo stared at the upturned bed. He was surprised by a soft voice beside him. It was Fyodor.

'You'd do all this. Search through your wife's clothes, turn your bed upside-down, rip up your floorboards—pull your own life apart. And yet you would not investigate the death of my son? You would not spare an hour to look at his body, to see his stomach cut open, the dirt shoved in his mouth?' Fyodor was calm, his voice soft. His anger was no longer raw, it had turned to ice.

'Fyodor, you didn't see his body either.'

'I spoke to the old man who found his body. He told me what he saw. I spoke to the eyewitness, the woman you scared away. A man was holding my son's hand, leading him along the tracks. She could describe that man. But now she's too afraid to speak. My boy was murdered, Leo. You were my friend. And you came to my home and instructed my family to keep our mouths shut. You read us a fiction and told us to commit those lies to our hearts, instead of looking for the person who killed my son.'

'Fyodor, I was trying to help you.'

'I believe you. You were telling us the way to survive. And in some ways I'm grateful. You saved us. That is why I'm here, to return the favour. Vasili is right. You must sacrifice your wife. Denounce her and you'll survive. Raisa is a spy, it's been decided. I've read Anatoly Brodsky's confession. It's written in the same black ink as my son's incident report.'

No, Fyodor was wrong. He was angry. Leo reminded himself that he had a simple objective—to investigate his wife and report his findings.

'I'm convinced the traitor's remarks concerning my wife were motivated by revenge and nothing more. So far my investigation supports that.'

Vasili had re-entered the room. 'Except that the other six names he listed have all been arrested,' he said. 'All six have already confessed. Brodsky's information has proved invaluable.'

'I believe he added my wife's name out of spite, to hurt me personally. It's an obvious, desperate trick. You're welcome to help with my search. As you can see'—Leo gestured at the ripped-up floorboards—'I've been thorough.'

'Give her up, Leo. You need to be realistic. On the one hand you have your career, your parents, on the other hand you have a traitor and a slut. You know she's a slut. That's why you had her followed before.'

Leo's anger was displaced by shock. They'd known.

'Did you think that was a secret? Denounce her, Leo. End this. End the niggling questions at the back of your mind. We'll go drinking together afterwards. By the end of the night you'll have another woman.'

'I'll report my findings tomorrow. If Raisa is a traitor, I'll say so. If she's not, I'll say so.'

'Then I wish you luck, comrade.' At the front door, Vasili turned. 'If you survive this scandal, you'll one day be running the MGB. I'm sure of it. And it would be an honour to work under you.'

Leo shut the door. Listening to them walk away, he noticed his hands were shaking. He returned to the bedroom and surveyed the mess. He replaced the floorboards, screwing them back down. He made the bed. He replaced all Raisa's clothes, folding them, conscious that he couldn't remember the exact order in which he'd pulled them out. An approximation would have to do.

As he lifted a cotton shirt, a small object fell out onto the floor. Leo bent down and picked it up. It was a copper rouble coin. He tossed it onto the top of his bedside cabinet. On impact the coin split in two, the separate halves rolling off opposite sides of the cabinet. Perplexed, he knelt down and retrieved the two halves. The inside of one had been hollowed out. When slotted together it looked like an ordinary coin. Leo had seen one of these before. It was a device for smuggling microfilm.

February 21

Present at Leo's deposition were Major Kuzmin, Vasili Nikitin and Timur Raphaelovich—the officer who'd taken Leo's place during Anatoly Brodsky's interrogation. Leo knew him only in passing; an ambitious man of few words and much credibility. The discovery that Raphaelovich was prepared to vouch for everything in the confession was devastating. This man was no lackey of Vasili, who by rank would have been the subordinate officer during the interrogation. Leo had been mistaken. Vasili wasn't behind this. The only person who could have organised the fabrication of such a confession backed up with such a high-ranking witness was Major Kuzmin.

It was a set-up, orchestrated by Kuzmin, his mentor. Leo had ignored his advice regarding Anatoly Brodsky and now he was being taught a lesson. The issue under scrutiny was Leo's suitability as an officer, it had nothing to do with Raisa. Why appoint a suspect's husband to investigate her unless the primary concern was how the husband would conduct himself during that investigation? Hadn't Leo been followed? Hadn't Vasili come to check whether he was searching the apartment properly? It all made sense. Vasili had goaded him yesterday, told him to denounce his wife, precisely because he hoped that Leo would do the opposite and stand up for her. It was a test. All he had to do was show Major Kuzmin that he was willing to denounce his wife, prove that his loyalties were absolutely with the MGB, then they'd all be safe: Raisa, his unborn child, his parents.

Yet why was he so sure his wife was innocent? After all, why did she befriend a dissident teacher? What was that coin doing in their apartment? Yes, she was a spy and the copper coin proved it. She was a threat to everything he'd worked for, everything he'd won for his parents and for himself. She was a threat to the country, a country Leo had fought to defend.

It was quite clear: if Leo said she was guilty, then this would end well for him and his parents. That was guaranteed. If this was a test of Leo's character, then Raisa would also be spared. And she'd never need to know. If she was a spy, then these men already had the evidence and were waiting to see if Leo was working with her. The only course of action was to denounce his wife.

Major Kuzmin began the proceedings. 'Leo Stepanovich, we have reason to believe your wife is working for foreign agencies. You personally are not suspected of any crimes. We've asked you to investigate the allegations. Please tell us what you have found.'

Leo had the confirmation he was looking for. Major Kuzmin's offer was clear. If he denounced his wife he'd have their continued confidence. What had Vasili said? *If you survive this scandal, you'll one day be running the MGB.* Promotion was a sentence away.

The room was silent. Major Kuzmin leaned forward. 'Leo?'

Leo stood up. 'My wife is innocent.'

THREE WEEKS LATER

The town of Voualsk, March 13

Basarov's restaurant was crowded. Ilinaya had heard drunken laughter fifty paces before stepping through the door. She'd guessed soldiers. She'd guessed right. There were often military exercises taking place in the mountains. Basarov, the manager, catered specifically for this sort of clientele. He served watered-down vodka, claiming, if anyone complained, that it was an attempt to limit drunkenness. But he made a tidy profit, selling the vodka he skimmed off. And if Ilinaya wanted to ply her trade on his premises, he wanted a cut. He was a speculator. He was scum.

By her reckoning, the soldiers were going to be drinking for another couple of hours. She surveyed the other customers, then straightened her dress and made her way to one of the back tables. The man sitting there was maybe forty. It was hard to tell. He wasn't handsome, but she reckoned he'd probably pay a little more because of that.

She sat down, sliding her leg up against his thigh and smiling. 'My name is Tanya,' she said.

The man lit a cigarette and put his hand on Ilinaya's knee. He tipped half his remaining vodka into a dirty glass and pushed it towards her.

'What's your name?' she asked.

He didn't reply, reaching into his jacket pocket, rummaging around. He pulled out his hand, his fist clenched shut. She tapped his knuckles. He turned his fist upside-down, slowly extending his fingers, one by one . . .

In the middle of his palm was a small nugget of gold. She leaned forward. Before she could get a good look, he closed his hand and slipped it back into his pocket. He still hadn't said a word. She studied his face. He had blood-shot, boozy eyes and she didn't like him at all. But if she wanted to get fussy she might as well call it quits and resign herself to staying in this town for ever. The only way she was going to return to Leningrad, where her family lived, where she'd lived all her life until being ordered to move here, was if she could save up enough money to bribe the officials. She needed that gold.

ILINAYA STOPPED WALKING. 'Hey, where are we going?'

It was freezing cold. Her legs were getting tired. He'd led her to the railway station on the edge of town. It was set in one of the oldest districts, made up of ramshackle one-room wooden huts with tin roofs, lined up along sewage-stinking streets. These huts belonged to the workers at the timber mill, who lived six or seven to a room, no good for what they had in mind.

'It's round the back of the station.'

'There's just forest back there.'

'You'll see.' He reached the side of the station. 'I'm an engineer. I work on the railways. That's a maintenance cabin. It's very private.' He was pointing at a small cabin not far from the edge of the forest.

Secrecy was one thing and she'd already presumed he was married. But since he didn't live in this town she couldn't understand what his problem was. Perhaps he was a high-ranking Party member. She didn't care. She just wanted the next ten minutes over. She began walking towards the cabin.

He took out a key, unlocked the padlock and stepped into the cabin. She heard the sound of a match being struck. Light flickered from a hurricane lamp. The man hung it from a hook sticking out from the roof. She peered inside. The cabin was filled with spare track, bolts, tools and timber. He cleared one of the work surfaces, then spread his coat across it.

Ilinaya stepped inside. 'Hope you don't mind if my jacket stays on?' She shut the door, though it was almost as cold inside as it was out. She turned.

The man was closer than she remembered. She caught sight of something metallic coming towards her—she didn't have time to work out what. The object connected with the side of her face. Pain shot through her body. She fell back against the cabin door, blood in her mouth.

He grabbed her arms. 'You do exactly as I say.'

She spat a mouthful of blood and phlegm in his eyes. He must have been surprised because he let go. She felt the door behind her and pushed against it—the door swung open and she fell onto her back in the snow. He grabbed at her feet. She kicked frantically; her heel caught his jaw. She heard him cry out. He lost his grip. She rolled onto her stomach, got up and ran.

Staggering blindly, it took her a couple of seconds to realise she'd run down the railway tracks, away from the station, away from safety. She checked behind. He was chasing her. She tried to scream but choked on the blood in her mouth, breaking her rhythm and losing some of her lead.

Suddenly the ground began to vibrate. She looked up. A freight train was hurtling towards them, plumes of smoke rushing out of the high iron front. She raised her arms, waving. The train gave no sign of slowing, no screech of brakes, no whistle. Seconds before a collision, she flung herself to the side, off the tracks into the thick snow. The engine and wagons roared past. Breathless, she peered behind her. Her pursuer had jumped to her side and was lying on the snow. He stood up and staggered towards her.

Spitting the blood from her mouth, she got up and started to run. She was at the edge of the forest when the man caught her. They crashed down into the snow. Then he was on top of her, squeezing her neck. She gasped, trying to break free, but his grip was too strong. She threw her weight sideways. They tumbled—rolling in the snow, over and over each other.

Inexplicably he let go, releasing her neck. She coughed, catching her breath. The man was still pinning her down, but his attention was on something else, something to the side of them. She turned her head.

Sunken into the snow beside her was the naked body of a young girl. Her skin was pale, almost translucent. Her hair was blonde. Her mouth was wide open and had been stuffed with dirt. The girl's arms, legs and face appeared uninjured, covered in a light layer of snow that had been disturbed when they'd rolled into it. Her torso had been savaged. The organs were exposed, ripped, torn, as though her body had been attacked by a pack of wolves.

Ilinaya looked up at her pursuer. He began to retch, doubled over and was sick. She got up and ran towards the station. She had no idea if the man was chasing her. This time she didn't slow down and didn't look back.

Moscow, March 14

Leo opened his eyes. A flashlight blinded him. He didn't need to check his watch to know the time. Arresting hour—four in the morning. He got out of bed, heart pounding. In the dark he staggered, disorientated, bumping into someone. The lights came on. He saw three officers: young men, armed. Leo didn't recognise them but he knew the kind of officers they were: low-ranking, unthinkingly obedient. They'd be violent without hesitation. They gave off a smell of cigarette smoke and alcohol. Alcohol would make them unpredictable, volatile. To survive these next few minutes, Leo would have to be cautious, submissive. He glanced at Raisa, who stood shivering in her crumpled nightdress, and hoped she understood that as well. But she was looking directly at the men, unembarrassed, defiant, angry.

One of the men left the room, to return almost immediately holding two small cases. 'This is all you can take. You can carry nothing on your person except your clothes and your papers. In one hour we leave.'

Leo turned to his wife. 'Wear as much as you can.' He glanced behind him. One of the officers was watching, smoking. 'Can you wait outside?'

'Don't waste time making requests. The answer to everything is no.'

They both got changed, putting on as many clothes as they could. It might have been comical, in other circumstances, their limbs swollen by cotton and wool. Then they grappled with the question of what belongings to bring. Each case was no more than ninety centimetres wide, sixty centimetres high and twenty centimetres deep. Their lives had to reduce to fit this space.

Leo made several quick calculations. Precious space had to be wasted with the inclusion of *The Book of Propagandists* and *The Short Course of the Bolshevik Party*, neither of which could be abandoned without it being construed as a subversive political gesture. He grabbed the books, putting them in the case. Their young guards were watching everything.

Leo touched Raisa's arm. 'Take our shoes. Pick the best, one pair each.' Good shoes were rare, tradable, a valuable commodity.

Leo gathered up clothes, photos of their wedding, his parents, but none of Raisa's family. Her parents been killed in the Great Patriotic War, her village wiped out. She'd lost everything. Leo's eyes came to rest on the framed newspaper clipping on the wall: the photo of himself, the war hero. With the signing of an arrest warrant, heroism had been made irrelevant. He took the clipping out of the frame, folded it and tossed it in the case.

Their time was up. Leo shut his case. Raisa shut hers. He wondered if they'd ever see this apartment again. It was unlikely.

Downstairs, there was a car waiting. Two of the officers sat in the front. One sat in the back, sandwiched in between Leo and Raisa.

'I'd like to see my parents,' Leo said. 'I'd like to say goodbye.'

'No fucking requests.'

THE DEPARTURE HALL was already busy. Soldiers, civilians and station workers were orbiting the Trans-Siberian express train. The engine was embossed on the side with the words HAIL TO COMMUNISM. While passengers boarded the train, Leo and Raisa waited at the end of the platform, flanked by their armed escort. Leo had no idea where they were going. This was unmistakably a passenger train, not the red cattle trucks used to transport prisoners to the Gulags. Were they going to escape with their lives?

After Leo's testimony he'd been sent home, placed under house arrest. On the way to his apartment, on the fourteenth-floor landing, he'd remembered that he still had the incriminating hollow coin in his pocket, and he'd tossed it over the side. Maybe Vasili had planted it, maybe not; it no longer mattered. Raisa had arrived back to find two armed officers outside their door. She'd been searched and ordered to remain inside. Leo had explained their predicament to her: the allegations against her, his own investigation and his denial of the charges. When he'd finished, her response had taken him by surprise. 'It was naive to think this wouldn't happen to us too.'

They had sat in their apartment, at the kitchen table, expecting the MGB to come at any minute. They had waited in silence. As the hours passed, Leo had realised this was the most time he and his wife had spent together, face to face, uninterrupted, for as long as he could remember. Neither of them had known what to do with it.

The knock on the door hadn't come that night. As it approached midday the following day, Leo had made breakfast, wondering why they were taking so long. When the knock finally came, he and Raisa had stood up, breathing fast, expecting this to be the end. Instead it was some trivial matter: an officer using their bathroom. Perhaps they couldn't find any evidence, perhaps they'd be cleared. Leo had only flirted with these thoughts briefly; accusations never collapsed through lack of proof.

A week into their confinement, a guard had entered the apartment, ashen-faced. He announced, in a voice trembling with emotion, that their Leader, Stalin, was dead. Only at this moment did Leo allow himself to contemplate whether they might just have a chance of surviving.

All he could gather was that Stalin had died peacefully in his bed. The newspapers had been hysterical. Everyone's sense of order and certainty had dissolved. Who would take over? How would they run the country? The absence of a leader would mean temporary paralysis. No one wanted to make a decision without knowing that it would be approved. Leo could imagine the muted panic within the corridors of the Lubyanka. In times like these the safest course of action was to do as little as possible. The case of Leo Demidov and his wife, Raisa Demidova, which had no doubt proved problematic, was best shunted to the margins. That's why there'd been the delay.

The last of the passengers had finished boarding. The stationmaster, seeing the uniforms clustered on the platform by the engine, was holding the departure for them. The train driver leaned out of his cabin, trying to figure out what the problem was.

Leo could see an officer walking towards them. It was Vasili. Leo had been expecting him. He'd hardly miss the opportunity to gloat. Leo felt a flicker of anger, but it was imperative he kept his emotions under control.

When Vasili finally reached them, he was smiling. 'I insisted that they wait, so I could say goodbye,' he said. 'And explain what has been decided for you. I wanted to do it personally, you understand?'

'I appreciate that,' Leo muttered.

'You've been reassigned. You're going to join the militia. Not as a detective, but as the lowest entry position, an *uchastkovyy*. You'll be the man who cleans the holding cells, the man who takes notes—the man who does as he's told. You need to get used to taking orders if you're to survive.'

This punishment was light. Considering the severity of the allegations, they could have faced twenty-five-year terms mining gold in Kolyma, where life expectancy was three months. They'd escaped not only with their lives but with their freedom. Leo didn't imagine that Major Kuzmin had done it out of sentimentality. The truth was that he would have embarrassed himself by prosecuting his protégé. In a time of political instability it was shrewder simply to relocate him. Kuzmin didn't want his judgment scrutinised; after all, if Leo was a spy, why had Kuzmin favoured him with promotions?

Understanding that any sign of relief would aggravate Vasili, Leo did his best to look crestfallen. 'I'll do my duty wherever I'm needed.'

Vasili pressed the tickets and paperwork into Leo's hands. Leo took the documents and moved towards the train.

As Raisa stepped up to the carriage, Vasili called out. 'It must have been difficult to hear that your husband had followed you. And not just once. On the other occasion it wasn't State business. He thought you were a slut. You must forgive him that. Everyone has their doubts. Personally, I don't think you're worth giving up everything for. I would have kept the apartment and had you shot as a traitor.'

Raisa remained silent. She opened the carriage door.

Leo followed her, careful not to turn round. There was a chance, if he saw Vasili's smirk, that he might not be able to control himself.

THE TRAIN DEPARTED the station. There were no seats available and they were forced to stand, cramped together. Neither of them spoke for some time.

Finally, Leo said, 'I'm sorry.'

'He would have said anything to get under your skin.'

'He was telling the truth. I had you followed. I thought . . .'

'That I was sleeping with someone else?'

'There was a time when you wouldn't talk to me. You wouldn't sleep with me. We were strangers. And I couldn't understand why.'

'Leo, how could I be unfaithful? I'd be risking my life. We wouldn't argue about it. You'd just have me arrested.'

'Is that what you think would happen?'

'You remember my friend Zoya? You met her once, I think.'

'Perhaps, I don't know.'

'You never remember anyone's name, do you? I wonder why. Is that how you're able to sleep at night, by blanking events from your mind?'

Leo was taken aback: he and his wife had never spoken like this before, never spoken about anything other than the household chores, polite conversation—they'd never raised their voices, never had an argument.

'You did meet Zoya,' Raisa continued. 'Perhaps she didn't register; she wasn't very important in Party terms. She was given a twenty-year sentence. They arrested her as she stepped out of a church, accusing her of anti-Stalinist prayers. Prayers, Leo—they convicted her for the thoughts in her head.'

'Why didn't you tell me? I might have helped.'

Raisa shook her head. 'Leo, how could you have helped? When you were like the men who arrested her—dedicated, devoted servants of the State? That night you didn't come home. And I realised you were probably arresting someone else's best friend, someone else's parents, someone else's children. Tell me, how many people have you arrested? Do you have any idea?'

'I refused to give them you.'

'They weren't after me. They were after you. Arresting strangers, you were able to fool yourself that they might just be guilty, that what you were doing served some purpose. But that wasn't enough for them. They wanted you to prove that you'd do whatever they asked even if you knew it in your heart to be wrong. They wanted you to prove your blind obedience.'

'Maybe you're right, but we're free of that now. We're lucky to get this second chance. I want us to start a new life, as a family.'

'Leo, it's not as simple as that.' Raisa paused, studying her husband carefully. 'The night we ate dinner at your parents' apartment, I heard you talking. I was in the hallway. I heard the discussion about whether or not you should denounce me. I didn't know what to do. I didn't want to die. So I went back down to the street and walked for a while, trying to collect my thoughts. Your father made a convincing case. Three lives weighed against one? It's hard to argue with those numbers. But what about three lives against two?'

'You're not pregnant?' Leo asked.

'Would you have vouched for me if I wasn't?'

'And you waited until now before telling me?'

'I was afraid you might change your mind.'

This was their relationship: stripped bare. Leo felt unsteady. The train, the people near him, the city outside—he could trust none of it, not even the things he could see and touch. Everything he'd believed in was a lie.

'Raisa, have you ever loved me?'

A short silence passed, the two of them rocking with the motion of the train. Finally, instead of answering, Raisa knelt down and tied her shoelace.

Voualsk, March 15

Varlam Babinich was sitting crosslegged on a filthy concrete floor in the corner of an overcrowded dormitory, using his body to shield from view the objects arranged in front of him. He glanced around. The thirty or so boys in the room weren't paying him any attention; most of them lay on the eight piss-sodden beds they were forced to share. Satisfied that he wasn't going to be pestered, he returned to the precious objects he'd collected over the years, including his most recent addition, stolen this morning—a baby.

Varlam was dimly aware that by taking the baby he'd done something wrong and that if he was caught he'd be in trouble. He was also aware that the baby wasn't happy. It was crying. But he wasn't worried about the noise; no one was going to notice another screaming child. As it happened, he was less interested in the baby itself than in the yellow blanket it was wrapped in. He positioned the baby proudly at the centre of his collection, among a yellow tin, a yellow-painted brick, a yellow pencil and a book with a yellow cover. The colour yellow was more important to him than anything.

For his first two years in Voualsk's *internat*, a State-run facility for children with mental deficiencies, he'd been chained to a bed frame. However, he was a strong, determined child, and over several months he'd managed to break the bed frame, pull the chain loose and escape. He'd ended up on the edge of town, chasing a train's yellow carriage. Eventually he'd been returned to the *internat* and locked in a cupboard. But that was a long time ago—the staff trusted him now he was seventeen and smart enough to understand that he couldn't climb high enough to pick the sun out of the sky. Instead, he concentrated on finding yellow closer to home, such as this baby, which he'd stolen by reaching in through an open window. If he hadn't been in such a hurry, he might have tried to unwrap the blanket and leave the baby behind. But now he noticed that the blanket made the baby's skin appear faintly yellow. And he was glad that he'd stolen them both after all.

Two CARS PULLED UP outside, and six members of the Voualsk militia stepped out, led by General Nesterov, a middle-aged man with the broad, stocky build of a farm labourer. He gestured for his team to surround the premises while he and his deputy, a lieutenant, approached the entrance.

The administrative office was open, a radio playing, a reek of alcohol in the air. No staff were to be seen. Nesterov and his deputy entered a corridor. The smell of alcohol gave way to the smell of faeces and sulphur. The sulphur was used to keep away bedbugs. There was shit on the floor and on the walls. The dormitories they passed were overrun with children, maybe forty to a room, wearing nothing more than a dirty shirt or a pair of dirty shorts but never, it seemed, both. They were sprawled on their beds, three or four layered across a thin, filthy mattress. Many weren't moving. Nesterov wondered if some of them were dead. Even though he had braced himself for terrible conditions, he found it difficult to comprehend how things could have got this bad.

The children in the rooms upstairs were older. Nesterov guessed that the dormitories were loosely arranged according to age. Their suspect was seventeen years old. They were coming to the end of the corridor. There was only one dormitory left to search. He stepped inside.

The suspect had his back to the door. Nesterov couldn't see what the boy was sheltering. He couldn't hear the sound of a baby crying.

'Varlam: stand up and turn round, very slowly.'

Varlam didn't move. All the other boys were sitting upright, fascinated.

'I'm not going to tell you again. Stand up and turn round.'

Nesterov stepped forward, approaching Varlam's position. Without warning, Varlam sprang to life, scooping up the baby. It started crying. Nesterov was relieved: the child was alive. But not out of danger; Varlam was holding it against his chest, his arms wrapped round the baby's fragile neck.

Nesterov checked behind him. His deputy remained by the door with curious children clustered around. He pointed his gun at Varlam's head, waiting for the order. Some of the children began screaming.

Nesterov spoke over the din. 'Give me the child.'

Varlam was beginning to panic. 'I'm in so much trouble.'

'No, you're not. I can see the baby's OK. I'm pleased with you. You've done a good job. You've looked after him. I'm here to congratulate you.'

'Can I keep it?'

'I need to check that the baby's OK, just to be sure. Then we'll talk.'

Varlam pulled the baby closer. Nesterov edged forward. There was no way he could extricate the baby by force—it could be crushed in the struggle. He glanced at his lieutenant, who nodded. Nesterov shook his head. The baby was too close to Varlam's face. The risk was too great.

Nesterov glanced at the yellow items on the floor. He'd encountered Varlam in a previous incident, when a yellow dress had been stolen from a clothes line. 'If you give me the child,' he said softly, 'I'll ask the mother if you can have the yellow blanket. I'm sure she'll say yes. All I want is the baby.'

Varlam relaxed. He stretched out his arms, offering the child. Nesterov sprang forward, snatching the baby. He checked that it seemed unharmed before passing it to his deputy. The lieutenant hurried out.

As though nothing had happened, Varlam sat down, rearranging the items in his collection to fill the space created by the absent baby. The other children were quiet again. Nesterov knelt down beside him.

'When can I have the blanket?' Varlam asked.

'You have to come with me first.'

Varlam continued rearranging his collection. Nesterov glanced at the yellow book. It was a military manual, a confidential document.

'How did you get that?'

'I found it.'

Nesterov picked it up, casually flicking through. There was something in the middle, pressed between the pages. He turned the book upside-down. A thick lock of blonde hair fell to the floor. He picked it up.

Varlam blushed. 'I'm in so much trouble.'

800 km east of Moscow, March 16

Raisa had just admitted to lying about being pregnant, so even if she'd said *Yes, I love you*, Leo wouldn't have believed her. If she'd answered truthfully—*No, I've never loved you*—the implication would have been that their marriage had been a trick played on him by her. But since when had love been part of the arrangement? He'd never asked before. He'd never said *I love you*.

She hadn't expected him to. He'd wanted a wife; he'd wanted her and he'd got what he wanted. Now that wasn't enough. Having lost his authority, he was choked with sentimentalism. And why was it her pragmatic deceit rather than his profound mistrust that had brought this illusion of marital contentment crashing down around them? After all, he'd set up that surveillance. He'd broken trust between them long before she'd been forced to.

Ever since they'd started seeing each other, she'd been conscious that if she displeased him he could have her killed. She had to keep him happy. When Zoya had been arrested, the very sight of him made her so angry she found it impossible to utter more than a couple of words to him. In the end the question was simple. Did she want to live? She was a survivor and the fact defined her. Indignation at Zoya's arrest achieved nothing. And so she'd got into his bed, cooked him dinner, washed his clothes.

Well, that time was over. She was no longer dependent on his goodwill. They were both in the same dire straits: their possessions reduced to one suitcase each, exiled to a far-flung town. They were equals as they had never been before. If he wanted to hear about love, the first verse was his to sing.

The train stopped at Mutava for an hour. Raisa broke the day-long silence between them. 'We should eat something.'

By which she meant that they should stick to practical arrangements. Surviving whatever challenges they had coming, that was the glue between them, not love. They got out of the carriage. A woman was pacing the platform with a wicker basket. They bought hard-boiled eggs, a paper pouch of salt, chunks of tough rye bread. Sitting side by side on a bench they peeled their eggs, sharing the salt and saying nothing at all.

THE TRAIN'S SPEED dropped as it climbed through black pine forests. In the distance, over the treetops, the Ural Mountains jutted upwards like uneven teeth. The tracks opened out into a clearing—sprawled before them was a vast assembly plant, tall chimneys, interconnected warehouse-like buildings suddenly appearing. This was their new home.

Leo's knowledge of this town came from propaganda and paperwork. Previously little more than timber mills and a collection of timber huts for the mill workers, the once-modest settlement of 20,000 inhabitants had caught Stalin's eye. The River Ufa ran nearby; there were the steel- and iron-processing plants in Sverdlovsk only 160 kilometres east and ore mines in the mountains, and it had the benefit of the Trans-Siberian railway. This, he decided, would be the ideal location to assemble the GAZ-20, a car intended to rival the vehicles produced in the West. Eighteen months after construction began, the assembly plant stood in the middle of the pine forests.

Thousands of workers had been vetted and transferred by compulsory writ from cities across the country to fill the newly created labour gap, the population rising fivefold over five years. Leo had done background checks on some of the Moscow workers transferred here. If they'd passed, they were moved out within the week. If they failed, they were arrested. Leo had been one of the gatekeepers to this town. The irony must have amused Vasili.

Raisa was asleep, her head resting against the window. Leo nudged her. She woke, looking at Leo, then out of the window.

'We're here.'

The train pulled into the station. They collected their cases, stepping down onto the platform. It was colder than Moscow, by at least a couple of degrees. They stood like two evacuee children, staring at their unfamiliar surroundings. They'd been given no instructions. They knew no one.

The station building was empty except for a young man at the ticket booth.

Raisa approached him. 'Good evening. We need to get to the headquarters of the militia.'

'You're from Moscow?'

'That's right.'

The man pointed towards the street outside. 'They're waiting for you.'

One hundred paces from the station entrance was a militia car.

As they got closer, Raisa and Leo could see two men sitting in the front. The door opened, one of the men stepped out.

'Leo Demidov?' he asked. He was middle-aged, broad-shouldered.

'Yes.'

'I'm General Nesterov, head of Voualsk's militia.'

Leo wondered why he'd bothered to meet them. But then he realised that the arrival of a former MGB agent from Moscow was going to put the militia on their guard. They wouldn't believe that he was merely here to join their ranks. They would suspect an ulterior agenda. Why would an agent travel hundreds of kilometres to join a small-scale militia operation?

The militia was a lowly subsection of the Ministry of the Interior: poorly paid, poorly respected. There was no need for a police force in a Communist state. The USSR's official crime rates were close to zero. As the newspapers frequently pointed out, the West was forced to waste vast sums of money on crime prevention, and employed many of its bravest citizens fighting crime. All that was needed here was a ragtag group of strong but otherwise useless men to break up drunken brawls. That was the theory. Leo had no idea what the real crime statistics were. But he knew his arrival was a striking anomaly.

Nesterov loaded their cases into the boot of the car before opening the back door for them. He climbed into the front passenger seat. The young officer behind the wheel put the car into gear, then pulled out into an empty road.

After a while, Nesterov glanced at Leo in the rearview mirror. 'We were told three days ago that you were coming here. It's an unusual transfer.'

'We must go where we're needed.'

'No one has been transferred here for some time. I certainly made no request for any additional men.'

'The output of the factory is considered a high priority. You can never have too many men working to ensure the security of this town.'

Leo's answers were deliberately enigmatic. Though he'd been tossed out of the MGB, it seemed sensible to make use of the fear it instilled.

'For the moment you'll stay in guest accommodation,' said Nesterov. 'Once an apartment has been found it will be assigned to you. I should warn you that there's a long waiting list. And there's nothing I can do about that.'

The car stopped outside what appeared to be a restaurant. Nesterov opened the boot and deposited the cases on the pavement.

Addressing Leo, Nesterov said, 'Once you've taken your cases to your room, please come back to the car. Your wife doesn't need to come.'

As Leo picked up both their cases, Raisa flashed him a look of irritation, then pushed open the door, entering the restaurant.

Inside it was dark; the shutters were closed and the air stank of stale smoke. Last night's dirty glasses cluttered the table. Leo put the cases down and knocked on one of the greasy tabletops. A man appeared at the door.

'My name is Leo Demidov. This is my wife, Raisa. We're from Moscow.'
'Danil Basarov.'
'I've been told by General Nesterov you have accommodation for us.'
Basarov scratched his stomach. 'Let me show you to your room.'
The room was small. Two single beds had been pushed together. Both mattresses dipped. The wallpaper was sticky with grease. The bedroom was directly over the kitchen, which could be seen, and smelt, through cracks in the floorboards. Raisa tried to open the window, but it had been nailed shut.
Leo felt tired. He'd been able to handle his humiliation while it had remained a concept but now that it had a physical form—this room—he just wanted to close his eyes and shut out the world. Obliged to go back outside, he put his case on the bed, unable to look at Raisa, not out of anger but out of shame. He walked out without saying a word.

LEO WAS DRIVEN to the telephone exchange. Inside, there was a queue of several hundred people waiting for their allotted two minutes. Since most of them had been forced to leave their families behind in order to work here, Leo could appreciate that these minutes were extremely precious.
Nesterov had no need to queue, heading into a cubicle. Once he'd set up the call, he handed the receiver to Leo.
'How's the accommodation?' It was Vasili.
'What is it you want?'
'To stay in touch so you can tell me about life over there and I can tell you about life here. Before I forget, the pleasant apartment you'd arranged for your parents, it's been taken back. We've found them somewhere more suitable to their status. It's a little cold, perhaps, and they're sharing with a family of seven. By the way, I didn't know your father suffered from terrible back pain. Shame that he has to return to the assembly-line floor.'
'My parents are good people. They've worked hard. They've done you no harm. What do you want from me?'
'An apology.'
'Vasili, I'm sorry. I treated you badly. I shouldn't have hit you. I'm sorry.'
'You're not trying hard enough. Convince me.'
'I don't understand what you want.' Leo was desperate, his voice trembling. 'You have everything. I have nothing.'
'It's simple. I want to hear you beg.'
'I'm begging you, Vasili. Leave my parents alone. Please . . .'
Vasili had hung up.

Voualsk, March 17

Having walked all night, Leo sat down on a park bench, put his head in his hands and wept. When Raisa had tried to talk to him last night, he'd ignored her. Unable to stay in their tiny stinking room any longer he'd gone downstairs, elbowed his way outside. He'd walked without any sense of direction, too angry to sit still and do nothing, although he realised that was exactly the nature of his predicament—he could do nothing. His parents wouldn't be shot in the back of the head; that would be too swift. Instead they'd be persecuted drip by drip. In their respective factories they'd be demoted, given the hardest, dirtiest jobs. They'd be goaded with stories of Leo's pitiful exile, his humiliation. As for the family his parents were forced to share an apartment with, there was no doubt that they'd be as unpleasant as possible, promised their own apartment if they stole food, argued and, through whatever means available, made home life intolerable. Vasili would break Leo from afar, systematically applying pressure where he was vulnerable—his family. With a little work, Leo could discover his parents' address, but all he could do, if his letters weren't intercepted and burned, would be to reassure them he was safe. He'd built them a comfortable life only to have it ripped from under their feet at a time when they could least handle the change.

He stood up, shivering with cold. With no idea what he was going to do next, he began to retrace his steps, back to his new home.

RAISA WAS DOWNSTAIRS, sitting at a table. She had been waiting for him all night. She knew that Leo now regretted his decision not to denounce her. But what was she supposed to do? Love wasn't something she could just conjure on demand. Still, she could have been easier on him. In truth, part of her must have relished his demotion. She wanted him to know: *This is how I feel every day.* Powerless, scared—she'd wanted him to understand.

Exhausted, she looked up as Leo entered the restaurant. She stood, approaching her husband, noticing his bloodshot eyes. She'd never seen him cry before. He turned away and poured himself a drink from the nearest bottle. She put a hand on his shoulder. It happened in a fraction of a second: Leo spun round, grabbing her by the neck and squeezing.

'You did this.'

Her veins constricted, her face flushed red—she couldn't breathe, she was choking. Her hands fumbled at his grip. But Leo wouldn't let go.

She reached towards a tabletop. She managed to grab a glass, swinging and smashing it against the side of Leo's face. As if a spell had been broken he released her. She fell back, holding her neck. They stared at each other, strangers, as though their entire history had been washed away in a second. A shard of glass was embedded in Leo's cheek. He touched it and pulled it out. Without turning her back, she edged to the stairs, then hurried up them.

INSTEAD OF FOLLOWING his wife, Leo downed the drink he'd already poured, then poured another and another, and by the time he heard Nesterov's car outside he'd finished most of the bottle. Unsteady on his feet, unwashed and unshaven, drunk, brutish and senselessly violent—it had taken him less than a day to sink to the level expected of the militia.

During their car journey, Nesterov didn't mention the gash down Leo's face. He spoke in short bursts. Leo wasn't listening; he was too preoccupied with what he'd just done. Another couple of seconds, a slight tightening of his grip, and his wife would have died. His provocation was that he'd given up everything—his parents, his career—on a false pretext, the promise of a family, the notion that there was some tie between them. But what he had done was unforgivable. He'd laid down his life for Raisa only to try to kill her. That was insanity. At this rate he'd have nothing, not even the woman he'd married. He wanted to say, the woman he loved. Did he love her? Leo sighed, rubbed his forehead. On the train he'd asked her to declare her love for him, to soothe him, reward him with a romantic fantasy in which he was the hero. It was pathetic. She was right to hold him in contempt.

They had stopped. Nesterov was already out of the car. Leo opened the door, stepped out and followed his superior officer into the militia headquarters. Introduced to staff, shaking hands, nodding, agreeing but unable to take anything in; names and details washed over him. Alone in the locker room he stripped, left his civilian clothing at the bottom of a locker and buttoned up his new uniform—coarse trousers with red piping and a heavy military jacket. He looked at himself in the mirror. There were black marks under his eyes, a weeping cut down his left cheek. He glanced at the insignia on his jacket. He was an *uchastkovyy*; he was nothing.

The walls of Nesterov's office were decorated with framed certificates. Leo discovered that his boss had won amateur wrestling competitions and rifle-shooting tournaments, and had received commendations as Officer of the Month on numerous occasions. It was an ostentatious display, understandable considering that his position was held in such low esteem.

Leo could see that his superior officer was studying him with an expression of distaste and suspicion. At last, Nesterov presented Leo with a file.

Inside there were black and white photographs of a young girl, lying on her back, surrounded by dark snow. There was something inside her mouth.

'Her mouth was stuffed with soil,' Nesterov explained. 'So she couldn't scream for help.'

Leo's fingers tightened on the photo. All thoughts of Raisa, his parents, himself, evaporated as his eyes focused on this girl's open mouth. The girl was naked; her midriff had been savaged, torn open. He flicked to the next photo and the next, not seeing a girl but instead Fyodor's little boy, a boy who hadn't been stripped naked, or had his stomach cut open, a boy whose mouth hadn't been stuffed with dirt—a boy who hadn't been murdered.

THE TWO INCIDENTS had nothing to do with each other, the death of Fyodor's young boy and the murder of this young girl—it was impossible. They'd taken place hundreds of kilometres apart. This was a vicious irony, nothing more. But Leo had been wrong to dismiss Fyodor's allegations. Here was a child murdered as Fyodor had described. Such a thing was possible. And there was now no way of knowing what had really happened to Fyodor's son, Arkady, because Leo had never bothered to examine the boy's body.

Nesterov was frank about the details of this murder, calling it by no other name—*murder*—and portraying it as a brutal and horrific crime. The victim's name was Larisa Petrova; she'd been found four days ago, in the forest, not far from the train station, by a drunken couple who'd retreated into the forest to fornicate. The body had been lying in the snow for several months, perfectly preserved. The girl was fourteen years old. The militia knew her. She had a reputation for having a disorderly sex life. Larisa had argued with her mother on the day she went missing. She'd threatened to run away, and it had seemed she'd followed through on her threat. No one had looked for her. According to Nesterov, her parents were respected members of the community. They were ashamed of their daughter and wanted nothing to do with the investigation, which was to be kept secret. The matter would be concluded swiftly because they already had a man in custody.

Leo was aware that the militia could only investigate after a criminal case had been opened and that a criminal case was only opened if it was certain it would be concluded successfully. Failure to convict a suspect was unacceptable and the consequences severe. If a case was difficult, ambiguous, it simply wouldn't be opened. For Nesterov and his subordinates to be this calm, they had to be convinced their job was done. Leo wasn't being asked to assist: he was being given a tour, expected to marvel at the efficiency.

The cell was small with concrete walls, a concrete floor. The suspect was seated, his hands cuffed behind his back. He was young, no more than sixteen or seventeen, with an adult's muscular frame but a child's face. His eyes seemed to roam with no particular sense of purpose. He was calm, though not in an intelligent way.

Nesterov pointed at the suspect. 'This is Varlam Babinich. We found him in possession of a lock of Larisa's hair. He has a history of stalking her—lingering outside her house, propositioning her in the street. Larisa's mother remembers her daughter complaining that he used to try to touch her hair.'

Nesterov turned to the suspect. 'Tell this man what you told me,' he said, speaking slowly. 'Tell us why you killed her.'

'I cut her. It was my fault. I liked her hair. She kept telling me to go away but I wanted her hair. I wanted it so bad. This is why I cut her. I'm sorry. I shouldn't have done that. When can I have the blanket?'

'Let's talk about that later.'

Leo interrupted. 'What blanket?'

'Two days ago he kidnapped a baby. It was wrapped in a yellow blanket. He has an obsession with the colour yellow. Fortunately the baby was unhurt.' Nesterov looked at Leo. 'Do you have any questions?'

Leo thought for a moment. 'Why did you stuff her mouth with soil?'

Varlam didn't answer immediately. He seemed confused. 'Yes, there was dirt in her mouth. I remember that now. Don't hit me.'

'No one is going to hit you,' Nesterov answered.

Leo continued: 'Explain what happened when you killed her.'

'I cut her.'

'You cut her body or you cut her hair?'

'I found her and I cut her. I should have said to somebody but I didn't want to get in trouble.' Varlam began to cry. 'I'm in so much trouble. I'm sorry. I just wanted her hair.'

Nesterov stepped forward. 'That's enough for the moment.'

Leo and Nesterov stepped outside. Nesterov shut the door to the cell.

'We have evidence that he was at the crime scene,' he said. 'Snow prints match his boots. You understand he's from the *internat*? He's a simpleton.'

Leo now understood Nesterov's bravery in addressing this murder head-on. They had a suspect who suffered from a mental disorder. Varlam was outside Soviet society, outside Communism. His actions didn't alter the truism about crime because the suspect was not a real Soviet.

'That shouldn't lull you into thinking he's incapable of violence,' Nesterov added. 'He's admitted killing her. He has a motive—an irrational one, but a motive. He has a history of committing crimes when he can't get what he wants: theft, kidnapping. His morality is undeveloped. It's sad. He should have been locked up a long time ago. This is a matter for the *sledovatyel* now.'

Leo understood. The investigation was over. This boy was going to die.

THE BEDROOM WAS EMPTY. Her case was missing. Leo ran down the stairs and into the restaurant kitchen. Basarov was cutting a joint of yellow meat.

'Where's my wife?'

'Pay for the bottle and I'll tell you.' Basarov pointed to an empty bottle, the bottle of cheap vodka that Leo had now finished.

'Please, just tell me where she is.'

'Pay for the bottle.' Basarov continued cutting the meat.

Leo didn't have any money. He was still wearing his militia uniform. He ran back upstairs, rifling through his case. In the back of the *Book of Propagandists* he had four twenty-five-rouble notes, an emergency stash. He ran back down to the restaurant, pushing one of the notes into the man's hand.

'Where is she?'

'She left a couple of hours ago. She was carrying her case.'

'How long ago, exactly how long ago?'

'Two or three hours . . .'

Three hours—that meant she was gone. Leo couldn't guess where. Basarov volunteered a little extra information. 'It's unlikely she made it for the late-afternoon train. There isn't another train till seven thirty . . .'

Leo had ten minutes.

He ran as fast as he could, but with only the roughest idea where the station was. He was running blindly, trying to recall the route the car had driven.

He turned the corner, only to be confronted by a dead end—a line of wooden houses. He was lost. As he tried to catch his breath, he remembered these ramshackle timber houses. He was close to the station, he was sure of it. He ran forward, entering the back of one of the huts, stepping into a family seated on the floor, in the middle of a meal. They stared up at him, silent, afraid at the sight of his uniform. Without saying a word he ran out, entering the street they had driven down on their arrival. The station was within sight. He tried to run faster but he had nothing in reserve.

He barged into the station doors, knocking them open with his shoulder. The clock showed it was seven forty-five. He was fifteen minutes too late. The realisation that she was gone, probably for ever, crashed across his mind.

He felt weak. He leaned forward, his hands on his knees, sweat running down the side of his face. Out of the corner of his eye he saw a man sitting on a bench. Why would a man still be on the platform? Leo straightened up.

Raisa was at the far end of the platform. It took an enormous effort not to run and grab her hands. Catching his breath, he tried to think of what to say. He glanced at himself—he was a mess, sweating, filthy. But she wasn't even looking at him; she was looking over his shoulder. Leo turned round. Smoke rose over the treetops. The delayed train was approaching.

Leo had imagined taking time over his apology, finding the correct words. Right now, however, he had a matter of seconds to convince her.

His words stumbled out. 'I'm sorry, I wasn't thinking. I grabbed you but that wasn't me—or it wasn't the person I want to be.' *Hopeless—slow down, concentrate.* 'Raisa, you're right to want to leave me. I could tell you how difficult it would be on your own. How you might get stopped, questioned, arrested. How you don't have the right paperwork. How you have no family to run to, no money. You'd be a vagrant. But that's not a reason to stay with me. I know you'd rather take your chances.'

'Paperwork can be faked, Leo. I'd rather fake that than this marriage.'

There it was. The marriage was a sham. All Leo's words dried up. The train came to a halt alongside them. Raisa moved towards the carriage.

Over the sound of grinding brakes, Leo raised his voice. 'The reason I didn't denounce you wasn't because I believed you were pregnant. I did it because my family is the only part of my life I'm not ashamed of. You don't love me, I know that. But there was a reason we got married, something between us, some connection. I've lost that. We can find it again.'

Carriage doors were opening, passengers were disembarking. Time was running out. Raisa looked at the carriage, clearly weighing up her choices. Then she looked at Leo, and put down her case. Leo smiled in relief.

She raised her hand, cutting short his smile. 'I married you because I was scared, scared that if I rejected your advances I'd be arrested. That story you tell about me pretending my name was Lena? You find that story funny, romantic? I gave you a false name because I was worried you'd track me down. What you took for seduction, I took for surveillance. Our relationship was built out of fear. You asked me to marry you and I acquiesced because that's what people do. They put up with things in order to survive. You never hit me or shouted at me, you were never drunk. So I reckoned that I was luckier than most. When you grabbed my neck, Leo, you removed the only reason I had for staying with you.'

The train pulled out. Leo watched it go, trying to digest what she'd said. But she gave him no pause. The words, now tapped, were flowing freely.

'The problem with becoming powerless, as you are now, is that people start telling you the truth. You're not used to it; you've lived in a world protected by the fear you inspire. But if we're going to stay together, let's cut the deluded romanticism. From now on I tell you the truth, no comfortable lies—we're equal. You can take it or I can wait for the next train.'

Leo had no reply. In the past he'd used his position to get better accommodation, better food. He hadn't imagined he'd used it to get a wife too.

Her voice softened a little. 'There are so many things to be afraid of. You can't be one of them.'

'I never will again.'

'I'm cold, Leo. I've been standing on this platform for three hours. I'm going back to our room. Are you coming?'

No, he didn't feel like walking back, side by side, a chasm between them. 'I'm going to stay here for a bit. I'll see you back there.'

Raisa returned to the station building. Leo sat on the bench, staring into the forest. He shuffled through the memories of their relationship, re-examining each one, adjusting his understanding, rewriting his past.

He'd been sitting there for he didn't know how long when he became aware of someone standing to the side of him. He looked up. It was the man from the ticket office, the young man they'd met on their arrival.

'Sir, there are no more trains tonight.'

'Do you have a cigarette?'

'I don't smoke. I could get you one from our apartment. It's just upstairs.'

'No, that's OK. Thank you anyway.'

'I'm Aleksandr.'

'Leo. Do you mind if I stay here for a bit?'

'Not at all. Let me get you that cigarette.'

Before Leo could answer, the young man had hurried off.

Leo sat back and waited. He saw a wooden hut set back from the tracks. That was near where the girl's body had been found. He could make out the edge of the forest, the crime scene—trampled snow.

Struck by a thought, Leo stood up, hurried forward, lowering himself off the platform, crossing the tracks and heading towards the trees.

Behind him a voice called out, 'What are you doing?'

He turned round and saw Aleksandr standing on the edge of the platform, holding a cigarette, and gestured for him to follow.

Leo reached the area where the snow had been trodden down at the edge of the forest. He walked to where he supposed the body must have laid and crouched down. Aleksandr caught up with him.

Leo looked up. 'You know what happened here?'

'I was the one who saw Ilinaya running to the station. She was badly beaten up, shaking—she couldn't speak for a while. I called the militia.'

'Ilinaya?'

'She found the body. Her and the man she was with.'

'Why was she beaten up?'

Aleksandr looked nervous. 'She's a prostitute. The man she was with that night is an important Party official. Please, don't ask me any more.'

Leo nodded. He pushed his hand through the snow. 'The girl's mouth was filled with soil. Imagine I am struggling with you, right here, and I reach out to grab something to stuff into your mouth because I'm afraid you're going to scream.'

Leo's fingers hit the ground. It was hard, like stone. He tried another place, then another. There was no loose soil. The ground was frozen solid.

March 18

Standing outside Hospital 379, Leo reread the main points of the autopsy report, which he'd copied longhand from the original: *Multiple stab wounds, blade indeterminate length. Extensive damage to torso and internal organs. Raped before or after death. Mouth full of soil but she did not suffocate, nasal passage clear. The soil was for some other purpose—to silence her?*

Leo had circled the last point. Since the ground was frozen the killer must have brought the soil with him. He must have planned the murder. But why bring soil? It was a cumbersome means to silence someone; a rag would have been easier. With no answers, Leo had decided to see the body for himself.

When he'd asked where her body was being kept, he'd been told to go to Hospital 379. Leo hadn't expected forensic laboratories, pathologists or a dedicated morgue. He knew there was no specialised apparatus for dealing with wrongful death. How could there be when there *was* no wrongful death? In the hospital the militia were forced to canvass for a doctor's spare moment. These doctors, with no training beyond their own medical qualifications, would take an educated guess at what might have happened to the victim.

At reception he asked if he could speak to a doctor, explaining that he needed help with the examination of a murder victim they had in their morgue. The man moved off to see who was available.

Leo's fingers tapped against the front desk. He was uneasy, glancing over his shoulder at the entrance. His visit was unauthorised. His job was to find evidence confirming a suspect's guilt, not question that guilt. Leo knew that even if he'd been the top-ranking officer he couldn't change the direction of the investigation. A course had been set, a suspect chosen. The system didn't allow for admissions of fallibility. What difference could he make?

The receptionist returned with a man in his early forties, Dr Tyapkin, who agreed to show Leo down to the morgue as long as it didn't involve any paperwork and his name didn't show up on any documents.

As they walked, the doctor expressed doubts as to whether the girl's body was still there. 'We don't keep them for long unless we're asked to. We were under the impression the militia had all the information they required. I thought you'd already caught the man responsible.'

'Yes, it's possible.'

The morgue was in the basement, built deep into ground that was frozen throughout the long winter. As a result, the corridors were naturally cold. Tyapkin led Leo to a large room with a tiled floor. The doctor unlocked a steel door on the far side and entered the morgue itself. Leo waited.

Tyapkin emerged from the morgue pushing a trolley. 'I've found your girl.'

Larisa Petrova lay on her back. Her skin was pale, crisscrossed with blue veins. Her hair was blonde. A large part of the fringe had been unevenly cut off: the part Varlam had taken. Her jaw was open, locked into position. Her mouth was empty, but her teeth and tongue were dirty, stained brown.

'There was soil in her mouth,' Leo said.

'Was there? I'm sorry, this is the first time I've seen her body. Perhaps the doctor washed it out in order to examine her throat.'

'It hasn't been kept?'

'I would think it very unlikely.'

Leo had never studied a dead body before with any forensic interest. But to his mind, the mutilation was so frenzied it could only be the work of someone insane. He'd seen enough. Varlam Babinich fitted the bill. He must have brought the soil for his own incomprehensible reasons.

Leo was ready to leave, but Tyapkin leaned closer. Using the tip of his pen he probed into the mangled midriff, examining the wounds.

'Can you tell me what the report said?'

Leo took out his notes and read them aloud.

Tyapkin continued his examination. 'That fails to mention that her stomach is missing. It's been cut out, severed from the oesophagus.'

'How precise, I mean in terms of . . .?'

'You mean did a doctor do this?' The doctor smiled. 'Possibly, but the cuts are ragged, not surgical. Although I'd be surprised if this was the first time. The cuts aren't skilful but they are confident. They're targeted, not random.'

'This might not be the first child he's killed?'

'I'd be surprised.'

Despite the cold, Leo found he was sweating. How could the two deaths—Fyodor's little boy and this girl—have anything to do with each other?

'Was her stomach not found nearby?' Tyapkin asked.

'No.'

It was either missed in the search, which seemed unlikely, or it had been taken away by the killer.

Leo remained silent for a moment, then asked, 'Was she raped?'

Tyapkin examined the girl's vagina. 'There's no trauma to her genitals. No bruising, no incisions. The injuries weren't targeted at her sexual organs. And there are no cuts to the breasts or to her face. The man who did this was interested in her guts. It looks savage but actually it's quite controlled.'

So this wasn't a frenzied attack. It was ordered, precise, planned.

'What is that?' Leo asked.

Round the girl's ankle was a loop of string, and a short length drooped off the trolley. There were marks where the string had rubbed the skin.

Tyapkin saw him first. General Nesterov was standing at the door. It was impossible to say how long he'd been there, watching them.

Leo stepped away from the body. 'I came here to familiarise myself with procedure.'

Nesterov addressed Tyapkin. 'Would you excuse us?'

Tyapkin glanced at Leo, as though wishing him luck, before moving away. Nesterov approached.

Leo tried to deflect attention. 'The original report doesn't mention that her stomach has been removed,' he began. 'We have a specific question to put to Varlam: why did he cut out her stomach and what did he do with it?'

'What are you doing in Voualsk?'

'I was transferred here.'

'Why?'

'I can't say.'

'I think you're still MGB.'

Leo remained silent.

'But that doesn't explain why you'd be so interested in this murder,'

Nesterov continued. 'We released Mikoyan without charge, as instructed. He had nothing to do with this girl's murder.'

Mikoyan must be the name of the Party official. He'd been protected. But was a man who beat a prostitute the same man who murdered this young girl? Leo didn't think it likely.

'I arrested Varlam because he killed that girl,' Nesterov went on, 'and because he's dangerous.'

'He didn't do it.'

Nesterov scratched the side of his face. 'Whatever you've been sent here to do, remember you're not in Moscow any more. If you undermine my authority, if you disobey an order, if you portray my officers as incompetent, if you make any denouncements regarding my men, I'll kill you.'

March 20

Raisa touched the frame of the bedroom window. The nails that had kept it shut had all been prised out. She opened it and glanced down. Directly below was a sloping roof, part of the kitchen. The snow had been disturbed where Leo had climbed down. She was furious. Having survived by the thinnest of margins, he was now gambling with both their lives.

Today had been Raisa's second day at Secondary School 151. The school's director had been more than happy with Raisa joining his staff, since she'd be taking over many of his lessons, enabling him, he'd claimed, to catch up with his paperwork. Raisa had been pleased to start work at once. From the classes she'd taught so far, she'd found the children less politically savvy than students in Moscow. They weren't competitive about proving their loyalty to the Party and generally seemed much more like children. They were made up of a patchwork of different backgrounds, families plucked from all corners of the country. Most of the teachers had also been transferred to Voualsk from different regions. They had experienced a similar upheaval to the one she'd just gone through and they treated her nicely enough. They were suspicious of her, of course. Who was she? Why was she here? But she didn't mind; these were questions everyone asked of each other. For the first time since arriving in this town, Raisa could imagine creating a life here.

She stepped back from the window, struggling to remain calm. Leo had begged her to stay with him. She had agreed for no other reason than this was her best bet. And now he was jeopardising their second chance. If they were to survive in this new town, they had to remain inconspicuous. Basarov was almost certainly an informer. Vasili would most probably have agents in the town spying on them, just waiting for a reason to upgrade their punishment from exile to internment to execution.

Raisa turned off the light and stood in the dark, staring out of the window. She could see no one outside. If there were agents working surveillance, they'd be downstairs. She put on her gloves and coat and climbed out of the window, lowering herself onto the icy roof. She closed the window behind her and clambered down to the ground. She'd made Leo swear to one condition: they were to be equals. Yet he'd already gone back on his word. If he thought she would silently stand by him—the obedient, supportive wife—while he endangered her life for his own personal reasons, he was mistaken.

AN AREA with a radius of roughly 500 metres from the point where Larisa's body had been found had been searched as part of the official investigation. That area seemed small to Leo. Nothing had been discovered except the girl's clothes, piled neatly some forty paces from the body. Why so far? The clothes showed no trace of blood; they bore no knife marks. Perhaps the killer had persuaded Larisa to accompany him into the forest, maybe offering money for sex. Once she'd taken her clothes off, he'd attacked. But Leo was finding it difficult to apply logic to this crime. He couldn't stop thinking about the incomprehensible details—the soil, the removal of the stomach, the string.

With little chance of finding anything new regarding Larisa's death, Leo was in the conflicted position of needing to find a second body. He had reason to believe that Larisa wasn't the first victim. The doctor had suggested the killer had a competence and assuredness that came from practice. And, of course, there was the death of Arkady.

Leo searched by moonlight and discreet use of his flashlight. Using a map stolen from the militia's office, he'd divided the forest surrounding the railway station into four areas. He'd found nothing in the first area, where the victim's body had been found. Even the bloody snow had been removed. But in the remaining three areas the snow was untouched. It had taken him an hour or so to cover the second grid, by which time his fingers were numb with cold. However, the advantage of the snow was that he could scan the ground for footprints, using his own tracks to mark sections he'd covered.

With the third area almost finished, he paused. He could hear footsteps—the crunch of snow. Turning the flashlight off, he crouched behind a tree.

'Leo?'

It was Raisa. He stood up. 'Were you followed?'

'No. Why are you here?'

'I told you. A little girl was murdered; they have a suspect but I don't—'

'You don't think he's guilty? Since when has that mattered to you?'

'Raisa, I'm just trying—'

'Leo, stop. I don't think I can stomach you telling me you're here doing the right thing, motivated by principles of justice, or honour. Let's be blunt. This will end badly, and when it ends badly for you it ends badly for me.'

'You want me to do nothing?'

Raisa became angry. 'I'm supposed to bow down to this personal investigation of yours? It's an unacceptable risk. You think if you can catch one genuinely guilty person all those innocent men and women you've arrested will just fade away? This isn't about any little girl, it's about you.'

Of course, everything she said was true. Their fates were stitched together; he had no right to embark on this investigation without her approval. And he was in no position to argue morality.

'Raisa, I don't believe they'll ever leave us alone. At a guess they'll wait a couple of months, maybe a year, between my arrival here and my arrest. I don't have long. And this is how I want to spend that time, trying to find the man who did this. He needs to be caught. I appreciate that doesn't help you. However, there's a way for you to survive. Just before I'm arrested they'll double the surveillance. At this point, you should go to them, feed them some story about me, make a show of betraying me.'

'What am I supposed to do until then? Sit in that room and wait? Lie for you? Cover for you?'

'I'm sorry.'

Raisa shook her head, turned round and walked back towards town.

Leo's energy was sapped, his movements sluggish, his thoughts no longer on the case. Was this just a selfish, futile enterprise? He hadn't gone far when once again he heard the sound of footsteps in the snow. Raisa had returned.

'You're sure this man's killed before?'

'Yes. And the evidence against Varlam Babinich is specific to this girl. If there's a second victim, the case against him falls apart.'

'They might just blame this boy Varlam for both murders.'

'That's a risk. But a second body is my only chance to reopen this case.'

'So, if we find another body, you have an investigation. If we don't, if we find nothing, you promise to let this drop.'

'Yes.'

'All right, then. You lead.'

Awkward, uncertain, they set off, deeper into the forest.

After almost thirty minutes, Raisa pointed ahead. Crossing their path were two sets of tracks, an adult's and a child's, side by side.

They walked for some time, following the tracks, with no sign of anything being amiss. Suddenly Leo stopped. Up ahead, an area of snow had been flattened, as though someone had lain down. Leo moved forward. The footprints became confused, as if there'd been a struggle. The adult had walked away from the disturbance while the child's tracks went off in the opposite direction, the footsteps unevenly spaced, ragged—the child had been running. From the impressions in the snow it was clear that the child had fallen over, there was a single hand print. The child had got up and continued to run. But the adult's footsteps were nowhere to be seen. Then, several metres ahead, they reappeared, emerging out of the trees. Yet something was odd— the adult was running in zigzags, inaccurately converging on the child's position. None of it made sense. Having walked away from the child, the man had changed his mind and run erratically back towards him.

Raisa stopped, staring ahead at the point where the tracks would meet.

Leo touched her on the shoulder. 'Stay here.' He moved forward.

He saw the bloody snow first, then the bare legs, the mutilated torso. It was a young boy, no more than thirteen or fourteen years old. He was on his back, staring at the sky. There was something in his mouth. Out of the corner of his eye, Leo saw movement. He turned to see Raisa behind him.

'Are you OK?' he asked.

Raisa lifted her hand to her mouth. She gave Leo the smallest of nods.

Leo knelt down beside the boy. Tied round his ankle was string, the skin red where it had rubbed. Leo turned to look at the boy's face. His mouth had been stuffed with soil. It gave him the appearance of screaming. There was no snow over his body. He'd been killed after Larisa, maybe in the last couple of weeks. Leo leaned over, taking a pinch of the dark soil. It was coarse and dry, with large, uneven chunks that broke apart when he rubbed it between his finger and thumb. It wasn't soil at all. It was bark from a tree.

March 22

Some thirty-six hours after he and Raisa had found the boy's body, Leo still hadn't reported the discovery. Raisa was right. Instead of throwing the case open, the second murder could be blamed on Varlam Babinich. The youth had no sense of self-preservation; he was open to suggestion—whisper something in his ear and he was likely to go along with it. Why look for a second suspect when there was one already in custody?

Leo couldn't simply announce the discovery of the boy's body. First he had to establish that Babinich knew nothing about it. Otherwise someone might decide that it was simpler and safer for everyone involved to amend the confession and spoonfeed the suspect the necessary details. On returning to the train station, Leo hadn't raised the alarm or called his superior officers. To Raisa's bewilderment he'd asked her not to say anything, explaining that he couldn't get access to Babinich until the following morning, which meant leaving the body out in the woods for the night. If the youth was to have a chance at justice, there was no other option.

Babinich was no longer in the militia's care—he'd been handed over to the lawyers from the procurator's office. By the time Leo made his request to speak to the prisoner, they were ready to go to trial. Leo had been forced to argue that the suspect might have killed more girls and that the militia and lawyers should jointly question him about that before he was taken to trial. Nesterov had cautiously agreed; it was something they should have done already. He had insisted upon joining the interrogation, which had suited Leo fine; the more witnesses the better.

Babinich had denied knowing about any other victims. Afterwards, the team had agreed that it was unlikely he had killed anyone else. There were no other missing girls with blonde hair, which was the motive for the murder. Leo had feigned uncertainty, claiming they should search again just in case, widening the search to include any part of the forest within a thirty-minute walk of the town's perimeter. Nesterov had seemed uneasy, but he had not opposed the suggestion, perhaps because he thought the order might be coming from Moscow. The search had been arranged to take place today.

Having recruited workers from the timber mills for the search, Nesterov split the men and women into seven groups of ten. Leo's team was assigned to search the forest on the opposite side of town from where the body was located. This was ideal, since it would be better if he didn't make the discovery. There was also a possibility that there were more bodies to be found.

The ten members of Leo's team broke into two groups of three and one group of four. Leo was working with Nesterov's deputy, a man instructed, no doubt, to keep an eye on him. They were joined by a woman, a mill worker. It took them the entire day to complete their portion of the search—several square kilometres through difficult snowdrifts, which needed to be prodded with sticks to make sure there was nothing underneath them. They found no body. Neither of the other two groups found anything either. Leo was impatient to know what was happening on the other side of town.

NESTEROV WAS STANDING by the edge of the forest, near the railway maintenance cabin. Leo approached, trying to seem unhurried and indifferent.

'What have you found?' he asked.

'Nothing. Nothing at all.'

Leo's poise of cool indifference left him. He turned away, trying to work out what could have gone wrong. Most of the teams were returning; there wasn't much time before the entire operation would be concluded.

Leo began questioning the returning men. Two militia officers searching the area closest to where the body lay admitted there'd been tracks but they'd appeared innocent since they were four sets, not two. Leo had forgotten that he and Raisa had made an additional set of tracks running parallel to those of the victim and the murderer. Fighting back his exasperation, he ordered the two men back into the woods to follow the tracks to their conclusion. The officers weren't convinced. And who was Leo to give orders?

Leo had no option but to go to Nesterov, illustrating with the use of a map that there were no nearby villages in that direction, arguing that the tracks were suspicious. But Nesterov agreed with the two young officers.

Unable to contain his frustration, Leo said, 'I'll go alone, then.'

Nesterov stared at him. 'We'll both go.'

Following his own footsteps deeper into the forest, Leo belatedly realised that he was in danger, alone with this man who wanted him dead.

Nesterov seemed calm. 'Tell me, Leo, what are we going to find at the end of these tracks?'

'I have no idea.'

'But these are your footprints.' Nesterov pointed to the tracks in front of them and then at the tracks Leo had just made. They were identical.

'We're going to find the body of a dead child,' Leo said.

'Which you've already discovered?'

'Two days ago.'

'But you didn't report it?'

'I wanted to establish that Babinich knew nothing about this murder.'

'You were worried we'd blame him for the murder?'

'I'm still worried.'

Nesterov continued walking. They said nothing more until they reached the body. Leo stood back, watching as his superior officer made an examination.

Finally, Nesterov approached Leo. 'I want you to go back, call the procurator's officer. I'll stay here with the body.' Remembering Leo's concerns, he added, 'It's obvious that Babinich had nothing to do with this murder.'

'I agree.'

'These are two separate cases. A girl has been sexually assaulted and murdered. A boy has been sexually assaulted and murdered. These are different crimes. These are different depravities.'

Leo stared blankly, bewildered by the assertion. 'We don't know the boy was sexually assaulted. The doctor I spoke to doesn't believe the girl was.'

'She was naked.'

'But they both had ground-up tree bark stuffed into their mouths. These children were murdered by the same man.'

'Varlam Babinich has admitted stuffing Larisa's mouth with soil.'

'Which is why he can't have killed her—the ground is frozen. If it was soil, where did he get it from? Her mouth was stuffed with bark just as this boy's mouth was stuffed with bark.'

'One child was murdered close to the station, barely out of sight. The screams could have been heard by the passengers. It was an idiot's crime and an idiot has confessed. But this child has been led almost an hour's walk into the forest, so no one could interrupt. This is a different man.'

'Why do they both have string round their ankles?'

'This is a different crime. The girl was killed for her blonde hair, by a sick man. This boy was killed by a different man, with a different sickness.'

March 23

It was eight in the evening by the time Aleksandr left the ticket office. He didn't have far to walk, as he and his parents lived in an annexe above the station. Technically, his father was in charge of the station. But his father wasn't well. No one at the hospital could say what was wrong with him, except that he was overweight and drank too much. His mother was in good health and generally cheerful. She had reason to be—they were a fortunate family. The pay for working on the State railway was modest. But they had sole use of an apartment with plumbing, hot water and insulation. In exchange they were expected to be on call twenty-four hours a day. A bell that could be rung from the station was wired to the apartment. If there was a night train or an early-morning train they had to be on hand. But these small inconveniences were more than offset by the comforts they enjoyed.

In his bedroom, Aleksandr changed out of his uniform, put on casual clothes and sat down to eat with his parents. After washing the plates, Aleksandr excused himself; he was going to the cinema.

There was only one cinema in Voualsk. Three years ago, a church had been transformed into a 600-seat auditorium where State-sponsored films were shown. It had become Aleksandr's favourite pastime. Arriving at the foyer he saw that *Nezabyaemy God* was showing. Aleksandr had seen the movie only a couple of nights ago and numerous occasions before that. He didn't join the queue, but headed instead towards the park.

Officially, Victory Park was closed at night. But there was no fence and the rule was never enforced. Aleksandr knew the route to take: a path away from the streets and hidden by bushes. He could feel his heartbeat quicken in anticipation, as it always did, as he took a slow lap round the perimeter.

There was a man up ahead. Aleksandr stopped. The man turned to face him. He was younger than Aleksandr, perhaps nineteen or twenty. A nervous pause communicated that they were here for the same reason. Aleksandr continued forward and the man waited for him. Side by side, they both glanced around, making sure they were alone, before looking at each other.

Aleksandr broke the silence. 'I know somewhere we can go.'

The young man looked around once more and then nodded.

'Follow me,' Aleksandr continued. 'Keep at a distance.'

Arriving back at the train station, Aleksandr entered the main building. Without turning on the lights he unlocked the ticket office and went inside, leaving the door open. He waited, wondering why the man was taking so long. Finally, the man stepped inside, and the two of them looked at each other properly for the first time. Aleksandr stepped forward to lock the door. They were almost touching, and yet not quite, neither of them sure who should make the first move.

Someone was hammering on the door. Aleksandr's first thought was that it must be his father—he must have seen. But then he realised it wasn't coming from outside. It was this man. He was calling out. Had he changed his mind? Aleksandr was confused. He could hear voices outside the office. The man was no longer meek and nervous. A transformation had occurred. He was angry, disgusted. He spat in Aleksandr's face.

Outside, a voice called, 'Aleksandr, this is General Nesterov. The man you're with is a militia officer. I'm ordering you to open the door.'

AS SOON AS THE DOOR was open, two militia officers reached in, pulling Aleksandr onto the concourse.

Leo looked at him, the first person he'd encountered after getting off the train, the man who'd fetched him a cigarette, the man who'd helped search the woods. There was nothing he could to do to help him.

Nesterov circled the suspect, weighing up his words. 'You've committed a very serious crime. A judge would give you five years minimum and he wouldn't care how many times you said you were sorry.'

'I haven't said sorry.'

'Brave, Aleksandr, but would you be so brave if everyone found out? You'd be humiliated, disgraced. Even after serving your five years in prison you wouldn't be able to live or work here. You'd lose everything.'

Leo stepped forward. 'Just ask him.'

'There is a way to avoid this shame. We need a list of every man in this town who has sex with other men, men who have sex with boys.'

'I don't know any others. This is my first time . . .'

'If you choose not to help us we'll arrest you and put you on trial. Work for us and you won't need to go to trial. Maybe this disgrace can stay a secret.'

'What is this about?'

'The murder of a young boy. You'll be doing a public service and making amends for your crime. Will you make this list?'

March 29

Leo sat on the edge of his bed, contemplating how his attempt to relaunch an investigation had instead precipitated a city-wide pogrom. Over the past week the militia had rounded up 150 homosexuals. Aleksandr's information came from conversations with the ten or so men he'd had sex with. Each man recounted liaisons with different men so that, added together, it was possible to draw a sexual constellation. Today alone, Leo had arrested six men. Some had been taken from their place of work, escorted out in hand-cuffs while their colleagues watched. Others had been taken from their homes, their wives pleading, convinced that there must be some mistake.

Nesterov had reason to be pleased. He'd found a second suspect he could call *murderer* without upsetting the social theory. Murder was an aberration. These men were an aberration. It was a perfect fit. Short of space, they had converted offices into makeshift cells and interrogation rooms. Every officer had been timetabled to work twelve-hour shifts, with suspects questioned constantly, twenty-four hours a day. Leo had been obliged to ask the same questions again and again, picking through answers for even the smallest variation. He'd carried out this task like a dull automaton, convinced that these men were innocent.

When Leo had shown photos of the young boy with his guts cut open, all the suspects had reacted in exactly the same way: they were horrified—or at least they appeared to be. Who could have done such a thing? Every man was resolute: they knew of no killer among them and they wouldn't protect him if they did. After a week the interrogations had yielded nothing.

Nesterov had been left with little choice but to initiate prosecutions against all 150 men, hoping this would make one of them speak. They would, if the judge was so instructed, receive twenty-five years for political subversion rather than five years for sodomy. Faced with this prospect, three men had begun pointing the finger. However, they hadn't picked the same person. Refusing to accept that his line of investigation was flawed, Nesterov considered himself up against criminal solidarity—honour among deviants.

Exasperated, Leo had approached his superior officer. 'These men are innocent.'

Nesterov had stared at him, puzzled. 'All these men are guilty. The question is which one is also guilty of murder.'

RAISA WATCHED as Leo kicked the heels of his boots together. Dirty chunks of snow fell to the floor. He stared down, unaware that she was in the room. She found his disappointment impossible to bear. He'd believed, sincerely believed, that his investigation stood a chance. He'd pinned his hopes on a fanciful dream of redemption, a final act of justice. It was an idea she'd mocked that night in the forest. But it had been mocked far more cruelly by the turn of events. In the pursuit of justice he'd unleashed terror. One hundred and fifty men would lose their families, their homes. And she realised, seeing her husband's hunched shoulders and drawn face, that he never did anything without believing in it. There was nothing cynical or calculating about him. If this was true, then he must also have believed in their marriage; he must have believed it was built on love. Steadily all the fantasies he'd created—about the State, about their relationship—had been shattered. She stepped forward, sitting beside him on the bed. Tentatively, she took his hand. Surprised, he looked at her but said nothing, accepting the gesture. And together they watched as the snow began to melt.

March 30

Leo drew his gun. They were on the top floor of Apartment Building 7; apartment 14 was at the end of the corridor. Leo was accompanied by Moiseyev, a thuggish militia officer. They'd gone to the local orphanage in an unsuccessful attempt to identify the murdered boy. But one of the teenage boys they spoke to had claimed he'd been propositioned by a man who worked at the hospital. The hospital staff had given them this address. The suspect had been off sick for the past week, since the first wave of arrests against the town's homosexual population, and hadn't been questioned before.

Leo knocked on the door. There was no response. He called out, stating their name and rank. There was no reply. Moiseyev lifted his boot, ready to kick at the lock. The door opened.

Seeing the guns pointed at him, Dr Tyapkin raised his hands and stepped back. Leo barely recognised him. This was the doctor who'd helped him with the examination of the girl's body. He'd lost weight. His eyes were wild.

Leo pushed the door open, surveying the apartment. 'Are you alone?'

'My baby son's here. But he's asleep.'

Moiseyev stepped in, smashing the butt of his gun against Tyapkin's nose. Tyapkin dropped to his knees, blood running into his cupped hands.

'Search him,' Moiseyev ordered Leo.

Moiseyev began searching the apartment. Leo helped Tyapkin to his feet, bringing him into the kitchen, where he sat him down on a chair.

'Where's your wife?'

'Buying food . . . she'll be back soon.'

'The hospital said you were sick.'

'That's true, in a way. I heard about the arrests. I knew it was only a matter of time before you came to me.'

'Tell me what happened.'

'I was mad, there's no other explanation. He was young, fifteen or sixteen. I wanted anonymity. I reasoned no one would ever listen to an orphan. I could give him a little money and that would be the end.'

Moiseyev re-entered the room. He grabbed Tyapkin's broken nose, twisting it, causing him to scream in pain. A baby began to cry in a nearby room.

'You fuck these boys then kill them?'

Moiseyev let go of Tyapkin's nose. The doctor dropped to the floor, curling up into a ball. It was some time before he managed to speak.

'I didn't have sex with him. I couldn't go through with it. I walked away.'

'Get to your feet. We're leaving.'

'We have to wait till my wife comes back—we can't leave my son alone.'

'The kid will survive. Get to your feet.'

'At least let me stop the bleeding.'

Moiseyev nodded. 'Leave the bathroom door open.'

Tyapkin lurched to the bathroom. He ran the water in the sink and pressed a towel against his nose. 'I'm very sorry for what I did,' he said, his back turned to them. 'But I never killed anyone. You must believe me. Because someone else murdered that boy, someone who must be caught.'

Moiseyev was becoming impatient. 'Come on.'

'I wish you the best of luck.'

Hearing those words, Leo ran into the room, spinning Tyapkin round. Embedded in his arm was a syringe. Tyapkin's legs went slack. He fell. Leo caught him, laying him down on the floor, pulling the syringe out of his arm. He checked his pulse. Tyapkin was dead.

Moiseyev stared down at the body. 'That makes our job easier.'

Leo looked up. Tyapkin's wife had returned. She was standing at the entrance to the apartment, holding her family's groceries.

April 1

Aleksandr closed the ticket office. As far as he was aware, Nesterov had been true to his word. The secret of his sexual activities had been contained. None of the customers glanced at him oddly, or whispered about him. His family still loved him. Aleksandr's life had returned to normal. However, he no longer went to the movies. In fact, he no longer went into the centre of town at all. He was fearful of who he might meet—perhaps a militia officer who would smirk knowingly at him. His world had shrunk.

He spent every moment wondering if the men who'd been arrested had guessed he'd betrayed them. The sheer number of arrests meant that they were probably forced into cells with each other. What else would they have spent their time doing except speculate on who'd written the list? And as he thought about those men, he'd found himself wishing that he could swap his freedom for the public humiliation of one of those cells.

He shut the door to the ticket office, locking it behind him, then he walked onto the platform. A couple were waiting for the train. He recognised them by sight though not by name. They waved to him and he waved back. He walked to the end of the platform and watched as the train approached. This one was on time. Aleksandr stepped off the platform and positioned himself across one of the tracks, staring up at the night sky.

NESTEROV HAD SPENT the last four years promising his family a better place to live. They lived on Kropotkinsky Street, on the outskirts of town. The houses here had been built haphazardly, and Nesterov, a competent carpenter, spent much of his free time making improvements. But no amount of tinkering could compensate for the property's shortcomings. There was no running water—the nearest well was a ten-minute walk. There was a pit toilet at the back of the house. His family lived cut off from advancements in comfort and hygiene, with no promise of a better future. He was forty years old. His pay was less than that of the twenty-something workers at the car assembly plant. His aspiration to provide a decent home had come to nothing.

There was a knock on the front door. It was late. Nesterov could hear Inessa answer the door. A moment later she appeared in the kitchen.

'It's someone for you. He's from your work. I don't recognise him.'

Nesterov walked into the hallway. Leo was standing outside.

Nesterov turned to his wife. 'I'll deal with this. It won't take long.' He stepped outside, shutting the door.

Leo was sweating and breathless. He'd clearly run all the way there. 'Aleksandr is dead. He killed himself, threw himself under a train.'

Nesterov dropped his head. 'I'm sorry to hear that. We gave him a chance to sort himself out. Maybe he couldn't. Maybe he was too sick.'

'We're responsible for his death.'

'No, he was ill.'

'He was twenty-two years old. He had a mother and a father. And now he's dead. And we're responsible. For his death and for Dr Tyapkin's.'

'Tyapkin killed himself because he was guilty. He had the surgical skill necessary to cut out a child's stomach. He gave a false testimony to you about the girl's murder to confuse us. He was devious, cunning.'

'He told me the truth. That little girl's stomach was cut out and her mouth was stuffed with bark, the same as the boy. She had string tied round her ankle and so did the boy. They were killed by the same man. And it wasn't Dr Tyapkin and it wasn't that teenager Varlam Babinich.'

'Go home,' Nesterov replied.

'There was a body in Moscow. A young boy, called Arkady, not even five years old. I was told that he was found naked, his stomach cut open, his mouth stuffed with dirt. I suspect his mouth was stuffed with bark.'

'Suddenly there's a murdered child in Moscow? That's very convenient, Leo. I don't believe it.'

'I didn't believe it either. I had the grieving family in front of me, telling me their son had been murdered, and I told them it wasn't true. We don't know how many other incidents have been covered up. Our system is perfectly arranged to allow this man to kill as many times as he likes. We're going to keep arresting innocent people, and he's going to kill again and again.'

Nesterov didn't trust this man. He'd never trusted him and he certainly wasn't going to be drawn into making criticisms about the State. He turned his back on Leo, reaching for the front door.

Leo grabbed him by the shoulder, turning him so they were face to face again. Without warning, he punched him. Nesterov's head cracked to the side. Then, slowly, he turned to face his junior officer. Nesterov's punch lifted Leo off his feet. He landed on the ground, on his back.

Nesterov stared down at him, touching his own jaw. 'Go home.'

Leo got to his feet. 'We've solved nothing.'

He threw a punch. Nesterov blocked, throwing one back. He was quick, despite his size. Punched in the stomach, Leo doubled up. Nesterov brought a second blow down across his face, dropping him to his knees and splitting open the skin on his cheek. Leo toppled forward, falling, then rolled onto his back, gasping.

Nesterov stood over him. 'Go home.'

In reply, Leo kicked him in the groin. Nesterov scuttled back, hunched over. Leo staggered to his feet. 'We've solved—' Before he could finish, Nesterov ran forward, knocking Leo to the ground and landing on top of him. He punched him, blow after blow. Catching his breath, Nesterov stopped. Leo wasn't moving. His eyes were closed—a pool of blood collecting in his right eye, fed by a cut to his brow. Nesterov got up and moved to the front door. As he reached for the handle he heard a sound behind him.

Leo had pulled himself up. Unsteady on his feet, he rocked from side to side. His voice was a whisper. 'We've . . . solved . . . nothing.'

Nesterov watched as Leo swayed. He walked towards him, fists clenched, ready to knock him down. Leo swung a hopeless, pitiful punch—Nesterov sidestepped and caught Leo under the arm just as his legs gave way.

LEO SAT at the kitchen table. Inessa had warmed some water and poured it into a bowl. Nesterov dropped a cloth in the water and Leo was left to clean his bleeding face. He couldn't open his right eye. Nonetheless, it was a relatively cheap price for getting Nesterov's attention.

'How many children do you have?' Leo asked.

'We have two boys,' Inessa replied.

'Do they walk through the woods on their way to school?'

'They used to. Now we make them walk through the town. It takes longer and they complain. We have to trust them not to slip into the forest.'

'Will they be walking through the forest now the killer has been caught?'

Nesterov stood up, pouring tea. 'Would you like something stronger?'

'If you have it.'

Nesterov took out a half-empty bottle of vodka, pouring three glasses, then sat down. 'Why are you in Voualsk?'

'I'm here to investigate the murder of these children.'

'That's a lie.'

Leo had to win this man's trust. He could do nothing without his help.

'You're right. But there was a murder in Moscow. I was ordered to sweep the matter aside. I did my duty in that respect. Where I failed was in refusing to denounce my wife as a spy. As a punishment I was sent here.'

'If you really are a disgraced officer, why are you doing this?'

'Because three children have been murdered.'

'You don't believe Varlam Babinich killed Larisa because you're sure that Larisa wasn't this killer's first victim. Am I right?'

'Larisa couldn't have been the first victim. He'd done it before. There's a chance the boy in Moscow wasn't the first victim either. The killer doesn't live in Voualsk. The murders were by the train station. He travels.'

'He travels? He murders children? What kind of man is this?'

'I don't know. But there's a woman in Moscow who saw him with the victim. She can describe this man to us. We'll need the murder records from every major town from Sverdlovsk to Leningrad.'

'There are no centralised records.'

'That's why you have to visit each town and collect their case files.'

The idea was outlandish. Nesterov should have arrested Leo. Instead, he asked, 'Why would I do that for you?'

'Not for me. You've seen what he does to these children. Do it for the people we live with. Do it for the children we don't know and will never meet. I don't have the authority to request those files. You do. Look for cases of murdered children, solved or unsolved. There'll be a pattern: their mouths stuffed with bark, their stomachs missing. Their bodies will probably have been found near train stations. They'll have string tied round their ankles.'

'I'd be taking a great risk.'

'Yes, you would. And you'd have to lie. You couldn't tell anyone the real reason. And in return for your bravery, you might end up dead. That is my offer.' Leo stretched out his hand across the table. 'Will you help me?'

Nesterov moved to the window and stood beside his wife. She didn't look at him, but swirled the vodka at the bottom of her glass. Would he risk his family, his home, everything he'd worked for?

'No.'

West of the town of Gukovo, April 2

Petya was awake before dawn. On the cold stone steps of their farmhouse, he waited impatiently for sunrise so that he might ask his parents' permission to walk into town. After months of saving he had enough to buy another stamp, which would bring him to the last page of his album. He'd been given his first set of stamps on his fifth birthday by his father, and it had become an obsession. Over the past two years he'd collected stamps from other families working on the *kolkhoz*—Collective Farm 12. He stuck them in a cheap paper album, which he kept in a wooden box. His father had made the box for him, because Petya had been unable to sleep at night, constantly checking that water wasn't leaking in through the roof or that rats hadn't eaten the precious pages. Every now and then his parents gave him the occasional kopek. In exchange he always made sure he did a little extra work around the farm. Last night he'd been given another kopek.

As the sun began to rise, Petya hurried inside. His mother insisted that he eat a bowl of oatmeal before going anywhere. He ate it as fast as he could. Finished, he ran out of the house, reaching the track that snaked through the fields on its way towards Gukovo, the nearest town.

In Gukovo, the kiosk that sold stamps and newspapers was still closed. Petya didn't know when it would open, but didn't mind waiting. He wandered the streets, then stopped by the *elektrichka* station. A train was due to leave, and he walked onto the platform and sat down to watch it. The *elektrichka* was a slow train that stopped at every destination on the way to Rostov. He and some of his schoolfriends occasionally boarded the train for no reason other than they knew they could do so for free. Tickets were rarely checked.

He was almost ready to return to the kiosk when a man sat down beside him. The man was smartly dressed and had a black case, which he put on the ground between his legs. Petya looked up at his face. He had thick square glasses, neat black hair, and was wearing a suit. He wasn't properly old, with grey hair. But then again he wasn't properly young either.

Suddenly, the man turned and smiled. 'Where are you travelling to today?'

'I'm not going anywhere, sir. Not on a train, I mean. I'm just sitting here.' Petya had been taught to be polite and respectful towards elders. 'I'm waiting to buy some stamps but the kiosk isn't open yet.'

The man turned his whole body towards Petya. 'You collect stamps?'

'Yes, sir.'

'I used to be a stamp collector when I was your age.'

Petya sat back, relaxing—he didn't know anyone else who collected stamps. 'Did you collect new stamps or used stamps? I collect both.'

'All of mine were new. I bought them from a kiosk. Just like you.'

'I wish all mine were new. But they're mostly used. Cut off old envelopes.'

'Do you look after your stamps?' the man asked.

'I take good care of them. I put them in an album. And my dad has made me a wooden box. That's to keep the album safe.'

'That's sensible.' The man seemed to weigh something up in his mind. 'Listen, neither of my daughters is interested in stamps. And I no longer have time for stamps—I'm busy with my work. Here's my idea: I'd like my collection to go to a person who'd take care of it, a person just like you.'

Petya considered the prospect of a book filled with new stamps. They'd date back for as long as this man had been collecting. It would be the collection he'd always dreamed of. He said nothing, unable to believe his luck.

'Well? Would that interest you?'

'Yes, sir. I could put it in my wooden box and it would be safe.'

'And you're sure you'd look after the stamps?'

'Yes, sir. I promise, sir.'

The man smiled. 'You've convinced me. You can have it. I only live three stops away. Come on, I'll buy you a ticket.'

Petya was about to say that a ticket was unnecessary but he swallowed the words. Until he got the stamps, he needed this man's good opinion.

SITTING ON THE WOODEN SEAT of the *elektrichka*, Petya swung his legs backwards and forwards. It now seemed unnecessary to spend his kopeks on a new stamp, considering the stamps he was about to acquire, and he decided to return the money to his parents. They could share in his good fortune.

The man interrupted his thoughts. 'We're here.'

The *elektrichka* had stopped in the middle of the woods. Petya was confused. This was a leisure stop for people wanting to get away from the towns.

He turned to his companion. 'You live here?'

The man shook his head. 'My dacha is here. I can't keep my stamps at home. My children might find them and touch them with their dirty fingers.'

He got off the train. Petya followed. No one else disembarked.

The man walked into the woods, Petya just behind. Having a dacha made a kind of sense. Petya didn't know anyone rich enough to have a summer home, but he knew they were often situated in woods or by lakes.

The man stepped off the path, walking through the undergrowth with quite some speed. Petya almost had to run to keep up.

'Sir, what's your name? I'd like to be able to tell my parents the name of the man who gave me the stamps, in case they don't believe me.'

'Don't worry. I'll write your parents a note explaining everything.'

'Thank you very much, sir.'

'Call me Andrei.'

After some time, the man stopped walking and bent down, opening his case. Petya couldn't see any sign of this dacha. Catching his breath, he stared up at the leafless branches of the tall trees that crisscrossed the grey sky.

ANDREI STARED DOWN at the boy's body. Blood ran down the side of the boy's head. Kneeling, Andrei felt for a pulse on his neck. He was alive. That was good. He rolled the boy onto his back and undressed him. He gathered the clothes in a bundle, picked up his case and walked away. After twenty paces he dropped the clothes beside a fallen tree, opened his case and pulled out a ball of coarse string. He returned to the boy, tying one end of the string round his ankle. Walking backwards, he carefully unwound the string. He reached the fallen tree, and lay down on the ground behind it.

He'd chosen a good spot. When the boy awoke, he'd be out of sight. There was still plenty of string left in his hand, at least another fifteen paces' worth. Andrei took off his glasses, slipped them into his jacket pocket and looked back. Now the child was just a blur. Andrei snapped a twig off the tree and began to chew the bark, his teeth turning brown.

PETYA OPENED HIS EYES. His head was sticky with blood. He touched it and looked at his fingers, beginning to cry. He was cold. He was naked. What had happened? Where was that man? Trembling, he sat up, hardly daring to breathe. He couldn't see the man anywhere. Raising himself into a crouch, Petya stared into the forest. The man was gone. He breathed deeply, relieved.

He peered around for his clothes. They were gone. He jumped up and began to run, his feet crunching across fallen branches, the soil wet from rain and snow melt. He wasn't sure if he was running in the right direction. All he knew was that he had to get away.

Suddenly his right foot was pulled back, as though a hand had grabbed his ankle. Petya toppled forward, falling to the ground. He rolled onto his back, looking behind him. He couldn't see anyone. He was about to stand again when he caught sight of the string tied round his right ankle. His eyes followed its trail into the forest to a fallen tree some forty paces away.

He grabbed the string, trying to pull it down over his ankle. But it was so tight it dug into his skin. The string was pulled again, harder this time. Petya was wrenched across the ground. When he came to a stop he looked up. There he was, that man, behind the tree, reeling him in. Petya concentrated on the knot. He couldn't undo it. He couldn't break the string. He had no choice but to tug it down, scraping the skin round his ankle. The string was pulled again, sinking into his flesh. He grabbed a handful of wet mud, lubricating the string. Just as the man pulled again, Petya freed himself from the noose. He leapt to his feet and ran.

THE STRING WAS SLACK in Andrei's hands. There was nothing at the end of it. He squinted but he couldn't see anything. Should he put his glasses on? No, he'd never had that option as a child. He'd been stuck like this—nearly blind, alone, stumbling through the forest.

He's leaving you behind.

Andrei followed the string. Reaching the end of it, he stopped and stared all around, squinting hard. He couldn't see him. The boy was gone. Andrei was alone, abandoned. Then, there, to the right, movement—a light colour, the colour of skin, a boy. Andrei ran, taking long strides, his jacket flapping. He collided with the boy at speed and they both fell to the ground. Andrei was on top, the boy wriggling underneath, scratching and biting his jacket.

Andrei muttered, 'It's still alive!'

He pulled out the long hunting knife attached to his belt. Closing his eyes, he jabbed the blade underneath him, only with the tip at first, small stabs, listening to its screams. He waited, savouring this moment. The blade went in further. When it was in up to the hilt, the child was no longer moving.

THREE MONTHS LATER

The Sea of Azov, July 4

Nesterov sat with his toes buried in the sand. This stretch of beach was popular with people living in the nearby city of Rostov-on-Don. Today it was crowded. Nesterov's two sons were playing in the shallow water; his wife lay beside him, her eyes closed. They had every reason to be relaxed—they were on holiday, allowed the use of an official militia car, with a State voucher for fuel, as a reward for the discreet and efficient handling of two murder investigations. He'd been ordered to take it easy.

The trial of Varlam Babinich had lasted two days. According to proce-dure, the defence were forced to rely upon the testimony of the same expert witnesses used by the prosecution. Since there were no psychiatrists work-ing at Hospital 379, the prosecution had selected a doctor with no specialist training. Called to make a judgment, this doctor had stated that he believed Babinich understood the difference between right and wrong and knew murder was wrong; after all, he'd said upon arrest: 'I'm in so much trouble.'

The defence then had no choice but to call the same doctor and attempt to prove insanity. Varlam Babinich had been found guilty. Nesterov had received a letter confirming that the seventeen-year-old had died on his knees, shot in the back of the head.

Dr Tyapkin's case had taken barely a day. His wife had testified that he was violent, described his sick fantasies and claimed that she hadn't come forward before because she'd feared for her own life and for the life of her baby. In exchange for this testimony she'd been transferred to the Ukraine, where she could continue her life without the stigma of her husband's crime.

With these two cases concluded, the court had processed over 150 cases against men accused of anti-Soviet behaviour. These homosexuals had received hard-labour sentences of between five and twenty-five years.

Several nights after the conclusion of the trials, as Nesterov lay awake, his wife had told him it was only a matter of time before he agreed to help Leo. She wished he'd just get on and do it. Had he been waiting for her permis-sion? Perhaps he had. He was gambling with his family's lives as well as his own. Independent action was always a risk, since it implied that the struc-tures put in place by the State had failed. All the same, he was confident that he could begin a quiet kind of investigation, which would appear to be no more than conversations between colleagues. If he discovered that there were no similar cases, no other murdered children, he could be sure that the punishments he'd been instrumental in bringing about had been just.

For the past ten weeks, Nesterov had operated on his own. Since Leo was almost certainly under surveillance, all he'd done was to scribble him a short note—*I'll help*—including instructions to destroy the note immediately.

There was no easy way of accessing regional criminal files. He'd made phone calls and written letters, mentioning the subject in passing, praising the efficiency of his department for the swift resolution of their two cases in an attempt to provoke similar boasts. He'd been forced to make several off-duty train journeys, meeting colleagues, drinking with them. It was an extraordinarily inefficient means of collecting information. Three hours of drinking might provide two minutes of useful conversation. After eight weeks Nesterov had called Leo into his office.

When Leo came in, Nesterov had checked the corridors and locked the office door. Then he'd reached under his desk and taken out a map of the Soviet Union, which he'd spread across the desk. He'd picked up a handful of pins and stuck two into the map at Voualsk, two in Molotov, two in Vyatka, two in Gorky and two in Kazan. These pins formed a row of towns that followed the train line west towards Moscow. Nesterov hadn't been to Moscow, fearing its militia officers would be suspicious of any enquiries. West of Moscow, Nesterov had found only one possible incident, in Tver. Moving south, he stuck three pins in Tula, two in Orel and two in Belgorod. Now into the Ukraine, he put three pins in Kharkov and Gorlovka, four in Zaporoshy, three in Kramatorsk and one in Kiev. Moving out of the Ukraine, there were five pins in Taganrog and finally six pins in and around Rostov.

Nesterov had understood Leo's reaction—stunned silence. He'd collected this information in a comparable frame of mind. The similarities were striking: the dirt in the victim's mouths, the mutilated torsos, the string round the ankles. The bodies were always naked, the clothes piled some distance away. The crime scenes were in forests or parks and often near train stations. No town had spoken to another, even though some crimes had occurred less than fifty kilometres apart. They'd been solved by blaming drunks, thieves or convicted rapists—undesirables, to whom any allegation would stick.

By his count there were forty-three in total. Nesterov had taken another pin from the box and stuck it into Moscow, making Arkady child 44.

NESTEROV WOKE to find the side of his face pressed against the sand. He sat up, brushing the sand off. He looked for his children, searching the beach. His elder son, Efim, seven, sat near the water's edge. But his younger son— only five—was nowhere to be seen.

Nesterov turned to his wife. 'Where's Vadim?'

Inessa had been slicing dried meat for their lunch. She looked up, her eyes finding their elder son but not their younger. She got up, checking behind her. They both moved forward and knelt down beside Efim.

'Where's your brother?' Nesterov asked.

'He said he was going back to you.'

'When?'

'I don't know. Not long ago. I'm not sure.'

Nesterov stood again. Vadim hadn't wanted to swim. He was on the beach, somewhere among these hundreds of people. Images from the case files rose into his mind. One young girl had been murdered off a popular riverside trail. Another young girl had been murdered yards from her house.

He took Efim's hand. 'Come with me. We'll both look for your brother.'

His wife went up the beach, in the opposite direction, while Nesterov walked down, weaving in and out of people, walking too quickly for Efim, so he picked his son up, carrying him. The beach came to an end, tapering off into long grass and reeds. Vadim was nowhere to be seen.

AT THE OTHER END of the beach Inessa called for her son. She'd read the documents pertaining to her husband's investigation. She knew what had happened to these missing children. Panicking, she blamed herself entirely. She'd encouraged her husband to help Leo. Tying their holiday into the investigation had been her idea. Since the greatest concentration of murders had taken place in the south of the country, the only way Nesterov could make a substantial expedition unnoticed would be to use his family holiday as a cover. Only now did she fully understand that she'd put her children in danger. She'd taken them into the heartland of this mysterious evil.

Short of breath, shouting for her son, her eyes filled with tears. People circled her. She begged them to help her.

'He's only five years old. He's been taken. We have to find him.'

'He'll be here somewhere,' said a stern-looking woman.

'You don't understand. He's in terrible danger.' She pushed the woman out of the way, turning round and round, calling his name.

Suddenly a man took hold of her arms. 'Why don't you calm down?'

'No, he'll be killed. He'll be murdered. You have to help me find him.'

The man laughed. 'No one is going to be killed. He's quite safe.'

She tried to break free. 'Let go of me! I need to find my son.'

Suddenly her husband broke through the crowd. He was carrying both their children, and explained that he'd found Vadim playing in the tall reeds. The man let go of Inessa's arm. She took hold of her younger son, clutching his head as though it were fragile and might break. They stood together as a family, surrounded, hostile faces all around.

They left the crowd, hurriedly collected their stuff and headed to the car.

ON THE BEACH, a thin woman with a touch of grey in her hair watched as the car disappeared. She'd made a note of the number plate, having decided this was a family that needed investigating.

Moscow, July 5

Until yesterday, there had been nothing directly linking Raisa to Leo's unauthorised investigation. She could have denounced him and there might have been a chance she'd survive. That was no longer true. On a train nearing Moscow, travelling under false papers, their guilt was indivisible.

They had no official business in Moscow. If caught they would die. The reason for their venture was a woman called Galina Shaporina, the eyewitness who could describe the killer, flesh him out—make him real. Leo and Raisa had as yet no idea of what kind of man they were searching for.

Raisa had also proposed talking to Ivan, her colleague from school. He had access to censored Western publications and might be aware of case studies about comparable crimes from abroad: random, multiple, ritualised murders. Leo appreciated that such material would be of benefit, but was keen to reduce their interaction to as few people as possible. He wasn't convinced that Ivan was worth the risk.

The train came to a stop at Yaroslavavski Vokzal. Leo glanced out of the window, waiting for everyone to disembark. All major transport junctions were patrolled by undercover and uniformed agents. Nowhere was layered in more levels of protection than Moscow.

Leo turned to Raisa. 'If you happen to catch their eye, a guard or anyone else, don't immediately look away. Don't smile or make any gestures. Just hold eye contact and then look at something else.'

They stepped down onto the platform, carrying their small bags. Leo tried to reassure himself that there was no chance any agents here were looking for them. Back at Voualsk, they'd got permission to go on a walking holiday in the mountains for a couple of days. They'd set off into the forest, trekking in a loop. Once they were sure they weren't being followed, they'd returned to the forest near the station. They'd changed out of their muddy clothes, buried them and boarded the train to Moscow. Should all go according to plan, they'd return to Voualsk, slip into the forest, change back into their muddy clothes and re-enter the town from one of the northern forest trails.

They were almost at the exit when a man called out, 'Papers.'

Without hesitating, Leo turned. He didn't smile or try to appear relaxed. He handed over his papers. Raisa handed over hers.

Leo studied the man's face. His eyes were slow, his movements sluggish. This was a routine stop and search. The papers, however, were fake. Nesterov had provided them, doctoring them with Leo's help. The agent's lips moved as his eyes scanned the lines, as though he could barely read.

Finally he slapped the documents against his palm. 'Let me see your bags.'

Leo and Raisa opened their bags. They carried little more than a change of clothes. The officer was becoming bored. He shrugged. In reply they nodded reverentially at him and moved towards the exit.

HAVING QUASHED Fyodor Andreev's own investigation into the murder of his son and then bullied him into silence, Leo was about to ask for his help. He needed Fyodor to take him to Galina Shaporina's apartment.

Leo was banking on Fyodor's loyalty to the memory of his son, and his desire for justice. But perhaps Fyodor had come to terms with Leo's assessment of the situation four months ago: an unauthorised investigation into the death of his son would put his entire family at risk. Would he decide to turn Leo over to the State? Leo knocked on the door. He was about to find out.

Apartment Block 18, fourth floor, an elderly woman opened the door—the woman who'd stood up to him.

'My name is Leo. This is my wife, Raisa.'

The old woman stared at Leo, remembering him. 'What do you want?'

Raisa answered, her voice low. 'We're here about the murder of Arkady.'

There was a long silence, the old woman studying both their faces before replying, 'You've come to the wrong address. No boy was murdered here.'

As she went to close the door, Leo put his foot forward. 'You were right.'

LEO EXPECTED ANGER. But instead the woman began to cry.

Fyodor, his wife and the elderly woman, Fyodor's mother, stood together, watching as Leo took off his coat, dropping it onto the chair. He pulled off his jumper and unbuttoned his shirt. Underneath, taped to his body, were the photos, descriptions, statements, maps—the evidence they'd accumulated.

'These are the details of over forty murders, children, both boys and girls, murdered across the western half of our country. They were killed in almost exactly the same way as I now believe your son was killed.'

Leo pulled the papers free. Fyodor took hold of them. His wife stepped forward, as did his mother. Soon all three were reading the documents.

Fyodor's wife spoke first. 'And if you catch him, what will you do?'

Remarkably, it was the first time Leo had been asked that question. Until now they'd concentrated on whether it was even possible to catch him.

'I'll kill him.'

Fyodor wasted no time with recriminations. He would take them to Galina's apartment immediately.

As THEY NEARED the building, Fyodor argued that Leo should remain outside; they couldn't risk him scaring her into silence again. Leo agreed.

Raisa followed Fyodor up the stairs, reached the apartment door and knocked. The door was opened by a woman in her thirties. Her eyes were nervous, taking in every detail of Raisa's and Fyodor's appearance.

'Galina, you remember me? I'm Fyodor, father of Arkady, the little boy who was murdered. This is my friend Raisa. She lives in Voualsk, a town near the Urals. Galina, the reason we're here is because the man who murdered my son is murdering other children, in other towns. That is why Raisa has travelled to Moscow, so that we can work together. We need your help.'

'How can I help?' Galina whispered. 'I don't know anything.'

'Fyodor isn't here as an officer of the MGB,' Raisa pointed out. 'We're a group made of fathers and mothers, any citizens outraged at these crimes. Your name won't appear in any documents; there are no documents. You'll never see or hear from us again. All we need to know is what he looks like.'

'But the man I saw wasn't with a child. I told you that. I can't help you.'

'Please, Galina, let us in for a second,' Fyodor said, becoming agitated.

Raisa touched his arm. They couldn't bully her. Patience was the key.

'OK, that's OK, Galina. You didn't see a man with a child. Fyodor explained that you saw a man with a tool bag, is that right?'

The woman nodded.

'Can you describe him for us?'

Galina considered. Raisa held her breath. They just needed a description, thrown away, deniable. Thirty seconds, that was all it would take.

Suddenly Fyodor cut through the silence. 'There's no harm in telling us what a man with a tool bag looked like,' he said. 'No one can get in trouble for describing a railway worker.'

Raisa stared at Fyodor. He'd made a mistake. People *could* get in trouble for describing a railway worker. They could get in trouble for much less.

Galina shook her head, stepping back. 'I'm sorry, it was dark. I didn't see.'

Fyodor put his hand on the door. 'No, Galina, please . . .'

'Leave.' Her voice became shrill with worry. 'Leave! Please, please . . .'

Galina's husband appeared. 'What's going on?'

Apartment doors opened; people were staring, alarming Galina further.

Sensing that they were losing control of the situation, Raisa moved forward, hugging Galina, as if saying goodbye. 'What did he look like?'

Cheek to cheek, Raisa waited, closing her eyes, hoping. She could feel Galina's breath. But Galina did not reply.

Rostov-on-Don

The cat perched on the window ledge, its tail flicking from side to side, its cool green eyes following Nadya round the room. She was six years old; the cat was nine. That might explain its superior attitude. According to her father, the area they lived in had a problem with rats, so cats were essential. Well, Nadya had never seen this cat do anything useful about the rats. It was a lazy cat, spoilt rotten by her father. And it never allowed her to touch it.

Unable to remain in the house with the cat staring at her, she decided to go for a walk. It was late and her mother was in the kitchen preparing *uzhin*. Knowing she'd be refused permission, Nadya sneaked out of the front door.

They lived on a bank of the River Don, her younger sister, her mother and father. The city's sewage and factory waste fed into the river just upstream. Nadya turned downstream, along a well-trodden path towards the country-side. Though there was very little light, she was confident of the route.

She'd been walking for a little while, humming to herself, when suddenly she saw a man walking towards her. He was tall and carrying some kind of case, but in the gloom she couldn't tell much else about him. Normally the sight of a stranger wouldn't have bothered her. But her mother had recently sat Nadya and her sister down and warned them not to talk to strangers. Nadya looked back towards her house. The thing was, she really wanted to climb her favourite tree further downstream. She decided she'd just walk straight past this man and, if he spoke to her, she'd say *good evening* but not stop.

She continued along the path. The man seemed to be walking faster. It was too dark to see his face. He was wearing some sort of hat. Nadya felt an inexplicable urge to hurry past him. She broke into a run. Concerned this would insult the gentleman, she called out, 'Good evening.'

With his free arm, the man grabbed her round the waist, lifting her frame clear off the ground, bringing her face close to his, staring into her eyes. She was terrified, holding her breath, her little body rigid with tension.

And then Nadya began to laugh. Recovering from her surprise, she put her arms round her father's neck and hugged him. 'You scared me.'

'Does your mother know you're outside so late?'

'Uh, yes. Why are you coming from this direction? Where have you been?'

'I've been working. I had some business in one of the villages just outside the city. There was no way to get back except to walk.'

'You must be tired.'

'Yes, I am.'

'Father, I'm glad you're home.'

STILL CARRYING NADYA, Andrei stepped into the kitchen. His youngest daughter ran over to greet him. He watched his family's pleasure at his return.

The cat jumped down from the window, rubbing itself against his leg. As Andrei lowered Nadya to the floor, she dropped her foot onto the cat's paw, causing it to screech and dart away.

Trembling with anger, he took hold of her wrist. 'Don't ever touch her.' Nadya bit her lip. Andrei let go of her wrist. He felt flustered and hot.

His wife smiled at him. 'Have you eaten?'

'I have to put my things away. I don't want anything to eat.'

'Was your work successful?'

'They want me to go away again in a couple of days. I'm not sure for how long.' Without waiting for a reply, he moved to the door leading to the basement. The cat followed him, its tail up high, excited.

He locked the door behind him and descended the stairs, feeling better now that he was on his own. An elderly couple had previously occupied this space but the woman had died and the man had moved out. The housing bureau hadn't sent anyone to replace them. It wasn't a nice room: a basement sunk into the riverbank. The bricks were always wet. In winter it was freezing. There was a *burzhuika*, a wood-fired stove, which the elderly couple had kept running for eight months of the year. But the basement had one advantage: it was his space. He had a chair in one corner and a slender bed. He occasionally slept down here. He lit the gas lamp, and another cat entered through a hole in the wall where the pipes from the *burzhuika* ran outside.

He opened his case. Among his papers was a glass jar. He unscrewed the lid. Inside, wrapped in newspaper, was the stomach of the girl he'd murdered some hours ago. Carefully he peeled the paper away. He put the stomach on a tin plate and cut it into cubes. Then he fired up the stove. By the time it was hot enough, there were six cats circling him. He fried the meat, then tipped it back onto the tin plate. Andrei stood watching the cats, holding the food, teasing them. They were frenzied by the smell of cooked meat.

After he'd had his fill of teasing them, he put the food down. The cats squeezed together round the plate and began to eat, purring with delight.

ON VOROVSKI STREET, Leo and Raisa joined the back of the grocery-store queue. Once inside, each person would place their order before being made to wait in a second queue to pay. After that, there was a third queue to collect the item. They could easily remain in these various lines for up to four hours, waiting inconspicuously for Ivan to come home.

Having failed to persuade Galina Shaporina to speak, they were in danger of coming away from Moscow with nothing. Their only achievement so far was to recruit Fyodor and his family into their investigation. They were no closer to identifying the kind of man they were looking for. Under these circumstances, Leo had reluctantly agreed that they had no option but to speak to the school teacher, Ivan. Raisa hadn't been able to get a message to him and so they'd taken a calculated risk, hoping that he'd be here.

They were almost at the shop door when they saw Ivan approach. They didn't call out or draw attention to themselves, watching as he entered his building. Leo checked the street for agents. After several minutes, he was confident there was no one following Ivan. They left the queue and entered the apartment building. Leo followed Raisa up the stairs. She knocked on the door. Footsteps could be heard inside.

'Yes?' asked a voice, nervous, through the door.

'Ivan, it's Raisa.'

A bolt was pulled back. Ivan cautiously opened the door. Upon seeing Raisa his suspicions dropped away and he smiled. She smiled in reply.

A couple of steps back, Leo watched their reunion from the gloom of the hallway. She was pleased to see him, her kindred spirit; they were easy together. Ivan opened the door, hugging her, relieved that she was still alive.

Then the teacher noticed Leo for the first time and he let go of Raisa, suddenly unsure, checking her expression for signs of betrayal.

'Why are you here?'

'We have a lot to explain. It would be better to speak inside.' Raisa touched his arm. 'Please, trust me.'

The apartment was small, well furnished, with polished wooden floors. There were books; at a glance they all seemed to be authorised texts, Gorky, political tracts, Marx. The door to the bedroom was shut.

'Are we alone?' Leo asked.

'My children are with my parents. My wife's in hospital. Tuberculosis.'

Raisa touched his arm again. 'Ivan, I'm so sorry.'

'We thought you'd been arrested. I feared the worst.'

'We were lucky. We've been relocated to a town just west of the Urals. Leo refused to denounce me.'

Ivan couldn't keep the surprise from his face. He stared at Leo, evaluating. 'Are you still MGB?'

'No, I was demoted to the militia, exiled.'

'You've travelled all the way to Moscow? Why?'

'We need help.'

At this, he was puzzled. 'What could I possibly help you with?'

Leo took off his coat, his jumper, his shirt—retrieving the files taped to his body. He summarised the case, offering the papers to Ivan.

Ivan didn't look at them, placing the evidence on the table. He collected a pipe and carefully filled it. 'And you two are working together now?'

Raisa blushed. 'Yes, we're working together.'

'You trust him?'

'I trust him.'

'And together you plan to solve this crime?'

Leo answered. 'If the State won't, then the people will have to.'

'Spoken like a true revolutionary. Except, Leo, you've spent your entire life murdering for the State. Now I'm supposed to believe you're thinking for yourself? I don't believe it. I'm sorry, Raisa. I think he's trying to win his way back into the MGB. He's duped you, and now he wants to hand them me.'

'He's not, Ivan. Look at the evidence. This is real, not some trick.'

'I haven't trusted paper evidence for a long time, nor should you.'

'I've seen one of these bodies, a young boy, his stomach cut open, his mouth filled with bark. I've seen it, Ivan. Someone enjoyed doing this and they're not going to stop. You have every right to be suspicious of us. But I can't prove it to you. If you can't trust me, then I'm sorry for coming here.'

Leo stepped forward, ready to collect up the files.

Ivan put his hand on top of them. 'I'll take a look. Both of you sit down.'

Raisa and Leo sat opposite Ivan and narrated the specifics of the case.

Leo summed up his own conclusions. 'Since it's very difficult to move about this country without a designated reason, he must have a job that involves travel. He must be integrated into society; he must be acceptable, respectable. The question we can't answer is why he does it. How can I catch him if I don't understand why? I have no image of him in my mind, no idea what kind of person we're looking for, beyond the basics.'

Ivan was smoking his pipe, absorbing everything Leo had said.

'I'm afraid I cannot help you.'

Raisa sat forward. 'But you have Western articles about these kinds of crime, murders that aren't conventionally motivated?'

'They wouldn't be enough to give you an image of this man.'

Leo slumped in his chair. This had been a wasted journey.

Ivan drew on his pipe. 'However, I know a man who might be able to help. His name is Professor Zauzayez, a retired psychiatrist, a former MGB interrogator. He lost his sight. Going blind gave him a change of heart, an epiphany, just like you, Leo. He's now active in underground circles. Perhaps he'd be able to shed some light on the kind of person who'd do this.'

'Where does he live?' Leo asked.

'He won't allow you to go to his apartment. He's very cautious. He'll come here, if he'll come at all. I'll do my best to convince him.'

Raisa smiled. 'Thank you.'

Leo was pleased: an expert was certainly better than some journalistic scraps. Ivan stood up, putting his pipe down, moving to the telephone.

The telephone.

This man had a telephone, in his tidy, well-furnished apartment. Leo took in the details of the room. Something was wrong. Why did Ivan and his family live in such comparative luxury? How had he managed to escape arrest after their exile? How had he evaded the authorities?

The call had been set up. Ivan was now speaking on the phone.

'Professor Zauzayez, Ivan Zhukov here. I have an interesting task I need your help with. Are you free at the moment? Could you come to my apartment? Yes, immediately, if that's possible.'

Leo leapt up, his chair flying back. He was across the room before Ivan had a chance to react, grabbing the phone and twisting its cord round Ivan's neck. Ivan's legs slipped on the polished floor; he gasped, unable to speak.

Stunned, Raisa got out of her chair. 'Leo!'

With the cord still wrapped round Ivan's neck, Leo lifted the receiver to his ear. 'Professor Zauzayez?'

The phone went dead. They'd hung up. They were on their way.

'LEO, LET HIM GO!'

Raisa stared in horror. Ivan's face was turning red.

Leo tightened the cord. 'He's an operative, he's under cover. Look at how he lives. Look at his home. There is no Professor Zauzayez. That was his State Security contact; he's on his way to arrest us.'

'Leo, you're making a mistake. I know this man.'

'He's a fake dissident, placed underground, flushing out anti-authority figures. Haven't all your friends been arrested, every one, except for him? That woman Zoya, where do you think the MGB got her name from?'

Raisa stared at Leo, then at Ivan. It was true: all her friends were dead or arrested, all except him. She caught sight of Ivan's hand reaching for the cabinet drawer. 'Leo, wait!'

'We don't have time!'

She opened the drawer. Inside was a letter-opener, sharp—the item Ivan was reaching for to defend himself. Behind that was a book, his copy of *For Whom the Bell Tolls*. She picked it up. A sheet of paper was inside. On it was written a list of names: people the book had been loaned to. Some names were scored through. Her name had been scored through. On the other side was a list of people he intended to loan the book to.

She turned to Ivan, raising the sheet of paper to his face, her hand shaking. No dissident would be foolish enough to write down a list of names. He loaned the book to incriminate.

She'd trusted him, solely on the basis of his books and papers, his musings on Western culture, his alleged plans to help dissident writers smuggle their works out to the West. All lies. She'd fallen for Ivan because of his obvious differences to Leo. The difference had been a disguise. The dissident had been the policeman and the policeman had become the counterrevolutionary.

Leo was struggling to hold Ivan. 'Raisa, turn away.'

She obeyed, walking to the other side of the room, crumpling the sheet of paper into her pocket, listening as Ivan's legs kicked the furniture.

BEFORE THEY LEFT the apartment, Leo had hurriedly gathered together the case file. He and Raisa had run down the stairs, then walked away, approximating calmness. As they'd reached the end of the street they'd glanced back. State Security agents were entering the building.

In their current predicament, trying to see his parents was an act of sheer brazenness. If Vasili wanted to catch Leo violating orders, then his parents were the perfect trap. But there was no train back to Voualsk until five in the morning, and this would be Leo's last chance to speak to them. Although he'd been refused contact with his parents, he'd acquired their address several weeks ago. He had to reach them without alerting the family they were sharing with, who were probably informers. He had to say goodbye.

They'd arrived on Ulitsa Vorontsovskaya. The house in question was an old, pre-Revolutionary building that had been sliced into a hundred tiny apartments, partitioned by nothing more than dirty sheets hanging from lengths of rope. There would be no running water, no indoor toilets. Pipes jutted out of the windows to release the smoke from the wood stoves. Leo turned to Raisa.

Before he could speak, she said, 'I'll wait here.'

Leo took her hand. 'I'd like you to come with me.'

The communal door was unlocked. The air inside was hot, stale, and they began to sweat. Upstairs, the door to apartment 27 was locked. Leo had broken into many properties. Using the tip of a flick knife, he unscrewed the plate. He inserted the blade into the lock mechanism. It clicked open.

The only light came from the window facing the street. Leo and Raisa could distinguish the outline of three beds, two containing adult couples. A smaller bed appeared to have three children sleeping in it. In the kitchen area two small children slept on rugs on the floor. Leo moved towards the sleeping adults. Neither of the couples were his parents.

Seeing the outline of another door, he moved towards it, the floorboards straining under each step. Raisa was of much lighter tread. The couple in the nearest bed began to stir. Leo paused, waiting for them to settle down. The couple remained asleep. Leo continued, Raisa following.

There were no windows in this room. Leo had to keep the door open in order to see anything. He could make out two single beds, with barely a gap between them. One bed contained two children. In the other bed there was an adult couple. He moved closer. These were his parents.

Leo returned to Raisa. 'Shut the door,' he whispered.

In total darkness, Leo felt his way along the bed until he was crouched on the floor beside his parents. He was crying. The room they'd been forced to share was smaller than the bathroom of their previous apartment.

He placed his hands over their mouths. He could feel them waking, startled, tense. 'It's me. Leo,' he whispered. 'Don't make a noise.'

The tension in their bodies disappeared. He removed his hands from their mouths. He could hear them sitting up. He felt his mother's hands on his face. Her fingers stopped moving when they felt his tears. He heard her whisper, 'Leo . . .' His father's hands joined hers.

Leo pressed their hands against his face. He had sworn to look after them and he'd failed. 'I'm sorry,' he muttered.

'You've nothing to apologise for,' his father replied. 'We would have lived like this all of our life had it not been for you.'

His mother interrupted. 'We thought you were imprisoned. We were told you'd both been arrested.'

'They lied. We've been sent to Voualsk. I was demoted. I'm now working for the militia. I wrote to you many times, asking that the letters be forwarded to you, but they must have been destroyed.'

The children in the nearby bed stirred. Everyone fell silent. Leo waited until he could hear the children's deep, slow breathing.

'Raisa is here.'

He guided their hands to her. All four of them held hands.

'The baby?' his mother asked.

'No,' Raisa said.

Not wanting to complicate this reunion, Leo added, 'Miscarriage.'

Raisa spoke again, her voice broken with emotion. 'I'm sorry.'

'This is not your fault,' Anna said sadly, then added, 'How long are you in Moscow for? Can we meet tomorrow?'

'No,' Leo said, 'we shouldn't be here at all. If we're caught we'll be imprisoned and you will be too. We leave first thing in the morning.'

No one spoke for a while, four sets of hands clasped in the darkness.

'I have to get you a better place to live,' Leo said eventually.

'No, Leo,' his mother replied. 'Listen to me. You've often behaved as if our love was dependent on the things you could do for us. That is not true. You must concentrate on *your* lives. We're old. It doesn't matter where we live any more. The only thing that has kept us alive is waiting for news from you. We must accept that this will be the last time we meet. Leo, I love you and I'm proud of you. I wish you could have had a better government to serve.'

Anna's voice was quite calm. 'You have each other, you love each other. You will have a good life, I believe that. Things will be different for you and for your children. Russia will be different. I feel very hopeful.'

Stepan took hold of Leo's hand, placing in it an envelope. 'This is a letter I wrote to you many months ago. I never had the chance to give it to you. It contains everything your mother and I wanted to say to you but were unable to for one reason or another. It contains all the things we should have spoken about a long time ago. Read it when you're safely on the train.'

'Father . . .'

'Take it, Leo, for us.'

Leo accepted the letter, and the four of them hugged for the last time.

July 6

Leo approached the train, Raisa beside him. Were there more officers than usual on the platform? Raisa was walking too fast; he took hold of her hand, briefly, and she slowed. They boarded the crowded train.

'Stay here,' Leo whispered to Raisa.

She nodded. He entered the cramped toilet, locking the door behind him. Taking off his jacket, unbuttoning his shirt, he removed the thin cotton bag he'd stitched to hold the case file. He found the letter. It was crumpled, dirty. His father must have kept it on his person day and night.

The train began to move, leaving Moscow. He opened the envelope and unfolded the letter. It was his father's handwriting.

Leo, neither your mother nor I have any regrets. We love you. We always expected there would come a day when we'd talk about this matter. We thought you'd raise it when you were ready. But you never did, you always acted as though it never happened. Perhaps it was easier to teach yourself to forget? This is why we said nothing. We were afraid that bringing it up again would only cause pain. We were happy together and we didn't want to ruin that. That was cowardly of us.

I say again, both I and your mother love you very much, and . . .

Leo stopped reading. Yes, he remembered what had happened. He knew what the letter would go on to say. And yes, he'd spent his whole life trying to forget. He ripped the letter into tiny pieces. He stood up, opening the small window, throwing the fragments out. Caught in the wind, the paper rose up into the air and disappeared from view.

16 km north of Rostov-on-Don

Nesterov had spent his last day in the *oblast* visiting the town of Gukovo. He was now on the *elektrichka*, travelling back to Rostov. Though the newspapers made no mention of these crimes, the incidents of murdered children had entered the public domain in the form of rumour. People outside the militia had begun to thread these deaths together. Unofficial explanations had begun to circulate. Nesterov had heard it stated that there was a wild beast murdering children in the forest, and supernatural theories abounded.

The people living in the Rostov *oblast* had no idea that there were similar crimes hundreds of kilometres away. They believed this was *their* blight, an evil that plagued *them*. In a way Nesterov agreed. There was no doubt in his mind that he was in the heartland of these crimes. The concentration of murders was far higher here than anywhere else. While he had no inclination to believe the supernatural explanations, he was in part seduced by the most persuasive of the theories, the notion that Nazi soldiers had been left behind as Hitler's final act of revenge, soldiers whose last orders were to murder Russia's children. These Nazi soldiers had been trained in the Russian way of life, blending in, while systematically murdering children according to a predetermined ritual. It would explain the scale of the murders, the geographical scope, the savagery. But he decided not to commit himself to one theory or another. Leo's mission in Moscow would be crucial to the speculation of the killer's identity. Nesterov had been tasked with the accumulation of facts regarding the killer's location.

Nesterov stood up, stretching his legs. He'd been on the *elektrichka* for three hours. He walked the length of the carriage, opening the window, watching the lights of the city approach. Having heard about the murder of a boy named Petya living on a collective farm near Gukovo, he'd travelled there this morning. Without too much difficulty he'd found the parents. Though he'd given a false name, he'd explained that he was investigating the similar murders of a number of children. Both parents had been refused access to their boy's body. But they'd heard what had been done to him. He'd been savaged as if by an animal, dirt thrust in his mouth. Nesterov had no words of consolation except a promise that the culprit would be caught.

The *elektrichka* arrived at Rostov. Nesterov disembarked. During their vacation, his family had been staying in his mother's apartment in the New Settlement. Nesterov checked his watch. He'd left at six this morning and it was now coming up to nine in the evening. Fifteen hours had been spent for the gain of no real information. Tomorrow they were returning home.

He entered the courtyard, and moved through the washing that hung from side to side. Opening the door of his mother's apartment, he went inside.

Inessa was seated on a wooden stool in the kitchen, her face bloody, her hands tied. Behind her stood a man he didn't recognise, wearing a uniform. Nesterov strode forward, overwhelmed with anger. He raised his fist. Before he could get close, pain engulfed his hand. Looking to the side he saw a woman, holding a truncheon. He'd seen her face before. He remembered now—on the beach, two days ago. In her other hand she held a gun.

'General Nesterov, you're under arrest.'

Voualsk, July 7

Leo and Raisa got off the train and waited on the platform until all the other passengers had moved into the station building. It was not yet dark, and they felt exposed as they climbed off the platform and hurried into the forest.

Reaching the spot where they'd hidden their belongings, Leo stopped, catching his breath. He stared up at the trees, wondering at his decision to destroy the letter. Had he done his parents a disservice? He understood why they'd wanted to make their peace. But Raisa had been right about him when she said, *Is that how you're able to sleep at night, by blanking events from your mind?* She was more right than she knew.

Raisa touched his arm. 'Are you OK?'

She'd asked him what was in the letter. He'd told her the truth: that he'd destroyed it. He didn't want to read it. His parents could rest easily, believing that they'd unburdened themselves. She hadn't questioned his decision.

Using their hands, they dug away at the cover of leaves and loose soil, unearthing their belongings. They took off their city clothes, intending to change into the trail gear they'd set out in. Undressed, they paused, naked, staring at each other. Perhaps it was the danger, perhaps it was opportunistic, but Leo wanted her. Uncertain about her feelings for him, he did nothing, afraid to make the first move. She reached out, touching his hand. That was enough. He pulled her towards him, kissing her. They'd murdered together, deceived together, plotted and planned together. It was time to consummate this new relationship. If only they could stay in this moment for ever.

THEY REJOINED the forest trail, walking into town. Arriving at Basarov's they entered the main room. Leo was holding his breath, but there was no one here, no agents and no officers. They were safe, at least for another day.

Upstairs, they unlocked their room. A note had been pushed under the door. It was from Nesterov, dated today.

Leo, if you're back as planned, meet me tonight in my office at nine. Come alone. Bring all the documents relating to the matter we've been discussing. Leo, it's very important that you're not late.

Leo checked his watch. He had half an hour.

THE BLINDS to Nesterov's office were drawn shut and it was impossible to see in. Leo knocked on the door. Almost as soon as he did, the door was opened, as though Nesterov had been waiting behind it. Leo was ushered in with inexplicable urgency, the door shut behind him.

Nesterov's desk was covered with documents from the case file. He took hold of Leo by the shoulders and spoke in a hushed, hurried voice.

'Listen very carefully and don't interrupt. I was arrested in Rostov. I was forced to confess. I had no choice. They had my family. I told them everything. I thought I might be able to persuade them to help, persuade them to elevate our case to an official level. They reported it back to Moscow. They've accused us of anti-Soviet agitation. They think this is a personal vendetta you have against the State, an act of revenge. They offered me a choice. They're prepared to leave my family alone if I give them you and all the information we've collected.'

Leo's world fell away. Even though he'd known danger was close, he hadn't expected it to cut across his path just yet.

'When?'

'Right now. The building's surrounded. In fifteen minutes, agents will enter this room and arrest you. I'm to spend this time finding out all the information you discovered in Moscow. I've come up with a plan. You're going to hit me with my gun, knocking me unconscious. Leo, are you listening?'

But Leo wasn't listening—all he could think about was: 'Raisa?'

'She's being arrested as we speak. I'm sorry but there's nothing you can do about her. You need to concentrate, Leo, or this is over.'

'This was over the moment you told them everything.'

'They had everything, Leo. They had my work. They had my file. What was I supposed to do? Let them kill my family? They still would have arrested you. Leo, you can get angry with me, or you can escape.'

Leo shook free of Nesterov's grip, pacing the office. He and Raisa had known this moment would come but they hadn't understood what it would mean. The prospect of never seeing Raisa again made it difficult to breathe.

'Leo!'

What would she want? She wouldn't want him to get sentimental. She'd want him to succeed, to escape, to listen.

'All right, what's your plan?'

'Knock me unconscious,' Nesterov replied. 'Then leave this office, go down one flight of stairs and hide in the offices to the right of the stairway. Wait until the agents enter the building. Once they've come up to this floor, descend to the ground floor and exit through one of the windows at the back. There's a car parked in a side street. They'll believe you're on foot. By the time they realise you've taken a car, you should be free.'

'Free to do what?'

'To solve these crimes.'

'My trip to Moscow was a washout. The eyewitness refused to talk.'

That took Nesterov by surprise, but he recovered. 'Leo, you can do this. You need to head to Rostov-on-Don. That's the centre of these crimes, I'm convinced. There are theories about who is killing these children. One involves a group of former Nazi—'

'No, it's the work of an individual. If the focus of murders is Rostov, then it's likely he lives and works there. He travels for his job. That's the connection between the locations. If we can work out his job, we have the man.'

Leo checked his watch. There were only minutes before he had to leave.

'There have been no murders east of Voualsk that we know of,' Nesterov said. 'That suggests this is his destination. What's the link with Rostov?'

'Voualsk has the car-assembly plant, but no other significant industries apart from the lumber mills. There are lots of factories in Rostov.'

Nesterov knew both locations better than Leo. 'The car factory and the Rostelmash tractor factory share close ties. The tyres for the GAZ-20 come from Rostelmash, while engine components are shipped south in exchange.'

Was that the connection? The murders followed the train lines up from the south and across into the west, point to point.

'The Rostelmash factory must employ a *tolkach*,' Leo remarked. 'Someone who travels here to make sure the car plant fulfils its quota obligations.'

'There have only been two child-murders here and they were the most recent. The factories have been working together for some time.'

'That means he's just got this job, or he's only just been posted along this route. We need the Rostelmash employment records to cross-reference with the murder locations. If we're right, we'll have the man.'

They could have discovered the killer's name by the end of the week. But they didn't have a week. They had four minutes. Leo had to leave. He took one document—the list of murders, with dates and locations—and folded it into his pocket. He moved to the door. Nesterov stopped him. He was holding his gun. Leo took it, delaying for a moment.

Nesterov saw the hesitation. 'Or my family will die.' He closed his eyes.

Leo struck him across the side of his head, grabbed the car keys from the table, then hurried into the corridor.

As he ran down the stairs, agents were entering the building. Leo could hear footsteps coming up towards him. Reaching the third floor, he darted to the right. The nearest office door was unlocked, as Nesterov had promised.

Leo could hear the clump of footsteps as he locked the door behind him. At least four agents were on this stairway. He stepped to the window and glanced out. A ring of men was outside the main entrance. Leo returned to the door, unlocked it and peered out. The corridor was empty. He ran to the next stairway. He couldn't see or hear anyone. As he raced down the stairs, shouting broke out on the top floor: they'd found Nesterov.

A second wave of agents entered the building. Abandoning Nesterov's plan, Leo ran along the first-floor corridor and entered a toilet at the back of the building. He opened the high, narrow window and clambered up. He couldn't see any officers outside. He was maybe five metres above the ground. He pushed through the window, headfirst, until he was hanging above the ground, supported by his feet. There was nothing to grab onto. He'd have to let himself fall, protecting his head with his hands.

He hit the ground with his palms, his wrists snapping back. He heard a shout. An agent was at the top-floor window. Leo had been spotted. Ignoring the pain in his wrists, he stood up and ran towards the side street where the car was meant to be parked. Shots rang out. Puffs of brick dust exploded to the side of his head. He turned the corner, out of the line of fire.

The car was there. He clambered in and slotted the key into the ignition. The engine spluttered and died. He tried again. This time it started and he pulled away. Since the car was a militia vehicle, he hoped that any officers who saw it would presume he was on their side.

He couldn't drive all the way to Rostov. It was several hundred kilometres away, he didn't have enough petrol and he had no way of getting any more. More importantly, once they figured out that he'd taken a car they'd shut down all the roads. He had to get as far away as he could, then dump the car and board a train. He accelerated onto the only major connecting road that led into and out of the town, travelling west.

Up ahead, there were men standing on the road, clustered round a parked militia car. It was a roadblock. If the road west was blocked so was the road heading east. They'd have closed down the entire town. His only hope now lay in punching through the roadblock, smashing into the car.

He picked up speed. The agents up ahead began firing. Bullets hit the car, sparking against the metal. One punctured the windscreen. Leo lowered himself behind the steering wheel, braced for the collision, no longer able to see the road. He just had to hold steady.

The car lurched down and to the side. Sitting back up in the seat, Leo tried to maintain control, but the vehicle veered left. The tyres had been shot out. There was nothing he could do. The car flipped onto its side and he was thrown against the door. The front smashed into the other car, and Leo was tossed to the roof as his vehicle rolled over. There he lay huddled as the car skidded off the road and finally came to a stop by the verge.

LEO OPENED HIS EYES. He wasn't sure if he could move and he couldn't muster the strength to find out. He was staring up at the night sky. His thoughts moved slowly. He was no longer in the car. Someone must have dragged him out. A face appeared above him, blocking the stars, looking down at him. Concentrating, Leo focused on the man's face.

It was Vasili.

Moscow, July 10

Leo's face was swollen and tender. His right eye remained closed, hidden beneath folds of puffy skin. There was intense pain down his side, as though he'd broken several ribs. The irony of ending up here—secured to a chair in a basement cell in the Lubyanka—hadn't escaped his attention. A guardian of the State had become its prisoner, a not uncommon reversal of fortunes.

The door opened. Leo raised his head. Who was this man with sallow skin and yellow-stained teeth?

'You don't remember me?'

'No.'

'I'm Dr Zarubin. I visited you when you were ill not so many months ago. I'm sorry to see you in this predicament. I say that not as a criticism of the action being taken against you; I simply mean that I wish you hadn't done it.'

'What have I done?'

'You've betrayed your country.'

The doctor felt Leo's ribs. Each touch caused him to clench his teeth.

'Your ribs aren't broken. They're bruised. No doubt it's painful. But none of your injuries requires surgery. I've been ordered to clean up the cuts.'

'Treatment before torture, a quirk of this place. I once saved a man's life only to bring him here. I should have let Brodsky drown in that river.'

Leo fell silent. Anyone could regret their actions once the tables had been turned. He understood, more clearly than ever, that his only chance of redemption had slipped through his fingers. The killer would continue to kill, concealed by his country's refusal to admit that such a man even existed.

The doctor finished patching up Leo's injuries. He leaned down and whispered into Leo's ear. 'I'm now going to tend to your pretty wife. She's tied up next door. Quite helpless, and it's your fault. Everything I'm going to do to her is your fault.'

Leo tried to stand up, lunging for the doctor. But his chair was secured to the floor and he was secured to the chair.

Dr Zarubin watched Leo strain against his restraints as though he were watching a fly trapped under a glass. He picked up his case and waited for the guard to open the door.

IN THE ADJACENT CELL, Raisa was secured in exactly the same way as her husband. The door opened and Dr Zarubin entered. He opened the grate on the wall, designed to carry sound from one cell to another. Then he put his case down and began examining her, even though she had no injuries.

'I need to study every part of you. For my report, you understand.'

Raisa tried to remain looking straight ahead as the doctor's hands crept across her body, as though he wasn't there. His fingers moved up the inside of her leg with awful and deliberate slowness. She felt tears in her eyes.

The door opened. Vasili entered. The doctor stood up, stepping back.

Vasili was annoyed. 'She's not injured. There's no need for you to be here.'

'I was just making sure.'

'You may leave.'

Zarubin took his case and left. Vasili closed the grate. He crouched down beside Raisa, observing her tears.

'Maybe you think you can hold out. It would be better for you if you told me everything immediately. You think I'm a monster. But do you know who I learned that particular line from? Your husband, that's what he used to tell people before they were tortured—some of them in this very room.'

Raisa stared at this man's handsome features and wondered why he appeared ugly. His eyes were dull, not lifeless or stupid, but cold.

'I'll tell you everything,' she said.

VASILI ENTERED Leo's cell, gesturing for the guard to place a chair opposite the prisoner. The guard obeyed, positioning it just outside Leo's reach. Vasili stepped forward, picked up the chair and moved it closer. Their knees were almost touching. He stared at Leo, taking in the way his whole body was straining against his restraints.

'Relax, your wife is unharmed. She's next door.' Vasili gestured for the guard to open the grate. 'Raisa, say something to your husband,' he called out. 'He's worried about you.'

Raisa's voice could be heard like a faint echo: 'Leo?'

Before Leo could answer, the guard slammed the grate shut.

Leo looked at Vasili. 'There's no need to torture either of us. I understand there's no point in holding out. Ask me any question, I'll answer.'

'I already know everything. I've read the files you collected. I've spoken to General Nesterov. Raisa confirms his information. I have only one question for you. Why? Why risk the little we allowed you to keep for this fantasy?'

Leo's fight was gone. 'I was wrong. I had a theory. It was wrong. I retract it fully. I'll sign a retraction, an admission of guilt.'

'You realise you're guilty of the most serious act of anti-Russian agitation. I could understand if you're working for the West. Maybe they promised you money, power, the things you had lost. Is this the case?'

'No.'

'That is what worries me. It means you genuinely believe that these murders were connected rather than the actions of perverts and drunks and undesirables. To be blunt, it is madness.'

'I had a theory. It was wrong,' Leo repeated.

Vasili stood up, mulling the situation over. State Security had been ordered, after Stalin's death, to cease all use of violence against arrestees. A creature of survival, Vasili had adapted immediately. And yet here was Leo in his grasp. Could Vasili just walk away and leave him to face his sentencing? Would that satisfy him? He could feel his usual caution giving way to something personal. He found it impossible to resist.

He gestured for the guard to approach. 'Bring Dr Hvostov.'

THE TREATMENT ROOM was exactly as Leo remembered it: small and clean, a red leather chair bolted to the white-tiled floor, glass cabinets filled with labelled bottles and jars, an array of steel surgical instruments. He was secured to the same chair Anatoly Brodsky had been secured to; his wrists, ankles and neck were fastened with the same leather straps. Dr Hvostov filled a syringe with camphor oil. Leo's shirt was cut away, a vein was found. He opened his mouth, waiting for the rubber gag.

Vasili stood watching the preparations. Hvostov injected Leo with the oil. Seconds passed. Suddenly Leo's eyes rolled back in his head. His body shook. They waited for the more extreme physical reactions to calm down.

Hvostov nodded. 'See what he says. Simple questions to start with.'

Vasili stepped forward and untied the rubber gag. Leo vomited gobs of saliva onto his lap. His head fell forward, slack.

'What is your name?'

No reply.

'What is your name?'

Leo's lips moved. He said something but Vasili couldn't hear.

He moved closer. 'What is your name?'

'Pavel.'

OPENING HIS EYES, Pavel saw that he was standing ankle deep in snow, in the middle of a forest, a bright moon above him. His jacket was made of coarse grain sacks, stitched together with care. He lifted one foot out of the snow. Wrapped round each foot were rags and a strip of rubber, tied together with string. His hands were the hands of a child.

Feeling a tug on his jacket he turned round. Standing behind him was a young boy, dressed in the same kind of coarse sacks. The boy was squinting. Snot ran down from his nose. What was his name? Clumsy and devoted and silly—his name was Andrei.

Behind him a scrawny black and white cat began to screech, struggling in the snow. It was being pulled into the forest. There was string round the cat's paw. Someone was dragging it across the snow. Pavel ran after it. But the cat, still struggling, was being pulled faster and faster. Pavel increased his pace. Looking back he saw that Andrei was being left behind.

Suddenly he came to a stop. Standing in front of him, holding the end of the string, was Stepan, his father, not as a young man but as an elderly man, the man he'd said goodbye to in Moscow. Stepan picked up the cat, snapped its neck and dropped it into a large grain sack. Pavel walked up to him.

'Father?'

'I'm not your father.'

OPENING HIS EYES, he found himself inside the grain sack, his head caked in blood, his mouth as dry as ash. He was being carried, bouncing against a man's back. His head hurt. He felt sick. Exhausted, he closed his eyes.

Feeling the heat of a fire, he woke. He'd been emptied onto the mud floor of a farmhouse. Stepan—now a young man, the man in the woods, gaunt and fierce—was sitting by the fire holding the skeletal body of a young boy. Beside him was Anna; she was young again too. They were crying. Anna stroked the dead boy's hair. Stepan whispered the dead boy's name: 'Leo.'

Finally Anna turned round, her eyes red, and asked, 'What is your name?'

He didn't reply. He didn't know his name.

'Where do you live?'

Yet again, he didn't know.

Anna continued: 'Do you understand why you are here?'

He shook his head.

'You were to die, so that our son might live. But he cannot be saved. He died while my husband was hunting. Since he is dead, you're free to go.'

Free to go where? He didn't know where he was. He didn't know where he'd come from. His mind was empty.

Anna stood up, offering him her hand. He struggled to his feet, weak and dizzy. She gave him a cup of warm water. The first sip made him feel sick, but the second was better. She took him outside, where they sat, wrapped up together under several blankets. He fell asleep against her shoulder.

When he awoke, Stepan had come outside. 'It's ready.'

They re-entered the farmhouse. The boy's body was gone. On the fire was a large pot, a bubbling stew. He sat down close to the heat, accepting a bowl filled to the brim. He stared down at the steaming broth: crushed acorns floated on the surface alongside bright white knuckles and strips of flesh.

'You were to die, so that our son might live,' Stepan said now. 'Since he has died, you can live.'

They were offering their own flesh and blood. They were offering their son. He raised the broth to his nose. He hadn't eaten for so long that he began to salivate. Instinct took over and he reached in.

'Tomorrow we begin our journey to Moscow,' Stepan explained. 'We cannot survive here any longer. I have an uncle in the city; he could help us. You can come with us, or stay here and try to find your way home.'

Should he stay here, with no idea of who or where he was? What would he do? These people were kind. They had food. They had a plan.

'I want to come with you.'

'You're sure?'

'Yes.'

'My name is Stepan. My wife's name is Anna. What is your name?'

He couldn't remember any names. Except for the one he'd heard earlier.

'My name is Leo.'

July 11

Raisa was shunted towards a line of tables, each manned by two officers, one checking a stack of documentation while the other frisked the prisoner. Raisa was pushed to one table, waved to another. She'd been processed so quickly her paperwork hadn't caught up. Something of an irritation, she was taken aside by the guard accompanying her, bypassing this part of the process.

These missing papers contained the statement of her crime and her sentence. All around, prisoners listened as sentences were called out: 'Five years! Ten years! Twenty-five years!' She observed the same reaction from almost every prisoner: disbelief. Was any of this real? It felt dreamlike, as though they'd been plucked out of the real world and thrown inside an entirely new world where no one was sure of the rules.

Raisa was guided out of the processing room onto the station platform, her arm held by the guard. She waited as thousands of other prisoners—some in fine, tailored clothes, most in rags—were loaded onto the converted cattle carts used to transport prisoners to the Gulags. They were being forced into carriages, hundreds being beaten into spaces that should take no more than thirty or forty. But in this new world, space was a precious commodity. The logistics of moving people were no different from the logistics of moving grain; pack it in and expect to lose five per cent.

As a matter of routine, families were broken up in the Gulags, and Raisa presumed that Leo would be sent to another camp. She saw Vasili coming towards her, leading an older man with a stooped back. Less than five metres away she recognised this man as her husband. She stared at Leo, bewildered at his transformation. What had they done to him?

Raisa placed her hand on his face, feeling his brow. 'Leo?'

It took him an effort to reply, his mouth shaking as he tried to say, 'Raisa.'

She was angry that there were tears in her eyes. Vasili would want that. She wiped them away. But they wouldn't stop.

'It's usual for husbands and wives to be separated,' Vasili said. 'But I thought you might like to take this journey together, a small act of my generosity.' He gestured at the guard, who shoved them towards the train.

Raisa helped Leo up into the carriage. They were the last prisoners to be loaded in. The door slid shut after them.

Vasili stood on the platform, his hands behind his back. 'Have arrangements been made?'

The guard nodded. 'Neither of them will reach their destination alive.'

100 km east of Moscow, July 12

Raisa and Leo had been crouching at the back of the carriage since boarding the previous day. The rough wooden benches that ran along the walls at three different heights had all been taken. On these benches, up to three people lay side by side. The only space Leo and Raisa could find was near a hole the size of a fist cut out of the floorboards—the toilet for the entire carriage. There was no partition, no option but to defecate and urinate in full view.

Initially, in this stinking darkness, Raisa had felt uncontrollably angry. The degradation was wilfully malicious. If they were going to these camps to work, why were they being transported as if they were intended for execution? She'd stopped herself from pursuing this line of thought; they wouldn't survive like this, fired up with indignation. She had to adapt.

Even without a watch, Raisa knew it must be past midday. The steel roof was being cooked by the sun, radiating an unrelenting heat on the hundreds of bodies. The train moved with such sluggishness that no breeze came through the small slits in the timber walls. Forced to let go of her anger, she found that the intolerable temperatures and smells became tolerable.

Raisa turned to Leo. He'd slept for most of the journey so far, resting against her. When he was awake he appeared calm, his mind elsewhere; his brow furrowed as though he were trying to make sense of something. She'd searched his body for signs of torture. Round his ankles, wrists and neck were red strap marks. She had no idea what he'd been through, but it was psychological and chemical rather than cuts and burns. She'd rubbed his head, held his hand—kissed him. This was all the medicine she was able to offer. She'd fetched his chunk of black bread and single strip of dried salty fish, their only meal so far, feeding it to Leo in small pieces.

Leo sat up, speaking for the first time since boarding the train. 'Oksana was a good mother. She loved me. I chose not to go back. My little brother always wanted to play cards. I used to say I was too busy.'

'Who are you talking about, Leo? Who is your brother? Who is Oksana? Are you talking about Anna?'

'Anna is not my mother.'

Raisa cradled his head, wondering if he'd gone insane.

Surveying the carriage, she was conscious that Leo's vulnerability made him an easy target. Most of the prisoners were too terrified to be of any threat, except for five men in the far corner, who were fearless, at ease in this world. Raisa guessed that they were professional criminals with sentences for theft or assault, crimes that carried shorter sentences than those of the political prisoners around them. This superiority came not only from their evident physical strength; she noted that power was conferred on them by the guards. Other prisoners were afraid of them. The men were able to leave their bench, use the toilet and fetch their water, all without fear of losing their prized spot. No one dared take their place.

The train came to a stop. Calls for water sounded out from every carriage. They were ignored. The door was opened. The guards called for the five men. They swung down from their bench and pushed through the prisoners.

Something was wrong—Raisa lowered her head, breathing fast. It was not long before she heard the men return. Slowly, she lifted her head. The men had climbed back into the carriage. All five were staring at her.

Raisa took hold of Leo's face. 'Leo, listen to me. We're in trouble.'

He didn't seem to understand; the danger didn't seem to register.

'Leo, please, I'm begging you.'

It was no good. She stood up, turning to face the approaching men.

The leader, the tallest of them, stepped forward and grabbed her arm. Raisa struck him in the eye with her free hand, her nails jabbing into the skin. The man tossed her to the floor. She landed on some prisoners, who scuttled out of the way. Trying to scramble away from her attackers, Raisa found that someone was holding her ankle. More hands grabbed her and flipped her onto her back. One man dropped to his knees, holding her arms, pinning her down while the leader kicked open her legs. In his hand he held a shard of thick, jagged steel, which, she realised, he'd been given by the guards.

Unable to move, Raisa turned to Leo. He was gone.

LEO'S THOUGHTS had shifted away from the forest, the cat, his brother. His wife was in danger. Struggling to assess the situation, he wondered why he was being ignored. Whatever the reason, he'd been able to stand without the men reacting. The leader was unbuttoning his trousers. By the time he'd noticed Leo, there was only an arm's length between them.

The leader swung round, punching him in the side of the face. Leo fell to the floor. His lip split, he listened to the men laughing. Let them laugh. The pain had done him good, focusing him. They were overconfident—strong but unskilled. Making a deliberate show of being shaky, he stood up, keeping his back to the men. He could hear someone moving towards him. Glancing over his shoulder, he saw the leader lunge at him with the steel shard.

Leo sidestepped, taking the man by surprise. Before he could recover, Leo punched the man's throat, winding him. The man gasped. Leo caught hold of his hand, twisting the shard free and jabbing the tip into the side of the man's neck. Leo plunged it all the way in, severing every vein and artery in its path. He pulled the weapon free and the man collapsed.

The nearest member of his gang stepped forward. Leo allowed the man to grab his neck, in reply pushing the shard into his stomach. Releasing his grip on Leo's neck, the man slumped to his knees. Leo locked the man's neck in a grip, choking him.

He turned to the remaining three men. They'd lost all interest in the struggle. Whatever deal they'd been offered wasn't worth the fight.

One of them took charge. 'We have no quarrel with you.'

Leo said nothing. The steel shard jutted out of his blood-covered hand.

The men pulled back. Leo helped Raisa up, hugging her.

'Those men were ordered to kill us by the guards,' she whispered.

Leo considered this. 'Our only chance is to escape,' he replied.

The train was slowing down. When it stopped, the guards would open the doors, expecting to find Leo and Raisa dead. When they discovered two of their assassins dead instead, they'd demand to know who'd killed them. Some prisoner would almost certainly speak up.

Leo turned to face the prisoners. There were pregnant mothers, men too old to survive the Gulags, fathers, brothers, sisters—ordinary people.

'Before I was arrested, I was investigating the murder of over forty children, from the Ural Mountains to the Black Sea,' he began. 'I know this is hard to believe, but I've seen the bodies for myself. I'm sure they're the work of one man. He'll murder any child, from any town. And he will not stop. My crime was to investigate him. My arrest means he is free to continue killing. No one else is looking for him. My wife and I must escape to stop him. We cannot escape without your help.'

There was silence. The train was almost at a stop.

'I'm from Rostov,' a woman called out. 'I've heard of such murders. Children with their stomachs cut out. When you find the murderer you'll kill him?'

'Yes,' Leo said.

The train stopped. The guards could be heard approaching.

'I've no reason to expect your help,' he added. 'But I ask for it all the same.'

Leo and Raisa crouched down among the prisoners. She wrapped her arms round him, covering up his bloodstained hands. The doors slid open.

Finding the two bodies, the guards called out, 'Who killed them?'

They were answered with silence.

The guards were shouting, pushing guns into the faces of an elderly couple. 'Who killed these men? What happened here? Speak!'

The woman wept. But neither of them replied. A guard moved towards Leo.

The man who'd told Leo there was no quarrel between them got down from his bench. 'Leave them alone. I know what happened. They killed each other, because of a card game.'

Leo understood that the *urki*, the criminal gang members, were prepared to rape and murder for a small profit. But they were not prepared to snitch.

The guards looked at each other. Unsure of what to do, they decided to do nothing. The journey to Vtoraya Rechka, on the Pacific coast, would take weeks. There would be plenty of opportunities. They'd await further orders.

One of the guards addressed the carriage. 'As a punishment we will not offload these bodies. Soon they will begin to rot and stink and you will all become ill. Perhaps then you will talk.'

The guards leapt off the carriage. After a while, the train moved again.

A young man whispered, 'How will you escape?'

In reply, Leo raised the bloody steel shard. The guards hadn't taken it back.

220 km east of Moscow, July 13

Leo was lying flat on the floor, his arm squeezed through the small toilet hole. With the steel shard he scratched at the iron nails fastening the plank. The three nails had all been hammered in from the underside of the carriage, accessible only through this small hole. Leo had taken the shirt of one of the dead men and cleaned the area as best he could. To reach the iron nails he was forced to bring his face down flat against the stinking wood, retching while blindly groping, guided by touch alone.

With a strip of shirt tied round his mouth and nose as limited protection from the stench, he picked at the third and last nail, gouging the timber and giving himself just enough space to wedge the tip under the nailhead and lever it out. It had taken many hours to remove two nails, since the work had to be interrupted by any prisoner needing the toilet.

This final nail was proving the hardest. Leo could get his fingertip under the nail's head but it wasn't coming loose. It felt crooked, as if it had been banged in at an angle. A wave of exhaustion came over him. His fingers were bloody and raw, his arm ached. Suddenly the train jolted to the side, he lost concentration, and the steel shard slipped from his fingers onto the tracks.

Leo pulled his hand out of the hole. Raisa was beside him.

'I dropped it. I dropped the shard.' He was furious at himself for having discarded the other nails. 'I need something to scratch through the wood and get out that last nail.'

'How long or sharp does it need to be?' Raisa asked.

'I've done most of it. I need anything harder than my fingertip.'

Raisa walked to the body of the man who had tried to rape her. He was lying on his back, his mouth open. She raised her shoe directly above the dead man's jaw, then hesitated, looking around. Everyone was watching. She closed her eyes, bringing her heel down against his front teeth.

Leo crawled over, feeling inside the man's mouth and pulling out a tooth, an incisor. He returned to the hole. Holding the tooth, he squeezed his arm through, found the remaining nail and continued to pick away at the wood.

When the nail was completely exposed, Leo wrapped his raw fingers in a shredded strip of shirt, then tugged at the nail, incrementally pulling it free from the plank. The nail removed, he sat up, pulling his arm out of the hole.

Raisa sunk her hands through the hole, gripping the plank. Leo added his hands. They both pulled. The top of the plank lifted up while the bottom remained secured. Leo lifted the end as high as he could. He could see the tracks below the carriage. There was now a gap of about thirty centimetres in width and over a metre in length, just enough for a person to get through.

Leo turned to his audience. 'I need people to hold this plank up while we drop through the gap.'

Several volunteers came forward, took hold of the plank. Leo assessed the space. After they'd squeezed through, they'd fall directly underneath the train. The distance to the tracks was perhaps a little over a metre. The train was travelling slowly but still fast enough for the fall to be dangerous. However, they had to go now, while the train was moving, during the night. When the train stopped at daybreak, they'd be seen by the guards.

Raisa took hold of Leo's hands. 'I'll go first.'

Leo shook his head. He'd seen the blueprints to these prisoner transports. They faced one more obstacle. 'On the underneath of this train, at the very end, there are hundreds of hooks that hang down on wires. If we fell onto the tracks right now and waited, as the last carriage passed overhead the hooks would snag us, dragging us with the train.'

'What are we supposed to do? We can't wait till the train stops.'

Leo examined the two dead bodies. 'When you drop down, I'll throw one of these bodies after you. Hopefully it will land somewhere near you. You'll have to crawl to it. Once you reach it, lie underneath it. As the last carriage passes overhead, the body will get snagged. But you'll be free.' He dragged the bodies close to the loose plank, adding, 'Do you want me to go first? If it doesn't work, then you should stay here.'

Raisa shook her head. 'It's a good plan. It will work. I'll go first.'

'When you're underneath the body, make sure no part of you is exposed.'

'Leo, I understand.' Raisa kissed him. She was shaking.

She squeezed through the gap between the planks and fell, disappearing from view. Leo grabbed the first body and squeezed it through the gap. The body dropped onto the tracks, out of sight.

RAISA HAD LANDED awkwardly, bruising her side. Dazed, she lay still for a moment. Too long; she was wasting time. She could see the body and began to crawl towards it. She glanced behind her. There were only three carriages until the end of the train. But she couldn't see any hooks. There were now only two carriages left. Raisa still hadn't reached the body. She tumbled over. With only metres before the final carriage passed over her, she saw the hooks—hundreds of them, all attached to fine wires, at different heights. They covered the entire width of the carriage, impossible to avoid.

Raisa got up, crawling again, as fast as she could. The body was lying face down. She lifted it up and crawled under her attacker, positioning her head under his face, staring into his dead eyes.

Suddenly the dead body was wrenched off her. She saw wires all around her, like fishing lines, each one barbed with many jagged hooks. The body lifted up, as though a puppet, no longer touching the tracks. Raisa remained flat on the tracks, perfectly still. She could see the stars above her. Slowly she stood up. She watched the train move away. There was no sign of Leo.

AS HE WAS LARGER than Raisa, Leo had figured that he needed the bigger of the two dead men to protect him from the hooks. However, this man was too large to fit through the gap between the planks.

Desperate, Leo lowered his head though the gap. He could see a body caught at the end of the train. Was it Raisa or the dead man? It was impossible to tell. Adjusting his plan, he supposed that if he positioned himself correctly he could escape underneath this body. He thanked the other prisoners and dropped onto the tracks.

Finding himself rolling close to the enormous steel wheels, he pulled himself away, facing the end of the train. The body in the wire was rapidly approaching, tangled up on the left-hand side. He positioned himself accordingly, making himself as small and as flat as possible. He lifted his head up off the ground just long enough to see that it wasn't Raisa. She'd survived. He had to do the same. He lay down flat.

The dead body brushed over him.

Then, pain—a single stray hook caught his left arm. The hook had cut into his flesh. With only a fraction of a second before the wire went taut, pulling him along, he grabbed hold of the hook and tugged it out, taking a clump of skin and flesh with it. Staggering to his feet, he saw Raisa hurrying towards him. Ignoring the pain, he put his arms round her.

They were free.

Moscow

Vasili wasn't well. He'd done something he'd never done before, something potentially dangerous—he'd taken time off work.

After Leo's exile to the Urals, Vasili had petitioned to move into Leo and Raisa's apartment; apartment 124. He'd got his wish. Some of the men who'd served under Leo now reported to him. Yet despite the delicious reversal of fortune, he felt empty. He no longer had anyone to hate. There were other men who he competed with, but the feeling wasn't the same.

Vasili got out of bed and poured himself a large measure of vodka. He stared at the glass, unable to raise it to his lips. The smell made him feel sick. He put the glass down. Leo was dead. Soon he would receive official notification that the two prisoners had died en route, as so many did, after getting into a fight over shoes or food or whatever. It was the final defeat of a man who'd humiliated him. So, then, why did he miss him?

There was a knock. He'd expected the MGB to send round men to authenticate his illness. He walked to the door and opened it.

A young officer stood before him. 'Sir, two prisoners have escaped.'

He could feel the dull ache inside him vanishing as he asked, 'Leo?'

The officer nodded. Vasili was feeling better already.

200 km southeast of Moscow

They were half running, half walking, constantly looking behind them, their speed depending on whether fear or exhaustion had the upper hand. The weather was in their favour: weak sunshine and thin cloud, not too hot. From the position of the sun, Leo and Raisa knew it was late afternoon, but they had no way of knowing the exact time. Leo's watch had been lost or taken. He estimated they had a four-hour head start on their guards at the most.

They broke out of woodland into open countryside. Seeing a small river at the bottom of an incline, they adjusted direction, picking up speed. It was the first water they'd come across. Reaching it, they dropped to their knees and drank greedily, cupping their hands, scooping it into their mouths.

Raisa focused on Leo's injury. The gash wouldn't stop bleeding. The strip of shirt they'd tied round it was now soaked with blood.

Leo unpeeled the shirt. 'I can put up with it.'

'It's leaving a powerful scent for the dogs.'

Raisa stepped out of the river and approached the nearest tree. A spider's web had been spun between two branches. Carefully, she transferred the web whole and laid it across the ripped flesh of Leo's upper arm. Upon touching the thin silver lines, blood seemed to solidify. She worked for several minutes, finding more webs and layering them, until the injury was crisscrossed with silky threads. By the time she'd finished, the bleeding had stopped.

'We should follow this river for as long as possible,' Leo said. 'The trees are the only cover and the water will hide our smell.'

The water was shallow, and not fast enough or powerful enough to enable them to float and drift with the current. Hungry and exhausted as they were, they had to walk. Leo knew they couldn't keep this up for long.

Since he and Raisa were classified as counter-revolutionaries, their escape would be of countrywide significance. Once the guards noticed the body caught up in the wire, the escapees' carriage would be identified; questions would be asked. Leo hoped that someone would be sensible enough to tell the truth immediately.

The hunt would begin along the tracks, using dogs. They'd been on the run for three-quarters of a day without sight of their pursuers, so Leo presumed that their scent trail had not been found. That meant that Moscow would be notified. Trucks, cars and planes would be mobilised; local military and security organisations would be informed. Leo hoped that they'd target the wrong area. Logically he and Raisa should be heading to the nearest border, the Baltic coast. A boat was their best chance of getting out of the country. But they were heading south—through the heart of Russia, towards Rostov, a direction with almost no chance of freedom at the end.

They'd been on the train for almost forty-eight hours. Leo guessed that they were now about 200 kilometres southeast of Moscow, travelling in the direction of Ryazan. Rostov was at least a twenty-four-hour journey south by train or car. But they had no money, no food; they were injured, filthy, and wanted by the entire national and local State Security apparatus.

They came to a stop. The river flowed in between two halves of a small village, a collective farm. They stepped out of the water some 500 paces upstream from the huddle of houses. It was late; light was fading.

'Some of the villagers will still be working on their land,' Leo said. 'We can sneak in, unnoticed, see if we can find some food.'

'You want to steal?'

'We can't buy anything. If they see us, they'll hand us in. There's always a reward for escaped prisoners.'

'We have hundreds of kilometres to cross. We can't do it alone. We have to convince strangers to help us—that's our only chance.'

'Harbouring us will get them shot, or twenty-five years' deportation.'

'You have a short memory, Leo. The inmates of that carriage helped us, all of them. They'll almost certainly face punishment. What did they do it for?'

Leo remained silent.

Raisa pressed her point. 'The people have no love of the State. If you steal from them, you'll be their enemy when we are in fact their friends.'

'So you want to walk into the centre of the village and greet them?'

'That's exactly what we're going to do.'

Side by side, they walked into the village. Men, women and children gathered round them. These people had nothing. Their houses were made of mud and wood. Their farm equipment was forty years out of date. All they had to do was turn them over to the State and they'd be richly rewarded.

Raisa spoke up. 'We're prisoners. We've escaped from the train transporting us to the Kolyma region. We're now being hunted. We need your help. We ask for this not for ourselves. Eventually we'll be caught and killed. We've accepted that. But before we die there is one task we have to perform. Please let us explain why we need your help.'

A man stepped forward, an air of self-importance about him. 'As chairman of this *kolkhoz*, it is my duty to point out that it would be in our best interests to turn them over.'

A man's voice called out, 'And what would you do with the reward, hand that over to the State too?'

There was laughter. The chairman went red, embarrassed, a comic figure. Clearly he wasn't the real authority.

From the back of the crowd an elderly woman spoke out: 'Feed them.'

As though an oracle had spoken, the debate was over.

They were led into the largest house. In the main room, where food was prepared, they were seated and given water. A fire was stoked. Soon the house was crowded. Fresh bread was brought from another house. They ate with their wet clothes steaming in front of the fire. When a man apologised for not being able to offer them a new set of clothes, Leo merely nodded, disorientated by their generosity. He could offer them a story; that was it. Finishing his bread and water, he stood up.

EVEN BEFORE he had finished his story, Leo realised that his audience's perspective on the world had been shaken. He apologised for introducing them to the reality of this killer's existence. In an effort to reassure them, he outlined the murderer's movements along the railways, through major towns. He killed as part of a routine that wouldn't bring him into villages like this.

Leo had been speaking for over an hour when a child ran into the house. 'I saw lights on the northern hills. There are trucks coming this way.'

Everyone got to their feet. Reading the faces around him, Leo knew that there was no chance these trucks could be anything other than the State.

'How long do we have?' he asked.

There were three trucks, three sets of headlights. The boy had seen them from the edge of his father's farm. They were coming from the north, several kilometres away. They'd be here in minutes.

There was nowhere to hide in these houses. The villagers had no belongings, no furniture to speak of. And the search would be thorough, Leo knew.

Raisa took hold of his arms. 'We can run. They'll have to search the village first. We can get ahead, maybe hide in the countryside. It's dark.'

Leo shook his head, feeling his stomach tense. There was no way to outrun these guards. They were rested, equipped to hunt—long-range rifles, telescopic sights, and dogs to pick up suspicious trails.

Leo turned to the young boy who'd seen the trucks. 'I need your help.'

THE BOY CROUCHED in the middle of the road in almost complete darkness, his hands shaking, a small bag of grain spilled before him. The trucks were approaching, coming fast, their tyres kicking up the dirt. There was a screech of brakes. The boy turned his head, caught in the beam of powerful headlights. He raised his arms. The trucks lurched to a stop.

A soldier called out, 'What the fuck are you doing? Get off the road!'

'My bag split. My father will kill me if I don't collect it all.'

'I'll kill you if you don't move.'

There was a metallic click. Panicking, the boy picked up bag and ran back towards the village. The trucks followed him, beeping their horns.

Leo and Raisa were hiding in the only place they could hope the soldiers wouldn't search—underneath their trucks. While the boy was distracting the soldiers, Leo had sneaked under the second truck, Raisa under the third. They'd wrapped their hands in shreds of shirt to ease the pain of holding on.

The trucks came to a stop. As the soldiers jumped off the back of the third truck, Raisa wedged her feet round the axle shaft. She was afraid but mostly she was angry. This plan was smart, but it depended on their ability to cling on. She didn't have enough upper-body strength. Already her arms were aching. She couldn't manage for much longer.

She had to think around this problem, find a solution that didn't rely on strength. The strips of the shirt—if she couldn't hold on, she'd tie her wrists to the axle shaft. That would be fine as long as the truck was stationary. But she'd have to lower herself to the ground while she bound herself, dramatically increasing the chances of her being seen. She looked sideways, left and right. The driver had remained guarding the vehicle. She could see his boots and smell his cigarette smoke. Slowly, Raisa lowered her legs to the ground. She unwound the strips of shirt, and fastened her left wrist to the shaft before partially tying her right wrist. Then she finished the knot with her already bound-up hand and lifted her feet up to the axle.

Tied under the truck, Raisa listened as the soldiers carried out their search: furniture was kicked over, pots upturned, objects smashed. It seemed to go on for an impossibly long time. Then the soldiers started returning, moving back to the trucks. They were about to leave.

Excited, she realised the plan had worked. Then the engine started. She was still tied to the axle. In a few seconds it would start spinning. She had to get free. But her wrists were bound and her hands were numb. She was struggling to untie the knots. The soldiers were in the trucks. They were about to drive off. Raisa leaned forward, using her teeth, tugging at the knot. It came undone and she dropped to the ground, landing on her back. She was in the middle of the road. In the light of the village she would be seen by the soldiers sitting at the back of the truck.

The villagers moved forward, clustering. As the truck drove off, they surrounded her. The soldiers would not have seen anything unusual.

Raisa waited, curled up on the road. Finally a man offered his hand. She stood up. Leo wasn't there. He wouldn't have risked letting go until the trucks were in the dark. She guessed he was worried about being seen by the driver of the third truck. But she wasn't worried. He'd know what to do. All of them waited in silence. And before long they heard a man running towards them.

Moscow

Despite the many hundreds of soldiers and agents now searching for the fugitives, no trace of them had been found. Vasili was not surprised. They were chasing a man who'd been trained to avoid detection and survive in hostile territory. So far, the search had focused on possible approach routes towards the Scandinavian border, the northern coastline and the Baltic Sea. It was taken for granted that Leo would try to cross into another country, probably using a fishing boat. Once in the West, he'd connect with senior government figures who'd gladly aid him in exchange for information. For this reason, his capture was a matter of the highest urgency.

Neither Leo nor Raisa had any family or friends in that area of the country—they should be alone, in rags, penniless. When Vasili had last spoken to Leo, the man hadn't even known his own name. Evidently he'd regained his wits. But Vasili didn't believe that Leo had any interest in fleeing to the West. Leo's agenda was rooted in the pages of this captured case file.

Vasili studied the documents accumulated by Leo and the local militia officer who'd helped him. During his interrogation, Leo had denounced this work. Vasili knew that denunciation was a lie. Leo believed in this fanciful theory that a single killer was responsible for all these motiveless murders, spread over many hundreds of kilometres in over thirty locations. It meant they could be heading anywhere. Frustrated, Vasili re-examined the map marked with each alleged murder.

One location appeared to have a larger number of murders than any other: Rostov-on-Don.

Southeastern Rostov Oblast, July 14

Leo and Raisa were in a crate one metre high and two metres wide, being smuggled south. The villagers had taken Leo and Raisa by truck to the nearest town, Ryazan, where they'd introduced them to friends and family. In a small apartment filled with an audience of nearly thirty and the fog of cheap cigarette smoke, Leo had told the story of their investigation. No one needed any convincing as to the urgency of the objective.

Plans were laid to transport them south. One member of the audience worked as a truck driver shuttling loads between Moscow and towns such as Kharkov, some 300 kilometres north of Rostov. Though driving into Rostov itself was too risky, since the driver had no business there, he'd be prepared to take them to the nearby town of Shakhty. He could legitimately pass off this diversion by claiming that he was visiting family. That same family would almost certainly agree to help Leo and Raisa travel into the city.

At the very least they had a day and a half cooped up in this crate. The driver was transporting bananas, luxury goods intended for the *spetztorgi*, the shops for high-ranking Party figures where Leo and Raisa had once bought their own groceries. There were breaks every three to four hours when the driver would stop, letting his human cargo stretch their legs.

In the darkness Raisa asked, 'What happens once this is over?'

'I don't know.'

'The West will want you, Leo. They'll protect you.'

'I'd never leave this country. If you want to defect, I'll do everything I can to get you onto a boat.'

'What are you going to do? Hide in the hills?'

'Once that man is dead, once you're safe, I'll turn myself in. I don't want to live in exile, among people that want my information. It would mean that everything these people in Moscow have said about me would be true.'

'And that's the most important thing?' Raisa sounded hurt.

Leo touched her arm. 'Raisa, I don't understand.'

'Is it that complicated? I want us to stay together.'

Leo said nothing for a moment. Finally he replied, 'I can't live as a traitor. I can't do it. I'm sorry.'

'We should make the most of this time together.'

'How do we do that?'

'We tell each other the truth.'

'The truth?'

'Secrets. I know I have some. Don't you? Things you've never told me.'

'Yes.'

'Then I'll go first. After I heard about Zoya's arrest, I was convinced you'd reported her. So, for about a week, I spat in your tea.'

'You spat in my tea?'

'For about a week. You didn't seem to care. So I stopped.'

'I didn't notice.'

'Exactly. OK, your turn.'

'I found a kopek among your clothes, a coin that could be split in two. It was a device for smuggling microfilm. Only an agent would have one.'

'That coin was mine . . .' Her voice drifted off, as though weighing up whether or not to continue. 'I didn't use it to carry microfilm. I used it to carry cyanide paste, when I was a refugee.'

Leo waited. Raisa had never spoken about the period after her home had been destroyed, the months on the road—the dark ages of her life.

'I'm sure you can imagine the kind of things that happened to women refugees. Soldiers, they had needs, they were risking their lives—we were their payment. After one time—and there were several—I hurt so much, I swore if it ever looked like happening again, I'd rub that paste across his gums. Maybe it would make them think twice about doing it to another woman. Anyway, it became my lucky coin because as soon as I started carrying it I never had any problems. Of course, it didn't cure the injuries I'd sustained. That's the reason I can't get pregnant, Leo.'

Leo stared into the darkness, at the place where he imagined his wife must be. As a soldier he knew such activity had been sanctioned by the State, considered an appropriate reward for a brave soldier. He rubbed the palm of her hand. What else could he do? Apologise? He'd hung that newspaper clipping on the wall, proud, oblivious to what the war meant to her.

'Leo, I have another secret. I've fallen in love with you.'

'I've always loved you.'

'That's not a secret, Leo. You're two secrets behind.'

Leo kissed her. 'I have a brother.'

Rostov-on-Don, July 15

Nadya was alone in the house. Her father was away on a work trip. Her mother and sister had gone to visit their grandmother. Nadya had feigned a stomachache and begged to be allowed to stay at home. Her mother had agreed. Nadya's plan was simple. She was going to open the basement door and find out why her father spent so long downstairs. She'd never been down there. It was strictly forbidden.

Nadya squeezed a knife between the door and the frame, lifting the latch. She pushed the door open. Excited, afraid, she took a step down. The door swung shut. Some light crept in under the door behind her, and through the ventilation hole for the stove below. She descended the stairs, her eyes adjusting to the gloom, then stood surveying her father's secret room.

A bed, a small table, a chest, a stove, an old lamp on the wall—there was nothing mysterious. Disappointed, she turned her attention to the chest. She put her hands on the top and lifted, just a little, to see if it was locked. It wasn't. She lifted it a little more.

Suddenly she heard a noise—the front door. There were heavy footsteps. Her father must have returned early. Light appeared as the door to the basement was opened. Panicking, Nadya lowered the lid. As his footsteps came down the stairs, she dropped to her knees and clambered under the bedspace.

Nadya closed her eyes, expecting when she opened them to see his furious face inches away from her. Instead, the entire bed creaked and sank. He was sitting on it. She watched as he untied his bootlaces. He didn't know she was here. The latch must have locked after the door had shut.

Her father stood up and fired up the lamp, which gave out a weak light. He walked towards the chest. Nadya could hear the top of the chest being opened. What was her father doing? Now he was sitting at one of the chairs, tying something round his foot. It was a strip of rubber. Using string and rags he seemed to be making some kind of homemade shoe.

Aware of something behind her, Nadya turned her head and saw the cat. It had seen her too, its back was arched, its fur stuck out. Scared, she turned to see if her father had noticed. He dropped to his knees, his face appearing in the gap under the bed. He stood up, and lifted the entire bed upright.

'Stand up.'

She obeyed, her head down, staring at her father's one bare foot and his other foot wrapped in rags. He lowered the bed.

'Why are you down here?' he demanded.

'I wanted to know what you do. I want to spend more time with you.'

Her father stepped away from her. He raised a finger to his lips.

'Father?' Nadya walked up to him and took his hand. 'Don't you like spending time with me?'

He wiped his brow. 'Nadya, why don't you like playing with your younger sister? When I was your age, I spent all my time with my brother.'

'You have a brother? Where is he?'

Her father pointed at the wall. Pinned up beside the lamp was a series of newspaper clippings. They were all the same: a photograph of a handsome Russian soldier standing beside a burning tank.

'What's his name?'

'Pavel.'

'Why doesn't he visit us?'

'He will.'

8 km north of Rostov-on-Don, July 16

They were seated on an *elektrichka*, travelling towards the outskirts of Rostov. The truck driver had taken them through several checkpoints and dropped them at Shakhty, where they'd spent the night with his mother-in-law and her family. For the third time, Leo had told the story of his investigation. They'd already heard of the child-murders, but they knew no facts. When told the estimated number of victims, the room had fallen silent.

This extended family had immediately set about making plans. Leo and Raisa had decided to wait until dusk before travelling into the city, since there'd be fewer people at the factory at night, and there was a greater chance the killer would be at home. It had also been decided that they shouldn't travel alone. They were now accompanied by three small children and two grandparents. Leo and Raisa were playing the parts of a mother and father. If the hunt for them had reached Rostov, State Security would be looking for a man and woman travelling together. They'd both cut their hair short, and had been given a new set of clothes. Even so, without the family surrounding them, they would have been easy to spot.

The train stopped. Through the window they could see several uniformed officers patrolling the platform—too many for an ordinary day in an ordinary station. They were looking for someone.

The seven of them got off the train. Raisa was carrying the smallest child, a young boy. All three children had been instructed to behave boisterously. The two older boys understood the nature of the deception and played their part, but the youngest was confused and merely stared at Raisa.

Fifty paces from the exit, two armed officers stepped in front of them.

'Where are you travelling from and where are you travelling to?'

For a moment Raisa couldn't speak. The words evaporated.

Leo stepped in. 'We've just been visiting her sister in Shakhty. She's getting married.'

'To a man who's a drunk,' the grandmother added. 'I told her not to do it.'

Leo smiled at her. 'You want her to marry a man who only drinks water?'

Both grandparents laughed. The officers did not.

One of them turned to the little boy. 'What's his name?'

The question was directed at Raisa. Once again her mind went blank. Plucking a name from her memory, she said, 'Aleksandr.'

The boy shook his head. 'My name is Ivan.'

Raisa laughed. 'I like to tease him. I'm always getting their names muddled and it drives them mad. This young man I'm carrying is Ivan. That's Mikhail.' Raisa now remembered that the eldest boy's name was Aleksei. But he'd have to pretend it was Aleksandr. 'And my eldest is called Aleksandr.'

The boy opened his mouth to contradict, but the grandfather quickly stepped in and rubbed his head affectionately. Annoyed, the boy shook his head. 'Don't do that. I'm not a child any more.'

The officers stepped out of their way. Raisa struggled to hide her relief.

Once they were out of sight of the station, they bade farewell to the family. Leo and Raisa got into a taxi. The plan was in place. Leo was going to enter the Rostelmash factory and break into the employment records. He didn't know how; he'd have to improvise. Raisa was going to remain with the taxi. The driver had been paid in advance, and generously, to keep him obedient. Once Leo had found the killer's name and address, they'd need the driver to take them to where the person lived. If he wasn't home, they would try to find out when he'd be back. They'd return to Shakhty and wait.

The taxi stopped. Raisa touched Leo's hand.

He was nervous, his voice barely a whisper. 'If I'm not back in an hour . . .'

'I know.'

Leo got out, shutting the door.

There were guards stationed at the main gates, though they didn't seem particularly alert. The MGB might have figured out that he was heading to Rostov, but Leo was almost certain that they hadn't guessed that this tractor factory was his destination. Walking round the back, he discovered a point where the wire fencing was sheltered from view by a brick building. He clambered up, straddled the barbed wire, then lowered himself down. He was in.

The factory ran a twenty-four-hour production line, employing several thousand people, Leo reckoned. But there weren't many people around, and with the split between day and night workers he doubted if anyone would recognise him as a stranger. He walked purposefully towards the largest of the buildings. Two men exited, smoking, heading for the front gates.

Leo waved, moving towards them. 'I'm a *tolkach* working for the car factory in Voualsk. I was meant to arrive much earlier but my train was delayed. Where's the administrative building?'

'It doesn't have a separate building,' one of the men answered. 'The main office is inside, on one of the upper floors. I'll take you there.'

Leo smiled. He couldn't refuse. The two men said goodbye to each other and Leo followed his unwanted escort into the main assembly plant.

Stepping inside, Leo briefly forgot himself. The sheer size, the high roof, the noise of the machinery—all created a sense of awe. Leo and this man walked side by side, making idle conversation. Leo was suddenly glad of his escort; it meant no one looked twice at them.

They climbed a flight of stairs to a corridor with views over the factory floor. The man knocked on the door. It was opened by an older man, a book-keeper perhaps, dressed in a suit, with sallow skin and a bitter expression.

'What do you want?'

Leo peered over the bookkeeper's shoulder. The office was empty.

Leo swung round, punching his escort in the stomach, causing him to double up. Before the bookkeeper had time to react, Leo had his hand tight round the old man's neck.

'Do as I say and you'll live, understand?'

He nodded. Leo slowly released his neck.

'Close all the blinds. And remove your tie.'

Leo pulled the younger man inside. He shut the door, locking it behind him. The bookkeeper took off his tie, throwing it to Leo before moving to the windows, shutting out the view over the factory. Using the tie, Leo secured the young man's hands behind his back, all the time keeping his eye on the bookkeeper. With the blinds closed, the man turned back to Leo.

'What do you want?'

'The employment records.'

Baffled but obedient, the man unlocked the filing cabinet.

Leo moved forward, standing beside him. 'Stay there, don't move and keep your hands on top of the cabinet.'

There were thousands and thousands of files, extensive documentation not just for the current work force but for people who'd left. *Tolkachs* weren't supposed to exist, since their necessity implied some fault in distribution and production. It was unlikely they'd be listed under that title.

'Where are the files on your *tolkachs*?'

The old man took out a thick file. The front was marked RESEARCHERS. As far as Leo could tell, there were five *tolkachs* on the payroll. He checked their employment history. Where had they been sent and when? He ran his finger down the list, comparing it to the dates and places of the murders, held in his memory. The first list didn't match. This *tolkach* had never been anywhere along the Trans-Siberian railway line. Leo opened the second file. This person had only started working last month. Leo pushed the files aside, opening the third file. It didn't match. He flicked to the fourth.

Voualsk, Molotov, Vyatka, Gorky—a row of towns that followed the train line west towards Moscow. Moving south from Moscow: Tula and Orel. Now into the Ukraine: Kharkov and Gorlovka. In all these towns there had been murders. Before he studied the personal details he'd check the fifth file. Barely able to concentrate, he ran his finger down the list. There were some cross-references but no perfect fit. Leo returned to the fourth file. He flicked to the front page and stared at the small black and white photo. The man was wearing glasses. His name was Andrei.

VASILI SAT on his hotel bed, smoking and drinking from the bottle. He was under no illusions: if he didn't hand his superior officers Leo and Raisa, he'd be held responsible for their escape. He had pushed through the process of getting the couple on the same Gulag transport without the proper paperwork. Embarrassed at their inability to catch the fugitives, the MGB were preparing for the fact that Leo was already in the clutches of Western diplomats. If Vasili could save them the trouble of launching a diplomatically complicated international manhunt, then his slate would be wiped clean.

He dropped his cigarette stub on the carpet and crushed it under his heel. He'd been in contact with the State Security in Rostov, a ragtag bunch. He'd given them photos. He'd told the officers to bear in mind that Leo might have grown a beard or cropped his hair. They might be travelling in a group, assisted by others. Officers should pay little attention to paperwork, all of which Leo knew how to fake. He'd ordered every officer to log all incidents, no matter how trivial, in order that he'd be able to check them himself.

There had been nothing so far. Would this prove another opportunity for Leo to humiliate him?

There was a knock on the door.

'Come in.'

A red-faced young officer stood to attention, holding a sheet of paper. Vasili gestured for him to give it to him.

Rostelmash factory. Two men attacked, employment files stolen.

Vasili got to his feet. 'He's here.'

THEY STOOD side by side, fifty paces from the front door. Leo glanced at his wife. She was unaware of this madness that had descended upon him. He felt giddy, as though he'd ingested some narcotic. He half expected that the feeling would fade and normality would return, that there'd be another explanation and this wouldn't be the house belonging to his little brother.

But that was his little brother's name: Andrei Trofimovich Sidorov.

And Pavel Trofimovich Sidorov had been his own name, until he'd shed his childhood identity. The small photo on the employment file had confirmed it was Andrei. The features were the same—a lost expression. The glasses were new. But that's why he'd been so clumsy; he was shortsighted. His awkward, shy little brother—murderer of at least forty-four children. It made no sense and yet it made perfect sense: the string, the ground-up bark, the hunt. Forced to concentrate on the memories he'd banished, Leo recalled teaching his little brother how to make a string snare; he'd told him to gnaw on the bark of trees to suppress hunger. Upon seeing the victims, these details hadn't registered any deeper in Leo's mind. Or had they? Had this been the reason he'd been drawn into the investigation when there was every reason to look the other way?

When he'd seen his brother's name, Leo had been forced to sit down, staring at the file, rechecking the dates. He'd been in shock, oblivious to the dangers around him. It wasn't until he noticed the bookkeeper sidestepping towards the phone that he snapped back. He'd secured the bookkeeper to a chair, disabled the phone, gagged both men and locked them in the office. He had to get out. But going down the corridor he hadn't even been walking straight. Outside, he'd instinctively turned towards the main gates, too late realising that it would have been safer to climb back over the fence. But the guards had let him go unchallenged. Once in the taxi he'd told the driver the address, ordering him to hurry. He'd been shaking, his legs, his arms—he'd been unable to stop. He'd been incapable of telling Raisa. She now knew of his brother; she knew his first name but not their full name. He'd watched her reaction as she studied the papers. She hadn't guessed.

Raisa sensed his hesitation now and asked, 'What's worrying you?'

'The other occupants of that house.'

'You've seen the photo. You can slip in and kill him while he sleeps.'

'I can't do that. I have to be sure. I have to talk to him.'

'He'll only deny it. The longer you speak to him, the harder it becomes.'

'That might be true. But I won't kill him in his sleep.'

They'd been given a knife by the truck driver's mother-in-law. Leo offered it to Raisa. 'I won't be using this.'

Raisa refused to take it. 'What if he defends himself? He must have a knife. Maybe even a gun.'

'He's no fighter. He's clumsy, shy.'

'Leo, how do you know that? Take the knife. How can you kill him with your bare hands?'

Leo gave her the knife, pressing the handle into her hand. 'You forget: this is what I was trained to do. Trust me.'

It was the first time he'd ever asked for her trust.

'I do.' She kissed him.

Leo moved towards the house, leaving Raisa hidden. The plan was already agreed. She was to watch and wait. If the man tried to escape, she'd intercept him. If something went wrong, if Leo failed, for whatever reason, she'd make a separate attempt on the man's life.

He tentatively pushed the door, which swung open. Before him was a kitchen area. He moved through the kitchen into the adjoining space. There were only two beds. In one, two young girls slept together. Their mother slept in the second, alone; there was no sign of Andrei. Was this his sister-in-law? Were these his nieces? A cat was staring at him, two cool green eyes. Though it was better fed than the cat they'd hunted and killed in the forest, it was the same colour, the same kind. Leo felt as if he was in a dream, with fragments of the past all around him. The cat squeezed through a second door, going downstairs. Leo followed.

The narrow stairway led down to a basement illuminated by a dim light. From the top step, most of the room was concealed. All Leo could see was the edge of another bed. It was empty. Was it possible Andrei wasn't home? Leo moved down the stairs, trying not to make any noise.

Reaching the bottom he peered round the corner. A man was seated at a table. He wore thick square glasses, a clean white shirt. He was playing cards. He looked up. Andrei didn't seem surprised. He stood up. Leo could see on the wall behind his brother a collage of newspaper clippings, the same photo over and over again, the photo of him standing beside the burning panzer, the hero of the Soviet Union.

'Pavel, what took you so long?' His little brother gestured at the empty seat opposite him.

Leo was aware that he was no longer in control of the situation. Far from being caught off guard, Andrei seemed prepared for this confrontation. In contrast Leo was disorientated, confused. He sat down. Andrei sat down. Brother opposite brother, reunited after more than twenty years.

'You knew it would be me from the beginning?' Andrei asked.

'The beginning?'

'The first body you found?'

'No.'

'What body did you find first?'

'Larisa Petrova, Voualsk.'

'A young girl, I remember her.'

'And Arkady, in Moscow, murdered on the railway tracks.'

'I remember him too. They were recent. I had perfected my method by then. Yet you still didn't know it was me? The earlier murders weren't as clear. I was nervous. You see, I couldn't be too obvious. It needed to be something only you would recognise.'

'What are you talking about?'

'Brother, I never believed you were dead. I always knew you were alive. And I have only ever had one desire, one ambition . . . to get you back.'

Was that anger in Andrei's voice or affection or both emotions together? Had his only ambition been to get him back or get back at him?

Andrei smiled. 'Your stupid, clumsy brother was right about one thing. I tried telling Mother that you were alive. But she wouldn't pay any attention to me. She was sure someone had killed you. I told her you'd run away, with our catch. I promised to find you. She wouldn't listen. She went mad. She would forget who I was. She'd call me Pavel and ask me to help her, as you used to. I'd pretend to be you, since that made her happy, but as soon as I made a mistake she'd realise I wasn't you. She'd become furious, until all her anger was gone. And then she'd mourn for you again. Luckily, the winter was coming to an end and things slowly got a little better. I looked after myself. I went hunting through the forest, every night, on my own. I followed tracks. I searched for you and called your name. But you did not return.'

As though his brain was slowly digesting the words, Leo asked, 'You killed those children because you thought I'd left you?'

'I killed them so you would find me. I killed them to make you come home. I knew you'd follow the clues from our childhood to me, just as you'd followed the cat's footprints in the snow. You're a hunter, Pavel. When I saw that photo of you, I spoke to the staff of *Pravda*. I asked for your name and division. I explained that we'd been separated and that I thought your name was Pavel. They said Pavel wasn't your name and that your details were classified. I knew from the secrecy that there was a strong chance you'd either be in the military or the State Security. You'd have access to the information regarding these murders. Of course, that didn't necessarily matter. If I killed enough children, in enough places, I was sure you'd come across my work, whatever your occupation. I was sure you'd realise it was me.'

Leo leaned forward. His brother seemed so gentle, his reasoning so careful. 'Brother, what happened to you?' Leo asked.

'You mean after the village? The same thing that happened to everyone: I was conscripted into the army. I lost my glasses in battle, stumbled into German hands. When I returned to Russia, having been a prisoner of war, I was arrested and beaten. But they let me go. I returned here. I concentrated my life on a single task—bringing you back to me. That's why I got a job as a *tolkach*, so that I could travel. You might have been anywhere. I needed to leave the signs spread across the whole of our country.'

'Signs? These were children.' Leo had been listening to his brother's soft voice as if it was a foreign tongue he could barely understand. 'Andrei, you have a family. I saw your children upstairs, children just like the children you've killed. Can you not understand that what you've done is wrong?'

Andrei banged the table with his fists. 'Don't take that tone with me! You have no right to judge me! You never bothered to look for me! You never came back! You knew I was alive and you didn't care! You left me behind with a crazy mother!' He wiped the sweat from his brow. 'The happiest moment of my life was when we caught that cat, together, as a team. When we were together I never felt the world was unfair. But then you went away.'

'Andrei, I didn't leave you. I was taken. I was hit over the head by a man in the woods, put in a sack and carried away. I almost died. That man who took me was going to kill me. They were going to feed me to their son. But when we arrived at the house, their son had already died. I was concussed. I couldn't even remember my own name. It took me weeks to recover. By that time I was in Moscow. I remembered you. I remembered our mother. Of course I did. But I had no choice. I'm sorry.'

Andrei picked up the cards and shuffled them. 'You could have looked for me when you were older. You could have made some effort. I haven't changed my name. I would have been easy to find.'

That was true, Leo could have sought his brother. He'd tried to bury the past. And now his brother had murdered his way back into his life.

'Andrei, I spent my whole life trying to forget the past. I grew up afraid to confront my new parents because I was afraid to remind them of the time when they'd wanted to kill me. I used to wake up every night, terrified that they might have changed their minds and want to kill me again. I did everything in my power to make them love me. It was about survival.'

'You always wanted to do things without me, Pavel. You always wanted to leave me behind.'

'Do you know why I've come here?'

'You've come to kill me. Why else would a hunter come? I'm not going to stop you. I've achieved all I set out to achieve. I've been proved right. You've been made to regret not looking for me sooner. If you had, think how many lives would have been saved.'

'You're insane.'

'Before you kill me I would like to play one hand of cards. Please, brother, it is the least you can do for me.'

Andrei dealt the cards. Leo looked at them.

'Please, brother, one game. If you play, I'll let you kill me.'

Leo took up his cards, not because of his brother's promise but because he needed time to clear his mind. They began their game. Andrei appeared perfectly content. There was a noise to the side. Alarmed, Leo turned round. A pretty little girl was standing at the bottom of the stairs.

Andrei stood up. 'Nadya, this is my brother, Pavel.'

'The brother you told me was coming to visit?'

'Yes.'

Nadya turned to Leo. 'Are you hungry? Have you travelled far?'

Leo didn't know what to say.

Andrei answered instead. 'You should go back to bed.'

'I'm awake now. I won't be able to go back to sleep. Can't I sit with you? I'd like to meet your brother too. Please, Father, please?'

Leo had to get rid of the little girl. He was here to kill.

'Perhaps we could have some tea, if there's any?'

'Yes. I know how to make that. I can do it by myself.'

'Yes, do it,' Andrei said.

Excited, Nadya ran back upstairs.

WHEN THE BASEMENT DOOR opened, Raisa was standing in the kitchen, holding the knife behind her back.

She had waited outside for what felt like a very long time. Something must have gone wrong. She'd have to finish this herself. As soon as she'd stepped through the door, she realised to her relief that there were very few people in this house. There were two beds, a daughter and mother. But who was this little girl in front of her? Where had she come from? She seemed happy and excited. There was no sense of panic or fear. No one had died.

'My name is Raisa. Is my husband here?' she asked softly.

'Do you mean Pavel?'

Pavel—why was he calling himself by his old name?

'Yes . . .'

'I'm Nadya. Pleased to meet you. I've never met any of my dad's family.'

Family—what was this girl talking about?

'Where is my husband? I just want to let him know I'm here.'

'Downstairs.'

Raisa moved to the stairs, placing the knife in front of her so Nadya couldn't see the blade. She pushed open the door and slowly descended the stairs, the knife in front of her, trembling.

Reaching the bottom, she saw her husband playing cards.

VASILI ORDERED HIS MEN to circle the house. He was accompanied by fifteen officers. Many of them were local and he had no relationship with them. Fearful that they'd do things by the book, arrest Leo and his wife, he would have to take matters into his own hands. He'd end this here, making sure he destroyed any evidence that might mitigate in their favour. He moved forward, gun ready. He gestured for the men to remain where they were.

'Give me five minutes. Unless I call for you, don't enter. Is that clear? If I'm not out in five minutes, storm the house, kill everyone.'

LEO STEPPED towards Raisa. 'I'll do it,' he said.

Her hand was shaking. 'Why are you playing cards with him?'

'Because he's my brother.'

Upstairs, there were screams. There was the sound of shouting, a man's voice. Before anyone could react, Vasili appeared at the bottom of the stairs, his gun raised. He surveyed the scene. He too appeared confused.

'You've travelled a long way for a game of cards. I thought you were hunting for a so-called child-killer.'

Leo had left it too late. There was no way he could kill Andrei now. If he made any sudden movement he'd be shot, and Andrei would remain free.

'Vasili, I need you to listen to me.'

'On your knees.' Vasili cocked his gun.

Leo dropped to his knees. 'Vasili, this is important—'

Vasili pressed the gun against his head. 'Raisa, kneel beside your husband, do it now!'

She joined her husband; they knelt side by side. The gun was moved behind her head. Raisa took hold of his hand, closing her eyes.

'Leo . . .' Vasili's voice trailed off.

Raisa's grip tightened round Leo's hand. Seconds passed; there was silence. Nothing happened. Very slowly, Leo turned round.

The serrated blade had entered Vasili's back and exited through his stomach. Andrei stood there, holding his knife, smiling proudly, happily.

Leo stood up, taking the gun from Vasili's hand. Blood snaked from the corner of Vasili's mouth. He raised a hand, placing it on Leo's shoulder as if saying goodbye, before collapsing. This man, whose whole being had been bent on Leo's persecution, was dead. But Leo felt neither relief nor satisfaction. All he could think about was the one task he had left to perform.

Raisa got up, standing beside Leo. Andrei remained where he was. Slowly, Leo raised the gun, taking aim, just above the bridge of his brother's glasses.

A voice cried out, 'What are you doing?'

Leo turned. Nadya was at the bottom of the stairs.

'Leo,' Raisa whispered. 'We don't have much time.'

But Leo couldn't do it.

Andrei said, 'Brother, I want you to.'

Raisa put her hand round Leo's hand. Together they pulled the trigger. The gun fired, recoiled. Andrei's head jerked back and he fell to the floor.

At the sound of the shot, armed officers stormed the house. They ran down the stairs. Raisa and Leo dropped the gun. The officers stared at Vasili's body.

Leo spoke first, his hand shaking as he pointed to Andrei. 'This man was a murderer. Your superior officer died trying to apprehend him.'

He picked up the black case. With no idea if his guess would prove correct, he opened it. Inside there was a glass jar lined with paper. He unscrewed the lid, tipping the contents onto the table. It was the stomach of his brother's last victim, wrapped in an edition of *Pravda*.

As the officers moved round the table, examining this gruesome discovery, Leo stepped back. Nadya was staring at him, fury in her eyes.

Moscow, July 18

Leo stood before Major Grachev in the office where he'd refused to denounce his wife. Leo wasn't surprised that someone new was in charge. No one lasted long in the upper echelons of the State Security force, and four months had passed since he'd stood here. This time there was no chance that they'd be punished with unsupervised exile or sent to the Gulags. Their executions would happen here, today.

In front of Major Grachev was the battered case file confiscated in Voualsk. He flicked through the pages, the photographs, the statements.

'In that basement, we found the remains of three stomachs, two of which had been cooked,' he said. 'They'd been taken from children. You were right. Andrei Sidorov was a murderer. I've reviewed his background. It seems he was a collaborator with Nazi Germany and was mistakenly released back into society after the war instead of being correctly processed. That was an unpardonable error on our part. He was evidently a Nazi agent. They sent him back with instructions to take revenge on us for our victory over the Fascists. That revenge has taken the form of these terrible attacks on our children; they targeted the very future of Communism. More than that, it was a propaganda campaign. They wanted our people to believe our society could produce such a monster when in fact he was corrupted and educated by the West.' He paused, looking at Leo. 'Was this not your thinking?'

'That was exactly my thinking, sir.'

Grachev offered his hand. 'Your service to your country has been remarkable. I've been instructed to offer you a promotion, a higher position within the State Security organs. We're in new times, Leo. Our leader Khrushchev considers the problems you faced in your investigation part of the unpardonable excesses of Stalinist rule. Your wife has been released. Both your records will be wiped clean. Your parents will have their old apartment back.'

Leo remained silent.

'You have nothing to say?'

'That is a very generous offer. And I'm honoured. But I would like permission to turn down your offer. And instead make a request of my own.'

'Go on.'

'I want to take charge of a Moscow homicide department. If such a department does not exist, I would like to create it.'

'What need is there of such a department?'

'I believe that murder will become a weapon against our society. Crime will become a new front in our struggle with the West. They will use it to undermine the harmonious nature of our society. When they do, I want to be there to stop it. I would like General Nesterov transferred to Moscow. I would like him to work with me in this new department.'

Grachev considered the request, nodding solemnly.

RAISA WAS WAITING outside the building. Leo took her hand, a brazen display of affection no doubt scrutinised by those staring out of the Lubyanka. He didn't care. They were safe, at least for the time being. That was long enough; that was as long as anyone could possibly hope for.

ONE WEEK LATER

Moscow, July 25

Leo and Raisa were seated in the director's office of Orphanage 12.

Leo glanced at his wife. 'What's taking so long? Something's wrong.'

Raisa shook her head. 'I don't think so.'

'The director didn't like us very much.'

'He seemed OK to me.'

'But do you think he liked us?'

'It doesn't really matter what he thinks. It matters what *they* think.'

'You're right. I'm nervous.'

'So am I.'

'How do I look?'

'You look fine. Relax, Leo.'

The door opened. The director, a man in his forties, entered the room. 'I've found them.' The man stepped aside.

Standing behind him were two young girls, Zoya and Elena, the daughters of Mikhail Zinoviev. It had been several months since they'd witnessed their parents' execution in the snow outside their home. The physical change had been dramatic. They'd lost weight, their skin had lost colour, their heads were shaved. They'd almost inevitably been infested with lice.

Leo stood up, Raisa beside him. He turned to the director. 'Could we have a moment alone?'

The director clearly didn't like the request. But he obliged and retired, shutting the door. Both girls positioned themselves with their backs against the door, as far away from them as possible.

'Zoya, Elena, my name is Leo. Do you remember me?'

No response, no change in their expression. Their eyes were alert, waiting for danger. Zoya took hold of her little sister's hand.

'This is my wife Raisa. She's a teacher.'

'Hello, Zoya. Hello, Elena. Why don't you both take a seat? It's much more comfortable sitting down.'

Leo picked up the chairs, putting them down near the girls. Reluctantly they sat down, still holding hands, still saying nothing.

Raisa and Leo crouched so that they were below the children's eye level.

Leo began. 'My wife and I want to offer you a home, our home.'

'Leo has explained to me the reason you're here. I'm sorry if this is upsetting to talk about, but it's important we say these things now.'

'I tried to stop the murder of your mother and your father, but I failed. Maybe you see no difference between me and the officer who committed that terrible crime. But I promise you, I am different.' Leo faltered. He took a second to regain his composure. 'You might feel that by living with us you're being disloyal to your parents. But I believe they'd want the best for you.'

Raisa continued: 'If you stay here, your lives will be tough and they're unlikely to get any easier.'

'My wife and I won't take the place of your parents. No one can. We'll be your guardians. We'll look after you, feed you and give you a home.'

Raisa smiled. 'We expect nothing in return. You don't have to love us, although we hope, eventually, you will. You can use us to get out of here.'

'If you say no,' Leo added, 'we'll try to find another family that will take you. If that would be easier for you, you can tell us. The truth is, I cannot fix what happened. However, we can offer you a better future.'

The girls sat in silence, staring at Leo and Raisa. They'd given no reaction.

'You are free to say yes or no,' Raisa said. 'It's entirely up to you.'

Leo stood up. 'My wife and I will go for a walk. We'll let you talk about it, alone. You'll have this room to yourself. Make whatever decision you like. You have no reason to be afraid.'

Leo opened the door. Raisa stood up and stepped out into the hallway, Leo followed, shutting the door behind them. Together they walked down the corridor, as nervous as they'd ever been in their lives.

BACK IN THE OFFICE, Zoya gave her little sister a hug.

TOM ROB SMITH

Born: London, February 19, 1979
Home: near London Bridge
Degree: English Literature, Cambridge

RD: Have you always lived in London?
TRS: London has always been my home, but I've lived in other places. I'm half-Swedish and used to spend school summers there, living with my Swedish grandparents, who were beekeepers. I grew up in Norbury, where my parents had an antiques shop. We moved to Purley briefly, and then to Dulwich. I've also lived and worked in Italy, Nepal and Cambodia.

RD: Do you think the capital has changed in the last few years?
TRS: London is a fantastic city. It's improved dramatically. One example is the South Bank: Tate Modern, the Globe. I think it's going to get even better. It's a great place to live.

RD: What was the starting point for *Child 44*?
TRS: The inspiration was the idea that in Stalin's Russia, the State denied the existence of evil, unpreventable crimes such as murder. In the novel, Leo suspects murders are taking place, but in the State's eyes, the only crime is that Leo believes there could be such a thing as a killer.

RD: Was it a hard to write this, your first novel?
TRS: 'Hard' is tricky word . . . I'm sure there are plenty of things that are much harder to do. What *is* hard is the knowledge that you might be spending years on something that might not get published, and you're not getting paid for it. I was buying research books that, from a financial point of view, I should've borrowed from libraries. But I wanted a shelf full of them staring down at me, demanding that I finish the novel. In a way, fear became a positive. It meant I worked harder and invested more time.

RD: Have been to the USSR and did that help with the writing?
TRS: During A Levels I spent about a week in Moscow and St Petersburg. Last year I visited Estonia, because I wanted to get a sense of a country that had been absorbed by the Soviet Empire. Tallinn has an interesting Occupation Museum; it also has a KGB headquarters that looks like any other building on the street. However, the primary research came not from travel but from other books. *Child 44* is a book built on reading, and the research has been incredible. Whenever I had a tough day, I'd find a great book on the subject and it would push me through.

RD: How did you get into screenwriting?

TRS: Quite simply I wrote a spec screenplay and sent it to my agent. Some people liked it; I got some commissions. I originally intended to write *Child 44* as a movie, but my agent argued it would be too hard to pitch an expensive-to-make, period thriller by an unknown writer. He suggested I write it as a book. I'm very grateful for the suggestion!

RD: And now Ridley Scott, director of *Blade Runner*, has bought film rights, which is fantastic. Have you met him yet?

TRS: Yes, we had breakfast in his incredible office surrounded by props from his movies. It was a dream meeting him. He's made a clutch of my favourite movies. And he was wonderful to speak to, generous, full of enthusiasm about the book.

RD: What would you most like to achieve as a writer?

TRS: I think it boils down to me wanting to give back the same pleasure I've always had from reading. My ambition is to write books people can't put down, that they clear a space in their day to finish—stories that make a crowded tube journey fun!

RD: Are you writing full time now? And, if so, how do you get away from that in terms of relaxation?

TRS: I've been writing full time for about three years. I don't get away! The book is always with me. I can't shut it down. But that's fine: it's never been a hardship.

RD: What three adjectives would you use to describe yourself?

TRS: I try to use as few adjectives as possible. In thrillers, the action is everything.

GUARDIANS OF THE OFFICIAL TRUTH

Josef Stalin (right) formed the MGB, or *Ministerstvo Gosudarstvennoi Bezopasnosti*, in 1944 to ensure the security of Russia's communist state under his strict governance. Officers of this branch of the Ministry of Internal Affairs—like Leo Demidov, hero of *Child 44*—were known as 'blue caps' because of their distinctive blue uniform. Their job was to crush undesirable political organisations, to fight against armed resistance, and to prevent infiltration by foreign secret service agencies. In 1954, the MGB was disbanded and the State Security Committee, the infamous KGB, was established in its place.

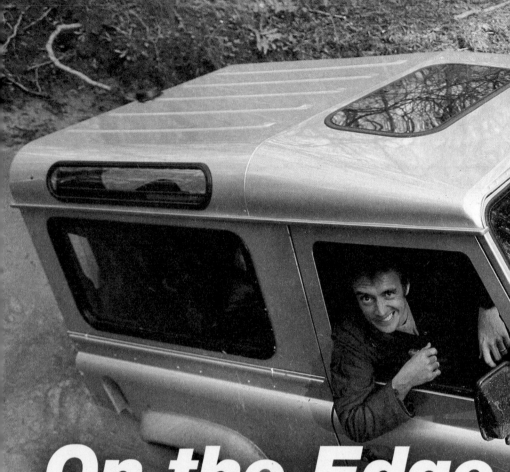

On the Edge
My Story

Richard Hammond
With Mindy Hammond

'I strode across the airfield: a man in his thirties,
living the dream he'd had since childhood.
I was walking confidently towards a
jet-propelled car that I would be driving in front
of millions . . . and the ten-year-old boy still
living inside me was giggling with excitement
and bursting with pride.'

Richard Hammond's exuberance was to be extinguished
only a few hours later, when the Vampire crashed at
232 mph, leaving him fighting for life.
This is his remarkable story.

Chapter 1

Instinct told me that I was watching one of those things that looked easy to do but that would, in reality, turn out to be difficult. My instructor glided across the frozen fields in an effortless sweep; her long, thin skis moving in a languid rhythm, until she seemed to ripple over the snow in a single movement. 'Bend the knees. You see? Bend, push, bend, push. You must get into a rhythm.' Even her voice, with its lilting, Swedish bounce, floated effortlessly across the open space. Her ski poles touched down gently with each stroke. She was demonstrating the classic cross-country-skiing style of her homeland and it looked as though she had spent her whole life doing it.

I knew that my efforts wouldn't look so good. I fell over, of course. I was discovering that cross-country skiing, or langlaufing, isn't just hard to perfect, it's almost impossible to get started.

Annoyingly, my first attempts didn't even amount to a hilarious, high-speed crash. I just slithered about for a few seconds, flopped onto my side and lay there, my nose inches from the frozen ground. But I wasn't learning this just for fun. In three months I would set off to the Magnetic North Pole on these same skis. Yet I couldn't cross a frozen playing field—and this was my third day of trying. I closed my eyes.

I was struggling because of the brain damage. It must be that. I'd always been good at things when I tried them for the first time. I mean, yes, after lesson one I'd get bored and fall to pieces. But I've always been good at the lesson one stage. A fast learner with a short attention span—every school report I have ever had said exactly that. I had a sudden memory of my first attempt at water-skiing on Lake Windermere. I had listened half-heartedly while the bloke droned on about the need to keep your knees together, to keep the rope tight, and a thousand other things that I had to know. Eventually I slipped into the freezing grey waters and grabbed the plastic handle at the end of the blue nylon rope. The boat started to pull away and then there was a firm tug on the rope. I gripped hard and rose up from the foam like a small, straggly Neptune in a borrowed blue wet suit. I was water-skiing; it was easy.

My wife, Mindy, can still hardly bear to talk about our first horse-riding trips together. She has been riding all her life: spent half her childhood being shouted at by women in polyester body-warmers about her leg position and posture in the saddle. Horse-riding is, for her, an art; something to be studied and perfected. She approaches it with the same respect that a test pilot might approach each flight. By contrast, I wandered up to the first nag I was going to throw a leg over, hopped on board, asked how you steered and braked it, and set off. There was no need to shout at me about leading legs or how I held the reins. I still ride horses the same way. It drives Mindy mad. I have always been like this; I love trying anything new and can usually make a decent go of it the first time. And then, if I have to learn how to do it properly, I get bored.

Lying on the snowy ground, I grew convinced that my inability to dazzle my instructor by slithering across the surface on my first attempt must be down to the aftermath of the jet-car crash. I knew that I was only struggling because I had damaged something important in my brain that would never mend. I must have dented my balancing gland or disconnected my coordination centre. Or something. The wet snow started to penetrate the damp fleece I had been issued with by the polar experts who had brought us here for our pre-expedition training. Somewhere, between the field I was lying on and Strasbourg airport, the rest of the guys were sharing a car, drinking petrol-station coffee and talking about home. They were flying back that morning; they'd no need to learn to ski; they were going to the Pole in a truck. Which meant right now, on this cold and lonely Austrian morning, they could go back home. I thought of Mindy, the kids, the dogs and our house. And I thought of that sodding crash and the pain it had caused.

THE EIGHT-YEAR-OLD ME silently weighed up the chances of actually becoming airborne. If the stunt went wrong and I hit the ramp too fast, there was a real chance that I might take off. I tightened my grip on the handlebars and swallowed hard. The crowd was big. I had better not look scared.

The bike looked brilliant, I knew that for a fact. I had tied two school satchels to the back and draped them over the rack to hang down on either side like motorcycle panniers. There was a fresh piece of cardboard in place, ripped from an old Weetabix packet and fixed to the chainstay. When I set off for the ramp, the cardboard would rattle away in the spokes and I would sound and look exactly like a California highway patrol bike on the telly, giving chase to a fleeing villain. At least in my imagination I would. I hoped I would to the assembled gang of neighbourhood kids, all watching and secretly hoping my attempt to leap into the history books would produce blood, and possibly a sighting of actual bone protruding through flesh, like that kid in the year above was rumoured to have done when he fell off a fence and broke his arm on an upended patio slab. We often spoke about that. We loved talking about gore.

My regular stunt activities were all just me showing off. It was a survival technique I had evolved. If you're a small guy and can't impose yourself on others physically, then think of something funny to say. When that fails, hit yourself in the face with a bicycle pump. Goes down a storm every time.

Comedy is a great way of making up for other shortcomings in your life. I learned my lesson pretty early on and by the age of eight, I was a master of the prat fall, the comedy trip and the pretend faint. It probably helped that I was small and light; when I dropped out of a tree there wasn't the kinetic energy generated by one of the big kids doing the same thing. When they fell, they broke bones and stuff. When I fell, I just bounced, laughed and checked someone was watching.

Other kids hung around after school and built models out of straws to try and impress the teachers; the bad kids set fire to trees or broke into school buildings. I set up ramps and tried to jump over stuff on bikes, attempted clearly impossible leaps across giant chasms, and climbed trees until I felt sure the air got thinner.

My first love, though, was my bike. I've always loved whatever two-wheeled transport I've owned at various stages of my life. I still do today, though now, of course, it has an engine. The walls of the bedroom I shared with my two brothers, Nick and Andy, were decorated with chopper bikes that I stared at until I fell asleep. Stunt legend and motorcycling hero Evel Knievel was my idol. It was the combination of showmanship, theatre and downright lunatic bravery that set my imagination on fire.

The bike I sat on now was styled to look like a racing bike, but sadly it didn't carry the look through into the technical department. I was proud of the glamorous yellow racing tape coiled around the dropped handlebars and fixed in place at the ends by blue plastic plugs. The most pressing concern I had was the lack of gears on my otherwise good-looking steed. That didn't stop me loving it though. My parents bought it second-hand from the huge bicycle shop near Robin Hood Island on the outskirts of Birmingham. It was the most exciting purchase I had ever been involved in.

Right now, my pride and joy felt unsteady. Way ahead in the distance—probably twenty or thirty feet—waited the ramp. We had made it from a piece of thin, shiny wood, probably a melamine cast-off from someone's kitchen. A couple of house bricks held it up. Beyond that was the pile of clobber I'd have to clear. And a ragtag band of kids from our suburban street in Shirley, West Midlands, were waiting for me to do it.

So, I decided to take the plunge. Needless to say, it was pathetic. I got a bit of a wobble on midway through the run-up to the ramp. Correcting the wobble used up precious momentum, the ramp itself was too bendy to hold the weight of the bike and just bowed to touch the pavement beneath as the front wheel rolled onto it. The leading edge of the ramp, supported on two bricks, couldn't bend and so stood proud immediately in front of my wheel. I stopped quickly and flopped over the side and onto the ground. It wasn't an exciting fall, there was no damage to the bike and there was no blood. By the time we had checked my knees for cuts one last time, the event was forgotten and we had moved on to talking about the kid who fell and chopped off both his arms and his head on an upended patio slab.

I DIDN'T JUST LOVE BIKES for what they could do; I loved them for how they worked. By the time I was ten or eleven, I was confident enough to strip them down to the last nut and bolt and restore them to smooth-running per-fection. I spent several weeks rebuilding my brother Andy's racer for him. It was a metallic-red Peugeot and had been in need of attention. After what seemed like months, the job was done. It was magnificent: a gleaming array of smooth-running, well-oiled efficiency. Every moving part had been removed, fiddled with, lubricated and replaced. Andy was delighted, though I now suspect he may have been humouring me. It had to be test-ridden and that, categorically, was a job for me. Test-riding was the best bit about being a bike mechanic.

Several houses down from ours a side road made its way round a triangular patch of grass known as 'the Triangle'. I used it for testing stuff. Residents along that stretch must have grown used to looking both ways twice as they left their front drives, because there was every likelihood that I might streak past while testing out a rebuilt bike, a scooter, or a tea tray with wheels and string to steer it. Today I was planning to break all records.

The bike was working beautifully and I shifted through the gears to check I had adjusted the cables correctly. The chainset ticked smoothly when I freewheeled, but mostly I just kept pouring on the power. It being a triangle, there were three corners in the road. I powered down the main straight, rounded the first corner, which was a gentle bend, then turned right and sped towards the last corner.

There was never much traffic on the triangle, which was why we were allowed by our parents to play there. It also meant that it took a long time for the loose chippings left after recent roadworks to be worn into the surface of the road. As I leaned the bike over to make the turn, I hit a deep patch of loose gravel. The front wheel started to slip away and I was into a crash. The first part of me to hit the deck was my right hand. I removed most of the skin on several fingers and a coin-shaped chunk of flesh from my right shoulder. In the hospital, they had to trim away the dead skin and tidy up the wounds. I swore blind you could see the white bone of my little finger's knuckle through the ripped flesh. It stung like hell when they painted it with iodine, but I couldn't wait to show my mates. I had seen the bone.

MY MUM AND DAD never encouraged the daredevil in me, but neither did they try to suppress it. With three sons to raise, they grew used to the fact that one of us would always have gravel rash on his knees, plasters on his elbows and a bruise on his face. It was usually me. They certainly never wrapped me in cotton wool. But they were dealing with the product of their genes and therein lay the problem. I say now, don't blame the parents, blame the grandparents. My father's father, George Hammond, was a tall, gentle man. While serving in the RAF during the Second World War, he volunteered for bomb disposal duty. While my father lay at home in Birmingham as a baby, Grandpa tinkered with German bombs and tried to stop them killing people. When the war ended, it must have been tricky for Grandpa to fill a considerable vacuum of excitement in his life. My father tells me now that not once did his father turn off the electricity when fixing a light switch or a plug socket. Occasionally, he would get the full force of the mains through his body. On one such occasion he was thrown backwards through the glass roof of the conservatory, on another he toppled off the banister and fell down the stairs. His response was to dust himself off and get back on with the job. There must have been a love of adrenaline deep inside my gentle grandpa. And I am equally sure that I inherited a strand of it.

From the other side of our family, from my mother's father, I inherited my passion for machines, engineering and, in particular, cars. He had trained as a cabinet-maker and later worked as a coachbuilder at the Mulliner factory in Birmingham. He went on to work at the Jenson factory, all the time expanding his considerable range of skills. He could carve wood, turn metal, work leather and improvise a way of making anything out of anything. The attic at the home he shared in Birmingham with my grandmother and great-grandmother was a place of magic for a six-year-old boy. Huge pillar drills glistened in dark corners and racks of cleaned-out jam jars and tobacco tins contained screws, bolts, washers and fittings of every size and nature. Nothing was wasted. He could make everything: pedal cars, sideboards, fancy-dress costumes, tables, cupboards and carvings emerged in a constant stream from his workshop. I stood in awe of his skill and it would be a proud thing indeed if today I could say I had inherited a fraction of it. But the evidence is clear. From these two gentlemen I inherited two things: a love of cars and engineering, and an almost equal passion for daredevilry and danger. So please, let's not blame my parents. Let's blame their parents.

LIKE ANY MAJOR ROAD, the A40 into London has many landmarks along its length. Among them is a pale, concrete footbridge extending over the four lanes of carriageway. Anyone queuing miserably along the stretch of road on the morning of February 19, 2002, searching the grey day for something to distract them, might have made out a small figure in jeans and a leather jacket sloping across the bridge. A lover spurned? A desperate man contemplating something dreadful on this Wednesday morning? No, it was me and I was crapping myself. At eleven o'clock, I was due to audition for a job on the all-new *Top Gear* programme.

At the time, I was working for Granada as a presenter on car and bike shows on satellite TV, and this was my dream opportunity. I had gone for a walk to steady my nerves. I stood at the top of the concrete steps and tried to convince myself that it was no big deal; I would either get the job or I wouldn't, and then I would go back home to Cheltenham and life would carry on as normal.

My whole life had been pretty much leading towards this moment. After a childhood dedicated almost entirely to fooling around on bicycles and obsessing about cars, I went to art college in Harrogate. I spent my time taking gloomy black-and-white photographs of scrapyards and painting pictures of American muscle cars. My photos and paintings can't have been very good; I finished art college and went to work in the least visual of all media: radio. My first job was at BBC Radio North Yorkshire. For an eighteen-year-old lad, a career in broadcasting seemed almost impossibly exciting. The station boasted a sophisticated luxury beyond my wildest dreams: a full-time receptionist, a kitchen where we could heat our own pasties in the microwave, and a production office in which every horizontal surface supported stacks of papers and reel-to-reel tapes.

Best of all, there were the studios. On my first visit, I was taken to stand in awe and look through the glass. A terrifying ON AIR light glowed red overhead as the presenter slid faders, pushed buttons and turned dials, all the time talking smoothly into an enormous microphone. He laughed confidently, flicked a fader downwards and introduced another caller to the airwaves. I was mesmerised and swore that, one day, I would do that. In the meantime, there was coffee to be made for the production team upstairs.

I spent the next ten years hopping from radio station to radio station, I lived in a series of bedsits and shared houses all over the North of England while honing my skills, interviewing, editing, dodging news meetings and running away from angry farmers who didn't want to talk about subsidies. I interviewed government ministers, authors, children's entertainers, celebrity chefs and adventurers. I spoke with people who had performed amazing feats, battled terrible illness and started successful businesses. I learned that all of us, each and every one, lives a life that is, in its own right, an epic.

At this point, on February 19, 2002, my own epic had brought me to the car park at the end of the footbridge over the A40. I bought a cup of coffee from the burger van in the car park and sat in the car to wait. I had ten minutes before I must head to the studios where the audition would take place.

I did eventually host a live show from that studio at BBC Radio North Yorkshire. I still have a taped copy. It wasn't brilliant. As the news ends and a station jingle is played, a tiny, thin voice does its best to rise above the dying chords of the jingle. I introduce myself and mistime the introduction to Dusty Springfield's 'Son of a Preacher Man', and, as my tremulous voice stomps all over the opening lyrics, my broadcasting career begins.

Now sitting in my car some thirteen years later, I still cringe at the memory of it. The car is a 1982 Porsche 911 SC. The red paintwork is far from perfect, the engine rattles ominously over 3,000 revs, the oil gauge doesn't gauge the oil, and the huge, tea-tray spoiler on the back reminds other drivers of stockbrokers in red braces and inspires them to gesticulate at me accordingly. It's the best car I have ever owned and I adore it.

On the day that I collected it, I drove it over to my parents' house in Leatherhead. It was a damp autumn day, but the rain had stopped briefly and I took in the lustrous red paintwork, admiring the way the raindrops formed silver pearls over the car's broad flanks. I twirled the key-fob in my fingers and hit the button to lock the doors—it was the first car I had ever owned with central locking. My parents sensed immediately that I was there on a showing-off mission and they 'oohed' and 'aahed' accordingly. This was a routine they had slipped into many times over the years—I would turn up in whatever set of wheels I had ruined myself financially to own and they would listen to my breathless demonstration of the car's finer points. They would bite their tongues and endure my manic attempts to justify the expense of such a vehicle when I could hardly afford a new pair of jeans. How they did this, time after time, I just don't know. But I thank them for playing along with my daft game, from the bottom of my heart.

Even when work was trickling along nicely, there was always a far-too-large chunk of my mind dwelling on cars and motorbikes. Whenever I reported for duty at yet another northern radio station I would secretly nip down to the garage to check out the radio car. Every station had one and using it was possibly the part of the job I liked best. The car, or sometimes a van, would be equipped with a mast that could, at the flick of a switch, rise up pneumatically from the roof and extend ten metres or so into the sky to allow the aerial on top to establish a broadcasting link. Every station had its legendary horror story concerning a rookie reporter who went out with the radio car, flicking the switch to send the mast up into the power cables suspended from a pylon immediately overhead. Depending on the humour of the sound engineer telling the story, it then became increasingly grisly.

Once the mast was successfully erected and the operator not fried, one could then feed live reports into the station's output. I reported on farm animal break-outs, carol concerts, jumble sales and sponsored swims. But for me, the job peaked when I pulled out of the garage. They were not, generally, glamorous cars. There isn't enough room for all the broadcast kit in a hot hatch and BBC budgetary constraints ruled out a radio-Lamborghini.

On my first day at Radio Newcastle, they sent me out in the radio van to report from what I did not at the time realise was a famously rough estate. I found my way to the school I was due to report from, parked the van and set up the mast. I unwound the drum of thick, green cable and attached the microphone and headphones to the end. I connected it to the van and threaded my way in through the gates, across the playground and into the school hall. I introduced myself to the teacher and the kids, popped the headphones on and prepared to hit the ground running when the presenter gave me the cue. Through the headphones I heard him announce my name and as soon as I spoke, the headphones went dead. I put it down to a problem with the tired old bakelite 'cans' and carried on regardless. When I went back to the van, I discovered that the end of the cable had been torn out and the interior stripped. I didn't work there for very long.

At Radio Lancashire I took over as producer and presenter of the weekend mid-morning shows. With the shows I inherited a range of regular contributors: editors of the local newspapers joined me to talk news, local politicians debated politics and Bill Scott, a restauranteur from Fleetwood, joined me every week to discuss food. But when the mics were off our conversation turned to other matters. Mostly, that meant cars. Fifteen years on, I still count Bill among my closest friends.

Another contributor opened my eyes to a whole new set of possibilities. Zog Ziegler, apart from boasting a unique name, fulfilled the role of motoring expert. He lived in Cheltenham and every week I would record a chat with Zog down the lines from his local radio station in Gloucester. He reviewed cars and discussed motoring-related issues arising in the week. This was the first time I had ever encountered a real live motoring journalist and I saw a whole new world open up.

The idea of driving new cars, formulating opinions on them and then sharing those opinions with an audience struck me as about the most wonderful way possible in which to earn a crust. I had watched *Top Gear* every week for as long as I could remember, devoured the car magazines and stalked the halls at every motor show I could visit. The idea of being involved in the world of motoring as a journalist was like being told as a kid that you could get a job as a jelly-bean taster when you grow up. From the moment I first opened a microphone to talk to Zog, I had a far better idea of what I wanted to do for a living.

Fortunately, the love of cars that I inherited from my grandfather didn't extend simply to a passion for posing in them. I'd also inherited a fascination for their innermost workings and a reasonable ability to fettle them when things got broken. Inevitably, every car that I bought was a supremely tatty example of its type; it had to be in order for me to afford it. I quickly found that a childhood enjoyment of fiddling with Lego and Meccano was easily translated into an adulthood ability to nurse along whatever rusty, broken old nail was the current apple of my car-crazed eye. I wrestled with changing my Mini's engine in a borrowed lock-up using a less sophisticated tool kit than I would expect to be delivered with a flat-pack chest of drawers. I lay in the mud to replace the gearbox under my Cortina-engined kit car through a winter so harsh I would lose all feeling in my back and have to crawl inside to get warm. Essentially, my life boiled down to two key activities: working as a radio reporter and presenter in order to pay for a procession of broken cars; the rest of my time I spent attempting to stick them together so that they could take me to work.

The Porsche 911, in which I now sheltered while waiting to audition for the new *Top Gear*, had never let me down. Though I often worried that, when it did, I would be ruined. But there was no more time for ruminating on the past. Right now I had to fire up the 911, drive about half a mile round the corner and walk into a TV studio with all the confidence I could muster to audition for the biggest job opportunity of my life.

Inside the studio I met the crew who would be filming the audition and was amazed how many people were involved. When we filmed stuff for Granada's Men and Motors channel there was me and my mate Sid who did the camera work, sound work and directing. Suddenly, I was in a world of dedicated camera operators, sound technicians, lighting technicians and assistants to the assistants. I was terrified. Then I was introduced to a man not much taller than me, with a face that somehow immediately engenders trust: it turned out to be Andy Wilman. Andy's the man who, along with Jeremy Clarkson, first came up with the idea for a whole new type of car show and persuaded the BBC that it was just what they wanted. He introduced himself with an amiable grin. I had already spoken to him on the phone but this was our first meeting. He took me aside and gave me a pep talk along the lines of: 'Try and keep your satellite-TV crap out of it, mate. Not too bouncy. This is grown-up TV now, not your toytown stuff.' The fact that he had given me a few hints about what was wanted filled me with confidence. As far as I was concerned, it meant he was on my side.

I had been asked to prepare a two-minute piece to present to camera, alone, about a car in the studio. I wandered around it, pointing out flaws and possible good points, trying to be funny and informative and not to trip over the wires on the floor. The next phase of the audition involved presenting a sequence rather like what is now the news section of *Top Gear*. For this I would be joined by a legend: Jeremy Clarkson.

To me, meeting Jeremy was comparable with a rookie racer being invited to drive with Stirling Moss. And I had to meet him for the first time and immediately begin messing about for the camera. He was turning up for every audition and so must have gone through the same process dozens of times, but he couldn't have made it easier. We argued about cars, discussed favourite motors, took the piss out of motoring stories in the news and generally acted up in precisely the way we do on telly now. He laughed at me for being short, I laughed at him for being tall, we both laughed at people who drive electric cars. It was like meeting up with an old mate.

Climbing into my car to begin the journey home, I felt no elation at how well it had all seemed to go, but instead had a sense of disappointment. I had enjoyed my time with the people in that studio so much that I knew whoever eventually landed the job was going to have a truly fabulous time. Apart from working on what promised to be a brilliant show, they were going to be teamed with a great bunch of people. I just took it for granted that I was never going to be given the role.

I rang Mindy on the way home and explained my feelings to her. She wasn't surprised by my pessimism. She's a patient woman, Mindy, and she understands me better sometimes than I understand myself.

It was because of my work that Mindy and I first met. After ten years spent trying to support myself and my various daft cars as a freelance radio presenter, I had finally caved in and got a 'proper job' in PR at a corporate headquarters on the outskirts of London. For a brief period, I enjoyed earning a reasonable wage. In the end, though, I returned to broadcasting. But not before I had found Mindy, who was working in the same office. I took one look at her curves and her long blonde hair, combined with her infectious enthusiasm, attitude to life and ever-present sense of humour, and I adored her. But I knew I didn't stand a chance. She has told me since that she took one look at the long-haired, pale-faced, skinny wretch in a cheap suit that turned up in the office one day and was, miraculously, given a job, and decided that I was 'interesting'. In fact, we fancied each other from day one.

We took to sneaking off together for fag breaks. It was, with hindsight, pretty pathetic; we had both made it fairly obvious that we were interested in meeting outside work, but we both lacked the courage to say anything about it. The breakthrough came when I was given a couple of tickets to a motorsport-related ball. I was determined to use them as an excuse to finally pluck up the courage and, like a lovelorn schoolboy, ask Mindy 'out'. Well, I didn't actually do the asking out myself, if I'm honest. I recruited the help of the boss's chauffeur, Terry. He was duly dispatched to Mindy's corner of the office to tell her I had a couple of tickets to some party and wondered if she would like to come with me. It was nothing more than the equivalent of one of those 'my mate really fancies you' conversations from school. It worked though. I picked her up from her flat in Northolt. She wore a skin-tight, figure-hugging blue dress and I nearly expired with desire when she answered the door. We spent the evening laughing, stealing cigarettes, talking about music and films and, eventually, snogging like a couple of sixth-formers.

For our fourth date, Mindy drove with her German shepherd dog and Border collie to where I lived on the edge of the Chiltern Hills. We walked, threw sticks for the dogs and on the way back shared a hug. In an instant, I fell in love with her and knew I had met my soul mate and best friend for life.

Mindy's friendship and support would be sorely tested from the start. She stayed with me when I gave up job security and went back to working in the media, presenting occasional car features on Granada TV's Men and Motors channel. I was once again broke. Mindy helped me with cash and kind words whenever things got tricky and she celebrated with me whenever something came good. We grew closer each year, eventually being blessed with our first daughter, Isabella, and getting married in May 2002. I still didn't have a 'proper job', and was now struggling to support us along with our first daughter and our first dog, Pablo, on whatever I could earn working freelance. We had moved to Cheltenham, because Mindy had family in the area and here was a place far enough from London to have its own sense of identity but not so far as to make travelling to the capital impossible. And now I was heading home with news of yet another audition for yet another job that I wanted more than anything in the world.

It would be several months before the decision was made. In the event, I was sitting at my desk in the cellar of our town house in Cheltenham when the call came. Mindy was down there with me.

The phone rang loudly and, for no reason, we were convinced immediately that it was the long-awaited call about the *Top Gear* job. Quite why we should have decided this, I have no idea, because the phone rang ten or twenty times a day. But we were right. Gary Hunter, the executive producer of the new *Top Gear*, got straight to the point:

'Hello, Richard. I was wondering—would you like to join our team?'

He was offering me the job but what I heard him say was, *I'm very sorry, but you haven't been lucky this time.*

I drew breath, ready to go into my usual speech about hoping that perhaps we might work together one day, and all the other stuff you say while your world collapses around you. And then I realised what I had heard: I had got the job. It had dominated our thoughts for the last few months. And now, finally, I had got the call and the news was unbelievably good.

'Wow, er, yes. Thank you. That's, er, brilliant.'

I put the phone down and looked across at Mindy.

'He said yes. They want me. I got it.'

Mindy was crying. I was shaking.

'Bloody hell. I got it. I actually got it. What do I do now?'

Then I realised that I hadn't asked a single intelligent question about what I would be doing, when I was starting or where I would be based. I called Gary back straight away. Mindy slipped upstairs and fished out a bottle of champagne, while I was gabbling on the phone.

We sat in the garden, drank the champagne and talked about what it might mean to us. We had, only a week earlier, agreed the sale of our Cheltenham house and the purchase of a crumbling little place in a remote corner of the nearby Gloucestershire countryside. Would this affect our plans to live in rural splendour with animals around us and space for our daughter—and maybe other children—to grow up? We had no idea. There was a lot to unfold with my new job. And most of it really would be brilliant.

'I'VE GOT A GREAT IDEA,' I announced. No one looked up and I carried on fighting my way through the piles of papers, radio-controlled cars and assorted props that blocked every path through the *Top Gear* office on the fourth floor of the BBC White City building in London. I had burst into the office to find the production team preparing for the ninth series of the show. It was four years since I'd got the call asking me to join *Top Gear*.

'It's a belter,' I panted. 'Really. Made for the new series. Perfect.'

Andy Wilman looked up from his desk and harrumphed—his normally friendly face creasing into a comically bad-tempered version of itself. As *Top Gear*'s editor, he is the man saddled with crafting the mishmash of fragile egos, dangerous enthusiasms and crazy schemes that float around the office, into a television programme. He is also the man who has to spend a lot of his time keeping BBC executives, the board of complaints, the pro-politically correct lobby, the anti-car lobby and, occasionally, the police at a discreet distance.

It was not by accident that his desk was to be found in this cluttered corner. He deliberately sited himself in the midst of the team of researchers, producers, production managers and runners. He had worked his way through the ranks and could do the job of every person in the room, if he had to. Which meant there was little they could get away with.

'Listen—' I tried to make it sound commanding but it came out like a plea '—I just want to go fast. That's it.' I shrugged what I hoped was a dramatic shrug and added in a fake American drawl, 'Jus' real fuckin' fast.' I had rehearsed the sales pitch on the motorway. It had gone better in the car. It's not a rare event for someone to try to persuade Andy that their scheme has the potential to make a great piece of telly. I wasn't nervous about chucking a proposal in, but in this case it was something I really wanted to do and I didn't want the idea to vanish without trace.

'I don't want to enter a race or do anything complicated. I think we should just do a piece on going faster than we've ever gone before. Straight-line speed, that's the thing. I've driven at two hundred mph in a car and on a bike. What does it feel like to go faster? A *lot* faster.' I ploughed on, warming to my subject. 'Speed can make us feel good. There's just something exciting about it. So all we need to do is find something that can go real fast in a straight line. I don't want to set a record. Well, maybe just a record for a car show. We can be the fastest car show on earth. What about that?' Andy nodded; the team saw the nod and registered his approval and I knew it would happen. Probably.

In fairness, it wasn't that unusual for one of the team to champion an idea that came from pretty far outfield. Someone had once suggested that we submerge a car in a tank of water to see how you really escape from a sinking car. That idea got the go-ahead and, one cold, damp winter's day, I found myself sitting in an old Vauxhall Carlton suspended from a crane over a water tank, about to film a demonstration of just how terrifying and disorientating it actually is when you find yourself sitting in a car as it sinks and the water laps up and over the windows.

In a moment of typical *Top Gear* genius, the director had shown me a video clip of someone else doing exactly the same thing. The seasoned stuntman involved had gone into a panic of such intensity that, watching the video, I feared he might die of stress before he got the opportunity to drown. He kicked the windscreen out and escaped to safety through the incoming flood of water. I climbed into the old Vauxhall, tried to remember how to breathe through the diving regulator hidden in the back of the car, gave the thumbs-up as cheerily as I could to the stunt crew, and hoped not to be meeting my maker any time soon.

To sit in a car and feel it begin to sink, watching as the water rises up the doors and then the windows is pretty frightening. Water rushed into the car with a threatening roar. The light from outside dimmed and turned green as the car sank beneath the surface, and the sense of claustrophobia increased as I sat, knowing that I must wait until the car filled entirely before I opened the doors and scrambled out. The Vauxhall continued to sink, the water now covering the windows completely and rising up the inside to chest height. I rehearsed again the moves needed to spin round and grab the ventilator and air tank hidden in the back. I hoped I wouldn't need them.

As the car filled, the water chased the last air pockets out of corners with explosive gurgles and hisses. The whole thing tipped forward as the weight of the engine took the front down first. My chest was soon completely submerged and the water rose up my neck. I had rehearsed in my mind the moment when I must push my mouth up to the roof to get a last lungful of air before the car filled with water entirely, but the reality was more frightening than I thought it would be. The thing that really had me pinned down with terror was the fear of panicking. If I passed out, if the locks wouldn't open, or if the windows caved in under the pressure, we had taken emergency precautions. I had the air tank in the car and a team of divers could reach me before I so much as looked uncomfortable. All I had to do was not panic. If I flailed around like an idiot, then it would be harder to rescue me and I would endanger the people around me. I would also look like an utter numpty and the rest of the team would never, ever stop taking the piss.

In the event, I sucked in a last breath of air, waited until the car was resting on the bottom of the tank, shoved the door, which opened smoothly, slipped out of the car and bobbed up to the surface like a cork. It was easy. Just don't drive your car into a canal.

The experts told me afterwards that it's all very well waiting until the car hits the bottom, but what if it ends up sitting next to an old fridge and the door won't open? Worse still, another told me that it's not uncommon for police divers to recover a vehicle from a lake and find the route to safety perfectly clear, but the driver still sitting there, dead, with their seat belt still on. That's how much of a problem panic can be.

In the four years I had worked on the programme, I had built a reputation for being happy to have a bash at the more risky-seeming stuff. I had absolute faith in the team around me and their ability to foresee problems. I was just lucky to be getting paid for exactly the kind of showing off I had been doing all those years ago on my bicycle. And so I enjoyed racing a

2CV around Snetterton Race Track for twenty-four hours, joining the Norwegian Olympic bobsleigh team for a full-speed run down the bobsleigh track in Lillehammer, and running with the bulls in Pamplona.

Someone in the team once suggested we record an item on what happens when a car is struck by lightning. Obviously, it would be time-consuming and expensive for me to sit in a car in a field. We needed a way to guarantee the lightning. We found it in Germany at a hi-tech research lab where they can generate artificial lightning. Sure enough, I volunteered.

The car sat in a compound surrounded by barbed-wire fences covered in warning signs indicating that trespassers would be fried with millions of volts of electricity before they were prosecuted. The film crew sat around the perimeter wire, the German boffins twirled knobs in the control room, and I sat in the car and wondered what being hit by lightning would feel like. We were about to demonstrate the Faraday cage effect, which dictates that the electricity from the lightning strike would travel not straight through the centre of the vehicle—frying everything inside, including me—but around the metal exterior, making the final leap to the earth from the wheels. The tyres would not be melted, the windscreen would not explode, my hair would not stand on end, and there would be no complicated forms for the director to fill in at the end of the day.

It was a scientific fact that this would happen, as guaranteed as any other scientific law. The lightning would behave in the way predicted because science said so. Nevertheless, sitting in the car as the machines outside hummed and the boffins read out the millions of volts being prepared especially for me, I felt the familiar grip of nerves. What if the rules of science suddenly and briefly changed that day? Then there was a loud crack, an eerie blue light outside the car—and it was over.

Several million volts of Germany's best homemade lightning had leapt from the wires overhead, covering the two-metre air gap in a fraction of a second, drawn to the car's metallic body and to the earth waiting below. I said something to the camera to the effect of, 'If I'm talking to you now without wings and a halo then we have demonstrated that the theory works.' It had, I wasn't dead, so we packed up and went home.

And now I was travelling home once more with news for Mindy of yet another stunt I might be attempting in the name of journalism, entertainment and paying the mortgage. I was, as usual, mobbed by animals and children as soon as I prised the front door open. We now shared our little house in the country with two daughters; Isabella had been joined by her younger sister, Willow, now three years old, along with five dogs, four cats, four horses, a small flock of sheep and a handful of chickens. It was a long commute to and from London, but the reward was a chance to really escape when I finally got home. We indulged our passion for horse-riding, dog-walking and taking the kids out for long rambles in the woods. Mindy had developed a passion for cars almost on a par with mine and we also, when time and children permitted, rode motorbikes. Mindy passed her bike test in 2005 and I had surprised her with a Harley of her own on her birthday the following July.

Work made its presence felt, though. There had been times when Mindy found it difficult to watch the footage of me doing stunts on *Top Gear*. When we watched the film of the car being dropped into the tank, I turned to see Mindy sitting with her eyes brimming with tears. She told me that she was terrified, even though I was sitting there next to her, weeks after the event, and very much not drowned.

We spoke briefly that evening about the 'real fuckin' fast' idea. But it was likely to be a long way off yet and might never become a reality.

Chapter 2

Within twenty-four hours, I would be deep in a coma as my brain expanded dangerously within my skull. But right now, I was in rural Bedfordshire, crouched in the lee of a Land Rover, picking burrs from my dog's coat. It was strangely soothing work and I let my mind wander back over the day's filming.

We were working on a sequence in which all three of us decided to go green by making our own bio-fuel. To do this, we would need to grow a field full of wheat, which could eventually be turned into something that worked very much like diesel. We would start by ploughing and that meant playing in tractors. James had managed to bury his in a boggy corner of the field; Jeremy had used explosives instead of a plough when he got bored with going slowly, and I had managed to tie my lengthy and very expensive plough in a knot behind my twenty-six-tonne caterpillar-tracked tractor with which, earlier in the day, I had blocked the main street of the village.

Top Gear Dog—or TG as she is affectionately known at home, where she lives with me and my family—had enjoyed her day hugely. We had wheeled her out for duty as a sheepdog, clearing the sheep before our ploughing attempts could begin. We were hoping she wouldn't be much good and that it would provide a moment of light relief for the viewer. She didn't disappoint: she was spectacularly bad. Half of the problem stemmed from the fact that with her pale, woolly coat, she looks rather like a sheep anyway, and so our targets felt perfectly at home in her company.

When Jeremy's explosives were due to be detonated. I took TG off to a safe distance. They went off with seven or eight dull thuds that you felt through the ground as much as heard. A shower of dirt and small stones rained down. TG lifted one eyebrow, looked up at me, put her head down on her paws and went back to sleep. She's not easily flustered. She was due to come with me to York after we finished filming that day; I'd thought it might add a rather jolly pilot-type flavour to the whole thing, having the dog standing on the airfield while I drove the jet car.

We had just finished filming the final sequence of the day and I went over to collect TG. I knew something was wrong as soon as I saw her. Her long woolly coat had picked up several million spiky burrs. These had so embedded themselves in her fur that they were causing her some discomfort. I picked as many from her as I could, but it was hopeless. I rang Mindy and we agreed that there was only one alternative. A member of the production team would drive her back home, where an expert would make sure all the burrs were removed. She wasn't going to be coming to York and she would miss the jet car. I would miss her.

The various crews were packing up their kit and readying themselves to head off to different locations for film shoots the next day. When we are getting ready for a new series, everyone is working hard to get as many of the films made as possible before we all get tied up with recording the studio element of the programme. Jeremy asked me what I was going to do. I told him it was the jet-propelled car thing up at Elvington.

'You're actually driving it, then?'

'Yes.'

'Goodbye.' He extended his hand with an air of absolute finality as one might extend a hand to a man walking to the gallows. It was a pretty standard joke really, the sort of thing we all do among ourselves on a daily basis. He was making out that I was sure to be 'killed to death' in a horrible crash.

'Yeah, whatever. It'll be fine.'

I phoned home and spoke to Mindy. She had picked up Izzy from school and Willow from nursery and we spoke about their day. I felt a pang as I pictured them in the kitchen. Sometimes, missing them becomes a real physical sensation in my chest that takes my breath away. On *Top Gear* shoots when we are all away from home, at about seven in the evening there comes a period when Jeremy, Andy, me and other members of the crew with young families can be found with mobile phone glued to our ears wishing our kids good night. No matter how much fun we all have when we are away working, there are moments when we all regret not being at home to give our kids a good-night kiss. Of course, we would never share this feeling in the hotel bar. But we all know it goes on.

It was at least three hours to the hotel in York. Because of my job, I drove a lot of different cars in order to write a script before filming them for *Top Gear* or to review them for my column in the *Mirror*. On this occasion, I had borrowed a Honda S2000 two-seater roadster and I was glad of the distraction of a test car to drive.

Settling into the driving seat, I turned my thoughts to the jet car I would be driving the following day. We had done a lot of research and prepared a great script. It wasn't about the absolute speed so much as the sensation of driving a jet-powered car with 10,000 bhp. I tried to imagine unleashing the power of eleven Formula One cars in one huge hit of adrenaline-fuelled speed. I watched the trees and lamp-posts whizzing by on either side and tried to multiply their speed by a factor of three or four. I couldn't imagine it. This would be a whole new experience and would, I suspected, for ever change my idea of what it meant to go fast.

Over the past few weeks, we had talked a lot about how to make the best of this opportunity to drive a pretty special machine. We had all agreed that it would be best not to get too caught up on the numbers. If I spent too much time staring at the speedo and trying to squeeze an extra couple of miles an hour out of the car before I ran out of runway to drive on, there was a real danger that I might get something wrong. The best way to go about it, we decided, was for there to be no speedo in the car. We would know the figures from the on-board telemetry system, which would record the speed, the acceleration, the g-forces and every single input I made into the controls as I drove. But that information would be referred to in the studio, after I had driven the car and put it safely away. I would be taught how to drive it by the man who had built it and drove it regularly. I would progress slowly, increasing the power and, of course, the speed as the day progressed and at a pace that both the owner and I were happy with.

A mate of mine, Colin Goodwin, a motoring journalist, had already driven the exact same car. Colin's down-to-earth explanation had been very useful in researching for the piece we were filming and, of course, in satisfying my curiosity about what lay ahead of me. It was, he had told me, mind-blowing. He had hit over 270 mph and never again looked at speed in quite the same way. He assured me that the machine was actually simple enough to operate and reckoned I was in for a pretty fantastic time and would love my day in a jet car. An expert had been dispatched from the BBC to give the car a thorough check and make sure everything was in order. It was; the car looked great and I was looking forward to driving it. By seven o'clock I was rolling into York and eventually found my way to the hotel. The next day's film crew had arrived and were settled into the bar for a last pint before bed. The team who had brought the car were also present. Colin Fallows, the guy who had built it, was in a corner and I sat next to him, eager to learn more about what was to come the following day.

As a technical man and a keen driver, Colin was someone I was bound to get on with. He had served extensively in the RAF, working with jet engines for decades, and was a fund of stories and technical insights on the subject of jets, planes and, of course, jet-propelled dragsters. We quickly settled into a friendly conversation about how he had built the car and why. I looked at him, a small, slightly portly chap, who looked more like a bank manager or quantity surveyor than a man who habitually took the helm of a dragster that propelled him to speeds in excess of 300 miles an hour. It goes to show that you never can tell about people until you talk to them.

I slipped away to bed early and rang Mindy. TG was booked in to visit the groomer the next morning. The girls were sleeping soundly. We wished each other good night. The following day was shaping up to be exciting and I was looking forward to the jet-car drive. But first, sleep.

I FISHED AN ARM under the bed feeling for my quarry. The car keys could have dropped off the bedside table in the night but I couldn't find them. I had got to the room door, my bags hanging from my shoulder, ready to go, before I realised something was missing. And now time was pressing. I had already decided to forgo the hotel breakfast; I knew that I could breakfast later at the airfield while the crew rigged their kit. All I had to do was find the flaming keys before dashing to the garage. I stamped over to the door and bent to pick up my shoulder bag. I knew it was the action of a nervous bloke, but I figured it was worth checking it just once more. Sure enough, I found the keys in the front pocket, jammed between my passport and my Moleskine notebook. I felt that surge of relief at finding something you had thought lost, closely followed by another surge of anger at myself for being such a disorganised clot. Grabbing my bags, I hefted the door open and ran.

It was not easy, but somehow our tiny convoy made it to Elvington. In the distance, surrounding the airfield, I saw stretches of dark green coniferous forest. The land was flat and broad and a light wind blew across it under a pale blue sky. I made my way towards the small crowd assembled round some sort of catering van. I recognised Scott, the director.

'Seen the car yet?' he asked.

'Nope. Can't wait. Where's Colin?'

'Getting it ready. They'll bring it over in a sec.'

I ordered a cup of tea and a bacon sarnie. We've adopted a sort of military approach to eating on these shoot days: if you see food, eat it now because you might not get any later.

I sought out Scott again and we got our heads together for a brief planning session. There was much to do, but for once we had to do it at the pace at which events unfolded. I had to be introduced to the car and taught how to drive it. This would take as long as it took. We had to film a few bits where I would talk to camera about the car, but we decided to do that at the end of the day. We only had the runway until 5.30 p.m., after which time noise restrictions would end our chances of driving the car. I grabbed another cup of tea and sat in the Honda, reading through the script. There's only so much that you can write before a feature like this one, but we could structure it pretty rigidly. The bits to be sketched in on the day would be my responses to driving the car. We wanted to record how it felt, what went through my mind, and how it compared to driving the other fast cars I have driven. I rang Andy Wilman in London. We stay in constant touch when we're out filming, and it's useful to speak with someone, away from the scene of the actual shooting, who can retain a sense of perspective. Andy reiterated the importance of not getting caught up in specific speeds. We agreed that this was all about the sensation of driving the thing. I told him that I would call him back as soon as I had completed my first drive.

Before I even got to sit in the Vampire, Colin was going to take it for a shakedown blast up the runway. It was the sort of hands-on approach you would expect from him. The car appeared and I got my first look at it. I was surprised by how long it was. This was more like the top-fuel dragsters I had loved when I was a kid. I would rummage about in my huge tub of Lego to build drag racers that looked exactly like Vampire, with its long, skinny body, big chunky rear wheels and skinny little front ones. But my models had never had the strange, cylindrical addition immediately behind the driver's head. This was the jet engine, the heart of the machine and the very reason for its existence. Colin was in the driver's seat and steered the thing into position on the start line. We had gathered a couple of hundred metres away. Colin's technical assistant busied himself making adjustments and checks. Our whole team watched in silence.

I could hear Colin and his assistant shouting instructions to one another and, eventually, I picked out the unmistakable whine of a jet engine starting up. The whine built to a shriek and hot air shimmered dizzyingly around the back of the car where the massive engine's thrust poured out into the crisp autumn morning. With no warning, the car leapt forward. There was a burst of flame from the engine's outlet at the back and a roar as the noise hit us. Colin was using the afterburners, so this would be a full-power run. I knew that much from our conversation the previous evening, and I tried to imagine what it must feel like, being hit in the back by a 10,000-horsepower engine and shooting up to 300 miles an hour in the time it takes a fast road car to hit sixty. Watching from the sidelines, the car's acceleration was endless. And then, only a few seconds after it set off, we could see the parachute mushrooming behind the car. Silence descended as the parachute collapsed to the ground behind the now stationary car, half a mile or so down the runway. I felt a twinge of nerves in the pit of my stomach. That had looked like a very great deal of power being unleashed to catapult a very small car up a very short runway.

It took half an hour for the car to be made safe and towed back up to the launch point at the top of the runway. While Colin and his team did technical stuff, we loitered by the burger van. The guys were asking how it felt, knowing that I was going to be driving the same car. I told them that I was nervous, but pretty sure I could manage it. I've spent too much of my life standing around waiting to do things that have made me nervous to be caught out now. It's best to be aware of the nerves, but not to let them take over. The nerves help by sending adrenaline flooding around your body, making you sharper and your responses faster; but if you let them take over your mind then you can lose focus.

Soon enough, the car was ready. Colin and I walked towards it together, leaving the crew behind. We would film a TV version of our briefing later on, but this was the real thing and best not interrupted by having TV cameras stuck in our faces. Colin began to fill me in on what the car could do. He explained that the engine was mounted in such a way that the thrust also pressed it down onto the tarmac. This put my mind at rest a little about the dangers of the engine suddenly trying to revert to its former life of sending an aeroplane hurtling around the skies. Then Colin indicated that it was time for me to climb in and I did.

The narrow aperture into the cockpit meant I had to slide myself in carefully, ducking my head beneath the protective bars of the rollover structure. Colin talked me through the controls. There were surprisingly few. Essentially, the car consists of an engine, a parachute and the seat. Because the engine does not transmit the power to the road, there are no complicated systems for sending the power through the wheels. It just revs up and sends the thrust out of the hole at the back. Because it's bolted to the engine, the car is thrown forward with it. So there is a control for turning the engine up to the required level in much the same way that you set the volume on a radio. The metal dial, about the size of the base of a teacup, sat on the right-hand side of the rudimentary dashboard.

Just below the engine control was a large metal lever, hinged beneath the dash. Colin explained that this cut the engine and deployed the parachute simultaneously. This, then, was my main braking system. Once under way the brakes on the wheels would be useless and I would rely on the 'chute to bring everything to a halt. In the centre of the metal dash panel was the steering wheel, made up of two small handles connected in the centre at a metal boss about four inches across. I rested my hands on the two handles, feeling the bare metal beneath them cool and strangely sensual. Through this wheel would be transmitted the power unleashed by the massive engine just a couple of feet behind my head.

These were all the controls I had to operate. There was no clutch pedal because there was no clutch. There was no accelerator because I dialled the power in before I set off. My right foot rested next to the footbrake, which was used only to hold the car stationary as the engine got up to speed. My left foot rested on a dead man's pedal, which would cut the engine the moment my foot lifted. This was a device that would come into action only in an emergency.

This was not the interior I'd imagined. I had envisaged rows of toggle switches controlling any number of intricate functions. I expected to see every surface sprouting more switches, with the gaps between them filled by gauges and dials. What I found in reality was a collection of controls as simple as the ones on the plastic dashboard I had stuck to the back of my dad's driving seat as a kid. There are more systems to monitor on a family hatchback. I was slightly disappointed, but also reassured that, if this was all I had to concentrate on, then there would be little to distract me from the business of steering and stopping at the right point.

I stared down the runway and imagined how it might feel. When Colin gave the signal, I would take my foot off the brake and feel the car surge forward with unimaginable force. Would it be smooth and steady, or would my head be jostled around, making it hard to see ahead? Would the G-force snap my head back? I asked Colin how I used the afterburner. He told me that we would not get round to using that until later but, when I did, it was just a case of thumbing the metal switch on top of the left-hand grip on the steering wheel. When I hit the switch, a flame would be sent shooting down the centre of the engine behind me, igniting the fuel in the engine and turning it into something like a cross between a standard jet engine and a rocket. The power would instantly be doubled. I wondered about the timing.

'You take your foot off the brake and then hit the button,' he told me.

'What if my foot is still on the brake?' I didn't want to get it wrong.

'Makes no difference. When you hit that button, you are going that way.' Colin pointed up the runway.

'Right.' I felt like a ten-year-old.

Before I did my first run, we would record a couple of bits of telly. It would be no good speculating on camera about how it might feel to drive the Vampire if I was dripping with sweat from having already done it. I would get changed into my driving kit, knock off a couple of pieces to camera, and then get on with the driving.

Another member of the *Top Gear* production team, Grant Wardrop, had joined us for the day. He passed me one bag stuffed with a set of racing overalls, and another containing a crash helmet. I protested that I had brought my own helmet, but he insisted that I use the one provided. He had realised early on that this was a pretty unique drive and had personally researched the best crash helmet for the job.

There was nowhere to get changed. I asked the paramedic guys if I could borrow their ambulance and turn it into a dressing room. They agreed as long as I didn't fill it full of flowers and blue M&Ms. I laid the silver-coloured racing suit out on the trolley bed and inspected the kit more closely. The suit was made of thick, fire-retardant material and the label told me that it was four layers dense. I pulled it on over a T-shirt and underpants and knew, instantly, that I looked ridiculous—more pixie than pole position.

At the bottom of the bag, I found the neck brace—a circle of padding that sits immediately below the opening of the crash helmet and limits how much your head can move in a crash. I put it on and doubted that the big blue circle just below my chin had improved an already shaky image.

The helmet, though, was a beauty: a plain white Arai, built specifically for car racing. I grabbed it by the chin-guard and hopped out of the ambulance's back doors. Predictably, the crew laughed when I came into view. I looked like an extra from an early episode of *Doctor Who*.

The car was waiting for me on the start line and it was time to get to work. The crew busied themselves getting cameras and sound-recording equipment ready. There were cameras on board the car too, tiny digital ones mounted so that they could look back at my face and forward along the length of the car.

As far as I was concerned though, this part of the day was not about the filming. My role now was not TV presenter but jet-car driver. I replayed Colin's thorough explanation of what I must do and put one hand on the side of the car, ready to climb in. Colin was there to remind me of the routine. I climbed over the side of the car. Colin glanced in to check that everything was OK, and stepped back to allow his technician to fasten the harnesses. They were pulled so tight that I could barely breathe. These guys were not taking any chances. And then Colin began fastening straps that connected my upper arms to the harness.

'What are they for?' I asked.

'If you have a crash, they stop your arms from flailing around.'

I looked to the side at the massive roll bars and winced as I imagined trapping an arm between one of them and the ground.

Colin asked me to run through the controls again. This time though, it was no dry run. When I asked for air and power, the engine would be started. I would be at the controls of a running jet engine for the first time in my life. Making a conscious effort to breathe steadily, I went through the motions one last time. With Colin happy, we were ready to do it for real.

I called for air and power. Colin flicked the switches. Immediately behind my head, an engine capable of delivering enough power to shove a jet fighter around the skies began to turn. I felt a surge of excitement mixed with fear as my mind was invaded by the close presence of a jet engine. The sound rose to the shriek familiar to airports across the world. But on this occasion, there were no other passengers and no one else to control the massive engine. The noise rose to a howl. Colin gave the thumbs-up.

I could feel the car straining against the brake. It had been transformed into a wild creature, held back just by my right foot. Colin signalled that I should go. This was it. I lifted my foot from the brake.

The acceleration was massive but I had expected a mind-warping blur of speed as I exploded away from the line. This was different, a firm and insistent shove that I had no choice but to go along with. The speed increased. Fast. Within 13.7 seconds of taking my foot off the brake, I had passed 205 miles an hour. But there was no way of knowing that inside the cockpit. And even if there had been a speedo fitted, I would have hesitated to glance at it. There was a lot to do. Because of the camber of the airfield and the crosswind, I had been told to apply a constant thirty degrees of steering input to keep the car going straight. I had not anticipated how much this was needed. Far from being the brave but pointless passenger I had thought I would be, I found that the driver was a very, very busy individual.

I tried to keep my eyes focused on the track ahead. Very soon, I would pass the traffic cones that signalled the point at which I must shut down the engine and deploy the parachute. It was hard to see. The runway surface communicated every bump and ripple through the wheel. The car shifted and vibrated. The noise was all-pervading. My senses were swamped by a constant scream as the engine hurtled me towards the horizon.

As we charged forward, my crash helmet was buffeted by a wind of unimaginable force. I wondered what would happen if I missed the cones. To make matters worse, my visor was steaming up. I couldn't lift a hand from the wheel to fiddle for the latch and open it. And even if I could, I didn't fancy a face full of wind at whatever speed I was now travelling. And then, through the mist, I saw the cones just ahead. It was time.

I moved my hand away from the pistol grip of the wheel and found the lever to the right. My fingers closed on the metal end. I pulled it. The jet engine changed from a shrieking monster to a more docile beast as its furious howls relaxed into a lengthy sigh. I wondered if the parachute had worked. And then I was shoved forward in my seat and I knew that the huge silk canopy had fired out of its tube at the back of the car and now grabbed at the air moving by at 206 mph.

The tug from the parachute was astonishing. At full acceleration, a car like this might shove the driver into the seat with 1.8g. That's 1.8 times the force of gravity. Under braking, though, the parachute can arrest the car so that the driver is thrown forward with 3.5 g, compared to the most a normal car driver is ever likely to feel, under braking of 1 g. It took my breath away. But it felt good.

In 9.3 seconds, the car had slowed to a more pedestrian sixty mph. I steered to the point where I knew the crew would be expecting me to stop. We had planned for the end of this first run. Having filmed the car as it hurtled up the runway, they would dash over to a pre-arranged spot where it would come to rest and I would deliver a few words about how it had felt. I didn't bother planning what I would say. This was one occasion when it is best to just open your mouth to allow whatever is in your mind to flood out. The results may not be considered and eloquent, but they will be heartfelt and honest. And as a viewer, that gives you something more special than the most polished speech. It's when TV really can take you somewhere.

The film crew dashed towards me. I blurted out words, trying to communicate how it had felt to be totally at the whim of something so incredibly powerful for a few brief seconds. My mate Colin Goodwin had told me how his drive in the same jet car had been a life-changing experience. I knew now what he meant by that. It was only 1 o'clock. I wanted to go faster.

I clambered out of the car and spent a moment or two with Colin. I looked into his eyes to try to catch a glint of recognition that we two had now visited a place not visited by many. It was an experience that I was due to repeat several times that day.

Over another cup of tea, I cornered Paul, the producer, and told him about the problems with the visor. We rang the production team and set them looking for a local shop where we could buy one of a number of products that you spray onto the inside of helmet visors to stop them steaming up. But I knew of a simpler solution. Smearing a tiny spot of washing-up liquid onto the surface of the visor has exactly the same effect. It's an old biker's trick.

I had recently taken up smoking after several years of abstinence. It had happened on another *Top Gear* shoot when we had been chased across Alabama by angry rednecks after we painted slightly rude slogans down the sides of our cars. They were offended and pursued us in pick-ups with shotguns. We fled across two states. I ended that day by sparking up my first cigarette in three years, and right now seemed like a good moment to indulge too. I slipped quietly into the solitude of the Honda, sparked up a smoke and sat back. I felt good. I had known all along that driving the jet car would be fine; that I would be nervous, but then elated and in control. And that was exactly how it had turned out.

There was much still to do. We had to film pieces to camera explaining how the car worked and more shots of the car in action. More to the point, I still had to progress to using the afterburner and do a full-bore run with all 10,000 bhp unleashed behind me. I was looking forward to the experience. Driving the same car with twice the power would be a huge buzz.

I rang home to speak to Mindy. I knew she was worried and tried my best to reassure her. I then phoned Andy Wilman to let him know that the first run had gone well and I had not flashed past the waiting cameras as a flaming fireball. We joked about, but I could tell that he was genuinely relieved that things were going well.

My second fag finished on cue, just as the team were done prepping the car. Duty called. I hauled myself out of the car and strode across the airfield: a man in his thirties, living the dream he'd had since childhood. I was walking confidently towards a jet-propelled car that I would be driving in front of millions of TV viewers the world over. It doesn't do to get too self-congratulatory in life—pride comes before a fall and all that—but as I walked across the smooth tarmac and slipped the neck brace onto the shoulders of my silver racing suit, the ten-year-old boy still living inside me was giggling with excitement and bursting with pride.

After a pep talk with Colin, I made my second run. I thrilled to the sensation of the power and the speed, and hopped about in front of a TV camera afterwards, trying to convey a sense of what I was experiencing. And then I did it again. By now, it was well into the afternoon. The next thing was for me to try a run with the afterburner lit.

I rang Andy Wilman again. He reminded me that I had to go at my own pace. I reassured him that I would only do what I felt safe to do.

Back in the jet car, I studied the switch that operates the afterburner. It is a tiny, metal thing but it would instigate a procedure that would unleash quantities of power that, for millennia, were seen as the preserve of the gods.

Colin described the process: a flame would shoot down the centre of the engine and ignite unburnt fuel; the power output of the mighty jet engine would, effectively, be instantaneously doubled. I rehearsed the moment: start the engine, hit the button as my foot came off the brake and then, seconds later, pull the 'chute and celebrate being alive.

The jet engine whined into life and built to a screaming crescendo. Colin gave me a confident smile. I took a deep breath, hit the button to fire the afterburner and lifted my right foot to release the brake. Suddenly, I was in a different car. I heard the roar and felt acceleration like I had never felt before. This time, the car exploded into action. I realised now that the jet engine, without the afterburner, was a friendly beast that put a hand at my back and pushed me gently up the runway as an adult might push along a child's toy car. This though, was a manic, violent thing.

I can't say that it felt any different from a fast drive in a supercar, but I was aware at the same time that it *was* different. I could sense that my mind and my senses were operating at optimum speed to act fast enough to cope and stay alert to what was happening.

Within just 17.2 seconds, I drew level with the cones. I pulled the lever to cut the engine and deploy the 'chute. Just twenty-three seconds after hitting that little button on top of the steering wheel, the run was finished. I had ridden a wave of power that ten Formula One cars together would struggle to achieve. I felt more alive than I could remember feeling in a very long time. Colin was happy, the crew were happy, the director was happy and I was ecstatic. On that run, I had hit 314.4 mph: faster than the official British Land Speed Record, though it would never be recognised as an official record because we had no official monitors present from the record books. And anyway, no one was going to tell me how fast I had gone, just in case I decided to try and go a little faster. Of course, I would anyway.

Back at the tea van, there was lots of excited chatter. Things were looking good; we had plenty of footage of Colin showing me around the car, shots of my first attempts without the afterburner and now, shots of my full-bore afterburner run, too. I rang Andy and we agreed that this was going to be a good, old-fashioned piece of family telly where a guy learns how to do something scary, and we all get to watch as he does it. It was now fast approaching 5 p.m. We only had permission to use the runway until 5.30. We talked it over. The car was running well, I was on top of controlling it, the weather was perfect. There was, we reckoned, just time for one more run.

While the guys prepped the car I chatted with the man in charge of the runway. He already knew that we wanted to do one more run, but I wanted to make sure he was happy. Back with the director, we reminded ourselves that we also had one more piece of camera to record. But that, we decided, could be done after the 5.30 curfew. Best use the noise-making time we had left to make noise.

Time: 17.25
After the crash, some doctors felt that the degree of recollection I had of events was unrealistically clear. Perhaps, they reckoned, these memories were the product of an active imagination that had cobbled them together as

I lay in a coma. But I remain convinced that they are real. And they tally perfectly with the records of the on-board telemetry system that can account for every millisecond of the crash.

Walking towards the car, my mind wandered briefly back to a conversation with a race technician a few weeks earlier. He had warned me never to race with a full bladder.

'You race when you need a piss, and there's a chance that, if you crash, your bladder could burst. Then you'll be dead before the medics get to you.'

Suddenly, just a few feet from the Vampire, I turned round and hiked back to the Portaloo. I do not believe that this was any sort of premonition of what was about to unfold. I just needed a piss and so I took one before I did something that would, I knew, demand a clear head and full concentration.

I looked at the car as I slotted my neck brace round my neck. The piece I would soon be delivering to camera dealt with some of the facts about its construction. The brakes had originally been from a Transit van. The fuel pump came from a cement mixer and the steering box from a Robin Reliant. This was a long way from the over-funded and corporate world of modern-day motor sport. And I loved it all the more for that. A bloke in a shed who knew exactly what he was doing had put this thing together.

I was, once again, strapped down under the harness so tightly that my breath came in ragged gasps. I looked at my blue race gloves as my hands gripped the wheel. One more crazy roar up the runway, a piece to camera about the car, and then I would be back in the Honda heading for home.

The engine began its slow spin. The noise built to the signature song of the jet engine as Colin stepped back and gave me the all-clear. This would be a full-power run and one I would enjoy. There was no fear of the unknown now.

Run starts: 17.30 and 16.89 seconds
I hit the button and release the brake. Inside the engine, a flame shoots through the middle of the spinning inferno and reaches the unburnt fuel exiting out of the rear venturi. The already awesome power of the mighty jet engine is instantly doubled and it throws itself, the car and me forward.

Time lapsed: 14.25 secs; 288.3 mph
I realise that something is wrong. This is not the usual push and pull of the steering as the front end scrabbles to keep the one-tonne car and its passenger heading in a straight line.

Time lapsed: 14.64 secs; 285.3 mph; cornering force: 2.1 g
I am counter-steering now and battling something. My brain would later remember a sense of struggling to keep it going straight ahead, of having an elemental fight to keep on going despite something trying to throw me off course.

Time lapsed: 14.64 secs; car drops 40 mm
The fight has just got a lot tougher. I register that something terrible has happened and that I am in trouble. In reality, the front right tyre has suffered a catastrophic failure. The resulting blow-out registers on the telemetry at 273 mph and, on video footage, the front of the car leaps high enough with the explosion to lift the other front wheel clear off the ground.

Time lapsed: 15.00 secs; 279 mph; 3.9 g
I am losing the battle. The car veers off to the right. My steering inputs and corrections, assessed later by experts, have been well inside the speed of reaction expected of modern-day fighter pilots. The telemetry records tell that I am inputting only the degree of steering required to correct the car's slewing path. My foot hits the brake—a futile gesture, instinctive but useless. I am not panicking, I am still fighting. But I am losing.

Time lapsed: 15.71 secs; 232 mph; deceleration 6 g
My last memory now. As the car veers to the right, I know that my steering efforts have not saved the situation. I am going to crash. I remember the parachute lever. I pull it. The car does not stop and begins to roll over. I register that it is off the road entirely now and is going to roll onto the roof. I can do no more. The next thing to happen, I am convinced, is that I die. There can be no other outcome. I am not scared, my life does not flash before my eyes, there is just a calm resignation. And also a strange relief at finally knowing the answer to a question that perhaps haunts many of us: *How will I die?*

Time lapsed: 16.17 secs
The car rolls upside down. The roll bars protect my head from the impact, but they dig into the grass. This acts as a ground anchor, slowing the car from 232 mph to 191 mph in just 0.46 seconds. My brain is thrown forward hitting the front of my skull. The force my brain experiences overstretches some of the nerves and causes them to break. The resulting injuries could

leave me paralysed, deaf, blind, or wipe out my personality, the person I recognise as me. But I am unconscious now and know nothing about it.

Part of the car touches down on the grass and digs in, sending the entire structure into another roll that turns into a flip. Were I conscious, I would briefly see a flash of blue sky before being plunged underground again as the car settles back onto its roof and begins its final stop. The avalanche of mud and stones kicked up by the roll bars ploughing into the field flips the helmet visor up, exposing my face. My left eye is damaged, the surrounding tissue pulverised. My mouth and nose fill with soil and mud as they are force-fed by the onslaught kicked up by the roll bar. As my head slews to the right, the side of the helmet is dented, cracked and caved in when it hits the crash structure. The right-hand side of my brain sustains more damage.

It ends just five seconds after the front right tyre blew. The car lies upside down. Inside, I am unconscious still, but changes are happening. My brain, thrown around inside my skull by the immense g-forces, is beginning to swell dangerously. My breathing is severely constricted by the soil in my mouth and nose. The arm-restraints have worked, keeping my limbs inside the relative safety of the cockpit. The harnesses have done their job too, keeping me pinned in place despite the battering as the car rolled and pitched across the field. But I am in a critical state. As far as I am concerned, I have just met my own death.

Chapter 3

Mindy's story

'OK, Ela, I'll be back in about an hour. Girls, be good and eat your tea and I'll be back before bathtime.'

I ran out to my Land Rover. Damn—I'd forgotten my riding hat. I threw open the heavy oak front door. 'Me again!'

Ela laughed, her arm outstretched, my riding hat in her hand. Ela was our Polish au pair. She'd arrived in June and had become such a friend. That summer we'd taught the children to swim in our tiny, previously frog-infested swimming pool. Every day after school the four of us—me, Ela, Izzy, our five-year-old, and Willow, three—would run to the pool and splash about until the sun disappeared behind the trees, forcing us back down the slope to the house and supper. Ela always helped with the animals, putting the pony in her stable, or—her favourite task—feeding the dogs (five) or cats (three). The children simply adored her. She was with us during her break from university where she was studying physiotherapy.

Riding hat in hand, I leapt into my nine-seater Land Rover, a G4 110 long-wheelbase Defender in a glorious bright yellow—love that car!—and set off for the stables to see my fabulous new horse.

I felt dizzy with excitement! All my life since memories began I dreamt of owning a horse. Then a few years ago Richard bought me a horse for Christmas. She was amazing, but when I took a break from riding her while she gave birth to a foal and weaned it, I lost my nerve. So I'd sold her, which left me devastated until a friend of mine suggested I look at a fantastic horse who she said would give me my confidence back.

I'd ridden him twice before this day, and on the last visit had decided to buy him. Today was to be my first 'lesson' on him. Thomas was the most incredible-looking horse I'd ever seen: he stood sixteen hands three inches, and was chestnut with a white blaze down his face and three white socks. I'm five feet one inch short and to even get on him was a bit of a performance as the saddle was about a foot above the top of my head.

I parked the car behind the equestrian college offices. Thomas occupied a large stable in a U-shaped courtyard lined by about fifteen boxes. As I walked through the gate into the yard, I could see him in the far corner.

It was about 5.30 p.m. and the sun was still warm on my back as I reached up and stroked Thomas's soft white nose.

'Hello, my boy.'

Wow! What a moment—he was finally mine. I fastened my hat and struggled to get my gloves on quickly enough.

'Mindy! Mindy! The phone—for you.'

'What?' My mobile didn't work in the yard, so Ela had rung the college.

'It's Richard. He's had an accident. You must ring Andy.'

'Oh God! No!' I hit the ground running and headed for the car. I threw my hat off, leapt in and stabbed the key in the ignition. I was almost airborne driving over the speed humps on the way out of the college.

At last a signal appeared on the mobile. I called Andy immediately but the line was busy. He was trying to call me.

'Arrggh!' I yelled. The tears were streaming down my face and as I turned into the main road, the phone rang—it was Andy.

'Mindy, Richard's had an accident.'

'How bad is it?'

'It's OK, he's moving his arms and legs. They're taking him to hospital.'

I let out a despairing cry: 'No, it's not OK, Andy. He's still got whiplash from the last one.'

Richard had suffered severe whiplash six weeks before when a van he'd rolled during a stunt had bounced on landing. I had no idea of the severity of this crash in comparison. It was only when Andy said, 'I'll meet you in Leeds,' that I knew it was serious. He was driving there from London.

My mind was in turmoil. I remember focusing on a huge oak tree in the middle of a field. It looked peaceful and full of life—and it broke my heart. Perhaps my world, our world, was ended . . . I snapped myself back to reality and phoned Richard's mum, Eileen. It seemed to take for ever for her to answer. She was her usual jolly self, but within seconds her world was changed too. Her first thought was for her grandchildren. 'We'll come and stay with the girls,' she offered.

After hanging up, I burst into tears again, screamed, yelled, wiped my face . . . and called my mum.

'Oh darling, no!' She'd been worried about Richard doing 'all these mad things' for a while. Poor Mum has had enough tragedy in her life to know how things can go wrong. Her ten-year-old son was killed by a 'careless' driver. Tim was holding Mum's hand under the bus shelter in front of his school when he was torn from Mum's grasp and slammed into a lamp post. She witnessed the whole thing, and his last look across at her before he died. She's always said 'things just happen'. She's right.

She said everything I needed to hear. So calmly, so gently, with such love. Another flood of tears exploded. I had to get myself under control.

As I turned into the lane leading to our house, I phoned Katrina, our PA, a quick-witted, intelligent girl who helped with all the logistical issues surrounding Richard's hectic work schedule. I knew she could be relied upon. I quickly told her what had happened and promised that I'd call again on my way to Leeds. She was upset, but instinctively knew I'd need her.

I rounded the last corner and pulled it together, knowing I had about three minutes to make myself look as normal as possible for the children. I ran upstairs calling Ela as I went. She joined me in the bedroom as I threw a case onto the bed.

'I have to go to Leeds—I don't know when I'll be back. Oh God!' Tears were running down my face as I threw ridiculous things into a suitcase.

'Oh, Mindy!' Ela hugged me and for a moment I slumped against her and wept. But I had to get moving.

What should I pack? Richard's pants and socks, a dressing gown—in hospital you always need a dressing gown. My wash bag, a change of underwear for me and a spare top. The dressing gown almost filled the small suitcase, but I didn't take it out. It was him. He'd like it.

I ran into my office and sent a one-line email to Richard's agent: *Richard's had an accident. SERIOUS. I'm on my way to hospital. Call me.* I looked at my watch—6.30 p.m. I must go!

Izzy and Willow were in the playroom.

'Girls! Girls!' I called. They appeared in the hallway, both staring up at me with a look of curiosity. I was sniffling, but smiling.

'Daddy's gone and bumped a car again.'

'Oh, not again!' said Izzy, rolling her eyes.

'Yes, I'm afraid so. And he's ripped some clothes, so I have to go and take him some new ones,' I explained.

'Oh, OK,' said Willow. 'He is silly.'

'Yes, darling, he is.' We hugged. Willow was easy. She was just three. But Izzy looked at me. Really looked at me. Her eyes filled with tears and so did mine. I knelt down, cupped her tiny shoulders in my hands and looked her straight in the eyes. 'It'll be OK. It will. I love you. Come on, Iz.'

She nodded, then threw her arms round me. 'I love you, Mummy.'

I gave that little girl such a hug, as her big brown eyes welled with tears, her brave face fighting them back. I will never know what went through her clever little head that day, but she knew something terrible had happened, and it had happened to her wonderful daddy.

It was time to leave. As I reached for the car keys I noticed Richard's spare mobile was on the table. I grabbed it, along with my spare. I dashed outside and realised my Land Rover would be too slow and too obvious. As a motoring journalist, Richard regularly has cars on loan to review and a press car had arrived that day. I knew I was insured to drive it in extreme circumstances, so I ran back in and swapped over the keys.

The girls were on the front step, both a little too quiet. I kissed them. 'See you soon. I'm sure I won't be long.'

'Will you be back tonight, Mummy?' asked Izzy.

'Well, maybe not tonight, but I'll let you know as soon as I can, and I'll phone you to say good night at bedtime—OK, baby?'

'Oh, OK.' Her lips were quivering and yet she managed to smile. We both knew she was being brave for her little sister's sake.

''Bye, Mummy,' said Willow, a bit confused by it all.

I had to turn away so they didn't see me crying. Then I ran to the car. I trusted Ela. I knew she'd look after them. In the meantime I had to get to Leeds. To Richard.

As I drove out of the gate the tears came again, but this time I took hold. I had to focus. There was no point in crying. I remember saying out loud, 'Come on. Pull up, for God's sake.'

I shoved the earpiece in and phoned Katrina. I had to organise things.

'I've borrowed a press car. Can you call the manufacturer? Explain what's happened. The pick-up address will need to be changed.'

Katrina told me one of the tabloids had already called Richard's agent. They knew he'd crashed. I asked Katrina to check what was happening with all the other papers. I knew Richard would want me to keep control of the situation. He wrote for the *Daily Mirror*. I must make sure they knew what was going on. He was adamant that, as his employer, the *Mirror* should always be kept in the loop.

While I was talking with Katrina, the phone was beeping; it was Jeremy and Francie Clarkson. At this stage we were oblivious to the severity of the crash. Francie was very sympathetic—she was one of the few people on the planet who could truly identify with what I was going through.

'It's what we all dread,' she said. The Clarksons insisted I call them if there was anything they could do. I remembered our holiday with them on the Isle of Man: we had all really relaxed—Richard had even painted for the first time in years. During our brief stay he'd surprised Jeremy with a beautiful watercolour . . . I wondered whether he'd ever be able to paint again.

I snapped at myself to stop thinking like that. He was the toughest man in the world. I'd get to the hospital and he'd be sitting up in bed with a few bruises and a sheepish look on his face, and I'd give him a hug and we'd carry on as usual.

Then, suddenly, reality hit. Katrina had just called back to tell me that every newspaper was following the story. The accident was big news. As I was talking to her, the BBC news came on the radio.

'*Top Gear* presenter Richard Hammond has had a serious crash in a jet car. The vehicle rolled and flipped at an airfield just outside York. He was transported by air ambulance to Leeds General Infirmary where he is in a critical condition.'

'Critical?' No one had used that word to me. And it flipped! The image in my head was of the *Bluebird* of the 1960s and I imagined it going tail-over-tip and then rolling at high speed. I wondered what state he was in. I imagined so many scenarios all at once. Our house was up for sale. Maybe we would just have to stay there and change things. If he was paralysed, we'd have to put in ramps and have things altered for wheelchair access . . . I'd get him a really fast wheelchair. It'd be OK. If he couldn't talk, I'd get him a great computer. Everything can be overcome. Just be alive. Just, please God, I beg you, please, please keep him alive for me.

All the while the phones rang. I didn't answer them every time. There are certain friends you know you'll open up to. You'll crumble. I couldn't afford that luxury. Richard needed to see me looking positive and strong.

I don't recall much of that drive. I know I spoke to Richard's parents several times. I remember checking Richard's phone to get a number for his editor at the *Mirror*. Katrina had heard nothing from them. When I got through they were amazing. They hadn't phoned me out of respect. I was so moved. 'Richard's a mate,' were his editor's words. 'If there's anything, absolutely anything we can do, call us, won't you?'

That had to be the blackest night—I distinctly remember looking at the road in front of me and it seemed blacker than black. The satnav displayed the number of miles left to travel. The miles just didn't seem to dwindle.

The bulletins on the radio repeated the news. I turned it off. I was shouting at the car in front to get out of my way. The traffic was slowing me up and Andy was calling periodically to see where I was. He was going to get there before me.

I'd tried to call the hospital but they were naturally cautious about giving details. I left them both my numbers while they checked out my details with the BBC. Trouble was that my phones were constantly busy. I stopped answering calls unless they were from Andy or Richard's parents, because I was desperate to hear from the hospital. Then 'unknown' came onto the phone. I answered it.

'Hello, Mrs Hammond—I'm a duty nurse from A and E at Leeds.'

'Oh, oh, hello.' My voice broke. I wanted to know about Richard, but at the same time I was frightened to death.

'Are you driving, love?'

'Yes, I am. Can you tell me how he is?'

'Not while you're driving. Can you pull over somewhere?'

'No, I can't. I'm on a motorway.'

'Well, can you see if you can find somewhere to stop and I'll call back in five minutes?'

I drove on. I couldn't stop on the hard shoulder—that was dangerous.

Richard had a thing about people doing that. I had to keep driving.

The voice called back three times, after which I was close to a complete breakdown. They were worried I might have an accident if they gave me the news while I was driving. The fourth time, I was screaming with frustration. 'Look, you'd better bloody well tell me or I'll crash anyway!'

'OK, love, OK. Your husband's had a blow to the head and he's sustained a serious brain injury.'

Serious brain injury—three words you never imagine hearing in connection with someone you love. It echoes through your soul. An injury to the brain. Not the head, the brain. And serious. My thoughts were spinning round: 'Flipped; crashed; critical; brain injury.'

My husband, my Richard, broken? It just couldn't be true.

'Where are you, love?' the soft Leeds voice asked.

I had no idea. I'd just kept driving. The miles never-ending. It was the longest drive of my life. I vaguely remembered seeing a road sign.

'Manchester, I think.'

'Oh, you won't be too much longer. You sure you're OK?'

'Yeah, I'll be fine.' I was shaky and crying. My funny, brave, beautiful, adorable husband was ahead of me. But maybe it wasn't him any more. Maybe it would never be him again. We'd cope. Whatever happened, we'd get through it.

'Enough now.' I remember saying out loud. Sniffing, I wiped my face and took a few huge gulps of air. I was getting close now, finally.

Andy called. 'Listen . . .' He spoke softly. 'There are a lot of TV crews and press here, so we need to get you in round the back, all right?'

'Yeah, OK.'

'Call me when you're a bit closer and I'll guide you in.'

I was pulling myself together. I wiped my face, blew my nose and pulled on my armour, ready for battle. It had to be good, that armour. I didn't know at the time, but it was to stay in place for many, many months.

As I turned that last corner to the back of the hospital and parked up, I remember thinking how bleak it looked. Andy came walking fast across the road towards the car. His appearance was shambolic as usual: baggy trousers and a grey T-shirt, dishevelled grey hair and a couple of days' beard growth on his chin. I gave him a half-smile as he hugged me.

'What a day, eh?' I said to him.

He was relieved. He genuinely thought I was going to get out of the car and belt him, but all I cared about was getting to Richard.

Andy was closely followed by a lady security guard. They were both on edge. The press were all over the place. Andy wanted to smuggle me in quickly without anyone noticing. I was escorted into the huge, dark building. Inside it looked old. Then, as we walked, it grew brighter, newer. The floors changed from stone and woodblock to lino and tile. It looked more like a hospital.

I felt numb. Few words were said. The pace was hurried. We turned a corner to two rows of lifts facing one another. I couldn't really hear anything. It was like being underwater. I had no idea how to get to Richard or even where he was, but I was close. Every step, brought me closer.

The lift stopped. We walked down a corridor. There were signs hanging from the ceiling. Ward names. We stopped. Double doors. An intercom.

I could hear my heart beating in my ears. Ahead was another pair of doors. The lights were dimmed inside. A nurse was smiling at me. Andy quietly disappeared.

The nurse said something. I saw a curtain drawn round a bed on my right. Was that him? No. We kept walking. Beeping noises. Intensive care. The next bed was him. Banks of machines. A ventilator pumping breath into his lungs; drips in both arms; monitors stuck to his chest and hand. His face yellowed with bruising, a bizarre lump the size of a fist on his forehead, and his left eyelid four times its normal size and deep crimson.

He was still. Not a flicker of life. The only movement came from the ventilator as it deflated, then filled again. I kissed his cheek.

'Hello, my darling.' The tears were dripping as I spoke, but I was half smiling. Awful as it was, I knew he was there. Knew with every ounce of my being. The spirit of this man, who was as tough as any warrior in a boys' storybook, was dormant . . . not dead. I'd just have to wait for him.

The nurse sat at a desk at the end of Richard's bed, recording everything. Percentage of air in his blood; blood pressure; heart rate and 'obs'— observations. But mostly she just sat at the foot of his bed, watching him like some guardian angel—a friendly woman with short, blonde hair and a kind face. Instantly, I felt reassured by her presence. She exuded calm.

I let my eyes examine Richard's face. It was the yellow-green colour that you get round the edge of a blue bruise. I could see how swollen it was but I'd expected a real mess. His left eye was really nasty and there was a lot of dried blood round his nostrils, mixed with earth, yet he looked like Richard. But Richard himself I sensed was a very long way away. This was a husk.

I sat holding his unresponsive hand . . . a hand you could squeeze, stroke, manipulate, but which gave not a millimetre of movement in return. There—but not there. It was so bizarre, so unreal, so awful.

The machines reminded me of my father in his last few days. He'd been diagnosed with cancer some years earlier. For the last three nights and two days of his life, I took turns with Mum, until she was exhausted. Her sister, my aunt Betty, was there too. The three of us in his little room, watching him die. My sister Sarah found it all too much and couldn't come to the hospital. She and Dad were extremely close, whereas I'd had a difficult relationship with my father until his last years. As Dad's breathing became more laboured, Mum and Aunty Betty exchanged glances. It was 11 p.m.

'Oh no, Bert. Not today,' Mum sobbed. It was the anniversary of their son Tim's death.

'Come on, Bertie, just a bit longer,' said my aunt.

And he responded. He drew a monumental breath and kept going 'til the following evening when, finally, my sister arrived.

Within moments of hearing her voice my father, who hadn't moved for days, lifted his head, opened his eyes and smiled at each one of us in turn, dropped his head back on the pillow, and died. His expression at rest had always been one of a mouth downturned, but when he died he had a look on his face I had never seen before. One of pure wonder and joy. But the thing is, he could hear. It is true what the doctors say in these situations. Hearing still works. I was blindingly aware of that with Richard.

Every thirty minutes the nurse would carry out observations, asking Richard to do various things. Open his eyes was the first task. Then say his name. She would place her index fingers in each of his hands, and ask him to squeeze her fingers, then wiggle his toes. He did nothing. She'd be talking sternly and loudly at him. Still nothing. Then . . .

'I'm going to have to cause you a little bit of pain, Richard.'

She explained to me that she had to gauge response from him, and she'd use her penlight on a pressure point between his eyebrow and his nose, pushing and twisting. He managed to flicker his eyes . . . little else. She held open his eyelids and shone the light in each eye . . . he didn't flinch. He didn't speak. It wasn't encouraging. The reality of a life with someone who doesn't improve from this stage is frightening. How do you cope? I wouldn't allow myself to think about it. It was early days. By God, if anyone could heave himself through, it was Richard. And I'd be there when he made it back.

At the scene of the crash, when the paramedics reached him, they were surprised to find Richard breathing. The visor on his helmet had been pushed open and then filled with earth as his head ploughed into the ground. They removed as much mud from his mouth and nose as possible before using a measure called the Glasgow Coma Scale to ascertain his condition. The GCS is scored between three and fifteen, three being the worst and fifteen the best. Richard scored three.

Since the accident, we've spoken with the air-ambulance crew who were on duty that day. One told me, 'When you go to scenes like that, you can usually tell straight away whether or not they're going to survive.'

I was expecting him to say, 'Of course we knew he'd be OK.'

Instead he told me, 'I didn't think he was going to make it.'

Once he regained consciousness, Richard stayed in the jet car while he was given verbal instructions on how to help the team get him out. According to those at the scene, he ignored everything the ambulance guys said, but when he heard a member of the *Top Gear* film crew, he obeyed.

Head injury is strange. The impact isn't felt immediately, which was why, once out of the car, Richard made protests that he needed to do a piece to camera, but then became steadily more aggressive on his way to A & E. His brain was swelling. At A & E he was completely anaesthetised to prevent him damaging his brain further. The drugs were soon switched off and their sedative effect ceased, but by then the effect of the injury had taken over.

A huge lump the size of my fist grew on his forehead due to fluid draining forward from his injury. He had suffered most damage to the right frontal lobe, the part of the brain that deals with recognition, the ability to judge distances, decision-making, problem-solving and personality. He'd damaged nerve cells in his brain. These are injuries that aren't detected on CT scans. Damage can range from paralysis, blindness or deafness, to depression, anger or seizures. We would just have to wait to see what permanent damage there might be.

We were told that he might never be the person he was before the crash. Some people no longer recognise their loved ones, or decide to change their whole way of life and simply abandon their family, their personality changed for ever. The future was, at the very best, uncertain.

Memories of that night, and of the next couple of days, are very confused. I soon understood that, when an alarm sounded, it was because the monitor had fallen off his finger. I'd also grown accustomed to the routine. My husband was lying next to me on life-support, and as far as I was concerned this was my foreseeable future. I'd accepted it because to be unaccepting is madness and to panic is pointless.

Richard's younger brother Nick arrived at about 1.30 a.m., having driven from Tunbridge Wells. Years ago, when Richard and I had been together just a few months, he was the first member of the family I met. I was surprised how little he resembled his brother. Nick was tall and slim with blond hair and sensible clothes. I worried he might be a bit stuffy, but as the afternoon passed into the evening I remember us sitting on the floor drinking wine, Nick with my collie's head on his lap as he told hysterically funny stories. Richard, Nick and I laughed 'til our sides ached. I quickly understood why Richard thought so fondly of him.

Nick now worked in the City, his free time as rare as Richard's. We hadn't seen each other for a while. As he hugged me, I explained what was going on and Nick digested the news. I can't imagine how it must've felt for him. They had grown up being daredevils and pranksters. Suddenly there was no fun. Just fear.

We sat briefly with Richard before Nick peeled me away. We checked with the nurse when the next obs would be and went downstairs. Leaving Richard was difficult. If he moved and I missed it, I'd feel dreadful. But I also needed a change of scenery. Nick was upset, but dealt with it by getting on with the practicalities. He made phone calls, spoke to everyone and was a kind of central liaison from the moment he arrived.

He'd bought a packet of cigarettes on the way down. We stood in a back courtyard to smoke. I've no idea what we talked about. I remember the cigarette tasted vile but I still smoked it. I suppose I needed that crutch.

At about 4.30 a.m., Richard's middle brother, Andy, arrived with his wife, Andrea. They'd driven from Devon and by the time they arrived they were exhausted. I remember they were surprised at the absence of really severe external injuries when they first saw Richard. On a drive such as theirs, the imagination has time to run wild and I'm sure they'd expected to see him in a far more broken state.

During the night, James May and Jeremy Clarkson had both driven from London. Jeremy had received a call while out at dinner explaining that Richard's condition had become life-threatening. He just got up from the table and said he had to leave for Leeds. Francie was worried that he might be in the way, and he'd said, 'I want to be there for Mindy.' And he was. James heard about the accident on the radio, then got into his car straight away too. As I walked into the reception area of the hospital, I could see the whole gang had taken over a corner. They were looking at the morning papers. Richard's crash was front-page news everywhere, and the

TV stations had been showing bulletins through the night. Meanwhile at our home in Gloucestershire, the press had started camping outside.

I remember vividly the first time the nurse caused Richard some pain and he reacted. It was terrifying. His arms flailing wildly, he tore off monitors and grabbed at the drips, all the while so disorientated he could scarcely lift his head from the pillow. The episode was brief but explosive. When he'd calmed a little, the nurse did the obs and made notes. He was trying to respond to commands, but he couldn't open his eyelids; couldn't speak. The nurse felt an almost undetectable movement with his right hand; his feet didn't move. I sat there and silently prayed. I felt desperate.

The next time she did obs it was worse. Again, he didn't respond, so she caused him more pain. This time he managed to tear a drip out of his arm and almost hit the nurse in the face. There was no coordination. His brain wasn't quite getting the messages right. As the nurse shone the light into his eyes, I saw for the first time the awful mess which was once his left eye. Beneath the lid there was no white—it was all red. Worse than that, the pupil wasn't recognisable—just a dark lumpy mass. He wasn't speaking. He just grunted. But what was really worrying was the lack of response from his left-hand side. There were small improvements with all of his other responses, but the left side of his body was essentially paralysed.

His nurse came over and explained that the lad in the bed next to Richard's was dying. His family had been called.

'Oh God, how awful.'

I took hold of Richard's left hand and spent the next few hours listening to someone die just feet away, and willing my husband to stay alive.

It was obvious when the terrible moment came, but when it did something strange happened: a cold chill brushed past me, as if it were the spirit of the lad next door coming to have a look at Richard. It was suspended there for a second or two. Then left. I'd like to think he was telling Richard it wasn't his time yet.

The nurses quietly asked all visitors to leave while they did what had to be done. When I returned, there was a fresh bed, and all the staff had moved on. I wondered how they could be so upbeat when someone had just died, but I suppose that's the only way for them to do their job. They really are amazing people.

I resumed my post next to Richard. The first forty-eight hours were vital. We'd know more about the damage to his brain after that. His obs improved slightly. He managed to actually lift one of the fingers on his right hand. It was such a breakthrough! I was elated. Then, about 4 a.m., he started to dip. He just wasn't interested. I looked at the nurse.

'It's bad, isn't it?'

'It's not good,' she admitted.

She'd tried causing him pain, but it hadn't worked. For the first time I really felt I was going to lose him.

'Can I shout at him? The way I do when he's drunk?'

'Try anything, love.'

I looked around me at the other beds. There were three other patients.

'I'll probably wake everyone up, though.'

'That doesn't matter. You go ahead.'

The way she spoke confirmed she was as worried as I was.

She had her index fingers inside his limp hands, but nothing was happening. Nothing.

I took a deep breath, got close to his face and yelled.

'Richard, you squeeze those fingers! Squeeze those bloody fingers!'

Tears were running down my face; both the nurse and I were hunched over him, watching his hands and, as I finished yelling, he made a very tiny movement with both middle fingers! Oh! The relief was so great! The only time I ever shout at him is on rare occasions when he's been on a boozy night out and decided to sleep on the sofa. It's the only way to get him to bed. He has confided since that he remembers thinking he was tired and there was a nice, easy route—he could just drift away . . . He remembers being jolted back. His mind suddenly recognised he was in trouble.

It is, I believe, no coincidence that we refer to people as 'pulling through', because that's precisely what Richard did. He has referred to the incredible determination and strength it took to 'pull himself back' at that moment. Remaining stationary meant certain death or disability. I'm so very grateful he made the effort.

After a few more sets of obs he was exhausted. I had to make some calls.

As I left the ward and rang for the lift, I was thrilled and excited. When the doors opened, Andy Wilman was facing me, ashen.

I smiled at that sad, crumpled human being. 'He moved both his hands.'

'Oh God!' Andy burst into tears and threw his arms round me. He remained there for the journey down in the lift. He felt so responsible, but not only that, he loved Richard. He said, 'What am I doing? I'm supposed to be supporting you, not the other way round!'

It didn't matter. Something magical had happened.

I called home and Richard's mum answered. I told her the good news and she was thrilled. We chatted about the girls and agreed that the TV and radio should be off while the children were around. We couldn't be sure how his condition would be reported. We decided not to send them to school or nursery, for fear of miscommunication about Daddy's condition.

I had a quick chat with both Izzy and Willow. It was hard to be jolly with them, but I tried to explain that Daddy needed me for a bit longer, and I'd be home soon. Izzy knew I was keeping things from her, and we both knew she'd made her mind up to humour me. Richard's mum told me there were reporters around the house. It was the first time we'd experienced big press attention. Sadly, it was Richard's parents who were having to deal with it all. The press were simply doing their job. But for the parents of a man lying in hospital, this was an added pressure which was hard to bear.

I called my mum to let her know that Richard had improved. She wanted me to get some sleep. 'Try and get an easy chair or something to doze in next to him, love, will you?' Mum understood her role as support at the end of the phone was vital and I needed her to be there for me. I wanted my mum as much as my girls wanted me.

As I approached Richard's bedside someone from the hospital administration was waiting for me. She felt it would be difficult for the *Top Gear* team to have any privacy in the reception area and volunteered the use of a boardroom in the old wing for everyone to use. She was eager to show me so, reluctantly, I accompanied her on the long walk to the old hospital.

She spoke the whole time but it was all I could do to try to memorise the route. We took so many turns along different corridors, I felt completely lost. I seemed to be miles away from Richard. I hated it.

Eventually we reached the room. It was unusually quiet, with people sitting around the edge facing a coffee table in the centre, which was buried beneath an array of paper coffee cups. Andy, Jeremy and James were there, along with the majority of the *Top Gear* crew. I sat down, trying to be positive as I told them about Richard. Everyone wanted to see him, particularly Jeremy and James. Apart from anything else, they're all very good mates. The newspapers were strewn around. Richard's crash was front-page news. I didn't want to see the pictures of the jet car, yet I had to look.

I couldn't stay for long though; my mind was elsewhere. It took every bit of composure I could muster to answer everyone's questions. As soon as I could, I was seeking out a route back to the new hospital. I followed the flow of the people ahead of me and was relieved to see a familiar tunnel.

When I arrived back at the ward I suddenly started shaking violently. I felt very light-headed and practically fell against the wall. The nurses had been warning me that it would all catch up with me. It had. I resumed my seat and a cup of sweet tea appeared next to me. I felt guilty. There I was, surrounded by a roomful of needy patients in intensive care, and the nurses were diverting their attention to some daft tart who had forgotten to eat. I suppose it's a kind of nursing instinct.

At 8 a.m., Richard's nurse handed over to her replacement, Jim. We didn't get off on a very good footing when he criticised me for putting the oxygen monitor back on Richard's finger when it dropped off. He was an older guy with glasses, very forthright, and I had the impression he'd stand no nonsense. His first obs with Richard were the most awful yet.

Within seconds, Richard was thrashing about. Two other male nurses came running over. Richard grabbed the ventilator tube and started yanking it from his lungs. He was gagging and fighting off the two nurses as he kept pulling the tube from his throat. His instincts had taken over. There was a tube in him that he wanted out. No one was going to hold him.

Jim shouted to the other nurses. 'Let him go! He'll hurt himself more if you try to stop him.'

They let go their hold and Richard gagged like an animal regurgitating food. But each time he retched, he yanked another few inches of tube out of his mouth. I felt as though I was watching my husband commit suicide. The tube had been keeping his lungs functioning and he was rejecting it. That pipe took for ever to finally come free of Richard's mouth. It was about a foot long. Once out, he coughed and moaned, then collapsed.

I asked Jim what would happen without the ventilator.

'We'll keep an eye on him and see if he can cope without it.'

I sat there for I don't know how long, watching the monitors like never before. His breathing was very weak; his chest barely moved. But then, unexpectedly, his right arm started to move around under the bedclothes and his hand found what it was seeking.

Jim was beaming. 'He's a scrabbler. It's a thing you see very often with men who've had this kind of injury. They regress. He's back to basics and he's checking his most important part is still there. It's a good sign.'

The consultant appeared with a neurosurgeon. They wanted to do another MRI scan to examine the spotting on his brain as his temperature had gone up slightly. I didn't want him to go. The porters came to take him and I was told he'd be back in about forty minutes and that was it—gone!

What if something happened in those forty minutes? What if he took a turn for the worse and I wasn't there?

It was awful. But I just had to accept it, calmly go downstairs and chain-smoke and drink strong coffee until his return.

Richard's obs weren't improving dramatically, but he'd try to open his eyes and make very small movements with his toes as well as his fingers. Admittedly, the left side was still weaker, but it was responding slightly.

I liked Jim. He took what the doctors said with a pinch of salt some-times; he'd been in the job for longer than many of them. When a young doctor suggested that one of Richard's drips could be removed, Jim acknowledged the advice. Then, after the doctor had left, he turned to me.

'I'm not going to do that,' he said. 'Bloomin' fool. And what? Put another one in the poor bugger tomorrow?'

He was right too, as it turned out. Trouble was, with Richard there was no telling how long anything would stay connected anyway. Later that morning, he decided to remove the catheter. It was another foreign body inserted where he didn't want it.

'Richard, no! Don't!'

I tried to catch his hand, but he pushed me away. As he did so, I realised his good eye was slightly open.

'Hello,' I said gently to him.

He looked straight at me, but there was absolutely no recognition whatso-ever. It was devastating. The tube that he'd removed was now leaking all over the bed. Jim told me to go and get a coffee while he sorted Richard out.

I walked to the toilets, sat on the loo and cried. 'Where are you?' I was whispering as I held my head in my hands. 'Please come back.'

I could hear voices outside. I had to pull myself together, go downstairs—coffee, cigarette. I took a deep breath, wiped my face and walked out.

THE FINGER MONITOR was always the first to go. I'd become very good at reattaching that one. However, the drips scared me. The last thing Richard needed was to break one of those in his arm. He proved pretty good at tug-ging them out, even with a ton of surgical tape securing each one.

Then there was the oxygen mask. This was a new addition following his dramatic rejection of the ventilator. Jim and I spent most of the time trying to reattach the mask. In the end, Jim decided that little tubes up his nostrils might work better. He was right, although we still had a battle to keep them on.

By this time, a great deal of positivity was building as Richard continued to make progress. He had started to move his limbs unprompted. Admittedly, it was either to grab a certain part of his anatomy or to pick his nose. But it was fantastic progress. I should mention, in Richard's defence, that his nose was, at the time of the accident, completely filled with mud, so his instinct was to try and remove it.

I was stroking his forehead gently when he mumbled something. I was so surprised, I nearly burst into tears. He repeated it, and I just made out the word 'gearbox'. I knew instantly what he was thinking about. A few days earlier something had gone wrong with my Land Rover. I was sure it was the clutch, and Richard had said it was the gearbox. The local Land Rover dealer had taken it in for repair and had told me the problem over the phone.

'No, it was the master cylinder,' I told him.

'Oh, OK.' He went back to sleep.

I was grinning like a Cheshire cat. Tears rolling down my face. He spoke, he was remembering a piece of life, recalling his world—our world.

Less than an hour passed and he spoke again. 'Where's the car?'

'What car?' I asked.

'The Morgan.'

'It's in the garage.'

'Where?'

'At home.'

He smiled slightly, nodded and was out. It was amazing—we'd had a conversation! But it was so heartbreakingly brief. Sadly, his next obs showed just how exhausted he'd made himself. He wasn't responding at all.

Chapter 4

I've no idea how the day passed, but I recall it was evening when James and Jeremy came to see him. They'd been waiting patiently downstairs for so long, and the nurses agreed that familiar voices might well help him. Andy came too. We all tried instinctively to be jolly. Jeremy sat next to Richard and told him he was a shit driver. He was acting as normal, and a corner of Richard's mouth flickered into a slight smile. Jeremy was elated.

Everyone was tiring though. Andy Wilman and James were talking about going back to Leeds, to the hotel that had been organised by the BBC. I was in the waiting room in the outer corridor with Andy and Andrea, when the door flew open and Jeremy burst in.

'Mindy, quick! He's awake! He's sitting up! C'mon!'

We were both running down the corridor, Andy and Andrea close behind. Jeremy was visibly moved.

'It was amazing! He just opened his eyes!'

We dashed through the doors, and there, incredibly, sitting on the side of his bed, his face bruised and battered, was my wonderful husband. He looked straight at me, a dopey grin on his face, his good eye half-open.

'Hello, baby.'

He knew me! Oh, thank God! How I loved to see that look I'd wondered if I'd ever see again.

'Hello, darling.' I was so thrilled to look him in the eye as I said it.

He wanted to have a pee. He was offered a bedpan, but wanted to go properly. I took one elbow and a nurse took the other, with a second nurse wheeling the drip as we headed towards the loo. Richard was surprised at his lack of coordination, but kept looking at me and grinning.

''Ello!' and then a few moments later, ''Ello.'

I thought my face would explode, I was smiling so hard.

It was like dealing with a drunk. We had to stay with him in the cubicle, or he would have fallen, but he was very cross at the nurse being there, so she had to agree not to look.

'This is gonna hurt,' I warned him, remembering that he'd ripped the catheter out.

'Oh shit!' His face was an explosion of unexpected pain.

We all shuffled back to his bed. He said a couple of words to Jeremy, 'Hello, cockface' to James, smiled and passed out.

The others left and I encouraged Jeremy to go home. Francie had to go away the next day and I knew he needed to drive back to Oxfordshire to look after the children, but he sat there, arms folded.

'I'm not going anywhere until you agree to get some sleep.'

'I'll be fine.'

'Well, so will I.' He crossed his legs defiantly.

I agreed to sleep on the sofa bed in one of the waiting rooms and thanked Jeremy for being so supportive, before he finally set off home.

The sofa bed almost filled the room. I felt so alone. I was accustomed to being by myself but I always knew Richard was at the end of the phone if I needed him. He was a part of my world even when he wasn't physically nearby. This time the reverse was true. He was only fifty feet away, but he could've been on Mars. I felt hollow. I spent a couple of hours dozing before I escaped back to the ward. Everyone was satisfied that I'd had some rest, so the nagging eased up.

Jim handed over to a new nurse at around 8 a.m. She thought it would be a good idea to clean Richard's teeth with a blue sponge on the end of a plastic stick. She tried to get it into his mouth, but he clenched his teeth.

'Shall I try?' I volunteered.

She handed me the sponge and I tried to get it into Richard's mouth.

'Geroff!' he mumbled.

'I'm just cleaning your teeth,' I said softly.

He opened his eyes and gave me the most venomous look. 'Bugger off!'

I smiled at the nurse, but inside I was heartbroken. He didn't recognise me. He'd looked straight through me. He'd forgotten again.

The consultants looked at his scans. They had been worried there might be some additional damage, but on examining the X-rays, he seemed to be free of other injuries. Given his improvement it was decided he could be moved to HDU (high-dependency unit) later that day. It was great news.

Since his big lavatory expedition, Richard had been very quiet. While he was semiconscious, the nurse thought it might be a good time to remove one of the catheters in his left hand. His drips were held on with very sticky tape. His poor nurse was trying, very gently, to peel this off his hand as he slept. Suddenly, eyes still closed, he snapped, 'Piss off!'

'I need to get the tape off, Richard,' she said softly.

'Fuck off!' He pulled his hand away, briefly opened his one eye and gave us both an evil glare.

'He must be feeling better then,' I said with a smirk to the nurse.

He was still cross when it came to the next set of obs. The nurse was trying to encourage Richard to squeeze her finger with the hand which had the catheter in.

'Come on, Richard—squeeze my fingers.'

'No,' he replied stubbornly.

'Come on,' she coaxed.

He yelled angrily, 'Fuck's sake! Ow!' and yanked the hand away.

'I think that's sore,' I said.

The nurse agreed. 'Sorry, Richard, I won't touch it again.'

He wasn't interested. He pulled a face, eyes still closed, and rolled over to turn his back towards us.

I left Richard briefly while the nurses prepared him for the move to HDU. It was great to see him after his wash and brush-up. He was all clean and lovely. The bed had been changed, there were new, crisp white sheets, just one drip left in his arm, and a catheter in his hand which was temporarily blocked off. He was ready to travel.

He must have come round for a couple of minutes because, although I was at the coffee machine at the time, when I returned his clean sheets were splattered with crimson, as were his chest, one of the nurses, and the wall opposite. He'd decided to see what would happen if he turned the green screw embedded in the back of his hand. (It was blocking off the tube which accessed his vein.) I think we all found out what that thing did, quite memorably. We arrived at HDU, me looking like a zombie and him my most recent victim. The nurse was apologising to all the staff for the shocking state of her patient.

I'd never been in a high-dependency ward before. That was really quite a shock. It seems to be the place they put all the really ill people who can cope without having a nurse each, as they have in intensive care. Richard's two closest neighbours were both breathing through holes in their throats, and one poor chap had been there for eighteen months.

The nurses were far more bustling and chatty in this ward. You instantly sensed you were with a gang of people who really enjoyed their work.

Richard was quite bewildered at his journey. He said, 'I'm sorry, I've made a bit of a mess.' He looked at me regularly for reassurance although I'm not sure he knew who I was.

The BBC had sent a car to our home to pick up Richard's parents and bring them to Leeds. Andy and Andrea had left to fetch their children, but planned to return as soon as possible. Nick would leave later that day to fetch his wife, Amanda, and his girls.

There were lots of flowers, cards and letters arriving from well-wishers. It was overwhelming. The sister bustled over. 'Just to let you know, we've locked this door.' She pointed to the door leading into Richard's bay. 'We're worried someone from the press might get in.'

Richard had suddenly become big news, I realised, and no one really knew how he was doing. Fortunately, his consultant, Stuart Ross, came by later that day and suggested he make a statement to the press on Richard's condition. It was reassuring to chat to him about his improvement. It seemed the medical team were all astounded by Richard's progress.

Every time Richard became lucid we asked him if he knew what had happened. He understood that he was in hospital but he had no idea why.

'You crashed, darling,' I explained.

'Did I?' He looked vaguely interested. 'Was it good?'

'Mmmm. Pretty impressive,' I told him.

'Oh.' His attention was drawn to a passing nurse with a cup and saucer in her hand. 'Shall we have a cup of tea?'

'Yeah. I'll go and get it.'

He smiled at me. 'Thank you.' He was too polite. He was talking to me as he would to someone he didn't really know. The move had tired him. His expression was becoming glazed.

I was aware that Richard's parents would be arriving at any moment and was hoping he'd manage to stay awake for their arrival. Andy had been in to assure me he was going to meet them at the door. He felt that Richard's mum and dad were entitled to be angry with someone, and he was volunteering for the job. I chatted with Nick and we agreed that would be ridiculous. Nick would make sure he was there first. Andy had been to hell and back with the rest of us, and it wasn't as though he could be held responsible for Richard's accident, even if he felt it was his duty to take the blame.

When his parents arrived, Richard was smiling, sitting up in bed and making jokes. It was a heart-warming picture for his mum and dad. Sadly, it was clear after three minutes or so that his memory of the present was gone. He'd repeat himself again and again, and get stuck. He'd ask his mum and dad, 'Did you drive here?' They'd explain that a driver had brought them, and Richard would take a sip of tea, then, 'So how did you get here?' We'd go round in circles. I warned everyone who visited that it would probably happen. Provided you drove the conversation and spoke about past experiences, or big plans for the future, Richard could stay pretty well focused and appear to be completely recovered. As he did when the Director General of the BBC, Mark Thompson, sneaked in to see him.

Richard has absolutely no recollection of the visit, but it's one I shall never forget. Mark was attending a conference elsewhere in Leeds and felt he couldn't be in the same city without checking in on Richard. Andy was running about like a headless chicken to make sure everything went smoothly, and when the DG arrived we'd all been well prepared. Richard was sitting up in bed grinning, and he became so animated, discussing programming and future plans with Mark, it was almost embarrassing. I wanted to interrupt, and say, 'I know you wouldn't think it, but he has got brain damage. He's just giving you a performance—honestly!'

Richard put on an incredible show and, as I walked him out of the ward, Mark commented on how amazing Richard was. I agreed, although secretly I was very worried about him.

When I arrived back, Richard was having a chat with his parents and suddenly looked exhausted. They noticed the signs. Richard fell asleep moments after they left. I went downstairs and turned the phones on.

I asked Ela if she'd accompany Izzy and Willow to Leeds on the Sunday. Izzy's birthday had just passed and we'd planned a big party at home. Instead we'd get all of Izzy's cousins together at the hotel and organise a birthday party there after she'd visited her daddy in hospital. Not quite what she'd expected for her sixth birthday.

The nurses had decided to move Richard into a side room. Just prior to the move, James May tumbled in.

'Erm, sorry to disturb . . . a newspaper has been on to the BBC to say that Richard was banned from driving for three months earlier this year.' He looked confused. 'He wasn't, was he?'

'No, he wasn't, what utter bollocks—how dare they?'

James grinned. 'I thought you might say that. I'll pass it on.'

At about 4 p.m. on Richard's first day in the room, I was sitting on his bed, when he said, 'This is very nice. You're very lovely.'

'Thank you,' I said.

'But I have to go now,' he said sheepishly. 'I've got to go back to my wife.'

That was a shocker! 'Darling, *I'm* your wife.'

'No, my wife's French.'

Just for a moment, a million thoughts went through my head—has he been having an affair with a French woman?

'Really, I am your wife.'

'But you can't be. I'm having too much fun with you. You're too lovely to be someone's wife.'

Phew. 'Well, aren't you the lucky one then?'

ALEX, ONE of the *Top Gear* researchers, had arrived upstairs with Andy.

'Alex is going to be your personal slave,' Andy said with a grin. 'Whatever you want, whatever you need, it's his job to get it for you.'

'Anything you want,' Alex agreed, smiling.

'Great.' I grinned. 'Pants.'

They both raised their eyebrows and laughed. But it was true. I desperately needed more knickers! Poor Alex was sent out with quite a list: knickers, bras, T-shirts, a pair of jeans and shampoo. He also had to buy Richard some clothes, as they'd gone walkabout at the airfield. Poor Alex—he'd joined *Top Gear* to work on exciting film shoots, and wound up buying underwear for the presenter's wife! Alex is a great bloke. I'd spoken to him innumerable times on the phone about filming issues, but this was the first time we'd met, and there he was writing down my vital statistics.

We huddled together in a side doorway to avoid causing disruption. As we talked, I saw a sweet, elderly woman with a dreadful gash in the top of her head held together with some serious-looking staples. It was sad watching her shuffle up and down with the aid of a nurse, her left arm outstretched, all the while calling gently, 'Puss, puss.' I could only surmise that when she received the injury she'd been looking for her cat. She had one of those delicate, friendly faces that are so rare. I had an overwhelming urge to take her home and look after her. As I watched her many emotions rushed through my head—pity, sympathy and then concern . . . were her actions a result of the head injury, or was some other illness to blame?

Would I cope with Richard if his grip on reality become so deeply affected by his injuries? How much further would he improve?

THE FOLLOWING DAY was very busy. With Richard conscious, everyone wanted to see him. His brothers had returned with their families, and of course Richard's parents were there too. But there was a problem. Richard was giving everyone an excellent rendition of the Richard he thought they'd like to see, acting the role of the perfect host—enquiring after their health and personal lives. Then he'd falter. He'd repeat himself, or take the conversation round in circles. I could see that he was getting more muddled as the day progressed, and he was very tired.

I'd left him momentarily and when I returned was horrified to find him on his knees, his hands cupped around the back of his head, his face buried into the pillows, rocking back and forth.

'Your head? Painful?'

'Yes! Oh God, help me! Arrgh!'

I ran straight to the nurses' station. 'He's in pain! Really bad pain!'

Two nurses ran back to the room with me. He was in such agony his face was unrecognisable. They fed some morphine into the catheter and I sat down heavily in the chair, watching as the expression on his face slowly changed, and the pain dropped away as he drifted into sleep.

It's strange how exhausting it is to watch someone you love in such misery. You go through every second with them. When eventually he fell asleep I thought I was going to be sick. I was shaking and needed to get some air. The nurses spent a disproportionate amount of their time encouraging me to rest, or leave Richard briefly. But whenever he was awake, I wanted him to see a familiar face.

When he woke, the doctor came. He asked Richard several questions and looked at his charts. I followed him out of the room. He confirmed that Richard's condition had deteriorated and suggested they keep him completely quiet for the foreseeable future. He'd been receiving far too much stimulus. He suggested I continue to be with Richard, but recommended only close family be allowed visits for fifteen-minute periods. Richard's determination to give everyone who visited him an enjoyable time had really taken its toll. He was extremely good at kidding everyone he was OK. He could fool just about anyone, and I knew he'd try to fool the nurses.

One conversation we had over and over again worried me, too. It went like this:

Richard: 'Do you know what I'd really like? I'd like you and me to go out there'—pointing to the window ledge—'and have a beer and a cigarette.'

Me: 'We can't do that, Richard. This is a hospital and you're a patient. They don't allow smoking, and there's definitely no beer.'

Richard: 'Oh c'mon, you could get some, I know you could. And I've got some Marly Lights.' He foraged in his camera bag.

Me: 'You haven't got any cigarettes, honestly.'

Richard: 'Yes I have, I remember. They were here.'

Me: 'No, Richard. Really, smoking isn't allowed anywhere.'

Richard: 'Do you know what I'd really like to do? I'd like you and me to go out onto that balcony and have a beer and a cigarette.'

Me: 'No, darling, we can't. It's not allowed . . .'

Whenever this conversation started I had to make sure it was brought to a satisfactory conclusion before I could leave him. Otherwise, left with the idea that the balcony was the ledge on the other side of the window, it could be dangerous to leave him. The other possibility was that he'd actually find some cigarettes and simply light up! I decided to stop smoking as the smell of cigarettes on me would just remind him of his own craving.

The cigarette conversation could take ten minutes or more to peter out and it was regularly revisited, with small alterations. The best one was in the middle of the afternoon.

Richard: 'I was just thinking; you know what would be really lovely?'

Me: 'No, what?'

Richard: 'If we go to the country and sit under a big tree, just you and me.'

Me: 'Mmm. That would be nice.'

In my head was a romantic picture of the two of us casually sitting against the trunk of a large oak, smiling at each other through dappled sunshine.

Richard: 'We could have a nice bottle of white wine resting in a stream.'

Me: 'Oh, how lovely.'

Richard: 'And a packet of Marlboro Lights.'

ONE OF THE LOVELIEST memories of this time with Richard was the overwhelming happiness that he had come back. He was childlike and forgetful and difficult, but he was undeniably Richard, and I think I probably loved him more then than I'd ever imagined possible. A part of me knew he could've been lost for ever. Yet he'd returned.

Throughout this period the pain in Richard's head was still intense and he was given morphine regularly, together with a cocktail of other drugs. He tried to manage the pain and forgo the tablets, but the nurses told him he should make life easier for himself. Unusually, he took their advice.

As Richard was so exhausted, the nurses were quick to tell me he'd be asleep all night. They were desperate for me to get some proper rest and, to be honest, I was starting to feel awful. So, at about 9.30 p.m., I left Richard and ordered a cab to take me to the hotel where the whole family were staying—visiting my room for the first time.

I joined Richard's parents for a bite to eat, and within an hour Richard's brother Nick and his family arrived. We should've all been happy to see one another, but of course this was no happy occasion. We were all worried, and there was only one place in the world I wanted to be: with him. And yet the mission was sleep, and I was soon on my way to bed.

I slept erratically and, by 6.30 a.m., I was dressed. I was in the taxi when the hospital phoned. Richard had woken up and was distressed because he didn't know where I was. Knowing that they'd felt it necessary to call me brought home to me how distraught he must have been. I would never sleep at the hotel again.

The taxi from the hotel seemed to take for ever. I was desperate. I had the money in my hand to give to the driver within minutes of taking my seat. My phone rang again. 'Hi, Mindy, Richard's getting quite agitated. I was just wondering when you might get here?'

'I'll be there within fifteen minutes. Please tell him I'm on my way.'

'I will, love, don't worry.'

But I did worry. I worried very much. To make him suffer any more was just unforgivable. I felt as though I'd been completely selfish and stupid. How could I put him through this? Every traffic light was hell and the second the car stopped, I was out like a flash. I ran to the lifts. Pressed the buttons on every one. Fidgeted as I waited. 'Come on!' I said out loud. The second a door opened, I dashed in.

HDU was on floor seven—it took an eternity. I half ran, half walked down past the nurses' station and opened the door to his room. 'Hello.'

He beamed at me. 'Oh, hello. I'm so glad you're back.'

We shared an enormous hug. It lasted longer than any other embrace I've ever known. I wonder whether, as everything was so very confused and mixed up for him, perhaps Richard didn't believe I'd return. Post-traumatic amnesia (PTA) is an alarming condition. For the majority of the time he had the memory of a goldfish (around five seconds). He could remember scraps of past history, just very little since the crash. I imagine he couldn't rely on his mind, which must be very frightening. He was described as being 'clinically confused'. The one thing he knew absolutely was that I was his ally. What he couldn't be sure of was whether I was simply a figment of his imagination. You're told of an accident you lived through, and by definition you should be dead. There are no serious injuries visible to support this 'crash' claim, yet you have a black eye and your head feels weird, as though you've been drugged. You vaguely recognise people, but you don't recall an awful lot of information about them, and you seem to be held prisoner in a small room with an en suite bathroom.

It's difficult to explain how our relationship emerged, and how scary the process was. Richard was stumbling through feelings and emotions and trying all the while to understand how they related to us. He'd accepted that I was his wife (I think), and I regularly held his face in my hands and told him, 'If you have any questions, any worries, ask me. I'll tell you the truth.'

I'd heard so many conversations with other visitors who hadn't realised the importance of talking straight with him. He'd ask a question they considered stupid, so instead of calmly setting him right, they made a joke out of it. For instance, when once he asked, 'Where's the party? Where's everyone going?' I overheard someone answer, 'Oh, it's upstairs. We're all having a great time.'

I immediately cut in, telling Richard there was no party. That sort of comment just compounded his confusion. I spent so much time with him I was aware of the importance of every single word. I thought very carefully before answering his questions, and developed a huge amount of patience. But it's impossible to expect everyone who comes into contact with a person suffering that type of injury to understand the complexities involved, particularly when the person they're talking to appears almost normal.

I'd quickly become the constant for Richard. After that morning I didn't leave his room unless he was asleep or with someone. Whenever he slept and I left the room, I'd always leave him a large note sellotaped to the TV screen, telling him where I'd gone and that I'd be back soon.

I would go downstairs and buy anything at the shop that he might like—Land Rover magazines, Curly Wurlys, Fry's Turkish Delight. James May had left him a copy of *Auto Trader*—their favourite game was fantasy car-shopping. They'd each have a copy and select their favourite cars (unlimited budget) and pretend they could buy them. It saddened me that, although I kept putting the magazine in front of him, he hadn't found his usual enthusiasm to go leafing through the pages. There was a big hole in Richard Hammond, and I was very worried we'd never find all the pieces.

On my return from one of my trips to the hospital shop, I had a shock. When I opened the door to Richard's room, he was on the phone! The little wotsit had rummaged in his bag and found his mobile (the battery from which I'd hidden). He'd taken the battery from my phone, which he'd found in my handbag, and put it into his own.

As I walked in, he finished the call and blushed.

'Who was that?' I tried to sound unconcerned.

'No one. Just a friend.'

'OK. Would you like to see what I've bought?'

I showed him the contents of the bag and avoided the subject of the phone call. Soon afterwards, the nurses came in and gave him some medication. He was exhausted and quickly fell asleep.

The second he was snoring, I grabbed the phone and quietly left the room. I turned both phones on when I reached reception. My phone instantly rang. There was a message from Richard's editor at the *Mirror*. We'd been in regular contact since the crash, but now he was calling because, as he put it, 'I've just had a chat with Richard, and wanted to check it out with you before we go to print.'

Richard had chatted long enough for his editor to realise it wasn't quite right. He did the decent thing and checked it out with me. He agreed not to write anything and promised that, should Richard call him again, it was to be kept between us. Thank goodness for honest newspapermen!

I went to find Alex. He'd been shopping and handed over several carrier bags. As I returned to the room a sudden wave of panic crept over me. Where on earth could I hide the clothes? Richard was still hell-bent on escaping for a cigarette, and I'd had to take his cowboy boots to the hotel as I'd twice caught him putting them on over his pyjama trousers.

I crept into the bathroom and shut the door. There was a mattress leaning against the wall opposite the shower—it was to be my makeshift bed on the floor next to Richard. I decided to hide the bags behind that. I shoved them out of sight and quickly flushed the loo.

As I walked back through the door, Richard was waking. He looked so lovable. His demeanour was one of someone just a little bit under the influence of a few sherries. He was smiley and affectionate and very forgetful, but mostly he was extremely tired. The nurses came in regularly to check his blood pressure, temperature, etc, and ask him questions. By the time they'd finished, he was finding it difficult to stay awake.

I'd asked Ela to come to Leeds with the girls and the BBC had kindly provided one of their drivers to fetch them. Alex came to the room to let me know they were getting close. So I dashed downstairs to wait at a side door. I'd missed the girls so badly.

When they arrived, I nearly burst into tears. I gave them huge cuddles and then hugged Ela. I asked the lady in charge of administration if there was a quiet room I could take the girls into before we went upstairs. She showed us to a large room with a boardroom table in the middle—there were probably twenty chairs around it. I picked up the girls and sat each of them on a chair facing me. I knelt in front of them.

'Now, you know where you are, don't you?'

Izzy, thumb in mouth: 'Yes, we're in a hospital.'

Willow nodded, straight-faced.

'Remember when I had to dash off because I needed to bring Daddy some new clothes?'

'Yes, because he broke his ones and they were all dirty,' Willow replied.

'That's right, poppet.' I smiled at them both. 'Well, when he tore his clothes he also banged his head a bit.'

Izzy pulled a face and nodded. 'Was there blood?'

'Just a little bit, where he banged his eye.'

'Oh! Has he got a plaster?' asked Willow, excitedly.

'Sort of. More like a bandage.'

'Wow! That's really good.' She was impressed. She was three.

I looked again at Izzy. Her thumb was planted firmly in her mouth and her face was as serious as she could muster. I waited for a moment.

'Because Daddy's banged his head, he doesn't feel very well. He's tired and a bit not like Daddy. But he just needs lots of sleep and then he'll be fine.'

'He probably needs a nap. He can have my dummy if he wants.' Dear Willow. 'I'll give him a big cuddle.'

'You do that, that'll make him feel much better.'

Izzy's eyes were looking watery.

'Did you make Daddy some cards?'

They were each gripping cards and paintings they'd made. Izzy had written him a letter too.

'Oh, you are clever girls.'

'Can we go and see him now?' Izzy asked.

'Yes. Let's go and visit your daddy.'

Ela didn't want to come into Richard's room. She waited outside. I'd already organised the nurse to help him with his eyepatch. We'd explained that he should keep the piece of gauze over his eye as it looked quite gory and might scare the girls. He was sitting on the bed when we entered the room. I'd prepped them just beforehand that we wouldn't be able to spend too much time with him, and they would be going to a party afterwards.

Richard was overjoyed when he saw them. But he'd completely forgotten why he had the eyepatch on and started trying to rip it off.

'Keep that on for a bit,' I pleaded with him. But he ignored me and tore it off. Thankfully, I'd prepared the girls.

'Oh, Daddy, that looks sore,' Willow commented.

Izzy was quiet, assessing the situation. Richard was over-excited. He got up from the bed and I dashed to grab the drip and follow him. He took the bag from me. 'I'm fine. I'm fine.' He hadn't managed to go to the loo unaided before this, but I understood that in front of the girls he would hate me to go with him. As he shuffled into the bathroom, he fell forward and saved himself by grabbing the emergency cord. Two nurses appeared like a shot and brought him back to the bed where he sat, grinning sheepishly.

Izzy was very subdued. She tried to talk to him about home but he wasn't able to concentrate. His eyes were heavy. The fall had exhausted him.

'Time to say goodbye,' I whispered to them.

Willow gave Richard a kiss. 'Bye bye, Daddy.'

Izzy's eyes started to fill. I mouthed, 'Say goodbye.'

'Bye, Daddy.' Her voice was breaking, but Richard was half asleep and didn't notice.

'Bye bye, darling,' he said. His eyes shut and we walked out as quickly as we could to the waiting Ela. She picked up Willow as Izzy exploded into uncontrollable sobs and I hugged her to me.

'Well done, Iz. You're a very, very brave girl. I'm proud of you.'

Poor Izzy. Daddy really wasn't Daddy, and if ever there was a little girl who worshipped her father it was this one. But she was also very clever and very trusting. I knelt in front of her.

'Iz, he will get better. He will, he's just tired.'

'OK, Mummy.' But I'm not sure she believed me.

Nick was waiting at the door. 'Hey! You've got a party to go to.'

'Aren't you coming, Mummy?' Izzy was pleading.

'Well, I need to be here for Daddy.'

'Oh, please, Mummy, please!'

'OK, I'll come a bit later. I'll come then.'

'Will you put us to bed? Will you be there for bedtime?'

'Yes, OK. I promise.'

It was really difficult, watching them walk down the corridor.

I wasn't quite sure how I'd manage to get away later, but it was important to the girls and I'd promised. Besides, I needed to see them. No, I *ached* to see them, to smell them, to play with them, to be their mummy again.

When I checked on Richard he was very deeply asleep. It was one of those rare opportunities to get away for a few minutes. I wrote a note and taped it to the TV screen in front of Richard:

Gone for coffee. Back in 15 mins. Love you lots. Mindy x

Seeing the girls had really knocked the wind out of me. I slumped against the wall of the huge metal lift as I went down to the ground floor.

I bought a coffee and sat down with my phone in a quiet corner. I was just dialling a number when a woman tapped me on the shoulder.

'Excuse me, are you Mrs Hammond?'

'Yes. I am. Who are you?'

'I'm afraid I'm from the press.'

I couldn't believe it. The one time I had snatched a few moments for myself. 'I'm sorry, I can't talk to you now.'

I scooped up my possessions and half walked, half ran towards the lifts. As I went I realised there were an awful lot of people sitting around with cups of coffee. The hospital was full of journalists.

The old lady was going for a walk with one of the nurses. She'd stopped calling her cat and the nurse was encouraging her to talk to people. I smiled at her as I passed and whispered out loud, 'God bless you.' I hope she's OK, I hope she went home.

Richard was just waking. 'Where are the girls? Where have they gone? They were here, weren't they? I didn't dream it?'

'No, you didn't dream it. They've gone back to the hotel.'

'Let's go and see them. We'll sneak out. No one will know.' He threw his legs over the side of the bed and I grabbed the drip bag before he pulled it out of him. 'Where are my clothes?'

'You have to stay here, darling. Shall I see what's on TV?'

'Oh, yeah, OK.'

He turned his head and relaxed a little. I hurried to get the TV on.

Thirty seconds later: 'Where are the girls?'

Me: 'They had to go back to the hotel. But they're fine.'

Richard, horror-stricken: 'Who's with them?'

Me: 'Ela's with them. It's OK, they're fine.'

Richard: 'Why don't we go and see them?'

He started to get up and I dashed round the bed to grab the drip.

Me: 'Darling, you really have to stay here. Shall I get a cup of tea?'

Richard, looking about him absent-mindedly: 'Yeah, OK.'

I was nervous about leaving him and rushed to the tea urn. When I got back I couldn't believe what I saw: he'd found another mobile phone in his bag and was dismantling mine and putting the SIM card into the spare phone. I tried to act calmly as I put the tea down.

Me: 'What are you doing?'

Richard: 'My phone doesn't work so I'm just swapping the SIM card.'

Me: 'Actually, I think that's my phone.'

Richard: 'No, I'm sure it's mine.'

He put his SIM card into the other phone and turned it on.

Richard: 'That's funny. I think it is yours. Where's mine then?'

He started searching through his bag. I felt dreadful. I'd taken his phone and put it in the safe. The doctors had impressed upon me that he shouldn't be making calls and he wasn't allowed to even think about anything work-related. That was difficult. The majority of Richard's friends were also involved in the industry. This was compounded by another problem: many journalists had Richard's mobile number and he'd be only too happy to chat with them, which could prove a bit tricky.

He looked weary. His brow was knotted; headache again. The headache, was always there in varying degrees of severity. He looked miserable.

Richard: 'Can we go home now?'

Me: 'No, darling, not yet. Not for a bit.'

Richard: 'Come on, let's just go, they won't mind.'

Me: 'Richard . . .' I looked him straight in the eyes. 'You've had an accident. You have to stay here until you're better.'

Richard: 'Yes, yes. Now, let's go.'

I was debating what to say next when, fortunately, two nurses walked in. They asked him if he was in pain and he was honest and asked for morphine. He really looked pretty dreadful. Seeing the girls had woken all sorts of emotions. The nurses were concerned he hadn't been drinking enough water, and he'd eaten barely a thing. His drip was almost empty and they decided to replace it.

Shortly after they left, he asked, 'Shall we have a cup of tea, then?'

'OK.'

His memory was so awful he'd eat breakfast and immediately after the last spoonful of cereal he'd ask, 'Shall we have breakfast now?' I didn't question him. He was, at this stage, clinically confused. I wouldn't have dreamt of making life any more complicated. I went to fetch the tea, and when I walked back into his room, Richard had fallen deeply asleep. I poured the teas down the sink and wrote him a new note:

Gone to put the girls to bed. Back soon. Love you, M x

I sped across Leeds in a cab to the hotel and was thrilled to walk into a roomful of happy children. Andy, Andrea, Nick and Amanda, together with Richard's parents, had gone to great lengths to make a really special birthday party for Izzy. But although I treasured each moment with the girls, my mind was constantly drifting back to the hospital, knowing how quickly Richard would become distressed if I wasn't there when he woke. Although I was smiling and chatting with everyone, inside me the panic was growing.

Ela and I took Izzy and Willow to their room. They begged me to stay and put them to bed. They hadn't seen me for two days, which was a first for them, and I felt overwhelmed by their love and desperately sorry watching them having to cope, even though they were doing so well. I was proud of them.

As I tucked them in, Izzy told me: 'I knew you'd come, Mummy. You said you would.'

I was so happy to hear those words. If I make a promise to the girls, I always keep it. I gave her a huge hug and felt her tears on my shoulder. She didn't want Willow to know how upset she was, and I held her there for a little while. I whispered to her: 'Are we OK now, baby?' She nodded. 'Well done, darling. You're a very brave girl. I'm proud of you.'

She nodded again, and wiped her nose on her sleeve.

I went over to Willow's bed.

'Mummy, where are you sleeping?' No flies on Willow!

'Oh, I'm going to go back to keep Daddy company.'

Willow was cross. 'But, Mummy, we won't see you!'

'Yes, you will.'

She became tearful. 'No, 'cos you'll be there and we're here, so we won't.'

I made a deal with them. 'I promise I'll be back in the morning in time for breakfast, and we'll all have breakfast together. How about that?'

They agreed. I kissed them both, had a quick chat with Ela and headed out of the hotel. I'd phoned for a taxi before bathing the kids and knew it was waiting. Leeds was very busy and the journey took longer than normal. I was really starting to panic. We drove up to the front doors of the hospital and I ran for it. When I opened Richard's door all my worries disappeared. He was just stirring.

The nurses came in for the usual tests and questions. When they left the room we snuggled up on the bed and chatted. After a while, I helped him to the loo.

As he got back into bed, he thought for a few moments and said, 'What're we having for lunch?'

I simply told him we'd had lunch and now it was bedtime.

'Really? Oh. OK.' He was very weary, and by the time I'd returned to the room after brushing my teeth, he was fast asleep.

I dragged the mattress in from the bathroom and laid it on the floor beside his bed. It was about 9 p.m., and after switching off the lights I was soon asleep.

I woke to a most strange sensation. The hair near my ear was wet and a bit sticky. Still half awake, I was trying to work out what it was when something landed plop! On my head. As I focused in the dim light, I noticed Richard's head over my side of the bed, his mouth against the safety rail and drool slowly leaving his mouth, trickling over the bar then landing on me.

'Ooh. That's nice,' I remember thinking. It did make me smile as I went to the bathroom to wash off my damp hair. As I walked back into the room, I remember looking at him and thinking, 'God, I love this man.' And in one of those brief, desperate moments, I whispered, 'Please, God, help him.'

I kissed his forehead and eased him away from the bars. I checked that his drip was still OK, kissed him again on the cheek, and watched a smile flicker across his face. Then I went back to my mattress. I knew I couldn't sleep too long. I needed to wake by five to get back to the hotel for the girls.

I tiptoed out of Richard's room at about 5.30 a.m. and told the nurses I would (hopefully) be back before he woke up. At the other end I dashed into the hotel, having sent a text to Ela to check they were awake. I'd ordered the breakfasts for 7 a.m. so we could have some time together.

We had a wonderful morning. To the girls this was more like an adventure. We tried not to talk about how poorly Daddy was, just how soon he'd get better and come home. Like most children, they're accustomed to time frames, and were very persistent about Daddy's going-home date. I had to be vague. Nobody knew how long it would take and I couldn't lie to them.

We were very silly and jolly during their breakfast. I couldn't thank Ela enough. She'd be returning home with the girls later that morning and we both knew it would be awfully difficult for them.

My phone rang. It was the hospital. Richard had called the nurse to ask where I was. 'Tell him I'll be there in twenty minutes.'

The girls looked crestfallen. 'Oh, Mummy. Stay here with us. Please.'

Izzy was pulling me towards her on the sofa. 'I won't let you go. I won't.' She hugged my arm as I sat next to her. This was so unlike Izzy. She was usually quite independent, but this experience was unnerving her.

'Listen, poppet, I need to go back and see Daddy because he's really not very well, and if I can help him to get better he can come home.'

She gave a deep sigh and the tears started. 'But I miss you, Mummy.'

'Oh, I miss you too, baby. So much.' I gave her a big cuddle, and Willow ran over and joined in.

Holding them both was wonderful and dreadful at the same time. Leaving them was the most heart-wrenching experience, particularly when I knew they needed me. But this time Richard needed me more, and I explained to them very honestly why I had to stay at the hospital, and why they were needed at home—to look after the animals, and make sure everything was ready for when Daddy came home. They sort of accepted this, and Willow began chatting about everything she'd do, but Izzy was quite reserved. Her thumb in her mouth, she simply nodded in agreement.

Reception called to say the car was waiting for me. I had to leave. I told the girls to get dressed and they could come to the hospital and say goodbye to Daddy before they started their journey home. I was all smiles and hugs as I left them. But once in the car I cried 'til I was halfway to the hospital.

Richard was sitting up in bed when I arrived. He was very pleased to see me. His face lit up. He was so excited about the girls coming to see him, but he tired easily and was soon dozing again.

The girls came later with Ela. Willow held Richard's hand and told him that he wasn't allowed to come home until his eye was better. OK?

Izzy was desperately upset but very brave. She smiled at him and then hid behind me. When we left his room, she burst into tears. I carried her to the visitors' room and once again told her how marvellous she'd been. Ela followed us with Willow, and the two girls stood silently, cuddling each other. When they stepped apart, they both put on their bravest faces. I was so overwhelmed by them. They behaved amazingly, careful to remember everything I'd told them, right to the end.

We went down to the waiting car and Ela and I helped them into their seats. With all my heart I wanted to go home with them. I missed them so very much. Still, I couldn't let them see me upset, so we chatted about how they must look after the animals and thank our neighbours, Anne and Syd, who'd been back and forth at home to make sure everything was OK.

I promised them that, as soon as I could come home, I would, and we'd talk all the time. I hugged and kissed them both, and Ela, who was looking after them so well. I'd been to the cashpoint in the hospital and handed her an envelope full of cash. She needed to buy food and supplies.

The second she saw the amount of money, she knew I wasn't planning on being home soon.

'Mindy, you're so brave,' she said to me as she hugged me goodbye.

'Oh bollocks!' I whispered, but I hugged her close and swallowed my tears.

I watched the car until it disappeared. I wanted to drop to my knees and wail, but I knew by now Richard would be fretful. I took a deep breath, straightened my back, then began the journey back to the ward.

FOR THE REST of the day, apart from Richard's brothers saying their farewells, I was the only visitor. He slept most of the time. Whenever he woke, he asked the same questions every five minutes:

'Where are the children?' He'd no memory of them leaving.

'Where do we go tomorrow?' He was convinced we were in a hotel.

'When are you meeting up with the others?' He thought there was some kind of party going on, which was understandable, as it was unusual for his entire family to be present unless it was a special occasion.

Then I'd explain (several times) that this wasn't a hotel, it was a hospital; there was no party. Eventually, he would accept what I'd told him. The problem was, no sooner had you answered one question than it would be followed by another, then seconds later the first question would be asked again. It was quite exhausting.

The worst one was, 'Where are my clothes?'

I'd explain that his clothes were cut off him at the scene of the accident, so he didn't have any.

'Are you sure? Have you looked?' was his standard reply.

Once I'd satisfied his questioning on that one, his next move would be to grab his bag. He'd start foraging through it, and I knew what for.

'I really want to go for a beer and a fag. Let's find a local restaurant/stare at the sea/sit by a stream and have a drink and a fag.'

When the sister appeared I asked that she explain to Richard why he couldn't have a drink and a cigarette.

'The hospital is absolutely no-smoking. And if you drank alcohol now you'd be at risk to fits and seizures. It's too dangerous.'

After she left the room, I spoke to him about why he was there:

'You had a crash, darling.'

'You keep saying that.'

'You still don't believe me, do you?'

'No, not really.'

Up to this point his memory of the crash hadn't seemed important. But sitting beside him on the bed, I felt the time had arrived. Should I tell him, yet again, my version of what had happened? No. It hadn't worked before so why would it work now? I could turn on the news and he could watch it on TV. No—too dramatic. Get one of the nurses to come and tell him? No. By the time I brought one of them to him, he would've lost interest.

Then it came to me. The newspapers. More particularly, Jeremy's piece in the previous day's edition of the *Sun*. He'd believe that, I was sure. There was a picture of the jet car, and him with TG.

I wasn't sure if it was the right thing to do because I was worried that he might react badly. I reached down behind the curtain and retrieved the newspaper. He sat propped up in bed. Our eyes met. I faltered. 'Are you sure you're ready for this?'

Why was I asking him? He had no idea. Was it better he didn't know? No, of course not; it couldn't be. He trusted me. I promised him I'd only tell the truth. This was the truth.

'It's a bloody big deal, Richard.' I knew my eyes were filling as I looked at his face. His expression had changed. Suddenly he looked quite serious, and as he laid the paper on the bed, he was taken aback by the headline:

Hamster walks . . . and I watched, says Clarkson.

'Fuck me! On the front page?'

I watched as he read. I knew the article well, and was feeling every emotion with him as he went through the text. When he opened the paper to the double-page spread, his eyebrows lifted. He was really surprised. There was a picture of the jet car, and a huge picture of him and Top Gear Dog.

He looked at me, panic-stricken. 'TG! Where's TG?'

'It's OK. She's at home. You sent her home the night before.'

'Oh, yeah. Thank God. When can we go home? Can't we just go?'

His attention had been broken.

'No, darling, you're in hospital and you have to stay here for a bit.'

'No, I can't. What time do we need to be at the restaurant?'

'We're not going to a restaurant, we're eating here.'

'But the others'll be waiting.' He was getting out of bed. I grabbed the drip bag. 'Where are my fags? Someone must have a fag. Let's go to the bar.'

He was up and heading for the door. I was close behind him.

'Richard, there's just a hospital corridor out there.'

'No, there isn't. This is a hotel.' He looked at me as if I was a fool.

I wasn't going to stop him. What was the point?

It was heartbreaking to watch him stumble the few steps to the door, intent on joining the others. In his mind, he was ready to have a good time. He opened the door and stopped dead in his tracks. A glimpse through the door revealed the bustle of the ward: nurses rushing back and forth; buzzers sounding, and patients wandering past wheeling their drips.

I caught him and helped him to sit back on the side of the bed.

It was so cruel. I knelt in front of him as he sat and stared at the door.

Quietly, he said, 'Shit.'

I held his hands. 'I'm so sorry. It really is a hospital, you see?'

He nodded, but looked so very upset. I hugged him. I held his head to my heart and kissed him through his hair. Wiping the tears so he wouldn't feel them drop. Feeling desperately sorry for him. He was lost and I didn't know how to help him to find his way back. Perhaps he never would.

He tugged at the newspaper he'd sat on. It was still opened to Jeremy's piece about the crash. He looked at the article. 'Bloody hell!'

It was a big surprise all over again, and I was grateful for the distraction.

For most of that day, the newspaper remained open on the bed. He read about the crash over and over. And each time the news came as a surprise.

Eventually, when he took a nap, I removed the paper and stored it back behind the curtains. He'd glimpsed a piece of evidence; whether anything would stick in his confused mind, I didn't know.

We had some wonderful chats that night. Several times, Richard asked me where TG was, which I found encouraging. Clearly, somewhere in his mind, he had connected with a small piece of new memory.

He didn't want me to sleep on the floor any more. He wanted me to lie with him. It was wonderful to be 'us'. I had been frightened. There are many people who've been through a similar experience, watching as the person they love claws their way back to life. You watch and pray for the sparks of recognition, a flash of memory to bring the pieces back together so that what used to be can be rekindled, but there's no guarantee. We were lucky. We were strong before the accident, and in that tiny room with boxes of cards and gifts strewn around us, pictures of cars drawn by children wishing 'The Hamster' better, emails and letters from all over the world from well-wishers, we fell in love all over again. My Richard remembered me.

We held each other all night, like our first time together. It was the start of the rest of our lives. I hadn't once enquired how he felt about me. Apart from explaining who I was and my feelings for him, there was never any reference to our relationship or life together. I knew it was possible he'd dismiss his life prior to the accident and wipe away all knowledge of our past. He could choose to love me or not. Thankfully—and I am for ever grateful—he fell in love with me all over again. Stronger, deeper, fuller. I knew then, whatever the future held, it embraced us together; we were one again.

The nurses all knew that I was sharing Richard's bed, but no one minded. All they cared about was the well-being of their patients. If having his wife with him made Richard feel better, then why not? I'm not sure whether we were unusual but I would imagine not. Anyone in my position would want to be with their husband, to help him, with every fibre of their being.

I slept little, but was able constantly to untangle his drip, chase him to the loo with the drip bag and prop him up as he took a pee; both of us always half asleep. He'd changed from the private, slightly self-conscious man who hated me helping him to a smiling, affectionate husband who appreciated my help, enjoyed my presence, loved my love.

The nurse from occupational therapy told us about post-traumatic amnesia. Essentially, we were playing a waiting game. Every brain injury is unique. Every patient dictates their own recovery time. She was careful not to voice what both she and I knew—there was no way of saying how much recovery would be achieved. He'd made amazing progress thus far, but no one can tell you if or when your loved one will recover.

IN THE OUTSIDE WORLD, a storm was brewing over the future of *Top Gear*. James and Jeremy, together with Andy, were adamant that the series was over if Richard wasn't able to return. In the media, some were vehemently opposed to the continuation of the show, accusing the BBC of being irresponsible and dangerous, and 'going too far'.

Reports in the papers that Richard had been trying to set a new land-speed record were untrue, but it was an understandable assumption. Jeremy was spending a great deal of time defending the programme, emphasising the significance of keeping Richard's job waiting for him. Richard himself was starting to ask about the show. He was eager to get back to work.

Imagine. You've suffered brain damage. You nearly died, heroically, you fought your way towards that huge goal—the first day back—and it doesn't matter, because no one's going to make the programme any more, and the job you loved has been abolished. And it's your fault. You killed it, because it didn't kill you. Had *Top Gear* been taken off air, I'm sure Richard's recovery would have been seriously affected. He would've felt guilty and miserable, and I daren't even imagine the depths to which his depression could've taken him.

Top Gear may seem a little gung-ho and dangerous but it's very carefully put together, and the group of people who run around like headless chickens in the production office are some of the hardest-working people I've ever known. They're also intensely proud of the end product. Jeremy, James and Richard are mates; Andy refers to them as a band. When Richard was in intensive care, I remember Andy turning away from the bed where Richard lay motionless. 'C'mon, mate,' he'd said in a broken voice. 'We can't go on without the drummer.'

RICHARD'S ESCAPE PLANS became even more complex. One night I found him trying to unhinge the bathroom window. There was only one sure-fire way to stop him: I hid his pyjama bottoms while he was asleep.

After showering the following morning, he began searching for fresh pyjamas. He found the freshly laundered jacket, then began looking about the room for the trousers. 'That's funny. No kecks!'

'Oh?' I called nonchalantly. 'Maybe they forgot.'

I awaited his response, but he'd climbed back into bed and was calmly looking at the kids' drawings.

Andy Wilman had contacted the Formula One neuro-doctor, Professor Syd Watkins, who'd designed the helmet that Richard had worn in the jet car. Undoubtedly it had saved his life. He'd also dealt with precisely the same injuries Richard had sustained many times before with F1 drivers. He had given Andy both his home and mobile numbers and suggested I call.

When we spoke he was reassuring. After asking a handful of questions, he calmly told me the future looked bright. He was convinced Richard would make a full recovery. He also told me that many patients in these situations think only of one thing: escape. He recalled one man who'd managed to escape from hospital. Syd had enquired whether any vehicles were missing. It transpired that an ambulance had gone.

'Go to his house. He'll be there,' Syd had told them.

They had found the ambulance parked outside.

I couldn't risk Richard escaping. Knowing his determination, it would be the fastest available car he'd choose for his getaway, not an ambulance.

Though Richard was desperate to leave the confines of his room, the nurses and doctors insisted that a controlled environment was essential. After a chat, we came up with a plan to get him into the fresh air . . .

A porter came to his room pushing a wheelchair; a security guard alongside. Richard (with pyjama bottoms now 'found') took his seat grinning from ear to ear. He was embarrassed at being forced to be a passenger, joking he was being bullied by all these women.

When he saw the security guard his first words were, 'Oh, come on, is this really necessary?'

The security guard laughed. 'I'm afraid so.'

We were all getting quite giggly. Richard's excitement was contagious.

The sister had given Richard a pair of sunglasses and put a blanket over his head. By this time, we really were close to collapse. Richard looked like a criminal about to be bundled into the back of a police van.

Once the giggles had subsided a little (after a 'sharp' word from sister), we made our way out of the ward—Richard making rude jokes, the porter laughing, the security guard trying to look tough but muffling giggles, and me casting the occasional stern glance at Richard. He was having a ball. Larking about and being naughty. Richard being Richard.

We reached the door of the memorial garden. It was a sort of roof garden and very concealed. The security guard insisted on hanging around by the door and the sister took the porter over to the other side, leaving us alone.

It was a warm, sunny day. Richard's chair was parked opposite me. He closed his eyes and turned his face to the sun, smiling.

'Good to be out?' I asked softly.

'Mmm. Sort of.' He held my hands in his. 'I'm sorry, Mind.' He looked me straight in the eye.

'Don't be silly.' I smiled. But he wasn't ready to stop talking.

'No, I'm really sorry. I love you.' He leant across and kissed me.

'I love you too.' Tears were dripping off my chin.

We looked out at the view across the rooftops in silence.

'So,' he said, 'shall we have a sneaky fag?'

I rolled my eyes. 'I don't believe you!'

He persisted for a few minutes with the usual argument. Then his mood suddenly changed. 'Can we go back now?'

Richard was far quieter on our return journey. I wondered whether this small interaction with the outside world had set him back a little. Perhaps he'd realised he really was unwell, and was in shock. He was certainly lost in thought when we got back to the room.

AS THE DAYS PROGRESSED, I had many discussions with the neurosurgeon, Stuart Ross. He was aware we were a long way from home and felt it would be better to move Richard to a special BUPA hospital in Bristol as soon as possible. We agreed to keep the plans from Richard until we had everything confirmed.

The time in Leeds was difficult for all of us but especially for Richard's parents. Although she hid it well, his mum was deeply upset to see her beloved son in such a terrible state. The lad she knew so well was very different, and no one could provide a definitive prognosis.

The doctors had decreed that visitors should be kept to a minimum. I was there constantly and the only other visitors were his parents. His dear dad took over whenever I left the room. It was a sort of tag team.

The day before Richard was scheduled to leave Leeds, his parents set off on their long trek back. It was a very emotional goodbye. Richard's mum put on her bravest face but had to leave quickly. His dad was steadfast to the last with encouraging words and a positive air.

That day, I started to assemble our worldly goods ready for departure; meanwhile Andy organised a fully equipped 'hospital plane' to take us from

Leeds to Bristol, as the neurosurgeons were concerned it was too far to expect Richard to travel by road. The Yorkshire air ambulance would fly us from the hospital to the local airport, and we'd be met by ambulance on arrival in Bristol.

Sourcing the right type of plane hadn't been easy, but then Andy's probably the best man on the planet when it comes to delivering the impossible—just watch a few of the *Top Gear* challenges and you'll see what I mean. Harrier jump jets, army vehicles, aircraft carriers—nothing is beyond him.

When I'd explained to Richard the plans for the move to a rehab unit in Bristol he was very excited. But his elation soon clouded.

'So we're going home tomorrow?'

'No, darling, we're going to Bristol. To the rehab unit.'

'Can't we just go home?'

'Not yet, darling. Hey! Guess how you've getting there? A helicopter is collecting you, then you're transferring to a little plane to fly you to Bristol.'

'You're coming too?' There was a slight air of panic in his voice.

'Obviously.'

'You won't leave me, will you, Mind?'

I knew straight away he wasn't referring to the journey. Richard had moments of great clarity when I believe he realised how unravelled he'd become. For a man who doesn't feel fear, he was genuinely scared.

'Never,' I whispered.

He squeezed me tight. I held him for a few moments more. I'd never seen him like this, and knew he'd be embarrassed if he had to face me. I felt physical pain as I held him. I couldn't collapse now.

'Cup of tea?' I asked softly.

'Yeah, that'd be good.'

I was careful not to look in his eyes as I made for the door. As I closed it behind me I drew a huge breath and exhaled slowly. A nurse gave me one of those looks which asks: *Are you OK? Do you need my help?*

I painted on a smile and said 'Tea!' She winked, and walked on.

I was returning when the sister stopped me. She explained that a nurse must accompany Richard on the flight and she was coming with us. We joked that she'd have to hitchhike back, so she'd better not bring much stuff.

She had followed me back to the room to check on Richard when another member of the team appeared with his medication.

'You won't believe what's been going on outside,' she reported.

A patient had arrived by air ambulance on the roof of the hospital, but the press had assumed it was Richard's lift. They'd caught wind of rumours about his imminent departure.

'The press are everywhere,' she told us. 'They're on the roofs, in other buildings—they all went rushing out of the reception area.'

'Blimey.' We were really shocked.

'It's as well they were flushed out today,' she continued. 'It'll make things easier tomorrow.'

'Oh God, I'm so sorry.' Richard shook his head. 'I'm not only a crap patient but you have to deal with all this other stuff as well.'

They replied, 'It's nice to have a bit of excitement.'

After they left, Richard continued to worry about it. We had a long chat about the air ambulance, the money that had been raised in his name, and of course his popularity (which he didn't believe).

'Everyone just wants to see how you are. Don't forget, the last time anyone saw you, you were upside down.'

'But they can't be *that* interested in me, for God's sake. I'm just the little bloke off a car show.'

'Ahem!' I pointed to the sacks and boxes strewn around his room, brim-full of cards, letters and gifts. 'You're the lovely little bloke off a car show. Don't underestimate how much people care about you.'

'But I'm just me.'

'Well, maybe that's why you're special.'

He gave me a quizzical look.

I DON'T REMEMBER what time we were leaving, but I recall waking early. It was strange seeing Richard in real clothes. The nurses were coming in regularly, checking he was OK. I was putting essentials into bags and making small talk. He was impatient. He just wanted to go.

'What time are they coming?' he asked every ten minutes.

'Don't worry, they'll let us know when the helicopter arrives.'

Andy and Alex were hovering in the corridor. Andy gave me a rundown on the plan of action. Alex had volunteered to clear the contents of the hospital room and transport it all to Bristol by car after we'd left. It was a monumental task. I thanked him for all his help. As I talked with them I felt quite choked.

Stuart Ross came in to say goodbye and told Richard how pleased he was at the progress made so far. But he was anxious to reiterate his advice: 'No work. Your continued recovery depends upon it.'

Both Mr Ross and I knew that Richard's promises to rest would be forgotten within minutes. I'd had endless battles, trying to prevent him from calling James and Jeremy and his colleagues at the *Daily Mirror*.

I explained to Mr Ross that what we were asking Richard to do was effectively cut himself off from his life. Mr Ross agreed a compromise: if I could ensure his conversations didn't turn to the subject of work, he could speak to his mates occasionally. Andy was only too happy to follow the plan, as were James and Jeremy.

I'd asked everyone involved in Richard's professional life at the BBC and elsewhere to write to him, explaining that nothing would happen until his return. I could put the letters in front of him whenever he became worried about work. He needed physical evidence.

The evening before we were due to leave, Richard had been fretting about work, as he often did. 'Can you get my phone? I need to call Wilman.'

This exchange had been repeated on and off all day.

'It's OK, Wilman's fine.'

'And I need to call the *Mirror*.'

'I've spoken to them, everything's OK.'

Suddenly, for the first time, Richard's whole persona changed. His face turned to anger.

'Look, I know you think you know what you're doing, but this is my career! My life! Stop speaking to me like I'm an idiot!'

I was so surprised, so overjoyed, I started to cry. Perspective had suddenly arrived. He remembered a previous conversation!!

'Richard—I'm sorry. Of course it's your career.'

But he still looked angry. 'Stop talking to me like that,' he snapped.

It was fantastic, but at the same time quite shocking. Taking care not to sound patronising, I said, 'I don't mean to talk down to you. I truly don't. But, darling, this is the first time you've remembered a conversation. You do remember us talking about this before?'

He looked at me like I was mad.

'Of course I do. Look. Just, just . . .' He paused, the memory gone but his anger still present. 'Just get on with what you're supposed to be doing.'

'OK.' I rushed into the bathroom and took a shower. During the five minutes under hot running water, my mind was in a frenzy. If his memory had returned, perhaps his anger would remain. Would I walk out to another uncomfortable evening? We'd had a few difficult nights when he'd refuse to leave a particular subject and got what the doctors referred to as 'stuck on point'. Moving the conversation on had become difficult, and he'd been very miserable.

Tentatively, I pushed open the door. He was in bed, gazing vacantly at the TV. As I walked through the door he shot me a loving smile.

"Ello! You were a long time. Have you shrunk?'

I felt a huge sense of relief. His memory was working its way back, and although still muddled he'd taken another huge step.

WE WERE TO GO by helicopter to Leeds–Bradford Airport. There, a small private plane equipped with stretcher, oxygen and medical equipment would fly us on to a small airport outside Bristol. An ambulance would be waiting to drive the final few miles to The Glen in Clifton, the only private intensive-care hospital in the area. It boasted a physiotherapy team and gym, and was close to the brain-rehabilitation centre in Frenchay. The team there would take over Richard's care during the weeks ahead.

I was nervous. Even though everyone—doctors, neurosurgeons, nurses, etc—assured me this was the best course of action, I was still worried. He'd improved so much in the now familiar surroundings of Leeds. I was frightened this huge upheaval might set him back.

When the time came to leave it was a bit of a scramble. Someone said, 'Time to go.' Richard was being difficult as usual, insisting he could walk.

'Oh no you don't, said the sister in her firmest tone.

A wheelchair was ready for him and, embarrassed or not, that was to be his mode of transport. I grabbed a couple of bags and was alongside. Andy came too. Richard kept trying to discuss work with him, but Andy was constantly changed the subject.

Such a positive moment, to be moving to a rehabilitation unit, and yet . . . somehow I felt we were leaving everyone behind. There wasn't time to thank them all. We just had to go.

Of course, it wasn't that simple. I knew Richard, he'd want to mess about or do something daft. In addition, I could see the helicopter. If he was in a wheelchair, he'd have to stand up and climb in. No way would he manage that. His confidence was high, which was fantastic, but I'd been warned that to step backwards while he was progressing so well could be catastrophic.

I didn't wait for the sister. 'Darling, you have to go on the stretcher.'

'No, I don't. Come on—'

The sister had cottoned on straight away: 'It's the only way they can carry you on the helicopter.'

'Oh, all right, then.'

So, thankfully, he was stretchered to the air ambulance. Then we discovered it was crewed by the same team who'd rescued him.

Richard thanked them for saving his life and set about reviewing the interior of the helicopter. He was joking with the crew, who were clearly delighted to see him so much better. I joined in, but was secretly petrified. He was putting on a show, and I'd back him up, but I was waiting to see what would happen as the trip progressed.

I should mention that I'd only ever been in a helicopter once before. In bad weather. It put me off for life; I was petrified. I sat alongside Richard and held his hand. The inside of the helicopter was quite spacious, and Richard wasn't fazed. As we took off, I was nervous he might react. But there was nothing, he simply admired the view.

We noticed that down below us a crowd of photographers had flocked to the front lawn of the hospital and were aiming their cameras skywards, but it was too late. The only photographer to get a shot of Richard leaving had been hiding on a roof opposite the hospital. When all the others had been discovered, he'd remained. We wondered later where on earth he'd hidden.

When we landed at Leeds–Bradford Airport, a small plane awaited us. Richard was soon settled on the stretcher aboard the plane. An oxygen monitor was clipped to his index finger. The sister and I sat opposite one another. As the plane took off, I watched Richard's face. He was clearly exhausted and looked distant.

'Are you feeling OK?' I asked.

'Yeah, yeah.' I knew he was trying to convince me.

I hated every moment of that flight. He received oxygen several times during the forty minutes in the air. I checked my watch minute by minute.

Richard pretended to be asleep but I knew him too well. He was trying to concentrate, dealing with his own demons. Several times during the flight, I had to wrestle with panic. If he was ill on the plane, what could be done?

I was so grateful when we touched down. Richard insisted on walking to the ambulance, a difficult few steps. The journey across Bristol was brief, and Richard resumed his cheery banter. He'd relaxed again. Thank God.

I've no idea what time we arrived at the hospital. I remember Richard fell asleep on contact with his bed. Bristol may have been another step towards recovery, but Stuart Ross warned me that the worst was yet to come. From a ludicrously quick recovery to date, it would all start to slow down. This was where the hard work began.

Chapter 5

Richard's Story

There is a scene in Stephen King's *Misery* where the main character wakes to find that his ankles, which his less-than-friendly hostess has recently broken for him with a mallet, are hurting badly. As I drifted between coma and consciousness in intensive care in Leeds General Infirmary that scene fixed itself at the front of my bleary mind. I could see a nurse holding a plastic cup. I couldn't understand who she was, why she was there, and why I was in bed. She offered me the cup. It was a dose of morphine. Did I want it?

In the Stephen King book, the character is offered morphine to dull the pain of his shattered ankles. This was why that particular scene had been tapping away at my mind like an insistent little bird at a window. The bloke with the ankles compares his pain to jagged, blackened piles of wood sticking out of the sea bed on the coast. The morphine is the sea and it washes over the pain, hiding it. I thought what a beautiful metaphor this was as the nurse leaned closer with the drugs. The morphine must have swept over whatever pain was troubling me and I drifted out of consciousness again.

The ground looked rough but friendly. The path twisted ahead, tempting me on. On either side, the mountains rose and the valleys between lay cool and dark. It felt like the Lake District, my favourite place in the world. I sensed tiny flowers on long, velvet stems bobbing in the grass nearby. The sky beyond the plateau was pale and white. There was no noise but the soft, occasional gusts of a breeze that set the grass waving. I was happy to be there and didn't want to give in to all the people who were a bit cross about my journey. But the pressure of their disapproval mounted. I could sense that their mood was changing to anger. Mindy was cross. So I stopped messing about and did as I was told. I came back.

Mindy was, indeed, cross. I didn't know it, but she had been standing over me, bellowing my name. I have learned since that things had been looking very bad for a while and Mindy had asked the nurse if she could shout at me to see if I responded. She told Mindy that it might help. That was all Mindy needed to hear and she launched into a barrage of shouting and yelling, urging me to come back. I did. The medical observations took a turn for the better; I was safe, though still unconscious.

I remember nothing clearly of being in Leeds General Infirmary. I owe my life to the people there but I can't remember being under their care. Time spent in a coma is time spent in an entirely different sort of consciousness. On many occasions, I am told, I woke, but I cannot distinguish those times from dreams and fantasy. It was a long time spent living between two worlds.

Bed was nice. I liked being there. But I had been in a crash. It was easier, finally, to believe it. Even though there was no evidence to support it. Apart from being in what, clearly, was a hospital, there was nothing else to back up Mindy's claims. I could move; there was no pain; everything worked. Something was wrong. I needed to sleep. So I did.

Distantly, in flashes, I remembered. The jet car had crashed. I had been fighting to save it. Something had gone wrong with the steering. I recalled the sense that I was on the point of losing my fight. There had been nothing more I could do but die. Now I was in hospital. I hadn't died. But I had hurt my brain; damaged the very place where I lived.

It's the most intimate way to be hurt. I was reduced to thoughts; to patterns and pictures but nothing solid. I had been forced back into the very cave that I came from and I had hidden at the back. I needed strength. I needed to sleep. So I did.

Mindy was talking to me again. The jet car had crashed and I had banged my head badly. I held her—or she held me—and I felt sad. But I believed her now. I was in hospital. I was the patient. Meals came and went. I slept when I wanted. A nurse came round now and then and stuck needles in me, but it was a small price to pay for being the centre of everyone's world.

A jet engine started up. It was right by my head. There were many people around me, busy doing important stuff. Mindy was with me. We were with a group of people. I was in a gang again. This was good. The jet engine screamed more urgently.

'Last thing I remember hearing was a jet engine,' I said. Someone laughed. I was showing off. That felt great. I had been in a crash with a jet engine. That was why I was up here on the roof getting into a helicopter. And then nothing.

Little flashes of consciousness meshed together out of sequence to make up a thread that I lived along. Finally, almost two weeks after getting into the jet car, I accepted that it had crashed. Mindy had explained it to me again and again and I had not believed her. But in the hospital room in Bristol, holding Mindy's hand, I accepted it. I felt guilty about the crash;

maybe I had done something wrong? Was it my fault? Did I go too fast? But at least now I believed what Mindy said. And that made things a lot easier to connect.

It was easy to accept in the end. If the last thing you recall is the sound of a jet engine starting up inches behind your head before being fired up a runway at 300 mph in a dragster . . . well, your mind is hardly surprised if you come out of a coma in hospital a week or two later. How much harder must it be for patients who come out of a coma to find they no longer recognise the woman everyone tells them is their wife and the last thing they remember is riding a bicycle to the shops for bread? I was lucky; I had hurt myself in such an exceptional set of circumstances that it was easier to accept.

Mindy had been a constant presence and I had come to rely on her as I rely on air and water. She was more than sustenance: she was my refuge, shield and strength. She was my interpreter, the conduit of my difficult and confusing emotions. How these roles drained her, I can only imagine. When she left the room, I stopped coping. She was living for two of us.

I had been a patient only once before when, as a six-year-old, I had stayed in hospital for a few days for minor surgery on my eardrums. The isolation, the loneliness and the homesickness returned to me in waves. The hospital's plumbing had been ancient and moaned all night, like a herd of spectral cattle wandering the wards. Their cries returned now to haunt the long nights in a hospital hundreds of miles and three decades away. I would sleep deeply until, for some unseen reason, I woke and lay silently, feeling once more the night-time dread of a scared six-year-old boy.

I would devote every waking hour to trying to persuade the doctors that I was ready to go home. I wanted to return to a life in which I went off to work and came home again to Mindy and the kids. My memory was still badly damaged. I knew who I was, I recognised my children, and I recognised my parents and brothers. But my day-to-day memory only extended to a few minutes. This added to the state of deep confusion that nagged away at me and, I suspect, made me difficult to be around.

Mindy

Richard was very tired after his arrival. The journey had taken its toll. As I was also tired it wasn't the easiest transition. Rick Nelson, the neurosurgeon taking over his care, came to visit.

Rick has a wonderful manner, calm and softly spoken, and he listened patiently to Richard's animated conversation, all the while glancing across at me. He was gauging the validity of the person in front of him, and guessed correctly that this wasn't the true Richard. At the end of the discussion, Rick asked Richard's permission to have a chat alone with me to discuss his progress as I saw it. He agreed.

I was Richard's ally; if I suddenly appeared to switch allegiance, all trust would dissipate. Rick had provided the ultimate solution. However, discussing my husband's condition behind his back felt terrible. I felt disloyal but I knew it was vital the medical team were aware of all the facts.

Rick immediately recognised textbook characteristics in Richard. He was desperately trying to demonstrate how well recovered he was, and yet . . . ask him what town he was in, and there was instant confusion.

Deep, deep sadness overcame me whenever we discussed his mental state. Richard was a very intelligent man, but his mind remained jumbled. The doctors compared the state of his mental function to a filing cabinet that had been knocked to the floor: all the files were scattered about, the papers spread all over the room. We were trying to help him put it back together. It was a slow and difficult task but patience was the key. And rest. His brain was exhausted and the best therapy was sleep. If he overtaxed his brain, it would set him back dreadfully, and Rick spared no punches—it would be hard to claw back.

There was little to compare my role at Leeds to that at Bristol. Although I slept with Richard every night we were close to home, to the girls, and clearly I should be with them, too. A routine was devised which allowed for a late afternoon nap for Richard. That was my time to rush home and return before he became too distressed. It wasn't terribly successful. Often the hospital would call my mobile before I'd even reached home. I'd try to enjoy a fun time with the girls, all the while preoccupied with a nagging sense of urgency to get back to him. The bedtime story was shorter and the 'good nights' more difficult. They'd phone Daddy to wish him good night and then I was off again. The second I left their rooms, I ran down the stairs, and then continued running to the car.

Journey time was taken up by phone calls. I had two phones, which was useful. At least one was always charging. I listened to messages and returned as many as possible. Conversations were timed to fit in the maximum. So many dear friends were desperate to know how he really was, but naturally my first call was always to his parents. My mum was next. Her words overwhelmed me, gave me strength and perspective. Always positive, always loving.

Occasionally, I'd feel tired, but determination drove me on, and the desperate longing to be back with Richard. It was like leaving a child in a strange place with kind but unfamiliar company. I sensed he was for ever fighting panic. Being brave.

Richard

Post-traumatic amnesia helped alleviate the boredom. I could happily read the same newspaper a dozen times, forgetting each time I picked it up that I had read it only minutes earlier. I would read the hospital menu, spot that cottage pie was available and exclaim that it was my favourite. When it arrived, I would forget that I had ordered it and be delighted as it was my favourite dish and ask how the staff could possibly have known.

By the time I understood post-traumatic amnesia, I was getting over it. But the confusion that remained, the fact that I could not trust my own perception of the world and my own thoughts, was a frightening state to be in. With every stage of increasing awareness, I grew more scared. At this point in the long process of recovery, I knew enough to know that there was something wrong, but I didn't know how to fix it, or how it might be affecting me. I could have been dreaming the entire thing. But at least now I accepted that I had suffered an injury and that I was in a hospital so that I might get better. And I still wanted to go home. Badly.

There is an expression that doctors wear when they come into your room, half-wary and half-defensive. As soon as they crossed the threshold, I would spring to attention and begin a torrent of talk as I tried to prove my return to health and sanity and regain my freedom.

'Morning, Richard, how are you?'

'Well, thank you. Much better. But worried about this weather though— looks like a spot of low pressure heading our way.'

I made a sweeping gesture to my right, meaning to encompass the window. Which was to my left.

'Did you know that swans mate for life?'

'No, Richard. Do you know what day it is?'

'No.'

And I didn't. I could recall stuff from years ago with incredible clarity. But I could get no grip on the present. My sense of time and place was badly distorted. Facts, ideas, meanings evaded my best attempts to pin them down. I became aware that there was something wrong with me that stopped me knowing or understanding. And I was scared. I had brain damage. It affected the way I thought about things. It might be affecting the way I thought about brain damage. And I didn't know what day it was. Or where I was. Only why. I was there because I had damaged my brain and these were the people who were going to help me make it better. The panic that rose whenever I failed to answer a question that I knew I should understand got in the way of my thoughts and made things worse. I would be screaming inside my head because I knew that this should be easy.

I shall never forget the days of struggling in a clinically confused state. It made me horribly self-centred; like a toddler who cannot comprehend that there can be a will in the world other than their own. My universe centred around me and so did that of everyone else around me. I shall try to keep these memories close, because it will change for ever the way I deal with other people who, for whatever reason, are likewise confused.

Sometimes it was rather pleasant to bounce along, wondering what was for lunch when I had only ordered it five minutes earlier. The distress arising from my condition was, sadly, to be felt by the people closest to me. It is far harder to visit someone you love and see them in a confused state than it is to be the one asking where the bar is in a hospital ward. But in those flashes of insight and awareness, there were some deeply frightening moments and my heart goes out to anyone now similarly afflicted and for whom the prognosis might not be so bright as mine proved to be.

As my mind relaxed into something closer to a normal state, there were some big emotions waiting to get hold of me. Early in my stay at Bristol, I was hit by an avalanche of guilt. I felt horribly aware of the worry and pain I had caused Mindy, my daughters, my brothers and, of course, my parents. The sense that I had done something very stupid and upset a lot of people hovered in the background of my jumbled thoughts.

I wanted to see my parents, to explain to them that something had gone wrong with the car and that I had not done anything wrong. I wanted to say that I was sorry and they mustn't worry. It was just like every time I had fallen off a bicycle as a child and felt both the pain of the accident and the guilt of knowing I would also be causing my parents pain. I never worried that they would shout at me when I hurt myself, but I knew that it would upset them. I remembered walking into the kitchen with my hand torn when I fell off my brother's bicycle. I remembered seeing my mother's face.

How did she feel now? This was worse. I had a better understanding of what a parent feels when they see their child hurt. I had children of my own and, once the switch of parenthood is thrown, it changes you for ever. I was lying in that hospital bed both as a ten-year-old child and as a father myself. I never managed to voice these feelings to my parents; somehow it just came out wrong when I tried. But I felt such a weight of guilt I thought it would crush me. This guilt is a common thing among people recovering from head injuries such as mine, and from many bodily injuries too. Much later, I would be hit by a second avalanche of guilt, this time centred on how I had been so lucky when many people are not. I would lie awake, pinned down by the knowledge that I had been through a massive accident and emerged alive when people are more badly hurt falling down the stairs. That guilt I still carry today. But right now, as I lay in bed in Bristol, the only guilt I felt was for the worry I had caused my parents, brothers and wife.

With my returning memory, the problem of filling my days became more pressing. But I was not lying in bed dreaming of getting back to work. I couldn't understand the concept anyway. I knew that work was something I did out there in the real world and that I had to be grown-up and that I had children and a wife and that my work paid for a house for us all to live in. But I couldn't imagine doing it. I wanted to play. I had regressed until I felt and thought like a child.

It was raining outside. I looked at the cars lined up below, studied the colours and shapes of them. I wanted to touch their metal curves, feel the raindrops on their thick-painted panels. I wanted to step out into the world and experience it for myself. Above all, I wanted to go to a shopping centre and buy something. I wanted to walk among familiar shop frontages, see their colourful signs. I wanted to hear the voices of other people echoing off the big plate windows, to see the hustle and bustle and be part of it all.

In my mind, I drifted back to childhood trips to the Bull Ring Shopping Centre in Birmingham. We were buying school shoes for a new term. We turned a corner and walked down some steps. There was a stand on a corner selling bags. I admired their shiny surfaces while my mum chatted to the man selling them. Suddenly I was in front of another stall selling food. I wasn't interested and I thought that, when I got home, I would make a model of Batman's car out of Lego. I wished I could think of a way of making the blade that the real Batmobile had in the front to cut through any wires that got in the way during a chase. I wondered if I could borrow wire Dad used sometimes to hold plants up. But no, it wouldn't look right. But the fins, the fins I would give this Batmobile would be fantastic.

Mum was calling me and my brother Andy. We had to go. In a flash, the scene changed. I was in Solihull now, closer to home. This was Mel Square, the centre of town, where the big fountains leapt from the square pool and splashed back into the shallow water. We ran down the ramp, which was cobbled with stones, causing us to take lots of tiny steps. We ran, and shouted, laughing as our voices wobbled. Mum thought it was funny too, and our voices echoed off the stony sides and filled the hall below.

I looked away from the window of my hospital room and I wanted to go outside. I wanted to walk into a shop and buy a new Lego set, to savour the moment when the tiny bricks tumbled out of the crinkly plastic bag ready to form into the picture on the front of the box. That was it. I wanted Lego. It had taken me through my childhood; I had spent nearly every waking hour trying to build the cars and bikes I dreamed of. My creations with their mismatched colours would set off on adventures through jungles under the coffee table or into the dark and threatening canyon between Dad's chair and the wall. I craved that escape now. I knew I wasn't a ten-year-old boy any more, that I was a thirty-six-year-old man in a hospital. But I knew also that I was ill and allowed to do things if they made me feel better.

Seldom do we have, as adults, the time to spend wondering about ourselves and our own lives. I had returned to a stage where I could while away hours thinking about life and my place in it. But maybe the process of recovery necessitated retreading old ground to remember who I was.

Dr John Holloway walked in and said hello. I recognised him now and could remember his name. I was happy to chat with him, enjoying his calm yet authoritative manner. We spoke about how I felt. I said I was fine. He stooped to pick up a book of prayer that had been sent in by a well-wisher.

'Are you reading this?' he asked gently.

'Er, well, I glance at it.' I wanted to show that I had big, spiritual thoughts. I wanted, as always, to show off.

He was sounding me out. I stayed silent. John waited. 'We keep an eye out for sudden, you know, surges of enthusiasm for things at this point.'

'I haven't suddenly found religion, if that's what you mean.'

'OK.' He seemed slightly relieved.

We knew each other well enough to talk about how accidents such as mine might affect people. I enjoyed these talks and, I suspect, John used them to gauge my recovery. He explained that sudden obsessions or compulsions can leap up from nowhere. They might be to give away all your money, give up a stressful job or to become fervently religious. It is, perhaps not surprisingly, common for people who have been near to death to return from that place with a new-found conviction. It was a subject I would relish talking about further, but this, perhaps, was not the time. After a few more comforting words, John left the room. I slipped into a deep sleep, eager to prove my prowess in at least this one aspect of life.

Mindy arrived. I came alive. We spoke about what was happening on the outside. Mindy had begun to explain that my crash had caused a bit of a stir. I don't remember her showing me the newspaper coverage and the doctors were still anxious that I should be protected from too many stimuli. Leafing through newspapers about my narrow escape might prove to be just that. This was still, as far as I was concerned, an intensely private matter.

I knew that the *Top Gear* team had been to see me when I was in Leeds General Infirmary, but I had no memory of the event. We are a close-knit team and I wasn't surprised. We have joked many times that we work in a playground for grown-ups. And one of us had fallen over in the playground badly. They all wanted to see how their friend was. The fact that they had visited meant a lot to me.

Mindy did allow a flow of letters, cards and gifts from well-wishers. They arrived at the hospital in sackloads, and each day Mindy would bring in as much of the post as I could cope with, until we got to the point where I could happily plough through them alone. And it felt wonderful. I did not open them as a celebrity soaking up the adulation of people he had never met. I read each card and letter just as a bloke, sitting in a hospital bed being wished well with real sincerity by thousands of kind friends.

Many of the letters were from people who had been similarly injured. They had faced similar battles to get well and were keen to share their experience with a fellow sufferer. I read an account from a teenage lad who suffered a head injury from falling off his motorcycle. He is, from his letter, clearly a young tough-nut who enjoys action. Yet he felt compelled to share the story of his accident, and how hard it was to recover.

He didn't write to the bloke off *Top Gear* to tell him about how fast he went on his bike; he wrote to tell him not to be scared that he had injured his brain, because he had done the same thing and got better. It was a source of comfort beyond words. His note, and the thousands of similar letters and cards written by people from all over the world, were the most touching acts of kindness I could have imagined. Each contributed to the restoration of my shattered confidence. My heart went out then, and does now, to those who are far more deserving of such help and do not have the benefit of it.

Mindy arrived carrying a box under her arm. It was a box of Lego. Mindy explained that James May had bought it for me. It was a model of a tractor. A big green one. The bags of bricks and plastic cogs felt as temptingly lovely as I had dreamed. The instructions were, for me at that point, complex enough to demand my full attention. I can only imagine what Mindy must have felt as she watched me throw myself into a project aimed at a child thirty years my junior. People came and went. I concentrated on the task. Dr Holloway agreed that, if I wanted to play with Lego, then I should. He said that the process of translating two-dimensional instructions into three-dimensional models might even be beneficial. It would, he explained, help me to rediscover my sense of spatial awareness and my concentration. This was all I needed to hear. I pleaded with Mindy to bring more Lego. She saw the enthusiasm in my face and ran to the shops.

Mindy

Richard was becoming increasingly frustrated at his confinement.

'I need to get out. I really want to go to a shopping centre and buy daft stuff, just go shopping. Please? Why can't I go bloody shopping?'

Richard *hates shopping*. Avoids it at all costs. So why on earth would he now have this uncontrollable urge?

He agreed to give me a list. I'd go. The list read: *Classic Bike* magazine, *Classic Cars* magazine, pen and paper for letter-writing, Lego set.

I dashed out to Cribbs Causeway, a large shopping complex just outside Bristol. The first three items were easy. The Lego, ridiculously, was a nightmare! I was jogging from one end of the enormous mall to the other to no avail. In desperation, I went into Boots. In the children's department there were just a couple of suitable models.

To compensate for my lack of Lego, I spent ten minutes in a sweet shop, buying Richard's favourites—sherbet fountains, jelly beans, and Turkish Delight. Constantly glancing at my watch, I knew time was passing far too quickly. I had an hour to get back to Richard, settle him and leave for home.

Shoppers stared at me as I ran at full tilt through the complex. I yelled at slow-moving traffic and made swift progress when the road cleared. I managed a fairly relaxed cup of tea with Richard as we looked through his goodies before leaving again on the return trip to Gloucestershire.

Richard

Within days, my room had filled with brightly coloured boxes of Lego as I buried myself in my new-found work. The place looked like a toyshop. Or, better still, like my childhood fantasy of a Lego-testing facility. And I was chief tester. Mindy arrived once more, stepping into the chaos where I was building a ship. She had brought the kids. My heart leapt and then steadied. I asked them if they would like to join me. They said yes and crouched down next to me.

With Izzy and Willow around, I knew my place again. I was their father; I was in hospital because I had suffered a head injury and I had to try not to upset them. With no sense of the passage of time, I was unaware how long they had been with me when Mindy announced that they must leave. I held the girls tightly; they clung to me and I to them. I walked with them into the corridor beyond. I was still unsteady on my feet, but was not going to show it. We walked to the lift and, too quickly, the lift arrived. In the pause before the doors shut, I smiled at them as they stood. They smiled back.

As the doors began to slide together, Izzy broke her gaze away from mine and turned to look up at Mindy. Her smile crumbled and her eyes filled with tears. She could hold them back no longer. She was a six-year-old girl missing her daddy very much, scared and worried. I looked at Mindy as the doors shut and I stared for some time at the blank space where my family had been. I wept too as I walked back to my room.

Mindy

The second the lift doors closed, Izzy burst into uncontrollable sobs. I was on my knees with her in an instant. I praised her bravery and was completely astounded by her. She instinctively knew how to help her beloved daddy. She was giving all her tiny body could muster solely for him. She even composed herself, without any encouragement, so that by the time we reached the back door two minutes later, she would raise a hand to the windows high above, knowing that Daddy was watching, and encouraging her little sister to do the same. Ela and I followed suit, the tears flowing down all our faces, save Willow, who thankfully didn't notice.

'Oh, Izzy, baby. Well done,' I told her.

She simply nodded, the tears dripping from her face.

'Are you OK, Izzy?' asked Willow.

Izzy nodded at Willow, and we drove home. Together, but without Daddy. For Izzy it was dreadful but she understood. This was the way it had to be. But as I told her again and again: 'He'll get better, Iz—I promise.'

She'd nod, and cry, and hug me. But she's from a tough stable and she believed me. She made Willow her responsibility, and I believe she determined to stay strong for her little sister.

One day she'll know what she went through, marvel at her own journey, and perhaps understand how she became the person she became. I only know this: a little girl decided of her own volition to become more than a daughter—she became, as Richard described her, 'his mate'.

It was wonderful to be home with them. As we drove through the gate, I could hear the dogs barking wildly from the kitchen, a sound I suddenly realised I'd missed. Home.

Ela and the girls opened the front door and we set the dogs free from the kitchen. I was surrounded by bouncing, barking, tail-wagging excitement, TG grabbing my hand in her mouth, Captain, our Jack Russell, leaping up at me, Pablo barking and Crusoe stretching forward and yowling; each of them desperate to impress their welcome upon me. Willow and Izzy laughed.

'I think they missed you, Mindy!' Ela smiled.

The girls and I ran outside with them and watched as they galloped up the hill next to our house. Barking, scampering, happy to be free.

We went over to see Hattie, our enormous outdoor dog. She slobbered and harrumphed and lay on her back for her belly to be scratched. Hattie is a guard dog, and she'd spent a great deal of the past week barking at the many strangers at the gate. She was at least three times Willow's size, yet with the children she was gentle as a lamb. They were her babies and she took her role as protector very seriously.

Apparently, when the children left the house she grew silent, awaiting their return, her front paws resting on the top of the gate at the entrance to her kennel area, watching for a car.

Ela made a quick supper for the girls while I dashed around upstairs, grabbing clothes for Richard. Izzy saw the suitcase. Her face fell.

'Oh, Mummy, do you have to go again?' She hugged my legs.

I carried her into the hall where Willow might not find us. I put her down on the stairs and sat next to her. We had one of our 'grown-up chats'. It was something Richard often did with her. We talked about Daddy, how she felt, and why I needed to help him now.

'I miss Daddy,' she sobbed, but she understood.

'Daddy misses you, baby. But we'll help him get better, won't we?'

She nodded, and wiped her face dry. 'I love you, Mummy.'

I held on to her. I couldn't prevent my own tears. But she didn't notice. Or at least, she pretended not to.

We joined Ela and Willow at the table for supper, but before it was finished the hospital called. My time at home was fast running out.

Richard

Like many people, I guess, I am never happy in an institution. But here, in Bristol, I adjusted to the new rhythm of life and became institutionalised. And I grew happier. I woke up, chatted with nurses, ate breakfast and played with Lego. At lunchtime, food was brought; I ate it, slept for a few hours, played with Lego again and wondered what was for tea.

In a sense, I was ten years old again. I began to miss my two brothers in a way I hadn't for decades. I wanted them sitting cross-legged on the floor with me, trying to decide what model to build next or wondering what was coming up on the telly. They have complicated adult lives but I had now drifted back into childhood and I wondered where my two best mates were.

I have spoken with them since and learned that, in many ways, they had been afflicted with similar emotions. Whatever happens to any of the three of us, part of us will always be the same three young tearaways who rode bicycles round the Triangle, made dens on the field at the back of the house, and played with toy cars in the ditch. They had visited me many times in hospital, but I held no memories of the early visits. On later occasions, they arrived to find me bewildered. I guess I was wondering who these two grown men were and where my brothers had gone.

But these thoughts, though intense, passed quickly. I could happily distract myself. I had, for a day or so, been building a model of the Batmobile, a big one brought by Mindy. Dr Holloway arrived and asked how the Batmobile was going. I began to explain that it was pretty tricky in places. I had taken his enquiry to mean that he too was in the process of assembling a Batmobile and I felt sure that he would benefit from my many years of modelling experience. It was only after a good few minutes of giving comprehensive instruction in the finer points of assembling the model that I realised he was humouring me. And I was embarrassed for the first time in a while. Which was probably a good sign.

At some point, someone had identified a need in me for physical exercise. I run nearly every day as a rule and, given that I had suffered pretty much no bodily injuries apart from those to my brain, I remained in reasonably good shape. But I had lost a lot of weight; a week or two of being fed through a needle in your arm will do that to you.

I was asked if I would like to go to the hospital gym and Mindy brought in my running kit. The physiotherapist lady was very friendly and I tried to show off by being really good at yoga. I wasn't. And then she asked if I would like to use the rowing machine. I pounced on it eagerly. After four minutes of pulling I was pretty much exhausted. It doesn't take long for whatever physical fitness you have to drain away. Mine had disappeared down the plughole the moment I took to a hospital bed. But it felt wonderful to be exerting myself again.

This was the first time I could really pit myself against something and be allowed to struggle. It was as much about the realisation that the doctors felt I was well enough to work up a bit of a sweat as it was about the exercise itself. The rowing machine suffered from a loud squeak. Over the next few days I would wonder if my frantic rowing and the accompanying squeak was keeping other patients awake. I felt bad but I rowed on, slowly increasing my stamina. Mindy did everything she could to encourage this gentle exercise, listening patiently when I explained proudly that I was up to seven minutes' rowing and was now being allowed to use the running machine too.

I dreamed of being able to take off on my own and run outside. As my trainers slapped down on the treadmill, in my mind, I crunched through golden leaves and breathed in the natural smells of the real world.

I was going to leave. It had been discussed, people had approved. I could leave the hospital but I couldn't go home. By now, it had been explained to me that our house was ringed by reporters and TV crews, and the doctors were worried how I might react. Because of the fragile state of my mind still, we had to be careful. There was no dipstick to slot into my brain and tell the doctors if I was now liable to convulsions or mental complications. But there were statistics.

Thousands of cases are recorded and examined, as much for the benefit of subsequent patients as the one under examination. And these statistics told the doctors that, with a brain injury of the severity of mine, there were real dangers associated with over-stimulation. Leaving the security of the hospital would be shocking enough, but to go home and be confronted with a horde of eager reporters, TV cameras and flashguns, could well provoke serious problems. But equally, Dr Holloway appreciated that I needed to begin engaging once more with the world.

And so a plan was hatched. We were going to slip away somewhere unnoticed. We needed to be guaranteed privacy and a safe place from which I could walk slowly and carefully back into the world. Mindy had found such a place. And we were going in a couple of days.

I hated the secrecy. No one must know where we were going, not even friends, because if it got out it would be terrible to find ourselves looking for someone to blame. And we didn't want anyone to be lumbered with the responsibility of keeping a secret that might well get out anyway.

I was told that I would be going to bed as usual on the evening of the great escape and would then be woken early in the morning. I had to have my bag packed and be ready to leave. I packed and repacked my bag every day to make sure I would be ready.

Mindy

Richard's medication became less intense as the days passed. His balance improved, he spent less time in bed and his physiotherapy sessions were increased to two per day. The physios concentrated on Pilates and aerobic exercise, together with relaxation techniques. They were a great team, concentrating on small achievements and helping him to regain his strength.

Once the sessions increased, he regained not only physical strength, but also a more positive outlook. Richard had always waxed lyrical about the buzz he enjoyed when exercising. If ever he was down, I'd encourage him to visit the gym or go out for a run. He invariably returned recharged and happy. I sensed he wasn't yet experiencing the buzz, but at least his body was starting to perform again. Because he was more mobile, daily injections could cease. Anti-clotting jabs in his stomach had left a chain of painful bruises. They wouldn't be missed.

Discussions with Rick Nelson had demonstrated Richard's 'increased insight' into his condition. This better understanding of his situation, what had happened to him, and how he was improving, was a very positive sign.

Richard was introduced to Dr John Holloway, Medical Director of the local Brain Injury Rehabilitation Centre at Frenchay, who was taking over his care. Richard instantly warmed to him, and quickly turned off his usual act. John was very adept at cutting through the crap and discussing the real issues. He gave Richard enough information to convey the severity of his injury without causing alarm. I listened to the exchanges between them with enormous relief—Richard would be guided by him. John would help us for many months. He was accessible night and day, and became an invaluable guide through the most difficult stages of recovery.

Every journey I took into or out of the hospital was met by a small group of photographers. They were respectful and didn't attempt to gain entry; similarly, the photographers at home weren't intrusive, they were just waiting to see if Richard emerged. However, we were really out of our depth with all the media coverage. I had no time to make sure the press were correctly informed—and that worried me. Richard's agent had been approached by various publications who were very interested in his story, and I had no idea what to do. Luckily I was put in contact with someone who did: Gary Farrow, a highly respected PR professional, became an important part of our lives. Initially, he was there to take care of media issues, but his role changed dramatically as Richard's condition improved.

Meanwhile, Richard was going stir crazy. He really wanted out, and was starting to get angry—to keep him in hospital for much longer would become counter-productive. However, the issue was how to get him out without massive press attention. The flashing lights from a bank of press photographers could quite possibly put him at risk of a seizure or epileptic fit. Then there was the attention we'd be in for when word spread he was at home. Our house abutted a country lane; the press could literally lean over the gate and see straight into the house.

The doctors suggested I try to get him away somewhere quiet where he could relax. Their one condition was that he shouldn't go on any long-haul flights. Gary and I discussed Ireland but it was too complicated. The Lake District was too busy. Then we hit upon Scotland. A cottage in the Highlands.

Perfect! But it had to be done very carefully. No one, not even Richard, could know the plan we were hatching. If anything reached the ears of the press, it would be all over.

Gary arranged for a group of ex-special-forces men to go into action on our behalf. Operation Joystick went like this:

> To minimise the number of people involved and the chances of being seen by third parties, we plan to move the family and the subject independently to a rendezvous point from where they will be driven in a large Winnebago to the ultimate destination.
>
> One person to fly ahead, hire a car to recce the location and act as a ferry vehicle in case the Winnebago cannot drive right to the final destination. Constant radio communication to be maintained at all times.

It was difficult to keep the whole thing secret from Richard, but he was incredibly excitable and would tell everyone he was getting out if even a whiff of it reached him.

I had to be at home Friday evening. Ela was leaving us. She'd extended her stay by two weeks to help us out, but had to return to university in Poland. Richard understood that I needed to say my goodbyes to her, and would have to remain with the girls once she'd gone. But he'd expect me to take the girls to visit him on Saturday, which was impossible, as the team had to come to our house to finalise plans for our departure on Sunday night. So I told him we were leaving in the early hours of Monday morning. I made him swear to keep the secret. He was excited but understood.

I called Richard's mum and told her we must 'disappear for a bit'. I asked her to buy a pay-as-you-go mobile phone and give me the number. I'd do the same. We would contact each other on the 'secret' phones.

Richard's brother Andy was due to visit him on Sunday afternoon. The visit would hopefully keep Richard's mind off imminent events, and make for an enjoyable afternoon.

Saturday
The two men in charge of the operation came to our house, accompanied by others in vehicles who were doing a sweep of the surrounding land. Members of the press had been camping in the woods opposite in full camouflage gear with long lenses focused, ready for any interesting movement. These guys planned to identify their whereabouts. I greeted them like friends at the door, as agreed. We chatted amiably in the kitchen over a couple of cups of tea and discussed the finer details of the plan.

Sunday
In the afternoon the daughter of one of the guys arrived. She was about eighteen years old and was there to get to know the girls. She was to play an important role the following evening. She played with them for hours and, when she left, promised to see them again soon.

I stocked the house with dog, cat and pony food, wrote notes to neighbours who'd be looking after the place, and started to assemble luggage while the girls were playing in the garden.

On Sunday night I put the girls to bed as usual, then started running up and down stairs collecting everything and packing bags and suitcases. The team was already in position around the house; they'd ensured no one was watching. Simultaneously, other members of the team were sweeping the area surrounding the hospital in Bristol.

At 11 p.m. the guys reversed their 4x4 so the back door of the vehicle practically opened into our hallway. There was a pile of luggage at the door.

Once the luggage was in, the young girl who'd visited earlier helped me to wake Izzy and Willow. 'Come on, we're going on holiday,' I told them.

They were sleepy but happy. They were each secured in their child seats before Captain and TG joined them, to giggles of delight. While we were gone the other dogs would be looked after by trusted friends and neighbours who generously offered their help.

I explained to the girls that I was going to fetch Daddy and meet them in a bit. They didn't once worry or question anything. There was nothing but smiles and laughter as they set off on their adventure and great excitement at the prospect of getting Daddy back.

I jumped into the second car and followed them down to the motorway where they headed north to a service station and a waiting Winnebago. We were going south to the hospital in Bristol.

Fifteen minutes before our arrival, I called the duty nurse as prearranged and told her our ETA.

'He's fast asleep,' she said. 'D'you want me to go and wake him?'

'No, thanks, it's OK, we'll get him up.'

Richard knew very well what time he was being sprung, and I was convinced there was no way he was asleep.

Richard

This was better than Christmas when I was five years old. In a few hours, I would go out into the world for what felt like the very first time. Lying on my back in the hospital bed, I was quivering with excitement, trying to control my breath. My brother Andy had been in to see me that day. The visit was fun; he indulged me by playing with Lego, and I told him, in secret, that we were going away tomorrow and that no one, not even most of the hospital staff, knew about it.

I trust him and every one of my friends and family entirely. It was enough for them to know that we would be safe, that we were going on the advice of the doctors and that help was on hand if we needed it while we were away. I would later wish I had simply told them where we were going and explained that we wouldn't blame them if it ever got out. But the doctors had decreed that we absolutely must keep it secret. The conspiracy didn't really help with my burgeoning paranoia.

When the knock at the door finally came, it didn't rouse me from sleep. I lay awake, tensed like a ski-jumper at the top of the ramp. Desperate not to appear too keen, I resisted the temptation to leap from the bed.

'Is it time then?'

'Yes, let's go.'

The lights were dim and the corridor opposite loomed dark and blank. I grabbed my bag. I had stuffed my treasured Lego sets into the holdall along with as many clothes as I could fit in. There was nothing else to take. We stepped out into the corridor and I experienced the grip of nerves. This felt somewhere between a scene from an action movie and leaving early on a holiday as a child. We walked the length of the corridor. Mindy held my hand.

Somehow I felt that the calm, dark-clad figure accompanying us might not be so moved by it all. He clearly knew the route exactly and he moved in a manner that suggested he was familiar with situations where taking a wrong turn down a corridor in a building at night might be more than a minor inconvenience.

We crossed a carpeted lobby and walked outside. The air hit me, wrapped about my face and blew through me. I wanted to yell and scream and run about. I didn't. A bird sang. The car waited by the entrance. The back door was open. I looked at the sky, at the buildings outlined against it, breathed some more of the cool night air into my shivering chest and climbed in.

'The girls are waiting for you, Richard. They're fine. And they've got a couple of the dogs with them too.'

I felt exhilarated; every moment that passed was important. I tried to preserve them. I would never do this again and I wanted to remember it. Nevertheless, I was asleep in seconds in the car and woke only when it pulled up alongside the motor home. I climbed out and a man grabbed my bag, passing it up to the open door.

The girls were sitting inside on a sofa. TG and Captain were there too. Suddenly, the world was in colour once more; I was home with my girls. I clutched them. They were excited to show me around inside the van. They took me to see a big bedroom at the back and their bunk, with its row of lockers overhead, and a place where TG insisted on sleeping.

Mindy studied what happened as I re-engaged with my children. She had taken us through one phase of recovery and now we were entering another. I was tired but too alive to sleep. Mindy sat next to me on the sofa bed, we cradled the girls' heads as they slept. TG curled up by their feet, protecting her flock.

We talked softly of our lives together, of how our experiences might change things. The doctors had reassured us that, though it would be long and difficult, I would recover fully. Right now, that felt like a very long way off. I was in too fragile a state ever to imagine feeling normal again. But we agreed on one thing: given a chance to carry on with our life together, we would do our level best to make the most of it.

We thanked and said goodbye to the team who'd seen us this far, and were introduced to our two drivers. They'd drive us from here to the Highlands of Scotland, and look after us the whole way.

The doctors had explained how seeing too many different stimuli might trigger convulsions. I closed my eyes, and waited for something to happen. I had no idea what an epileptic fit would feel like. I surveyed the bedroom from the sliding doors that led into the cabin. There were windows at the head and side of it, and through the blinds the lights of the motorway pulsed and flashed. I saw a similar pulsing as the overhead motorway lighting flashed by. Mindy looked up.

'Go to sleep, darling.'

Being scared had become an almost constant state for me over the weeks, but was made no more pleasant by its familiarity.

'Mind, I'm worried. They tell you that flashing lights can trigger epilepsy even if they're on the telly. If they can do that to normal people sitting at home, what about me now?' It sounded petulant and ungrateful. What did I know anyway? 'And if I sleep in there'—pointing to the warm bedroom behind me—'the lights are flashing even more.'

Mindy reached across the bed and pulled the curtains together. The room was dim now and Mindy looked at me through the gloom. 'You'll be fine. The doctors said you'll be OK. What you need is sleep. Remember, they told you that the risks increased the more tired you get. Come on.'

She pulled the bedcover back and stepped to the side to make room for me to fall on to the bed.

'I'm sorry, I'm just scared. To come this far and then to . . .'

I tailed off. I understood sleep could make all the difference to my recovery. I closed my eyes but sleep would not come. I lay and waited for a seizure to start, tried to access the remote extremities of my body to see if I could detect any warning sensation.

The axle of the van thumped heavily as it dealt with a ripple in the motorway surface. I threw the covers off and got up.

'I can't sleep. I just don't think I should be doing this.'

'Do you want to go back?'

'No. God no. But I just . . . This is a stupid idea. For God's sake, they said no flashing lights, no sudden noises. Listen to it, when the camper goes over a bump there's a huge noise. I'm going to have a fucking fit and then

I'll be stuck with them for life and I'll lose my driving licence and we won't be able to earn a living and we'll be fucking ruined. Why didn't you just book a flight? Who cares if some bloke off a car show who banged his head gets on a plane? This was the worst thing you could have done to me.'

She stood, gripping the edge of the door. I was blaming her for everything. The doctors had warned that patients recovering from head injuries can suffer problems with rage. Maybe this was what was happening now. We both knew it and the knowledge made me angrier. I wasn't cross because of the bang on my head, I was cross because everyone wanted to kill me, to ruin all the hard work I had done in making myself better. It was all going to go wrong, and it was just because people didn't think.

'Darling, get some sleep. Please.'

Her voice was soft and warm as she placated me. I pulled the cover over my head to block out the lights and waited to be gripped by a seizure. I wondered what it would feel like. Would Mindy know, or would I just seize up and die? The road rumbled past below the bed as we travelled further from one world and into another.

Mindy

The girls cuddled up together on the bed in the living area with TG lying in front of their feet, edging them into the safest corner of the bed. She took on the role of a nanny dog from the moment the journey started.

Richard couldn't settle in the bedroom and he was petrified he might suffer a seizure. There was very little light coming through the windows; it was one-way security glass covered by blinds, which were covered by curtains, but that didn't matter. I understood enough to know reasoning with him was not the answer. Eventually he returned to the bed and pulled the covers over his head.

As I left the room, I realised he'd broken the sliding door off its runners. I tried to fix it back on, but it was quite heavy and he heard me and grew angry. I wouldn't be able to fix it and I needed to stay close to him. I couldn't join him in the bed; the door would slam. I had only one option. I put my hand between the door and its closing point and leant up against the wall at right angles to it, my right foot braced against the opposite side of the Winnebago to avoid sliding down if I fell asleep.

I stayed there through the night, sometimes grappling with the door when it escaped my grasp on a sharp bend, other times wincing as it trapped my fingers on a right-hand turn. When dawn came it offered no respite.

I couldn't leave my post until Richard woke. At last the scenery became visible, with the promise of a sunny day.

We were all together, a family again. Richard had been nervous the previous night but that was understandable. The external stimuli had suddenly overwhelmed him but he'd overcome it. He'd be OK. I yearned to climb into the bed next to him, but he needed as much rest as possible. The best I could do was to remain there, with my crumpled fingers in the door.

Richard

I woke to find that the van was still ploughing on but the terrors of the night were gone. Izzy and Willow were still sleeping on their bunk with TG. Mindy was standing outside my door looking tired but she kissed me when I slid the door open.

"Morning, darling. You finally got some sleep, then?'

Despite last night, she sounded warm. I knew how much she cared.

'Yes. Thank you. Sorry about shouting. I was scared.' I hung my head.

'I know. It's fine. We're in Scotland. The guys have done brilliantly.' She motioned to the two drivers up at the front.

'Oh, yes. Good morning, lads.'

On either side of the road ahead, the land swept back and grew to become gentle, rolling hills. Beyond, lining the edge of the horizon to our right, were mountains, huge and green against the pale blue sky.

'What time will we get there?'

'The guys reckon by four thirty. Depends on the traffic. You hungry?'

'Yes. What have we got?'

'We can stop. We can get whatever you want.'

Suddenly, I felt gripped by a new worry. I didn't want to see anyone. The idea of meeting people I didn't know made my stomach churn. I didn't even want to have two strange guys driving the truck. I was terrified of anyone I didn't know. Mindy must have seen the fear on my face.

'Darling, we can pull over at the services and park out of the way. We've got to stop to let the dogs have a pee. You can stay here and the guys will get us whatever you want. How would you like a bacon sandwich?'

I wasn't really hungry any more; the thought of meeting strangers had killed my appetite. But I wanted a bacon sandwich at the service station because that's the sort of thing you did, out in the real world.

'Yes, please. I'd love one. Let's do it, let's pull over.'

After a while, we drew up in a large car park and I hid in the bedroom.

Peering under the curtain, I saw car wheels parked around the place. I shuddered and felt the tension through my shoulders. Mindy gave TG and Captain over to one of our chaperones and they took them outside. I couldn't imagine just striding down the steps like that, taking it all in and being taken in by other people. By strangers. I pressed myself into the gloom at the back of the bedroom. This was an important step: doing something because we had to. I had a job list again. And I ran away from it.

Mindy

We all ate a full Scottish breakfast, or at least we all ate a bit of it. Richard was visibly on edge at being stationary. The girls were running about and getting restless and I noticed Richard closing his eyes against their high-pitched voices on a couple of occasions. This was difficult for him. He'd been living in a different world since the crash and had been dropped back into the bedlam of a young family.

I asked him if he'd like to lie down, but he was adamant: 'I've done enough lying down to last a lifetime. I want to be here with you and the girls.'

He sat with Willow on his lap. Izzy was happy with her colouring book, the dogs at peace on the floor, as if knowing instinctively the world needed to hush a while, to give Richard time to acclimatise.

As we moved off on the final leg of the journey, Richard was careful not to look out of the windows for longer than a few seconds at a time. His brain couldn't cope with the complexities of the view. Whenever the Winnebago slowed down, he'd enjoy admiring the view again, and point out interesting things to the girls. We saw streams, babbling and chasing as they cut their way through mountainsides, the thickest of forests, standing tall on the hillsides, and there in the distance our destination—the Highlands.

Just after 4.15 p.m. we arrived at a five-bar gate. A young woman was there to greet us and lead the way in her car to the cottage we'd rented for three weeks. The Winnebago just made it along the narrow winding tracks; we turned a final corner and there it was, in a clearing surrounded by wood-land—a staggeringly beautiful little house. A Land Rover was standing out-side. I'd ordered it to use as our transport and Richard was thrilled. We were escorted into the house and Richard was instantly besotted. A roaring fire had been lit in the living room and mugs of hot tea greeted us. The lads carried our bags inside. Richard excused himself and quickly disappeared into the master bedroom. He was exhausted. I was so proud of him. He was thrilled with the place; he was ready to relax. He just needed a bit of privacy.

Chapter 6

Richard's Story

I knew I had never been to the cottage before, yet there was a comforting familiarity to the place. The rooms were large but not overwhelming. Underfoot, warm, red carpets swirled contentedly as I padded from room to room. On every wall hung watercolours capturing the textures and colours of the hills and forests that surrounded the cottage. This was not an ostentatious house but a warm and friendly one, perfectly suited to a family wanting to spend time in a wonderful place and enjoy it to the full. It felt like the safe place we needed in which to hide away. And then I found the door at the back of the cottage. It was not inherently sinister but it looked out of place. In the wall to the right of it was another door that opened onto the bathroom. But where did this one go?

Mindy was in the kitchen, busily rooting through the provisions. I asked her about the door. She explained that we had been lucky enough to employ someone to cook for us once a day, so that we could have more time together as a family. The cook lived next door with her husband, and the door went through to her house. It was locked but it was a connecting door. I froze with fear. This safe little place by the woods had a door in it that opened up into another house with strangers in. I walked slowly back down the corridor to look through the window into the yard. The walls around it were built of the same dark stone as the cottage and had grown darker still with the steady rain. Out past the yard, the looming conifers braced themselves on the mountainside and dripped rain into the pine-needle carpet below. I could hear the rain hissing and a slow wind shouldering through the trees. I looked back to the door. The friendly familiarity of the cottage had been replaced by my unfriendly but no less familiar companion: fear.

Mindy

I'd called ahead a week before to order an enormous list of groceries and I'd agreed a list of casseroles and pies, which the cook would prepare and store in the freezer. From bitter experience, I knew holiday arrangements rarely went to plan, but this time we'd struck gold. Everything was as promised. The house was comfortable, clean and welcoming; the children were outside with the dogs, running around, exhilarated to be free. I watched their obvious excitement as they discovered two Highland ponies in the paddock. They both came running in.

'Mummy! Mummy! Quick, come and look!' Willow cried, her cheeks flushed and eyes wide as she grabbed my hand and led me outside.

'Oh, Mummy, they're so beautiful!'

'What are?' I pretended not to know.

'Just wait, you won't believe it,' Izzy continued.

We rounded the corner from the front door and walked towards the side of the cottage. 'Oh, girls, aren't they gorgeous!'

The two grey ponies nonchalantly wandered towards us. They were big softies and allowed the children to stroke them through the fence. I left them there, as I returned to make tea. Watching the scene through the window I was moved to tears. To me, that was all we needed, two little girls lost in the joy of ponies. If only everything could be so simple.

Richard appeared at my shoulder and put his arm round my waist.

'Well done, Mind.' He smiled. 'This place is fantastic.'

I sighed. 'Good. I'm glad you like it. I was worried you might not.'

'I'm a difficult bugger to please but you've done us proud.' He sounded calm, but I sensed an air of unease; I didn't pursue it.

He glanced out of the window. 'Oh, wow—look at the girls.'

Willow was on her haunches, deep in conversation with her pony, while Izzy leaned against the fence, stroking the mane of the other. We watched them for a few minutes, until they noticed us, and the biscuits we were eating, and ran inside.

Richard

Breakfast would be enormous—it always was. Each morning, we were presented with thick bacon and chubby sausages with mushrooms, beans and tomatoes. I would wolf it down, my appetite returning fast. Now, I lay in bed and listened to the sizzles and splashes from the kitchen. Mindy must be in the kitchen too, because the bed beside me lay empty. I could hear that the girls were up; giggles and light voices came through the door, though the girls themselves did not. They were still cautious around me, aware that the usual rough and tumble of our lives together had to be put on hold for a while.

I would get up and dress. Mindy had brought a few shirts and pairs of jeans and hung them in the wardrobe that stood next to the window. I looked at it and considered how much better it was to be in charge of my own life again. I could get up and dress myself now, even choosing the clothes I wore and what I did with my time afterwards. I pulled on jeans and a rough blue shirt and walked into the living room.

The girls were playing in front of the fireplace, Lego pieces scattered to every corner of the room. I had given them a set of their own; the picture on the box depicted a garage with five cars customised with flames. I had had a similar set as a child, though not so sophisticated. I was happy now that the girls wanted to do the same.

A fight broke out. Izzy was cross because Willow wanted to build the green car. She shouted that it was hers and Willow must build the white one. And why did she have to spoil everything? My face grew tense. The argument turned into noisy bickering and the sound of it rattled about me.

'Izzy, can you let Willow build the green one? She'll give it back to you afterwards. Go on, she's only small.'

Izzy pushed the green pieces towards her sister.

'Say thank you, Willow.'

'Thank you.' She muttered it but then looked up to her sister and smiled.

The argument was over. But it had left me drained. This was hard, looking after the kids. I could happily have joined in and played their games all day, but to bear even a slight responsibility for them while they played and I watched was very uncomfortable. I felt like I had when we first took Izzy home from hospital as a one-week-old baby. We sat on the sofa cradling her tiny form and waited for someone to come and tell us what to do. There were no instructions, no rulebook and we realised that, for the first time in our lives, we really were properly in charge. That feeling came back to haunt me now and I felt dizzy with the pressure. I didn't want to be in charge, I wanted to play.

'Girls, let's build it together. Here—I'll build the green one.'

The routine had established itself. After breakfast we went for a 'whatever the weather' walk, a practice we had established years before in which, once a walk was decided upon, we would go whether it was raining or not. The kids loved it and were splashing along happily as Mindy and I tailed them in our heavy Drizabones, rain dripping from the brims of our hats.

It was, I declared, 'very wet' rain. Mindy laughed and we held hands and watched the girls play. Behind us, TG and Captain snouted along, sniffing the hollows where sheep had slept and deer had chewed the grass.

'Where are we going?'

'To the picnic place, of course,' Mindy answered.

'Ooh, that's too far. It's miles away.' Izzy stopped as she moaned and I saw Willow tense as she prepared to join in.

'It's just up there, past the bridge. Come on.'

'Yes, it's not far,' I chimed in, trying to help placate them. 'You've walked there loads of times. Come on, race you.'

We set off, covering the last piece of open ground to the edge of the forest in short time. The girls ran as hard as they could and I staggered about in mock tiny steps to stay alongside them.

'Let's walk now,' Izzy said in the forest's silence and she slipped her hand into mine. It curled in my palm.

'Come on, Willow, let's hold hands for the last bit.'

Willow grasped the fingers of my right hand. The dogs came past and TG barged into Willow as she overtook.

'Oh, no! TG! She hurt me, she pushed me.'

'Willow, you're fine, She's just clumsy, silly dog.' I made fun of TG, sticking out my tongue and rolling my eyes and panting to make the girls laugh.

'She's really clumsy,' Willow giggled.

Our picnic place was a clearing on a bend of the path between the dark conifers. Logs on the ground made perfect seats, tables and climbing frames. We sat with our backs to the hill and looked out over the tops of the trees sloping away to the valley. We would eat sandwiches, drink coffee from a flask, play games and fill our time laughing and talking. When the girls wandered off, Mindy and I spoke about the future and the past.

Mindy

Richard would confide his innermost feelings out there in the woods. The log where we sat at picnic times had become his talking place.

'I've been really ill, haven't I? I'm still bad.'

'You've improved so much. You should be proud of yourself.'

'I kept thinking there was nothing wrong with me and everyone was being nice to me under false pretences. But they weren't. I know that now.'

He was so sad. Surrounded by all this beauty, yet he still felt so awful.

I'd packed his watercolours and pastels. As I looked about us I was bombarded with a thousand different hues of green, incredible dappled sunlight piercing the forest canopy and dancing off every rock.

Richard refused to paint; he even refused to take a photograph. He confided in me: 'I'm scared I'll get stuck where I was when I was at college. I hated those years. I want to get past that.'

I nodded, I understood.

At times, huge blocks of memory would just fall, suddenly, into his head. It was quite alarming. He'd explain that within a second a gap was filled with years of experience in amazing detail.

If he didn't want to explore his artistic talents yet, that was fine.

On our return from a walk one afternoon we noticed a strange car outside the house. Richard became agitated. He refused to walk further than the woods until I'd investigated. The girls came with me into the house. Straight away, the smell of cooking reached my nostrils. The cook had turned up and was preparing our food for the following week. It was her car outside. She lived in the cottage next door and she'd just returned from a trip to the shops; unloading was easier from outside our house. Richard was relieved when he heard who our visitor was, but his dislike of unpredictability was apparent. It occurred to me the doctors' advice about structure and routine had been wisely enforced. As long as we stuck to routine and he knew how his day would unfold, it was OK, but had we gone straight home, with the likelihood of unexpected visitors, he would certainly have struggled.

The following day it seemed ridiculously busy on our walk. We had to leave the track several times in order to let Land Rovers pass, and each time Richard would pull down his hat and walk with his back to them. There were many walkers on the footpaths too, which added pressure. It ruined the day for him and he remained in a foul mood. The only light relief came as we ate our supper, a casserole that I noticed contained one ingredient Richard detested—celery. I was nervous about even offering the meal to him, but, to my amazement, not only did he devour it with relish, he asked for seconds.

That evening he was quiet. I watched his expression as he fought unknown battles in his mind. I was powerless to help. All I could do was offer support in whatever way he would take it. We spoke long into the night and I reassured him all would be well, but as I lay awake, for the first time I felt really sorry for myself. I had no one to share this with. There seemed to be no gentleness, no softness any more, just difficulty.

Richard

This was a moment to savour. I pulled the laces on my trainers and fastened them tightly.

'You won't overdo it?'

'No. I shall be sensible. Honest.'

Mindy, standing behind me in the hallway, smiled.

'Really? You'll be sensible? How long are you going to be?'

'About twenty minutes should do it.' I stretched my calf muscles as I spoke. 'I'll go up the hill towards the picnic place. Tell you what, I'll just run in that direction for ten minutes, turn round and run back.'

'Take care, baby.'

Turning round to face the open space in front of the cottage, I tugged my lightweight running jacket down a little and pinched the peak of my black baseball cap between finger and thumb to adjust it. And I trotted off up the track towards the woods and the hills.

The sense of freedom was immense; I could go where I wanted. Running into the forest, it felt like an embrace as I passed under the thick-needled branches. Inside, the air was tangy and heavy with the scent of pine needles, damp undergrowth and peat. I heard the stream pouring down from the hilltops, crashing over the stones. Jogging past the picnic place, I thrilled to the sensation of being somewhere familiar but on my own, just a bloke out for a run passing a place he took the kids for a picnic. It was normal. My legs strained as I crested the hill, but not so badly I needed to slacken off the pace. In fact, the slight pain felt good; I was making myself work for the first time in what felt like years. I pushed on.

The thrill now was building to euphoria. I measured my breathing against my paces and enjoyed the double beat as my chest reverberated to every footfall. The trees went past me faster. I wondered what would happen if their flashing, flickering trunks acted as a sort of stroboscope and triggered a seizure. Would I collapse and die immediately? Or would I fall to the ground, to die slowly of exposure before a hill walker stumbled across my grisly remains? But I felt no fear at the prospect. Right now, I was running and it felt good. If it caused something bad, well, so be it.

As the endorphins released by the exercise flooded my system, my confidence rose. I laughed out loud, swung my arms wildly over my head and took a path that dropped off to the right into the muddy woods. Ahead lay a wooden fence in which was set a wooden gate. I swung the gate open and closed it carefully behind me before I carried on, pumping my legs to take me over the rise where the fence line lay and then to follow the path that took me down towards a small valley floor. As I ran, my thoughts grew calmer. This was what I needed, this would help more than anything else. Just one tiny thought floated in to disturb my new-found calm. Had I closed the gate? Yes, I remembered carefully latching the metal clasp, just as I have closed tens of thousands of other gates on other runs. But I didn't trust my memory. Had I really closed it, or was I imagining it?

And then another thought arrived: was this paranoia? The doctors had warned that paranoia might rear its head along with compulsive behaviour patterns. Was I being compulsive? Was this now-burning desire to run back up a substantial hill to check a gate that I knew for a fact I had closed only minutes earlier compulsive behaviour? Was I being paranoid about my compulsion? I turned round. Bugger it, I thought, if it's going to send me mad worrying about it, I'll go and check the gate anyway, whether it's paranoia or compulsive behaviour that compels me to do it. I ran back up the hill. The gate stood, firmly closed. I felt broken and shamed.

Mindy
Richard had been too long. He'd promised to be back within twenty minutes. Thirty had passed and I was worried. I was sure he'd either overdone it and was lying in pain somewhere or had got lost, which was even more of a worry as it was starting to get dark.

I told the girls we were going for a drive in the Land Rover. They had just started to argue over who would sit in the front, when the cottage door opened and a sweaty, muddy Richard stood in the doorway.

'Did you have a good run?' I started to take my coat off.

'It was OK. Where are you off to?'

'I was about to come and look for you. You were quite a while. Where did you go?'

Richard recounted the episode with the gate, concerned he was chronically paranoid.

'Y'know, I couldn't begin to tell you the number of times I do stuff like that. It's the lost-key syndrome. Every time you've lost your keys in the past you haven't instantly assumed you've got permanent brain damage, you've simply lost your keys. You just had to check the gate. Simple.'

He seemed a little appeased, and went off for a shower. Meanwhile, I had to take the girls round the block because I'd promised them a ride in the Land Rover.

Richard
Sitting on a bench to take in a view and daydream is not something I do by accident or without meaning to. As I lowered myself onto the wooden slats of the bench to the front of the cottage, I looked across to the mountains

and readied myself for a relaxing, thoughtful pause. Mindy and the girls were busy and I had stolen outside to take stock.

I breathed in slowly and relaxed my mind, ready to let my thoughts wander where they would. And nothing happened. I gazed at the greens, blues and purples of the mountains and the forest. I let my eyes unfocus and blur the image to a tinted smudge. I couldn't daydream. I thought about where we were, what we were doing, why we were there. I thought about who else might have sat on this bench and looked at the same scene. But my thoughts wouldn't wander. Like a faithful but irritating dog, they kept returning to my heel to look up and ask for direction.

I looked at the tree in front of me. I knew that it had roots that ran into the ground and brought moisture and nutrients up the trunk. I knew that the leaves spread to capture the energy of the sun and that their greenness was to better facilitate the photosynthesis that brought the thing to life. But there was no poetry, nothing fantastic or mystical about the tree.

I could not daydream. The thought of it took hold of my mind and, like the dominating beech trees, shaded every other thought out of existence. I felt thinner, made less because of the loss of this simple act. I could not daydream and maybe I never would be able to again.

Mindy

The evenings in Scotland were my most feared part of the day. I'm not sure whether it was fatigue or boredom, but often Richard would be in a bad mood. He couldn't watch television, because at the slightest hint of confrontation he'd have to leave the room. Instead, we spent evenings playing Top Trumps, or leafing through car magazines. Once the girls were in bed we whiled away an hour before climbing into bed ourselves. We were both exhausted.

Richard could lie in late every morning, before he joined the girls and me in the kitchen. We were at the breakfast table one morning when he suddenly stopped eating. His face contorted into so many different expressions it was really very strange to watch.

'You OK? What's up?'

I watched his face go through change. He looked different. He didn't look like Richard. His face was ashen and aged ten years. Had I seen this man in the street I wouldn't have recognised him. When it ceased, moments later, he was bewildered and confused. All I could do was hug him. Richard explained that, as he'd sat there, from nowhere about ten different emotions hit him all at once. He was bombarded by them from deep in his psyche.

I felt we were being reminded: it was going to be difficult. Very difficult, but we'd get through it.

Richard

Someone was out there. I was sure of it. I leaned round from behind the wall to look outside. The rough track that ran in front of the cottage disappeared to my right. But I saw no one. Izzy and Willow played happily on the carpet behind me, their pencils and felt-tip pens scattered in front of the fireplace. I had heard a car drawing up and leapt from the floor where I sat with them. My motivation had come from a desire to protect them and to hide from whoever was approaching. What would I do if they came to the door?

'What is it, Daddy?'

'Oh, just the rain. Just looking at the rain.'

I saw a van emerge from the bend in the track. It was dark green and old. I slid further away from the window, leaving just enough room for my right eye to watch as the van rolled in front of the cottage. It stopped.

'What are you doing, Daddy?'

'I'm just seeing what's out there.' I suddenly felt angry. How could Mindy have left me alone? I didn't feel ready for the responsibility of looking after the kids on my own. I watched the shape of the driver moving round from the front of the van. I was too scared to look directly at him. He might see me. Through the blurry bottom edges of the window I could make out the shape of him walking towards the front door. If he thought there was nobody in, he would go away. And then the letterbox rattled. If he was leaving a letter, it meant he was going away. I breathed out and felt my shoulders sag. But I was angry still; angry that I was left alone, angry that I was scared, angry that I was hiding under the window sill. Izzy and Willow were still playing by the fireplace. I shuffled over to them.

'How's it going, girls? Let's have a look.'

As the girls showed me their colouring and chatted about what they had done, my anger faded to sadness.

Mindy

Our grocery stock began to dwindle midway through the second week; I'd have to go out to get more supplies. I could take the girls.

Richard disagreed. 'Don't be silly, I'll look after the girls; you go shopping, have a break.' He was trying to sound matter-of-fact, but it was very unconvincing. I was concerned about leaving him, but he wasn't taking no for an answer. He promised to call the cook if he had any problems.

I jumped into the Land Rover, waved goodbye as I drove past the sitting-room window, and worried myself half to death over the next fifty-seven minutes. On my return I was relieved to find them all happily playing in the living room. However Richard could bear no more and as soon as he saw me, escaped into the bedroom. I took him the customary cup of tea.

'How was it?'

'Oh, Mind . . .' His voice was shaky as he cradled the mug in his hands; he seemed fragile. 'It's scary being on my own with them now; being responsible.' He paused, sensing my concern. 'But it was fine, honestly. We had a lovely time. I'm just tired.'

'I shouldn't have gone.' The trip had caused him unnecessary stress; I felt terrible.

'No, Mind, I'm their father. I just need to get used to it, that's all.'

He was disappointed. He'd been brutally reminded of his new limitations.

'Get into bed and have a nap. I'll wake you in a couple of hours. You're doing really well, you know. I mean *really* well.'

'Yeah, I know, but it doesn't feel like it. I hate being like this.'

I cuddled up to him on the bed. 'You get better every day. We'll get through this, y'know.'

'We will, won't we?' There was doubt in his voice.

'Oh Christ, yes. We'll come back the new, improved, stronger us. The same as before, only more so.'

'God, I love you.'

'I love you too.' I kissed him. 'Now, get some bloody sleep.'

Outside the light was fading, but just as dusk approached I saw through the hall window, no more than eighty feet away, a large stag. We'd heard them roar every night but we'd seen nothing this close. I wanted to wake Richard, to share the moment with him, but to wake him would be selfish. I found the girls though, and the three of us watched that magnificent creature for some minutes before he disappeared back into the mist.

Richard

We were going home tomorrow. We had packed our bags and they lay scattered about the cottage. I wanted to go out for one last run in the hills. Crouched by the front door, I pushed my feet into my trainers. This place had been everything we needed. We had enjoyed peace, tranquillity and a chance to regroup as a family. But I had also learned more about how I had damaged myself. As every day passed, I looked back over it and realised how unwell I had still been that day and how much better I now was. And then another day would pass; I would look back on that one and realise that I was still unwell. But now was not the time to slop about, fretting. I was going for my final run through the beautiful, wooded Highlands and I was determined to savour it.

The letterbox rattled as the door shut behind me. I ran the length of the rough road in front of the house and felt the surface turn to broken stone as the road gave way to a track. My legs felt stronger now; I was running every day. I passed into the forest. Crossing the footbridge, I smiled at the sound of the stream dashing underneath. I leaned to the left as I turned to run past the picnic place. I would miss our time there together as a family and the hours that Mindy and I had spent, holding hands on an old log—two people who love each other talking over an experience that nearly parted them for ever and making plans for the future.

I pressed on. I had worked hard to get my fitness back. This was something I could do for myself. It was something I could be proud of achieving and that pride mattered more than the achievement itself.

I was running across the hillside now. To my right, the forest stood dense and busy until it gave way to a clearing that opened back from the track. Emerging from the edge of the trees to walk confidently into the clearing was a stag.

It saw me, or caught my scent, and it stopped. From where I stood I could see the curves of muscle stretching across its brown flanks. I could see the awkward joints of its hips and the strong legs tapering down to slender points. And I could see its deep brown eye swivelling below the woody turrets of its antler crown. The shooting season had ended several days ago and the local gamekeepers believed that the deer knew, to the day, when this happened, and grew braver. In front of me now, the stag surveyed this interloper in his forest kingdom.

I breathed slowly, a privileged observer not knowing quite what to do. The stag turned and walked back into the forest, breaking into a trot as it reached the trees, all the time carefully balancing its antlers. I stayed where I was for some time. My moment had found me: a moment I couldn't understand or read, an encounter in which I was the one without language or purpose. And a moment I knew would stay with me for ever. I felt blessed as I broke into an easy trot back to the cottage.

Mindy

The day before we left Scotland, I took a drive in the Land Rover to savour my last memories of that amazing place. I drove across the hillside and through the forests, drinking in every last detail: the enormous pine trees, the colours of the heathers at their feet, and the grace and majesty of those beautiful deer. I was suddenly overcome by a desperate longing to stay. I burst into tears and had to pull over. I didn't want to face the complications of our life at home. It was peaceful here; safe, friendly. But I knew that we had to face our demons and overcome them. Even so, saying farewell to the place which had become our sanctuary, was one of the saddest journeys I've ever known.

The car arrived to take us home just after lunch. We'd calculated to arrive home around midnight. There wouldn't be any press around at that time of night. None of us was particularly thrilled at going home—even the dogs had acclimatised—but as we reached the outskirts of Gloucestershire we all started to pick up. For the girls it was returning to their rooms and their faithful pets. For me it was the familiarity of my home, and knowing that when Richard crossed the threshold the picture, finally, after so many weeks, could start to get back to normal.

I watched him as he sipped his tea, slumped on the sofa in the sitting room. I loved him so very much. I was so grateful he was alive, so proud to be home together, shoulder to shoulder, ready to carry on.

Richard

This didn't feel the same as a homecoming after a long holiday. I had felt a gentle surge of warmth and excitement at crossing the threshold, but something was different. I had been away for just five weeks.

The next morning I stood at the top of the stairs as Izzy and Willow dashed about. I could see the painting of a horse that I'd bought Mindy for Christmas two years ago. I studied the wooden trunk we had picked up from a junk shop. Behind the trunk stood the wooden staff I had collected on a walking trip across the Lake District twenty years ago. I was surrounded by memories. It should have been comforting but something was still wrong. Why did this not feel like the joyous homecoming I had dreamed of?

Finally, I had made it home, back to my own hearth. Despite the pain, the confusion, I was back. The doctors had said it might take me years but I had done it in just a few weeks. And now, standing here in my own house with my family and dogs around me, I felt sad.

I was, for the first time, in an environment familiar to me from a time before the crash. I had lived in this house, laughed, shouted, argued and played. I remembered hundreds of little incidents with incredible clarity. And I knew why I felt sad. This was the first time I had been somewhere I could remember being before I damaged my brain. This was the first time I had met myself. And I knew that while the house was the same, I would never be the same again. Everything that had gone on in this house before would feel different if I went through it again now. My reactions, my interpretation of it, would be different. The home was familiar. But I was a stranger. Everything was the same, yes—everything except me. The sameness in the things around me just served to illuminate the strangeness in me.

I found Mindy and we held each other. I didn't need to tell her that I was sad or why. She knew. We had made it this far and we were sure as hell going to carry on.

'You OK?' She spoke softly, her head on my shoulder.

'Yes. Just feels a bit . . . weird, that's all.'

'I know.'

'Where are the girls?'

'Putting their boots on. We're going to say hello to the pony.'

'Come on, then. I'd like to do that too.'

'You sure you're OK?'

'Yeah. I'll be fine.'

IT'S NOW ELEVEN MONTHS since I sat on a bench in Scotland and wept when I realised I could not daydream any more. I can daydream now; my mind roams as freely as ever it did. I'm no longer terrified of strangers and I can get through a day without needing a nap. My emotions remained tricky for a while. I wandered across my garden some months ago and saw my old battered Land Rover. Seconds later, I was overwhelmed with a great flood of love. I had, briefly, fallen in love with my Land Rover. It was a sincere, deep-rooted response but it was a phantom emotion. I was lucky; I could recognise it for what it was and untangle myself from it. My emotional checks and balances are back now and I hope not to fall head-over-heels with a rusty 4x4 again.

As each week has gone by since I came out of hospital, I have looked back and realised how far I still have to go. It is a long process. The medics saved my life. But I then had to relearn subtle lessons in how to use the fully functioning brain they had given back to me. It's still going on. A year after

I started out, I am still trudging along that road to recovery. And I thank every one of my lucky stars that I am able to make that trudge.

I did get out to the Arctic in the end. My skiing improved, though hardly to Olympic standards. I battled on through temperatures of minus forty, covering thirty or forty miles a day on foot and on skis. And yes, there were times when I battled also with demons inside that, perhaps, would not have been there before. But I had, by then, accepted that the damage to my brain would sometimes mean I struggle with things that were easier before, but it no longer scares me. It was no more frightening than feeling the occasional twinge from a once-broken arm.

I got back to the *Top Gear* studio too. The boys cooked up a few gags for my return and we played it partly for laughs. But at the same time, we knew that we were dealing with something sensitive, not just for me and the team, but for anyone else affected by the thousands of car crashes that happen every day. We could not gloss over the whole event and pretend to the world that, in the fantastic TV world of *Top Gear*, things don't go wrong. They do. Standing once more on the *Top Gear* stage, I silently thanked every member of the team for ensuring, through their diligence and professionalism, that when I was hit by disaster I stood a chance of making it through.

This is not a sad story, not by a million miles. The lessons I have learned, about myself and the world around me, have far outweighed the personal discomfort. I do feel for my family though, who had to watch and worry when they were told I might die or be changed for ever; that is not a lesson to be embraced; it is just a very hard thing to have to do. Perhaps though, by coming through it together, we are closer and stronger than before.

Of course, there are thousands who are not so lucky. Visiting the Brain Rehabilitation Unit in Bristol for check-ups, I saw many other brain-injury victims. People for whom the last memory before their world was turned upside down really was of riding a bike to the shops for a loaf of bread. The bravery, determination and sheer force of humanity of them and their families is difficult to contemplate but inspiring nonetheless.

I've learned too that it can be tricky for people recovering from brain injury, if only because often there is no external sign that anything might be wrong. Both the best and the worst thing was when people would look at me, assume I was fine, and carry on as if nothing had happened. It was great to be able to forget about the accident, but, at the same time, I needed people to understand the trouble I might be having doing ordinary stuff.

The one thing that has never been a pain though, is when people come up and ask how I am. They will often worry that perhaps I am tired of people asking. Why would I be? Every time a middle-aged lady I have never met before puts her hand on my arm and asks how I am, it's as though an aunt has given me a big hug and asked the same question. It's comforting, if only because it's a reminder that it's good to be a human being after all. And so I will never be able to thank enough the people who wrote to me and thought about me when I was ill. It contributed, I'm sure, to my recovery.

And so life gets ever closer to returning to what was normal for us. Of course, as our 'normal' includes days when I set out to try to reach the North Pole by dog sled, cross the English Channel in a floating van or even drive a jet car up an airfield in Yorkshire, we can never entirely relax. When my driving licence came back, I grabbed the keys to my trusty Morgan and, with Mindy by my side, cruised the country lanes near our home. The doctors had been worried about possible flashbacks and repercussions when first I drove. In fact, it never crossed my mind. If I had fired up my Morgan and heard a jet engine start, I might have had a bit of a moment. But this was just driving, and I loved it. We laughed a lot. So did Izzy and Willow when I first took them for a drive a few days later.

'Daddy?' they both asked together in their sing-song voices.

'Yes?'

'Don't go upside down and bang your head again, will you? We'll all have to go to hospital then, and who will look after the horses?' They laugh and laugh and laugh.

It's a routine we still go through every time we all get into Mindy's yellow Land Rover and set off on a family trip. And in answer I always say, 'No, no, I won't go on the roof again.' And if I can help it at all, I shan't.

And sitting beside me when I say that, as she has been beside me now through the highest and lowest points in my life and the moments when it looked like it very well might end, is Mindy. The impact of any such accident is felt initially by the patient. But from that point on, it becomes a burden to be carried by those closest to them. And so I thank my parents, my brothers and my friends for being there when I needed them. I am sorry for putting them through a tough time. My daughters were largely shielded from the hurt of it, but they missed their daddy and one day, I'll be able to say sorry to them too. And to Mindy, I can only ever say a simple thank you. And dedicate the rest of my life to her.

ON THE EDGE : MY STORY

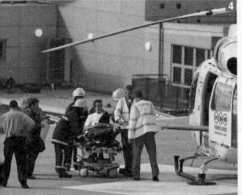

Top (left to right): **1** Richard Hammond, art student. **2** Cutting a dash in the Lake District. **3** The jet-propelled Vampire dragster, owned and built by Colin Fallows. **4** After his initial spell in hospital at Leeds General, Hammond was taken by helicopter to a private hospital in Bristol. **5** The *Top Gear* team, from left: James May, Jeremy Clarkson and Richard Hammond. **Bottom: 6** Together again: (left to right): Izzy with her dad, Captain, the Jack Russell, and Mindy Hammond with Willow.

the
CRYStaL
SKULL

MANDA SCOTT

Deep in a Yorkshire cave, Stella Cody
finds a crystal skull of
exquisite beauty and extraordinary
power, which has lain hidden for four
centuries. Ancient texts record that
the skull has the potential to prevent a
catastrophic end to the world and, as
its new 'keeper', Stella must decipher
its final resting place . . .

PROLOGUE

To Dr Barnabas Tythe, visiting professor, Balliol College, Oxford, written this 13th day of July, in the year of Our Lord 1556, greetings.

My dear friend—I write in haste and with regret that I must depart without a proper leave-taking. Cambridge is alive with accusations of heresy. Poor Thom Gillespie is already arraigned and faces death by burning for nothing more than questioning the use of a prayer book to mend a fractured wrist.

All those of us who practise medicine in accordance with the highest science, abjuring the superstitions of the Church, are in like peril. With a secret such as mine, I am doubly in jeopardy. Already there is a pamphlet circulating which states that I am in possession of 'a blue stone skull in the shape of an unfleshed man's head' and that I use it to gaze upon the stars. In our current climate, even so much would see me burn, but it cannot be long ere someone links the heart-stone with my healing of the sick which would, I greatly fear, lead to the stone's destruction as well as mine.

I leave, therefore, on the evening tide in the company of others who share my peril. But, before I go, I must tell you that I have been in communion these past three weeks with Dr John Dee, who has lately been astrologer to the Princess Elizabeth in her exile at Woodstock and has become the second of my teachers, behind only yourself.

As you know, it has long been my belief that if ever I have success in my physic, it is down to you alone. More than any other, you have taught me the rigours of anatomy and how observation of the patient is of paramount importance. But these last weeks Dr Dee has been

*most assiduous in showing me how the twin sciences of medicine
and astrology may be brought together to hasten the restoration of
the afflicted.*

*He has looked long and deep into the tissue of the blue heart-
stone that has been my family's heritage and is of the opinion that it
is of an age far greater than the oldest relics of Christendom. It is,
he thinks, one of many that were birthed together in the temples of
the heathen ancients, and sent forth to the world for the greater
benefit of Mankind. He believes that there are those who fear the
greater good that will be wrought by these stones in years to come
and therefore seek their destruction. Thus I have enemies of whom
I know naught, who will seek me out where ever I may go and will
threaten the core of my life.*

*I am ashamed to confess that I have been in possession of the
stone for a decade and yet am ignorant of its true nature, and this
ignorance may be my death. It is pursuit of learning, therefore, as
much as fear, that drives me from England to seek the help of any
who might educate me as to the stone's purpose and my own.*

*In this regard, Dr Dee has observed my Part of Fortune, and the
turning of my natal sun, and assures me that I will return to England
at some future time when the climate is less dangerous.*

*I wish to believe him, and shall do so, knowing that only thus may I
see you again. Until then, I must take my fortunes in France, carrying
from Dr Dee his letter of recommendation to a friend whom he would
trust with his own life and mine.*

*I have no knowledge of where this adventure will lead me, but am
heartened by the scatter of the Constellations; on this day, Venus has
come to rest on the fourth degree of Virgo, in near trine to Mars, as
she did on the morning of my birth. Every felicitous part of my life
has taken place under the good auspices of this star and her position
now cannot but aid my cause.*

*With that to cheer us both, I take my leave. Know that I miss
you greatly and will return to Bede's, and to you, when time and
life allow.*

*For now, I am your most humble servant, honoured student and
honest friend,*

*Cedric Owen, Physician, Master of the Arts (Bede's College,
Cantab, 1543) and Doctor of Philosophy (1555).*

1
Beneath Ingleborough Fell, Yorkshire Dales

May 2007   Because it was her wedding gift, Stella came first out of the tunnel. Filthy, wet and shivering hot-cold from the effort of the last fifty-metre uphill haul, she crawled on her belly into the blackness beyond.

She moved slowly, keeping taut the umbilical line that linked her to Kit, and shuffling forward no further than the spilled light from her head-torch. Like the tunnel, the cave was of chalk. Her torch showed bright trickles of damp everywhere, washing over flat, undulating stone. Beyond the splash of yellow light was unknown territory, unmapped, unexplored, as likely to be a ledge and a bottomless fall as a flat cave floor.

With cold-stiff fingers, she set a bolt into the wall by the mouth of the tunnel, clipped into it, and tugged the rope to let Kit know that she had stopped and not to pay out more rope. By the light of her head-torch she checked her compass and her watch and marked the incline and her estimate of its length with wax pencil on the chart that she kept in her chest pocket. Only after she had done all these things did Stella turn and look up and send the thread of her torch into the vast cathedral space Kit had found for her.

'My God . . . Kit, come and look.'

She spoke to herself; he was too far back to hear. She tugged twice on the rope, then felt the single answering twitch and then the sudden slack as he began to move towards her. Switching off her head-torch, Stella stood in the roaring silence and let Kit's gift stand still in all its vast, black perfection around her, so that she could remember it for the rest of her life.

Marriage is fine for the rest of the world, but I want to find you a present that will last us for ever, something to remember when the magic of now has grown to quiet domesticity. What is it in the world that you want most, my lovely woman, that will let you love me for eternity?

He had said it in Cambridge, in his river room that sat proud above the Cam, with the river running glassy green below, on the morning before they had gone to the registrar with their two witnesses and made themselves legal in the eyes of the world.

She had known him little more than a year; he the Bede's scholar, she the Yorkshire lass with a degree from a metropolitan university. Yet they had found a meeting of minds that had carried them, in fourteen dizzying months, from discussions on string theory to marriage.

Then, lying at peace with herself and the world, it seemed there was nothing she wanted from him that he had not given, but it was a beautiful day and she was thinking of rock and how little of it there was in the flat fenlands of Cambridge.

Find me a cave, she had said, without thinking particularly, *a cave no one else has ever seen. For that, I will love you for ever.*

He had come to kneel by the bed, to a place where his complex green-brown eyes could see and be seen. He had kissed her on the centre of her brow and smiled his driest, most knowing smile. *What if I were to find you a cave with buried treasure that no one has entered for four hundred and nineteen years?* he had said. *Would that be almost as good?*

Four hundred and nineteen . . . ? She had sat up, too fast for the heat of the day. Always, he had surprised her; it was why she was going to marry him. *You've found Cedric Owen's cave? Why didn't you tell me?*

Because I wanted to be sure.

And are you now? Stella had studied his eyes.

As sure as I can be without going there to look. It's all in the cipher in the ledgers: the hanging thorns, the falling river. It had to be somewhere Owen knew like the back of his hand and the only place is Ingleborough Hill up in Yorkshire. He was born on the side of it. The thorns are gone by now but I found references to them in an old diary and there's a river that falls into Gaping Ghyll.

Gaping Ghyll? Kit, that's the deepest pothole in England. The cave system running out from it goes for miles.

It does indeed. And there are bits of it that haven't been explored yet, possibly a cathedral of the earth that no one has been in since Cedric Owen wrote his poem. Would you like to go, as our present to each other? To find the cave and search out the hidden pearl entombed therein?

Stella had known, then, that the gift was for him as much as for her. Cedric Owen's blue heart-stone was Kit's life's love, the great treasure of his college that had been sought by the high and mighty down the ages but never found.

They had not known where to look, the great and the good; they had not read between the lines for the hidden words and phrases as Kit had. It was his greatest accomplishment, and his greatest secret; by marrying him, she became a part of it.

Even so . . . I thought the skull had killed all those who ever held it?

He had laughed and slid his part-dressed body over hers and said, *Only if they fell into the sins of lust and avarice. We won't do that.*

They were close then, eye to eye, nose to nose, heartbeat to heartbeat, sharing each breath. She had looked up into his green-brown eyes and, quite truthfully, said, *I could fall into lust for the first descent of an undiscovered cave. You can't begin to imagine what kind of gift that would be.*

But I can. You're a caver: it means to you what finding Owen's heartstone would mean to me. It's why we can do it, you and me together . . .

She was the caver; hers the responsibility to bring the dream to reality. Which was why she had persisted after she had found the rock fall that blocked the route, and why, when she had discovered an opening that might lead to where they wanted to go, she had gone first along the long, claustrophobic tunnel, where she had become a snake and then an eel and then a worm in order to bend round the corners and slide under the overhangs and creep, inch by pulling inch, up fifty metres of a one-in-ten incline that had brought her at last to the exit and the cavern beyond.

The rope went tight in her hands and then slack again as Kit rounded the final bend. She switched on her head-torch to give him something to aim for. Like a flickering cinema, her beam picked out random lengths of stalactites and stalagmites, closing like shark's teeth from floor to roof and back again. She eased the camera from her pack. The flash reached out and splashed colour across the rising, falling calcite, drew rainbows from the sheen of water, sprinkled brilliant, living diamonds across the rock.

Only as Kit was easing out of the tunnel to stand beside her did she follow at last the thunderous noise and turn west, to shed light on the cascading torrent of the waterfall.

'My God . . .'

'The cathedral of the earth. You clever, clever girl. I thought the rock fall had finished us.' Kit's arm wrapped her waist and she leaned in to him, drysuit to dry-suit, then turned her light up to his face. He was filthy and euphoric at once; a man on the brink of a promise.

She said, 'I can't think Cedric Owen knew about this route; you'd never get a Tudor physician in doublet and tights along that tunnel.'

'Nor any sane man, without his lady love to guide him.'

Laughing, she said, 'Have you a flare? It'd be good to see it all properly.'

'I have.' He was already rummaging in his pack. 'And then we have to find out where Owen came in when he walked the easy route.' Kit locked the flare in a high cleft and lit it with his hand covering his face.

White!

Blistering incandescence spilled from the cavern wall. Under its magnesium light, the cave's roof was finally visible, a greying white limestone arch halfway to the heavens.

'How high is it, do you think?' Kit asked.

'A hundred metres? Maybe a bit more. We could climb one of the walls and find out if you're feeling keen.'

Kit grinned, weakly. 'I'd rather find the skull.' He leaned back on the wall, bit his glove off one hand, delved into the hidden pockets of his backpack, and came out with the precious folded paper. The print of Cedric Owen's cipher, the pinnacle of three years' work.

'Read it to me again.'

He was a poet at heart, for all he buried his head in hexadecimal code and computer languages. He turned so that the flare cast his shadow behind him and read aloud:

'*That which you seek lies hidden in white water. Stone will be rendered unto stone, made safe in a place of hallowed beauty against the Enemy that seeks its destruction. Search north and then east, fifteen and twenty, behind the hanging thorns within the curve of the bow, in sound of the falling river.*

'*Enter with courage. Go forward as far as the dark allows. Step through night's arch and come to the cathedral of the earth. Face the rising of the sun, and its setting, pierce the curtain to the well of living water and discover at last the pearl there entombed.*

'*Find me and live, for I am your hope at the end of time. Hold me as you would hold your child. Listen to me as you would listen to your lover. Trust me as you would trust your god, whosoever that may be.*

'*Follow the path that is herein shewn and be with me at the time and place appointed. Do then as the guardians of night foretell. Thereafter, follow your heart and mine, for these are one and the same. Do not fail me, for in doing so, you fail yourself, and all the worlds of waiting.*'

He lowered the paper. Softly, he said, 'We have come to the cathedral of the earth.'

'We have. So next we have to face the rising and setting sun. But we didn't step through night's arch to get here; we crawled through a tunnel that wasn't there before half a ton of rock fell into the route Cedric Owen took. We need to find out where he came in before we can work out where he went next.'

Stella stood at the margins of the magnesium white and turned in a slow circle. Her head-torch cut a horizontal line along the wall until it fell into a tall slice of darkness. 'There.' She ran to a jaggedly asymmetric cleft in the rock and followed it cautiously, rounding a bend, moving into a narrower passageway.

'This is it,' she shouted. 'The rock fall's up ahead. It must be at least twenty metres thick. Our crawl-tunnel looped out and round to come out further along the cavern's wall.' She reversed back towards Kit, playing her torch over the passage walls. Here and there were smudges of colour that barely held her torchlight.

'I think there are cave paintings on the wall.' She could hear the awe in her own voice as she backed out into the cavern, to where there was light enough to look around, to search the high walls for signs of ancient life. 'God, Kit . . . I take it all back. There *are* better things than finding a cave no one has ever been in.' She grinned at him, her blood fizzing in her veins.

'Stell?'

The flare was fading fast. In the yellowing light, she saw him pull off his head-torch and strip back the black neoprene hood. His hair glowed like gold in the poor light. She saw what he was going to do and yanked off her own cap as he had done. He was near and warm and he smelt of sweat and fear and excitement and she loved him.

They closed the kiss in darkness, with no head-torches and no flare, and Stella was afraid, suddenly, for both of them, that from these heights there was only a long slope down.

He caught the swoop of her feeling. Hoarsely, he said, 'Are you ready to face the rising of the sun and its setting?'

She checked the compass on her wrist. 'I think that means we need to go east of the entrance and then west. There's a river over by the north side of the cavern. Can you set another flare somewhere up there, so that it shines on the wall and the water together?'

They had three flares. He wedged their second one between two stalag-mites at the side of the water-cut channel in the chalk. The magnesium spat and flared and the black ribbon of the river became a thread of silver.

Stella said, 'It's too wide to jump. We're looking for a stepping stone, or a bridge, where we can cross. It's the only reason why we'd go east before we go west along the north wall. The waterfall is a curtain and there's a pool at its foot that's as close to a well of living water as we're likely to get. Owen didn't want his heart-stone to be easy to find, but not impossible either.'

Kit was ahead of her, searching. He was back in neoprene with his lamp set at his brow. 'Then we'll cross here, will we?' he said. 'On the stepping stones that look like marbles?'

The stepping stones also rolled like marbles underfoot, so Stella set another bolt and strung out two lines at right angles to give maximum security before she tried again. She was glad of them when the third stone rolled under her feet and she felt the strength of the black current.

'We're going to have to dive for it,' she said.

'You don't have the gear to dive.' He sounded anxious, which was not at all like him; the currents had unnerved him.

'I've got a mask and an underwater light. They'll do.'

'We might need the third flare.'

'No. We don't know what's ahead. We might need it to get out. Come on, let's have a look at the waterfall.' Already, she was regretting the profligate waste of the earlier light.

'*Face the rising of the sun and its setting, pierce the curtain to the well of living water and discover at last . . .* et cetera, et cetera.'

She tilted her head back to guess the height of the cataract. Her beam did not reach a point where there was no water, although at the limit of its reach was turbulence, and a spray that reached far out into the cavern and danced like fairy lights so that she could believe the river's head might be there.

'*Pierce the curtain,*' Kit said. 'How?'

'I don't know, but Cedric Owen did it without flares or a neoprene drysuit and he came out alive, so we have to assume that it's not as terrifying as it looks. If we—'

'Stell?'

'—take a look at the rock face where the waterfall ends, then we—'

'Stella . . .'

'—might find that there's a hollow in the space behind the water that will let us— What?'

'I don't think he did.' Kit's voice was flat.

'You don't think who did what?'

'I don't think Cedric Owen made it out alive. There's a skeleton here, with not a bit of flesh on it, and a huge amount of limescale deposit, which suggests it's been here for a very long time.'

STELLA KNELT by the skeleton and sent her light over the bones made thick and uneven by layers of chalky deposit that welded it to the floor.

'There's nothing obviously broken,' she said. 'No fractured spine or legs bent at bad angles.'

Kit stood back a little at the other side. His torch lit only the skull; a real skull, not the one of coloured stone that they had come to find. 'It's so peaceful,' he said. 'It's laid out like a knight on a tomb, everything in straight lines and its hands folded over its chest. All he needs is a sword and—'

'I think he's got one. Look.' Stella had a multi-function climbing tool strong enough to prod stubborn climbing gear from its wedged place in rock. She used the end of it to scrape the crumbling chalk from the thing that might have been a sword. She said, 'And he was carrying something round his neck.'

Beneath the maybe-sword was something soft that had not rotted away, but grown a shell of chalk. She wriggled it out and rolled it between her hands to break the stone.

'It's a leather bag, lined with something that's kept the water out.' With an effort, she teased apart the neck and tipped the contents into her hand. 'It's a pendant. Bronze, maybe.' She rubbed the silt from the face and held it up. 'It's got Libra scratched on the back.'

'Show me?' Kit's torch angled down her shoulder.

'It's been scratched on with a nail, or the point of a knife—see? If we turn it over'—she did just that—'there's a crest, one of your ancient medieval cryptic sigils, on the other side. Have a look.'

As he lifted it into the light of his head-torch, she saw the colour bleed from his face. 'It's a dragon under the risen half-moon.' He was as Irish as she had ever heard him. 'That's the Bede's College crest. It's on the stained-glass window outside my bedroom; it's above the gate to the Great Court and the door to the Master's suite. As a medallion like this, it's only worn by the Masters of Bede's or their emissaries, when they had emissaries.'

He dangled it over his finger like a rosary and its shadow swept in arcs along the length of the skeleton. 'This can't be Cedric Owen. He was never anyone's emissary. In any case, he died at the gates to the college on Christmas Day, 1588, everyone knows that. I wonder if someone else came here to try to find the skull-stone?'

'How? No one broke the code before us.'

'No one that we know of.' He handed her back the pendant. 'Will you keep this? We'll try to find out whose it is later.'

'If it's not Cedric Owen, then someone else died within reach of the heart-stone, exactly as the legends promise. You told me that: *everyone who has ever held this stone has died for it.*'

'Do you still want to try to find it?'

'Definitely.' She swept her light up the length of the cataract and down again. 'Just let's try not to add to the statistics.'

STELLA HAD TO DIVE in the end. Kit held the rope and paid it out slowly as she breathed in half a lungful of air and dipped under the churning water.

On a good day, in a river, with sun above, she could hold her breath for three minutes. Underground, in temperatures this low, she hoped for maybe half that. She sent the narrow beam of her diving head-lamp past the churning edge of the water to where the currents cut alcoves and potholes in the rock. She could see nothing but white: white water, white rock, white light.

Three times she came up for air. Three times the eddies pushed her back, before she could reach the place where an anomaly of the current held the water still and the white rock lay wide and round as a cauldron.

She had a rule: always try three times and then stop. It had kept her alive in caves where 'one more try' would have left her too exhausted to turn round and climb out. She was ready to stop now, but for the encouragement that made her take more rope from Kit and duck down again to kick forward hard through the wall of white turbulence to the black space beyond.

There, in the dizzy light of her head-lamp, was the lip of cavitied rock.

They had come looking for the blue stone in the shape of an unfleshed man's head. What lay in the black water before her was a blob of chalk; a lumpen, misshapen pearl with barely a shadow of eyes and nose and mouth to suggest the skull within. Stella leaned down to reach it.

Blue!

A blinding intensity of blue that made her gasp even as her heart leapt in her chest. She lost a mouthful of air and came to the surface in a flurry of panicked coughing.

Kit was at the water's edge. 'Stell, you've been in too long. Come on out. No piece of stone is worth dying for. We can leave it.'

'No!' She waved an arm high over her head. 'It's there! I can get it!'

Once more she ducked down into the black water. Stiff with cold, her hands reached into the churning dark, to the pearl beyond price that was Cedric Owen's skull-stone. The blue was less intense a second time, and she was waiting for it. The skull-stone came to her hands, singing its welcome.

'STELL, YOU'RE FREEZING. We have to get you moving, get you out, get back into sunlight.'

'Give me chocolate and hold me and I'll be fine.'

She was stupidly, insanely cold. She sat in torch-eating darkness, ten feet from a skeleton, clutching an uninspiring lump of limestone that was barely identifiable as a skull—and she was as happy as she could ever remember. She let Kit fold his arms and his legs and his whole body around her.

'Kit?'

'Yes?' He had not asked to see the skull-stone yet, which surprised her.

She said, 'This is the best wedding present in the world. Thank you.'

'We're not out yet.'

'No, but it won't be long. The draught is all from east to west. If we go left of the waterfall, I'll bet there's a walk-out that joins up with the White Scar complex and takes us out near the car.'

'If it's an easy walk, people would have been in here by the hundreds.'

Stella wriggled from his grasp and wrestled with her pack, setting the skull-stone safe inside, close to the bronze pendant on which a dragon unfurled its wings beneath a high half-moon.

'OK, so there might be a bit of a climb. And maybe a tiny bit of a crawl through an entrance so small nobody's been dumb enough to try it yet. But the poem said, *Find me and live*, so we have to do exactly that. Come on, we'll make a caver of you yet.'

THEY HAD CLIMBED and crawled and were on the second pitch of a downward climb when Stella heard a stone fall in the darkness. She was at the belay point, winding in the rope. She looked up, letting her torch beam catch Kit's feet.

'Did you hear something?' she asked him.

'Other than the blood rushing in my ears, the chattering of my teeth and the premonition of my screaming body falling into the centre of the earth down this devil's climb you've magicked out of nowhere? No.'

For a non-climber, Kit was coping astonishingly well. And he was cheerful again, which was little short of a miracle.

Stella stood to one side of the ledge, keeping the belay safely taut, but not so tight it pulled him off the rock. His feet reached her first and then he was down beside her.

'Where now?'

She tipped her torch onto her plastic map pocket. 'If the charts are right, this ledge is part of the White Scar complex that was only opened up nine months ago. It's not surprising nobody found the way into the chamber. We'll be fine as long as we don't stray into Gaping Ghyll.'

'The pothole with the river falling into it?'

'The pothole with the longest waterfall in England falling into it.'

The Ghyll was her home territory. She traced a line with her index finger. 'As far as I can tell, this ledge carries on for about half a mile to a fork where we take a left. After that, the ledge gets narrower and the drop deeper. If we're lucky, there'll be bolts and a rope to hold on to but even if not, as long as we don't go near the edge, it's a cake walk.'

'A cake walk . . .' Kit let his light play over the side wall and the black nothingness below. Experimentally, he kicked a stone from their ledge. It rattled briefly against the side and then fell in absolute silence to a faraway floor. 'And you do this for pleasure. Stella Cody, you are insane.'

He dug out his water bottle and drank, then passed it to her. The slosh of water very nearly covered the clatter of a distant stone.

She said, 'There!'

'What?'

'A rock fell.' She said nothing more. How to tell him that the skull-stone was coming alive, that she could feel its presence on the edges of her mind, and that it sensed danger nearby? 'There was one earlier,' she said. 'Before you came down.'

'In the middle of a mountain, made of rocks piled on rocks, you heard a rock fall? Is that unusual?' He flashed his head-lamp at her face, dowsing her with light.

His buoyancy was infectious so she smiled, to bring him down gently. 'It is, actually. You only ever hear rocks fall in caves when there's somebody sending them down, like you just did. I think we have company.'

'Do we mind company?'

'Possibly not, but we're in an unmapped cave and we've just picked up an artefact that people have been hunting for the past four hundred years. I think we should keep moving, and try not to make too much noise.'

'STELL, THAT WAS definitely a rock bouncing on another rock.'

'I heard it. And the one before. They're coming at thirty-second intervals.'

The ledge on which they walked had narrowed to less than fifty centimetres across. Stella kept her torch beam angled so that the light overlapped her feet and she never stepped further than she could see. There were no bolts and no rope to hold on to. She said, 'Whoever's following wants us to know he or she's there.'

'What do we do?'

'If I said that the skull-stone thinks we should run like hell, would you divorce me?'

'Pass. I need to have notice of that question. Does it say why?'

Kit was making such an effort to sound calm. She loved him for that. She said, 'It doesn't want to meet whoever is behind us.'

'Let's run, then. Or at least let's walk a bit faster.'

'*KIT!*' It came out muffled, into neoprene. His hand was over her mouth, the other switched her light off. His own light had already gone. His whole body held her against the rock. Somewhere, not far back round a left-hand bend, a rock tumbled to nowhere.

'Whisper.' Kit's voice in her ear. 'We're being herded, not hunted. Is there something bad we're going to blunder into up ahead or does this ledge simply run out and leave us nowhere to go?'

The chart was burnt into her mind. 'There's a pinch point two hundred metres from here. There should be bolts and a rope by then.'

'But if we're pushed too fast, we'll miss them and then we'll go over.' Kit's lips were on her forehead, beneath her lamp. There was no fear in him now, only a bright, sharp anger. 'So here's what we'll do. I'll take your spare light so it looks like there's two of us and go ahead fast and messy. You wait until the bastard has passed you and come up behind. If he's trying to push us off, he won't get both of us, and if we're lucky you'll get a good look at who it is. Just don't do anything about it till we're safely back in daylight.'

'Kit, that's madness. Which one of us is the caver? If we're going to split, let me go ahead.'

He shook his head and the shiver of it ran through his shoulder to hers. 'You can climb up the wall and get out of sight. I couldn't do that if my life depended on it.'

She had no answer to that. Taking silence for agreement, he said, 'How far after the pinch point before we see daylight?'

'About half a mile of easy going and then you're in the main chamber. From there it *is* a walk-out.'

'Sorted.' His hands clasped her face and he hugged her. They clashed, head-lamp to head-lamp, and sketched the barest kiss. 'I love you. Now, give me your underwater light and I'll see you back at the car.'

SHE LOVED HIM. She gave him her second light and listened to him make noise enough for two, if those two were trying to be quiet.

The dropping of stones halted for a moment and then came along faster. *You can climb up the wall and get out of sight.*

It was madness. Blindly, she felt for handholds in the rock wall at her side, making herself a gecko, a squirrel, able to adhere to wet limestone and never fall back into the swooping, sucking dark. Footholds came to her hand and then her feet. She turned her face sideways and glued her cheek to the damp surface and did not allow herself to think how she would get down.

He came soon, whoever he was, a passing solidity of flesh and breath and the smell of male sweat and neoprene and mud that moved fast and sure-footed, with only a pinprick of light. He did not look up to where she was, even when the skull-stone screamed a warning and flashed a spark of pure blue lightning that existed, as far as she could tell, only in her mind.

She waited a long time, holding to wet rock with fingers that were locked with fear as much as cold. The sound of padding feet died to nothing.

'Kit, please God, Kit, be safe.'

Silence answered her, with no falling stones.

When she had counted a thousand, she risked her light, then lowered herself down onto a ledge that was exactly the width of her two feet set toe to heel. Beyond it, her light probed the darkness and saw nothing. She turned her lamp forward, and began the long walk out.

2

Paris

August 1556 Paris lay asweat under the pall of summer. Smoke from the cooking fires hung as a blanket over tiled rooftops and the stench of sewage clogged the narrow streets. Life had slowed almost to a halt.

Some things took no notice of the heat: birth and death among them. Thus did Cedric Owen, known to those around him as Monsieur David Montgomery—ostensibly a Scot loyal to France's serene majesty and his ally the Pope—find himself up to his arms in the slime and gore of a difficult childbirth. It was his fourth since coming to France. The first had gone well and so earned him a reputation among the street folk to whom he ministered. The second was for the wife of a tailor who had once sewn the points onto the hose of Monsieur de Montpelier, who was something small at court. The third came at night and he was called from his bed by a man who rode a horse and carried his own sword. The woman brought to bed was his mistress and her white linen sheets were ripped up to make staunching pads when she bled. Her survival was considered a minor miracle. The woman's lover, it transpired, was a cousin of Monsieur de Montpelier and something rather more substantial at court.

And so, without any wish or effort on his part, other than to follow his chosen profession, less than three weeks after his arrival in France, Cedric Owen came to attend a chambermaid to the Queen, gone into labour nearly a month before her time.

Naked to the waist, Owen lay on floorboards at the foot of her birthing-bed with his eyes shut, the better to see with his fingers, which were at full length inside, at the place where the babes lay. He felt bad news.

'My lady, you are about to be delivered of twins,' he said in passable French. 'The two babes are evenly placed in your womb. I must send one back to allow the other to advance. Have I your permission, and that of your husband, to choose which of your children is to be born first?' It was not a trivial question; lives had been made or broken on the order of birth.

Opening his eyes once more, he looked about and saw the sign of the cross being made over and over on the breasts of those who stood in attendance, most particularly on the breast of Charles, the ashen-faced youth come early to manhood who had introduced himself as the father.

Owen had never been greatly impressed with the combination of youth and money that infected all courts. He allowed an edge in his voice. 'Sir? God may guide my hand, but I need your permission before I act,' he said.

Dully, the young courtier said, 'The Queen had twins in June, both girls. One died at birth. The other lies in the care of the best physicians in the land. Most believe she will not live. We cannot have twins as did the Queen. The King will see it as ill luck.'

Owen eased his hand out of the tight confines of the birth canal and looked up to the woman in labour. The fear in her eyes was more for her children and the racking pain than for any superstitions of the court.

'Madame? There is nothing to be done but let the children within you see the light of day. King Henri is not known for his illogic. I doubt if he will truly see you as an ill omen for his child.'

He saw her mouth move and could not make out the words. She wet her lips with a dry tongue and tried again. 'Choose well by your own lights.'

The raw courage in her gaze was what had first brought Cedric Owen to his calling and what kept him there in the face of idiocy, superstition and plague. With a strange, familiar ache swelling his breast, he sent the most coherent of the serving women out for more hot water and then he turned his attention on the woman and the two new lives he had felt.

'MONSIEUR MONTGOMERY?'

He heard the voice from a long way off. He sat on the scrubbed wooden floor, still damp from the wash-mops of the serving girls, and listened to the one living child suckle its mother. He was lost in the world beyond exertion where the cramping pain in his arm had become something sweet to be treasured and the closeness to new life was a gift that transported him beyond the fears and hopes and trivia of those around him.

It also temporarily caused him to forget the pseudonym he had taken.

'Monsieur Montgomery? The Queen requires your presence.'

'The Queen?' He remembered very suddenly who he was and where. Catherine de' Medici was not known for her patience. 'Why?'

Charles, the young father, was now a sick shade of grey. He bared his teeth in a grimace that made pretence of a smile. 'Word has reached her majesty of our . . . felicity. She wishes to see the young Scottish doctor who has brought a healthy girl-child into the world.'

They had both been girls. The living one, perforce, had been named Victoire after the daughter who had come to grace the lives of Queen Catherine of France and Henri II, her husband.

Therein lay the problem. Not only had the King's sister married James V of Scotland, but James's daughter, the young Mary, Queen of Scots, was betrothed to Henri's eldest son. The French court was home to as many Scots as Frenchmen—any one of whom would discover in the first minutes of conversation that the carroty-haired young Scotsman had precious few memories of Scotland, its people or its politics.

If they discovered he was English, they might invite one of the representatives of His Holiness Pope Paul IV to try him for heresy; the Inquisition was as active in Paris as any other place in Europe. Then he would die at the stake if he were lucky, and under torture before that if he were not.

Cedric Owen pushed himself to his feet and reached for his shirt. He looked down at his homespun breeches. They were clean, which was the best that could be said for them. He had a cloak of good velvet, but he had left it at his lodgings, together with his cap.

He looked up and found Charles staring at him. 'The Queen will make allowance for your dress. It is your skill she seeks.'

Owen bowed low and gestured to the door. They passed the small casket containing the dead child on the way out.

CEDRIC OWEN was ushered into an antechamber to the ailing infant's bedroom, an oak-panelled place that smelt of sulphur and rosemary oil and more faintly of rosewater and sickness.

At one side of the room stood a clutter of middle-aged men who shared the belief that long beards and black gowns gave them an air of studious learning. But it was the Queen who held the better part of Owen's attention; a vision of ivory silk with primrose-yellow bows about the waist and hem, and diamonds worth an emperor's ransom set about her throat and hair. She had been weeping, and the part of him that was always professional admired her fortitude. Catherine de' Medici was two months past her confinement and the entirety of her court knew that her husband, the King of France, was in love with his mistress, Diane de Poitiers. That she could look as regal as she did in such circumstances was a testament to her breeding.

Owen bowed as low as he knew how and then stood awkwardly, not knowing how to deport himself before a queen.

'You may view us.' She spoke her French richly and with only the trace of an Italian accent. 'And then you may view more closely our daughter. For how else may you heal her?'

'My Lady . . . Your Highness'—Owen's French came out in poor order—'I am a bringer to birth and a giver of such medicines as I might find useful. I can scry the heavens for their wisdom, but I regret that I have no skills in the treatment of children. Your Majesty has in this room physicians far more skilled than I.'

The Queen said, 'We have men who have so far not permitted our child to thrive. We would have a fresh eye assess the case. They say you do not consider the four humours to be chief in aiding your diagnosis.'

This was controversial and had nearly cost Owen his studies in Cambridge. The pressure in the room became delicately brittle and, somewhere beyond the hearing of others, Owen heard a high, bright whine, which was the warning sound of the blue heart-stone. Though concealed beneath a floorboard in his lodgings, still its sound reached him. Always, when he heard it, his life took a new turn.

He took a breath and smoothed his sweating palms on his shirt tails and said, 'Your Highness, I believe the physician Paracelsus was correct and that life is better measured by the balance of the three elements: salt, sulphur and mercury. The estimation of humours has its place, but it is not the full explanation of life.'

They hated him for that, the crow-garbed men, and they were not stupid; they could sense falsehood as easily as they could smell putrefaction. By the law of averages, at least one of them was likely to be a Scot, and so able to unearth his deception.

Owen was turning his back on them when one, a small man and the youngest by a good ten years, looked across the room at him and offered a subtle, but perfectly clear, inclination of his head. The Queen saw it. 'Michel, *mon ami*, you have an ally.'

'And gladly so.' The man bowed deeply. His voice was surprisingly delicate. 'In which case, perhaps between us we may begin to—'

A wail began in the bedroom beyond them and rose to a shriek. Another joined it. The Queen spun round and when she flung open the door to her daughter's chamber the grief spilled out, enveloping them all. The young princess, clearly, had died.

The small man with the gentle voice slipped unnoticed through the chaos and came to stand with his shoulder pressed tight against Owen's, moving them both back, closer to the far wall. 'When we can leave, we should do so. You have lodgings nearby?'

'On the south bank. Maison d'Anjou.'

'We should go there forthwith, with but a small detour to my own lodgings en route. I have in my effects a letter addressed to me by a young man, which contains within it a letter of recommendation from Dr John Dee, a gentleman of great renown. Would you know anything of it?'

In the heat of the day, a ball of ice formed in Cedric Owen's guts. 'I have sent a letter to a physician of even greater renown in Salon,' he said. 'None to Paris.' His voice, he was glad to hear, remained level.

He looked up into eyes that laughed and warned together. 'I was summoned here three days ago from my home in Salon. Your letter followed me, and a second one from my friend, Dr Dee, giving the description of a young man of great talent who was in possession of a particular stone,' said Michel de Nostradame, physician, astrologer and prophet. 'We should—'

The Queen had stepped back into the antechamber, spitting orders, cat-like, at anyone and everyone in her path. The failed physicians stood bunched in a corner like crow-caped cattle.

Catherine de' Medici raked her gaze across them. 'You will attend us,' she said, icily. 'Now.' It did not sound like a kind offer.

By fate and the fortuitous sideways step made by Michel de Nostradame, neither Cedric nor the physician-astrologer was anywhere close to them, and the Queen, it seemed, had forgotten their existence.

Owen felt a tug at his sleeve. 'We should go now,' said the gentle voice. 'I, too, had not yet examined the infant; her blood is not on my hands. I would be honoured if you would join me for wine, perhaps, and some dinner at your lodgings. There is much to talk about. In particular, I would see the stone you have, which has been the inheritance of your family.'

'DOES IT REQUIRE your death, this stone?'

Michel de Nostradame asked his question casually, towards the end of the meal. The blue heart-stone lay on the table, a third interlocutor in a conversation that was both comforting and unsettling at once.

Madame de Rouen's dish of pigeons roasted with almonds and port had been the equal of anything offered in the palace. She had served it herself in Cedric Owen's chamber on the first floor of the Maison d'Anjou, accompanied by red wine served in cups of good boiled leather.

Owen had dared show the stone only to those few men whom he trusted with his life. Most, on seeing the likeness of their own unfleshed heads, stepped away in fear, but others—and these were the more dangerous in his view—had begun to view it with a passion bordering on lust, so that he must needs take steps to avoid them.

Not the Queen's physician; Nostradamus had laid his napkin flat that Owen might set the stone down cleanly, had got up to check that the lock on the door was secure, and then opened wide the westerly shutters, the better to let in the evening sun.

The light had stirred the fires in the depths of the blue stone, so that the empty eye sockets filled with it, and the arch of the cheekbones sharpened.

Nostradamus had said, 'May I touch it?' and, on a nod, had done so, silently laying his hand at the nape of the neck. It was then, moving his hand away and raising his wine, that he had asked his curious question. 'Does it require your death, this stone?'

Owen took his time in finding an answer. Presently, he said, 'I have the stone from my grandmother. It should have come to me on my twenty-first birthday, but my grandmother was slain on the orders of King Henry's counsellors. She was to be hanged for heresy, but fought the men who came for her and was slain at sword-point. My great-uncle, who was keeper before her, died in like manner and his mother before him was killed by a thrown knife from a thief who desired to possess the stone. None of the previous keepers died at less than the age of sixty. This, therefore, is both the gift and the curse of the stone: it gives a long life of great joy but the end must come in violence.'

Nostradamus made a steeple of his fingers and viewed him over the top of it. He blinked, owlishly. With the same soft care, he said, 'Nevertheless, you care for your stone, do you not?'

Owen had not expected the question, and so had not prepared an answer. His heart spoke for him, without censure.

'It is the core and light of my life, my greatest love.'

Even to himself, he had never made it so plain. He wrapped his hands on either side of the stone. It was the size and exact shape of the human skulls he had handled so often during his training. The lower jaw moved freely but was hinged somehow so that it could not be disarticulated and removed as could a true human relic. The surface was polished to perfection and the blue that suffused it was breathtaking, the pale, sharp, cool clarity of a sky seen at noon over an open sea. Looking into it was to gaze into infinity.

Michel de Nostradame said, 'It is no shame to love this thing; it is at least as marvellous as the pyramids of Egypt, as old and as wise. And yet it is more vulnerable than any of these; for there exist in our world those who would destroy it, to rid the earth of the promise it carries. You have done well to have come this far unscathed.'

Owen said, 'Dr Dee was of the belief that this stone is not alone, that there are others and they will be called together at some time long hence, to keep man's greatest evil from afflicting the world. Would you concur?'

Unconsciously the two men had migrated to classical Greek, the language of physicians. In that language, and with his gaze resting somewhere in the blue of the heart-stone, Nostradamus said, 'I have here another bottle of Madame de Rouen's wine. If you were to pour for us both, we might perhaps begin to speak the unspeakable.'

They rinsed the old wine into the hearth and poured new. Its fruited scent filled the air.

Inhaling his appreciation, Nostradamus said, 'I concur with all that Dr Dee has told you and can add to it what I have learned from the teachings of Egypt. Your stone is one of thirteen that were created together after the flood that drowned the great cities of Atlantis. Those who survived wished

THE CRYSTAL SKULL | 455

to preserve their wisdom against the tide of ignorance sweeping the earth. To this end, they brought together stones of different hues from the different lands that circle the earth, and carved them with the skill and beauty you see here. Nine are coloured and are shaped for the races of men. Four are clear as glass and are made for the beasts that walk, crawl, slide and fly. Remember this. You will need knowledge of it later.

'After many generations, when the task was complete, each skull-stone was returned to the place of its birth to be held in trust until such time as all are needed to avert the catastrophe that Man will wreak on God's earth. In each land was set a lineage of keepers who guard the knowledge of what must be done with the stones in that end time.'

Owen broke into a sweat. 'Then I have failed at the start,' he said. 'My grandmother died before she could pass to me all that she knew. Too many of our family have died in the stone's name. If that knowledge was ever ours, it has not reached me, and thus I cannot pass it on.'

'Not true!' Nostradamus's hand slammed the table. 'What has been lost can be found again! This is your life's work. Three tasks have been set you, Cedric Owen: to find the wisdom of the heart-stone, to record it in such a way that it can never be lost again and last, to hide the stone so that none might come across it by chance or ill design until the end times are near.'

Michel de Nostradame then leaned forward and reached across the table for Owen's hands. 'You must do this. If any one of the thirteen skull-stones is lost before the end times, then the whole cannot be made from the sum of its parts and the world will descend into such darkness and infamy as to make our current sorry state seem like heaven by comparison.'

Letting go of Owen's hands, Nostradamus continued. 'Make no mistake, the attacks on your family were not accidental. There is a force at work that does not wish our world made better; it feeds on death and destruction, fear and pain, and wishes these things to continue into the nadir of Armageddon. It bends men to its will—intelligent, thoughtful men, who believe that they can take the power they are offered and wield it only for good. But the nature of power is otherwise; it breaks them, always, and its greatest desire is that the thirteen stones might never again conjoin to deliver our world from misery.'

'You speak of the Church?' Owen asked, whispering.

'Ha!' The Queen's prophet spat a flurry of wine into the hearth. 'Yes, I speak of the Church, though the Church is but a vehicle for those who crave power. In centuries to come, the State will become as powerful and men will arise with power we can only dream of. Then your stone will be in even greater danger than it is now. This is why the lineage of skull-keepers must be broken and your heart-stone hidden from the avarice of such men.'

'I don't understand.'

'Wait.' The prophet held up his hand. 'We must draw the blinds before we speak of such matters, but first there is a thing you must see while we yet have the sun. You must understand what it is that you hold. Dr Dee will have shown you how the light of the sun might be split by a crystal?'

'He did indeed.'

'Excellent. Then we shall perform that feat now.'

Nostradamus pulled a small shard of clearest crystal from an inner pocket and set it on the white napkin on the table at a place where the sun sent its last rays. He paused a moment, then moved his hand away. There was shed a bright, brilliant rainbow, no wider than the palm of his hand, onto the white of the table napkin.

Owen gave a soft exclamation; he had seen it once before, but it was not a thing of which a man might tire.

Gratified, Nostradamus said, 'Thus is the sun's light revealed to be made of seven colours. By this means also is a rainbow fashioned when light meets falling rain.'

Owen said, 'And the fifth colour is the blue of the noonday sky, which is also the blue of the heart-stone. In my earliest childhood, my grandmother showed me this.'

Nostradamus smiled and nodded. 'The colours of the world are nine in total: the seven of the rainbow, plus the black of no-light and the white of all-light. Blue is fifth of the nine, the fulcrum about which all turns, the keystone of the world's arc. The ancients knew this, which we have forgotten. To the blue was given the heart of the beast, and the power to call together the remaining twelve parts of its spirit and flesh so that the whole may be joined again.'

Owen frowned. 'What beast?'

'The Ouroboros, spoken of by Plato, the ultimate beast of all power, which embodies the spirit of the earth and will arise at her time of greatest need. What else could free the world from the wrath of Armageddon?'

Seeing the incomprehension on Owen's face, the little man stood, his added height giving weight to his words.

'The flesh of this great serpent is made from the four beast-stones. I know not the nature of these beast-stones, nor how they may be brought together—you must find this. What I can tell you is that the life-spirit of the beast comes from the nine rainbow stones that encircled the earth.

'The ancients knew of the lines of force that flow around us, unseen and unfelt. They mapped them and built on them great artefacts: pyramids and stone circles; tombs where the dead guard the points of deepest power. At nine of these points, they fashioned sockets to receive the stones and hold them on the earth. At the appointed time, when the stars are in propitious alignment, if all nine are set in place, then can the coloured stones of the rainbow arc join with the four beast-stones to become the Ouroboros.'

Owen stared at him, trying to imagine such a thing. 'But why?' he asked. 'To what end? What can such a beast do?'

Deflated, Nostradamus sat. 'That we do not and cannot know, for the circumstances are not yet upon us that would require it. If man is indeed the instigator of all evil, then it may be that the only answer is to cleanse the earth of our sorry presence. I would hope that this is not so, that it is possible for so great a thing as the earth-serpent to find hope in the race of men and thereby turn the tide of devastation, but we cannot say for certain.'

The sun was all but gone. The rainbow faded to nothing. The heart-stone drew in the light of the fire and shed it blue across the table. Heartsick, Owen said, 'Then it may be that I hold the end of mankind in my hands.'

'But you may hold its saving. Do not deign to judge.'

The Queen's physician rose to close over the shutters, then used his flint and tinder to light the two tallow stubs left on the table. New light and new shadows furled about the skull-stone, dancing with the fire at its heart.

In the changed atmosphere, Nostradamus poured more wine. 'Let us review your tasks in reverse,' he said. 'When the time comes, you must hide the stone so that it cannot be found by any until the end times. Before then, your task is to recover the wisdom that your ancestors knew, and to preserve it for those who come after.'

Frustrated, Owen threw himself back in his chair. 'How? Who is left who will teach me this when all of Europe is under the thrall of the Inquisition?'

Nostradamus pulled his seat round to sit with his shoulder pressing Owen's. Heavily, his eyes black, he said, 'You will not remain in Europe. Now is the time of revealing. You, Cedric Owen, ninth of that name, are the one chosen to make the bridge between past, present and future. This stone does require your death, but it offers a life lived full and long.

'You will go to the place south of here where the Mussulman once ruled. From there, you can take ship to the New World, therein to find the oldest part of the Old World and there to meet those who understand the nature of the battle that will be fought at the end of time, and the ways in which we might survive it. It is they who know the heart and soul of your blue stone. They will tell you how best you may unlock its secrets and preserve them for all eternity. You must return at last to England, and find the place of white water and stone. Hide your secret there and ensure that those who follow may understand what they have and what they must do.'

Owen waited a long time for the life to return to the other man's eyes. He watched as the Frenchman came back into himself and viewed him.

'Good. It is done.' Nostradamus smiled. 'I have fulfilled my part of our bargain. Now, you are a physician and you will need to gain some knowledge. I have in my lodgings a monograph by Dr Giovanni da Vigo, who was surgeon to the Pope himself, and several from the Moor El Zahrawi, who is, in my belief, the best man to bring the sciences of medicine, surgery and astronomy together. Do you speak Spanish?'

'Yes. As part of my studies, I spent half a year in Cadiz, learning the ways of the Moorish physicians there.'

'Excellent. All Paris must enter mourning for the young princess. You will be unable to leave for at least a ten-day. If you will come to my lodgings at six of the clock tomorrow morning, I will give you these two books and you may read them in my company. You may ask me what you will, and at the end you will know enough to perform such surgery as might be needed. Amputations, particularly, should be your field of study.'

3
Ingleborough Hill, Yorkshire Dales

May 2007   Stella wanted to go into the cave again, but the rescue team would not let her. She had reached the car at eighteen minutes past three. By half past, when she had stripped out of her dry-suit and changed into shorts and a clean T-shirt, wet-wiped her hands and face, drunk half a bottle of water and eaten some sandwiches, she had called Kit's mobile.

By quarter to four, when there was still no answer, she had called the hotel and Bede's College in Cambridge and told all of them she could not find Kit. She had not told any about the skull, or the pearl-hunter.

At four thirty, she had called the police, who had called Cave Rescue, who had come out in force; a dozen efficient, well-equipped men and women who lived for the chance to go underground.

They left her in the charge of the young woman police sergeant who was working the radio and had been asking all the right kinds of questions. All the time, the skull-stone lay in her backpack, whispering its warning.

For the skull-stone, for its urgent insistence, and for Kit, because he had risked his life for it, she did not say why they had been in the cave or what they had found in the cavern, or that she had no idea where he had fallen or even if he had fallen at all because she was too far behind; she simply said she thought it most likely to be the pinch point, and prayed she was wrong.

Half a dozen experienced cavers offered themselves in to the dark on her behalf, for an untruth, poorly told. She smiled for them and went down to stand by the car.

'MRS O'CONNOR?' A new police officer came for her, a tall man in a flat hat with more polish to his uniform than the young WPC she had left at the cave's mouth. He strode down the hillside, alive with urgency.

'Mrs O'Connor—' Breathless, the officer bent and placed his palms on his braced knees and fought to make his straining lungs work. 'Mrs O'Connor . . . we need you to . . . come up the hill. The caving team are . . . on the radio. They think they've found—'

A car door slammed, solidly. 'Her name's Cody. Dr Stella Cody.'

'*Tony!*'

She swayed. Tony Bookless was a tall man, with an impeccably tailored suit and short silvery hair. He caught her arm and held it.

'I didn't call to ask you to come . . . It's such a long way.'

He hugged her close. 'I didn't come from Cambridge. I was in Harrogate, at the conference. The office phoned me just after you'd called them and I left as soon as I could. Tell me what you need me to do.'

Tony Bookless, forty-third Master of Bede's College, Cambridge, was old enough to be her father, solid, certain, sure, with the bearing of long-ago military heritage. He had been one of the two witnesses at her wedding. Stella gripped the hand he offered and felt human again.

'Make Kit be alive?'

'Oh, Stella . . .'

He drew her in to his chest, where the world was safe. Over her shoulder, he held out his hand and introduced himself to the officer behind her. 'Professor Sir Anthony Bookless, Master of Bede's College, Cambridge.

I am Dr O'Connor's employer. If I can be of assistance, please tell me.'

'Detective Inspector Fleming, sir. Our caving team is at the bottom of a four-hundred-foot wall and they believe they have found . . . what they were looking for.'

Four hundred feet. Gravity sucked at Stella again, the yawning blackness, the sliding slope of the ledge to an unknown drop. She looked up. Two men were looking back at her. Numbly, she said, 'What do you need me for?'

Fleming stared at his feet. 'At some point, we'll need an . . . identification, but not until they come out, which won't be for a bit yet.'

She said, 'You've found Kit? Is he all right?'

'My dear, we are rarely asked to identify the living.'

Tony Bookless had never treated her as less than an equal. While Fleming tried to think of new ways to obfuscate, Kit's mentor took Stella's shoulder and turned her away, bringing himself down so that his eyes and hers were level. In the simple, steady compassion of that act was the truth she could not face.

For the first time in her life, Stella felt reality break apart around her. From a great distance, she saw Tony Bookless's mouth open and close, like a fish under water. She heard him ask a question. 'Inspector Fleming is asking if there was someone else in the cave, someone who may have wished you harm. Can you remember?'

A part of her that could still function said, 'I was looking down on him. Perspective does strange things, but he looked big.'

'There was a man, then, you're sure of that?' Fleming asked.

'Yes, I think it was a man but I couldn't be certain. I was on the wall above the ledge. Kit took my spare light and went on ahead—he thought he could get out faster alone than with me. I climbed up the wall above the ledge to get out of the way. Whoever it was passed beneath me.'

'You climbed a cave wall in the dark, with no lights?' Tony Bookless looked at her in awe. 'Stella, that's . . . immensely dangerous.'

It was a compliment, of sorts. She flushed. 'I was desperate.'

Fleming was not so easily impressed. He came to stand over her, with his hand on the car roof. 'There must be something you can give me. We're four hours past the time of the event. Every passing hour loses us evidence.'

She stepped out from under his gaze. 'I had no light. I was holding on to rock with a ten-degree overhang. I was trying not to fall off and die.'

'We'll see if we can send in anybody to find any prints, then, aye?' Fleming turned away and spoke into his radio.

Tony Bookless sighed and said gently, 'I don't understand why someone would be chasing you in a cave. You and Kit are the last people on earth to have upset anyone that badly.'

'He wasn't after us. We found—'

She was about to shrug off her pack to show him the stone, but as the words were shaping on her tongue, the heart-stone stole them and slid in others of its own.

Glibly, she said, 'Kit had Cedric Owen's blue heart-stone in his pack. Whoever it was wanted the stone, I'm certain of that.'

'The crystal skull?' Tony Bookless's eyes were sudden windows to his soul and it ached. 'It went over the edge with him? It's lost?'

To hide her own face, she gave him another hug. 'I'm sorry. It was in Kit's pack. It won't have survived a four-hundred-foot fall onto rock.'

As ALL LIES DO, this one grew roots and became real.

With Tony Bookless and DI Fleming tracking behind, she retraced the path to the cave's exit, where Sergeant Ceri Jones bent over the shortwave radio, playing with the reception. 'They're pulling him up on a stretcher. There was water at the base of the wall . . . The medics think . . .' Kind eyes met hers. 'Don't hope too much.'

'Do they have his pack?' Tony Bookless asked. His hands were on Stella's shoulders. 'I'm sorry, but it *is* Cedric Owen's stone.'

Ceri Jones stared at him, flatly. 'They didn't say. Probably not high on their list of priorities. They'll be here in ninety minutes, give or take. You can be patient till then.'

Stella saw Bookless was discomfited. He stepped away from her and sat on a rock. 'I wish I'd known you were going for the stone. Perhaps I could have helped.'

'It was Kit's present to me, that we should do it together, alone. After Friday . . .' On Friday they had married, with Tony Bookless casting rice in handfuls over their heads.

'Ah.' His smile was brief and sad. 'Private.'

Professor Sir Anthony Bookless had made his name cowriting the definitive biography of Cedric Owen. More than anyone else, he was linked to the blue stone and all it represented. The hurt in his eyes was tangible.

Gently, Stella said, 'Kit wanted to bring the stone back to show you as a surprise. You were so clear in your reading of the legends, about the dangers that attended the stone, but he thought you'd change your mind if—'

'Stella.' Bookless edged off his rock and, holding her two hands between his own, looked up at her earnestly. 'It's not about changing my mind, it's about the integrity of scholarship. Owen's skull-stone has not been seen since his death. Sir Francis Walsingham, spymaster to Elizabeth I, searched the length and breadth of England looking for it and failed to find it, as have at least three dozen others in the time since. Could you tell me, then, what Kit found that four hundred years of scholarship failed to uncover?'

The truth was harder to tell than the lie, knowing it would rock this man's foundations. Quietly, distinctly, over the crack and hiss of Ceri Jones's radio, Stella said, 'We broke the cipher in the ledgers Owen bequeathed to Bede's. It wasn't written by Cedric Owen. Kit thinks it was written by Francis Walker after Owen's death.'

Tony Bookless frowned. 'I'm sorry?'

'The ledgers are fakes, Tony. At least the last half-dozen are.'

There was no way to say it kindly and Stella did not try. Bookless stared at her. His eyes were a pale brown, made richer by the descending sun. They searched her face now.

Patiently, she said, 'When Kit finally got his software to work, he wanted to test it on the Owen ledgers: thirty-two volumes, written by the same man over thirty-two consecutive years, with almost a fifty-fifty mix of text and numbers. He thought that if the algorithms could make sense of a medieval accountancy manuscript, they'd chew through our modern attempts at scribbling signatures in seconds.'

'I know this. He asked me for permission to enter the archives.'

Tony Bookless looked up to Ceri Jones and Fleming and explained. 'Bede's College has some of the most advanced archiving facilities in Europe. The Owen manuscripts are a set of accountancy ledgers dating back to his time in the New World. We keep them locked in a sealed archive with temperature, humidity and atmospheric controls. Kit was commissioned to write a program that would analyse and compare any handwriting by any individual at any point in their life and verify it as authentic. He only started the analysis in January of this year. He's been very quiet since. I thought—forgive me, Stella—I thought he was preoccupied with other things.'

Other things. You.

She tried to imagine Kit distracted from his life's joy, and failed.

To Tony Bookless, she said, 'No. He was preoccupied with how to tell you that Bede's entire academic basis is a sham. The ledgers were written in five years, not thirty, and by two different people. Cedric Owen wrote the first two dozen or so volumes; someone else wrote the remaining six. They tried to copy his handwriting and to the untrained eye it looks the same. But when Kit scanned it in, it blew his program out of the water. The handwriting matches a letter sent to Barnabas Tythe after Owen's death, acknowledging a christening present and signed by someone calling himself Francis Walker.'

'Why?' Bookless was standing now, pacing a swath through the bracken. 'The ledgers are the rock on which Bede's stands. Owen knew they would be, it's why he hid them from Walsingham. Why, *why*, would he do this to the college he loved?'

They had asked themselves that, Kit and Stella, in the solitude of the river room. And out of the asking had come an answer.

'To hide the skull where only someone like Kit would find it,' Stella said simply. 'There's a code in the ledgers. On the last twenty pages of the last volume, there's shorthand of the kind used by John Dee, the Elizabethan astrologer. It told us where to look for the skull-stone, in the cathedral of the earth, in the white water. We went to look for it, and we found it, and Kit had it, and if they don't bring it up with him, then it really has gone.'

Find me and live, for I am your hope at the end of time.

In the quiet afternoon, the radio hissed and popped. Ceri bent to her headphones and came away, smiling uncertainly.

'They're ten minutes from the entrance. They've asked for a helicopter. They think they have a pulse.'

THEY BROUGHT HIM OUT to her in the evening sunshine, strapped by arm and leg and head to an aluminium stretcher. His hands were folded over his chest in peaceful repose. His legs were bound straight, hiding the break that Ceri had told her was there. His eyes were shut. A graze-bruise down one side of his face leaked up to a bloody mess in his hair above his left ear.

One of the team was a medic who was cutting Kit's dry-suit and sticking on patches for an ECG. 'We think he hit his head on the side of the wall before he fell over,' he said. 'He was probably unconscious when he hit the water. His pack saved him; he had a plastic lunch box in there that held air and kept him up.'

'No stone?' Tony Bookless asked from just behind her.

The medic stared through him and said nothing. He fixed the wires to the patches and set the screen on the end of the stretcher. The green line blipped . . . and blipped . . . and blipped.

Stella stared at it, stuffing her knuckles in her mouth.

'Thought so.' The medic reached for her arm and patted it, smiling tightly. 'Your man's alive. Whether he'll regain consciousness, or when, is another question entirely. We need to get him warmed up and on oxygen.'

Behind, on the hillside, the blast of a rotor flattened the bracken. 'Can I come with you to the hospital?' she said.

'Sure.' The medic glanced past her. 'And your father, if he wants to.'

STELLA'S LIE UNRAVELLED in the hospital later that night, with only Tony Bookless to hear it.

Kit lay in a white room with a white curtain drawn about. Wires and drips rose from him like cobwebs. His face was white, except at the left temple, where a great black bruise spread down towards his jaw. He had not yet opened his eyes or spoken. The medics did not know if he ever would.

Miraculously, the right half of his face was almost untouched. If she looked at that alone, Stella could believe him to be sleeping. Tony Bookless had gone out to make a phone call, and she sat alone, holding Kit's hand. To lose love—to lose Kit—was unimaginable to her. She focused on the right half of his face and recounted for herself the full litany of shared memories, from first meeting to last parting in the cave.

When Tony Bookless came back from his phone call, he rested his hand lightly on her shoulder, and said, 'Would it help to talk?'

'I was just thinking that I'm the caver. I should never have let Kit go on ahead. He'd only been caving with me once before.'

'But you thought you were being chased and he was the better runner.' Bookless found a chair and pulled it up. 'As long as you're sure there was someone there? DI Fleming, I feel, may well write this off as an unfortunate accident with you as the paranoid hysteric.'

'There *was* somebody there, Tony. He was hunting Owen's skull-stone.'

She felt stupid saying it, here, with everything so starkly white and perfect. She stared a long time at the cardiogram. When she looked up, Bookless said, 'What did he do, this . . . hunter?'

They were edging closer to the truth. The stone still occupied a part of her mind, keeping her watchful and wary.

'He threw stones, so that we could hear them—one every thirty seconds, so that there was no chance it was random. Kit said we were being herded and that, if we separated, he could draw off the danger. He took my under-water lamp and went ahead.'

'And he fell off that ledge and took the skull-stone with him. One final

THE CRYSTAL SKULL | 465

death added to its toll of dozens.' Tony Bookless sat back, deflated. He had not been the same since she had told him the Owen ledgers were a fake. She wanted to give him something worthwhile, so ignoring the warnings of the skull-stone she offered her only gift.

'No. He fell and left the stone with me. He was only ever the decoy.'

It took all her will to say it. The stone screamed and screamed, a nail driving into the soft parts of her brain.

She put her head in her hands.

'What is it?'

'The skull. We should never have touched it. It's become part of me. It's driving me mad and there's some lunatic out there who wants this thing badly enough to kill for it.'

She reached for her bag. Tony Bookless's hand caught her arm. 'Please don't. I don't want to see it.' He smiled wanly and lines etched patterns on his face. 'This is probably the greatest artefact our college could have. It would make the truth of the ledgers a victory, not an abject failure. But all that we know, all of its history, says that everyone who has ever held it has died. No stone is worth dying for and this one carries the blood of too many people already. Get rid of it, Stella.'

'How?'

'Take it back into the cave and throw it into the water where it should have gone this afternoon. When you've done that, we'll organise for Kit to come to Addenbrooke's, where they have some of the best minds in coma medicine in the world. I'll push through the fellowship you were going to get anyway, and you'll make of your life the very best that it can be until Kit is well enough to join you, whenever that may be.'

'I can't . . .'

He gripped her hand. 'Stella, you're a caver. You can do anything you want to. Kit will still be here when you get back. I'll watch him.'

'It's not that. I can't go back to that cave tonight. I haven't got the bottle, Tony. I'm not sure I'll ever try a cave again.'

He had the good grace not to argue. 'Is there somewhere else, less . . . intimidating?'

'Gaping Ghyll maybe. It's the first wet cave I ever went down and the entrance isn't far from here. But I don't want to go in the dark.'

'I'll take you there tomorrow morning, then. And afterwards we'll head back to Cambridge.'

'Don't you have a conference to go to?'

'Some things are more important than listening to a hundred earnest professionals discuss how the government is eroding our civil liberties. Now, will you let me drive you back to your hotel? Kit's not going to wake in the next twelve hours. The consultant was quite clear on that. You'll be better able to make decisions in the morning if you've had a good night's sleep.'

It was not a time to argue. She leaned in and kissed Kit's cold, plastic cheek and let Tony Bookless drive her back to her hotel. From its place in her backpack, the skull-stone sang to her sadly, in waves of quiet blue.

4
Seville

Late August 1556 'Señor Owen, my ship is ready to sail with the dawn tide. She will take me to New Spain, where I will make my fortune. For the duration of the trip, she will be part of a small convoy which includes two warships that will keep us safe from privateers. You want me to take you with me, but then so does half of Seville. I have refused to take any man, however wellbred, unless he can prove himself of use to me. None has so far done so. Can you give me one good reason why I should take you?'

'I can give you three,' said Cedric Owen flatly, 'and you can choose for yourself which one finds the highest favour.'

Wind and tide and the gentle nudgings of the blue heart-stone had brought Owen here, to this table with this primped Spanish popinjay. Fernandez Alberto Garcia de Aguilar had an expensive taste in doublets and a quite catastrophic affectation to do with gold jewellery that dangled from the lobe of his left ear. Owen had expected to be welcomed and he was tired of the word-joust. Only his English manners held him in his seat. Behind them, the high white walls of the Moorish fortress made scimitar curves against the too-blue sky. Seville was only three centuries from her release back into Christendom and she was still proud of her battles.

Fernandez de Aguilar was certainly proud of his city's history, and of its battles, past, present and future. He was proud also of his family and his ship, possibly in equal measure, although it seemed to Owen that he was proud chiefly of himself.

The Spaniard tapped his finger to the perfect bow of his lips and said, 'Your three reasons, señor?'

'For the first, I am a physician of some worth, for the proof of which I travel with a letter of affirmation from Michel de Nostradame, physician to the Queen of France. I am prepared to minister to the sick and injured on your ship for no charge for the duration of our voyage.'

'*Our* voyage?' The Spaniard had the flawless, sun-olive skin of his race, with the blackest of black hair that fell in coiled, oiled ropes to his shoulders. Only his eyes set him apart from his countrymen: they were wide and grey-blue and just now they were brimful of affronted dignity.

'You are presumptuous,' declared Fernandez de Aguilar. 'And arrogant. The Queen of France, they say, lost both of her daughters within months of their birth, and their loss does not say much for his wife's physicians. I value my crew highly. I would not want such a man as you to tend them if they were sick, and, in any case, a ship has more need of a surgeon than a physician. I am not filled with admiration. Your second point?'

'For the second, my mother's father sailed with Admiral Sir Edward Howard, who served King Henry of England, our Queen's late father. I have from him a deep and abiding understanding of the sea.'

'So perhaps you will also try to captain my ship? I will tell you that my father's uncle, Geronimo de Aguilar, sailed with Juan de Valdivia, the bearer of His Majesty's most sacred purse. Their ship sank off the coast of New Spain and my great-uncle was one of only nineteen who survived to join the lifeboat. They were taken captive by savages and held as slaves until, eight years later, my relative escaped and became translator to the great Hernán Cortés, conquerer of the Aztecs. He wrote back to us, his family, of how barren was the landscape and how poor the people, and yet he stayed to live and die there, when he could have come home and been a hero. Do you not think that strange, Englishman? I do. So I am taking a ship to see why he chose to stay there, and to make the fortune he did not see in the green gold around him. I have as yet heard no reason why I should take you with me when I have turned down so many.'

The Spaniard reached a long, lazy arm and poured himself some more wine without offering any to Owen. In England, men had died for insults less starkly made than that, although none of them at Owen's hand: he had been the bane of his swordmaster's existence, sent packing with the advice never to risk the ignominy of a duel.

De Aguilar grinned savagely and said, 'I am not greatly taken by your first two reasons. For your third, you are not, I hope, going to suggest that I should take you on because my King has these past two years been married to the unloveliness that is your Queen Mary? All true Spanish men pity him that he must endure this marriage for the betterment of us, his people.'

Cedric Owen rose to his feet and bowed stiffly. 'Señor, I am wasting your time and mine. I apologise for interrupting your day and offending your hospitality. If you will allow me to pay for the wine . . . ?'

He had not expected that offer to be accepted. The fact that it was, and that the tavern owner charged ten times what the wine was worth, left him with a much reduced purse and a foul temper.

Some hours later, in the evening, Cedric Owen found a tavern where his imperfect Spanish was greeted with warmth, and the fish soup was rich and plentiful and did not lighten his pockets too much further. He fell to talking with an actuary who had once been an employee of the Medici bankers and the conversation meandered from the New World to the Old and back again, with detours into the many ways a man might make himself rich. None of it touched on the 'green gold' of de Aguilar's dreams, but it was interesting and stimulating nonetheless.

Owen took more wine than perhaps he should have done, but it was the first time he had relaxed in amenable company since leaving France and it was a cheerful man who left the tavern to return to his lodgings up near the Moorish walls that warm night.

'Help! Murderers! *Help!*'

The cry was in Spanish and came from his left. Without thinking, Cedric Owen ran towards it, skidding round a corner to enter a narrow, unlit alley-way between two neighbouring rows of white-limed villas.

The dark ate his shadow and turned the ground into a lightless void. He hurtled into a barrel of old fish, which upended, sending him to the ground.

'*Aaaayeeeeh—!*'

The scream started low, rose fast to a screech, and then stopped, abruptly, to be followed by the discordant rhythm of wood beaten on flesh.

Owen thrust himself to his feet. Bracing both hands against the side walls of the alley for support and direction, he hurried as fast as he could round the elbowed bend towards the sounds. A spill of light from a part-open door revealed a huddled shape on the ground and two others bent over it. A long iron blade flashed dully in the poor light.

'Stop! Stop now!'

Outnumbered, unarmed, and against all the urgings of his fencing master, Cedric Owen flung himself on the figure holding the knife.

The fight was brief and painful and the first surprising thing about it was that Cedric Owen did not die immediately. The next surprising thing was that, though he lay in the gutter with his head cracked open and that same knife poised high above him, the blade never struck home. As Owen stared out into the blue, he felt a hand grasp his shoulder and lift him to sitting.

'Well, that was intriguing, was it not, Señor Owen? I am attacked by cut-throats in my home city and the only person who comes to my cry in the whole of Seville is a drunken English doctor.'

The bruised and bloodied face of Fernandez de Aguilar grinned at Owen. With one hand, the Spaniard helped him to his feet. De Aguilar's other arm hung limp at his side, with the hand turned out at an unnatural angle.

Through swollen lips, Owen said, 'Your arm needs to be set.'

'It does indeed. Is that within the purview of a physician?'

'I can do it, yes.'

The Spaniard was in high spirits, such as men are who have fought against heavy odds and won, but his eyes were steady and the soul behind them was not the self-opinionated popinjay that Owen had met that afternoon.

'If you would care to assist with its setting, then perhaps afterwards we could review our conversation of this afternoon? We sail in two weeks' time. It is my turn, I believe, to buy the wine.'

ITS POSITION FIGURED by the night method, the Part of Fortune crossed from the Goat to the Water Carrier and lay in wide squares to both Venus and Saturn, which lay in mutual ill-omened opposition.

Accordingly, a steady drizzle smeared the sky into the sea and the fish were not biting. Cedric Owen was sitting with his feet over *Aurora*'s stern, holding a useless fishing line in his hand, feeling seasick and sorry for himself. He was not, however, feeling sick enough to keep to his cabin as he had for the first ten days of the voyage.

Fernandez de Aguilar, as ship's captain, had shown no sign of illness at any point, nor did he now, as he leaned both elbows on the stern rail and looked out along the long, silvered tail of the ship's wake, showing off his perfect profile. He was, Owen decided, more Latin than Spanish, a youth-ful, vigorous Trajan, lacking only the beard to cement his authority. His caustic grey-blue eyes were thickly lashed, like a girl's, and even soaked to the skin, he managed to look regal.

De Aguilar said, 'Now that you're well enough, you should go barefoot. It makes moving on deck far easier.'

The comment was so unexpected that it took a moment before Owen realised it had been addressed to him. Stiffly, he said, 'You do not.'

'Hose and boots are the penance of the captain and his mate, but not those unbound by the restrictions of rank. If you abandon your shoes and your jacket and change your shirt once in a while, the men will still think you dress a world above them. Thus you will not lose your dignity.'

'I see.'

They fell back into an awkward silence.

De Aguilar stared thoughtfully at the sea and the three boats of the convoy that sailed just far enough back to be visible. The rain was almost gone and the cloud was lifting. The sun leaked through patchily, sending intermittent shadows aft along the ship's length. Finally he said, 'When we spoke of your coming on the voyage, we never considered your family and how it might affect them. Have you a wife who is mourning your absence?'

'I have no wife.'

'For one so talented? I find that hard to believe. A lover, then?'

That was very much too close to the bone. Owen flushed rarely, but when he did it was spectacular, such as now, when hot blood breached the wall of his neck and flooded his face.

Stiffly, he said, 'I have no lover, nor any desire for one. At some point, I may hope to have a wife, but in the meantime, I remain content. It may not be fashionable in these days but I have no wish to make the demands of intimacy upon any woman without the benefit to her of marriage. If you find that risible, I would ask you to keep your humour private.'

Peaceably, de Aguilar said, 'I apologise for offending you. You are that rare thing, a nobleman in the true sense of the word. I had thought it, but was not certain.' So saying, he nodded amiably and left.

The next day, Owen abandoned his hose and stout shoes and went barefoot. Nobody commented, but he found by noon that he could walk more easily, and by dusk that he could stroll as he might have done along the banks of the Cam.

CEDRIC OWEN SPLIT his lip open on the heaving deck and tasted hot salt in all the cold salt of the sea. The slop bucket broke free of its moorings and the stench of a night's shit and piss slewed around the cabin before the storm smashed over the bulkheads and everything was wet and cold and smelt of seaweed and harsh, unforgiving air.

He woke, gasping, and brought his hand to his mouth. There was no blood and no pain. *Aurora* swayed on the benign seas as gently as she had when he had first fallen asleep. The blue heart-stone that shared his bunk rolled a little with the tilt of the waves and came to rest against his ribs, a warm thing in a warm night. He felt its presence as a sleeping lover, but that it was not asleep, and it had a message for him that broke the night apart with its urgency.

Owen was already upright, fumbling for buttons in the dark, tucking in shirt tails so that he might present himself as a gentleman. Grimacing, he stepped out into a wide, black night, lit by a dish-faced moon that flooded light across the flat sea.

Behind them sailed three other merchant ships of a similar size to *Aurora*, and far out on the port bow was a naval warship laden with cannon, set there to ward off privateers by her presence alone, even though it was well known that the privateers set their targets on the rich ships returning from New Spain, not those going out.

From the start, Owen had seen the warships as an insurance, not a necessity. With the perspective of the blue stone, he saw them newly as a burden to be shed, though he was not certain why or how.

'Sir?'

Owen knocked on the captain's door. 'Don Fernandez, are you there?'

'Señor Owen? Wait—I will come out.'

The astonishing thing—one of the several astonishing things—about Fernandez de Aguilar was the speed with which he could don his outrageous doublets. Even as he thought it, the captain emerged decently sober in midnight blue with only a small prince's ransom in his ear.

'A beautiful night.' De Aguilar braced a hand on the starboard rail and studied the Englishman. 'May I ask what it is that has brought you out in it so late, and me with you?'

'There's going to be a storm.' It sounded lame, there, under the flawless stars. 'Bigger than anything we've seen already. It will break the convoy apart, possibly sink us. We need to . . .'

Owen struggled for words. His Spanish was much improved, but he would have hesitated now in any language.

'Things need to be done but I don't know what they are. Only that you must do them so that we come through alive and so that, at the end of it, we are no longer part of the convoy.'

'Not part of . . . ? I don't understand.'

At least de Aguilar was listening to him, not sending him to his cabin with a draught of laudanum to keep the night-fears at bay.

Owen said, 'We must not cling to the other boats. If we can steer clear of them we have a chance. We *must* make our way to New Spain alone, without those who might hamper us, or alter our judgment.'

'So? I said once you might try to captain my ship. I did not believe you would do it in truth.' De Aguilar spoke thoughtfully, without the sharp pride of which he was capable. 'Will you tell me how you know this?'

It was Owen's turn to stare at the sea. The lie came less easily than he would have liked and left a bad taste on his tongue.

'As I told you once, my grandfather sailed with Sir Edward Howard. He spoke to me as a child of the peculiar smell the sea makes when a storm is coming—like iron that is made white hot then plunged into water. I have smelt that now, coming from the port bow. The storm will come from that direction. As to the rest, I thought to compare your natal chart with that of the present moment, setting our location here on the ocean, as best we can. I should have seen this far sooner and deeply regret that I did not.'

This part, at least, was true. More confidently, Owen said, 'The Part of Fortune for this night lies conjunct now to Saturn and is in quintile aspect to your Part of Fortune, which lies in wide conjunction to your moon. If these two sat in opposition, I believe we would see such a catastrophe as to die. Because they lie quintile one to the other, we may prevail.'

De Aguilar stared out over the starboard bow. The sea rocked them a long time before he spoke again.

'Perhaps one day you will honour me by sharing the truth. For now, we will believe there is a storm coming and wake the men and tie down the rigging and alert the other boats so that they may do the same. Afterwards, if it proves not to be true, I will call the crews of all six ships together so you can tell them the story of your grandfather, and I will let them cast you overboard if they do not like your tale.' He grinned as he spoke. There was room to believe that he might have been in jest.

With nothing at all he could do, Cedric Owen retired to his cabin and listened as the crew set to work on making *Aurora* bend to the captain's bidding. The blue heart-stone lay under the blankets on his bunk. He felt a fresh alertness in its waiting, such as he might have felt from a hound at the start of a night's coney-catching, knowing that it sensed beasts he would never see until they were retrieved to his hand, soft, warm and quite dead.

Owen turned on his side and stared at the moonlight that came through the cracks in the doorway. Quite soon after that, the wind began to thrum faster on the rigging.

5
Ingleborough Fell, Yorkshire Dales

May 2007   Stella was alone with the sheep and the skull-stone on the slopes of Ingleborough Fell. The night was cool, but not cold. Threads of cloud drew fine lines between the stars. High up, Fell Beck poured its black water into the blacker hole that was Gaping Ghyll. The stone was light in her backpack. She was beginning to understand the different feel of it. Here, now, neither she nor it were in danger.

The low path by the stream gave way to a left-handed climb. As she trod lightly through the bracken Tony Bookless's words sounded over and again in her ear. *No stone is worth dying for . . . Get rid of it, Stella.*

She had gone to sleep hearing him and woken to his voice in the black heart of the night. The skull had made no protest as she rose and dressed and drove out along the unlit lanes to the car park in the village at the foot of the train.

She walked up now, feeling the night air tight on her skin. Here, in the high place above the village, the air smelt of night-dew and bracken. Sheep stepped sleepily out of her path as she took the last steep rise and then walked over the elbow to the flatter landscape beyond. In a world of greys and deep, sucking blacks, she sat on a slope of grassy earth, well back from the lip of the pothole. Ahead, the waterfall threw spray up into the starlight. She took the skull-stone from her pack and held it in her hands for the first time since she had sat shivering in the cathedral of the earth with its first blue flash still searing her brain. It was quieter now, and in this light, shadowed and white, it looked enough like Kit's bruised, broken face for her truly to hate it and the destruction it had wrought. Tony Bookless's voice whispered in the rush of the water. *Get rid of it . . .*

And yet . . . It was hard to surrender the passion with which she had first held the stone. Even underwater, cold and close to drowning, the sense of homecoming, of welcome, of a pact long made, which she had forgotten and was only now remembering, had been overwhelming.

Get rid of it!

She balanced the weight of the skull-stone in her hands and raised them for the throw. The shard of blue lightning in her mind was so far away, so old and worn, so nearly spent of all its reserves.

Stella lowered her arms. With unexpected care, she cradled the stone to her, feeling its rough chalky coating through the thinness of her T-shirt. Her heart beat for it, as it had only ever beaten for Kit. Suddenly she yearned to protect this lump of mucky limestone. Aloud, she said, 'We should clean you up, make you whole again.' Still holding it close, Stella stood up and looked around. Dawn was near. The sheep were waking. Gaping Ghyll yawned more blackly and Fell Beck dropped as fast. They waited, these two, with the same ancient intelligence as the stone she held. Instinct said they must be fed.

She set the stone in her backpack, swaddled in a towel, and set to looking for a stone the same size and shape. She found what she needed beyond the wire fence and brought it back. With the rising sun behind her casting a shadow across the water, Stella bowled the new-found stone into the centre of the gap. Some time later, she heard the shatter of breaking rock.

'Well done,' said Tony Bookless from behind her. 'I wasn't sure you'd be able to do it.'

She stood still. He completed his ascent of the fell. His shadow welded to hers so that their twinned heads fell over the pothole.

She said, 'I dreamt of Kit. It seemed as if the stone . . . that it needed to come here.' In a corner of her mind, the thing that had become a part of her held its breath, waiting.

He said, 'I heard you get up. When you didn't come back, I thought you might need help.'

'Thank you.' She was back in the lie again, and this time the stone had not made her do it. She had no regrets.

Bookless lifted his phone. 'I just had a call from the hospital. Kit has regained consciousness. He's asking for you.'

6

Aurora sailing in the Caribbean Sea

September/October 1556 The sea lay calm on all sides. For the first time in the week since the storm, *Aurora* dared full rigging and ran ahead of the wind. The air was alive with the hiss of the waves on the bow and the flagging of sails on the three masts, and somewhere in the distance the long, forlorn cry of a seabird.

Cedric Owen rose before dawn and came to stand with his back to the foremast. As the blue heart-stone had warned, *Aurora* had become separated from the rest of the convoy in the chaos of wind and rain that had ripped at least one of the other boats apart. Against all sanity, de Aguilar had spent two days in savage, spiralling wind, sailing in circles, searching for a sign of flag or sail or, more frantically, for living men among the wreckage that danced on the waves.

Finding no one, they had reluctantly set a westerly course again, not knowing if the other ships were searching for them in like manner or had fallen to the wrath of the storm. In the beginning, Owen had found the sense of isolation unnerving, but the quiet assurance of de Aguilar's captaincy had changed that and now he never wanted it to end.

Only the blue heart-stone wanted more. Its urgings had woken him before dawn, bringing him out to this place at the masthead where he could look out across the black void of sea and sky, to the place on the undefined horizon where they merged. Ahead and a little off the port bow, an orange light flickered occasionally in a way that mimicked fire.

He was watching that, and wondering as to its nature, when the blackness broke apart, letting the first knife-edge of sun streak out across the water. Displayed for his admiration alone was the priceless moment when the sea abandoned the inky mystery of the night and opened to the blinding blue and gold of the dawn. It was heart-stopping in its beauty.

'It is worth it all, just for this, is it not?'

Owen found he was not entirely unhappy to have shared the moment with his captain. He said, 'If I were to die now, having seen this, I would not feel my life ended too soon.'

De Aguilar clucked his teeth lightly in reprimand. 'You should be careful what you say. An invitation to death is not a thing to give lightly. We will make land by nightfall, did you know?'

'I thought as much. Do you know where we are headed, now that the storm has sent us so far from our original course?'

'I would be a poor captain if I did not know where I had brought my ship,' the Spaniard said. 'We were due to berth north of here, in Campeche. However, as we have not food and water left to reach there, we are headed instead for the city the natives call Zama, which means "dawn", and I suspect we have just seen the reason why. At night, those who live there keep the coasts safe by warning ships of the rocks. If you look across the port bow, you will see the fire they keep burning in the tower that looks over the sea.'

'It is a fire, then? I had wondered. I had not imagined the savages to understand the concept of a lighthouse.'

'They understand a lot more than you might imagine. They keep the coasts safe by an effort of engineering that would leave our architects weeping with envy. The lighthouse whose fires you see is not a rude column such as mars the coastlines of England and Spain, but a square-sided pyramid, of a size and grace that would match any of our cathedrals. The carvings and murals are of a complexity to outdo Egypt, and their writing is as opaque to our understanding as the paintings on the walls of the pyramids. The beauty of it is that these people are alive and may teach us what their carvings mean, when all of Egypt's antiquity is beyond our ken.'

'And will they teach us? Or do they offer war, as they did to Hernán Cortés?'

De Aguilar turned to look at his companion for a moment, before returning his gaze to the horizon. 'I hope they will not offer war, but have no certainty. I would like to believe that being bathed in the light of a sunrise such as this on every day of one's life predisposes a man to reflection and farming, rather than war, but I may be wrong.'

Owen closed his eyes and tilted his face to the sun. He said, 'However they guard their coasts, I think the natives are not our only danger.'

'No. If my information is correct, there is a priest in Zama who is second only to the bishop of Yucatán in his desire to bring the Inquisition to New Spain. In his letters home, this Jesuit writes that he seeks to bring heathen souls to God and so save them from an eternity of burning. To do that, he will inflict on as many of them as is necessary the more temporal burning of death at the stake.'

There was a pause. Owen heard a rustle of cloth as de Aguilar turned to face him fully. Then came the quiet, eloquent voice: 'You should be careful, my friend. Many of those who have died have not had such a thing as a skull of pure crystal to carry with them into the executioner's fires.'

There had been no warning. Owen opened his eyes and stared up at the impossible blue of the sky.

'How long have you known?' he asked.

'Nearly a week. If you remember, there was a night of calm before the second, worse part of the typhoon. I excused myself then from dinner. I do not expect your forgiveness, but you must know that I could not risk taking my ship and its men on an unplanned, poorly charted leg of the voyage without knowing for whom, or for what, I was doing it.'

'And so you went to my cabin and sought out the stone?'

'It was lying in the open, waiting to be found. I did not touch it.'

Owen turned to the Spaniard. 'Every man I have met, with the exception of Nostradamus, has either feared that stone or desired to possess it. Has the skull lost its power to command the minds of men?'

The slapping of waves on the hull was the only sound. Presently, de Aguilar said, 'If I had a wife of exceptional beauty and wisdom, such that you saw in her everything you had ever desired in a woman, would you wish to take her from me?'

'I would take nothing from you, especially not a heart, freely given.'

'So, then, why would I not feel as you do? The stone is clearly yours in all ways. I choose not to desire it.'

Owen said, 'Your integrity shames me. You are captain of this ship and I owe you my life. More than that, I have seen how you treat your men and respect you. I would not have kept the knowledge from you, but—'

'But it is hard to know whom to trust, I know. And perhaps you would not wish so to burden a friend?'

Owen had not thought of Fernandez de Aguilar as a friend, nor imagined he might be considered so in return. Spoken aloud now, after all that had just passed, he saw the truth of their friendship.

'I have lived my life under the weight of the stone's existence. I love it and all that it brings, but I would not inflict that burden lightly on another, particularly not on a man I admire. And yet . . . That night, when I came to dinner, I did not leave it in the open—it was well hidden.'

'The stone let me see it?'

'It would seem so.'

The two men fell silent for a while, then de Aguilar reached into his shirt and brought from a hidden pocket something of gold.

'By all accounts the priest at Zama, Father Gonzalez Calderón, is a fanatic who revels in the pain of others and I believe we should tread very carefully in his presence. At the least, we should appear to be men of God. If it does not offend you greatly, perhaps you could accept this?' A small gold crucifix of quite exceptional workmanship dangled from his fingers. 'It was my mother's,' said Fernandez de Aguilar simply.

The sun caught the cross as it turned slowly in the breeze. Cedric Owen reached for the crucifix and the blue stone, which had recoiled from every other artefact of religion, did not flinch.

'Thank you,' Owen said. 'I would be most honoured.'

ON CALM WATER that sparkled under a noon sun, *Aurora* slid slowly into the small natural harbour at Zama in New Spain.

High white limestone bluffs stood as sentinels of purity, drawing them in to a city of startling blood-red stone, walled on three sides and faced on the fourth by the vast, red, pyramidal tower that was its lighthouse.

When the captain finally brought his ship to a place where he could safely anchor, he set down the small-boat for himself and his favoured companions to make first landfall.

Their arrival was not unannounced. For the last hours, since they had been able to see the harbour, they had seen also the growing crowd of natives awaiting them, dressed in colours bright as birds and with a quantity of green feathers set about their headdresses. At least a dozen in the foremost rows held guns; the rest bore spears or wooden clubs made black at the edges.

'They call them *maquahuitls*,' said de Aguilar quietly. He stood at Owen's side in the bow of the small-boat with a coiled rope in his hand, ready to leap ashore. Behind him, six men rowed in trained synchrony. 'My great-uncle described them as the greatest hand-held weapon he had ever seen in action. They're made of hardwood with blades of obsidian set along the edges. The warriors of the Maya wield them two-handed, which gives more force to the strike.'

'The natives do not look to me welcoming, however bright their clothing or their feathers,' Owen observed.

De Aguilar nodded peacefully. 'Then we will die swiftly, having seen that blazing dawn. I would prefer it to a European death of torture and fire. What does your blue stone say?'

'That it is nearing home and cannot reach land soon enough,' said Owen. 'It says nothing of how welcome we may be when we take it there.'

THE BLACK-ROBED PRIEST stood at the end of the jetty and deftly caught the rope that de Aguilar threw to him. Two native men stood a pace behind. Alone among their brethren, their trousers and smocks were of plain, uncoloured cloth and they bore no weapons.

The priest leaned back on the rope and made it taut. There was a moment's drifting impact and then Fernandez de Aguilar jumped lightly to the wooden planks and swept the lowest, most courtly bow Cedric Owen had ever seen performed by any man.

'I present myself, sir, Fernandez de Aguilar, a ship's captain of little worth, but I bring with me Señor Cedric Owen, our ship's physician and astrologer. He comes with a recommendation from Catherine de' Medici, the Queen of France herself. I commend him to you and your friends. You, of course, are Father Gonzalez Calderón, priest of the mother church in Zama, New Spain. May we set down a plank so that the good doctor can come to land?'

'No.'

The priest was an ox of a man, broad of back and girth and all of it sinew and muscle. His neck was thickly corded with a layering of chins. Across the broad, black sweep of his chest lay the largest and heaviest crucifix Cedric Owen had ever seen.

His single word held all the harbour still and silent. Watched now by every man on boat and land, the priest threw the rope at Owen's feet.

Raising his voice to be heard, he said, 'We have had smallpox here. It has passed now, but before it did so, God took to Himself over half the men, women and children of our city. Can your esteemed physician swear to me in the name of God that you carry no such disease?'

The sudden scream in Owen's mind's ear was of a different pitch from any he had ever heard. In an effort to escape it, he lifted his gaze beyond the black-garbed priest and onto the two native men who stood behind and stopped, because thought had become impossible.

The two men behind the priest were dressed in trousers and smocks of unbleached cotton. The one on the left fingered a wooden cross at his chest and stared without interest at *Aurora*. The one on the right had a broad zigzag scar coursing down his left cheek and was staring directly at Cedric Owen—and straight through him into the blue of the heart-stone. When the man turned his gaze away, the scream in Owen's ear fell almost to nothing. He was able to hear things in the outer world again, chief among which was the priest saying, 'Señor Owen? You are a physician as well as a caster of charts. Can you swear before God that your ship brings us no disease?'

'No,' Cedric Owen replied at length. 'I can promise nothing and would certainly not swear so in the name of God. I can say that I have been at sea with these men for two months and that there has been nothing beyond the usual intestinal instability and a single case of a torn shoulder when a man held too long to a lanyard. I can say that we stopped in Panama to take on more food and water, but it is my belief that if there were any disease on board we would have fallen ill by now. In view of that, I will swear in any way you like that I have seen nothing to indicate illness, but no more than that. If you wish us to put back to sea, with our hold full of guns and powder, lead and steel, then you may do so. I am sure that the followers of King Philip at Campeche will welcome us.'

He had planned none of that. The words fell out of his mouth and he heard them with as much surprise as the others.

The priest inclined his head as if in prayer, then said, 'Well argued, Englishman. If you had sworn by God that your men were clean, I would have had you shot and your ship burnt in the open sea.'

'And all in vain,' Owen said. 'You have been close enough to Don Fernandez to be a source of infection if he did indeed harbour disease. You would have spread plague wherever you walked.'

'Except that I would not have walked among them at all. My clerk here, Diego'—the wave of his hand indicated the scar-faced native—'has orders to cut my throat and then his own. Domingo'—a lifted finger indicated the quieter of the two clerks—'would have walked into the sea, this being his choice of death. With us gone, the second rank of warriors would set the fire arrows to your ship. No child willingly shoots his father, but they would kill me on my command; this much I believe in them.'

Owen saw Fernandez de Aguilar sharpen. 'These people see you as their father?' he asked.

Gonzalez Calderón's face was unreadable. 'I see myself as their father under God,' he said. 'I believe that if I tell them that you come bearing gifts and knowledge, they will allow you to land your ship. What happens thereafter is in God's hands. I cannot guarantee your safety any more than your physician can guarantee the clean health of your men.'

7

Bede's College, Cambridge

June 2007 A stem of white lilies left over from the wedding decorated the low ash-wood table in Kit's river room. By a feat of Tudor engineering, over half the room's length projected out over the Cam. Windows on three sides let in the strong summer sun and the river ran greenly beneath. Kit stood swaying by the table, taking in the sky and the thin strips of cloud.

Stella watched as he came back to himself; to the memory of what he had been, and what he had become. His turbulent eyes met hers, full of new passions she could not read. 'I remembered the lilies,' he said.

'Kit . . .' She could not move. From the moment she had visited him on the ward, he had been cold and withdrawn. Now she saw him gather himself to deliver something prepared that she did not want to hear.

His face was a harlequin's: greenly bruised on the one, still side, and alive, mobile and white on the other. With that half alone, he made himself smile. 'You should leave me. Now, while the memories are all good ones.'

'Don't . . .' She was weeping, which she had promised herself not to do. 'You don't mean it. You married me less than a month ago. I married you. It's not time to give up.'

He frowned and shook his head. His hands were unsteady on the walking sticks. She wanted to step forward and catch him, to find him a chair, to reach for the electric wheelchair and make it ready for him.

He lifted his one good shoulder in a shrug. 'I don't want to be with you as less than I was.'

'Kit . . .' She wiped her face with the heel of her hand and struggled in the pocket of her shorts for a tissue.

He was not what he had been, that much was indisputable. Even so, he was not as bad as the medics had predicted at first. That he was able to walk at all was testament to the skill of the neurology team at Addenbrooke's.

What they were not able to do was perform further miracles and give him back to her fully mended, so they had sent him home half done, a man prone to falling asleep without warning, who could only smile with half his face, who could not move his left leg fully, who had only partial use of his left arm. They sent him with sticks and a wheelchair and a regime of exercises from the physiotherapist. They thought, with time, he might be able to dispense with one of the sticks, but they could not say whether he would walk normally, or run, or if the full quirk of his smile would come back.

They could not say, either, whether he would ever recover his memory of the cathedral of the earth, of the white limestone skull they had found, of the crawl along the ledge and the fall that came after it, with enough clarity to be able to persuade DI Fleming to reopen the case as attempted murder.

Quietly, he said, 'You know I'm right.'

'No.'

Desperate, she reached into her backpack and drew out the crumbling white stone that had been Kit's life quest and set it on the table. She felt nothing from it now, no sense of the vulnerability that had so moved her by Gaping Ghyll. For three weeks, she had not been able to look at it.

She said, 'I didn't throw it away.'

'Clearly.' His face had become quite still; this once, it was symmetrical. 'Perhaps I should sit down?' He swayed on his sticks and cursed, then shuffled round to his wheelchair.

She wanted him to be glad of her help, but he tolerated it with bad grace, letting her bring him to the chair and settle him as the hospital had taught her. For too long, he stared at the skull in cold silence.

'If you hate it that much, we can throw it in the river now.'

He frowned. 'Would that keep us safe?'

'Is that what this is about? Safety? It feels deeper than that.'

His face twisted. 'Someone tried to kill me for this, Stell. How much deeper do you need?'

'So throw it away.'

'You told me you'd already done that.'

They had never fought before. This sharp, edgy friction was new and unexpected and terrifying.

'Tony Bookless told me to,' she said. 'I tried. I couldn't do it.'

'But you let him believe you had. And me.'

'I thought you'd be pleased. I was saving it as a surprise for you.'

'Tony didn't believe you'd thrown it away. He thinks you're in love with it. It does that to people, apparently. It's why they die.'

The sound of his voice stopped her more than what he said—a soft throatiness she had never heard before. She turned. His eyes were rimmed red.

'Are you crying?'

'I'm trying not to.'

'Oh, Kit . . .' She had to lift him out of the chair to hold him properly. In that long, wordless moment was more connection than they had managed in all the weeks since the accident.

'When did Tony tell you?' she asked.

'Last night. He came back again after you'd left.' His hand teased out her hair. He said, 'I promised him I'd get you to destroy it. I've lost so much chasing after a pipe dream, Stell. I don't want to lose you too. I couldn't bear that.'

She lifted her head away from his chest. 'Why would you lose me?'

'Because Cedric Owen didn't write his verse for its poetry alone, he wrote it as a guide and a warning.' He closed his eyes and spoke from memory. '*Find me and live, for I am your hope at the end of time. Hold me as you would hold your child. Listen to me as you would listen to your lover. Trust me as you would trust your god, whosoever that may be.*' He opened his eyes again. 'Stell, everyone who has ever cared for that stone has died because of it. I would have done if there hadn't been water in the cave. You're in even more danger. You're in love with it.'

Bringing her closer, he ran the tip of his finger over the arch of her ear, in a way that sparked down the length of her spine. For three weeks she would have given anything to feel that. Now, she caught his wrist and held it.

'Kit, listen to me. It's not the stone that kills people. It's people who kill to get hold of it, or to destroy it. In the cave, the pearl-hunter wanted to destroy the stone, not you. I really believe that.' She sighed. 'Not that the police believe us. They think what happened to you was an accident.'

Kit laughed unevenly. 'So whoever did this is still out there. He knows exactly who we are and we haven't the first clue who he is.' Clumsily, he turned Stella round, so they were both looking out of the window, and hugged her in to his chest. There was a long moment's wait, time to feel the warmth of the one thing he said that she could hold on to. *I don't want to lose you . . . I couldn't bear that.*

'Stell, I made this happen,' Kit said at last. 'It was my pipe dream, my idea for a wedding present. If you want to go on with it, you can take responsibility from here on in, but this far, it's mine. Deal?'

'Deal.' Then, with ice gnawing her stomach, Stella said, 'If you stay here and I go away to find what the skull's about, it doesn't mean I don't love you, or you're losing me. You do know that, don't you?'

'I do. And you need to know that if I come with you, it doesn't mean I'm jealous of a stone.' A spark of laughter grated in his voice. He kissed the top of her head. 'You are a very brave woman. I do love you, did I mention?'

'Not since the cave.'

Her cheek was against his chest. She raised her head and slowly, not quite accurately, he bent to kiss her.

THE NEED FOR SLEEP caught him soon afterwards and he lay back in his wheelchair, his face childlike in its peace. Stella sat cross-legged on the bare oak floor and looked at the skull-stone on the table. Then she propped her elbows on her knees and brought her eyes level with the skull's.

'Before his death, Cedric Owen hid you in a place where time and hard water could have kept you secret for ever. But someone wanted us to find you so badly that they usurped Owen's manuscripts to plant their own code. *That which you seek lies hidden in white water.* Why did they do that?'

Why?

Kit had asked it first, when he had analysed the ledgers and found them written by two different hands.

Why? Everything we know about Cedric Owen says he was a decent, honourable man. He planned everything else so carefully; he hid his money and the ledgers, and left a letter with a lawyer, to be opened a century after his death so there was no way the Crown could confiscate his estate. Once it was safe for them to be found and brought to the college, he left orders that the ledgers be kept available to the public. He knew how much they would enhance the college's status. If they're fakes, there has to be a reason.

It had been raining that day with a dense mist lying over the Cam. The river room balanced on the shelf of it, a place of grey-green light and the hypnotic drumming of water on water.

Without undue thought, Stella had said, 'There must be something else hidden in the text. You're the cryptographer. Why not crunch the numbers and see what comes out?'

He had loped across the room and kissed her on the forehead. 'You're a genius, did I mention?'

In the weeks that followed, Stella studied the difficult looping manuscript until she began to dream of cramped, crabbed Elizabethan handwriting every time she closed her eyes. Then, while looking at the last ledger, she realised that the smears and errors, which had always been thought to be the result of writing on board ship, were actually the deliberate masking of a known shorthand. It had taken her less than two hours to transcribe it and half of that was spent in the library finding notes that led her to the contemporary translations of John Dee's shorthand.

That which you seek lies hidden in white water . . .

Stella had found the text, but Kit was the one who had understood that it directed them to Cedric Owen's heart-stone; Kit who had cared enough to plan the trip and make it happen. But it was Stella who had come to care for the ugly mass of white lime. She stared at it emptily. 'What am I missing?'

She walked over to the far corner of the room, to where Kit kept his files. She pulled out a box file containing printed copies of the first three ledgers, a pad and a pen, and took it all back to the table in the window.

'HELLO? ANYONE AT HOME?'

The sun was leaning far to the west, sending amber light to glance off the river. Stella sat cross-legged in the late afternoon's quiet light chewing a pen and making notes on her A4 pad.

'Am I not welcome?' A stocky figure stepped in through the doorway.

'Gordon! Of course you're welcome. Come on in . . .'

Professor Gordon Fraser, BSc, MSc, CGeol, FRS, was a sedimentary geologist and caver of international renown; he was also one of Stella's closest friends in Cambridge, and the second witness at her wedding. A short, wide man, he bore a carroty beard and a head of wild curls that would have been the envy of any woman. He stood awkwardly on the threshold now, holding a bunch of freesias. The skull-stone was not in his line of sight. Stella slid her pack over it before she stood.

'I'm sorry, I was lost in the ledgers. Let me make you coffee and then we'll wake up Kit. He'd be sorry to miss you.'

From his wheelchair by the window, Kit said, 'Kit's awake.'

He spoke in the lazy slur that made it impossible to know if he were still half asleep or had been awake for the past three hours. A whine of batteried wheels turned the chair. He shrugged his better shoulder.

'I'm sorry. I should have said something sooner. It was good to watch you work.' He answered the look on her face, then continued lightly, 'I need to pee. If you make coffee, I might be done by the time it's ready and then you can show the two of us what you've made of Cedric Owen's ledgers.'

While he was gone, Stella went to the galley kitchen in the corner of the room and set Gordon to grind the beans while she boiled some milk in a pan. Kit's wheelchair whined back from the bathroom as she carried a tray of coffee mugs to the table.

'I watched you in the window all the way across Jesus Green.' Gordon wrapped his fingers round the mug Stella gave him. 'You were lost in something that looked as if it must be important. What have you found, lass?'

Stella swirled her coffee and said, 'I found the second cipher in the ledgers. The one "that is herein shewn".'

Kit, smiling broadly with the half of his mouth that could manage it, said, 'You clever, clever girl. I thought it was a lot of work for two men just to leave us a page of poorly cadenced poetry. What does it tell us?'

'I don't know. It's a hieroglyph. I've spent half the afternoon on the web trying to find out what it is. Look—'

She made a stack of her notes and set them on the table.

'It's like the shorthand: each page has half a dozen marks that look like random slips of the pen, except these ones are better hidden. See here near the bottom of the page . . .' She picked up a volume at random and ran her finger under a line. '*August 21, 1573, To Imagio, son of Diego,*

For: 2 brayce hunted fowl: 2d. If you look closely under the figure three of the year, and again in the "s" of son and the "y" of brayce, there are curls and lines. If I copy these across the page . . .' She laid a sheet of thin tracing paper on top and copied them to it. 'And then repeat again for the next line . . . *August 22, 1573, To Father Calderón, For: rent for 2 persons, viz, myselfe & don Fernandez.*' As she spoke, Stella picked out marks and copied them. 'That finishes this page. It's not very coherent yet.'

'It's gibberish.' Kit picked up the sheet, frowning.

Stella took the page back and picked up three others. 'It's a composite. If we fit the pages together in groups of four, and match these dots down in the bottom left-hand corners . . .'

Four pages of tracing paper came together to make an array of strange curling glyphs, of half-seen goggle-eyed men and animals, of gaping mouths and suns and trees and moons and coiled snakes and jaguars.

Stella said, 'I think they're old Mayan glyphs. Cedric Owen was in the Mayan lands for thirty-two years of his life, so I'd bet on that.'

'Can you read them?' Gordon asked.

'Not a chance. We need someone who's already steeped in this stuff.'

'Of which I imagine there are very few.' Kit was looking at her in the way she remembered. 'But you've found someone who knows all about it?'

She grinned. 'Maybe. I googled "Cedric Owen" and "skull" and "Mayan" and all the links seemed to lead to Professor Ursula Walker of the Institute of Mayan Studies, part of Oxford University. This woman's amazing; the institute is based at her home, which is a Tudor farmhouse in Oxfordshire and also happens to be the place where the Owen ledgers were found. So you could say she has something of a family interest. She got a first in anthropology—'

'From Bede's?' Kit said.

'Yes, and then she spent four postgraduate years writing a biography of Cedric Owen—with Tony Bookless.'

Gordon smacked his hand on his head. 'I thought I'd heard the name.'

'Exactly. But after they got their PhDs, he joined the army and became a military historian, and she became a field anthropologist. I sent her an email and we have an invitation to go and visit her tomorrow afternoon.'

We. Stella was watching Kit as she spoke, trying to read him. He saw her looking and smiled unevenly. With great care, he reached across to the table and snapped a single bloom off the stem of white lilies. She sat very still as he manoeuvred his chair round and slid the flower in behind her ear. With his hand on her shoulder, he said, '*Follow the path that is herein shewn and be with me at the time and place appointed.* We've got this far. Do we want to be at the time and place appointed?'

She wanted to cheer out loud. She said, 'We have to find them first. That's why we're going to Ursula Walker's.'

'Knowing somebody else will be dogging our every step?'

'We have to be careful; we know that. And the stone will warn us if there's real danger. We have to believe that.'

She had not mentioned the stone in company before. Kit looked at her, surprised. 'So . . . can we show Gordon what we've got?'

'I don't see why not.' Experimentally, Stella said, 'Gordon, we have something to show you.'

There passed a short silence, in which Stella braced herself against the protests of the skull-stone—which did not come. Gordon sat on the floor opposite her and she held it for him, as she might have held a newborn child. He sat and looked at it with quiet awe. 'My . . . that's a bonny thing.'

'Can you clean it?' Stella asked. 'Can you do something to remove the limescale and take it back to what it was?'

Gordon flicked a glance from under his caterpillar brows. 'We can give it a shot. It would be a very lovely thing to see.' He looked at his watch and at them both, then just at Stella. 'You and I could go over to the lab now, maybe, while everyone's out?'

THE GEOLOGY DEPARTMENT early on a summer evening was a quiet place. Stella followed Gordon down three flights of stairs into air-conditioned dryness that smelt, like laboratories the world over, of unnamed acids and alkalis and chromatography gel.

In this subterranean aridity, they came at last to a white-tiled laboratory, which had a space-age fume cupboard on one wall with an electronic control panel fit for a fighter jet at the front.

'This is Maisie. She's the real thing.' Gordon stroked the cabinet's glass front fondly. 'Before this beastie came along, what we're planning would have taken six months of slow tedium waiting for the lime to dissolve into an acid bath. Now, thanks to Maisie, it'll all be done in the blink of an eye, more or less. Do you want to put him in?'

He slid open the glass and let Stella set the skull-stone on a plastic stand on the base of the cabinet. Fine tubes angled down from all directions.

The front of the cabinet closed with a pneumatic thud. Gordon was a man in his element. He began moving his hands over pressure-sensitive controls at the front. Lights flickered. The array of tubes moved closer to the skull. A needling whine began to eat at their ears.

Stella said, 'How long will it take?'

'Maybe a couple of hours.'

'So I could go back to Kit? If there's a way to get him down here, I'd like him to see the result when you're finished.'

'I'll call you. There's a lift you can use. I just don't like it much,' said the man who had led climbs in some of the hardest caves in Britain. 'It's too claustrophobic.'

KIT WAS ASLEEP again when she returned. She made a salad and set it aside for when he woke.

She was sitting on the floor by the low ash table, drinking green tea and watching the sun gild the trees on Midsummer Common, when Sergeant Ceri Jones, the young radio operator who had talked Kit's rescue party out of the cave, rang her mobile.

'I'm on Ingleborough Fell again.' At 200 miles' distance, her accent seemed broader. 'We finally got a police team together to look inside your killer cave. We just came out. I thought you'd like to know.'

'Thank you. What have you got?' Stella asked.

'Two things. The easy bit is the skeleton. You remember there was a body holding a sword lying in the cave? Well, we had a forensic pathologist on the team and I can tell you that your skeleton was a man, five foot ten and in his sixties when he died. The important bit is, they think the body's at least four hundred years old, so he died around Cedric Owen's time. And the sword he was holding cleaned up enough for us to see that the hilt was bronze, or brass, and the blade was iron. I thought you'd like to know.'

'Thanks. If that's the easy bit, what's the rest?'

Picking her words, Ceri said, 'We've just been along the nightmare ledge again. We set up bolts and a rope so it's safe now, but we went along it twice to get it set. There's nowhere for someone to hit their head hard enough to smash their skull open like Kit did.'

She waited. When Stella said nothing, she said, 'It proves that you were right; there was someone else there with you.'

'He might have hit it as he fell.'

'No. The wall angles inwards below the ledge where he fell; there's no way he could have hit himself on the way down. Our forensic pathologist is sure that it wasn't an accident. We're trying to work out a motive for an attempted murder. If we find one, DI Fleming will be the first to know.'

'Thank you, I'll pass that on to Kit. I'll mail you with anything we get.'

They closed the connection. The sun was a red globe deep in the west. The bars and pubs up near Magdalene Bridge were coming to life, spilling multicoloured reflections on the river. Some time later, into the quiet evening, her phone rang again.

'Your stone's ready,' said Gordon Fraser. 'I hope you are.'

NOTHING COULD have made her ready.

An unusually subdued Gordon met her and Kit at the elevator and ushered them into the fluorescent hush of his laboratory.

'Dear God . . .'

Kit whispered it hoarsely, in awe, or fear; Stella could not tell which.

Blue. All she could see was crystalline, perfect, unblemished sky-blue. Colour flooded the space: dense, dazzling, lucent colour.

Stella crouched down, bringing her face level with its eyes. Freed from its limestone carcass, the skull was heartbreakingly beautiful, a thing of flawless crystal that drew the light inwards in curves to make a soft, blurred flame at its heart.

On the outside, the smooth arc of the cranial vault gave way in front to two tunnelled eye sockets above sharply angled cheekbones. The nose was a clear triangle. The lower jaw looked separate, so that the mouth could open and shut if one chose to play such games with it.

Stella did not wish to play games of any sort. Softly, she said, 'Kit, have you got the bag?'

'Are you sure you want to do that?'

It was Gordon who spoke. He stood at the far side of the room, white and wide-eyed, and had not come near her.

'What do you mean?'

'I'm not sure. Just that it's a thing to steal the soul and I'm not sure I want mine stolen. It's too beautiful. To be honest, I think you'd be safer putting it under a pile driver. We have one, if you need it.'

There was silence. Stella looked at Kit instead of the stone. 'What do you think? Do you think it has stolen my soul?'

'Honestly?' He glanced up at her. 'I think you're stronger than that. If you weren't, we wouldn't be having this conversation.'

'Are you not afraid of it?' Gordon asked.

Kit pursed his lips. 'Not that I'd noticed. It's . . . striking, but I can't see what's to be afraid of.'

'You're a stronger man than me, then.' Gordon eased back his shoulders and came forward to open the cabinet for her. 'And you might like to know that what you're looking at is a single piece of blue quartz, better known as sapphire. And it's probably the biggest gemstone ever dug out of the northern hemisphere.'

He slid open the cabinet door. Stella lifted up the stone. Blue light enveloped her. A sense of welcome, of homecoming, of friendship rekindled soaked her soul. Distantly, she heard Kit ask, 'Where exactly is it from?'

Gordon answered, 'Scotland. I've seen one or two of that colour from the basalt layers at Loch Roag on Lewis, but never one that big without flaws in it. It's been cut against the grain of the crystal, which is hard to do without breaking it into a thousand tiny pieces.'

Stella was only half listening; all her attention was on the skull-stone. She cradled it in the crook of her elbow. *I am your hope at the end of time. Hold me as you would hold your child. Listen to me as you would listen to your lover. Trust me as you would trust your god, whosoever that may be.*

Gordon was saying, 'See how the zygomatic arches pull in the light? And the eye sockets are lenses, to focus it into the cranium? Nobody knows how to cut quartz like that today.'

He took a step across the room and stood at his computer rattling his big fingers across the keys. 'I took the liberty of analysing the deposits encasing the stone and I think I can safely say that your rock has been sitting in water of high calcium carbonate content for four hundred and twenty years, give or take five per cent.'

Kit said, 'So it *is* Owen's.'

'It's in the right time frame. That's as much as geology can do for you. The rest is up to you.'

'We're no further forward, really, are we? We're still trying to stay alive long enough to find the time and place appointed, if we had the first clue what they were,' Kit said. 'Trivial.'

'We need to know who it is first,' Stella said.

'I recognise that voice.' Kit turned his chair the better to see her. The humour left his face. 'What's up?'

Stella shook her head. 'I don't know.' It was hard to explain, a certain coalescence of mist, of flame and light. 'I keep seeing a face, but not clearly. It comes and goes when I look at the stone.'

'The face that goes with the skull?'

'I think so. It feels like it. Is there anyone we can trust who would be able to build the face?'

'Not my field.' Kit looked up. 'Gordon?'

'There's only one that I know of.' The Scotsman regarded Kit doubtfully. 'Did you know Davy Law went into forensic anthropology?'

There was a moment's silent pause that Stella did not understand, then, 'No,' Kit said flatly. 'Not him.'

Gordon flushed, which was almost as surprising. 'He's a Bede's man, and he knows what he's doing.'

'Oh, *please*.'

'Guys?' Stella looked from one to the other. She felt the beginnings of a warning creep under the base of her skull.

Kit sighed. 'David Law was a medical student who pulled out of his training and ran off to do something less arduous. He's a runty little shit who coxed for the first boat the year Bede's came last.'

Stella laughed. 'That's hardly a hanging offence.'

'He assaulted the stroke of the women's team the night before the race.'

'*What?*' She swept round. 'Gordon, is this true?'

'No, it's slander and you know it, Kit O'Connor.' Gordon was looking flushed and angry. 'It was a rumour, there's no proof. But even the rumour wrecked Davy's career. He ducked out of his clinical training and ran off to join Médecins Sans Frontières and cut his teeth bandaging bullet wounds in Palestinian refugee camps. When he came back, he trained as a forensic anthropologist. He's spent the past five years in Turkey pissing off the government in Ankara by putting names and faces to the bones in Kurdish mass graves, which isn't something just anyone could do. If Stella needs someone who'll keep his mouth shut while he puts a face on the bones of her stone, Davy's the man.'

Kit raked his good hand through his hair. He looked for a moment as if he might argue, then shook his head and let all the tension drop from his body. 'This isn't my call. Stell? What do we do?'

She slid the skull-stone into her backpack and closed the fastenings. She said, 'Can we go and see Tony Bookless and take all that we've got? If he thinks it's a bad idea to go and see Davy Law, we'll give it a miss. If not, we'll go first thing in the morning and then go on to Ursula Walker's. Deal?'

'Deal.' Only because she knew Kit well did she see the hesitation before he spoke.

THEY MOVED SLOWLY through the warm evening streets of Cambridge, chose the less crowded route past King's, Trinity and John's, left before the Round Church and right before Magdalene Bridge to the path that led along the riverbank. Kit was learning to handle the chair. Away from the town, he took more risks, moving faster. They slid along the edge of Jesus Green with its sporadically unquiet couples exploring each other in the grey-green grass. At Midsummer Common, they stopped under the trees.

'He's not in,' Stella said.

Bede's College lay on the far side of the river, a place of sandstone and granite, of Tudor extravagance and Georgian austerity, where the library dwarfed the chapel and was, in turn, overshadowed by the square tower that held the Master's suite. Here and there, muted lights shone from uncurtained windows, but not from the leaded lights of Tony Bookless's study.

'But the porters will be there,' said Kit, grasping her hand. 'They're not supposed to pass on the Master's itinerary to anyone short of the police, but I bet you a kiss to a coffee that if I show my bruises and my wheelchair, they'll tell me when he's due back.'

It was hard not to follow him in this mood, even though the tingles of warning had returned. She hugged him, briefly. 'If you win, do I get the kiss or the coffee?'

'Both.' He leaned forward in his chair. 'Race you to the porter's lodge?'

'Kit— No!' But he was already gone.

FOR HIS BRUISES and his wheelchair and his reputation in the college, the porters did, indeed, give Kit all that they knew: the Master had been expected back to his rooms from a formal dinner thirty minutes ago, but had not appeared. They had no idea where he might be.

They offered coffee or tea and the chance to sit and catch up with college gossip. Kit was relaxed in their company, open and expansive and discussing the cave as if it were all a heady adventure.

Stella would have sat all night listening, had the skull allowed it. She held out as long as she could. When the shards of bright yellow panic became blinding, she tapped the back of his wrist.

'What's up?'

She shook her head to clear it, and failed. 'There's something wrong, but I don't know what. It's something to do with us being here when we should be . . .' A certainty took her. 'We need to go back to the river room. Now.'

Stella left Kit in the care of the porters and ran ahead, ducking under the archway to the Lancastrian court, where a dragon in painted glass faced an unarmoured swordsman by the light of a high half-moon. The electric-yellow crisis in her head had exploded into showering stars as she ran towards Kit's room and, stopping in the hallway outside it, saw the broken lock and open door; she already knew what she would find inside.

It was hard to feel anything but rage and horror as she stood in the chaos of opened drawers, spilt coffee beans and scattered papers. Kit's shrine to neatness had been desecrated with a venom that frightened her.

'Stell?'

She had heard the whine of his chair and now returned to the doorway and reached out to catch his hand. Their clasp was wordless and she waited for the sick taste in her mouth and the heart-crushing outrage to subside.

'Stell?' Kit squeezed her hand. 'What is it?'

'He knows you,' Stella said. 'Only someone who knows you would do this.'

'And hates me.'

Stella let his hand drop. 'He wasn't just looking for the stone. Your computer's gone and all the ledgers and files. All this afternoon's work.'

Woodenly, Kit said, 'The insurance will buy a new Powerbook.'

'What's the point if we've got nothing to put in it? The ledgers have gone, the code, the shorthand. Everything.'

Kit managed half a smile. 'Sweetheart, you're talking to a computeroid. The machine backs itself up three times a day to the server in the library and once daily offsite. I can download the latest from back-ups in the morning and we can take them with us to Oxford.' He glanced at her sideways. 'If we're still going?'

'Definitely.' She had control of the anger now, so that it no longer paralysed her, but instead rode over the swelling ocean of her fear. 'Tonight—this minute—we're going to call the police and see if they'll take us seriously now. Tomorrow, we're going to Oxford and we're going to find out what the skull-stone's about. And when we know that, we're a step closer to finding who did this and making him sorry.'

ONLY LATE IN THE NIGHT, lying together for the first time since the accident, did Stella begin to shake. They were on the single bed the porters had found for them in the visiting academics' accommodation. She had thought Kit asleep and only realised otherwise when he rolled over and reached his one good hand for hers. 'Stell?'

'Mmm?'

'Gordon was right. The skull has entered part of your soul. You're not the woman I married.'

She held on to him, shuddering uncontrollably. 'Is that a bad thing?'

'I don't know.' He pressed a kiss to the soft skin of her neck. 'I'm worried for you. Will you make me another promise? Will you swear never to go anywhere you can't come back from?'

It was not so great a request. She held him and kissed him and when the shaking had grown less consuming, she said, 'I swear I will not go anywhere I don't think I can come back from.'

It was not exactly what he had asked, but it was close and he was already half asleep. It was only as she sank into sleep herself that she saw the void between what he had asked of her and what she had promised, and by then it was far too late to change it.

8
Zama, New Spain

October 1556 'In their ignorance, my children believe that we are not the first of God's creations, but the fifth and final race to inhabit the earth. They make their ornaments in testament to this, such as the one you behold now. I have preserved it exactly as it was when I first made landfall here and took this, their temple, as my home. If you would care to enter? Diego will serve you with what wine we have, unless you have brought your own . . . ? Thank you. I had thought you might.'

It was becoming apparent that while Father Gonzalez Calderón, priest to the natives of Zama, had the physique of a hired thug, it was wrapped round the mind and manners of a prelate. It was equally apparent from the spartan furnishings of the place that the father was not a man given to enjoying the delights of the flesh.

Nor, evidently, did he find de Aguilar's flamboyance amusing, which was unfortunate given that the Spaniard seemed to be in a particularly expansive frame of mind. At this moment he was crouched in the centre of the priest's house, examining a coloured mosaic that took up half the floor.

Owen watched the priest make an effort to look away from the vulgarity of de Aguilar's earrings and felt a stab of remorse for his own earlier prejudice. Seeking harmless conversation, he said, 'This building is not painted red like all the others I have seen in this place. Did you ask for it so?'

'Of course. I had it painted with limewash when I took it as my own.'

'But I cannot help observing that the remainder of the city is painted the colour of blood. Is it a reminder of human sacrifice, or—'

Owen spoke in innocence, repeating only what all of Spain knew of these people. He regretted it at once, as thunder blackened the priest's features.

'My children do not seek, and never have sought, the death of others in appeasement of their gods. They were untutored, but not barbarians. Being more thoughtful and less savage than their neighbours, the Aztecs, the people of Zama came upon the idea that if they paint their buildings blood-red, they will appear similar to the temples of the devil-worshipping barbarians whose steps are slick with human blood. By mimicking them in this way, my children hope to deter any attackers who may— Thank you, Diego. Please do come in.'

On the order, the scar-faced native entered bearing on a tray three clay beakers and an opened bottle of wine.

The priest treated him as any lord might treat his servant: as an obdurate child, to be seen but not heard. Cedric Owen would have been glad to do likewise, but that the piercing eyes carved holes in his mind and made deafening the background song of the stone.

With an effort, he fixed his attention once again on the priest. 'Does it work?' he asked. 'Painting the houses red?'

'I have been here nearly seven years and the only enemy we have fought has been the pox. Therefore we can conclude that it works,' said the priest, with glorious illogic. 'And now we must deliver your captain from his knees, for otherwise there will be no part of the floor free on which to place the table. Have you found the riddle of the mosaic yet, señor?'

'I regret not.' Fernandez de Aguilar stood with evident reluctance. 'I think perhaps I have the beginnings of it, but it is opaque to my mind. Señor Owen, will you bend your physician's logic to the puzzle on my behalf before our host divulges its secret?'

Thus, inattentively, and with his mind set all awry by the unsettling gaze of the scarred native, did Cedric Owen come to stand before the image that changed for ever the trajectory of his life.

From a distance it had looked like a child's painting done in stone, a haphazard collection of pebbles, picked for the clarity of their colour, showing goggle-eyed men and fantastical beasts entwined in an eternity of conflict. On closer inspection, the shapes proved to be more complex. In the centre a fire was laid out in red and yellow stones, with an encircling rim made of green leaves woven thinly. About the perimeter in a deep, wide band was a map of the heavens, and between fire and sky stood the two futures of Man, held in eternal balance. To the one side, conflict, war and misery stood depicted in fierce and warring figures. To the other stood the battle's antithesis, a summer meadow carpeted with coloured flowers too beautiful to name. A child knelt in the centre of it, peaceful in the solitude.

Separating these two was the barest thread of a dividing line, an erratic rift of black and white tiles with a thread of fat, coloured pearls strung along it, in the seven colours of the rainbow, with black and white set together at the end.

From nowhere, Owen remembered an upstairs room in a lodging house in Paris, and a gentle voice: *The colours of the world are nine in total; the seven of the rainbow, plus the black of no-light and the white of all-light . . . To the blue was given the heart of the beast, and the power to call together the remaining twelve parts of its spirit and flesh . . .*

'What do you see, my friend?' Fernandez de Aguilar asked quietly. If the priest wondered at the change in the Spaniard and his English physician, if he planned their deaths by fire and rack as a result, neither of them cared.

The question freed Owen's tongue. He said, 'I see the moment before the world's end, before the onset of Armageddon. I see a map of the heavens that gives us the date and time exactly. And I see the means by which there may be hope to avert the ultimate evil.'

He looked up at the priest. Father Calderón lifted his silver cross and kissed it. 'Pray continue.'

Owen drew breath. 'I see first the sun, greatest light of all, shining down a long, dark tunnel to the place from whence all matter is born. I see Venus, the Morning Star, in wide embrace to Mercury, the Messenger, and these two dance in opposition to Jupiter, the Golden Benefactor. I see Jupiter—'

The words snagged in his throat. 'I see the planets and constellations set in a pattern that will not happen in my lifetime, nor in many yet to come.'

The scar-faced native gazed at Owen with pitiless knife-eyes, but it was Father Gonzalez Calderón who said softly, 'This shape is not made in God's heaven for four hundred and fifty-six years. What is it that the stars and planets herald?'

Owen bent back to the wonder before him. 'The image shows a frozen moment in time, as if the world has been caught on the brink of disaster and there is but this single thread of hope to save it. To the west, we see the conflict of the final Desolation, where men fight against all creation, each one consumed with greed, lust, avarice, the lack of care for others, the willingness to inflict pain on them, heedless of their plight and, in the end, to trample on all that exists. This is the force that will lead to the destruction not only of all that is good in the world of men, but of the world.'

'And is there no redemption?' asked the priest.

'There may be, for set against the horror is a place of peace.' Owen laid a hand on the southern quadrant. 'Here, in the east, a girl child kneels in a summer's meadow playing knucklebones. She is the epitome of Innocence, of the unstained human soul that might yet be saved, and so save the future of the world.'

'It is a girl, not a boy?'

'I believe so.'

'And therefore not the young Christ. A mistake, clearly.' The priest jabbed at the image with his silver cross. 'You have spoken only of the background. What can you say about the four beasts who make the greater part of the image?'

'Ah . . .' What could he say of such things? Owen had not seen them at first, such was the wonder of the mosaic, where images hid within others. But now, the four beasts dazzled him, in all their might and wonder. Here was the animation, the power, the light to brighten the darkest of worlds.

'I spoke of a thread of hope in the picture and, in truth, the greater part of the mosaic is given over to the manifestation of that hope. Here we have four beasts. Up here in the northeast corner is a spotted lion, a hunter to exceed all others. Next, in the southeast, is a serpent, long as a ship and thick as a man's waist. Opposite these two an eagle sits to the northwest, its wings as wide as this house, its eyes of sharp gold. Last, in the southwestern corner sits a lizard as large as a horse, with teeth that could tear a man in half. When these four join together . . .'

Even as he spoke, the beasts erupted from the mosaic and met. Limbs entwined with wings, heads with hearts, talons and tails together. For one luminous, heartbreaking moment, the four became one, to make a beast that was infinitely greater than all apart. It was too bright. Owen closed his eyes against the blinding light. When he opened them again, the earth serpent was gone and all sign of the beasts that had made it.

Dizzily, Owen risked a look to the shadows beyond the priest and was not surprised to see that the scar-faced native was no longer there. Where he had been, a single bright green feather lay on the floor.

Owen stood, feeling light-headed and a little foolish. De Aguilar was studying him in silence. A shadow crossed them both, breaking the intensity of the moment. Father Calderón stood in the doorway, his ox-bulk blocking both entrance and exit.

'Are we to die, Father?' asked de Aguilar quietly.

'Possibly, but not at my hand. I have lived in Zama nearly seven years and in that time I have tried to learn the ways of the natives that we might better teach them the clear path. Yet I have only lately come to perceive what your ship's physician has so clearly seen at first sighting.

'With my greater knowledge, I can tell you that the spotted beast is not a lion but a jaguar, which is sacred to my children, the Maya, as are the three other beasts: the eagle, which represents the air, the serpent, which is fire, and the crocodile, which is water. The jaguar, of course, holds power over the earth. The Maya are taught that at the End of Days these four will come together to form one beast. Can you imagine, sir, what might arise out of the union of these four?'

The presence of Nostradamus cooled the shining light in Owen's mind that he might speak calmly of what he had seen. 'Plato named it the Ouroboros,' he said. 'The many-coloured serpent that encircles the earth in endless compassion and swallows its own tail that it might never be separated. In my land, we would know it rather as a dragon, a beast with the body and claws of a jaguar, the head of a crocodile, the tail of a serpent and the wings and grace of an eagle. I was sent here to find how these four might join to make one, and now, having seen it, I cannot remember.'

The priest smiled thinly. 'Such things are not for us to know, although we may praise their happening. In the lands of my children, the four-in-one is the feathered or rainbow serpent known as Kukulkan, or also Quetzalcoatl, a beast which would make a fitting mount for Christ, were He to return to save us from our own ruin.' Father Calderón bowed to each of them fluidly, then stepped aside from the doorway. 'Now I have committed as great a heresy as yours, and we are in each other's debt. It will make for an easier evening, I believe, which is as well, for here is Domingo with our meal.'

'THIS, MY FRIEND, is the green gold that will make us the richest men in Europe, and our children and grandchildren after us.' Fernandez de Aguilar squatted on his heels in the dust and grit of a barren landscape. A mule stood behind him, flapping its ears and flicking its tail at the insects. It had been a gift, or at least a loan, from Father Gonzalez Calderón.

Cedric Owen studied the plant that had taken his companion's eye: a fist-ful of leathery, sword-blade leaves sprouting from a thickened husk of a stem, seemingly designed to be inedible by man, beast or insect. He took the opportunity to dismount and stood in the shade cast by his gift-mule. He sat down on a rock with his back to the high, hot sun and skipped a pebble across the desert. He tried to imagine and failed.

'How?' he asked. Heat was teaching him an economy of language.

'There are two kinds of these plants, my friend,' said de Aguilar. 'One can be distilled to a kind of spirit-drink more potent than the best of brandies. The other kind is used by the natives to make a type of rope, like hemp. Cortés used this on his ships as he sailed home.' He went to his mule and lifted from it the coiled rope that hung across the pommel. 'This is what can be made with this plant. They call it sisal and it is better than hemp and stronger, coarser and hardier than anything we produce in Europe. You and I will grow this plant and we will make ropes to fit the navies of all Christendom and beyond. We will be the richest men in Europe. Look to my birth stars and tell me I am not bound for greatness.'

Only a very confident man tempted fate with such hubris. In truth, de Aguilar's chart was, indeed, one of brilliance, marred by a single hard square from Mercury to Jupiter, on the cusp of the third house. His Sun/Venus conjunction rising in Aries less than one degree above the ascendant saved that square from misery.

'Fernandez, I trust you with my life, but perhaps not with my money. To grow these plants in quantities such as you dream of would need torrents of water and there is precious little here. I walked around the fields outside the town this morning while you were unloading the ship. The people have barely enough to keep their peppers from shrivelling on the stalk.'

'This is because they do not have my great-uncle as their adviser. He had travelled the whole land in his time as a slave to the natives and he told me things that even they have forgotten—that the natives of old chose the sites of their ancient cities for the great underground reservoirs that exist natu-rally here. He never put these two facts—the aquifers and the rope plants—together; nor did any of my family.'

Owen stretched his full length lazily along the warm rock, ironing out the kinks in his back. Presently, he said, 'That sounds good. You can use the water to irrigate the plants and then if we can get Father Gonzalez to organ-ise a monopoly on the rope trade for all of New Spain, we'll—'

'*Cedric!* Don't move!'

It was the first time in the entirety of their acquaintance that de Aguilar had used his Christian name. Frozen, Owen lay staring up into the crown of his hat. Sweat soaked his shirt so that the cool of it swamped his chest.

'What?'

Evenly, Fernandez said, 'There's a snake behind the rock. One of the dangerous ones that Father Gonzalez told us of, with the red bands on yellow with black between. It hasn't seen you yet. If you can stay still a while longer, I will kill it with my sword . . . Lie still while I . . . bring my blade from its sheath and position it . . . so . . . and then I will— Ah! *No!*'

'Fernandez!' Owen sprang to his feet and spun round.

The snake hung by its teeth from the snowy-white linen of the Spaniard's shirt cuff, thrashing viciously. Small speckles of scarlet blood scattered about it, fat as rowan berries; its teeth had punctured flesh as well as linen.

De Aguilar stood rigidly still with his eyes white all round the rims. His sword dropped from his fingers, noisily.

Owen grabbed a blade and, with no thought for his own safety, he swept the borrowed sword high and sliced it down again, severing the head of the snake. The body fell to the ground, writhing and pumping thin, dark blood. The front part of the head, with the teeth and all the venom they contained, remained fixed to de Aguilar's wrist.

Like a puppetmaster manipulating a doll made of wood and horse sinew, Owen manoeuvred de Aguilar to sit on the rock. The snake had ground its teeth deep into the flesh of the Spaniard's forearm. Owen drove his eating-knife's point into the pinch of skin below the dead eye and wriggled it up and down to separate the upper and lower jaws.

De Aguilar sat through it white-faced. At the end, he looked down to the four deep puncture marks in his arm. 'I know of this snake. Its venom stops a man's muscles from working. In time, he can neither walk nor stand and then his chest ceases to move and his heart stops. The only way to stop it is to remove the limb. Few men live through that, so I am dead.' He said it without sentiment. His eyes were bright and level. 'We should go back to Zama. There is much to be arranged. If I am correct, I have half a day in which I might function as a whole man and I would not waste it. Tomorrow . . .' His gaze rested on the sea beyond the limestone bluffs. 'I should like to see that dawn again. Will you sit through this last dawn with me, Cedric Owen?'

'No.' Owen was weeping, a thing he had not done since the blue stone became his at the age of thirteen. 'It will not be your last dawn. I believe amputation could save your life.'

'But you, as you have often told me, are not a surgeon.' It was said gently, as an elder brother might chide a youth for an excess of zeal.

Owen cursed. 'You don't understand. Nostradamus made me spend ten days reading books on surgery and answering his questions. I will perform the surgery and you will not die.'

'But, Cedric, with all due respect—'

'Don't. Just don't . . . Just get on your mule now and come back with me. You may lose your sword arm, but I will not let you lose your life. Not when you are about to make me one of the two richest men in Europe.'

9
Law Forensic Laboratory, Oxford

June 2007 Stella walked alone through a corridor of white tiles and concrete, through doors of brushed aluminium, to a laboratory of steel tables and glass cabinets that smelt of chemistry, cigarette smoke and death.

Dr David Law met her at the door. He did not look as bad as Kit had described, but there was enough to build the caricature. She faced a small, wiry man with straggling, mouse-tail hair and chisel teeth that pushed his upper lip from his face. They were stained brown by years of tea and tobacco so that when he smiled his breath preceded him into the corridor.

'Dr Cody.' He wiped his hand on his white coat and thrust it out. 'Professor Fraser called to say you were on your way. Any friend of Gordon's is welcome to my time.' His grip was firmer than Stella had expected, with an impression of underlying strength that made five years spent exhuming Kurdish mass graves seem more plausible. His eyes drifted past her to the corridor. 'Kit isn't with you?'

'He's asleep in the car,' she said. It was true, but sounded like an excuse. 'Actually, we've rented a van so we could bring his wheelchair,' she added, feeling strangely uneasy.

'Right.' Walking away from her, he held open the door of his lab. 'Gordon told me you had a skull and needed to build the face from it?'

He turned to look pointedly at her backpack. The blue skull-stone slept in it, silently. Since the warning of Kit's room, it had been quiet. She reached for it now and felt nothing, no instinct to go or to stay.

'It's not a bone skull. It's carved out of stone. Gordon thought we could

trust you to keep it private,' she said, unzipping the backpack. Without ceremony, she lifted the skull-stone into the harsh lights of his lab and held it
out, letting its blue cast lighten the clinical cold of his room. 'We found
this,' she said. 'There was a cipher in Cedric Owen's ledgers that led to it.'

She was expecting a short moment of shock, of a breath taken in and let
out again slowly, at first sight of the stone. She did not expect the surge of
rage, or grief, or pain—she could not tell which—that warped Davy Law's
gargoyle features as his eyes flicked between the stone and her face.

He shuddered. 'Who else has seen this?'

'Besides me and Kit? Only Gordon. Tony didn't want to look. He said it
carried the blood of too many people he respected.'

Law's smile was full of acid irony. 'Gordon wouldn't tell me what it was
you were bringing. There's not many could keep a secret like this.'

'He's a good friend.'

With shaking hands, Law rolled himself a cigarette and lit it, staring at
the redly glowing end. 'This is Cedric Owen's blue heart-stone, yes?'

'We think so.'

For the first time, he looked at her full in the face. 'Men have killed for
this. They killed Cedric Owen, and everyone else who held it, back up the
line of his ancestors.' He pursed his lips. 'Were you followed, coming here?'

'I don't think so. I'm not sure I'd know.'

'Stella!' He was angry with her, and did not know if he was allowed to
show it. 'Tell me you understand the danger you're in?'

'Am I in danger from you?'

'No.' He could laugh now, and did so, coughing at the end. 'Not now.
I've seen beauty and grabbed for it once in my life. I'm not going to make
the same mistake twice.'

Carefully, she said, 'Is this the reason Kit and you fell out?'

He shrugged, loosely. 'He's your husband. I can't answer for him.'

'But he was a friend of yours? A good friend?'

'Once. Not now.' His bloodshot eyes were hard. After a while they flickered from Stella to the skull-stone and back again. 'It's modelled on a
Caucasian woman,' he said. 'Did you want to know more than that?'

'If I can. I keep seeing a face—half seeing it—I think it matters to see it
properly. If you can make that happen, I might be a step closer to understanding why this is worth killing for and who is trying to destroy our lives.'

'Fine.' Davy Law pinched his cigarette out. 'OK. Let's build ourselves a
face and see if you like what it tells you.'

FOR THE SECOND TIME in two days, the skull-stone sat on a small plinth in a cabinet with lights shining in from different angles. Here, the work was done not by acid projected under pressure, but by pencil-thin lines of red light that streamed in from all possible angles in all possible planes.

In goggles and thin gloves, Davy Law puffed in streams of dry ice from a hand-held probe to make them visible and ensure their positioning.

'It's all done with lasers,' he said. 'The scan takes half an hour, though it might be longer given the nature of the quartz.'

He screwed shut the door to the tank and took off the goggles. 'The screen's on my desk next door. I have an espresso machine. It's not quite Starbucks, but it's drinkable. Or you could go and sit in the car.'

It was neither an offer nor a request, just a statement. Stella found she was beginning to enjoy Davy Law's quiet refusal to play the social game.

'Coffee would be fine,' she said.

DAVY LAW'S OFFICE was small, with barely enough room for two chairs and a desk, on which sat two oversized computer screens and a phone.

From his seat behind the keyboard, he lit a new cigarette, then he tipped his chair back. 'Skulls are my obsession. And since we're going to have to wait a while to find out what face we can build, there might be something to be discovered in exploring some of the skull legends from around the world. What do you know about the Mayan prophecies of 2012?'

Of all things, she had not expected that. She brought her coffee to his desk and sat down. 'I got half a million hits on Google yesterday when I searched under "Mayan" and "skull". Most of them had 2012 in the title. There wasn't one that made sense.'

Law raised his brow. 'Cultural imperialism has a lot to answer for.' He leaned forward and turned his attention to one of the screens.

Stella studied the second screen. The skull-stone revolved on it clock-wise, no longer blue, but digitally converted to a solid grey set against a pale background and crisscrossed by a thousand tangential lines in shades that ranged from bright, arterial red through magenta to a range of vibrant greens and yellows. Between these the matt grey surface was changing as flesh grew between the coloured hair lines, yet the face was barely human.

Law came to lean on the back of her chair. 'If you can guess who it's going to be, you can have a job.'

'Female? Caucasian? Around at the time of Cedric Owen?' Stella snatched name from history. 'Queen Elizabeth the First?'

He grinned wide, like a fox. 'Nice try. No, these skulls were made at least three thousand years before Elizabeth was born.'

'Skulls?' Stella spun her chair round. 'Are there others?'

'Allegedly.'

'How do you know?'

'I did a degree in anthropology after I screwed up my medical career.' He moved back to his seat in front of the other screen. He put his hand on the top, ready to turn it for her to see. His eyes were brown, sharp and serious. 'You could still walk away,' he said. 'It might be easier.'

His change of mood caught her off balance. 'David, someone tried to kill Kit in the cave where we found the stone. Someone else—or maybe the same person—trashed his room last night in a blatant act of intimidation. I can't walk away. I'm not ready to get out the hammer yet.'

'Davy,' he said absently. 'Not David; Davy. And don't give up on the hammer. When your life's at stake, it's always good to have an exit strategy.'

He finished his coffee and his cigarette and tilted the screen towards her. She expected mandalas, or Mayan gods, or the other skulls. What she saw instead were Mayan glyphs, exactly like those she had found in the ledger.

'That's the Dresden Codex,' he said. 'One of the sacred texts of the Maya. Of the thousands they wrote, only four survived the spiritual vandalism of the Jesuits. This one ended up in the Sächsische Landesbibliothek in Dresden. This and the three others are the surviving remnants of a civilisation that makes ours look infantile. And according to this document, the world is going to end on December the 21st, 2012.'

'Very funny.' Stella spun her chair away from him.

He caught the armrest and spun her back. 'Listen, this isn't a joke. The codex is the product of a civilisation that could map out the planets with an accuracy that would make NASA envious.'

'Don't try to blind me with science,' she snapped.

'Stella, I'm trying to open your eyes. Look—' Stabbing at the keys, he opened other pages. Block upon block of glyphs flowed across the screen. 'The whole of the Dresden Codex is a table of Venus and Mars progressions as accurate as anything that can be done today. It's the foundation of the Mayan calendar. Back in Cedric Owen's time, while we were still pissing about in the transition from Julian to Gregorian calendars, trying to find a system that didn't leave Christmas in midsummer, the Maya had already lived for a thousand years with a calendric system that could predict a lunar eclipse to the nearest 0.0007 of a *second* for eight millennia either way. The

Dresden Code is the key to Mayan cosmology. They divided time into ages of five thousand, one hundred and twenty-five years each. We are living in the fifth age. According to their legends, each of the previous four ended in a cataclysm that destroyed the nascent races of men: fire, earthquake, storm or, in the case of the last one, a flood.'

'Are you quoting scripture at me?'

'Not particularly. There are one hundred and thirty-seven culturally separate flood legends besides the one where the animals go in two by two; every civilisation currently on the planet remembers that they were born out of flood water. The Maya, however, are the only ones who left us with a timetable for the next disaster. The end of the fifth age isn't just the end of an age, it's the end of an era, as defined by the precession of the equinoxes. An era begins and ends when the sun lies over the Galactic Centre at twenty-eight degrees of Sagittarius, a place the Maya called *Xibalba be*, the Road to the Underworld. When the sun walks along that path, we'll see catastrophe on a grand scale—Armageddon. In the Mayan calendar the date of this is 13 Baktun, 13.0.0.0.0. In our calendar, it's December the 21st, 2012.'

He threw his hands behind his head and stared at her, unblinking.

Stella drank her coffee. After a while she said, 'What's it going to be? Global warming? Eco-catastrophe? Nuclear annihilation?'

'All of the above, I should think. The Maya destroyed themselves in the space of about fifty years, an entire culture wiped out by a mix of warfare and overuse of local resources. We're doing the same on a planetary scale.'

'I don't see what this has got to do with the skulls.'

'Because, according to the legends, the Mayans made a group of thirteen crystal skulls which, when brought together, will help us find a path out of this catastrophe. You have one of those skulls.'

'The skulls will stop Armageddon?' She was incredulous.

'No, they'll find us a way through. A gateway, if you like.'

'Do you actually believe this?' She stared at him, disbelieving.

He did not smile, only shrugged and tapped again at his keyboard, to no obvious effect. 'I'm telling you what's in the old texts.'

'Don't dodge the question, Davy.'

He turned his chair away from the desk and lifted one shoulder in half an apology. 'Yes, I believe it. These people knew things that we lost a long time ago when we took a wrong turning. I'm not the only one. There are a lot of other folk out there who think the same.'

'Oh, for God's sake.' She was out of the chair, pacing the length of the small room. 'There are plenty of others who believe in the Second Coming of Christ, and the nightly perambulations of the Tooth Fairy. You're a medic, Davy. You deal in flesh and blood and bone, not this kind of . . . inane transcendental crap.'

He said quietly, 'A failed medic. I didn't complete my clinical training.'

The anger left, as fast as it had come. She sat down again. 'Sorry.'

'Don't be. It doesn't matter. Stella, what brought you to me?' He was not joking now. His hard eyes held her.

'I wanted to see the face of the skull.'

'You were already seeing it, that's why you came, remember? "I keep seeing a face." Your words. And it sings to you. You *hear* a stone in your head. Tell me that's not inane transcendental crap.'

She said nothing; there was nothing to say. He leaned forward and gripped the arms of her chair. His face was inches away.

'What else? What else makes it more than just a pretty lump of rock that men will fight over?'

She stared past him to the glyphs on the computer screen.

Dully, she said, 'The skull warned me of danger in the cave; it's why Kit and I separated, why he was pushed off the ledge when I was not. Last night, it warned me of what was happening in Kit's room, I just didn't understand in time. And . . . there's a cipher in the ledgers. I think I'm the only one who can see it, but it looks exactly like this.' She jabbed her thumb towards the screen. 'It's page after page of Mayan glyphs. Another codex.'

'There's a codex hidden in Owen's ledgers? Please, you *have* to let me . . .'

He was close enough for her to feel the heat of his face. His hand was on her arm. The words locked in his throat, too many, or too urgent, or too desperate, to find their order and come out.

Before Davy could utter them, something metal cracked against the door post and an acerbic voice said, 'Am I interrupting something? Do say. I can always go away again.'

'Kit?'

He was in the doorway, leaning on his sticks. He looked through her, and at Davy Law beyond. 'Having fun?'

'Kit! He's trying to help.'

'I can see that. What kind of help this time, David?'

'Not what you think.' Law stepped back to his own side of the lab. Looking back at Stella, he said stiffly, 'You were leaving, I believe? Though it might be worth looking to see if we've put a face to your skull-stone first.'

The other screen was turned away, where none of them could see it. Law walked behind both seats to turn it back so they could all see it.

'That can't be right.' Stella shook her head, and kept on shaking it.

Kit looked from her to the screen and back again. 'Is this a joke?'

'Computer software,' said Davy Law, 'has no sense of humour.'

There was no ambiguity; Stella's own face stared out at them from the screen, plastic and still, as if in sleep. She remembered the first flick of Davy's eyes from the stone to her face and back.

She turned on him. 'You knew it was me all along.'

He smiled emptily. 'I've been in this job a long time.'

'But you've added the hair and eyes. You've no proof they were the same.'

'Of course not. You can have black hair and blue eyes if you want, but it'll still be you. Like bone, stone doesn't lie. Whoever made this skull, they based it on someone who carried the same facial characteristics as you, probably a distant ancestor.'

Stella shook her head and held up her hand for him to be quiet. She needed time and a clear head to think and had neither.

She said, 'Davy, what do we do?'

He shrugged, loosely, without energy. 'Keep the skull hidden. Keep yourselves safe,' he said at last.

'We were going to see Ursula Walker. Is she safe?'

Sharply, he turned back and his eyes met hers. He laughed aloud. 'As safe as anyone can be. She's one of the very few people alive today who has seen one of the other skulls.' He reached into a desk drawer for a business card with his name and three numbers. 'Land line, mobile and international mobile. Take it, Stella. It doesn't mean you have to use it.'

10
Zama, New Spain

October 1556 'We don't have ice,' Owen said. 'We don't have mandragora or hemlock, or any of the other things the Islamic doctor and philosopher Ibn Sina described as necessary to keep a man at peace for the removal of his arm.'

'But you do have the opium poppy that Nostradamus gave you? Perhaps that will be enough.'

De Aguilar sat in the cool of the priest's stone-built, single-roomed former temple, which had been offered as the best place for the surgery partly because it was a house of God and therefore sanctified, but more importantly because it had stone floors and walls and could be scrubbed clean as the Moor El Zahrawi had said it should be before major surgery.

Walking to the table, de Aguilar still moved with the fluid balance of the trained fencer; the venom had not yet hampered his brain or his grace. 'We will follow my first plan to take dinner together, then sit through the night and watch Zama's dawn rise. I can think of no better way to end a life.'

'Fernandez, don't give up on me so soon.'

Father Gonzalez Calderón filled the doorway of his house as an ox fills a stall, followed by the scarred native.

'Diego understands that you are in want of something—a drench or similar—that will work together with the poppy so that the surgical process may go forward more smoothly, is that so?'

Owen answered, 'It is.'

Father Gonzalez nodded. 'My clerk is ashamed that so noble a visitor as Don Fernandez should be inconvenienced by the prospect of death when he has clearly come here to help the people of Zama. He offers you a drench—perhaps "drink" is the better word—his people use to bring themselves closer to . . . God as they understand Him. He believes that it will combine with the poppy in the way that you need it to and that—'

A torrent of mellifluous sound interrupted him. Diego spoke urgently, staring at Owen all the while.

At a pause in the word-flow, Father Gonzalez said, 'He would have you know that this offer comes because of you, Señor Owen, in part because you read aright the mosaic that shows the End of Days, but also because of what you bring to Zama that is as yet unnamed and unshown. You should know that this . . . drink is used only in the most sacred ceremonies before God. Diego believes that what you attempt is such a rite and that you will understand what it is that he offers. Do you?'

Cedric Owen took a long time to consider, during which he reached for the blue stone and was reassured. 'Yes,' he said at length, 'I believe I do.'

'DEAR GOD . . . a man would have to want very badly to come closer to his eternal soul to drink this. It's foul.'

'How do you feel?'

'Sick. Horribly swimmingly sick. Diego did say that I would . . . But also very . . . peaceful. I think that I could sleep even in sight of your black stone knives and that is a miracle in itself.'

De Aguilar's good hand reached out for Owen's and missed, grasping at nothing and falling back. 'Good night, my friend. Do what you can. Know that I hold nothing against you and—'

'Fernandez . . .' Owen took the good, warm hand. 'Fernandez . . .? God in heaven, he's asleep.' He lowered the limp arm to the table.

The priest said, 'I would encourage you to act swiftly, if you would have him feel nothing. Do you wish my assistance in applying the tourniquet?'

FOR TWO DAYS and nights Fernandez de Aguilar slept without cease, watched by his friend and surgeon, Cedric Owen, who did not sleep at all. At first, Owen had been relieved at his patient's ability to rest; every learned text he had ever read recommended sleep as the best restorative following the devastation of surgery. Thus encouraged, Owen tiptoed his way through the dressing changes in an effort not to disturb his patient to wakefulness. Fernandez de Aguilar's arm was gone, and Owen had fastened the last strip of flesh and skin in place with the cactus thorns he himself had picked in the frenzied planning before the surgery, when it had seemed that even to succeed in cutting the bone would be a miracle. Now he dared to hope that such a thing might come from what he had done.

Some time in the second day, Owen reviewed the charts he had cast of the constellations and movements of the stars. In doing so, he found that Diego was a better source of information than his notebooks on the current position of the three healing planets, Mercury, Venus and Mars. Consulting the redrawn wheels, he found them all to be at least partly favourable. With that and good pulses in his friend's remaining arm to support his cause, he made an effort to rouse the sleeping man that he might drink.

His effort failed. Fernandez de Aguilar could not be woken. Frustrated, Owen abandoned his attempt and, with Diego's help, found a way to raise the patient and pour water into his mouth, massaging his neck to ensure that he swallowed and did not inhale. When Diego went from the temple to attend to his own needs, Owen set the blue stone on the table at de Aguilar's head, so that its eyes faced down the length of his body. He found a small stone lamp and two candles and set them to the sides and base of the skull, moving them a hair's breadth until the three uncertain lights were drawn in and sent out as two certain beams along the length of de Aguilar's body.

Satisfied, Owen brought a stool and placed it at the Spaniard's feet, resting his chin on the table so that his eyes could look into those of the skull-stone. Sitting thus, he said aloud, 'My friend, what we do now is outwith the realms of what you know. If you trust me, I will find you and bring you home. If you wish not to be found, that is your choice and I will honour it.'

So saying, he closed his eyes, and sought once again the place of still, high blue that was the heart-stone's song.

'Wait.' A word, spoken in Spanish. 'Your stone will be stronger elsewhere.' Owen's eyes snapped open.

Diego looked at him across the room, waiting. The skin of Owen's scalp prickled. Quiet in the dark night, he heard Nostradamus's whisper: *Go to the place south of here where the Mussulman once ruled. From there, you can take ship to the New World, therein . . . to meet those who know the heart and soul of your blue stone. They will tell you how best you may unlock its secrets . . .*

'Where must we go?' he asked. 'How far?'

'A place I know. We can take mules. Two days, maybe three.'

BATS. EVERYWHERE BATS. A shrieking, flittering tide that filled the clearing from treetop to treetop, blotting out the afternoon sun and bringing on such darkness as would have been unbearable, but that the heart-stone cast blue light into the false dusk.

'This is the place,' Owen said, straightening. 'I can feel it.'

'Then we make camp.'

Already, Diego was crouched on his heels, cutting turf for a fire. Carlos and Sanchez, his brothers, who had accompanied them on this three-day journey into the jungle, tied the mules and went to find firewood. They passed Owen without a word, although he thought that all three native men looked at him more favourably since he had lifted de Aguilar and carried him on his back these last few miles up an ever-steepening jungle path.

Checking for snakes, he lowered Fernandez de Aguilar to the ground and set the satchel with his heart-stone at his side. Around him, the tide of bats dispersed whence they had come and life returned to the jungle, noisy and colourful. Everywhere, small jewelled birds flitted among the branches, sharpening the air with their calls.

Somewhere, a jaguar coughed. Owen chose to ignore it. His heart-stone did not augur danger. Owen caught at Diego's arm. 'This is the place,' he said again. 'We must act. Fernandez will not live long if we tarry.'

Diego shook his head. 'The time is not yet right. First, we light a fire. Then we eat a little corn and wait.'

'But why, when this is the place?'

Diego smiled a little. 'Cedric Owen, do you know where to go or what to do with your blue heart-stone? No? Neither do I. But one comes who does, and until then, we wait.'

THE JAGUAR CAME in the early evening, when the shadows of the trees sawed across the clearing in sharp-edged stripes, like the bars of a cage.

Cedric Owen sat at the fireside, cradling his heart-stone in its satchel with de Aguilar's senseless body lying supine beside him. The scarred native sat with his two brothers on the other side of the fire.

When the waiting had stretched beyond endurance, Owen rose and walked to the centre of the clearing to a place where an irregular wink of yellow kept catching his eye. He scuffed at the dead leaves with his foot and saw a smear of something hard and bright, the colour of celandines. Falling to his hands and knees, he cleaned away the gritty earth. A small rectangle of buttery stone winked up at him in the last of the evening light.

Others spread out from it, of different yellows, some brighter, some deeper, and at their margins deep blood-reds and flame-orange and the occasional sparkle of green. Soon a full circle of mosaic-fire, banded by red and blue snakes, lay before him.

'My God . . .'

He stood and swept his foot across and across, cutting arcs through the sward. Spreading out from the tiled fire were the outlines of men and animals laid out in a mosaic far larger than the one in the priest's house in Zama. Yet it portrayed the same image of Armageddon.

'Diego?'

Even in his passion, the silence caught him. Owen turned round, and saw that the three native men now stood with their backs to the fire, staring out into the velvet shadows between the trees.

His guts clenched and he ran back to the fire. 'Diego?'

'Hush.' He was a child, to be quieted with a flap of the hand. Owen bit back the retort that leaped to his lips and turned instead to look where the brothers were looking—

—and met the face of the jaguar level with his own face, and stared into a pair of bright eyes that knew him, and all that he had ever been.

The jaguar snarled and its mouth gaped wide. Cedric Owen stared death in the face and tried to scream but could not; his voice had abandoned him. He managed to raise one hand and pressed it uselessly against the soft, bepatterned fur.

'Welcome,' said the jaguar, in Spanish.

Cedric Owen fainted.

11
Lower Hayworth Farmhouse, Oxfordshire

June 2007 Kit asked, 'Why are we stopping?'

'Because I want to know if the green Audi that's been on our tail for the past twenty minutes is following us.'

Stella pulled the van into a field's grassy gateway. Tall hazel hedges reared on either side, dangling late, dried catkins. A sleek green Audi slid past, slowed at the T-junction at the foot of the lane and turned left.

After a moment, Kit said, 'Tell me we're turning right?'

'We're turning right,' Stella said. 'At least I am. You don't have to. I can take you to the station and put you on a train back to Cambridge, if you want.' She turned to face him. 'Is that what you want? You haven't said a word since we left Davy Law's lab.'

He folded his laptop shut. 'I was working. I thought . . .'

'Working?' She laughed.

Kit flushed. 'I've written you a program that'll take the squiggles in Cedric Owen's ledgers and fit them together to make the Mayan glyphs. If you can get your head round using a graphics tablet, it should halve your time to translate the second cipher.'

Stella said nothing, only leaned back and let him drift into silence.

He shook his head. 'I don't want to fight. Not over Davy Law.'

'He told me you were friends once. So why won't you tell me about it? It's not good, Kit. We're supposed to be on the same side.'

'OK, but there's very little to tell you that Gordon hasn't already said. Mistakes happened and someone I cared for was hurt. Doubtless I carried my share of the blame and I only noticed Davy's. I was young and arrogant and angry and I should have let it go then and I certainly should be big enough to let it go now.' He raised his eyes. It was impossible to read his expression when only half his face was under his control. 'I'm scared, Stell.

I just wanted to tell you that. Being nice about Davy Law is more than I can handle at the moment. Does the stone think we're in danger here?'

'No.' The heart-stone lay in her backpack behind her seat. It was comfortably alert, watching the world with the newborn–ancient wisdom she had felt before. She said, 'It's happier here than it was in Davy Law's lab.'

He smiled at that. 'A stone with good taste. I like it better already.'

THE FARMHOUSE WAS OLD, all sloping black beams and layers of whitewash with a cottage garden at the front and roses in an arch over the gate. A small path led to an oak front door flanked on both sides by hanging baskets. Stella parked close by the gate and began to open her door.

Kit caught her arm. 'You could go in on your own, but if we've kissed and made up, then you might like company?' He leaned over and kissed the side of her cheek. 'I love you, did I mention?'

'You did. And I'm still getting over my luck on that one.' Stella caught his hand and held it. 'Come on, we'll go bravely and together.'

At the end of the path, a brass plate on the wall beside the door read: THE INSTITUTE OF MAYAN STUDIES, OXFORD. DIRECTOR: PROFESSOR URSULA WALKER.

Stella rang the doorbell and several moments later the door was opened by a tall woman with dark hair and steel-grey eyes. She stood in the doorway and smiled at Stella. 'I'm Ursula Walker. You must be Dr Cody.'

'That's right.' Stella smiled back, then turned to Kit, who was seated in his wheelchair. 'This is my husband, Dr Kit O'Connor.'

Ursula Walker bent down and shook Kit's outstretched hand. 'Please come in. I'm sure you could do with some refreshment.' She led them through to her kitchen, which was a haven of cool peace with a flagged stone floor and stone walls four feet thick that kept out the heat of the day.

By the time they sat down at the large oak table, Kit had already fallen asleep in his chair. Stella placed her backpack, containing the heart-stone, at her feet. Ursula slid squat tumblers of homemade elderflower lemonade across the table and sank onto a chair between Stella and the sleeping Kit.

'Well, as you have already discovered, this is the place where Cedric Owen's ledgers were found,' she said. 'One of my ancestors unearthed them a century after Owen's death. They were bricked up in the bread oven to the right of the fireplace, together with the diamonds that made Bede's College wealthy. Her son wrote the first thesis on their contents in 1698 and the obsession has run in the family ever since. I've given my life to understanding the things that Cedric Owen did and to trying to locate his crystal skull.'

Stella said, 'Dr David Law told me that you are one of the few people alive to have seen one of the other crystal skulls.'

'Did he?' Ursula Walker stared into her lemonade a moment, then stood up and reached behind Kit to where a bookcase lined the wall. She selected a slim notebook, from which she pulled, in turn, a photograph printed to full A4. She slid it along the table to Stella and sat down again.

'I went to Lapland to do some research. I'm a scientist. It is sometimes difficult to believe . . . the various properties, for instance, of this—'

Ursula Walker was in the background of the photograph, half hidden by the draped reindeer hides, with the starry sky over her left shoulder, but she was not the focus of the image, nor the point where Stella's eye fell. It was the white crystal skull-stone, held between the hands of an old man dressed in reindeer skins and wearing a headdress of flattened, velvet-covered antlers. His eyes were cataract-white and he looked straight at the lens, and through it, to Stella. The skull-stone he held shed white light from its eyes, which focused on the backpack at Stella's feet.

Ursula said, 'This is the white spirit-stone of the Sami. I was not allowed to hold it. I was instructed, however, to bring back this one picture, and to show it to the new keeper of the blue heart-stone, that she might recognise the face of the white stone-keeper should they ever meet. His name is Ki'kaame. I saw him heal a child with the beams of light from the eyes of his skull-stone. Have you ever tried anything similar with yours?'

There was a long silence. Stella looked down into her glass. White petals of elderflowers floated on the top, the same colour as the skull-stone in the picture. She had not mentioned the heart-stone to Ursula. It still lay mute in the bag at her feet, but it was vividly alert now, sharpening her mind.

'How did you know?' she asked at last.

Ursula shrugged. 'A lucky guess?' She ticked the evidence off on her fingers. 'You're from Bede's. You're married to Kit O'Connor and he's been sniffing around the origins of the heart-stone since he first learned of its existence. You contact me out of the blue telling me you've found some Mayan glyphs in the ledgers. And when I rang Tony Bookless last night to find out who you were—he was most flattering, by the way—he asked me to do whatever I could to make sure you broke the item that had recently come into your possession.' She sat back and lifted her glass, eyeing Stella over the top of it. 'Were you going to tell me?'

Stella, too, leaned back in her chair and let out the breath she had been holding. Carefully, she said, 'Someone has tried to kill Kit at least once.

They—or someone else—wrecked his room yesterday and took his computer. As far as I can tell, everyone who has ever seen Cedric Owen's blue heart-stone has wanted either to possess it or to destroy it. It seems sensible, therefore, not to rush into showing it around. And it has my face. I can't tell you how much that scares me.'

She thought Ursula might ask how she knew. Instead, she said, 'Good. Then you truly are the skull's keeper. In which case the rest of us have a duty to keep you safe long enough to do what is needed.'

'Which is what, exactly?'

'According to the Sami, you have to place your stone on the heart of the earth at the moment of sunrise on the Day of Awakening, at which point it will join with the other twelve stones that will have been set in place by their own keepers. The full array, once linked, will bring to life the dragon of the winter snows, freeing it to fight the source of all evil and thereby heal the woes of mankind and the earth.'

'The dragon of the winter snows?' Stella laughed harshly. 'This is anthropology?'

It was hard to tell if Ursula was angry, offended or amused. 'You could call it the Ouroboros, or Quetzalcoatl, or the rainbow serpent, or Arthur's dragon of Albion, or the fire-dragon of China. And yes, the comparative cultural studies of this are written up in a dozen peer-reviewed journals. For the Sami, it is part of an oral legend that has remained intact for four hundred and eighty-seven generations. At the start of the ceremony, Ki'kaame invoked each of the spirit-skull's former holders by name. You can't begin to understand the power of that.'

'I'm sorry.' Stella closed her eyes. Distantly, she said, 'There was a poem in the Owen ledgers that led us to the stone. Read right, it's a set of instructions. It tells us to find "the time and place appointed", exactly the same as Ki'kaame's legend. It just doesn't tell us where to go or when.'

'Has the skull not told you?'

'I wouldn't be here if it had.' Stella lifted her pack from the floor, took out the skull and set it on the table next to the picture of the white stone. Ursula was not afraid of it; nor, it seemed, did she lust for it. She folded her arms on the table and laid her chin on them and, for a long time, faced the skull on its own level. She neither spoke nor moved for a long time.

'Are the other stones held by people similar to us?' Stella asked at last.

'I have reason to believe there's one in Hungary and one in Egypt, both held by families who understand what they're for and what's needed. I would like to believe the rest are held by people who also know what to do.'

'So the Sami could tell us where to go and when?'

'I think so,' Ursula said. 'The problem is how to ask them without going there. When you contacted me yesterday, I sent an email to Lapland asking for help, but I'm not holding my breath for a reply. It's a seven-hundred-mile trek from the herding grounds to the internet café in Rovaniemi in Finland and only one of Ki'kaame's great-grandsons is able to use a PC.'

Kit had woken. 'How long would it take you to get to Finland?'

'Too long. The stone wouldn't risk coming out of hiding unless we were very close indeed to the Day of Awakening.'

'And I thought we'd been so clever finding the code.' The irony in his smile, at least, was real.

'You were,' Ursula said warmly. 'If there had been no one left with a strength of heart and mind to match it, it would have stayed hidden for the rest of eternity. Our problem now is how to begin to find the answers when we don't even know how long we've got.'

'We have the codex we found in Cedric Owen's ledgers,' said Stella. 'It must have the answers, surely?'

It was worth a lot to see the world crash to a stop in Ursula's face. She said, 'I don't understand.'

Stella opened her bag and spread everything across the floor: the original copies of the ledgers, the prose poem they had found from the shorthand in the final volume, and her attempts at re-creating the Mayan glyphs.

'I told you that we'd found some glyphs,' she said. 'They're part of a code I built up from marks in the ledgers.' Stella spun the opened file across the floor. 'Can you read them?'

Ursula was already on her hands and knees, pulling the pages into a line across the flagstones, reading as she went. '*I, friend of the . . . jaguar-woman . . . I write this . . . account of my life, my knowledge, my learning*—That one isn't clear, I'll need to look it up. *I begin in . . . the city with the great river*—that would be Paris. He was never in London—*and my meeting with the . . . star-gazer and teller of . . . true futures*. That has to be Nostradamus; they shared a lodging in Paris . . .' Ursula's eyes were alight. 'Stella, this is a gold mine. Somewhere in here will be the detail of where we have to take the stone and when. How fast can you transcribe this?'

'Faster than I could have done now we've got Kit's software.'

'What are you waiting for?' Ursula was flushed. 'You write, I'll translate. We could conceivably have all thirty-two volumes done within a week.'

12
Southern Mayalands, New Spain

October 1556   Cedric Owen woke to rain that was not rain, but Diego standing over him flicking water at his face. His heart-stone, safe in its satchel, dug into the small of his back where he had fallen on it. He rolled over to find that the jaguar was at his side, gazing at him curiously.

From this new angle, he could see that the gape of its jaw was the large pelt of a beast, with the still-boned head set atop wiry native hair, that the lines flaring back from the bared teeth were not whiskers, but scars gouged deep into the cheeks of a dark native face, that the great white jaguar teeth below were not set in the jaws of a beast, but only threaded onto a necklace, and beneath them, pushing them out in two gentle curves, were . . .

Very much too late, Cedric Owen came to understand that the beast which now stood up beside his prone form was a woman, and that beneath the spotted beast-skin cape she was naked.

From the place he no longer cared to look, a deep voice said, 'Cedric Owen, are you afraid to set your eyes on me?'

He was afraid, but not as he had been. He stood, now, and made himself look. The jaguar-woman was a head shorter than Diego, but she was as well muscled as any fighting man. She stepped closer then to him and he saw the fine-branched lines at her eyes and he believed her close to forty. The belief made her no less terrifying, or beautiful.

'Do you not know me?' she demanded.

'I regret not, madam. I came in search of help for my friend, who is dying.'

'Only that?'

. . . therein to meet those who know the heart and soul of your blue stone. They will tell you how best you may unlock its secrets and preserve them . . .

'No, madam. I came also to find the knowledge of how best to use my blue heart-stone. If I find the secrets of my stone, I may heal my friend.'

Raising a brow, the jaguar-woman took a step back. 'I am Najakmul. And I have known you since before you were born, and since before you last died, when you were not Cedric Owen, and I know who you will be when next you walk upon the earth. We have little time. Are you prepared?'

'I don't know.'

'My sons have not told you what is required?'

'Your *sons*?' Owen spun with all the force of an aggrieved and injured pride. 'Diego!'

The scarred native shrugged sheepishly. 'What could I say that you would have believed? Only those of us who still live in the jungle, by the ways of the jungle, understand the power of the she-jaguar. When she talks, we listen. What she needs of us, we give her.'

'Of course.' He turned to Najakmul and bowed. Fernandez de Aguilar breathed painfully at their feet. Owen knelt and lifted the sleeping man's hand, that they might all remember why he had come. 'Perhaps, then, you can tell me what is required to achieve the healing of my friend?'

Catlike, the jaguar-woman came to kneel at the Spaniard's side, bringing her face close to his. Her eyes shone, dazzling him. 'Can you light a fire, Cedric Owen, keeper of the blue heart-stone? Light it on the fire circle of the mosaic in the clearing. As keeper of the stone, it must be your fire.'

She handed him the loose-strung bow and charred rod that the natives used with such ease and which Cedric Owen had never used at all. Under the gaze of Najakmul and her three sons, he crouched in the sweating heat and bent his back to slide the blackened tip of the stick into its socket. He did his best to draw the bow back and forth as deftly as Diego had done.

None of them laughed, for which he was grateful. He sweated and swore and cursed and slowly he saw a reddening glow come alive in the tinder and fed it small fragments of dried moss and grasses.

The smoke was rich with the scents of the jungle. Diego and his brothers gathered at his back and, in the shelter of their bodies, his single flame became many. When they matched the fading sun, Diego pressed a knot of grasses and leaves into his hand. 'Burn this. Drink the smoke.'

The bundle burnt with a high, blue flame, and the smoke slid down his throat and spread through his chest, warming him, lightening him. Before, he had thought the jungle blindingly iridescent. Now, he saw the colours within the colours and was dazzled. Light-headed, he might have launched himself into the sweep of saffron yellow flaring out from the sun's globe, letting go the fragile boundaries of his body, but that Fernandez de Aguilar coughed, and that chaotic sound was followed by a deep, bubbling in-breath.

Owen reached forward for his friend's wrist, and found it, and read the truth in the three pulses. 'He is dying. We must act now!'

Najakmul answered, 'Then look at me. The time is right.'

She sat in shadow. Two beams of light came from between her hands and Owen squinted at the bright space between her bony fingers. Slowly, a shape grew: the silvering outline of a jaguar skull crafted from perfectly clear, colourless stone.

So it was, in the throbbing night, that Owen saw for the first time another skull wrought of stone and shaped by hands that knew the secrets of the stars. He felt his soul rise to his eyes. 'What have you done to me?'

'Opened the eyes and ears of your heart. You are fit now to walk the rift between the worlds, to bind the four beast-stones and join together the nine stones of the races of men.'

A half-remembered shadow rose to him from the mosaic, and a chance remark by the priest: . . . *at the End of Days these four will come together to form one beast. Can you imagine, sir, what might arise out of the union of these four?*

Afraid, he said, 'You want me to raise the dragon Kukulkan, the rainbow serpent? The end times are not yet upon us, surely?'

Najakmul shook her head. 'Not yet. The nine stones of men must be joined in the hoop that will girdle the earth before the four beasts come together as one. Only you can find the piece that is yet missing from our knowledge.' She leaned forward over the fire. Thick smoke furled about her head. 'Will you believe me, Cedric Owen, if I tell you that time is a path along which you may walk if we open the gates and send you?'

Something in her dark eyes warned him, and a simple question from Nostradamus. 'Does death attend the trying?' he asked.

'Death attends all things.'

'And yet, if I succeed, will the death that presently attends Fernandez de Aguilar depart so that he might live?'

She nodded, and it was almost a bow. 'If you can do this, it is possible your friend may be healed. But if you fail, Desolation will spread over all the earth. Are you willing to risk all for the life of the one you care for?'

'I am,' he said with certainty.

'Then look down, Cedric Owen, and see the world at your feet.'

SOME TIME BEFORE night fell, de Aguilar had been brought to lie on the very centre of the mosaic that mapped the end time. At his right hand was devastation, grief, destruction and death, made so real Owen could hear the soul-death of those who struggled simply to survive. At his left, a girl-child played knucklebones in a meadow with wild flowers scattered around.

Caught in the rift between these two was the string of many-coloured pearls: a thin thread of hope for Fernandez de Aguilar and for the world.

With the care of a father to his firstborn, Owen brought out his blue stone and delivered it into the firelight. Tilting his hands, he played with the light until the stone gathered enough of fire and moon to weave them together and send them out to meet and match the clear, uncoloured crystal of Najakmul's snarling jaguar. In their meeting was an alchemy of tone and light he had not witnessed before. Lifting his skull, he directed the shine from its eyes and the thread of its song onto the tiled rift in the mosaic.

He began in the south, with the red stone, colour of the fire's heart. The rift widened as he sent the blue song of the heart-stone onto it, so that what had been a red-stained pearl became a skull-stone of deepest carnelian, and what had seemed a single line of plain black obsidian pebbles set into the earth became instead a widening place of night-time shadows.

Drawn by his blue heart-stone, he moved on and in. Now the rift was a broad valley in a sandy desert. Owen looked up to a crisp night sky with stars he had never imagined and could not name.

The red fire-stone was held by a woman with skin black as pitch who sat before him. She nodded to a log on which a visitor might sit. As Owen bent to take his seat, he heard a slither on the sand behind.

The blue skull-stone sang a bright note of warning and he spun on one foot and hooked the toe of the other under the red-bellied black snake that struck for him. As he sent it sailing far into the night he felt no fear, only a strange, dry exhilaration. Turning back, he found the black-skinned woman standing. Her skull-stone was the colour of blood, of birth, of raging, red-fanged death, the colour of the snake's belly. It took in the light of the fire and spilt it out again in a scarlet song-line that stained the earth to make a path. Owen turned his blue stone the same way and the paths wove together to make something greater than either apart.

'Come,' said Cedric Owen. 'Ours is the time, the joy and the duty.' The words were not his; they came from the night and the earth and the place beyond the scuffing shadows of the fire whence they must walk.

In silence they followed the red-blue path into the darkness, and presently came upon a rock that reared out of the desert. High on its side was a rounded cleft the size of a man's head.

Owen said, 'Your stone must join with the soul of the earth.'

The woman was already reaching up. Her stone slid home to its place in the root of the earth with a sound like the birth of a star. A blinding, deafening implosion that robbed Owen momentarily of his senses so that he did not see the second snake, which came for the black-skinned woman.

She was dying when next he opened his eyes, but gladly so. She smiled as he fell backwards onto earth that opened to let him through.

'That was the first,' said Najakmul. 'You faced the serpent and lived.'

Cedric Owen was already in a new place by the time he realised she was speaking to him.

Eight times in all did he cast his song-line along the rift that held back the Desolation. Eight times he met a skull-holder, each with a stone of a different colour, who gave it to the earth, that its song might join with the song of the blue stone, which was also the song of all that had gone before, and greater. Eight times did he face death in its many guises, from a scorpion at the foot of a pyramid to a charging boar in the forests of a wet, windy plain. Eight times did he see the skull-holder greet the same death he had just avoided after the stone had been given to its place in the earth.

He came last to the all-light that he remembered Nostradamus describing in Paris. An old, old man with a hooked nose and an antlered headdress held the white skull-stone in a place of snow and ice. Death came for Owen as an avalanche, which he ran from, returning later through thigh-deep snow. The cleft that joined the skull to the earth was dug deep into the living ice and bedrock and the old man had to be lowered in on a rope and lifted out afterwards, when the white stone was set. Then the old man was swept away unresisting, in an avalanche.

Alone, and untouched, Owen stood on the boundary between white snow and black night and his own blue stone sang to him, spinning and holding at once the complex thread of eight colours that encircled the earth.

Only eight.

The shadow of Nostradamus whispered in his ear: *Nine are shaped for the races of men. Remember this. You will need knowledge of it later.*

Owen looked down at the blue stone. Thinking back, it came to him that there had been no chance on this journey to go to England, whence the blue stone had come and must return.

Over the thousand leagues of snow and ice Najakmul's voice came to him on the razor wind. 'You must set your will to go there.'

Aloud, he said, 'But where? I know not the place.'

'The place will call you. Care for your friend, and follow the song of your heart.'

To his shame, Owen had all but forgotten Fernandez de Aguilar, lying flat on the mosaic with one arm gone and the fluid rattles in his lungs that were killing him. He smelt the smoke of the fire, suddenly sweetly pungent.

Najakmul said, 'You have staked your life on your friend's life. *Think and remember.*'

With a grinding effort, Owen trawled his mind and found at last something he could hold to: the image of de Aguilar looking out at the dawn before Zama, offering friendship without attachment or condition. *Perhaps you would not wish so to burden a friend?*

The light, acerbic voice reached Owen across the wastes, and the burn of the sun and the salt-sour wind, and the sway of the ship underfoot. Even as he matched it, the ship swayed less. The wind grew warmer and did not cut him so. The mewling cries of a distant gull came closer, and were instead the tremulous call of a tawny owlet. Owen opened his eyes, only then aware that he had closed them. He was in England; he knew it by the smell of damp turf and the sway of the beech trees in the moonlight. Most, he knew it by the silence of the blue stone, which had come home at last.

He did not know the place to which he had been brought. A circle of tall standing stones made the forefront to a low mound of barrowed earth, grown over with grass. At its end, facing Owen, was a stone-lintelled entrance, into which a tunnel bored, guarded by the four sentinel stones.

The owl called again, more harshly. Owen felt the skin on his back shrink from an unknown threat. His blue stone gave no warning, but sat in the silence of a held breath, waiting. *Does it require your death, this stone?*

The owl called for the third time. Owen lifted his blue stone that it might better catch the moonlight at his back and send it forth to light his way. For the first time, the colours it sent forward were all nine of the races of men, woven together to make the shimmer on the surface of water, or of the ice on a high mountain, split and re-formed, a colour that had no name, but was precious beyond imagining. Along the ghost-light of this path, Cedric Owen walked into the mouth of the grave mound, which opened to receive him, and down the length of the tunnel beyond.

THE LIGHT WAS SWALLOWED by the dark. Owen stood at the blind end of the grave mound. There were bones on the floor. Kneeling, he felt the length of them, and the curved ends, and knew them for parts of human and horse, more than one of each. His fingers brushed against something metallic: a brooch or a coin. He dropped it into his satchel and felt on for the socket into which the heart-stone must be seated.

A noise made him turn: the sound of voices, arguing. Swaying back against the tomb wall, he found an alcove and pressed himself into it. In the black, his eyes made shapes that could not be there. A young woman passed him, outlandishly dressed, speaking words in a language Owen did not recognise. She reached the end of the grave mound and looked about and, in the light of her presence, he saw the socket that would take the blue skull-stone.

Without wishing it, Owen gave a small and breathless gasp.

The woman turned, and Owen saw that between her hands she held a blue stone like his own. In the curved mirror surface of its cranium, he saw himself reflected exactly as now, but that his hair was silver. The shock of seeing these two things—the stone and his hair—rendered him mute.

The young woman peered at him and frowned. He saw his grandmother in her face and was likewise recognised. He might have spoken, but that she turned and looked back behind her in alarm, and ran on to the end of the mound, and knelt, and lifted her stone towards its resting place.

Urged by his own fears, Owen said, aloud, 'Do not delay.'

She turned to him, shocked. He reached out to help her as he had helped the others. Before his hands could find flesh, there fell a dense fog that swallowed both woman and stone. From outside came a crack, like thunder. In the darkness there was a stifled scream and the sound of a body falling.

Owen did not believe the woman had set her stone as was needed. Fog-blind, he felt his way forward to where she had been. By touch, he found the socket, and would have set his own blue stone into it as he had seen done eight times already, but that his skin pricked a warning.

He turned. There, in the dark, where there had been a blank wall, was a wide space. In the centre, Fernandez de Aguilar lay on a mosaic, lit by a dying fire. His breath rattled.

'Fernandez?' Owen knelt to take a pulse that fluttered and leaped under his fingers in a way he knew well, and had always hated. 'Fernandez, no! You cannot die!'

Owen still held the blue stone and it sang for him. The boundary between life and death was a tangible thing that shaped the air between him and his friend. Thrusting his free hand through the barrier to the place where de Aguilar's body lay in the worlds of death, he felt a flesh-scorching heat, paired with a bitter, aching cold, as he strained to touch his own life to the dark place of de Aguilar's death.

Death came for him, faster than the serpent, more crushing than the rocks of an avalanche. As a fist of dark ice, it sprang up the full length of his arm, clutching for his heart—

—and met the song of the blue heart-stone, in the core of his own soul.

The world exploded into shards of blue and black and scarlet.

Cedric Owen fell backwards, striking his head on stone. Fire scorched him on one side, cold on the other. A small, terrified part of his mind told him that he had entered hell. The rest of him knew only that the blue heart-stone was lying heavily on his abdomen and that he needed urgently to be sick. At last, retching on nothing until he thought the lining of his stomach would fall to shreds, he sat up and opened his eyes to find which god or devil, or some monster in between, was now his keeper.

He turned his eyes towards a half-seen figure in a white shirt who sat near the fire with one arm draped across its knees.

'Welcome back,' said Fernandez de Aguilar peacefully. 'It would seem that, once again, I am in debt to you for my life.'

For the second time that night, Cedric Owen fainted.

HE WOKE IN DAYLIGHT, in that cool part of the morning when the fire was still welcome. He lay on grass, not on the mosaic, and there were trees overhead, full of coloured birds. He sat up and was sick again. This time, Najakmul held him. The cone she handed him had water in it.

Owen said, 'I failed you.'

Najakmul seemed exhausted. 'You did not fail.'

'But I am alive, when the others all died.'

'You think that failure?' She smiled her disbelief.

He was not in the mood to be taunted. 'I thought only of Fernandez. I did not marry the blue heart-stone to the earth; I have it here with me still.'

'It was not up to you to set it, only to find where it should be. This is yours, as proof of it.'

Najakmul pressed a coin into his hand. On closer inspection, through blurry eyes, he saw rather a bronze medallion, with a dragon worked into its front face. The wings were an eagle's, the body lithe as a jaguar; the gaping jaws were of the crocodile and the tail curled up after the manner of a serpent. The whole thing stood with the rising sun at its back and a half-moon high above. A man stood before it in the west, small, insignificant.

A leather thong of a hide he did not recognise made the coin something to be worn. Najakmul took it from him and hooked it over his head.

Owen looked up, holding it to the sun. 'Is this Kukulkan?'

'It is indeed; that which will arise from the four beasts when the arc of the nine comes together. Only the keeper of the blue stone may wear such a thing, and must do so at the end times. Ensure that it stays with the stone.'

He felt his brow furrow along its length. 'But I did not set my stone. Kukulkan will not arise. Will Desolation rule the land?'

Najakmul sat on her heels at his side. 'The time of Desolation will not come upon us until the sun treads the path to the Underworld four hundred years from now. You moved across more than miles in your journeys, Cedric Owen; you moved also across centuries. You have travelled the song-line of your stone, which is not only distance, but also time. This is why you did not place the heart-stone. In that distant time—many years from now—another will be asked to place it, and may do so, if you can leave true word of where it must go and when.'

'Then I have truly failed because I don't know where the place was. I could search the length and breadth of Britain and never find it again.'

'You will find it.' She nodded to make them both believe it. 'It is the second of your three tasks. You have completed the first: to find the secret of the heart-stone. The second is to find where the stone must be placed at the end times, and the third is to hide the stone safely, leaving word of where it must go at the time when Kukulkan arises. The fate of the world rests on you, Cedric Owen. Therefore you will find the place. It must be so.'

'And I will die when all is done?'

'The keeper always dies. It is the way of things.'

Owen looked down at the blue stone. He said, 'I had silver hair in the grave mound.'

Najakmul leaned in to touch his brow. 'Show me. Make a picture in your head and show it to me in the stone.'

He brought forward the memory of his own reflection in the blue stone: a scar lay across one cheek that he did not presently have, and his hair was silver, almost to white. He struggled to hold the mirrored image.

'Enough.' Najakmul sat back. 'You should sleep now. Where you have been and what you have done is not easy.'

He was already half sleeping. Thickly, he said, 'In the time-yet-to-come I saw a young woman in the grave mound. She carried a blue stone, but I did not see if she placed it in its seating. A fog came and my sight was taken from me. I saw nothing of her after.'

Najakmul chewed her lip, nodding slowly. 'Then it is not certain that she will succeed. We can only do our best to make it so.'

She picked a stick and stabbed it into the fire to good effect; sparks flew high into the cool blue sky. 'You excelled yourself, and we are proud of you, we who brought you to this. Not one of us could have done better.'

WHEN OWEN WOKE NEXT, Najakmul was no longer watching over him. Instead, Diego and his brothers fussed with the mules a short distance away. De Aguilar was nearby, dressed in a white linen shirt, with the empty sleeve pinned up. He had cut a long stick and was practising fencing moves, left-handed. He saw Owen and threw his stick away, then came to sit by the fire.

'Welcome. I had thought perhaps you would sleep until the snows come. Would you like food? I can cook corn pancakes now.'

'Thank you, yes.'

One-handed, de Aguilar cooked them both a pancake. The moves had the fluent look of sustained practice.

'How long did I sleep?'

'Perhaps best that you do not ask. It is a great thing you have done, even so little as I understand of it.'

'It did not seem so at the time.'

'Then it will not lead to arrogance, which is a good thing. I could not bear to be so indebted to an arrogant man.' There was a new calm in de Aguilar's eyes as he rolled the pancake and passed it across.

Owen said, 'You are different.'

'I have seen death and stepped past it. There is little to be afraid of now.'

Owen felt the warm press of the bronze dragon on his chest. He lifted it and rubbed it lightly with his thumb. 'I suppose we should return to England now and seek out the place of the stone circle.' He rubbed his face. He had no real wish to abandon all that he had found in the jungle.

Circumspectly, de Aguilar said, 'Would you care to go back to your homeland a rich man or a poor one?'

'Do I have a choice?'

'I believe so. Najakmul has been called into the jungle to tend a woman in childbirth but she gave me to understand . . . that you had grey hair in your journeys?'

'I did. Bright silver, like pewter. It was a strange thing to see.'

'She said as much. It would seem that we are given some grace to rest and enjoy each other's company before we must return to England to fulfil your destiny.'

'Some grace? How long? A week? A month? A season?'

'Until you have silver hair, my friend.' De Aguilar leaned forward and with exaggerated interest, studied the roots. 'Unless you have a bad shock, I would say perhaps thirty years.'

'Thirty . . . ?' Owen stared at him, and laughed, and went on laughing, knowing himself a fool but enjoying the feel of it. 'Half a lifetime and then you will come with me to England? Really?'

De Aguilar let a smile stretch to his eyes and beyond. 'To England, I insist upon it. But not yet. First, we will live out the best parts of our lives in paradise, and make our fortunes in doing so.'

13
Lower Hayworth Farmhouse, Oxfordshire

June 2007 On the laptop in front of Stella were a few more lines of text to end the page.

Julye 3, 1586, From Jan de Groot, trader, For: three shyps' hold of Sisal unmade into rope and one shyp of rope readie-made: diamonds to the value of £100 (one hundred pounds).

Julye 3, 1586, Also from Meinheer de Groot, ane sword for a left-handed manne, craftit with grate skylle by the Brothers Gallucci in Turino, Italy, to the worth of £5, a gift.

In the four days she'd been at Lower Hayworth Farm, the transcription of the ledgers had become her obsession. She was in Ursula Walker's study, from where French windows opened onto an orchard and herb garden. Ursula worked under the apple trees outside.

A dragging footstep sounded from the doorway to the kitchen.

'Coffee?' Kit asked.

'Thank you.' She did not lift her head. 'What time is it?'

'Half past five. You've been at it for eleven hours. You should take a break.'

'Soon. I'm nearly done.'

'Gordon rang,' said Kit. 'He's finished the analysis of the limestone section. He thinks the skull was immersed in the cave in the spring of 1589—*after* Cedric Owen died.'

'So we still don't know who the skeleton was?' Stella said. And then, 'How's the translation going?'

'Slowly.' Kit swayed on his two sticks. He was walking better than he had been, but he still needed Stella's help to dress and undress. Now, he leaned against a wall for stability. 'Cedric Owen is in the Mayalands, drinking smoke in the jungle with a woman who is also a jaguar. I think we forget how impenetrable Elizabethan writing can be even when it hasn't been warped through the prism of ancient Mayan glyphs. Ursula's asked her cousin Meredith Lawrence to come and help. He's a Classics man at Oxford.'

'I know.'

They spoke as strangers and could not change it. Since they'd arrived at the farmhouse the hairline crack between them had become an unbridged, unbridgeable divide. They talked to each other only when they must. What shocked Stella most was how fast they had fallen apart. She could remember that she had loved him, but she could not remember how or why. The cold in Kit's eyes had become a steel wall and he no longer tried to pretend he was letting her in. Nor did he make any effort to hide his loathing of the blue skull-stone. He would not have come into the room now if she had not put the skull into the backpack hidden under the desk.

Stella pressed a key to open a new page and was more relieved than sorry when she heard Kit leave.

MEREDITH LAWRENCE came in from the garden, where he'd been helping Ursula transcribe the glyphs. He was a tall man, no older than his cousin, a man in his academic prime. He leaned against the French windows, with his tie gone and his shirt sleeves rolled up. 'Can you take a break, Stella?'

'If you can give me a good enough reason.'

'Not the one you want.' He smiled an apology. 'No date and time appointed, but possibly some pointers in the right direction. If you'd care to join us for some iced tea, we could show you what we've got.'

The garden was small and wild, with a roughly mown lawn and borders filled with kitchen herbs and straggling tomato plants. Ursula worked on a tartan blanket beneath an apple tree. She sat up and cleared a space as Stella approached. 'Sorry, it's a bit rustic. Would you like a chair?'

'The blanket's fine.' Stella stretched out in the sun on the red and black tartan, resting her forearm across her eyes for shade. Kit was nowhere to be seen, for which she was grateful.

Some while later, Meredith brought out the iced tea. Stella was warm and mellow by then, and not inclined to get up. Still with one arm over her eyes, she asked, 'What have you got?'

'A dog and a bat,' said Ursula. 'To be more accurate, we have a pair of recurring glyphs that have no obvious bearing on the narrative, but they are almost certainly Oc and Zotz, part of a date in the Long Count of years.'

Stella lifted her arm from her eyes. 'And in English, that would be . . .?'

Meredith was in her field of view. He spread his hands. 'If we knew that, I'd have come to you a little more cheerfully.'

'Without numbers, the glyphs are meaningless,' Ursula said. 'It's like saying today is a Tuesday in June. If I don't say it's Tuesday, June the 19th, 2007, you're none the wiser.'

'Is that it?'

'So far. We're working on it.'

'Great.' Stella rolled over onto her stomach. 'Four days' work for a Tuesday in June. Why didn't Owen just give us the date in plain text?'

'He didn't know which calendar to use,' Meredith said and, when Stella looked at him questioningly, 'Owen had just lived through the administrative chaos that was the transition from the Julian to the Gregorian in which some Catholic countries in Europe had cut nine days from their calendars while the Protestant ones, including England, chose to ignore the deviations of a Catholic pope. Half of Europe didn't know what the date was and nobody could have predicted which version we'd be using five centuries later, if either. He had no choice but to use a system that he knew was accurate.'

'And Mayan calendrics is accurate to 0.0007 of a second for sixteen thousand years, so he'd be safe with that,' Stella said, remembering something that Davy Law had told her. 'So where do we go from here?'

'We make an effort to think as Owen thought.' Ursula reached for a pile of papers.

Meredith said, 'One obvious route would be to break up the information into fragments and hide each part in a different place. It's what I would do, in Owen's place. Which leads us directly to the medallion you found in the cave of the skull-stone, the one with the mark of Libra on the back.'

'This?'

Stella reached into her shirt, pulled the thong over her head and held it out to him. Ursula bent over Meredith to look at the medallion.

'No numbers,' Meredith said, disappointed. 'Not in English, not in Roman numerals, not in the Mayan counting system, not even notches on the rim.'

Ursula took the medallion, turning it over in her hand. 'And nothing to link us to Libra, either, unless we can find a date in October that fits with Oc and Zotz. But that's five months away, and Ki'kaame said the stone would only dare to show itself in the last weeks before the date.' She held the medallion up. There was a pause, and then a sudden catch of breath. 'Meri, when was the last time you saw a dragon facing right instead of left?'

'Apart from every other vertical surface at Bede's?' He cocked his head. 'Hardly ever. Pretty much every other dragon ever painted in the canon of European art points left, facing a knight in the left foreground.'

'Not on a hillside, less than half an hour's drive from here?'

'Ah.' A broad smile of understanding dawned on his face. 'The horse that might not be a horse. Well done, cousin mine. Stella, have you ever seen the White Horse of Uffington?'

Stella sat up. 'Not that I know of.'

'You'd know.' He grinned cheerfully. 'It's a Neolithic monument, at least five thousand years old. Our ancestors carved the shape of a horse into the hillside, taking away the turf to show the white chalk beneath. The best place from which to sit and look at it is called Dragon Hill. Take your medallion and your skull and see if they think it's a good place to be. And take Kit while you're at it.'

'I can't—'

'You can. You're four volumes ahead of us in your transcriptions. You deserve an hour or two off.'

The misunderstanding was deliberate. Stella might have argued, but Kit was there, standing at the French windows, blocking her route back into the study. For a moment, she believed it was a coincidence, then remembered the length of time Meredith had taken to bring the iced tea.

Feeling leaden, she stood up. She could think of nothing to say.

Woodenly, Kit said, 'I've been there once, a long time ago. I know the way, but you'll have to drive.'

'Do you want to go?'

He shrugged. 'Do you?'

'Oh, for God's sake,' said Ursula. 'Just go. Go together. Walk up the hill together, sit at the top together, and for heaven's sake talk about something other than the weather when you get there. It'll be worth it, trust me.'

'THERE ARE STEPS,' Stella said. 'You don't have to crawl up the hill.'

'I don't want to use the steps. They're an affront to the wildness of the place. Just go ahead and stop looking at me. It doesn't help.'

Already the sun was a lavender bruise on the western horizon with washed veils of tangerine above. A waxing half-moon hung high overhead.

The car was parked illegally at the roadside. The small, flat-topped hill grew out of the road, and Stella used her hands to pull herself up the steep, tussocked slope, suppressing the urge to look back at Kit and help him.

He found he was more agile on all fours and put on a burst of speed at the end and reached the top before her. In silence, he offered his hand to haul her up the last strides. Uncertainly, she hooked her fingers through his and drew herself up. The top was a place of sun-dried turf and they sat down together, staring at the grass. The silence stretched.

Kit said, 'Have you looked at the horse yet?'

'Not yet.' She did not think he had, either. A shared perversity kept them both from it.

Kit lay back on the turf. The late sun cast spears of gold across his face. The green bruises were a faded remnant of his fall.

'Is this the appointed place?' he asked.

'No. The skull-stone feels safe here, but no more than that.' The backpack that held the stone lay at her side. For the drive and all the way up the hill, Kit had ignored it. Stella was surprised that he mentioned it now.

When the silence became too thick to break, she, too, lay back and let her eyes rest on the sky. Kit was warm at her side and she remembered other summer days, on other grass, when a blue sky didn't hurt like this.

She said, 'I should have thrown the stone away.'

'I don't think so. You are the skull's rightful keeper. I don't want to be responsible for the end of time just because I can't handle how you feel about a stone.' He was silent for a while. The sun had deepened to amber. The high moon brightened with it. 'I'm trying to imagine what might happen to end the world and how a scary lump of blue crystal might change it.' He touched his lips to her cheek. 'The sun's nearly gone. Shall we look at the horse while it's still there to be seen?'

Stella rolled away from him and got up. 'Go on then.' Later than him, she looked up. 'My God . . .'

It was only a horse, carved in simple, flowing lines from a green hillside to show the white chalk beneath. It was only chance that the sun and the moon spilled even light across it, so that the white glowed as liquid fire. The horse on the hillside was almost exactly the same as the dragon on Cedric Owen's medallion, alive in all its wild beauty. All it lacked was wings.

'Kit, do you see . . . ?'

He dragged her hand to his lips and crushed them with it. 'Don't speak. We're here at the balance between day and night and no one can take it from us. It's perfect. Please don't speak.'

For full thirty seconds, she held herself silent against the breaking ocean within. Then, 'Kit, say that again?'

He huffed amused frustration. 'It's perfect. Please don't—'

'No, before that, about balance.'

He frowned, caught by her tone. 'I don't remember.'

'*We're here at the balance between day and night.* It isn't Libra on the medallion. It's the scales in their own right.' With one hand, she was scrabbling in her shirt, pulling out the medallion; with the other, fighting to get into her pockets for her mobile. 'Why did we not see this before? Meredith was right, Owen *did* leave us what we needed in more than one place.'

'Stell, you're not making sense.'

'Hush.' She flapped one hand. With the thumb of the other, she speed-dialled Ursula's number. When the call was answered, she said, 'Ursula, it's the summer solstice! The day after tomorrow! The scales on the stained-glass window at Bede's and the sign of Libra scratched on the back of the medallion show the same thing. They're weighing day against night, not sun against moon. Does that fit with the dogs and the bats?'

'Wait, I'll check.' There was a tight, cluttered moment, filled with the rattle of keyboard, then a pause.

Hoarsely, Ursula said, '9 Oc, 18 Zotz is June the 21st, 2007. The day after tomorrow. I can't think why we didn't look before.'

'It doesn't matter, we have it now. And we've got the time of day to go with it. The stained-glass window shows the dragon arising at dawn on a day when there's a waxing half-moon in Virgo. So the time appointed is about thirty-six hours from now. All we need is the place.'

'Is it not the white horse?'

'The skull-stone doesn't think so. It feels safe here.'

'Then we're still stuck because it's nowhere in the manuscript and we've translated all you've transcribed. Meredith's gone into town to check some of the glyphs against the dictionaries in the Bodleian, but I don't hold out much hope. In the last bit we've translated, Owen has just come back from the New World to England. But it's clear he doesn't know the location of the place he's looking for. He says so clearly in the text.'

'Well, he must have found it before he died. We'll come home now and I'll finish transcribing the last four volumes. It has to be in there.'

IT WAS TEN O'CLOCK on the night before the solstice and Stella had one more page left to transcribe. She was alone in the study; Kit had gone to bed and Ursula was working upstairs in her bedroom. Outside, the half-moon was setting. It lay on the far horizon, bright against a backwash of stars.

The last page wavered on the screen: *March 12, 1589, From Francis Walker, who was once another man, my thanks for all you have done . . .*

She could not focus. The skull-stone sat on the desk in plain view; Kit had asked her to put it there. The blue eyes observed her, too much like life for comfort. Aloud, she said, 'You look like my grandfather.'

For sixty years, Stella's grandfather had raised sheep on Ingleborough Fell, through summer heat and winter snow. From the hollows of her memory, he said, *You should wake, child. It is not a time for sleeping.*

'I'm not sleeping. I'm working. It just feels like sleep.'

No. The voice was different. Stella blinked again. Where had been her grandfather was a younger woman, like her and yet unlike, with darker hair braided to her elbows. *You dream and should wake, else it was all for nothing. Wake now!* The woman clapped her hands and Stella woke.

In the study was smoke, sliding at floor height, coiling up the legs of the chair. In the blue place of her mind, the skull-stone awoke as if from a deeper dreaming. The scything yellow of its panic met the force of her own terror. She grabbed the laptop and ran for the door.

'*Fire!*'

14
Trinity Street, Cambridge

Christmas Eve 1588 Dr Barnabas Tythe, reader of physic and philosophy and Vice-Master of Bede's College, Cambridge, was enjoying the blaze and crackle of his own fire, alone in his lodgings, when the rap came at the door. He ignored it, being lost in contemplation of a letter. Solitude had slowly become him since his wife's death and he had come to realise that he loved his college more than he might ever love another too-mortal woman.

His house, a short distance from the college, was not difficult to manage. Thus it was that this Christ's Mass, he had given leave to those of his serving staff who wished it to visit relatives, that they might be in the company of their loved ones when they gave thanks to God that the English forces had this summer so roundly defeated King Philip of Spain's Armada.

Tythe had not been called up to arms in defence of the realm. His position as one of the country's foremost academic physicians, added to his age and the old injury to his left knee, ensured he was not required to strap on the sword he could barely use and stand shoulder to shoulder with others equally unsuited to warfare. Thus had summer given way to a good, rich autumn, full of relief and relaxation. Little of real worth had been taught or learned that Michaelmas term but there was no great harm in that, and the holidays had come and the snow had followed soon after and Cambridge had passed quietly into Christ's Mass, pleased to remember that God loved the Puritans more than the Catholics and, by way of evidence, had left their Queen Elizabeth to blaze in all her glory on the throne.

Nobody, in all of this, thought greatly of Sir Francis Walsingham, secretary and spymaster to the Queen. Nobody, that is, except Walsingham himself, and his extensive network of spies.

Nobody knew the full count of those in Walsingham's pay, yet it was well known what happened to men with whom the Queen's secretary was displeased, and no man in his right mind would choose to risk ending his life in the Tower of London by so doing. Which made it unsettling, therefore, to have received a letter in Walsingham's own hand, demanding action that was, in Tythe's opinion, impossible to take. Three feet of snow combined with the onset of Christ's Mass gave him grace to consider his reply, and he had been doing just that for two days, since the letter arrived.

He threw another log on the fire and read the letter for the fifth time that evening, then drank a sip of good Greek malmsey and shook his head.

The second knock rattled the door on its hinges. A voice he had not heard for years hissed, 'Barnabas? Barnabas Tythe. If you would not have us perish on your doorstep, would you open up and let us in?'

The malmsey spilled all over the hearth, sending aromatic vapours into the air. The goblet received a dent that would take the town's silversmith some skill to repair. Tythe paid attention to neither, but stared in shock at the letter lying across his hand and tried to understand how that which had been impossible was rendered otherwise, and how, in God's name, Sir Francis Walsingham could have known it aforehand.

The dark shadow of the Tower loomed suddenly darker as the Vice-Master of Bede's stood up and hobbled forward to open the door.

'*WRITTEN THIS 20TH DAY of December in the year of Our Lord et cetera, to Sir Barnabas Tythe, from Sir Francis Walsingham, greetings.*

'*The most momentous year in our history draws to a close. We have fought off the Spanish evil and kept whole the sovereign borders of our land and the rights and sufferance of our most Beloved Queen.*

But the Papists never rest and nor must we. I have it on good authority that one Cedric Owen, formerly of your acquaintance, is travelling in the company of a Spaniard and is carrying with him certain items of witchcraft that must be taken and held for further examination.

'I believe that he will endeavour to reach you within the closing days of the year. You are to apprehend him with all necessary force and deliver him alive to London with all speed. Should you require assistance, raise your own banner above your house and those who are our friends in this matter will come to you.

'"Deliver him alive to London."' Barnabas Tythe lowered the letter he had been reading and stared across the top of it to his friend. 'Whatever you have done to make an enemy of Francis Walsingham, Cedric Owen, you should undo it if such is in your power, or flee England to escape him.'

'That's one option. I would like to think there might be others, though.'

The night, which had been strange, was descending rapidly into unreality. The first of the two men standing warming themselves in a steam of damp riding habits by the fire was sixty years old, almost to the day. Barnabas Tythe knew this because he had attended Cedric Owen's twenty-first birthday celebrations thirty-nine years before. It was a matter of some concern, therefore, that Owen should look so exuberantly healthy, when all accounts had laid him dead in a French dockside tavern thirty years before.

And he had brought an accomplice, a one-armed popinjay with an astonishingly inappropriate nugget of gold at his left ear lobe, who spoke now, in a soulful not-quite-English. 'Have I not said already that Walsingham is the agent of the Enemy? You should listen to your swordsman, my friend, for your life is mine to protect, and I scented danger before ever we left Sluis.'

Manifestly more disconcerting than the presence of a once-friend whose death he still mourned every Twelfth Night was the growing understanding that the accomplice was both a Spaniard and Cedric Owen's friend.

Tythe was neither a weak man nor a coward. Nevertheless, he felt sick in every part of his body and soul. He had been in the Tower once and had caught a whiff of the stench of utter despair.

He said, 'Cedric, I have loved you like a son, but I ask you now to leave. Please. I beg of you. Go now while the streets are empty and the falling snow will cover your tracks. I will tell no one you were here, I swear to it.'

'Barnabas, it is Christmas Eve. We can stay safely for two days, I think, before anyone considers it necessary to call on you, and even then, surely you can trust the men of Bede's?'

'No. That's just it. The Master, Robert Maplethorpe, is Walsingham's man as much as I. More so, if the truth be told.'

'Barnabas?' Cedric Owen blinked at him. 'Can we assume that Sir Francis does *not* know that you are still a Catholic at heart?'

There was a choking noise in the quiet that was Barnabas Tythe's answer. The bejewelled Spaniard said softly, 'That was not kind, my friend. Now you have made your friend sick with fear. He believes himself undone and in the company of witches, or at least of blackmailers.'

Barnabas Tythe watched mutely as Owen opened his riding pack and unwrapped a spare cloak. A corner of the cloak fell away and the placid amber light of his fire was warped to a cold ice blue. It was thirty years since he had seen its like and it still haunted his dreams.

'Not the blue heart-stone. Please God, Cedric, in thirty years, have you not had the sense to rid yourself of that? Queen Mary may have wanted to burn you for it, but Walsingham will do far, far worse.'

'Ha!' The Spaniard had startling grey-blue eyes and long, glossy hair. 'My friend, Dr Tythe is right; we should be gone from here. If Walsingham knows where we are, the birth of Christ will not keep him from us.'

'No, but the snow will. And it gives us time to plan. In any case, I have more wealth than he has.'

Walsingham was one of the richest men in England, so Tythe assumed that Owen was speaking in allegory. It was with some surprise, therefore, that he saw the other corner of Cedric Owen's riding cloak fall back to reveal a life-sized mask of a woman's face cast of gold with a crusting of diamonds at both ears that made the Spaniard look positively restrained.

'Cedric?' Barnabas Tythe found his mouth gone dry. 'Where did you get this? Does it carry men's blood?'

'It carries a woman's blood, certainly. It was cast from the face of a woman for whom I had the highest respect. Her son made it on the occasion of her death, as our leaving gift. I will be sad to see it go, but if anyone can gaze upon Walsingham and cause him ill, it is Najakmul.'

'But why? This would buy you freedom if you used it wisely.'

Owen tilted a smile. 'If I sought freedom, and if it were all that I had, I might consider your suggestion. But I seek more than freedom, which makes it fortunate that this is not all that I have.'

Tythe gaped. 'There is more?'

'Indeed. Clearly I do not choose to carry it all with me. The rest is largely in gemstones, which are more easily hidden. They are in the false bottoms of barrels housed in a cellar near the port in Harwich. Given that I must die soon, we must find a way for you to reach it, and then for you to hide it until such time as Walsingham and all like him are gone.'

The wine sat unexpectedly sour in Tythe's mouth. 'Why must you die?'

'Walsingham has issued a warrant for my arrest. I am a traitor, to be arrested on sight and taken to the Tower. Only if I am dead will he desist.'

'But if you are a traitor and die, your estate becomes forfeit to the Crown.'

'Which is why I must die a pauper and the wealth be hidden for your lifetime and beyond.' Owen smiled and cocked his grey-tinged head. 'What is your greatest love, Barnabas?'

That answer was easy. 'Bede's,' said the Vice-Master.

'Then will you help me to give my diamonds to the college in such a way that Walsingham cannot get his hands on them? Even if it means my death?'

Tythe felt great sorrow. 'Would you fall on your sword for this man, Cedric?'

Owen grinned. 'Well, I would fall on somebody's sword. My own might not be public enough for Walsingham's tastes.' Then, with a new hardness to his voice, he asked, 'Who else is in Walsingham's pay?'

Tythe said, 'Besides Maplethorpe, I cannot say for certain. I doubt there's a master of any college in Cambridge, or Oxford for that matter, who isn't taking money from him in some form. And there will be others, too.'

'Then we must be doubly cautious.' Owen stared into the blue stone and then turned to the Vice-Master. 'Barnabas, if I were to offer you the Mastership of Bede's as my Christmas gift, what would you say?'

Tythe laughed, with little humour. 'That you should sleep and we should begin again with the clean slate of forgetfulness on the morrow.'

'You don't want to be Master?'

'Of course I do! I have given my life to my college and am vain enough to want her to grant me her ultimate accolade in return. But Maplethorpe is not a man to cross lightly. He hides behind a veil of abstinent piety and sends his three manservants to murder those who stand against him. It's one of the reasons he was elected Master; none of us dared do anything else.'

The Spaniard flashed a ferocious smile. 'A challenge! At last!'

Cedric Owen ignored him, saying, 'Now would be a good time, then, for you to go to Maplethorpe and tell him that you have unexpected visitors. Show him the letter and tell him we came to prevail upon your Christian charity. It is Christmas and the roads are blocked. We cannot therefore be dispatched to London and so you seek his advice on what best to do.'

'He'll kill you,' said Tythe flatly.

Owen bowed. 'Then you will have done your duty and will fly high in Walsingham's favour. If I cannot give you the Mastership, what better gift than this, that we have not endangered your life or your standing?'

BUT FOR THE DRIFTING echoes of the night bell, the streets of Cambridge were softly quiet and absolutely dark. The young moon had fallen below the earth's edge, leaving only a scattering of stars by which to see.

'What if your subterfuge with the torches fails?' Tythe asked, as he led his visitors through the lightly falling snow to Midsummer Common.

'It worked in Sluis and twice before that,' Owen said, 'it will work again. Men fight more poorly if they do not know the true numbers they face.'

'He has three men to guard him and he can fight as well as any of them.'

'There were six in Rheims. All are dead. Keep out of the fighting and you will remain safe.'

Owen watched Tythe screw up his courage. The flame of the old man's torch progressed to the gates of the college and was presently drawn inside.

Owen and de Aguilar were left alone in the dark. 'Thirty years of preparation and all for this,' de Aguilar said softly. 'It does not seem so long.'

'It was long enough,' Owen said. 'The heart-stone gave us three decades' gift. All that remains is to find if we can fulfil the tasks it requires of us, for if we fail it has all been for nothing.'

THERE WAS NO SOUND from the porter's lodge of Bede's College, but the side door opened and three torches appeared where there had been one.

'Only three. Maplethorpe has not come,' de Aguilar hissed.

'He will. I knew him as a student. Even then, he baited bears for pleasure. He will not miss a chance to kill men now for the sport of it.'

The torches came forward in a line abreast. At a certain moment, a shaft of light blazed as the porter's door opened and shut on the candles within. Two shapes stepped out into snow and were lost in the cloaking dark.

'Now,' said Owen.

He struck flint against tinder to light a single torch, and then two others from it. Handing one to de Aguilar, he emerged from the line of trees at the edge of the river walking crabwise, bearing a torch in each hand. De Aguilar followed in like manner, his torch held behind him so that it might seem as if three or four men walking line astern had crossed the small arched bridge and entered the college grounds.

At the porter's door, Owen let out an oath in Fenland brogue and doused his torches. In more of an academic voice, he said, 'God's bones! Did you not bring a better light on such a night as this?'

'Hush now. Silence about the Master's work.' In thirty years, de Aguilar had learned English as if born to it, perfecting both the scholar's drawl and the nasal East Anglian vowels. In these latter, he said, 'We'd best douse the torches. There's no need for more than one when all we're hunting is a one-armed man and a fop.'

'No need even for one, when we have three.' The authority in the voice that came from the porter's lodge exceeded that of any porter.

Robert Maplethorpe stepped out into the crescent of churned snow that marked the gateway to Bede's College. The blade of his sword flickered naked in the grey snowlight. His three men came behind him, each bearing aloft a lit torch in one hand and ironwood cudgels in the other.

Barnabas Tythe stood framed in the doorway and called out over the heads of Maplethorpe's three thugs, 'Joseph, is that you?'

Cedric Owen said, 'Aye,' and hawked and spat into the snow. 'At your service, Master Tythe. We are come as you asked, bringing all we could muster. Your enemies remain in your rooms making free of your hospitality.'

He thrust his own torch into the snow, creating a darkness that engulfed him; by chance, he and de Aguilar stood beyond the circle of light cast by Maplethorpe's men. De Aguilar cursed, and appeared to stumble.

'*You're drunk!*' Maplethorpe hissed it with venom.

'N-nay, Master.' De Aguilar staggered backwards in evident terror. As far as anyone could see, he was not armed. The three men behind Maplethorpe leered knowingly as their Master brought his blade up to fighting height. He was a fit man. In three strides he was beyond the arc of the blazing torches.

'Hold! I will have no man of mine drunk at any time, and least so on the day of Our Lord's birth.'

From the dark, coarsely, Cedric Owen said, 'Master, is it not the Spaniard that we seek, not the death of your loyal servants?'

'I will not kill him, only . . . teach him a . . . lesson.'

The sentence was twice punctuated by the scuffling of feet and the sleek whistle of a sword blade slashing air. All of those listening heard that sound, partway between a grunt and a squeal, that is the earnest signature of death, and all heard a body fold to the ground.

Maplethorpe's voice said, 'A pity, but a lesson learned.' His shape loomed in the darkness, cloak a-flying. 'Why are we still lit like a festive bonfire? Can you not find your way to Tythe's lodgings by starlight?'

His three thugs doused their lights. The man they still believed to be Maplethorpe strode to the nearest—who had just time to see that his assailant was thrusting left-handed before the sword thus deployed slid in up a line from the sternum to pierce his heart. He fell back, choking blood. Barnabas Tythe, with a surprising courage, knifed another of the thugs in the back and kicked his legs out from under him so that he fell to the snow.

The third of Maplethorpe's three mastiffs had the speed of reflex to leap forward, swearing, and advanced on de Aguilar. Breathing hard, he swung at the Spaniard. Cudgel met blade—and broke it. De Aguilar threw himself sideways, rolling, and rose with the stolen cloak already off his shoulders and spinning round his only arm. He danced on the snow, dodging and ducking the swinging cudgel. His assailant cursed and drew his eating dagger. He had two weapons against a one-armed, disarmed man. He moved fast and in three moves had jabbed his dagger into de Aguilar's thigh and swung the cudgel at his head. Owen watched as the Spaniard crumpled to the snow and the cudgel-man stepped in to finish his work.

'No!'

A long time ago, Cedric Owen had vowed never to wield his own sword in anger. In the Jesuit bloodbath at Zama that had seen Najakmul dead, in Rheims, in Sluis, in the harbour at Harwich, where they had nearly been taken by Walsingham's agents, he had used his knife, or a club, and let the Spaniard set his serpent-fastness against other men's flesh and blood. He had seen it strike against greater numbers so often now that he had begun to believe his friend invulnerable.

He had no sword now, but a dead man's cudgel lay at his feet. He swept it up and waded forward through the snow and let the heavy wood carry him past his incompetence.

He was not too late. That was the thought that filled him as the cudgel-man struck back. The first blow took him in the ribs and he felt three of them crack. The reverse swing struck his head, with the full, skull-cracking force of the big man's arm, and felled him.

In the long, long moment of falling, Cedric Owen heard Barnabas Tythe shout his name and fancied he saw his old tutor hobble up to stab a dagger into the back of his assailant—his murderer, in fact, because he had no doubt that he was dying.

His one thought, as the snow received him into its embrace, was that he was about to meet Najakmul and that she would know that he had failed.

15
Oxfordshire

June 2007 In a small side room off the intensive-care unit in the Radcliffe
Infirmary, Oxford, a consultant physician in a white coat spoke to the senior
nurse, ignoring Stella and Kit who sat at the bedside.

They smelt of smoke and hurt and fear but were not in need of medical
aid. Ursula Walker, by contrast, lay bandaged and unconscious. A ventilator
breathed for her through the endotracheal tube that poked out of the side of
her mouth. Plasma expanders dripped into the veins in her arms.

The consultant signed a note and left. The nurse drew the curtains round
the bed. Left alone with Kit in the clinical whiteness, Stella pressed her fingers to her eyes. The skull was quiet now.

'Why did I let her go back in?'

'You couldn't have stopped her,' Kit said.

'But I didn't try. She said she knew what she was doing, that she had
found something vital in the diaries. I *believed* her.'

'I didn't stop her either, Stell. If we're going to fall into recrimination, we
should at least split it equally.'

'You were barely conscious. I don't think—'

The nurse pulled the curtain again. 'Mrs O'Connor? Your brother's here.'

'My bro— *Davy?*'

David Law, dressed in a white coat, embraced her briefly, drily. He shook
hands with a shocked and silent Kit. He said, 'You shouldn't beat yourself
up about it. Nobody could stop Mother when she set her mind to something, you know that as well as I do.' He nodded to the nurse. 'Thank you.
Can we be alone with her for a while?'

The nurse stepped backed neatly. Before leaving she said, 'I'll let you
know the blood results when we get them.'

Davy stood at the foot of the bed and studied the monitors. Tonelessly, he
said, 'There was chlorine in the smoke. This wasn't just arson, it was
designed to kill whoever was in the farmhouse. Ursula—that is, my
mother—seems to have realised the danger in time. Apparently she had
wrapped a linen tea towel soaked in lemonade over her face to act as an acid
barrier. It's probably the only reason she's still alive.'

He was speaking automatically, in the clinical rhythms of the medics.

Stella took his shoulders and guided him to a seat and pressed gently, until he sat. 'Will she get better?' she asked.

'If she lives through tonight, she'll probably survive, though she may end up as a respiratory cripple dragging an oxygen bottle everywhere she goes.' Davy Law dragged his gaze from the monitors and looked across the bed at Kit. His eyes were rimmed red. He said, 'I heard what happened in the cave. I'm sorry.'

Kit said, 'So am I. But I'd rather be here, the object of everyone's pity, than not be here at all.'

After a moment, Davy Law said, 'I think I would rather be hated than pitied. But it goes hardest when there's both together.'

'I never pitied you, Davy.'

'But you did hate?'

'What else was left?'

The curtains contained them, soft veils that kept the world at bay while something broken was mended, or not; Stella could not tell. On the bed, Ursula Walker's chest lifted and fell with the sigh of the ventilator.

Kit said, 'Why did we not know Ursula was your mother?'

Davy Law smiled crookedly. 'You didn't see the family resemblance?'

'There isn't any.'

Davy laughed. 'You're right. My mother wanted a beautiful, striking, intelligent child to carry on the line unbroken since before the Romans landed and what did she get but a runt of a son. She didn't often acknowledge me, but she let me come back home to the farmhouse when I screwed up at Cambridge and couldn't go on with medicine, and she opened doors for me in anthropology, so in the end I followed in her footsteps after all.' He reached out and smoothed a finger down her cheek. 'She took me with her to Lapland, where she and I found mutual respect out there in the ice and the snow. I would like for it not to be taken from us just yet.'

Through a tight throat, Stella said, 'If there's anything we can do . . .'

He shook his head. 'All you can do is find the heart of the world and take the heart-stone there at the right time. Her whole life has been pushing to this.'

Kit said, 'The time appointed is dawn tomorrow, but we still don't know the place. Unless someone else can translate the last two volumes, we're finished. Can you read Mayan script?'

'I can, but not without my mother's dictionaries and they were all in the farmhouse. We must—' It was the ring tone that stopped him. His eyes flashed. 'Please tell me one of you hasn't left your mobile on here in ICU?'

'It's yours. It's a text,' Stella said, turning round to catch hold of his coat, which he had taken off and hung on the back of her chair. She lifted the phone out of a pocket and handed it to him, then watched as the blood fled from his face. 'Davy?' she said, alarmed.

He sat down heavily. 'It's from my mother. Timed at ten twenty-seven this evening. The fire brigade pulled her out at ten fifty-one so she must have sent this when she was still in the house.'

Gently, Kit said, 'What does it say, Davy?'

'"Now is the time to open that which was closed in the fire's heart. Please."' He was weeping. 'I have to go to the farmhouse.'

'Then we're coming with you,' Stella said.

THERE WERE NO FIREMEN, no flames, no orange sky at Ursula Walker's farmhouse, only a dark night lit by half a moon and sharp stars and the smell, everywhere, of smoke and ash. Stella parked the car and she and Davy helped Kit out. They walked together towards the ruins of the house.

'Ursula was in the kitchen when the firemen found her,' Kit said.

'Best try the back door, then.' Davy forced a grin. 'I don't suppose you happened to bring a torch?'

'Use your phone,' Stella said, switching hers on. Along two faint beams of light, they picked their way round the side of the house. The back door was gone, the door frame warped and scorched.

Davy said, 'Whoever did this knew what they were doing.' Behind him, Stella swept the light of her phone in an arc across charred remains. Absently, Davy added, 'Can you wait here a moment?'

They waited in the dark with the noise of settling timbers going off like firecrackers around them.

'Scared?' asked Kit.

'Terrified,' Stella said. At that moment, a sound came from the broken doorway and Stella looked up. 'Davy? What's that?'

'A lump hammer. There's been one in the garden shed for as long as there's been a garden shed, which takes us back to 1588, or thereabouts. Martha Walker had the first shed built. She was the woman who married Francis Walker to found the dynasty. She left a rather strange instruction in her will that the hammer was never to be beyond reach of the kitchen.' Davy turned the hammer over in his hand.

'What are you going to do?' Kit asked.

'What she told me to do: open that which was closed in the heart of the fire. It does make sense, but you have to know the family history fully to understand, which was why it was safe to put it in a text. If I didn't get it, nobody else would figure it out.' He lifted his head. 'Could you shine the light from your phone here, on the hearthstones?'

He swung the hammer even as he spoke, aiming it at the solid stone floor where it met the wall in the heart of the inglenook fireplace.

Three times, the hammer rebounded off solid stone. On the fourth, the sound was different. Davy rained softer, more precise blows against the opening gap. Between each one he said, 'Cedric Owen's ledgers were . . . found in the bread oven a century after his death but . . . nobody has ever opened this . . . for the obvious reason that my family's history required that it not be opened until the time of . . . final reckoning, which my mother . . . clearly considers to have— Damn. Could you make more light?'

'Can't,' Stella said. 'The mobiles are running low. Kit, kill yours. We need to keep the batteries for later.' He did and they stood in darkness lit by stars. She said, 'Davy, are there any candles?'

'Under the sink. On the left. There's a box of matches on the shelf above. If we're lucky, the stone of the sink will have protected them from the fire.'

Stella felt her way there and found a pack of six misshapen candles and the matches, not burnt in the heat. She took three, set them in a triangle on the floor and lit them. Next, she held the skull-stone over the triple flame and caught the centre point, where the firelight became blue heart-light, shining softly from the skull. She directed the light at the place on the floor where the hammer had hit. 'Go on, Davy,' she said. 'Finish it.'

He did, chipping at a rectangular gap. Carefully, he pushed against the stone at its edge, then stepped forward uncertainly and angled the light of his phone into the hole below.

'Oh, yes. Oh, very, very yes.'

From the denser dark he withdrew a scroll of parchment tied about with a scrap of linen, and a small notebook.

Stella said, 'Tell me that's a map?' She set the stone down. The yellow candle flames changed the colour of the night.

'I think so, I hope so,' Davy said excitedly. He held up the parchment. 'I think this was old when Cedric Owen was alive. While this'—he held up the book—'was hidden for a very good reason and I badly want to know what it was.'

Stella fumbled with the knots in the linen threads that bound the scroll and it came undone. With unsteady hands, she eased it open. 'I'll break it.'

Davy Law said, 'Stella, we have less than six hours until dawn. If we can see where it shows, breaking it doesn't matter.'

She did break it, but side by side, the two pieces made a whole—a sketch of a landscape, showing a circle of stones with a grassy mound inside and a shaped stone gateway. Trees swayed behind and a quarter-moon stood overhead, with the sun sketched as an arc on the horizon.

Stella looked at Davy. 'Do you know where it is?' she asked.

'It's Weyland's Smithy,' he said. 'The Saxons believed that if you left a horse there overnight with a silver piece, the god-smith Weyland would have shod it again by the morning. It's only ten minutes away.' His eyes were shining. 'We'll make it before dawn, no problem. And we still have time to look at the book.'

On the front cover it bore the letters *BT, YULE,1588* in spidery capitals. Davy opened it with a finger's end, touching only the corner. He said, 'They never found Barnabas Tythe's first diary.' And then, 'Read it for us, Stella. You're the one practised in reading Elizabethan script.'

And so she did, slowly, by the light of the three candles.

'Written this 26th day of December, in the year of Our Lord 1588.

'I, Barnabas Tythe, have this day become Master of Bede's College, Cambridge, most honoured position of our land. To my great shame, my first act in this post was a lie. May God and my college forgive me, for I have performed a funeral for a living man. Cedric Owen is not dead.'

16
Lodgings, Trinity Street, Cambridge

December 28, 1588

Written this 26th day of December, in the year of Our Lord 1588. To Sir Francis Walsingham, from Sir Barnabas Tythe, Master of Bede's College, Cambridge, greetings.

It is with regret that I inform you of the deaths, not only of your loyal servant Sir Robert Maplethorpe, but also of the traitor Cedric Owen.

Owen did indeed come to my lodgings for succour as you had
suggested. I went with all haste to the Master of my college to ask his
assistance in taking him prisoner. Professor Maplethorpe came with
armed men, intent on taking him alive, but in such we failed; Owen
fought with a ferocity unknown to us, and had clearly been most
succinctly tutored. The man who killed him has been punished for
his recklessness, but not by our hand—he died of his wounds.

The Spaniard of whom you wrote was also wounded. His body
has since been burnt. Owen's corpse has been consigned to the
paupers' graves at Madingley. I searched the corpse myself and found
not one whit about it to tell us of his purpose, but I found in his saddle
bags an item in gold—herewith enclosed for your perusal—
of quite exceptional workmanship.

Owen died as a traitor and thus all of his property belongs now to
the Crown. I would ask, however, that for the sake of the college,
Cedric Owen be known to the future as a good man. It would sit ill
with us to have nurtured a traitor, however unwittingly.

I await your further instructions on all matters.

I remain, sir, your most humble and loyal servant before God,
Professor Barnabas Tythe, Master-Elect, Bede's College, Cambridge.

'ARE YOU SURE you want to give it to him?' Barnabas Tythe's fingers strayed
across the gold funeral mask. He said to Cedric Owen, 'Walsingham does not
expect it. I could write the letter again and say that your saddle bags were
empty save for a few gold coins from New Spain.'

From his fireside chair, Owen shook his head. 'If he thinks there is more,
he may chase down the means of our arrival from Sluis. I do not want to draw
down Walsingham's pursuivants on Jan de Groot's head.' Owen spoke thinly;
in the two days since his injury he had found that if he gave rein to his voice,
the pain in his head became unbearable. He said, 'The mask will buy
Walsingham a great deal of information. My hope is that he puts his energies
into spending the revenues it generates, not into hunting for more.'

In the chaotic aftermath of the fight outside the college, Tythe had certainly
believed Owen to be dead. Fernandez de Aguilar, whose own wounds were
fortunately superficial, had been alone in believing otherwise, but had not let
his care for his friend overtake the necessities of the moment. He it had been
who had arranged the bodies that anyone else with an eye for a fight might
see how Owen, the master-swordsman, had slain Maplethorpe and one of

his henchmen before losing his own sword to a cudgel. How, immediately thereafter, the traitor had taken a like weapon from the ground, allowing him to defeat the last of Maplethorpe's men, before Barnabas Tythe, hero of the hour, had taken his knife and finally killed him.

The good fortune of it was that the third man did bear some passing resemblance to Owen. They moved swiftly to clothe him in Owen's cloak and boots, and for the rest, the falling snow had covered the battle site, concealing any inconsistencies that might have given the lie to their tale. De Aguilar, then, had carried Owen to safety, sending Barnabas Tythe to convey the two parts of good news to his fellow scholars: they were free of Maplethorpe, and Cedric Owen, enemy of the State, had been slain.

For the greater part of Christmas Day, while Barnabas Tythe had cemented his authority on the college, Fernandez de Aguilar had wrapped a bandage about his own leg before tending to the unconscious Owen.

For a man with only one arm and no medical training to speak of, he had bound the broken ribs and skull with a dexterity that Tythe envied when finally the old man returned to tell of his unopposed election as Master and the successful passing off of Maplethorpe's thug as Cedric Owen.

In this they had been lucky; the men of the college council had better things to do than to stand in the mortuary examining bodies on the day of Christ's Mass. When Tythe himself, the only physician present, had hinted that there was a risk of infection from the ill humours of the dead, they were all too grateful for his offer to arrange for the appropriate burials.

That had left the issue of Maplethorpe's remaining henchman. A rumour arose that shortly before his death Maplethorpe had confided to his Vice-Master that the wretch, who now had gone missing, was a suspect in the matter of some missing silver, and it was quickly accepted that he had seized the opportunity to flee with his ill-gotten treasure. For the preservation of the college's good name, no hue and cry was raised. As for Owen's accomplice, Tythe had ordered his personal servants to dredge the Cam, and, when they returned with a body—a not unlikely outcome, and one that Tythe had banked on—had identified it himself as the Spaniard. The Master's sword could not be found but that was of no great moment.

The twelve men of the council had given vent to a collective sigh of relief at an ugly matter neatly closed, agreed a memorial to the memory of a 'much beloved and sadly missed' Master and unanimously voted the blood-stained hero, Barnabas Tythe, as their new Master, granting him the professorship he should have had long before.

'WHAT DO WE DO NOW?' the new Master of Bede's asked of his guests.

'We wait,' said Owen, 'and we hope most fervently that we are both fit to mount a horse and ride by the time the snow stops falling.'

Tythe grimaced. It occurred to him that his question had not been answered. 'And what are you going to do when the snow stops falling?'

'I don't know.'

It came as a hard admission from Cedric Owen, who leaned back and directed his attention to the blue heart-stone sitting on the hearth. Presently, he said, 'I have certain tasks to perform in this life, the first of which was to find the secrets of the stone and record them in such a way that only one truly wedded to the stone might find them. Fernandez and I have together done just that; we have left in hiding in Harwich a set of volumes that will marry past to future and some time soon we must find a safe place to hide them. Somewhere that was sacred to our forebears. To my shame, and great distress, I know not where to look.'

'How will you recognise that which you seek?'

'I have dreamt it. The first time was thirty years ago, but the dream has remained with me since. It is a wild place, in a flat wooded plain with a circle of standing stones and the wind howling around. It could be a hundred places from the southernmost coast of Cornwall to the far north of Northumberland. We cannot search them all.'

Tythe pressed his fingers to his lips. A memory danced somewhere just out of reach. He was trying to see its form and substance when he became aware of the blue stone that sat so crisply on his hearth and shed its light into the room. In the space of two breaths, there was a change in the texture of the flowing blues—their boundaries had spread out to reach him.

Barnabas Tythe watched this alchemy and felt the hairs rise along his forearms, then suddenly a gateway opened and the elusive memory stepped up to meet him, sharp and clear.

'I have a cousin, recently bereaved, who lives in a farmhouse near Oxford. Before the late king destroyed the monasteries my cousin's father was retained by the Abbot of Glastonbury to maintain the ancient byways and paths of the ancestors that pass through the abbey and assorted other churches. The Catholic Church was not as ignorant of these things as the Puritans prefer to be, and my cousin's father was the one among them who understood the old ways best.'

Owen's eyes fixed on Tythe's face. 'Would your cousin's father help us?'

'He will be ninety-three in June, so it may be that he has died. But if he still lives, there is no other man who knows more of the standing stones and the dragon-ways of England than he.' Tythe stood up briskly. 'I will give you a letter of introduction to my cousin. You must leave as soon as the snow stops, preferably tonight. If you and de Aguilar can ride well enough to allow you good speed, you will reach Oxford before ever my letter to Walsingham reaches London.'

ENGLAND LAY in a wash of melting snow. Trees dripped steadily onto grey, slush-ridden pathways. Horses stumbled and slipped on patches of hidden ice. Travelling at night had proved dangerous and Owen relied for secrecy on the fact that no one ventured abroad without exceptional reason.

They came to Lower Hayworth Farm at nightfall on December 30. It was a prosperous-looking place of timber, stone and thatch. Smoke rose from the chimneys and the smell of roasting meat scented the air.

Cedric Owen dismounted, with some difficulty. He was wet to the skin and shivering. Beside him, de Aguilar sat blue-lipped on his horse. He kept his cloak pulled tight, with Robert Maplethorpe's plain blade in his hand.

'Knock,' he said. 'We have nothing to lose. If Tythe's cousin turns us down and we sleep outside another night, we will both die.' He essayed a feeble grin. 'The warmth of hell would be a blessing after this.'

'We haven't come this far to die,' Owen said, and tried to believe it. He rapped on the farmhouse door.

He was too cold to move fast, and too blinded by the wet hair that streaked across his face to see the club that angled down at his head in time to avoid it. He heard de Aguilar shout hoarsely in Spanish and was trying to frame an appropriate reaction when his brains fell to water and his knees ceased to hold him up a moment longer.

THE WARMTH in his feet was Owen's first sense on waking, the unutterable luxury of dryness and tingling heat when he had ridden the last three days believing he would never again feel anything but cold and wet.

He lay a while, restricting his attention to his nether regions in an effort to avoid the bruising pain in his cranium or the waxing and waning of his consciousness. In one of his more lucid moments, he thought he heard mellifluous Spanish spoken in two voices, which was, of course, impossible. But it was there again when next he surfaced. Raising himself half to sitting, he opened his eyes.

'Ah. Señor Owen awakens. And not before time.'

Against the protestations of his body, Owen made his head turn towards the source of speech. He was in a large, comfortable farmhouse kitchen, with flagstones upon the floor and a vast stone-built inglenook fireplace currently burning what appeared to be an entire oak tree in sizable logs. Seated at a long oak table was Fernandez de Aguilar and beside him a figure robed in black. *I have a cousin, recently bereaved . . .*

That one rose now, and came to where Owen lay before the fire.

'I'm sorry, sir. I live alone but for my widowed father and England in this weather is not a place where honest men choose to travel. I took you for brigands, come for what little silver we have saved. Had not your friend shouted in Spanish, I might have done you more damage. You have his exhaustion to thank for that; had he not been tired and fevered almost to insanity, he would have manufactured a shout in English and I fear it would have been the end of you.'

Owen stared, dizzily, trying to focus on the face before him. The eyes were a dense steel-grey and catlike, teasing and savage together. The lips were perfect and framed about by deeply etched lines of laughter that put their maker on the wrong side of forty, but cheerfully so. The overall effect was of a fierce, intelligent face, framed about by hair the same colour and curl as Barnabas Tythe's. It was this, then, that identified the speaker incontrovertibly as Tythe's cousin. Which posed the question of why Tythe had omitted to mention that his cousin was a woman, or that she was quite astonishingly handsome.

Owen said, 'How long have I been asleep?'

De Aguilar said, 'Not long. It is evening of the day we arrived. Martha has spoken to her father. He knows that we are fugitives from Walsingham's pursuivants but he has insisted that we must stay. Moreover, he has asked to see the blue stone. We waited until you were awake to show him.'

Martha . . . We . . . De Aguilar appeared—with perfect reason—to be infatuated with the woman beside him. The greatest change was not in his language, but in the texture of his voice, which had become soft and rich.

'May I know to whom I am speaking?' Owen sat up too fast, and closed his eyes against the pain in his head.

'I am Martha Huntley, daughter to Edward Wainwright, who sits yet by the fire, and wife to Sir William Huntley, who died aboard ship this summer defending England from the enemy.'

Owen opened his eyes. He said, 'And you speak Spanish like a native. Did that set you apart from your neighbours when the Armada threatened?'

'My neighbours know that I am fully loyal to Queen and country. My family fled to Spain in my youth when Queen Elizabeth first came to the throne. My parents feared that the burnings would start again except that they would be of Catholics this time, not Protestants.'

'You came back because you were wrong?'

'My father missed England and my mother, who was not of robust health, wished to die here. She was granted that wish.'

'I'm sorry,' Owen said. 'With your mother and husband both dead, you are doubly bereaved.'

The frankness of her gaze acknowledged his courtesy and yet denied the need for it. 'My mother died many years ago. I am more concerned now that my father is also fast approaching his final communion with his Maker. He remains tied to this life because he will not leave me as a woman alone, who will be forced to marry to keep my good name and my home.'

Owen switched his gaze from her to de Aguilar and back again. Artlessly, he asked, 'Do you fear his imminent death?'

She flushed, but did not lower her gaze. 'I do, but for other grounds than those you think. He holds to life for a second reason: he has had dreams of a certain blue crystal stone fashioned in the shape of a skull, which he must see before he dies.'

Owen did not answer at once, but waited in vain for the stone to speak to him. Risking the knifing pain in his head, Owen turned to search the room.

For thirty years, Fernandez de Aguilar had divined whatever Owen wanted. Yet again, he was there at his side, holding the saddle packs, his eyes speaking complex messages of apology and reassurance. He wanted Owen to know that nothing had changed, that the widow Martha Huntley was not going to come between them, but that the sun had risen in his life in a new way and he craved the freedom to enjoy it.

Owen said, 'Fernandez, let us bring the blue heart-stone into the light of the fire and perhaps we can find why it has fallen silent.'

The stone was asleep, or it seemed so to Owen. The firelight barely leaked through the passive stone. 'I'm sorry to interfere with your repose,' Owen said to the thread that wove songs in his head, 'but there is one who would meet you.'

'Thank you.' The voice responded to a thought he had spoken only inwardly.

Owen turned towards Edward Wainwright, who sat close to the fire in his armchair, swaddled in fine-woven blankets. He was stronger than he appeared and now reached out to grasp Owen's wrist. 'Have I your permission to look at your jewel?'

'Of course.' The stone gave no warning as Owen set it down, nestling it on the bony knees. The old man's skeletal face was a study in awe. Slowly, in wonder, his clawed fingers closed around its smoothly perfect temples.

At the moment of their meeting, the stone wept, or so it seemed to Owen. Certainly, the old man was weeping. Sparse tears made tracks of living gold down his cheeks, as if all the fluids of his life were saved for this.

Nonetheless, his eyes were dry when eventually he raised them to Owen again. 'There is a place in this land that was fashioned to hold this stone at the end times. Do you know where it is?'

Owen felt his heart stop, and then start again, erratically. 'I have dreamt of this place every night for the past thirty years, but do not know where it is. I have been sent to England to find it.'

'Then my last year has not been wasted.' A warmth lit Wainwright's face. 'For my daughter's joy and for your arrival have I waited, and today both are fulfilled. And yet we who walk the old, straight tracks were never told which of the five places we guard was the one that mattered most. Could you draw for me the place of your dream?'

Like a flood tide, racing, the blood flowed too fast in Owen's veins. 'If you furnish pen and paper, I can try.'

At her father's direction, Martha fetched a goose quill and black ink and a sheet of good, flat paper. Owen sat by the fire with a wooden tray invented as a resting board on his knees. He talked as he drew. 'The place is shrouded by mist; when I first come to it, all I can see are the half-shapes of beech trees all along one side. And yet the moon gazes upon it, a week before full, so that the shadows of the standing stones are crisp.'

'There are stones, then? Will you describe them to me?'

'As I approach, I come to a row of four upright stones, each one taller than a man. They surround a long, low mound, bowl-like in its shaping, and there are lower, rounder stones in a circle before it. The mound itself is made of stone covered with earth and turf that hides a tunnel at its heart. It has lintel stones, squared at the edges and ends so that they fit together as a joiner fits timber to make a door frame.'

From the far side of the inglenook, Edward Wainwright said, 'It is well done.' He looked beyond Owen to where Martha Huntley sat. 'For this we have lived, you and I. Now is the time of revealing.'

Wordless, Martha took her candle to the great fireplace and with some skill she dismantled the blazing fire. Then, kneeling near the back of the fire, she performed a minor miracle, pushing her hand through the thick stone hearth to a cavity beneath. Owen took his own candle closer, and by its light found that it was not so much a miracle as a sleight of hand; one stone in the midst of the hearth was balanced around a mid-pin, so that, when pushed, one side slotted inwards while the other rolled outwards, leaving a gap such as a man's arm might fit through.

From the hollow space thus hidden, Martha brought out a bundle of scrolls, rolled and tied with braided horsehair. With reverence she laid them on her father's knee. He sorted through them and held one out to Owen.

'Would you do me the honour of opening this? It has been in my family for a little over one hundred generations,' said Edward Wainwright. 'I could name them for you, but fear my life would end ere I was finished.'

As he untied the binding with unsteady fingers, Owen said, 'In my family also, we can name the generations of those who have held the blue stone. It is the first thing I learned from my grandmother.'

'Of course, for you are the keeper and your line is as unbroken as ours. We are the walkers of the trackways. To us has fallen the task of keeping the life in the old places.'

Owen unrolled the parchment and it was some time before he found sufficient spit to speak. 'This is unquestionably the place of my dream, but even now I don't know where in England it is.'

Wainwright looked at him, shocked. 'Of course not! Only by keeping stone and knowledge separate are we safe in a world where fire and torment are used to pull the truth from unwilling minds.' He took the parchment back and began carefully to fold it. 'And still, there is no need for you to know, for it is many years before your stone must be set there, to form the heart of the beast that will arise from the land. As we have done since before the birth of Christ, we who walk the trackways will hold this knowledge safe until such time as man's evil requires that it be drawn forth in the earth's defence. Your task is to hide the skull in a place of great secrecy that will thwart all those who seek its destruction, while yet leaving it to be found by the one who must bring it here.'

Owen nodded. 'My grandmother described the place to me, and a wise Frenchman spoke of it again, long ago, in the summer of my youth. It is in Yorkshire, where I grew up, a good ten days' ride from here.'

'Then we can each fulfil our tasks. I will hide again the map that my family may keep the secret of it, and you must set forth to York that you may keep the final part of your bargain with the stone. Martha? Will you return the scroll to its resting place?'

His daughter did as she was bid, closing over the hidden place and returning the fire to its bed.

'Thank you.' With no small regret, Wainwright handed back the heart-stone to Owen. 'Sirs, it has given me untold pleasure to see the stone and yourselves in the last days of my life. By all rights, I should send you swiftly to complete your final task, but tonight is not a night for travel and the morning will suffice. In the meantime, we can set the beds to warming and we have food enough for four.'

NOT FAR AWAY, a church bell tolled midnight.

Cedric Owen lay awake, staring up at the dark ceiling. Cobwebs draped thickly across the corners of the roof beams. The mattress was of uneven horsehair with ends that poked out to stab through his shirt to his skin. With all of this, it was luxury compared to where he had slept in the journey from Cambridge, and he was glad of it. He listened to the breathing of the man on the bed next to his own. Presently, into the dark, he said, 'Fernandez, if you cannot sleep, why do you not go to her? Likely she is as awake as you.'

There was a silence, then de Aguilar said, 'She is a lady. I would not sully her good name.'

'And if Walsingham's men come tomorrow? Would you not rather at least have let her choose what she does with her good name? You can be married in days if you and she wish it.'

'And if she does not?'

'Then you will have your answer. Go to her. You have nothing to lose.'

A bed creaked in the dark. He heard the slide of starched sheets and the subtle noises of de Aguilar's dressing, broken by a pause.

Amused, Owen said, 'You need not change your doublet. If she does not love you in the tawny velvet, she will not love you better in the blue. You will wear neither for long if she feels as you do.'

'I had thought to find something with less mud on it, but you are right, there is nothing to be gained by dissembling.' For a man who had never been uncertain, there was a shadow of doubt in de Aguilar's voice now. 'If she does not want me, we may have to leave before morning.'

'Then so be it.'

Soft-footed, de Aguilar left. Owen lay awake in the dark and heard, presently, the murmur of voices and the scrape and rattle of the hearth as the fire was roused. He smelt its smoke and the cinnamon sweetness of wine newly mulled and let himself drift into a doze.

He woke some time later to the baying of bloodhounds, a sound to rouse the moon and make it flee from its course. The heart-stone sang with them, a song of alarm that had penetrated the clouds of his dreams.

Owen sat bolt upright in the dark, reaching with one hand for his knife and with the other for de Aguilar, and only when he had found neither did he remember where he was and to what purpose.

He rolled out of bed and ran along the corridor to the room where slept his host's daughter. 'Fernandez? Are you there? We are assaulted!'

'Wait for me downstairs.'

The three of them met downstairs in front of the red-ashed fire. Fernandez was sharply awake, his eyes alight with the life of newly consummated love. He buckled on his sword belt one-handed.

'Walsingham?' he asked.

'I believe so. The heart-stone sounds a warning to match the hounds. We are too close to the end to risk failure now. Fernandez, take the stone. I will leave first and ride north from here and thus lead them away. When they have followed me, you can return to Martha in safety.'

'No.' Moving closer to Martha, de Aguilar said, 'Cedric, you have the blue heart-stone and I still have my sworn duty to protect your life and that of the stone. Therefore, I will trust you to guard Martha and her father, and I will be the one to act as decoy. They will tell me now which trackways I may follow that will most confuse those who hunt us. Please—this is our only hope, and thus the hope of the world for all eternity.'

He held up his hand against the chorus that came against him, brooking no argument.

'Pack what little you must carry and leave the rest. Take sufficient diamonds to keep you in good heart for half a year and hide the rest. Leave a little of the gold where it might appear to have been hidden in haste; if it is found, it may be enough to buy us freedom. If we live, we can come back for the rest later.' When he stopped firing instructions, de Aguilar caught them each, Owen and Martha, with his one arm. 'I am not seeking my death, only to buy life for us all. You must trust me to do this, both of you.'

Martha was the braver of the two. She moulded herself to de Aguilar's embrace and received a brief, chaste kiss. Stepping back, she said to Owen, 'Name a place where he may meet us when he has lost them,' and thus was the decision sealed.

THEY MOVED SWIFTLY, goaded by the worsening sound of the hounds and the frantic urgings of the heart-stone. The candle had burnt down less than a quarter of an inch by the time they embraced their last goodbyes. Their diamonds and as much of the gold as they dared was hidden in the resting place at the back of the fire; the rest of the gold was left in a place where searching men might find it and think they had come across a hoard. Owen was packed and ready with Edward Wainwright and his daughter. De Aguilar had committed to memory, but not written anywhere about his person, the name of the place where they might meet.

He was mounted on the grey gelding that had been Owen's since they left Cambridge. Owen reached up a hand to the bridle. In the dark, his friend was a bare outline. 'We will wait for you ten days from now, and every alternate day for a month. After that, we will return monthly, in case you have been there. If you come and we are not there, tie a square of linen to the hawthorn tree near the ford and we will come every day at dawn. If you are taken and made to talk, tell them to tie white wool and we will know we must flee.'

De Aguilar leaned down from his horse. His breath was misty in the greying air of morning. 'I will not be taken. Wait for me there. I shall join you as soon as I may.'

His parting from Martha was brief and heartfelt. They stood together, Owen and Martha, in the sharp cold of the stables, and listened to de Aguilar make noise enough for three. The bloodhounds bayed and, too soon, they heard a shout and the sound of many horsemen and the whistle that was de Aguilar's signal that he had been spotted. Very soon the sound of the hunt grew loud and fell away into the night.

'We should go now,' Owen said gruffly, to Martha and her father. 'It is a ten-day ride north to York and we must travel circumspectly.'

17
Near Weyland's Smithy, Oxfordshire

June 21, 2007: 4.00 a.m. 'We're being followed.' Stella turned to look out of the back window of the car. Somewhere behind in the black night were twin points of light.

Kit was in the back seat. He leaned forward. 'Davy, can you drive without the lights?'

'Not unless you want to die before dawn.' Davy knew the way to the grave mound and so he was driving.

'How far to go?' Kit asked.

'Another two or three miles.'

'Then stop the car and go ahead without me. I'll catch you up.'

'Kit?' Stella turned to catch his hand. 'You can't walk.'

'I can walk, I just can't run. You can, and it's you two who need to be there. Davy knows where you need to go, you have the stone. So leave me behind. Don't piss about, Davy. Just do it.'

Davy kept his eyes on the road. After a moment, he said, 'Junction coming up. There's a field just past the turning where we can park the car behind the hedge. Stella, there's a torch in the glove compartment. We'll need that. Kit, if you're walking, stick to the road. Go up the hill to the white horse car park and turn right onto the Ridgeway. Head for the line of beech trees. Hold tight. Here's the turn.'

He flicked off the headlights and pulled hard left on the wheel. In the blinding darkness, only hope and luck kept them safe. Stella found the torch and shone it out through the windscreen. Davy cut the engine. In silence they bounced over rutted ground into the field.

'Out,' Davy said. 'Fast.'

He had been in war zones; it showed in the way he moved, keeping close to the hedge line, away from the grey starlight.

Standing knee deep in uncut barley, Stella gave Kit the torch and her phone. They stood in the dark, with stars above showing outlines of faces, hands and eyes. Somewhere, not too far back, a car paused, then came on.

Kit said, 'It's like the cave, but this time you're running ahead.'

'I have nowhere to fall.' She felt him falter, and sit. 'Kit—'

'I'm fine. I'll sit here a bit and catch you up. Go on. Tonight is about you and the stone. Afterwards, we can find the balance.'

She found his shoulders in the dark, and then his face and his lips, and kissed him. 'I love you, did I mention?'

'Not today.' His eyes were wet. He made himself smile. 'Thank you.'

'I'm not choosing between you and the stone.'

'I never really thought you were. Please go.' His voice was steadier. He drew back and gave her a small shove between her shoulders. 'I'll catch you up, I promise.'

Davy caught her arm. 'Run, or we'll lose the advantage.'

In the dark, under sharp stars, with cold night air on her face and the first hint of dawn dew, with the heart-stone bouncing in her backpack, urging her faster onward, she followed Davy up the hill and onto the track that led to the Ridgeway. No car lights followed.

'Davy—' She had to stop. She leaned forward, with her hands on her knees. He came back to her and stood, breathing in a whistle. 'How much further?' she asked.

Wordless, he pointed. Ahead, in a cornfield, a circle of trees blotted out the stars. He said, 'Nearly there. No need to run now.'

They walked the last quarter of a mile until they reached the place of the ancient drawing Cedric Owen had hidden in the heart of the fire. It was not a spectacular place; it had neither the majesty of Stonehenge nor the artistry of the running horse at Dragon Hill, but in its very simplicity was a power each of these lacked.

Ahead, a circle of ground rose in a squat, flat mound, covered in turf. Its circumference was bounded by stones. At the front, facing her, four tall, sharp-topped stones reared into the black night. Between these, a low channel led to the squared stone entrance. Inside that, only black.

Davy came to stand beside her, his shoulder warm on hers. Here, this close, it was the smaller, carved stone in the entrance that held Stella. It spoke to her in the same tongue as the heart-stone sang, but she could not understand the words. Presently, she said, 'I had thought there would be more of a tunnel.'

'It'll open when you need it to. You have to believe that.' Davy stepped in front of her, blocking the route to the doorway. 'It's too early to place the stone in its setting,' he said. 'If I understood anything in Lapland, it was that timing is crucial. If you set the stone before dawn, or too late, you might as well not have bothered.'

'Once we're in, how do we get out?' Stella asked.

'The same way we went in. There's only the one entrance.'

'Then it's a death trap.' Something was tugging at Stella's mind, fainter than it had been in the car, but enough. She said, 'We're still being followed. Don't ask me how I know that, but if we go into the mound and can't get out, we're dead.'

With no edge to his voice, Davy said, 'What do you want to do?'

'Find somewhere among the trees where we can see but not be seen.'

They stepped back under the whispering beeches. Stella hunched her shoulders against a tree, hugging her knees to her chest for warmth. She lifted the heart-stone from the backpack and pulled it into the foetal circle of her abdomen, keeping the backpack to sit on. Davy sat beside her.

The stone crouched in her mind, waiting.

Slowly, Stella said, 'Davy, do you know who's hunting us?'

It was growing lighter, not yet dawn but with a greyness that lit his eyes. Now, they met hers, unwavering. He said, 'I might be wrong.'

She felt sick. The stone was sharpening her senses, and she replaced it in her backpack. 'Who, Davy?'

He shrugged. 'Is it important to find a name? Every mass grave I've ever exhumed has been dug by someone who's crossed the line to a place where the ends justify the means; where one person's life, or ten, or a thousand, is a fair price for what they believe is right.'

Stella said, 'I read your mother's translation of the ledgers. If she's got it right, Nostradamus said the same sort of thing to Cedric Owen when they met in Paris: there's a force that feeds on death and destruction, fear and pain, and needs these things to continue into the nadir of Armageddon. But none of that brings us any closer to who's doing it.'

'Oh, come *on*.' He turned his head and his gaze scoured her face. 'Who knew where you were going to look for the skull? Who knew you were coming to see me? Who knows my mother so well she won't even countenance the possibility that he's spent his *entire life* working to keep the blue heart-stone hidden?' He stood up. 'Who served with the King's Troop in Northern Ireland and knows how to make the kind of chlorine bombs that destroyed my mother's farm and put her in hospital? Who—'

'Who is walking down the Ridgeway, now, towards us?' Stella said. She did not need the stone's piercing warning to tell her that the hunter had found her. With a sudden lucidity, she saw past, present and future come together. 'Davy, dawn can't be more than half an hour away. You know what needs to be done. Take the stone into the mouth of the mound and wait until the tunnel opens. I'll stay outside and keep whoever it is occupied.'

'No.' He was smiling in a way that froze her blood. For a heart-stopping moment, she thought she had made the ultimate mistake and that he was the hunter. She raised the backpack, her only weapon.

'Stella, don't.' He held up a hand. 'I said I would die for it. I meant it. But *you* have to place the stone, only you. It has your face and you are the one it speaks to. So go into the mound. I'll do whatever it takes to keep him away.'

'But I'm the one they're looking for. They'll go straight through you and I'll be trapped.'

'They?'

'There are two of them and they have a gun. Go to the woods at the back of the mound, Davy, and stay there. I'll tell them you've already left. Go! You're the only wild card we've got.'

'OK.' In one more astonishing moment in an astonishing night, Davy Law hugged her and was gone, running quietly. Stella walked forward, along the circle of beech trees to the narrow green avenue that passed through the barley. A figure was limping slowly along it.

'Kit!' She reached for him, smiling.

'Hey.' He leaned on her shoulder and ruffled her hair. 'Where's Davy?'

The lie came easily. 'He's gone back to the hospital. He's worried about Ursula and I didn't need him once I knew where to go. The mound's here, in the clearing. It's amazing. Come and see.' She turned, tugging him by the wrist. He came slowly, using both sticks. The heart-stone had not ceased its warning. 'You're not walking well. Did you hurt yourself?'

'No. I'd never have made it like this. I got a lift.' He stopped and leaned against the first of the upright stones to catch his breath. 'Tony brought me. I know what you think, but you have to trust him. He's come to help. He's just parking the car. He'll be here any moment.'

She said, 'He's here now.'

A thin torch beam bobbed along the track. The figure behind it emerged slowly from the pre-dawn mist, distorted and shrunken and not at all like Tony Bookless. She stepped forward. 'Tony?'

'Not Tony,' said Gordon Fraser grimly. He stopped at the edge of the clearing, a small, stumpy dwarf of a man, her friend, the best caver in Britain. 'He's a yard or two behind. It's going to be one big grand reunion when the sun comes up, and then won't the fireworks be spectacular?'

18
Near Ingleborough Fell, Yorkshire Dales

April 1589 Easter was past and a late frost rimed the scar of turned earth. Cedric Owen, now named Francis Walker, trader and would-be farmer, bent and laid a wreath of catkins on the grave of his wife's father. At his side, Martha Huntley, now Martha Walker, four months pregnant, bent also, and laid a lace of freshly picked daisies on the raw earth, which was what the old man had asked of her when he knew his final hours had come.

They stood together a while, a man and the wife with whom he had not lain, and had no intention ever so to do. At length, Martha said, 'He is dead a week. We gave our word that the heart-stone would be delivered to its place of safekeeping within a ten-day of his death. There is nothing to be gained by waiting.'

'Except that Fernandez might come.'

'He will not.' She said it sharply, a poor disguise for the grief that still caused her nightly to weep in her sleep. 'We should not wait.'

'But still, the route to the cave's mouth leads past the hawthorn. We can look on the way.'

He held the chestnut gelding for her to mount. Of the three good horses they had brought north with them, one had died of colic soon after they arrived, and the bay mare, gift of Barnabas Tythe, had surprised them all by giving birth to a weedy, undernourished colt foal on the last day of the spring's snowfall, a week to the day before Edward Wainwright's death.

Martha settled her skirts and clucked for the horse to move on. Cedric walked at its shoulder in easy silence. They had not chosen each other, but their shared grief over the loss of Fernandez, and Owen's obvious care for Edward Wainwright in his dying days, had brought them together much as a man might be with his sister, or she with her brother, so that each knew what the other thought without need to ask.

Their route took them out of the tiny churchyard past the well and the grey hard-stone inn that marked the ending of the village and out to the grey-green moorland, where only sheep could thrive.

From above his shoulder, Martha said, 'We could begin to sell the diamonds slowly now, I think, saying they were my legacy from my father. That would not arouse comment.'

'As long as it does not arouse Walsingham's interest, we will be safe. I would not relish having to flee again as we did that night.'

'No.' Martha shuddered and pulled her shoulder cloak tightly about her. The journey had killed her father. Edward Wainwright had never recovered from the cold and misery of ten days spent on the roads in the January snows. Neither of them said it; they had never indulged in recriminations, but it was there between them as yet another thing to keep them separate. Owen kept his thoughts for the growing child, whom he must rear as his own.

The path rose up Ingleborough Fell. They picked up a new river and followed its bank to the ford Owen had remembered from his childhood. The hawthorn tree that was their marker had neither linen nor a square of white wool tied to it, to show any hint of the fate of Fernandez de Aguilar.

Owen watched the shadow of hope pass from Martha's face and he saw her set her jaw. He feared that the weight of disappointment might one day crack her.

She turned the horse away from the thorn bush. 'We should go to the cave,' she said. 'I brought candles and a skein of wool and a pitch torch.'

The mare was sure-footed and Owen let her pick her own way up the hill. A buzzard made wide lazy sweeps overhead. Half a mile to their right, a handful of crows erupted from behind a gorse thicket and sprang upwards.

'It would seem we are not alone on this hillside, even though the morning is so newly broken.' Owen slowed the horse to a stop. The blue heartstone lay heavy against his side. He heard from it the faintest warning. 'It might be a shepherd, but we should take no chances. You should go back, Martha. If we are betrayed, it will do no good for both of us to be caught.'

'If we are betrayed, I would rather be caught in the open than die in the Tower at Walsingham's pleasure.' She shuddered. 'No, we go together. Fernandez left you in my care as much as me in yours.'

He had tried to argue with her once or twice before in their four months together and had found her almost uniquely intransigent. He gave way with what grace he could muster and helped her down from the gelding, setting hobbles about its forelegs that it might not wander too far.

'Let us go, then. The opening to the cave is upwards and to our right.'

THE HEART-STONE did not want to go into the cave, that much was obvious. Owen felt from it the same fierce, wordless grief he had sensed from women dying in childbed: knowing that something worthwhile must come of their ending, but grieving that they cannot live to see it.

'We'll wait here a while,' he said, breathing heavily from the climb. 'If anyone is following, we shall see them before they see us.'

The entrance to the cave was a slantwise crack in the wall of rock ahead of them, half hidden by a stand of thorns. Owen caught Martha's elbow and drew her sideways, to a dry, flat place hidden from without by the trees. At their back, a tunnel sloped into darkness, wide enough at its start for them both to pass together.

He waited, letting his eyes adjust to the grey light, but when nobody came and there was no further excuse for delay, he did what he had done as a youth exploring these caves: he brought to mind the evening his grandmother had taken him to the quiet room to the north of their house and shown him what might be done with candles to make the light come from the skull's eyes. Later that evening, she had described how to find the cathedral of the earth. She had not asked him to go, only mentioned where it was, believing that, however great his fear of small, cramped places, he would go one day to see it.

He had not gone that autumn, but waited until spring, which was too late to tell her of the beauty he had found for she was dead by then.

Martha was at his side now, watching him knot the wool and fix the end in a crack where it would not pull out, that he might find his way out to daylight again safely.

Owen said, 'If you wish to remain here, I will come back to you as fast as the tunnel permits.'

'I would gladly accept, but I promised my father I would see the place where the heart-stone lay,' she said grimly. 'We who walk the trackways have our own fates to fulfil.'

She had his grandmother's courage. As they turned towards the dark, he saw the colour leak from her cheeks and he gave her a chaste hug. 'Just imagine you are walking the corridor in your house at night with no candles.'

Their route in was as bad as his childhood memories had told him. At length, they stood side by side on flat ground, with the roof too high above their heads to feel, and no walls pressing in on either side. The sound of a waterfall surrounded them, so that it seemed as if they must stand within it.

'Here, we can light the candle and the lantern,' Owen said, and then, with a child's love of mystery, 'Would you close your eyes?'

He lit the lantern and said with unexpected shyness, 'If it please you, would you look now?'

'Oh, Cedric . . .'

It was worth the dark and the cold and the fear. He moved close and hugged her again. 'Look and remember, so that the generations after may know that the cathedral of the earth is worth the route they must take to find it.' He gave her the lantern and lit from it the candle. 'If you will stay here, I will place the heart-stone in its resting place.'

He lit four more candles and set them on ledges about the arched entrance, that she might sit in ample light, then he left her and retraced the steps he had taken once before: east for twenty paces and then across the river on stones that rolled unsteadily underfoot. Turning west again, he followed the line of the river's edge to the astonishing, soul-lifting beauty of the waterfall. Caught in the sooty light of the lantern, it cascaded as living gold into the wide stone crucible at its foot, where the white rock caught it and made it quicksilver. His grandmother had described the place as the well of the living water and he could think of no better words.

Balancing the lantern on his knee, Owen sat on the edge and drew the heart-stone at last from the leather satchel. It rested quietly between his hands, silent now that the end had come. He felt its mourning as a heaviness about his heart, and all sense of beauty, all joy in his own success drained from him. In the heart of the cavern, his world emptied of light and colour, scent and touch, song and love. In this new deadness, he understood for the first time how his life must be with the stone gone. He could not bear it.

'Why must it be so?'

He cried aloud and looked back at his life with a bitter wonder that he had not thought to ask the question until it sprang now to his lips. In his childhood, his grandmother had told him of the stone's resting place and he had accepted it without question, as he had when later Nostradamus had spoken this destiny.

Najakmul had trained him for this moment through thirty years in paradise and he had thanked her daily for it. He had come to England driven only by the need to bring the skull to this place for its safekeeping, that future generations might find it when the world had greatest need.

Cedric Owen did not care about the world's need now. He wept for his own pain and for Fernandez, for Martha and for the stone.

You would undo all that we have done?

The voice was one he knew most intimately, else he would not have looked up. Najakmul was there, standing in the power of the waterfall. She reached a hand for him. *If I tell you that the stone will be here, where I am, would that ease for you the pain of parting? You will not be long without it.*

A spray of water reached him, lighter than rain. Najakmul said, *Give the stone to the living water, son of my heart. Your life's work is near to done.*

Son of my heart. So she had called him in her last days alive. It was this that gave him the courage to rise, to lift the heart-stone so that it might hold for one last moment the cascading silver of the waterfall.

The well of white water boiled beneath, and opened, as a heart opens, to show the still black of its core.

'*Cedric!*'

Bright searing yellow sliced across his mind, with Martha's voice twined through it, from the far side of the chamber. In the candlelight he saw her struggling with two assailants.

His need balanced on a knife edge, his two duties opposed. With a courage unmatched, Cedric Owen launched the stone that carried his soul into the bowl beneath the cataract. And then he was running, lantern in one hand, eating knife in the other, back across the river to where Martha battled with the men who would take her life and that of her unborn child.

19
Weyland's Smithy, Oxfordshire

June 21, 2007: 5.00 a.m. Dawn came slowly to the Oxfordshire countryside. The stones about the grave mound were the first thing to show colour; splashes of grey lichen became, as Stella watched them, more subtly green. Overhead, a crow barked from the highest beech.

Branches cracked near the road. Tony Bookless was a formless shape, striding up the avenue of trees towards Weyland's Smithy.

'Stella, you're there!' He fairly ran the last few yards, crashing into the open space before the mound. 'And Kit. And Gordon. That's good.' He named them off like a roll call, but his eyes never left Stella and the blue stone that lit the air around her. His right hand was jammed awkwardly in his pocket. 'Where's Davy?'

'He went back to Oxford,' Stella said. 'I didn't need him here once he'd shown me the mound, and he's worried about his mother.' She could lie to him now with a clear conscience. It gave weight to the words.

'Of course. Kit told me there had been an accident.'

An accident? Stella stared at Kit. His eyes flashed a frantic, silent warning. *Trust me. Danger! Please trust me!*

Flatly, she said, 'An accident, yes.' She no longer knew who to trust. Gordon was nearest. His fear of the stone was a palpable thing, but even so he had stood up when Tony Bookless arrived and taken a protective step towards her. Kit was in the open away from the mound, swaying on his feet.

Whatever his silent pleas, he and Tony Bookless were both moving now, edging round, slowly, absently, with no obvious place to go, except that Bookless came closer each time to Stella, and Kit further away.

The stone gave no help. It offered nothing but a desperate need to enter the tunnel. Stella lifted it level with her own head. Gordon made a small, hurt noise in his throat.

Abruptly, Tony Bookless stopped moving. 'I know you think the fate of the world hangs on the stone going in there,' he said, 'but I remain of the belief that no stone is worth dying for. I promised Kit I'd keep you alive. I am doing my best to achieve that.'

He was so plausible. The fragile safety of the morning hung on the fiction that she believed him. Too late, Stella took breath to answer, to keep the fiction going.

To her right, Gordon Fraser had already lost the last threads of control. 'You did your best to murder Ursula Walker, you hypocritical bastard. Don't pretend you're here to help.'

Tony Bookless ignored him. With perfect diction, he said, 'Stella, what *exactly* happened to Ursula—'

'Don't pretend you don't know, Anthony Sir fucking Bookless. I worked you out days ago. You're a cold-blooded killer. You—'

'Gordon, stop.'

Once started, the small Scotsman was all but unstoppable. Propelled by his own rage, he took the final bound towards Stella, making of himself a wall between her and Tony Bookless. He was her friend, her mentor. In the silence of her heart, she thanked him even as she reached out to catch his arm and hold him silent.

She said, 'It's kind, but I don't need you to fight my battles for me. I'll do this for myself.'

She directed her coolest smile at Tony Bookless. 'Ursula's on a ventilator in the Radcliffe ICU suffering from smoke inhalation. She stayed in the farmhouse too long after Kit and I got out. The fire caught her in the kitchen. There was chlorine in the smoke. The police *will* be investigating this one as attempted murder.'

'*Chlorine?!*' Bookless was an exceptional actor. He raised his head to look past her. 'Kit, why did you not tell me this in the car?'

They had all his attention. If ever there was a time to act, it was that moment. Stella gave a silent call, and was answered the same by the shifting leaf patterns in the woods behind.

'Stella, go to Kit, *now.*'

Tony Bookless snapped in a way she had never heard before. The time for pretending was past. Stella did not move. 'Why?' she asked. 'So you can kill us both as you tried to kill Ursula?'

'Quite the reverse, so that I can do my utmost to keep you safe while— *Davy Law, don't do it! You've got the wrong man!*'

He took his hand from his pocket. He did not hold a gun, but a bunch of keys. He threw them, hard, straight at Stella, who ducked sideways with a speed she did not know she had, and rolled, holding the stone.

Tony Bookless filled her spinning world, and Gordon, closing in on him, and at last Davy Law, running low and hard from the encircling trees from quite another place than she had expected.

The morning was lost in a brutal collision of flesh and the crack of a shattered bone—and after it, a gunshot. Someone grabbed for the skull. Stella clutched it, kicking, and was pulled clear by her elbow.

Davy Law stood over her, one arm hanging useless at his side. With the other, he shoved the small of her back.

'It's dawn. The mound's waiting. *Go!*'

Gordon Fraser shouted, 'Stay where you are!'

'*No, Stell, go for it!*'

She trusted Gordon with her life, but she would not have stopped for him, whatever he had shouted. It was the unrooted terror in Kit's voice, even as he urged her forward, that cut through the pull of the stone. She tripped to a halt and turned.

Kit was standing rigid. A gun held at his temple.

Gordon Fraser said, 'Step back from the tunnel.'

'Gordon?' Stella stared at him. His red hair was everywhere. His eyes fed on the skull and it was not fear that fired them, but yearning.

Floundering, she said, 'Is this a joke?'

A grunt from the ground made her look down. Tony Bookless lay there. Blood spread in a narrow band, staining the dawn turf. He shrugged something that might have been an apology. 'First rule of warfare,' he said, drily. 'Always do what the man with the gun tells you.'

'Right.' Gordon gestured with his free arm. 'So put it down and step away.'

She could not; the stone would not let her.

She said, 'What do you want?'

'The stone, what else?'

She gaped. 'But you're scared of it. You could hardly go near it the day you washed the chalk off.'

He flushed a sore, angry red. 'We just need time to get to know each other, it and me.' His hand was steady if his voice was not. 'It'll be different when this dawn's past and it's lost its hope. Just keep clear of that doorway until the sun's well up and we'll all be happy.'

Flatly, Davy Law said, 'What makes you think the stone will be anything but a piece of flashy sapphire when the dawn's past? If you stop it from going into the mound now, you'll break its soul, then what will you have?'

'I'll still have the biggest gemstone in the Western world at no risk to myself. But I don't think it'll let go of its power that easily. And don't even try to say you wouldn't do the same if you had the guts.'

'I would never have pushed someone off a cliff for it.' Even as he spoke, Davy was moving slowly towards Stella.

Gordon laughed. He sounded perfectly sane. 'I've been looking for Cedric Owen's blue heart-stone since I came up to the college thirty years ago. Kit O'Connor had barely been in a real cave in his life. What right had he to find the stone for half a day's looking? I'll have it now and there'll be justice done for once.'

As if to commend him, the band of sun to the east broke through a thin strap of cloud. Gordon gave a short nod and squared his shoulders, as Stella had seen him do in countless caves before the big descents.

With military sharpness, he said, 'David, if you move another muscle, Kit dies and you after him. Stella, put the stone down by the count of three or he's a dead man anyway. *One.*'

'Don't do it, Stell.' Kit had more colour, suddenly. 'He can't kill both of us in time to stop you.'

'You're welcome to try me. *Two.*'

'Stella, you have a choice: me or the stone. You *know* which matters more.'

Suddenly, unexpectedly, she did.

'*Thr—*'

Against the scything panic in her head, she bent and set the blue skull-stone on the earth before the mound.

'Have it, then.' She stepped back. 'It won't give you what you think—Kit! *No!*'

He was unsteady and half maimed and he made the choice she had just turned down. She saw him wrench to his left, heard the gunshot, louder than thunder, saw blood, and did not know if it was his or Gordon's before they fell together to the ground.

From the hard earth, Kit shouted, 'Stella, run!'

He was alive; it was all she needed. She was already snatching up the skull, running like a hare over the stone that blocked the entrance to the mound, down the short tunnel into the embracing darkness.

20
Ingleborough Fell, Yorkshire Dales

April 1589   Owen had not known that Martha carried a knife, but in the time it took him to cross the water, he saw her use it once to good effect. Even so, he thought he was too late. There were at least two of them fighting her, Walsingham's men beyond doubt, and only one wounded by her knife. He had hold of her hair with his one good arm and was pulling her head back and round, towards the tunnel. The other seemed intent on grabbing her feet, but that her kicking was stopping him. By the half-light of the candles, Owen saw him abandon that endeavour and reach for his sword.

'*Martha!*'

The sound of her name, or the closeness of the shout, caused her to cease her struggling and temporarily spared her life. The sword-bearer spun, snarling, to face the new danger. At the sight of Owen and his three-inch knife, he barked a laugh.

'They said you were no swordsman.' The man was black-haired and bearded and spoke with a Devonshire accent. 'Drop your knife, *Doctor*,' he went on. 'Be sensible and we'll let you live.'

'In the Tower? I would rather be dead.'

The man grinned, showing white teeth in the fuzz of his beard. He said, 'Join your friend, then, the one-armed Spaniard. Though he died slowly enough. We only need one of you and we'll have the wife if we can't have the husband.'

At the mention of Fernandez, Owen saw the fight go out of Martha. Before Blackbeard could turn, he dropped his knife. The clatter was lost in the rush of the waterfall. 'Let her go and I'll come with you.'

The man advanced. 'Or we'll take you both, since you've so kindly offered.'

Owen kicked the knife sideways. It skittered across the floor and splashed into the river, taking Blackbeard's attention with it for the moment Owen needed to scoop up a large stone from the cave's floor.

He was no swordsman, but he had spent thirty years in New Spain playing 'catch-and-throw' with generations of children. In Zama, it was the beginnings of the hunt and Owen had found a flair for it.

'What of Fernandez?' Owen asked. 'Did he tell you to come here?'

Blackbeard sneered. 'He told us everything we asked of him.'

Owen wanted to disbelieve him, but he knew Walsingham could make any man reveal his soul if asked aright.

'When did he die?' he asked, not daring to look at Martha.

'February,' Blackbeard said, 'near the end of the month.' He was wary of the stone, and began to circle, pushing Owen away from the candle's light with the point of his sword.

Owen stepped sideways and flung his stone as well as he had ever done. Not well enough. Instead of hitting Blackbeard's head, the stone sank into his shoulder, biting deep into flesh and sinew and bone.

Some men retreat when injured; others are roused to fury. Blackbeard was of the latter mould. He raised his sword before him like a lance and ran at Owen, roaring fit to drown the river.

Slow as a dream, Cedric Owen saw his death approach. Somewhere far away, at the tunnel's mouth, he heard Martha scream his name and then a man's shout and then Blackbeard was on him and he heard the iron pierce his shirt, his flesh, his lungs, and felt the wet gush of blood.

Owen's body crashed against the limestone wall. His left elbow shattered; in his new place of distant objectivity, he could count the pieces and knew it would never mend. His knees buckled and he felt his back slide down the wall, and was surprised to see Blackbeard topple also, but in the other direction.

And then he knew he was truly dying, for Fernandez de Aguilar was standing in front of him, with Robert Maplethorpe's dark-wet sword in his hand. He tried to lift his hand and failed. 'Your presence gives me great joy. I had not thought that death would be so forgiving as to bring us both together.'

'Cedric . . .' De Aguilar was weeping openly, a thing Owen had never seen from him in life. He lifted Owen's hand and the touch of his skin was surprisingly warm for a dead man. He said, 'I was as fast as I could. I have been playing cat-and-mouse with my pursuers across the length and breadth of England this four months. I could not leave the linen square because it would have led them to you. I lost them just before they entered the cave. I heard the blue stone cry out once, loudly. Only that brought me to you.'

The world was beginning to sway. Owen frowned. The meaning of the words strayed into his mind and out again. He grasped at them, as at passing fish. 'Fernandez? You're alive?'

'Alive and unhurt, against all my vows to protect you.'

'I had to see if . . . I could . . . fight just once.' He managed to grin but stopped at what it did to Fernandez. 'Martha?'

'Hurt, but not badly so. I can tend her. I cannot tend you, my friend. I am so, so sorry. You should not have died now when you have achieved your life's tasks.'

'Not . . . finished. Need to . . . finish ledgers. Must leave record for . . . those who come.'

'I will bring to pass all that you and I and Barnabas have planned, I swear it. The college shall have its legacy and the world shall see the ledgers, but not while Walsingham lives. It will all be done.'

'Thank you.' The feeling in Owen's fingers was leaving. His head fell back and struck the limestone, but he felt no pain. He could sense the blue heart-stone waiting for him, as if it straddled the line between life and death and could ferry him across. A moment's lucency struck him. He grasped again for Fernandez's hand. He said, 'Sell the diamonds . . . for you. Make your . . . daughter . . . a wealthy woman.'

'She shall be. In your name shall the Walkers keep open the trackways. I swear it. Goodbye, my friend. Do not forget me where you travel; I would meet with you again, if we may.'

Owen could not speak. He felt a warm hand on his brow and fingers on his eyelids that made the world black and gave him peace, so that he could turn now and see a chalk-riven hillside, on which waited an arc of colour and four beasts becoming one.

Najakmul was there, glorious in her majesty, as she had promised she would be. She swept open her arms and there came a rush of welcome and choice and one final request.

21
Weyland's Smithy, Oxfordshire

June 21, 2007: 5.12 a.m. The tunnel into the grave mound was not long, and it did not muffle the noises from the clearing outside. Another shot rang out, and another. The part of Stella that could still think clearly knew that Gordon Fraser was free now to follow her. That same part grieved for Kit, even while the rest held the blue stone and knew that he had made the right choice where she had not; it mattered more than her life or his for the stone to be in the heart of the earth at sunrise.

At the tunnel's end was a fire, with shadowy figures about it. One was clearer than the rest: a lean man with a quirked smile and gold in his ear. Bowing, he said, 'My lady, we who are here as guardians cannot guard for long. The place is known to you. Will you set the stone into it?' He bore a sword that she recognised in his one hand. She looked for a medallion about his neck but did not see it.

A recess in the back wall glowed with a blue light all its own. With too-slow fingers, Stella fumbled the heart-stone to the lip of the recess that had been made for it at the dawn of time. There was no warning from it now, no flashes of colour in her mind, only a need that went beyond words. Behind her, a figure of flesh and leaking blood blocked the entrance to the tunnel.

A voice she had never heard before spoke from the earth: *Do not delay*.

Stella stepped over the fire and lowered the stone down to the place that had waited for over 5,000 years.

The gunshot came afterwards, or before, she could not tell which, only that her world exploded in damaged flesh and blue light and pain.

She was blinded a moment by the fire and Gordon Fraser was there, looking dazed, and an old man with a nose like a ship's prow who stood with his staff raised, and so they were all dead together, which explained why she saw the dragon of the winter snows rise up from the side of Uffington Hill and unfurl its wings and tip back its head and roar out its yearning to turn back the tide of all evil and save the world from ruin.

And yet, it could not fly; only eight colours made its form. The sky-blue of the heart-stone was missing. Stella looked down. In the lands of the dead, the stone was more alive than she, vibrant in ways she had never seen before. On the hillside, twelve people stood in an arc about the dragon. At their head, Ki'kaame asked her, 'Will you join us, last of the keepers, and return the heart of the earth?'

'Of course.' She was already walking.

From the other half of her heart, Kit said, 'Stell? Please don't go.'

Stella stopped. Ki'kaame stopped.

The air parted and came together again. To her left was now a man of medium height with silvered hair. The medallion about his neck was the image of hers. His smile was old as time. He said, 'You are the latest and the youngest. Your life has not been shaped for this. If you wish, I will take the stone to the heart of the dragon. You have that choice.'

The dragon called to her once, with all the yearning of the stone. From another, less bright place, Kit's voice whispered, 'Stella?'

'*Kit.*' The word came from her soul, an answer and a choosing.

Already the cold was inside her, welling upwards.

'Thank you. We have followed our hearts, you and I. There must always be love, as well as duty.' Cedric Owen reached for her and for the skull together. His hand was a clear sky-blue.

In the core of Stella's heart, a fist of ice met the song of the blue stone. Her world exploded into shards of blue and black and scarlet.

'STELL?'

She was in sunlight, lying on grass with birdsong quiet around. Her shoulder was on fire. Kit was leaning over her. His face was a kaleidoscope of grief and wonder.

'Stell. God, Stell . . .'

With both arms, he lifted her. The pain in her shoulder was blinding, so that she was slow to understand.

'You're whole!' she said presently, in wonder. 'You can walk.' He was carrying her to a place where the sun fell on the grass. 'And you're alive.'

He said, 'You've been shot, but the bleeding's stopped, and the hole's not a hole any more. And your medallion has changed.'

He lifted it up. On the flat surface was a dragon alone, with no man to raise it. On the other side, the scales that balanced sun and moon had gone.

Unsteadily, he said, 'As a scientist, I'd rather not ask how this happened.' And then, because she needed to know, 'Gordon Fraser's dead; Tony got the gun and shot him. Davy's cracked his arm, but otherwise he's OK.'

'Ursula?'

'We don't know yet. Davy's calling the hospital.'

She let Kit help her to sitting. She said, '*Thereafter, follow your heart and mine, for these are one and the same.* Cedric Owen was there. He gave me the choice. I followed my heart. I came back to you.'

'I felt you do it. I can't tell you how glad I am.'

In a daze of pain and sunshine, she held his hand. '*Do not fail me, for in doing so, you fail yourself, and all the worlds of waiting.* I don't know what the worlds are waiting for, but we didn't fail, either of us.'

Kit smiled again, and the world was perfect. 'I know.'

MANDA SCOTT

Star sign: Virgo 'with ascendant in Scorpio'
Favourite authors: Mary Renault, Robert Wilson
One wish? An end to global warming

RD: You spent fifteen years as a vet before you turned to writing as an alternative, less sleep-deprived profession. Is the life of a novelist pretty much as you had imagined?

MS: Not at all. I still work the same seven-day week, I have far less time off, but the difference is that if I work late and at weekends it's because I choose to, not because someone has picked up a phone and called me out. Getting used to being calm when the phone rang took a long time. The biggest change is that I have time to have my own animals now, which I never had before. Getting my own dog was the first huge step into a new life. I wouldn't swap writing for anything else.

RD: Do you enjoy the research that you do for your books?

MS: Yes. It's a constant source of surprise and a kind of hidden joy that I can spend days immersed in texts pulling out tiny details. But it's vital that the research never runs the book. Books are about people and are driven by the emotions of the moment.

RD: In *The Crystal Skull* you have combined a contemporary mystery with a historical narrative set in Tudor times. What led you in this direction?

MS: It became clear that I couldn't write *The Crystal Skull* without a foot in the past to give a perspective on the skulls and where they came from. And I realised that I needed to write it from the viewpoint of the first Europeans to meet the descendants of the ancient Maya. I never thought I'd be interested in Elizabethan England, but the Cedric Owen thread was a joy and almost wrote itself. Elizabethan Cambridge was immensely interesting. I'd lived in Cambridge for so long but hadn't really researched its history. And then everything came together at Weyland's Smithy, which is timeless and made a good place to bring the narrative threads to a single point. Writing the scenes in the Yorkshire caves was completely adrenaline-filled, particularly at the end.

RD: Has the success that has come with your four *Boudica* books changed you?

MS: Living has changed me. Not being a vet has changed me. Teaching the dreaming [see www.mandascott.co.uk] has changed me out of all recognition—you teach best what you most need to learn—if all of these are brought by success then, yes, it has, but what has changed me most is having the time and space to push my own boundaries.

RD: What do you like most about living in the country now that you've moved to Shropshire?

MS: I love the lack of noise, the lack of light (I live on a lane with no streetlights for miles); at night I can see all the stars. I love the fact that my dog can go out without a collar or lead and we can walk for miles and not meet anyone. I love being able to sit in the garden and listen to the buzzards and the crows. I love all of it, actually.

RD: Do you see something of yourself in the character of Stella?

MS: There has to be a part of me in all of the characters or they can't be alive. But, yes, there's a lot of Stella in me. She won't let go until she's found the core of something, which is so very true to (my) type.

RD: Do you believe the Mayan prophecy that mankind is plummeting towards the end of the world in 2012?

MS: I don't believe the date 21.12.2012 is a precise end point, but I do think we are definitely moving towards an ending and that it is man-made. The message of the skulls is that we can change—it's not too late to turn everything round—but we have to listen to the warnings and let them influence what we're doing. If *The Crystal Skull* brings the concept of change a little closer to the surface of our collective consciousness, I'd be very pleased.

FAKE OR FOR REAL?

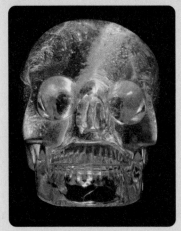

In *The Crystal Skull*, the Mayan prophecy that the world will end on December 21, 2012 triggers a desperate race to avert apocalypse. Legends of the Mayan and Aztec civilisations tell of thirteen carved skulls scattered in various parts of the world and promise that at a time of global crisis, if all the skulls can be reunited, Quetzlcoatl, the serpent god, will arise to save the planet. The British Museum owns a crystal skull (left) similar to the one in Manda Scott's novel, but there is heated debate over its authenticity. Some claim it is from the ancient Aztec civilisation in what is now Mexico, but this has been discredited by scientists who argue that the carving is too sophisticated. Furthermore, the skull was acquired from Eugene Boban, a 19th-century antiques dealer, who may have faked its origins. Nevertheless, many New Age followers still believe in the skull's mystical powers.